THREE

COMPLETE

NOVELS

Lilian
Jackson
Braun

THREE
COMPLETE
NOVELS

Lilian Jackson Braun

The Cat Who Moved a Mountain

The Cat Who Blew the Whistle

The Cat Who Said Cheese

G. P. PUTNAM'S SONS
NEW YORK

G. P. Putnam's Sons
Publishers Since 1838
a member of
Penguin Putnam Inc.
200 Madison Avenue
New York, NY 10016

Library of Congress Cataloging-in-Publication Data

Braun, Lilian Jackson.
    [Novels. Selections]
    Three complete novels / Lilian Jackson Braun.
      p.   cm.
    Contents: The cat who moved a mountain—The cat who blew the
whistle—The cat who said cheese.
    ISBN 0-399-14364-5
    1. Detective and mystery stories. American.   2. Qwilleran, Jim
(Fictitious character)—Fiction.   3. Journalists—United States—
Fiction.   4. Cats—Fiction.   I. Title.
PS3552.R354A6   1998   97-18197 CIP
813'.54—dc21

Printed in the United States of America
10   9   8   7   6   5   4   3   2   1

Book design by Patrice Sheridan

Dedicated to
Earl Bettinger, the Husband Who . . .

Contents

THE CAT WHO
MOVED A MOUNTAIN

CHAPTER 1

A man of middle age, with a large, drooping moustache and brooding eyes, hunched over the steering wheel and gripped the rim anxiously as he maneuvered his car up a mountain road that was narrow, unpaved, and tortuous. Unaccustomed to mountain driving, he found it a blood-curdling ordeal. On one side of the road the mountain rose in a solid wall of craggy rock; on the other side it dropped off sharply without benefit of guardrail, and it was narrowed further by fallen rocks at the base of the cliff. The driver kept to the middle of the road and clenched his teeth at each hairpin turn, pondering his options if another vehicle were to come hurtling downhill around a blind curve. A head-on collision? A crash into the cliff? A plunge into the gorge? To aggravate the tension there were two passengers in the backseat who protested as only Siamese cats can do.

It was late in the day, and the gas gauge registered less than a quarter full. For almost two hours Jim Qwilleran had been driving on mountain passes, snaking around triple S-curves, blowing the horn at every hairpin turn, making the wrong decision at every fork in the road. There were no directional signs, no habitations where he might inquire, no motorists to flag down for help, no turn-outs where he could pull over in an effort to get his bearings and collect his wits. The situation had all the elements of a nightmare, although Qwilleran was totally awake. So were the two in the backseat, bumping about in their carrier as the car swerved and jolted, all the while airing their protests in ear-splitting howls and nerve-wracking shrieks.

"Shut up," he bellowed at them, a reprimand that only increased the volume of the clamor. "We're lost! Where are we? Why did we ever come to this damned mountain?"

It was a good question, and one day soon he would know the answer. Meanwhile he was frantically pursuing a nonstop journey to nowhere.

Two weeks before, Qwilleran had experienced a sudden urge to go to the mountains. He was living in Moose County, a comfortably flat fragment of terrain in the northernmost reaches of the lower Forty-eight, more than a thousand miles away from anything higher than a hill. The inspiration came to him while celebrating a significant event in his life. After five years of legal formalities that had required him to live in Moose County, he had officially inherited the Klingenschoen fortune, and he was now a certified billionaire with holdings reaching from New Jersey to Nevada.

During his five years in Pickax City, the county seat, he had won over the natives with his genial disposition and his streak of generosity that constantly benefited the community. Strangers passing him on the street went home and told their families that Mr. Q had said good morning and raised his hand in a friendly salute. Men enjoyed his company in the coffee houses. Women went into raptures over his flamboyant moustache and shivered at the doleful expression in his hooded eyes, wondering what past experience had saddened them.

To celebrate his inheritance, more than two hundred friends and admirers gathered in the ballroom of the seedy old hostelry that called itself the "New" Pickax Hotel. Qwilleran circulated among them amiably, jingling ice cubes in a glass of ginger ale, accepting congratulations, and making frequent trips to a buffet laden with the hotel's idea of party food. He was an outstanding figure, standing out from the crowd: six-feet-two and well-built, with a good head of hair graying at the temples, and a luxuriant pepper-and-salt moustache that seemed to have a life of its own.

Chief among his well-wishers were Polly Duncan, administrator of the Pickax library; Arch Riker, publisher of the *Moose County*

Something; and Osmond Hasselrich of Hasselrich, Bennett & Barter, attorneys for the Klingenschoen empire. The mayor, city council members, chief of police, and superintendent of schools were there, as well as others who had played a role in Qwilleran's recent life: Larry and Carol Lanspeak, Dr. Halifax Goodwinter, Mildred Hanstable, Eddington Smith, Fran Brodie—a list longer than the guest of honor had imagined. None of them dared to hope that this newly minted billionaire, city-born and city-bred, would continue to live in what urban politicians called a rural wasteland. None could guess what he would do next, or where he would choose to live. He had been a prize-winning journalist in several major cities before fate steered him to Moose County. How could anyone expect him to remain in Pickax City?

Kip MacDiarmid, editor of the newspaper in the adjoining county, was the first to ask the question that was on everyone's mind. "Now that you have all the money in the world, Qwill, and twenty-five good years ahead of you, what are your plans?"

When Qwilleran hesitated, Arch Riker, his lifelong friend, hazarded a guess. "He's going to buy a string of newspapers and a TV network and start a media revolution."

"Or buy a castle in Scotland and go in for bird watching," Larry Lanspeak contributed with tongue in cheek.

"Not likely," said Polly Duncan, who had given Qwilleran a bird book and binoculars in vain. "He'll buy an island in the Caribbean and write that book he's always talking about." She spoke blithely to conceal her feelings; as the chief woman in his life for the last few years Polly would feel the keenest regret if he should leave the north country.

Qwilleran chuckled at their suggestions. "Seriously," he said as he loaded his plate for the third time with canned cocktail sausages and processed cheese slices, "the last few years have been the richest in my entire life, and I mean it! Until coming here I'd always lived in cities with a population of two million or more. Now I'm content to live in a town of three thousand, four hundred miles north of everywhere. And yet . . ."

"You're not living up to your potential," Polly said bravely.

"I don't know about that, but I'll tell you one thing: Taking it easy is not my idea of the good life. I don't play golf. I'd rather go to jail than go fishing. Expensive cars and custom-made suits are not for me. What I do need is a goal—a worthwhile direction."

"Have you thought of getting married?" asked Moira Mac-Diarmid.

"No!" Qwilleran stated vehemently.

"It wouldn't be too late to start producing heirs."

Patiently he explained, as he had done many times before, "Several years ago I discovered I'm a washout as a husband, and I might as well face the truth. As for heirs, I've established the Klingenschoen Foundation to distribute my money—both while I'm alive and after I've gone. But . . ." He stroked his moustache thoughtfully, "I'd like to get away from it all for a while and rethink my purpose in life—on top of a mountain somewhere—or on a desert island, if there are any left without tourists."

"What about your cats?" asked Carol Lanspeak. "Larry and I would be glad to board them in the luxury to which they're accustomed."

"I'd take them along. The presence of a cat is conducive to meditation."

"Do you like mountains?" Kip MacDiarmid asked.

"To tell the truth, I haven't had much experience with mountains. The Alps impressed me when my paper sent me to Switzerland on assignment, and my honeymoon was spent in the Scottish Highlands . . . Yes, I like the idea of altitude. Mountains have a sense of mystery, whether you're up there looking down or down here looking up."

Moira said, "Last summer we had a great vacation in the Potato Mountains—didn't we, Kip? We took the kids and the camper. Beautiful scenery! Wonderful mountain air! And so peaceful! Even with four kids and two dogs it was peaceful."

"I've never heard of the Potato Mountains," Qwilleran said.

"They're just being developed. You should get there before the influx of tourists," Kip advised. "If you'd like to borrow our camper for a couple of weeks, you're welcome to it."

Arch Riker said, "I don't picture Qwill in a camper unless it has twenty-four-hour room service. We used to be in scouting together, and he was the only kid who hated campouts and cook-outs."

Qwilleran was quaking inwardly at the thought of condensed living in an RV with a pair of restless indoor cats. "I appreciate the offer," he said, "but it would be better for me to rent a cabin for a couple of months—something Thoreau-esque but with indoor plumbing, you know. I don't need any frills, just the basic comforts."

"They have cabins for rent in the Potato Mountains," Moira said. "We saw lots of vacancy signs—didn't we, Kip? And there's a nice little town in the valley with restaurants and stores. The kids went down there for movies and the video arcade."

"Do they have a public library? Do you suppose there's a veterinarian?"

"Sure to be," said Kip. "There's a courthouse, so it's obviously the county seat. Neat little burg! A river runs right along the main street."

"What's the name of the town?"

"Spudsboro!" the MacDiarmids said in unison with wide grins as they waited for Qwilleran's incredulous reaction.

"We're not kidding," said Moira. "That's what it's called on the map. It's right between two ranges of mountains. We camped in a national forest in the West Potatoes. On the east side there's Big Potato Mountain and Little Potato Mountain."

"And I suppose the Gravy River runs through the valley," Qwilleran quipped.

"The river is the Yellyhoo, I'm sorry to say," said Kip. "It's great for white-water rafting—not the Colorado by a long shot, but the kids got a thrill out of it. There are caves if you're interested in spelunking, but the locals discourage it, and Moira is chicken, anyway."

"Where do the Potato Mountains get their name?"

The MacDiarmids looked at each other questioningly. "Well," Moira ventured, "they're sort of round and knobby. Friendly mountains, you know—not overwhelming like the Rockies."

"Big Potato is in the throes of development," said her husband. "Little Potato is inhabited but still primitive. In the 1920s it was a haven for moonshiners, they say, because the revenuers couldn't find them in the dense woods."

Moira said, "There are lots of artists on Little Potato, selling all kinds of crafts. We brought home some exciting pottery and baskets."

"Yes," Kip said, "and there's a girl who does those tapestries you like, Qwill." When his wife nudged him he repeated, "There's a *young woman* who does those tapestries you like . . . How do you bachelors manage, Qwill, without a wife to set you straight all the time?"

"It's a deprivation I'm willing to suffer," Qwilleran replied with a humble bow.

"If you're really interested in mountains, I'll call the editor of the *Spudsboro Gazette*. We were roommates in J school, and he bought the newspaper last summer. That's how we found out about the Potatoes. Colin Carmichael, his name is. If you decide to go down there, you should look him up. Swell guy. I'll tell him to have a rental agent contact you. Spudsboro has a chamber of commerce that's right on the ball."

"Don't make me sound like a Rockefeller, Kip. They'll hike the rent. I want something simple, and I want to keep a low profile."

"Sure. I understand."

"How's the weather in the Potatoes?"

"Terrific! Didn't rain once while we were there."

For the rest of the evening Qwilleran appeared distracted, and he kept fingering his moustache, a nervous habit triggered by a desire for action. He made quick decisions, and now his instincts were telling him to flee to the Potato Mountains and resolve his quandary. Why that particular range of mountains attracted him was something he could not explain, except that they sounded appetizing, and he enjoyed what he called the pleasures of the table.

Arriving home after the reception, he was greeted at the door by two Siamese cats with expectancy in their perky ears and waving tails. He gave each of them a cocktail sausage spirited away from the hotel buffet, and after they had gobbled their treat rapturously and washed up meticulously, he made his announcement. "You guys won't like this, but we're going to spend the summer in the mountains." He always conversed with them as if they were humans with a passable IQ. In fact, he often wondered how he had lived alone for so many years without two intelligent beings to listen attentively and respond with encouraging yowls and sympathetic blinks.

Their names were Koko and Yum Yum—seal-point Siamese with hypnotically blue eyes in dark brown masks and with brown extremities shading into fawn-colored bodies. The female was an endearing lap sitter who was fascinated by Qwilleran's moustache and who used catly wiles to get the better of him in an argument. The male was nothing short of extraordinary—a genetically superior animal gifted with senses of detection and even prognostication in certain circumstances. His official cognomen was Kao K'o Kung, and he had a dignity worthy of his namesake. Koko's exploits were by no means a figment of Qwilleran's imagination; the hard-headed, cynical journalist had documented them over a period of years and intended eventually to write a book.

Before he broke the news to his two housemates he anticipated a negative reaction. They could read his mind if not his lips, and he knew they disliked a change of address. As he expected, Yum Yum sat in a compact bundle with legs tucked out of sight, a reproachful expression in her violet-tinged blue eyes. Surprisingly, Koko seemed excited about the prospect, prancing back and forth on long, elegant legs.

"Have I made the right decision?" Qwilleran asked.

"Yow!" said Koko spiritedly.

In the next few days Qwilleran proceeded with plans, arranging for a summer-long absence, plotting an itinerary, choosing motels, and making a packing list. For good weather and the quiet life he would need only lightweight summer casuals. It never occurred to him to take rain gear.

Soon the mail began to arrive from Spudsboro. The first prospectus invited him to buy into time-share condominiums, now under construction. A realty agent listed residential lots and acreage for sale. A contractor offered to build the house of Qwilleran's dreams. Several rental agents sent lists of cabins and cottages available, no pets allowed. The Siamese watched anxiously as each letter was opened and tossed into the wastebasket. Yet, the more disappointing the opportunities, the more Qwilleran was determined to go to the Potatoes.

The situation improved with a telephone call from Spudsboro. The person on the line was friendly and enthusiastic. "Mr. Qwilleran, this is Dolly Lessmore of Lessmore Realty. Colin Carmichael tells us you want to rent a mountain retreat for the entire summer."

It was a husky, deep-pitched voice that he identified as that of a woman who smoked too much. He visualized her as rather short and stocky, with a towering hair-do, a taste for bright colors, a three-pack-a-day habit, and a pocketful of breath mints. He prided himself on his ability to personify a voice accurately. Yes, he told her, he was considering the possibility of a mountain vacation.

"I thought I'd call and find out exactly what kind of accommodations you have in mind," she said. "We have a lot of rentals available. First off, do you want the inside of the mountain or the outside?"

The choice stumped him for only a second. "The outside. I'll leave the inside to the trolls."

"Let me explain," Ms. Lessmore said with a laugh. "The inside slope faces the valley, overlooking Spudsboro, and you have spectacular sunsets. The outside faces the eastern foothills, and you can see forever. Also, it gets the morning sun."

"Do you have anything at the summit?" he queried.

"Nice thinking! You want the best of both worlds! Now, if you'll tell me your birthday, it will help me match you up with the right place."

"May twenty-fourth. My blood type is O, and I wear a size twelve shoe."

"Hmmm, you're a Gemini, close to Taurus. You want something individual but practical."

"That's right. Something rustic and secluded, but with electricity and indoor plumbing."

"I think we can do that," she said cheerfully.

"I like a firm bed, preferably extra long."

"I'll make a note of that."

"And at least two bedrooms."

"For how many persons, may I ask?"

"I have two roommates, a male and a female, both Siamese cats."

"Oh-oh! That poses a problem," she said.

"They're well-behaved and not in the least destructive. I can vouch for that," he said. Then, recalling that Koko had once broken a $10,000 vase, while Yum Yum would steal anything that was not nailed down, he added, "I'll be willing to post a bond."

"Well . . . that might work. Let me think . . . There's one possibility, but I'll have to check it out. The place I have in mind is rather large—"

"I was hoping for something small," Qwilleran interrupted, "but under the circumstances I'd compromise on large." He was currently living in a converted apple barn, four stories high, with balconies on three levels. "What do you mean by large?"

"I mean *large*! It was originally a small country inn. It was converted into a home for the Hawkinfield family quite some time ago. There are six bedrooms. The last of the Hawkinfields really wants to sell—not rent—and it has great potential as a bed-and-breakfast operation. If you expressed an interest in eventually operating it as a B-and-B, Ms. Hawkinfield might consent to rent it for the summer. How about that?"

"Are you asking me to perjure myself? I have no interest in a B-and-B . . . now or at any time in the future."

"This is all off the top of my head, of course. I have no authority. Ms. Hawkinfield lives out of state. I'll have to consult with her and get back to you."

"Do that," Qwilleran said encouragingly. "As soon as possible."

"By the way, we haven't talked about the rent. How high are you prepared to go?"

"Tell me how much she wants, and we'll take it from there. I'm not hard to get along with."

Within a week the deal was sealed. The owner, who was asking $1.2 million for the property, graciously consented to rent the premises for the summer, fully furnished, to a gentleman with references and two cats, for $1,000 a week. Utilities would be provided, but he would have to pay his own telephone bills.

"It wasn't easy to convince her, but I did it!" Ms. Lessmore said proudly.

Still unaccustomed to limitless wealth, Qwilleran considered the rent exorbitant, but he was determined to go to the Potatoes, and he agreed to take the inn for three months, half the rent payable in advance. Later he would wonder why he had not asked to see a picture of the place. Instead he had allowed himself to be captivated by the agent's bubbling enthusiasm: "It's right on top of Big Potato! There's a fabulous view from every window, and gorgeous sunsets! Wide verandas, eight bathrooms, large kitchen, your own private lake! The Hawkinfields had it stocked with fish. Do you like to fish? And there are lovely walking trails in the woods . . ."

Koko was sitting near the phone, listening, and when the conversation ended Qwilleran said to him, "You'll have a choice of six bedrooms and eight bathrooms, all with a fabulous view. How does that strike you?"

"Yow," said Koko, and he groomed his paws in anticipation. Yum Yum was nowhere about. She had been sulking for days—pretending not to be hungry, sitting with her back turned, slithering out of reach when Qwilleran tried to stroke her.

"Females!" he said to Koko. "They're a conundrum!"

With the agreement signed and the deposit made, he paid a formal visit to the walnut-paneled, velvet-draped office of Hasselrich, Bennett & Barter for a conference with the venerable senior partner. A meeting with Osmond Hasselrich always began with the obligatory cup of coffee served with the formality of a Japanese tea ceremony. The attorney himself poured from an heirloom silver coffee pot into heirloom Wedgwood cups, his aged hands shaking and the cups rattling in their saucers. Their dainty handles were finger-traps, and Qwilleran was always glad when the ritual ended. When the silver tray had been removed and the attorney at last faced him across the desk with hands folded, Qwilleran began:

"After much cogitation, Mr. Hasselrich, I have decided to go away for the summer." Even after five years of business and social acquaintance, the two men still addressed each other formally. "It's my intention to distance myself totally from Moose County in order to plan my future. This agreeable community exerts a magnetic hold on me, and I need to escape its spell for a while in order to think objectively."

The attorney nodded wisely.

"I'm going to the Potato Mountains." Qwilleran paused until the legal eyelids stopped fluttering. Fluttering eyelids were the old gentleman's standard reaction to questionable information. "No one but you will have my address. I'm cutting all ties for three months. Mr. O'Dell will look after my residence as usual. Lori Bamba handles my mail and will refer urgent matters to you. All my financial affairs are in your hands, so I anticipate no problems."

"How do you intend to handle current expenses while there, Mr. Qwilleran?"

"Apart from food there will be very few expenses. I'll open a temporary checking account, and you can transfer funds to the bank down there as needed. The bank is the First Potato National of Spudsboro." Qwilleran waited for the eyelids to stop fluttering and the jowls to stop quivering. "As soon as I know my mailing address and telephone number, I'll convey that information to your office. My plan is to leave Tuesday and arrive in the Potatoes by Friday."

Although often disturbed by Qwilleran's seeming eccentricities, Hasselrich admired his concise, well-organized manner of conducting business, little realizing that his client was merely in a hurry to escape from the suffocating environment.

On Monday there was a bon voyage handshake from Arch Riker after Qwilleran promised to write a thousand words for the *Moose County Something* whenever a good subject presented itself. On Monday evening there was a farewell dinner with Polly Duncan at the Old Stone Mill, followed by a sentimental parting at her apartment.

Then, early on Tuesday morning Qwilleran packed his second-hand, three-year-old, four-cylinder, two-tone green sedan for the journey. Despite his new wealth he still spent money reluctantly on transportation. Included in the baggage were his typewriter and computerized coffeemaker, as well as a box of books and the cats' personal belongings. The Siamese observed the packing process closely, and as soon as their waterdish and pan of kitty gravel disappeared out the back door, they made themselves instantly invisible.

CHAPTER 2

When the compact four-door pulled away from the apple barn, both cats were in their carrier on the backseat, reclining on a cushion befitting their royal status, and Qwilleran was at the wheel contemplating a new adventure that might change his life. He planned to keep a diary during the journey, using the small recorder that was always in his pocket. It would capture his thoughts and impressions while driving, along with yowling remarks from the backseat, and he could add commentary when they stopped at motels. The following account was recorded on tape:

TUESDAY . . . Left Pickax at ten-thirty, a half hour later than planned. The car was packed, and I was ready to take off, when the Siamese vanished. Nothing is more exasperating than delay caused by a last-minute cat hunt. First I found Koko on a bookshelf, doing his ostrich act behind the biographies, with six inches of tail protruding from the hiding place. With him it was a game, and the tail was intended to be a clue, but Yum Yum was in deadly earnest. She was huddled on a beam under the roof, accessible only by a forty-foot ladder. Curses! Rather than call the volunteer fire department, I opened a can of cocktail shrimp with an ostentatious rattling of utensils and remarks such as "This is delicious! Would you like a *treat*, Koko?" In our household the T-word is taboo unless a treat is actually forthcoming, so it always works. After a minute or two a series of soft thumps told me the princess was on her way down from her ivory tower.

Having enjoyed their impromptu feast they hopped into their carrier, ready to hit the road. Did I say impromptu? I daresay the entire episode was plotted by those two incorrigible connivers!

To avoid tiring my passengers, who are confined to 360 square inches of cushioned luxury, I plan to limit each day's driving. At rest stops I release them from the carrier, giving them freedom to hop about the car interior, have a drink of water, and use their commode, which is placed on the floor of the backseat. At least, that's the general idea; they usually ignore their commode until we arrive at a motel. Tonight we'll stop at the Country Life Inn, which not only welcomes pets but supplies a friendly cat to any guest who wants feline company overnight. Extra charge for this, of course.

TUESDAY EVENING . . . Here we are in room 17 of the Country Life Inn. I paid for a room with two beds, and the cats immediately went to sleep on the one I intended for myself. Meanwhile, I went out and had a decent steak at a so-called family restaurant where the waitresses wear granny dresses. More families are dining out these days. I was surrounded by broods of four or six children who screamed, spilled drinks, raced up and down the aisles, threw food, and otherwise made themselves at home. A spoonful of mashed potato and gravy narrowly missed my left ear, and I determined then and there to boycott wholesome family restaurants and patronize murky dives where the waitresses wear mini-skirts and fishnet tights, where sleazy characters hang around the bar, and where all the potatoes are french fried.

WEDNESDAY . . . I gassed up and pulled away from the inn after a breakfast of buckwheat pancakes, eggs, and country sausages. (We have better sausages in Moose County.) Last night after I turned out the lights, the cats started roaming. I could hear their claws scurrying around the bathtub, and I assumed they were wrestling and having a good time. Later I discovered there was more to that caper than met the ear . . . Anyway, I fell asleep and didn't hear another sound until the car doors started slamming at 7 A.M., at which time I opened one eye and looked over at the other bed. It was empty. Both cats and one dead mouse were in bed with me! Tonight we're going to have separate rooms.

We are now approaching urban areas and driving on freeways,

and the furry folks in the backseat seem to be lulled by the steady rate of speed and drone of traffic. Or they may be drugged by the diesel fumes and broken-down oil burners on the highway.

For lunch I stopped at a fast-food restaurant and parked at the rear near the dumpsters, thinking the garbage aromas would entertain the Siamese during my absence. After releasing them from the carrier, I took care to leave the windows ajar for ventilation and lock all four doors before going in for a quick burger and fries. When I left the restaurant fifteen minutes later I could hear a horn blowing—the continuous, annoying wail of an automobile horn that's stuck—a short in the wiring or whatever. Imagine my embarrassment when I realized it was my own car! That roguish Koko was behind the wheel, standing on his hind legs, with his paws planted firmly on the horn button. As soon as he saw me, the rascal jumped into the backseat. I said, "That's a clever trick, young man, but we could all be arrested for disturbing the peace."

It was only when I fastened my seat belt and turned the ignition key that I noticed an unauthorized object on the floor. It was below the window on the passenger side. Until I reached for it I couldn't identify the thing. It was a piece of bent wire from a coat hanger. Car thieves—or worse, cat thieves—had tried to break in! I apologized to Koko . . . Was it a coincidence? Or is he now functioning as a burglar alarm? I can never be sure about that cat!

WEDNESDAY EVENING . . . We checked into our motel at four-thirty. This time I paid for two rooms, both singles. The three of us are spending the evening together in room 37, the cats huddled on the bed watching TV without the audio, while I start a Thomas Mann novel I haven't read since college. At bedtime I'll turn out the lights and slip into room 38.

THURSDAY . . . Now we've left the freeways behind. The scenery is more picturesque, but the forested hills are spoiled by billboards advertising discount stores and warehouse outlets. I went into one such store in a town called Pauper's Cove and bought a pair of slippers, having left mine in Pickax. They had two thousand pairs but only one in size twelve. The slippers weren't the color I wanted, but they were a rare bargain. Then I stopped for lunch at a local eatery and had some very good vegetable soup and cornbread. While I was eating, a guy rushed in and shouted something, and the entire place emptied—customers, cashier, cook, everyone! I followed, thinking it was an earthquake or a forest fire. But no! They were all standing around my car, peering in at the Siamese, who were leaping gracefully about the interior and striking magnificent poses. Whenever they know they have an audience, those two are shameless exhibitionists.

Before starting to drive again, I went into another discount store, just to browse. They had a good price on driving gloves, so I picked up a pair to use in Moose County next winter—that is, if I'm still in Moose County next winter. Time will tell. I may be in Alaska. Or the Canary Islands.

THURSDAY EVENING . . . Tonight I paid for two rooms at the Mountain Charm Motel, which would be improved by better plumbing and mattresses and fewer ruffles and knickknacks. When I put on my new slippers, I found out that the one I had tried on in the store was size twelve, all right, but the other was size eleven. That led me to inspect the driving gloves. They were both for the right hand! There's one thing I like about Moose County: Everyone's honest . . . Tomorrow we arrive in Potatoland.

FRIDAY . . . Last leg of our journey. Koko and Yum Yum have just had their first experience with a tunnel through a mountain. They raised holy hell until we emerged into the sunlight . . . They're getting excited. They know we're almost there.

Directional signs are beginning to assure me that Spudsboro really exists. The purplish ridges in the distance are turning into rounded mountains of misty blue, and the highway is heading toward a gap between them. Now and then it runs close to the Yellyhoo River . . . Just caught a strong whiff of pine scent from a truckload of logs coming out of the mountains . . . It's been raining here; there's a rainbow . . . We're passing a well-kept golf course, a new hospital, three fast-food palaces, a large mall. Judging by the number of car dealers, Spudsboro is booming! . . . Here we are at the city limits—time to stop talking and concentrate on my driving.

Upon arriving in the small but thriving metropolis of Spudsboro, Qwilleran found it to be a strip-city, a few blocks wide and a few miles long, wedged between two mountain ranges. Three or four winding but roughly parallel streets and a railroad track were built on a series of elevations—like shelves—following the course of the river. On one shelf a locomotive and some hopper-bottom cars were threatening to topple over on the buildings below. Qwilleran imagined the whole town might wash away downstream if hit by a hard rain.

At the residential end of Center Street a conglomeration of Victorian cottages, contemporary split-levels, and middle-aged bungalows coexisted peaceably—with the usual hanging flower baskets on porches, tricycles on lawns, and basketball hoops on garage fronts. Next came the commercial strip: stores, bars, gas stations, small office buildings, barbers, two banks, and one traffic light. Naturally Qwilleran's eye was quick to spot the newspaper office, the animal clinic, and the public library. In the center of town a miniature park was surrounded by the city hall, fire hall, police department, county courthouse, and post office. Pickets were parading in front of the courthouse, which had a golden dome too grandiose for a building of its modest size, and a police officer was issuing a parking ticket. Altogether it was a familiar small-town scene to Qwilleran, except for the mountains looming on each side of the valley.

Somewhere up there, he kept telling himself, was the hideaway where he would be living and meditating for three months. It was comforting to know that he could rely on police and fire protection; that he could take his cats to the veterinarian and his car to the garage; that he could have his hair cut and his moustache trimmed. Although he wanted to get away from it all, he was reluctant to get too far away.

At the Lessmore & Lessmore office on Center Street he angle-parked and locked all four doors, having rolled down the windows two inches with confidence that he would find no bent coat hanger on his return.

There were two enterprises sharing the building: a real estate agency and an investment counseling service. In the realty office a woman with a husky voice was talking on two telephones at once. She was on the young side of middle age, short and rather pudgy, dressed in bright green, and coiffed with an abundance of fluffy hair. On her desk was a sign that destroyed Qwilleran's preconceived notion of Dolly Lessmore: THANKS FOR NOT SMOKING.

"Ms. Lessmore?" he inquired when she had finished phoning. "I'm Jim Qwilleran."

She jumped up and trotted around the desk with bubbling energy and outstretched hand. "Welcome to Spudsboro! How was the trip? Have a chair? Where are the cats?"

"The trip was fine. The Siamese are in the car. When did you give up smoking?"

She darted a puzzled glance at her client. "How did you know? Last March a charming young doctor at the hospital gave a class in not-smoking."

"Spudsboro seems to be a lively town," he said approvingly, "and right up to the minute."

"You'll love it! And you'll love your mountain retreat! I'm sure you're anxious to see it and move in, so as soon as I make one more phone call, I'll take you up there."

"No need. You're busy. Just tell me where it is."

"Are you sure?"

"No problem whatsoever. Just steer me in the direction of Big Potato Mountain."

She pointed across the street. "There it is—straight up. Little Potato is farther downriver. I have a little map here that you can have." She unrolled a sheet of paper. "Here's Center Street, and over here is Hawk's Nest Drive. That's where you're going, although you can't get there from here—at least, not directly. When you reach Hawk's Nest Drive, just keep going uphill. It's paved all the way. And when you can't go any farther, you're there! The house is known as Tiptop, which is the name of the original inn."

The map was a labyrinth of black lines like worm tracks, peppered with numbers in fine type. "Don't any of these mountain roads have names?" Qwilleran asked.

"They don't need names. We always know where we are, where we're going, and how to get there. It may be mystifying at first, but you'll get used to it in no time. Hawk's Nest Drive is the exception to the rule; it was named by J. J. Hawkinfield when he developed Tiptop Estates."

"Is there anything I should know about the house?"

"All the utilities are connected. Bed linens and towels are in a closet upstairs. The kitchen is completely equipped, including candles in case of a power outage. There are fire extinguishers in every room, but all the fabrics and carpets are flame retardant." Ms. Lessmore handed over three keys on a ring. "These are for front and back doors and garage. We had to make some minor repairs in preparation for your arrival, and a Mr. Beechum will be around to do the finishing touches. He's one of the mountain people, but he's an excellent worker. If you need anyone to clean, there are mountain women who are glad to earn a little money. We had one of them fluff up the place yesterday. I hope she did a satisfactory job." While speaking she was swiveling and rocking her desk chair with a surplus of nervous energy.

"What's my mailing address going to be?" Qwilleran asked.

"There's no mail delivery up the mountain. You can have a rural mailbox at the foot of Hawk's Nest Drive if you wish, but for your short stay, why don't you rent a post office box?"

"And where do I buy groceries?"

"Do you cook?"

"No, but I'll need food for the cats. Mostly I prefer to eat in restaurants. Perhaps you could recommend some good ones."

At that moment a roughly handsome man in a business suit rushed into the investment office, threw a briefcase onto a desk, and started out again. "Gonna play some golf," he called out to Ms. Lessmore.

"Wait a minute, honey, I want you to meet the gentleman who's renting Tiptop. Mr. Qwilleran, this is my husband, Robert . . . Honey, he was asking about restaurants."

"Give him the blue book," he said. "That has everything. Don't plan dinner, Doll. I'll eat at the club. Nice to meet you, Mr. . . . ."

He was out on the sidewalk before Qwilleran could say "Qwilleran."

"Robert's a golf nut," his wife explained, "and we've had so much rain lately that he's been frustrated." She handed over a blue brochure. "This lists restaurants, stores, and services in Spudsboro.

If you like Italian food, try Pasta Perfect. And there's a moderate-priced steakhouse called The Great Big Baked Potato."

"And how about a grocery?"

"You'll find a small but upscale market at Five Points on your way to Hawk's Nest Drive. From here you go down Center Street until it curves to the right, then take a left at the Valley Boys' Club and wind around past the old depot, which is now an antique shop, and go uphill to Lumpton's Pizza, where you jog left—"

"Hold on," Qwilleran said. "It sounds as if you have me going west in order to go east. Run through that once more, and let me take notes."

She laughed. "If you think about east and west in the mountains, you'll go crazy. Just concentrate on left and right, and up and down." She repeated the instructions. "Then ask anyone at Five Points Market how to reach Hawk's Nest Drive. It's very well known."

"Thank you for your assistance," he said. "If I get lost I'll send up a rocket."

She escorted him hospitably to the door. "Enjoy your stay. Be sure to walk through the woods to your private lake. It's enchanting! In fact, you'll love everything about Tiptop and want to buy it before the season's over."

"If I do," Qwilleran said, "my first move will be to change its name."

Unlocking the car, he said to his passengers, "Sorry for the holdup, but we're on our way now. It won't be long before you can have a good dinner and a new house to explore."

For answer there was some stoic shuffling and squirming in the carrier.

As he started to drive, Big Potato was on his left; soon it was ahead of him; next it was on his right. Yet, he was not aware of having made any turns. It was quite different from downtown Pickax, where streets were laid out north and south and every turn was ninety degrees. He found the market at Five Points, however, and loaded a shopping cart with food for the Siamese, plus ice cream, doughnuts, and a can of pork and beans for himself.

At the checkout counter the cashier surveyed with undisguised curiosity the ten cans of red salmon, six cans of crabmeat, five frozen lobster tails, eight cans of boned chicken, and two packages of frozen jumbo shrimp. "Find everything you want?" he asked helpfully, glancing at the oversized moustache.

"Yes, you have a fine store," Qwilleran said. "Do you take traveler's checks?"

"You bet!" The young man's badge indicated that he was the manager, filling in at the cash register, and he was briskly managerial—a smiling, rosy-cheeked, well-scrubbed, wholesome type. Qwilleran thought, He runs in marathons, pumps iron, coaches basketball at the boys' club, and eats muesli. There's such a thing as looking too healthy.

"We have a good produce department," the manager said. "Just got some fresh pineapple."

"This is all I need at the moment, but I'll be back. I'm staying in the mountains for three months."

"Where are you staying?" The young man seemed genuinely friendly and not merely interested in selling pineapples.

"At a place called Tiptop. Can I get these things home before they thaw? I'm a stranger here."

"You'll be up there in ten minutes if you take the Snaggy Creek cutoff. Did you buy Tiptop?"

"No. Just renting."

As the manager totaled the array of salmon, crab, lobster, chicken, and shrimp he asked politely, "Are you with a group?"

"No, we're only a small family of three, but we like seafood and poultry."

The man nodded with understanding. "Everybody's worried about cholesterol these days. How about some oat bran cookies?"

"Next time. Tell me about this cutoff."

The manager closed the checkout counter and accompanied Qwilleran to the exit. Pointing up the hill he said, "Okay. This street winds around for half a mile and dead-ends at a pond. That's really Snaggy Creek, swollen by the heavy rain. Turn left there and go to the fork. Okay? Take the right spur. It goes downhill, which may look wrong, but don't try to figure it out. Just remember: the *right spur*. Okay? After you cross a culvert—the water's pretty high there—watch for some wet rocks on the left and immediately turn right across a small bridge. Okay? About two-tenths of a mile farther on, there's another fork . . ."

Qwilleran was scribbling frantically.

"That's the simplest and fastest way to go," the manager assured him. "You won't have any trouble. By the way, my name's Bill Treacle. I'm the manager."

"I'm Jim Qwilleran. Thanks for the directions."

"Hope we have some good weather for you."

"It's more humid than I expected," Qwilleran said.

"That's very unusual, but the weatherman has promised us a nice weekend." Treacle helped load the groceries into the trunk, exclaimed over the Siamese, and said a cheery "Hurry back!"

Two hours later Qwilleran was cursing the friendly Bill Treacle and his Snaggy Creek cutoff. Either the man had misdirected him, or someone had moved the spurs, forks, culverts, bridges, and wet rocks. There was nothing remotely resembling a paved road that might be Hawk's Nest Drive. There were no road signs of any kind, and for the last hour there had been no signs of life, on foot or on wheel. He could no longer see Spudsboro down in the valley.

"Don't tell me I'm on the *outside* of the mountain!" he shouted in exasperation. "How did I land on the other side without going over the top or through a tunnel? Does anybody know?"

"Yow-ow!" said Koko with the infuriating authority of one who has all the answers.

The dirt road Qwilleran was now following was merely a narrow ledge between a towering cliff and a steep drop-off, with no guardrails even at hazardous hairpin turns. Gouged by tires during the recent wet spell, it had been blow-dried by mountain winds into treacherous ruts, bumps, and potholes. The ice cream was melting in the trunk; the frozen shrimp were thawing, but Qwilleran cared little about that. He simply wanted to arrive somewhere—anywhere—before dark and before the gas tank registered empty. Suddenly visibility was zero as he drove into a low-flying cloud. And all the time the Siamese were howling and shrieking in the backseat.

"Shut up, dammit!" he bellowed at them.

At that moment the bouncing, shuddering sedan emerged from the cloud and headed into someone's front yard. Qwilleran jammed on the brakes.

It was only a rough clearing. An old army vehicle and a rusty red pickup with one blue fender were parked in front of a weatherbeaten dwelling that was somewhat more than a shack but considerably less than a house. Two nondescript dogs came out from under the porch with a menacing swagger like a pair of goons. If they had barked, someone might have come forth to answer Qwilleran's question, but they watched in threatening silence from a distance of ten feet. There were no other signs of life. Even in the backseat there was a palpable silence. After a reasonable wait he opened the car door cautiously and stepped out in slow motion. The watchdogs continued to watch.

"Good dogs! Good dogs!" he said in a friendly tone as he proceeded toward the house with his hands in his pockets. Through the open windows and half-opened door he could hear a sound of muffled beating. With a certain amount of suspicion he mounted three sagging wood steps to a rickety porch and rapped on the door. The beating stopped, and a shrill voice shouted some kind of question.

"Hello there!" he replied in the same amiable tone he had used to address the watchdogs.

A moment later the door was flung wide and he was confronted by a hollow-cheeked, hollow-eyed young woman with long, straight hair cascading over her shoulders. She said nothing but gave him a hostile glare.

"Excuse me," he said in a manner intended to be disarming. "I've lost my way. I'm looking for Hawk's Nest Drive."

She regarded him with indecision, as if wondering whether to reach for a shotgun.

"You're on the wrong mountain!" she snapped.

CHAPTER 3

The mountain woman with hollow cheeks and sunken eyes stood with her hands on her hips and glared at Qwilleran. Assuming—from his astonished expression—that he had not heard the first time, she screamed, "You're on the wrong mountain!" Then, half turning, she shouted something over her shoulder, after which she pushed past him, grumbling, "Follow me." She was wearing grubby jogging shoes and a long, full skirt, and with skirt and long hair flying she leaped off the porch, ignoring the steps. Before Qwilleran had sense enough to return to his own car, she had started the sputtering motor of the pickup.

The ordeal of the last two hours had been stupefying, but now he gathered his wits and followed the other vehicle gratefully as it led the way back down the narrow road to a fork, where it turned onto an upbound trail. The lead vehicle was a modified pickup with the chassis elevated high above the wheels to cope with rough terrain like this, but Qwilleran's sedan bounced in and out of ruts, causing non-stop complaints from the backseat.

"Quiet!" he scolded.

"Yow!" Koko scolded in eloquent rebuttal.

The route meandered left and right and dipped in and out of gullies. There was one hopeful sign, however; Spudsboro was again visible in the valley, meaning they were back on the inside of the mountain. When they finally reached a paved road, the woman stopped her truck and leaned from the driver's seat, shouting something.

Jumping out of his car, Qwilleran hurried in her direction, saying, "How can I thank you, ma'am? May I—"

"Just get out of my way," she growled, revving the motor and making a reckless U-turn.

"Which way is up?" he called to her as she drove away. At least he was now on solid blacktop, and if "up" proved to be "down," he had only to turn around and drive in the opposite direction, assuming there was gas enough in the tank. This was the route he should have discovered two hours ago. There were hairpin turns, but the road's edge was marked by white lines and protected by guardrails, and double yellow lines separated the upbound and downbound lanes. The speed limit was posted, as well as warnings about dense fog, fallen rocks, and icy bridges. A creek, rushing alongside the road, occasionally disappeared and emerged somewhere else. At one point Qwilleran met a sheriff's car coming downhill, and he returned the stare of the officer behind the wheel.

Around the next bend he came upon a handsome house in a carefully landscaped clearing, its many levels ingeniously designed for a hillside. Large glass areas overlooked the valley. The russet stain on the board-and-batten exterior looked appropriately woodsy but failed to conceal that this was an architect-designed residence with a three-car garage and a swimming pool. In slowing down to observe the details, Qwilleran was able to read a rustic signboard: SEVEN LEVELS ....THE LESSMORES.

Farther up the mountain another impressive house was designed with cedar boards applied diagonally to form a herringbone pattern. A satellite dish faced a wide swath cut in the forest. The rustic signboard read: THE RIGHT SLANT ....DEL AND ARDIS WIL-BANK.

Hawk's Nest Drive climbed higher and higher, hugging roadside cliffs crowned with trees that were losing their footing and leaning precariously over the pavement. With every turn Koko yowled vociferously and Yum Yum made threatening intestinal noises as their bodies swerved left, right, left, right . . .

Suddenly Tiptop burst into view, brooding above them on a rocky knoll. The clamor in the backseat stopped abruptly, and Qwilleran stared through the windshield in disbelief. He had expected it to be more cheerful, more hospitable. Instead, Tiptop was a dark, glowering, uninviting building in a gray-green stain, the upper floor sided in gray-green fishscale clapboard. The main floor windows were shaded by a gray-green wrap-around veranda, while second floor windows and attic dormers were darkened by deeply overhanging roofs.

"Great!" Qwilleran muttered as he parked in a blacktopped area large enough for ten cars. "Don't go away," he said to his caged passengers. "I'll be right back." It was his custom to check for hazards and feline escape routes before introducing the Siamese to a new environment. Slowly, noting every dismal detail, he walked toward a gray stone arch inset with a mosaic of darker pebbles spelling out TIPTOP INN—1903. From there a broad flight of stone steps—he counted eighteen—led up to the inn, and seven wooden steps painted battleship gray led up to the veranda.

Unlocking one of the French doors that marked the main entrance, Qwilleran walked into a dark foyer—a wide central hall running the length of the building and ending in more French doors at the rear. Their glass panes did little to lighten the foyer, and he switched on lights—three chandeliers and six wall sconces. He flipped switches in the surrounding rooms also—a cavernous living room, a dining room that seated twelve, a hotel-sized kitchen—thankful that electricity was included in the rent.

Next he opened a window to freshen the deadness of the atmosphere and discovered there were no screens to keep the Siamese from jumping out. This was another mark against the place. They liked to sit on a windowsill sniffing the breeze, yet not a single window was screened. In each room he lowered the sash a few inches at the top for ventilation. This done, he brought the cats and their baggage into the kitchen, fed them a can of salmon hurriedly, and pointed out the location of their waterdish and commode in the pantry.

For himself he brought in the computerized coffeemaker without which he never left home. Although he had been obliged to swear off alcohol and had been convinced by an attractive woman M.D. in Pickax to give up smoking, he still insisted upon his coffee; he liked it strong and he liked it often. Carrying a cupful of the brew and with apologies to the Siamese for leaving them in the kitchen, he now wandered through the house with a critical eye. During his days as a roving news correspondent, checking in and out of hotels, his environment had meant little, but his changing circumstances in recent years had given him an awareness of pleasant living quarters.

The interior of Tiptop, though obviously redecorated not too long ago, was depressingly gray: gray plush carpet, gray damask draperies, wallcoverings predominantly gray. Certain items of massive furniture, circa 1903, were appropriate in sixty-foot rooms with ten-foot ceilings, but they were grotesque in design. More attractive were the sofas, chairs, and tables added by recent owners, and yet the rooms looked bleak, as if deliberately stripped of all small objects. There were sculpture pedestals without sculpture, plant stands without plants, bookcases without books, vitrines without curios, china cabinets without china, and lamp tables without lamps. Pictures had been removed, leaving hooks and discolored rectangles on the walls.

And for this, Qwilleran thought, I'm paying $1,000 a week!

Only one picture remained, a painting of mountains, hung in the foyer over a chest on which were a telephone and a phone directory. He looked up the numbers of the Lessmore office and residence and left the identical message in both places: "Tiptop has been burglarized!" Hurried visits to the six bedrooms upstairs and the recreation room on the lower level confirmed the fact. Even the three fireplaces were stripped.

Meanwhile, impatient cries were coming from the kitchen. "Sorry! Sorry!" he apologized to the rampant Siamese. "Now it's your turn to explore. I hope you like it better than I do."

They entered the dining room warily, slinking under the table in search of crumbs, although the house had been empty for a year. Then Yum Yum sniffed an invisible spot on the carpet in front of the massive buffet while Koko rose effortlessly and silently to the serving surface. Once upon a time, Qwilleran imagined, it had groaned under platters of roast pheasant, chafing dishes bubbling with lobster thermidor, and eight-gallon bowls of brandy punch. That was almost a century ago, but it was no secret to Koko.

In the foyer Yum Yum discovered the balustered staircase and ran up and down like a pianist practicing scales. Koko was attracted to the painting of mountains and jumped to the top of the chest in order to rub his jaw against a corner of the frame.

"Please! Let's not move any mountains," Qwilleran pleaded as he straightened the picture. He had never decided whether Koko had an appreciation of art or a perpetually itchy jaw.

The staircase was wide and well-proportioned for the spacious foyer, which had a group of inviting chairs around a stone fireplace. On either side of the entrance were two old-fashioned hat-and-umbrella stands with clouded mirrors, a couple of tired umbrellas, and some stout walking sticks for tramping about the woods. The most conspicuous item in the foyer, however, was the bulky and unattractive chest holding the telephone. Alongside it were a pair of Queen Anne side chairs matching the ten in the dining room, and above it hung the painting of a mountain range. A very good painting, Qwilleran thought; it expressed the mystery that he sensed about mountains.

Yum Yum had now ventured into the living room and was stretched on an upholstered chair in what Qwilleran called her Cleopatra pose. Koko followed her but went directly to a tall secretary desk that had empty bookshelves in the upper half. He craned his neck and mumbled to himself as if questioning the absence of books; he was an avid bibliophile.

"Okay, let's go!" said Qwilleran, clapping his hands for attention. "Let's go upstairs and see where you guys are going to bunk."

Neither of them paid the slightest heed. He had to carry them from the room, one under each arm. When they reached the staircase, however, Koko squirmed out of his grasp and headed toward the rear of the foyer. First he examined a Queen Anne chair, passing his nose up and down the legs, and then the frame of a French door, which looked newly painted.

"That's enough. Let's go," Qwilleran insisted. "You've got three months to sniff paint."

On the second floor there were two bedrooms at the rear that would get the morning sun, and the view was a breathtaking panorama of distant hills, a panorama unbroken by billboards, power lines, transmitter towers, or other signs of civilization. One of the rooms had a giant four-poster bed, a good-sized desk, and a pair of lounge chairs that appealed to Qwilleran. The back bedroom across the hall would be good for the Siamese. He put their blue cushion on the bed and left them there to explore their new surroundings while he made up his bed and hung towels in the bathroom.

Then he turned his attention to the upstairs hall, a kind of lounge where guests of the inn, once upon a time, may have been served their morning coffee. Here the gray walls were covered with memorabilia in the form of framed documents and photographs, items of no value to the thieves who had stripped the house. In old, faded photos (circa 1903) there were stiffly formal men in three-piece suits and derby hats sitting in rocking chairs on the porch, while women in ankle-length dresses and enormous hats played croquet on the lawn. Also exhibited in narrow black frames were photographs of present-day celebrities with inscriptions to "J.J."

Of chief interest to Qwilleran was a clipping from the *Spudsboro Gazette* dating back only a few years. It was a column called "Potato Peelings" written by one Vonda Dudley Wix in a cloyingly outdated style. Yet it contained information of historic importance. The copy read:

The fashionable past of our lush and lovely mountain is about to be revived, gentle reader, in a way unheard of in 1903. In that memorable year the Tiptop Inn opened its snazzy French doors to a galaxy of well-heeled guests. Those were days of pomp and circumstance (ta-da! ta-da!), and the gilt-edged elite arrived by train from New York, Washington, and Chicago, some of them in their poshly private railway cars. (Sorry. No names.) They were transported up the mountain to the exclusive resort in sumptuous carriages driven by Dickensian coachmen in red velvet coats and top hats.

There they spent a gloriously sybaritic week in salubrious surroundings (look that up in your Webster, dears). The emphasis was on dining well (no one had heard of calories), but they also strolled along mountain paths or played battledore and shuttlecock (fun!) after which they relaxed on the endless veranda or repaired to the game room for some naughty gambling. Throughout the week they were pampered by an attentive staff, including an English majordomo, a French chef, and a bevy of Irish maids. (Oh, those Irish maids!) During the ten-course dinners a violinist played "Barcarolle" and Schubert's "Serenade" (what else?), after which the evening musicale featured art songs by an oh-so-lyric soprano.

So, you are asking, what happened? . . . Well, the stock market went *boom,* and the richly rich stopped coming to Tiptop. A prolonged Depression and World War II delivered the *coup de grâce* to the poor old inn. After that it was owned by a Philadelphia bank for many cruel, cruel years, during which it was boarded up and sadly forgotten.

Then, in the 1950s, the inn was purchased, along with most of Big Potato Mountain, by Otis Hawkinfield, the highly respected owner òf the *Spudsboro Gazette*, as a summer retreat. After his death his son (whom we all know and love as J.J.) refurbished the inn as a permanent home for his lovely wife and their four beautiful children. Fortune did not smile on them, alas, but let us skip swiftly to today's happy news.

J.J. Hawkinfield has announced his intention to share Big Potato Mountain with the world! (Bless you, J.J.!)

"For two generations," he announced in an interview today, "the Hawkinfields have been privileged to enjoy this sublime mountain environment. I can no longer be selfish, however, about the spectacular views, the summer breezes, the good mountain water, the wooded trails, and the breathtaking waterfalls. The time has come to share it with my fellow citizens." (Cheers! Cheers!)

Yes! J.J. and a syndicate of investors plan to develop the inside of Big Potato for family living. The approach road has already been paved, and architects are working on plans for year-round homes to be built on lots of no less than three acres, in designs integrated with the mountain terrain.

Boasted J.J. with excusable pride, "I believe that Frank Lloyd Wright would approve of what we are about to do." (Hear! Hear!)

Future plans call for a campground for prestige-type recreation vehicles, offering such facilities as a swimming pool, hot tubs, and tennis courts. (That's class, my friends!) Condominiums and a mountaintop high-rise hotel with helicopter pad are also envisioned by J.J.

"Eventually," he revealed, "the outer slopes of Big Potato will have a ski lodge and several ski runs. What I have in mind is the economic growth and health of the entire valley, as well as an opportunity for all to share in sports, recreation, and the joys of nature."

"Oh, sure," Qwilleran said aloud, huffing cynically into his moustache. "Frank Lloyd Wright was probably throwing up in his grave!" He had another look at the framed photographs of celebrities. Many of them were posed with a man having a prominent nose and a high forehead. That, he guessed, was J.J. Hawkinfield "whom we all know and love" and who probably died of an overdose of compassion for his fellow citizens.

At that moment he was summoned to the telephone.

"How's everything at Tiptop?" asked Dolly Lessmore's cheery voice.

"Didn't you get my message? The place has been ransacked," Qwilleran said.

"Sorry, I neglected to tell you, but Ms. Hawkinfield was very close to her mother and wanted some family mementos—things that her mother loved so much."

"Like the television? That's gone, too."

"I didn't realize that. Well . . . we have an extra TV you can borrow for the summer."

"Never mind. I don't watch TV. The cats enjoy it, but they can live without the summer reruns."

"But you do understand about the accessories, don't you? Ms. Hawkinfield couldn't bear the thought of her mother's favorite things going to strangers who might purchase the house."

"Okay, I'll accept that. I just wanted you to know that they weren't here when I moved in. Not even any fireplace equipment."

"Is everything else all right?"

"One question," Qwilleran said. "When we discussed this place on the phone, did you say it was *roomy* or *gloomy*? Either you're going to run up an enormous electric bill, or the cats and I are going to turn into moles."

"Today wasn't terribly sunny," the realty agent explained, "and you have to remember that twilight comes earlier in the mountains. Ordinarily the light is so bright on the mountaintop that you'll be glad the windows are shaded by a veranda. Did you find the bed linens and towels all right?"

"I went through the entire linen closet," Qwilleran said irritably, "and there was not a single plain sheet. They're all loaded with lace!"

Ms. Lessmore's voice registered shock. "You don't like it? That's all handmade lace! Those bed linens were Mrs. Hawkinfield's pride and joy!"

"Then why didn't her daughter take them?" he snapped. "Sorry. Forget I said that. You'll have to excuse me. I'm tired tonight. I've been traveling for four days with two temperamental backseat drivers."

"You'll get a good night's rest and feel better tomorrow," she said encouragingly. "Mountain air is great for sleeping."

After hanging up the phone Qwilleran had an overwhelming urge to call someone in Moose County. Whether he knew it or not, the loneliness of a mountaintop and the emptiness of the house were making him homesick. Polly Duncan's number was the one that came promptly to mind. The chief librarian was the major link in the chain that bound him to Moose County, although the link had been weakened since her acquisition of a Siamese kitten named Bootsie. Her obsessive concern and maudlin affection for that cat made Qwilleran feel that he was sharing her with a rival. Furthermore, he considered "Bootsie" a frivolous name for a pedigreed Siamese with the appetite of a Great Dane, and he had told Polly so.

Now, consulting his watch, he was inclined to wait until the maximum discount rates went into effect. Despite his net worth and his extravagance in feeding the Siamese, he was thrifty about long-distance calls, and phone service was not included in the rent. He invited the Siamese into his bedroom for a read.

"Book!" he announced loudly, and they came running. They always listened raptly as if they comprehended the meaning of his words, although more likely they were mesmerized by his melodious reading voice. Being unable to find an ottoman anywhere in the house (that woman, he was sure, had taken the ottomans, too), he pulled up a second lounge chair and propped his feet on it.

Then, with Yum Yum on his lap and Koko on the arm of his chair, he read about a fellow who went to the mountains for a few weeks and stayed seven years.

He read until eleven o'clock, at which time he telephoned Polly Duncan at her apartment in Pickax City. It was a carriage house apartment, and he had spent many contented hours there—contented, that is, until the unfortunate advent of Bootsie.

"Qwill, I'm so glad to hear your voice," she said in the pleasing, well-modulated tones that made his skin tingle. "I wondered when you were going to call, dear. How was the trip?"

"Uneventful, for the most part. We had a little difficulty in finding the top of the mountain, but we're here with our sanity intact."

"What is your house like?"

"It's an architectural style called Musty Rustic. I'll be able to appraise it more objectively when I've had a good night's sleep. How's everything in Pickax?" he asked.

"Dr. Goodwinter's wife finally died. She was buried today."

"How long had she been ill?"

"Fifteen years, ten of them bedridden. Just about everyone in the county attended the funeral—as a tribute to Dr. Hal. He's dearly loved—the last of the old-fashioned country doctors. We're all wondering if he'll retire now."

Qwilleran's mind leaped to Melinda Goodwinter, the young doctor with green eyes and long lashes, who had cured him of pipe smoking. Had she returned to Pickax for her mother's funeral? He hesitated to inquire. She had been Polly's predecessor in his affections, and Polly was inordinately jealous. Approaching the question obliquely he remarked, "I never knew if the Goodwinters had many children."

"Only Melinda. She came from Boston for the funeral. There's speculation that she might stay and take over her father's practice."

Qwilleran recognized the possibility as a hot potato and changed the subject. "How's Bootsie?"

"You'll be glad to know I've thought of a new name for him. What do you think of Bucephalus?"

"It sounds like a disease."

"Bucephalus," Polly said indignantly, "was the favorite horse of Alexander the Great. He was a noble beast."

"You don't need to tell me that. The name still sounds like a disease, although I agree that Bootsie eats like a horse. Back to the drawing board, Polly."

"Oh, Qwill! You're so hard to please," she protested. "How do the cats like the mountains? Does the altitude affect them?"

"They seem happy. We're reading *The Magic Mountain*."

"Do you have a good view? Don't forget to send me some snapshots."

"We have a spectacular view. The place is called Tiptop, but if I owned it, I'd name it Hawk's Nest."

"You're not thinking of buying, are you?" she asked with concern.

"I make quick decisions, but not that quick, Polly! I arrived only a couple of hours ago. First I have to get some sleep, and then go into Spudsboro tomorrow to do some errands. Also I've got to learn how to drive in these mountains. One drives south in order to go north, and down in order to go up."

The two of them chattered on with companionable familiarity until Qwilleran started worrying about his phone bill. They ended their visit with the usual murmur: "À bientôt."

"That was Polly," he said to Koko, who was sitting next to the telephone. "Bootsie sends his regards."

"Yow," said Koko, batting an ear with his paw.

Qwilleran went outdoors and paced the veranda that circled the entire house, wondering why he was here alone when he had been so comfortable in Moose County among friends. From the front veranda he could see across the dark treetops to the valley, where pinpoints of light traced the city of Spudsboro. Directly below him the mountainside was dotted with the high-powered yardlights of the houses on Hawk's Nest Drive. One bank of lights flooded a swimming pool like a baseball diamond illuminated for a night game.

Elsewhere, the view was one of total darkness, except for a circle of light toward the south. It appeared to be on a nearby mountain, and the circle appeared to be revolving. Qwilleran went indoors for his binoculars and trained them on the circle. It was definitely moving—a phenomenon that would bear investigation.

A chill wind was stirring, and he retired for his first overnight on Big Potato.

CHAPTER 4

Qwilleran took a few precautions before falling into the arms of Morpheus. It was June, and the sun would be rising early; that meant the Siamese would be awake at dawn, clamoring for their breakfast. Fortunately there were blinds on the bedroom windows—opaque, room-darkening roller blinds. Qwilleran pulled them down in the cats' quarters as well as in his own—four in each room. He also took care to leave their door open so they could go downstairs to the pantry and the turkey roaster that served as their commode. It was a long walk to the pantry, and they really needed a second commode, he thought. He added "turkey roaster" to his shopping list for the next day. There was nothing like a turkey roaster, he had discovered, for a non-tip, rustproof, easy-to-clean, long-lasting litterbox.

He expected to sleep well in the fresh mountain atmosphere. There were many claims made for living at high altitudes, he recalled as he started to doze off: People who live in the mountains are nicer . . . They live longer because the water and air are so pure . . . Heavy drinkers have fewer hangovers in the mountains . . .

He slept fairly well, considering the strange bed and the lace on the sheets and pillowcases. Whenever he shifted position he felt an alien substance under his chin. Nevertheless, he managed well enough until about five-thirty. At that early hour he was jolted awake.

Was it a gunshot? It brought him to a sitting position even before his eyes were open. At the sound of the second shot he was wide awake! The realization that it was happening *inside the house* catapulted him from the bed just as the third shot rang out! He dashed for the door, fearing for the cats and unmindful of his own safety. He yanked open the door in time to hear the fourth shot!

At that moment he realized it was not gunfire. Two Siamese were walking triumphantly from their sleeping quarters, tails waving. Early morning light was streaming into their room, turning everything rosy. All four window shades were raised!

"You devils!" Qwilleran muttered, shuffling back to his bed. One of them—no doubt Yum Yum the Paw—had discovered how to raise a roller blind with an explosive report. Simply insert a paw in the pull-ring . . . release it . . . and BANG! Up it goes! He had to admit it was a smart maneuver.

Two hours later it was the noisy motor of an aging truck that disturbed his sleep. Checking the parking lot from a second floor window, he saw a bearded man stepping out of a red pickup with one blue fender. His beard was untamed, and he wore old-fashioned striped railroad overalls and a wide-brimmed felt fedora that was green with age. Collecting paint buckets from the truck bed, he walked slowly toward the stone steps with a hitch in his gait. Hurriedly Qwilleran pulled on some clothes and met the workman on the veranda.

"Good morning," he said to the stranger. "Nice day, isn't it? A bit coolish, but fresh." He had lived in Moose County long enough to know about weather as a form of introduction.

"Gonna rain, come nightfall," said the workman. "Gonna be a gully-washer."

"How do you know?" The air was crisp; there was not a cloud in the sky; the mountains were sharply defined. "What makes you think we'll get rain?"

"Earthworms comin' up. See'd a black snake in a tree." The man's face was a crinkled, weatherbeaten tan, but his eyes were keen. "Gittin' too doggone much rain in these parts."

"Are you Mr. Beechum?"

"Dewey Beechum, come to finish up," he said as he started around the veranda toward the rear.

Qwilleran followed. "What needs to be finished?"

They had reached the rear of the house, and Mr. Beechum nodded toward the railing of the veranda. "That there back rail, and that there glass door." He nodded toward the French door that Koko had sniffed the night before.

"What happened to the door?" Qwilleran asked.

"Busted." He applied a final coat of stain to a section of railing and then painted the framework around the small glass panes of the door—without using a dropcloth and without a spill or a smear.

"You do good work, Mr. Beechum."

"Don't pay to do bad. See that there chair?" He nodded toward the Queen Anne chair in the foyer. "Legs was busted, but I fixed 'em. Never know they was busted."

That explained Koko's interest in the chair and the French door; one of them had recently varnished legs, and the other had new glass and a coat of fresh paint on the frame. Clever cat! He never missed a thing. He even knew that the tall secretary desk in the living room was supposed to have books in its upper deck.

"Do you live around here?" Qwilleran asked.

Beechum jerked his head to the south. "Yonder on L'il Tater. That there's a real mount'n."

"Big Potato looks pretty good to me."

"Ain't what it was, years back."

"What happened?"

"Folks from down there"—he nodded toward the valley—"they come up here and rooned it, cuttin' down trees, buildin' fancy houses, roonin' the waterfalls. No tellin' what they'll be roonin' nextways. But they won't git L'il Tater iffen we hafta hold 'em off with shotguns!"

"Good for you!" Qwilleran always agreed heartily with anyone he was trying to encourage, and already he envisioned Mr. Beechum as a colorful subject for a column in the *Moose County Something*. "I've been thinking, Mr. Beechum, that I'd like to have a gazebo built among the trees."

"A what?"

"A small summer house—just a floor and a roof and screens on all four sides. I don't think it would ruin anything."

"Don't need no screens up here. No bugs."

How could Qwilleran explain to this mountain man that the

gazebo was for the cats, so they could enjoy the outdoors in safety? "Just the same," he said, "I'd feel more comfortable with screens. Could you build it for me?"

"How big you want?"

"Perhaps ten or twelve feet square."

"Twelve's better. No waste."

"May I pay you in advance for the materials?"

"Ain't no need."

"I'd appreciate it if you'd use that treated lumber that doesn't need painting."

"That's what I'm aimin' to do."

"Good! We're on the same wavelength. When can you start, Mr. Beechum?"

"When you be wantin' it?"

"Soon as possible."

The workman raised his green fedora and scratched his head. There was a line of demarcation across his forehead—weather-beaten tan below, pasty white above. "Mebbe Monday," he said.

"That sounds good."

"Mebbe Wednesday. All depends. Could rain." Beechum started back to the pickup with his paint buckets and brushes.

Accompanying him down the steps Qwilleran took another look at the red pickup with one blue fender and said, "I believe I stopped at your house last night, Mr. Beechum, when I was trying to find my way here. A young woman kindly came to my rescue. I'd like to thank her in some way."

"Don't need no thanks," the man mumbled as he started the reluctant motor.

Qwilleran returned to the house to feed the cats, prepare some coffee for himself, and dress for a shopping trip to Spudsboro. Saying goodbye to the Siamese he inquired, "Will you characters be all right if I go out for a while?" They regarded him with a blank feline stare capable of undermining self-esteem. He knew that look. It meant, Just be sure you come back at dinnertime.

Before descending the twenty-five steps to the parking lot, he stood on the veranda and absorbed the view. Directly below him were treetops and an occasional odd-shaped roof or turquoise swimming pool. In the valley the dome of the courthouse glistened in the sunlight, and a meandering line of trees marked the course of the Yellyhoo River. Across the river the West Potatoes rose majestically. He snapped a few pictures to send to Polly and then walked down the steps, wondering if his car would start, and if he still had a jigger of gas in the tank, and if one could safely coast down the mountain to a gas station in the valley.

There was no cause for concern; the small car could run on a thimbleful. Maneuvering it around the curves of Hawk's Nest Drive he was thankful for the smooth pavements, the guardrails, and the white and yellow lines. He passed the Wilbank and Lessmore houses and other contemporary dwellings with glass where one would expect walls—and walls where one would expect glass. All had neat, circular drives, blacktopped. In one large area cleared of trees a new house was being built, and a powerful backhoe was gouging out the hillside. At the bottom of the hill the entrance to Hawk's Nest Drive was marked by two stone pylons and a sign: TIPTOP ESTATES . . . PRIVATE ROAD.

Qwilleran filled his gas tank and asked for foolproof directions to Five Points—without shortcuts—and was amazed how easily he found the star-shaped intersection. At the Five Points Café he sat in a booth, ordered ham and eggs, and perused the *Spudsboro Gazette*, in which the headline news was Friday's excessive rain, seven inches in two hours. The river was running high, and the softball field on the west bank was too wet for play. Otherwise, Colin Carmichael's newspaper was similar to the *Moose County Something*, although it surprised Qwilleran to learn that the "Potato Peelings" column was still being written by Vonda Dudley Wix. She was gushing about Father's Day.

The radio at the restaurant was playing country music and advertising a sale of recliners at a local furniture store, and in an adjoining booth three men were arguing over their coffee.

A voice with a nasal twang said, "I see the damned pickets came crawling out of the woodwork again."

"They're there every Friday afternoon and Saturday," said another man with a high-pitched voice. "They're trying to embarrass the city when the weekend tourists arrive."

"There oughta be a law!"

"Ever hear of freedom of speech, Jerry?" This voice sounded somewhat familiar to Qwilleran. "It's their constitutional right. I'd carry a picket sign myself if I had a legitimate beef. Okay?"

The second speaker said, "The trouble is—things are going so good in this town. Why do they have to make waves?"

"They're a bunch of radicals, that's why!" said Jerry. "That whole crowd on Little Potato is radical to the eyebrows!"

"Oh, come off it, Jerry. Okay?"

"I mean it! Always trying to sabotage progress. Just because they live like bums, they don't want the rest of us to live nice and make a little money."

"Listen, Jerry, there should be a way to live nice without spoiling it for everybody else. Okay? Look what happened to the road up Big Potato! They call it Hawk's Nest Drive and put up a sign to keep people out. That's no private road! That's a secondary county highway, and they can't legally stop anybody from driving up there. When I was a kid, my dad used to drive us to the top of Big Potato where the old inn is, and we'd have picnics at Batata Falls. That was before they dammed it and made it Lake Batata. In those days it was nothing but a dirt road. Then J.J. pulled strings and got it paved at taxpayers' expense, after which they try to call it a private drive. I'm gonna get a picket sign myself one of these days. Okay?"

"Bill's right, Jerry. J.J. started it, and now his cronies are selling timber rights and slashing the forest for a motel or hotel or something. Investors, they call 'em. Not even local people!"

"Whoever they are, it's good for the economy," Jerry insisted. "It creates jobs and brings more people in. You paint more houses, and Bill sells more hot dogs, and I sell more hardware."

"Speaking of hot dogs," Bill said, "I've gotta get back to the store. See you loafers next week—okay?" As he paid for his coffee on the way out, Qwilleran recognized the manager of the Five Points Market and would have relished a few words with him about the Snaggy Creek cutoff, but Bill Treacle slipped out too quickly.

Qwilleran himself left the café soon afterward and drove downtown. He parked and walked along Center Street, noting the new brick sidewalks, ornamental trees, and simulated gaslights. Approaching the Lessmore agency, he thought of stopping to ask a couple of questions: Would there be any objection to a gazebo? What were the revolving lights on the mountain? The office was closed, however. Generally, Center Street had the deserted air of a downtown business district on Saturday when everyone is at the mall. There was no one but Qwilleran to read the picket signs in front of the courthouse: SAVE OUR MOUNTAIN . . . NO MORE SLASHING . . . STOP THE RAPE . . . FREE FOREST.

At the office of the *Spudsboro Gazette* a Saturday calm prevailed, and when he asked for Mr. Carmichael, the lone woman in the front office pointed down a corridor.

The editor was in his office, talking to a law enforcement officer, but he jumped up exclaiming, "You must be Jim Qwilleran! I recognized the moustache. This is our sheriff, Del Wilbank . . . Del, this is the man who's renting Tiptop for the summer. Jim Qwilleran used to cover the police beat for newspapers around the country. He also wrote a book on urban crime."

"Am I intruding?" Qwilleran asked.

"No, I was just leaving," said the sheriff. He turned to the editor. "Don't touch this thing, Colin. Don't even consider it—at this time. Agreed?"

"You have my word, Del. Thanks for coming in."

The sheriff nodded to Qwilleran. "Enjoy your stay, Mr. . . . ."

"Qwilleran."

The editor, a fortyish man with thinning hair and a little too much weight, came around the desk and pumped his visitor's hand. "When Kip told me you were coming, I flipped! You were my hero when I was in J school, Qwill. Okay if I call you Qwill? In fact, your book was required reading. I remember the title, *City of Brotherly Crime*. Dolly told me you were renting Tiptop. How do you like it? Have a chair."

"I came to see if I could take you to lunch," Qwilleran said.

"Absolutely not! I'll take *you* to lunch. We'll go to the golf club, and now's a good time to go, before the rush. My car's parked in back."

On the way to the club Carmichael pointed out the new public

library, the site of a proposed community college, a modern pap-
ermill, a church of unconventional design. "This is a yuppie town,
Qwill. Most all the movers and shakers are young, energetic, and
ambitious."

"I noticed a lot of expensive cars on Center Street," Qwilleran
said, "and a lot of small planes at the airport."

"Absolutely! The town's booming. I bought at the right time.
The furniture factory is being automated. An electronics firm is
building downriver and will be on-line this year. Any chance you'd
like to relocate in Spudsboro? Kip said you took early retirement.
There's plenty to do here—fishing, white-water rafting, golf, back-
packing, tennis . . . My kids love it."

"To be frank, Colin, I plan to be the solitary, sedentary type this
summer. I have some serious thinking to do, and I thought a mountaintop would be ideal. How about you? What brought you and
your family to Spudsboro?"

"Well, my wife and I had been hoping to find a smaller, healthier
community to bring up our kids, and then this opportunity popped
up. I'd always wanted to manage my own newspaper. Don't we
all? So when the owner of the *Gazette* died and it went on the
block, I grabbed it, although I may be in hock for the next twenty
years."

"Are you talking about J.J. Hawkinfield?"

"He's the one! It's his house you're staying in. My kids wanted
me to buy that, too, but they were asking too much money for it,
and we don't need all that space. We're better off with a ranch
house in the valley. And who knows if the school bus could get
up the mountain in bad weather—or if we could get down?"

When they arrived at the golf club, groups were pouring into
the clubhouse. Saturday lunch, it appeared, was the accepted way
to entertain in Spudsboro. Men wore blazers in pastel colors.
Women dressed to outdo each other, one of them actually wearing
a hat. Altogether they were far different from the sweaters-and-
cords crowd that patronized restaurants in Moose County. There
were club-shirted golfers as well, but most of them walked through
the dining room to a noisy bar in the rear, called the Off-Links
Lounge.

Carmichael ordered a Bloody Mary, and Qwilleran ordered the same without the vodka.

"How do you like Tiptop?" the editor asked.

"It's roomy, to say the least. Something smaller would have been preferable, but I have two cats, and no one accepts pets in rental units. Dolly Lessmore twisted an arm or two to get me into Tiptop."

"Yes, she's quite aggressive. As they say at the chamber of commerce meetings, he's *less* and she's *more* . . . Cheers! Welcome to the Potatoes!" He lifted his glass.

Qwilleran said, "What do you know about your predecessor?"

"I never met J.J., but people still talk about him. They're thinking of naming a scenic drive after him. He was quite powerful in this town and ran the *Gazette* like a one-man show, writing an editorial every week that knocked the town on its ear. Mine must sound pretty bland by comparison."

"What was his background?"

"J.J. grew up here. His family owned the *Gazette* for a couple of generations, but he wanted to go into law. He was in law school, as a matter of fact, when his father died. He dropped out and came back here to run the paper, but he was a born adversary, from what I hear. He stirred things up and made a lot of enemies, but he also spurred the economic growth of Spudsboro—not to mention the circulation of the *Gazette.*"

Qwilleran said, "From a conversation I overheard in a coffee shop this morning, there's divided opinion about economic growth."

"That's true. The conservatives and old-timers want everything to stay the way it was, with population growth at zero. The younger ones and the merchants are all for progress, and let the chips fall where they may."

"Where do you stand?"

"Well, you know, Qwill, I'm exposed to both viewpoints, and I try to be objective. We're entering a new century, and we're already engulfed in a wave of technology that's going to break the dikes. And yet . . . the environment must be understood and respected. Right here in the Potatoes we've got to address such issues as the stripping of forests, damming of waterfalls for private use, population density, pollution, and the destruction of wildlife habitat. How are they handling it where you live?"

Qwilleran said, "In Moose County we're always thirty years behind the times, so the problems you mention haven't confronted us as yet. We haven't even been discovered by the fast-food chains, but the situation is going to alter very soon. The business community is pushing for tourism. So I'll watch the situation in Spudsboro with a great deal of interest. Who are the pickets in front of the courthouse?"

"That's an ongoing campaign by the environmentalists," Carmichael said. "Different picketers show up each weekend—all hill folks from Little Potato, some of them with a personal ax to grind. There are two kinds of people on that mountain, living quite primitively, you might say. There are the ones called Taters, whose ancestors bought cheap land from the government more than a century ago and who still cling to a pioneer way of life, and then there are the artists and others who deserted the cities for what they call plain living. We call them New Taters. They're the ones who are militant about protecting the environment. Strange to say, some of the conservatives in the valley are afraid of the Taters, even though they're on the same side of the fence politically. It's not a clear-cut situation."

Two golfers walking through the dining room to the lounge attracted a flurry of interest from women who were lunching. One had a shaggy head of sun-bleached hair and the other was neatly barbered. Qwilleran recognized the latter as Dolly Lessmore's husband.

"That's Bob Lessmore and Hugh Lumpton, top guns in the club," the editor explained. "Champion golfers have a certain look, don't they? Their build, their walk, even their facial set. It comes from concentration, I guess. Do you play golf?"

"No," Qwilleran said. "I never thought that anything smaller than a baseball was worth hitting. Baseball was my game until I injured a knee. I was too short for basketball, too cowardly to play football, too poor to play polo, and too sane to play soccer."

Carmichael recommended the poached flounder, saying that the new chef was introducing a lighter menu to a membership hooked on corned beef sandwiches and sixteen-ounce steaks. Qwilleran ordered the poached flounder, although he noticed that his host ordered a corned beef sandwich and cheddar cheese soup. It proved to be a small piece of fish, lightly sauced and served on an oversized plate along with three perfect green beans, a sliver of parboiled carrot, and two halves of a cherry tomato broiled and sprinkled with parsley. It was accompanied by the starch of the day, mashed turnip flavored with grated orange rind.

Gingerly Qwilleran forked into this repast, and as he did so, he was aware that a woman at a nearby table was staring at his moustache. She had the embalmed look that comes from too many facelifts, and she was wearing a voluptuous brimmed hat that zoomed up on one side and swooped down on the other.

"Who's the woman in the hat who's giving me the eye?" he asked under his breath.

"That's Vonda Dudley Wix," the editor said without moving his lips. "She writes the 'Potato Peelings' column. She's spotted your moustache, I'm afraid, and she'll be nailing you for an interview."

"She'll have to catch me first. I've read her column. What do you think of her style?"

"Overripe, to say the least. I tried to kill the column when I bought the paper, but the readers rose up in protest. They actually like it! Newspaper subscribers are unpredictable."

Helping himself to a third mini-muffin, Qwilleran was glad he had eaten a substantial breakfast at the Five Points Café. He maintained an amiable composure, however. "How long does it take to learn your way around the mountains, Colin? All I've got is three months." He related his experience of the previous day: how he wound up on the wrong mountain and how he was rescued by one of the Taters. He said, "Her manner was definitely hostile, and yet she went miles out of her way to help me find Hawk's Nest Drive. I don't understand it."

"They're not easy to understand," said Carmichael. "In fact, there are some weird characters in them thar hills."

"The MacDiarmids told me the artists have a community where they sell their handcrafts. Where's that?"

"Potato Cove. It's on the outside of Little Potato. It was a ghost town that they resurrected."

"Is it difficult to find?"

"It's on a dirt road, but the route is well marked because it's a tourist attraction. Go to Five Points and then follow the signs."

Qwilleran said, "I saw something strange last night. It was around midnight. I went out for a lungful of fresh air before turning in and walked around the veranda. On a mountain toward the south there was a circle of light, and it was revolving."

"Oh sure, we see that once in a while."

"Is it some kind of natural phenomenon? I have friends in Moose County who'd insist it was an alien aircraft from outer space."

The editor chuckled. "Are you ready for this, Qwill? . . . They say there's a witches' coven up on Little Potato. Apparently they celebrate certain phases of the moon—or whatever."

"Have you ever done a story on them?"

"Are you kidding? Even if we could find them in that godforsaken wilderness, no outsider could get close enough to take a picture or spy on them. But if you want to take a whack at it, we'll buy the story," Carmichael added in a jocular vein.

"No, thanks," said Qwilleran, "but I think it was one of the witches who came to my rescue last night."

They ordered coffee, and Qwilleran had a slice of double chocolate fudge cake that restored his interest in the golf club. On the way out, at the editor's urging, he signed up for a social membership that would permit him to use the dining room. They gave him a card with the club logo: SGC in embossed gold, on a brown oval representing a potato.

"And now where do you want to be dropped?" Carmichael asked.

"At a furniture store, if there's one downtown. I left my car on Center Street."

"Didn't you rent the place furnished?"

"Supposedly, but I need an ottoman. I like to put my feet up when I read. I also need a small radio for weather reports."

"The hardware store at Five Points is the best for that. Get one that can operate on batteries in case of a blackout."

"Do you lose power often?" Qwilleran asked.

"Only when a tree blows down across a power line."

As they drove back downtown, the editor pointed out some local attractions: the Lumpton furniture factory, offering guided tours every afternoon; the historical museum in an old house on Center Street; the scenic drive about to be named after J.J. Hawkinfield.

"How old was he when he died?" Qwilleran asked.

"Not old. In his fifties."

"What happened to him?"

Carmichael hesitated. "You haven't heard? He was murdered."

Qwilleran put his hand to his moustache. "Ms. Lessmore didn't tell me that." He had sensed something sinister, though.

"Well, you know, Qwill . . . small towns are sensitive about serious crimes . . . and with the emphasis on tourism here, murder is never mentioned to vacationers."

"I had a hunch that something irregular had happened to the owner of Tiptop. What were the circumstances?"

"He was pushed off his own mountain. You can read about it in our files if you're interested. The murderer is in prison, although there's an element here that thinks they convicted the wrong man, but that's par for the course, isn't it? . . . Well, here's your furniture store, Qwill. It's great to have you here. Don't be too solitary. Keep in touch."

Chapter 5

According to signs plastered on the windows, the furniture store was having a sale of recliners, a fact corroborated by the lineup of chairs on the sidewalk. Qwilleran walked in and asked to see some ottomans.

"Did you see our recliners on sale?" asked a pleasant elderly woman, eager to be of service.

"Yes, but I'm interested in an ottoman."

"All the recliners in the store are twenty-five percent off," she said encouragingly.

"Do you have any ottomans?" he asked with exaggerated politeness.

"Harry!" she shouted toward the rear of the store. "Do we have any ottomans?"

"No!" Harry yelled. "Show the customer the recliners!"

"Never mind," Qwilleran said. "Show me a telephone book."

Consulting the classified section, he found a likely source of ottomans just two blocks away: Peel & Poole Design Studio. It was a juxtaposition of names that appealed to his fancy for words.

At the Peel & Poole studio he was greeted by a smartly suited young woman who reminded him of Fran Brodie, a designer in Pickax. They had the same suave buoyancy and the same reddish blond hair.

"May I help you?" she asked cordially. Her hair flowed silkily to her shoulders, and long, straight bangs drew attention to the blueness of her eyes.

"I need an ottoman," he said. "I'm renting a furnished place for the summer, and I like to put my feet up when I read. I do not— want—a recliner!" he said with measured emphasis.

"You're quite right," she agreed. "I'm a firm believer in ottomans, and we have a nice one that we can order for you in any cover."

"How long does it take for a special order?"

"Six to eight weeks."

"That won't do. I'll be here only three months. I'm renting Tiptop for the summer."

"Really?" she asked in surprise. "I didn't know they were willing to rent. What condition is it in?"

"The building's in good repair and has all the essentials, but it's rather bleak and full of echoes. Someone has cleaned out all the bric-a-brac."

"The Hawkinfield daughter," the designer said, nodding. "When J.J. died, she took everything in the way of decorative accessories to sell in her shop in Maryland. I helped her appraise the stuff. But now, if you'd like any help in making the interior comfortable for the summer, I'm at your service. I'm Sabrina Peel."

"Qwilleran. Jim Qwilleran, spelled with a QW," he said. "Are you familiar with Tiptop?"

"Definitely! Our studio helped Mrs. Hawkinfield with the interior a few years ago—just before she went into the hospital. The poor woman never returned to enjoy it."

"What happened?"

"She was committed to a mental hospital, and she's still there—doesn't even know that her husband is dead. Would you like a cup of coffee?"

"I never say no to coffee," he said.

"Or a glass of chardonnay?"

"Coffee, if you please."

While she prepared the beverage he wandered about the studio, admiring the Peel & Poole taste. He also found the ottoman she had mentioned: large, cushiony, inviting, and labeled "floor sample." After the first sip of coffee, he regarded her with the beseeching eyes that women could rarely resist and asked, "Would you consider selling me your floor sample?"

She took a moment to react, pushing her hair back from her face with an attractive two-handed gesture. "On one condition—if you'll let me spruce up your summer residence. I can use small rugs and pillows and folding screens to make it more livable and without a large investment on your part. You owe it to yourself to have a pleasant environment when you're vacationing."

"Sounds good to me!" he said. "Would you like to drive up and look it over?"

"How about Monday afternoon at one-thirty? I'll take along some accessories for your approval."

"Tell me something about the Hawkinfields," Qwilleran said. "Why did they want such a large house?"

"They had several children and did a lot of entertaining—originally. Then all of a sudden their life went into a tailspin. Three of the boys were killed within a year."

"How?" Qwilleran was always quick to suspect foul play, and since their father had enemies and was a murder victim himself, the possibilities were rife.

"There were two accidents a few months apart, both related to outdoor sports. It was a crushing blow for the parents. After the second incident Mrs. Hawkinfield couldn't cope and had a nervous breakdown. We all felt terrible about it. She was a nice woman, although she let her husband keep her under his thumb. Everyone wished she'd stand up for herself . . . I don't know why I'm telling you this, except that it's Tiptop history, and it goes with the house, along with the carpet and draperies."

"I appreciate knowing," he said. "I've been getting negative vibrations."

"Is that true? How interesting!" the designer said, leaning forward. "I'm very sensitive to the aura of a house. When I visit a client for the first time, I get a definite feeling about the family's past and present."

"Mrs. Hawkinfield seemed to be hooked on gray, if that signifies anything."

"Hooked is the right word! We tried to warm it up with antique gold and Venetian red, but she loved gray and always wore it. Actually it was becoming. She had lovely gray eyes—and prematurely gray hair, which we all blamed on her husband."

Qwilleran was about to inquire about the murder, but a chime at the front door announced another customer, and he drained his coffee cup. "I'll look forward to seeing you Monday afternoon, Ms. Peel."

"Sabrina," she corrected him.

"Don't bring anything gray, Sabrina. And please call me Qwill."

Driving away from the design studio with the ottoman in the trunk, he felt a bond of camaraderie with Sabrina Peel. He liked designers, especially those with that particular roseate hair tint, which he thought of as "decorator blond." When he stopped at the Five Points Market to stock his bar for possible guests, he included chardonnay with the usual hard and soft drinks.

The friendly Bill Treacle, who was bustling about the store with managerial urgency, saw Qwilleran loading a shopping cart with scotch, bourbon, vodka, rum, sherry, beer, fruit juices, and mixes. "Having a party?" he asked cheerily. "Looks like you found Tiptop okay."

"No problem," Qwilleran replied. After meeting Sabrina he was feeling too good to quibble about the Snaggy Creek cutoff and the thawed seafood and the melted ice cream.

At the same intersection he went into Lumpton's Hardware and asked for a turkey roaster.

"What size?" asked a man with a nasal twang.

"I thought one size fits all."

"We've got three sizes, top of the line. From Germany. How big a turkey are you talking about?"

"Just a small one," Qwilleran said. He was staggered by the price, but he could afford it, and the cats deserved a second facility. He himself had eight bathrooms at Tiptop; why should they be limited to one commode? He also bought a radio with more features than he really wanted, the control panel having several switches, six knobs, and seventeen buttons. Even so, it cost less than the cats' commode.

Upon leaving the hardware store Qwilleran saw a barnwood sign advertising mountain crafts and handmade gifts at Potato Cove. He followed the arrow, thinking he might find a gift for Polly and a ceramic mug for himself. The coffee cups at Tiptop had finger-trap handles and limited capacity; he could empty one in two gulps.

The road to Potato Cove was the kind that map makers call "unimproved," meaning that it was gravel with teeth-rattling bumps and ruts. It was marked at every turn and every fork, however, and it wound through a dense forest where the pines stood tall and straight, as close together as pickets in a fence.

On the way to the cove Qwilleran saw a few dwellings, poor excuses for housing, and yet there were more signs of life than he had found around Tiptop Estates. He saw children chasing each other and climbing trees, two women laughing as they hung diapers on a clothesline, cats and dogs sunning, a man chopping wood, a white-haired woman sitting on the porch of a log cabin, peeling apples. There was something poetic about this humble scene: her placid demeanor as she sat in a rocking chair with a bowl cradled in her lap, leisurely wielding the paring knife as if she had all afternoon. Qwilleran's camera was on the seat beside him, and he would have snapped a picture if it had not been for the shotgun leaning against a porch post.

Farther along the road there was an enterprise that called itself

"Just Rust." A long, low shed was jammed with rusty artifacts that spilled over into the front yard: bed frames, parts of sewing machines, plows, broken tools, folding metal chairs, wash boilers, scythes, bathtubs, bird cages, bed pans, frying pans, wheelbarrows . . .

Next came a streetscene that might have been the set for a low-budget Hollywood western: crude buildings of weathered wood, spaced haphazardly along the road and connected with wooden sidewalks. Yet, even in this ramshackle environment the hand of an artist was evident in the signs painted on barnwood. The first was a parody of small-town hospitality: WELCOME TO POTATO COVE . . . POPULATION 0. Similar signs nailed to the buildings identified the shops of Otto the Potter, Vance the Village Smith, and specialists in woodcraft, leather goods, hand-dipped candles, baskets, and the like. There was wit in some of the signs. The chair caner called his shop The Bottom Line.

Among the visitors who walked up and down the wooden sidewalks there were townspeople wearing Saturday casuals and doing a little shopping, as well as tourists in shorts and sandals, gawking and snapping pictures. Qwilleran followed a few who were walking briskly toward a shed behind Otto's pottery.

"What's going on?" he asked one of them.

"Kiln opening," was the hurried answer.

In the shed, lighted by sunshine streaming through holes in the rusted metal roof, twenty or more bystanders were watching eagerly as a soft-spoken man in a canvas apron removed pots from a large oven, holding them up one by one. "This is my new decorated platter," he said modestly. "And this is a weed holder with the new glaze I've been working on."

Responses shot out from the onlookers: "I'll take it . . . Let me see that one up close . . . Do you have three more like that plate? . . . Oh! That's a pretty one! . . . I'll take that, Otto."

The potter continued his commentary in a quiet monotone. "The ones closer to the fire may have some variation in color . . . This bowl's imperfect. It got a little too hot and started bloating. Like we say, the kiln giveth and the kiln taketh away. Here's one of my new pitchers with pine tree decoration."

"I'll take that!" said a man in the back row, and the pitcher was passed over the heads of the others. In a low voice he said to his companion, "I can sell it in my shop for three times the price."

Qwilleran noticed that men in designer shirts and gold jewelry and women in pastel pants suits and expensive cologne were grabbing four-dollar mugs and seven-dollar candleholders, handmade and signed by the potter. He himself found a mug with a handle that accommodated his fingers comfortably, and when he learned it was one-tenth the price of the cats' commode, he bought four. At last the kiln was emptied, and a groan of disappointment went up from the audience.

"Sorry I don't have more," the potter apologized. "I really tried to pack the kiln this time, using miniatures to fill up the corners."

As the purchasers stood in line to pay, voices filled the small shed with social hubbub—exulting over their finds, greeting friends, sharing local gossip. Qwilleran overheard two women saying:

"Did you hear about Tiptop? Some crazy fella with a big moustache and a lot of cats is renting it for $2,000 a week!"

"Is he a Canadian or Japanese or what?"

"Nobody knows. The Lessmores made the deal. He's supposed to be a writer."

"That could be a front for something else."

"Anyway, it doesn't sound good."

Qwilleran hustled away with his mugs wrapped in newspaper and stashed them in the trunk of his car before joining the parade up the wooden sidewalk. He stopped to watch a man making sandals and a woman caning chairseats. Then, hearing the ring of hammer on metal, he followed the sound to the smithy. Within a barn with doors flung wide there was a glowing forge, and red hot metal was being hammered on an anvil by a sinewy young man with full beard and pigtail. He wore a leather apron and a soiled tee with the sleeves cut out.

"Howya," he said when he saw Qwilleran watching intently. Picking up a rod with tongs, he thrust it into the glowing coals, checked it for redness, fired it again, and finally hammered it into shape. When the hot iron was plunged into a tub of water to cool, the sizzle added to the show of sights, sounds, and smells.

Qwilleran examined the hand-wrought objects for sale: hooks, tongs, pokers, spikes, and cowbells, but his eye was taken by an item in a shadowy corner of the barn. It was a wrought-iron candelabrum, seven feet tall and branched to hold eight candles. An iron vine twisted around the main stem and sprouted a few tendrils and leaves. "Is that for sale?" he asked.

The smith looked at it dubiously. "Guess so," he said.

"How much are you asking?"

"Jeez, I dunno. It was just somethin' I hadda prove I could do. Mosta the time I'm a mechanic down in the valley."

"It's a spectacular hunk of iron," Qwilleran said, thinking of it for his apple barn in Pickax. "Set a price and let me buy it."

"Uh . . . two hundred?" the blacksmith suggested hesitantly.

"Sold! If I pull my car up, will you help me load it? How much does it weigh?"

"Plenty, man!"

By reclining the passenger seat they were able to pack the candelabrum lengthwise inside the car. Next, Qwilleran amazed the candle dipper by buying three dozen handmade, twelve-inch beeswax candles. Pleased with his purchases and hoping to find a cup of coffee, he trudged up the hill. He had a few words with the quiltmaker and a woman making cornhusk dolls, and then he spotted a building that looked like an old schoolhouse, with a sign saying: THE BEECHUM FAMILY WEAVERS. An old army vehicle was parked alongside.

The open door revealed a veritable cocoon of textiles: shawls, scarfs, placemats, pillows, tote bags, even hammocks hanging from the ceiling. Two customers—tourists, judging by their sunglasses, sun hats, and cameras—were fingering placemats and asking questions about washability and price. They were being answered curtly by a tall young woman with hollow cheeks and long, straight hair hanging to her waist. She turned around, caught sight of Qwilleran's moustache, hesitated, then turned back to the shoppers.

At the same moment he heard soft thumping and beating sounds at the rear of the shop. A woman with gray hair pulled severely into a bun at the back of her head was sitting at a loom, rhythmically operating the heddles, throwing the shuttles and pulling the beater. He watched her work—watched her with fascination and admiration—but she never looked up.

Examining the products in the shop, Qwilleran found it difficult to believe that they had been woven, thread by thread, on that loom. One was a capelike jacket, incredibly soft, in the new brighter blue that Polly now liked. The pricetag read $100, and he made a quick decision to buy jackets for four other friends as well. His chief joy in having inherited money was the pleasure of giving it away. During his days as an underpaid journalist, generosity had been a luxury beyond his means, but now he was enjoying the opportunity to be munificent. Buying capes for Polly, Mildred, Fran, Lori, and Hixie in Moose County would also be a way of expressing his gratitude to the aloof young woman who had rescued him the night before.

He heard her say to the shoppers, "These are woven by hand on that loom. If you want two-dollar placemats you'll find them at Lumpton's Department Store in Spudsboro." She made no attempt to be tactful, and they walked out.

"Hello again," Qwilleran said amiably.

"Howya," she said in a minor key without smiling.

"Is this all your own handwork? It's beautiful stuff!"

"My mother and I are the weavers," she said, wasting no thanks for the compliment.

"I'm very grateful to you, Ms. Beechum, for steering me to the right mountain last night. I don't know what I'd have done without your help."

"We aim to be good neighbors in the mountains." There was no trace of neighborly warmth in the statement.

"I'd like to buy this blue—this blue—"

"Batwing cape."

"I'd like to send it to a friend of mine up north. Do you have any others? I could use four more in different colors."

"They're a hundred dollars," she informed him, as if he might have misread the price tag.

"So I noticed. Very attractively priced, I would say. May I see the others?"

The weaver relaxed her stern expression for the first time. "They're not here. They didn't sell well, so I took them home. Most of the shoppers are looking for things under five dollars. But I could bring the capes to the shop if you want to come back another day." She looked at him dubiously as if questioning his sincerity.

"Are you open tomorrow?"

"Sunday's our biggest day."

"What hours?"

"Noon till dusk."

"Very well. I'll be here first thing. My name is Qwilleran. Jim Qwilleran, spelled with a QW. And what's your first name, Ms. Beechum?" She told him, and he asked her to spell it.

"C-h-r-y-s-a-l-i-s."

"Pretty name," he said. "I met a Dewey Beechum this morning. He's going to build a gazebo for me."

"That's my father. He's an expert cabinetmaker," she said proudly. "He was one of the best hands at the furniture factory before they automated. He's looking for work now. If you know anyone who wants custom-made furniture—"

"I'll be glad to recommend him." As she wrapped the blue cape in tissue and a Five Points grocery bag, he said, "Pardon my ignorance, but why is this called Potato Cove? I've just arrived in these parts. What is a cove?"

"A cove is smaller than a valley but larger than a hollow," she said. "Are you going to live here?"

"Only for the summer."

"Alone?"

"No, I have two Siamese cats."

"What brought you here?" she asked suspiciously.

"Some friends from up north camped in the national forest across the river last summer, and they recommended the Potatoes. I was looking for a quiet place where I could do some serious thinking."

"About what?" Her blunt nosiness amused him. He was nosy himself, although usually more artful.

"About my career," he replied cryptically.

"What do you do?"

"I'm a journalist by profession . . . Tell me about you. How long have you lived in the mountains?"

"All my life. I'm a Tater. Do you know about Taters? We've

been here for generations, living close to nature. We were environmentalists before the word was invented."

"If you'll forgive me for saying so, Ms. Beechum, you don't talk like a Tater."

"I went away to college. When you go into the outside world, you gain something, but you also lose something."

"Can you make a living by weaving?" he asked. If she had license to pry, so did he.

"We don't need much to live on, but we do fairly well in summer. In the winter I drive the school bus."

"You mean—you maneuver a bus up these mountain roads? You have my admiration . . . I'll see you tomorrow," he said as more tourists entered the shop. "Is there any place in the cove where I can get a cup of coffee?"

"Amy's Lunch Bucket," she said, pointing up the hill. Although she didn't smile, she had lost the chip on her shoulder.

Qwilleran waved a hand toward the silent woman at the loom. "Good afternoon, Mrs. Beechum, and compliments on your weaving!" She nodded without looking up.

Amy's Lunch Bucket was aptly named, being large enough for four old kitchen tables and some metal folding chairs obviously from the Just Rust collection. But it was clean. The floorboards were painted grass green, and the white walls were decorated with an abstract panorama of green mountains against a blue sky. A plump and pretty woman with the healthy radiance of youth presided over a makeshift kitchen behind a chest-high counter. "Nice day," she said.

"Are you Amy?" Qwilleran asked.

"Sure am!" she replied cheerfully. "What can I dish up for you?"

The menu posted on the wall behind her offered vegetable soup, veggieburgers, oat bran cookies, yogurt, apple juice, and herb tea. "Do you have coffee?" he asked.

"Sure don't. Only coffee sub and herb tea."

There was a sudden squawk behind the counter, as if from some exotic bird.

"Goo goo goo," said Amy, leaning down.

Qwilleran peered over the counter. On a table was an infant in a basket. "Yours?" he asked.

"Yes, this is our Ashley. Two months, one week, and three days. He's going to be an ecologist when he grows up."

Qwilleran accepted coffee substitute and two oat bran cookies, which he carried to a table near the front window. The only other patrons were the candle dipper, who was eating yogurt and reading a paperback, and the blacksmith, who had ordered everything on the menu and was tucking into it with ravenous gulps.

"Howya," he said with his mouth full, and the candle dipper looked up and smiled at the man who had bought almost a hundred dollars' worth of beeswax.

A moment later Chrysalis Beechum burst into the restaurant in a hurry, waving a ceramic mug. "Apple juice for Ma," she told Amy. "How's Ashley? Is Ashley a good boy today?"

"Ashley is an angel today. How's business down the hill?"

"Surprisingly good! Put the juice on our bill, Amy."

As Chrysalis started out the door with the brimming mug, Qwilleran stood up and intercepted her. "We meet again," he said pleasantly. "Won't you join me for a cup of coffee substitute and an oat bran cookie?"

She hesitated. "I've left my mother alone at the shop."

The candle dipper spoke up. "I'm all through eatin', Chrys. I'll stay with her till you git back."

"Aw, thanks, Missy. Take this apple juice and tell her I won't be long." Chrysalis turned back to Qwilleran. "My mother doesn't speak, so I can't leave her in the shop alone."

"She doesn't speak?" Sympathy was masking his curiosity as he held a rusty chair for her.

"It's a psychological disorder. She hasn't said a word for almost a year."

"What may I serve you?"

"Just some yogurt, plain, and thank you very much."

In that small restaurant Amy heard the order and had it ready by the time Qwilleran reached the counter.

"How do you like Potato Cove?" Chrysalis asked him.

"Interesting community," he said. "Very good shops. I like everything except the tourists."

"I know what you mean, but they pay the rent. How do you feel about what's happening to the mountains?"

"Having arrived only yesterday, I'm not ready to make a statement, I'm afraid. Are you referring to the land development?"

"That's what they call it," she said aggressively. "I call it environmental suicide! They're not only cutting down trees to ship to Japan; they're endangering life on this planet! They're creating problems of erosion, drainage, water supply, and waste control! They're robbing the wildlife of their habitat! I'm talking about Big Potato. And the Yellyhoo—one of the few wild rivers left—is in danger of pollution. I'm not going to have children, Mr. . . ."

"Qwilleran."

"I'm not going to have children because the next generation will inherit a ravaged earth."

He had heard all this before but never with such passion and at such close range. He was formulating a reply when she demanded:

"You're a journalist, you say. Why don't you write about this frightening problem? They're ripping the heart out of Big Potato, and they'd like to take our land away from us, too. Little Potato will be next!"

"I'd need to know a lot more about this subject than I do," he said. "Are you connected with the group that pickets in front of the courthouse?"

"I take my turn," she said sullenly. "So does Amy. So does Vance." She nodded toward the blacksmith. "Who knows whether it does any good? I get very depressed."

"Answer one question for me," Qwilleran said. "When I was downtown today, there was a picket sign I didn't understand: Free Forest. Are you campaigning for a national park or something like that?"

Her thin lips twisted in a grim smile. "My brother is Forest Beechum . . . and he's in the state prison!" She said it bravely, holding her head high and looking at him defiantly.

"Sorry to hear that. What kind of term—"

"He was sentenced to life! And he's innocent!"

Qwilleran thought, *They always say that.* "What was the charge?"

"Murder!"

Amy called out from behind the counter, "The trial was a pack of lies! Forest would never hurt a fly! He's an artist. He's a gentle person."

They always say that, Qwilleran repeated to himself.

The blacksmith, still speaking with his mouth full, said, "There's lotsa Spuds that coulda done it, but the cops never come up with a suspect from the valley. They made up their mind it hadda be one of us."

Qwilleran asked, "Did you have a good attorney?"

"We couldn't afford an attorney," Chrysalis said, "so the court appointed one for us. We thought he'd work to get my brother off, since he was innocent. We were so naive. That man didn't even try!" She spoke with bitterness flashing in her eyes. "He wanted Forest to plead guilty to a lesser charge, but why should he? He was totally innocent! So there was a jury trial, and the jury was rigged. All the jurors were Spuds. Not one Tater! It was all so wrong, so unjust, so unfair!"

"Ain't nothin' fair," said the blacksmith.

There was a minute of silence in the little restaurant, a moment heavy with emotion. Then Chrysalis said, "I've got to get back to the shop. Thank you for the yogurt and for listening, Mr. . . ."

"Qwilleran."

"Do you really want to see the batwing capes tomorrow?"

"I most certainly do," he said, rising as she left the table. No one spoke until Ashley made his lusty bid for attention.

"Goo goo goo," said Amy.

"The cookies were delicious," Qwilleran told her. "Did you make them?"

"No, they're from the bakery up the hill. They have wonderful things up there."

"Good! That will be my next stop."

"It's after four o'clock. They're closed. But you should come back and try their Danish pastries made with fresh fruit, and their sticky buns made with whole wheat potato dough."

"Amy, you've touched the weakest spot in my character." Qwilleran started out the door and then turned back. "About this murder trial . . . who was the victim?" he asked, although a sensation on his upper lip was telling him the answer.

"Big shot in Spudsboro," said the blacksmith.

"He owned the newspaper," Amy added. "Also an old inn on top of Big Potato."

Qwilleran patted his moustache with satisfaction. All his hunches, large and small, seemed to emanate from its sensitive roots. Right again!

CHAPTER 6

Qwilleran stood in front of Amy's Lunch Bucket and gazed at the sky. The heavens refuted Beechum's prediction of rain. With the sun shining and the sky blue and the mountain breezes playing softly, it was one of those rare days that June does so well. There were dragon-like clouds over the valley—sprawling, ferocious shapes quite unlike the puffy clouds over Moose County. They looked more dramatic than threatening, however, and the meteorologist on the car radio had promised fair weather for the next twenty-four hours.

As he stood there he doubted not only Beechum's prediction but also the story he had just heard. How many times had he interviewed the parent, spouse, or neighbor of a convicted felon and listened to the same tale! "My son would never harm anyone! . . . My husband is a gentle, peace-loving man! . . . He was a wonderful neighbor, always ready to help anyone!"

Whatever the facts about the Hawkinfield murder and the conviction of Forest Beechum, Qwilleran was beginning to understand his negative reaction to Tiptop. It was not only the gray color scheme and the barren rooms; it was an undercurrent of villainy. Exactly what kind of villainy had yet to be discovered.

Then he remembered that the Siamese had been left alone all day in unfamiliar surroundings, and he drove back to the inn. Hawk's Nest Drive, so smoothly paved and so expertly dished on the curves, made pleasant driving after the discomforts of the road to Potato Cove.

To unload his purchases it was necessary to make several trips up the long flight of steps—with the ottoman, the supply of liquor, the turkey roaster, his new radio, Polly's batwing cape, three dozen candles, four coffee mugs, and a very heavy iron candelabrum. After transporting them as far as the veranda, he sat down on the top step to catch his breath, but his respite was brief. A feline chorus inside the French doors was making imperative demands, Yum Yum saying, "N-n-NOW!"

"All right, all right, I know it's dinnertime," he called out as he turned the key in the lock. "You don't need to make a federal case out of it!"

It was not food that concerned them, however; it was an envelope that had been pushed under the door. Qwilleran ripped it open and read, "Cocktails Sunday at Seven Levels. Come around five o'clock and meet your neighbors. Very casual. Dolly." He pocketed the invitation and carried his acquisitions into the house.

"I've brought you a present," he told the Siamese. "You'll be the only cats in the Potato Mountains with a state-of-the-art commode imported from Germany!"

Koko, who had to inspect everything that came into the house, was chiefly interested in the liquor supply as it was lined up on the bar. The sherry particularly attracted his nose. This was Polly's favorite drink, and it would be astounding, Qwilleran thought, if the cat could make the connection. More likely it was the label. Koko had a passion for glue, and the Spanish wine industry might use a special kind of seductive adhesive in labeling bottles.

After opening a can of crabmeat for the Siamese and a can of spaghetti for himself, he checked the house for catly mischief; they could be remarkably creative in their naughtiness when they felt neglected. Surprisingly everything was in order except for the painting of mountains in the foyer, which had been tilted again.

As he straightened it, Koko came up behind him, yowling indignantly.

"Objection overruled," Qwilleran said. "Why don't you go and massage your teeth on that half-ton buffet in the dining room?"

The painting, which had an indecipherable signature in the lower righthand corner, hung above a primitive cabinet built low to the floor on flat bun feet. It was crudely decorated with hunting symbols and a cartouche on which was inscribed "Lord Archibald Fitzwallow." There were two drawers (empty) and cabinet space beneath (also empty). It was no beauty, but it was a handy place to keep the telephone and throw car keys. As Qwilleran was examining the cabinet, Koko impudently jumped to its surface and moved the mountain for the third time.

"Are you trying to be funny?" Qwilleran shouted at him. "We'll put an end to that little game, you rascal!" With this pronouncement he lifted the picture from its hook and placed it on the floor, leaning it against the wall. Koko stayed where he was, but now he was standing on his hind legs and pawing the wall.

"What's that?" Qwilleran exclaimed. Hanging from the picture hook was an old-fashioned black iron key about three inches long. Koko had sensed its presence! He always knew when anything was unusual or out of place.

"Sorry I yelled, old boy. I should have realized you knew what you were doing," Qwilleran apologized, but now he combed his moustache in perplexity. What was the key intended to unlock? And why had it been hung behind the painting?

It was clear, he told himself, that the Tiptop Inn had catered to a wealthy clientele who traveled with their jewels, making security an important consideration. All the bedroom doors were fitted with old-fashioned, surface-mounted brass locks, the kind requiring a long key. Other doors throughout the house—with the exception of cylinder locks at front and back doors—retained the old style as part of the quaint authenticity of the historic building.

Carrying the key and marveling at its inconvenient size and weight, Qwilleran began a systematic check of the house from the fruit cellar on the lower level to the walk-in linen closet upstairs. He found no lock that would take the key, not even the door to the attic stairway. The attic stairs were steep and dusty, and the atmosphere was stifling, but he went up to explore. It was a lumber room for old steamer trunks and cast-off furniture. There was also a ladder to the rooftop, which he climbed. Upon pushing open a hatch, he emerged on a small railed observation deck.

This was the highest point in the entire mountain range, close to the dragon-like clouds that rampaged across the sky as if in battle, the sun highlighting their golden scales. Below were the same views seen from the veranda, but they were glorified by the extra elevation, and there were unexpected sights. To the north, the top of Big Potato had been sliced off, and an extensive construction project was under way. To the south, there was a glimpse of a silvery blue mountaintop lake, and the beginning of a footpath pointed in that direction.

Forgetting his mission, Qwilleran hurried downstairs, threw the key in the drawer of the Fitzwallow eyesore, and grabbed a sturdy walking stick from the umbrella stand in the foyer.

"I'll be back shortly," he called over his shoulder. "I'm going to find Lake Batata. If I don't return in half an hour, send out the bloodhounds." The Siamese followed him to the door in ominous silence and then scampered into the living room and watched from a window when he headed for the woods, as if they might never see their meal ticket again.

A wooden shingle daubed with the word "trail" was nailed to a tree, and from there a sun-dappled path carpeted with pine needles and last year's oak leaves made soft footing. It wound through a dense growth of trees and underbrush, and the silence was absolute. This was what Qwilleran had hoped to find—a secret place for ambling and thinking. The trail meandered this way and that, sometimes circumventing a particularly large tree trunk or rocky outcrop, sometimes requiring him to climb over a fallen tree. It was descending gradually, and he reminded himself that the return walk would be uphill, but he was not concerned; in Moose County he walked daily and rode a bike, and he was in good condition.

Every few hundred yards there was another chip of wood nailed to a tree to reassure him that this was the trail, but Lake Batata had not appeared. Could it have been a mirage? The decline was becoming steeper, the woods more dense, the footing less secure. There were slippery leaves that had not dried in this deep shade, and there were half-exposed roots that made the trail treacherous. Once he tripped and went down on his bad knee, but he pressed on. The inn was no longer visible on its summit, nor was the valley. This was real wilderness, and he liked it. Now and then a small animal scurried through the underbrush, but the only birds were crows, circling overhead and cawing their raucous complaints. Where, he asked himself, are the cardinals, chickadees, and gold-finches we have in Moose County?

Walking downhill put more of a strain on his knee than walking uphill, and he was glad to stumble upon a small clearing with a rustic pavilion, a circular shelter just large enough for a round picnic table and benches. Qwilleran sat down gratefully and leaned his elbows on the table. The wood was well weathered, and the pa-vilion itself was rotting. It was a long time since the Hawkinfields had picnicked there. He sat quietly and marveled at the silence of the woods, unaware that this was the silence before a storm. Even the crows had taken cover.

After a while his watch told him it was time to start back up the trail . . . if he could find it. From which direction had he come? All the trees and shrubs looked alike, and there were several tram-pled areas that might be the beginning of a path. While sitting in the circular pavilion he had become disoriented. The sun would be sinking in the west, and the inn would lie to the north, but where was the sun? It had disappeared behind clouds, and the woods were heavily shaded. Beechum's prediction might be ac-curate.

Without further delay Qwilleran had to make a decision. One path ascended slightly, and the others descended. Common sense told him to take the former, so he started out, but soon it rose over a knob and sloped abruptly downhill. Returning to the clearing he tried another trail, which soon became no trail at all; it led into a thicket. Still, it was ascending, and Tiptop was up there—some-where. In the long run how could he go wrong? He struck out through low underbrush, catching his pantlegs on thorns, picking his way among shrubs that snapped back in his face and threatened to jab him in the eye. The walking stick was more of a hindrance than a help, and he tossed it aside. All the while, it was getting darker. He could go back, but which way was back? He had a fear that he was traveling in circles.

He stood still, closed his eyes, and tried to apply reason. That was when he heard something plunging through the underbrush. It sounded like a large animal—not one of those small scurrying things. He listened and strained his eyes in the direction of the rustling leaves and snapping twigs. Soon he saw it through the gathering darkness—a large black beast lumbering in his direction. A bear! he thought, and a chill ran down his spine. What was the advice he had heard from hunters? Don't make a sudden move. Keep perfectly still.

Qwilleran kept perfectly still, and the black animal came closer. It was advancing with grim purpose. Cold sweat broke out on his forehead, and then he realized it was a dog—a large black dog. Was it wild? Was it vicious? It was not starving; in fact, it was grossly rotund, and it seemed to be wearing a collar. Whose dog would be up here on this desolate mountaintop? The trimmed ears and tail suggested that it was a Doberman, out of shape from over-eating. With relief he observed that it was wagging its tail.

"Good dog! Good dog!" he said, keeping his hands in his pockets and making no sudden move.

In friendly fashion the Doberman came closer and leaned against his legs. The collar was studded with nailheads, spelling a name: L-U-C-Y.

"Good dog, Lucy," he said. "Are you Lucy?" He patted the black head, and the overfed dog leaned harder, applying considerable pressure. She was pushing him to one side. Qwilleran stepped away, and Lucy pushed again.

My God! Qwilleran thought. She's a rescue dog! Where's her brandy keg?

When he started to move in the direction she indicated, she bounded ahead, looking back to be sure he was following. Lucy could penetrate the thicket better than he could, and when he made too little progress, she returned to investigate the delay.

Eventually they emerged onto a carpet of pine needles. "This is the trail!" Qwilleran exulted. "Good dog! Good Lucy!" She bounded ahead. Now he recognized a certain fallen tree and a certain giant oak circumvented by the path. When finally the great gray-green hulk loomed above the treetops, he let out an involuntary yelp, and Lucy raced for the inn. She arrived first and waited for him on the veranda, close by the kitchen door.

Incredible! Qwilleran thought; she wants food, and she knows exactly where to go. Two yowling voices could be heard indoors. "Too bad, Lucy," he said. "I can't invite you in, but I'll find you some chow. Stay here." On the porch she appeared much smaller than she had when first lumbering out of the dark woods. Gratefully he gave her four hot dogs he had bought for himself. The Siamese disdained hot dogs with withering contempt, but Lucy gobbled them and took off—on another errand of mercy or in search of another handout.

Indoors the Siamese sniffed Qwilleran's pantlegs and made unflattering grimaces.

"Don't curl your whiskers," he reproached them. "Lucy brought me home just in time." Rain was obviously on the way. The wind was rising, creating a menacing roar around the summit of Big Potato, and the dragon sky was raging.

For no reason at all, except relief at being rescued, Qwilleran felt a need to talk with someone in Moose County. This time he phoned Arch Riker, hoping he would be at home. It was Saturday night, and the middle-aged editor of the *Moose County Something* might be dining out with his cranky, middle-aged friend, Amanda—that is, if they were on speaking terms this week.

When Riker answered, Qwilleran said, "Just checking to see if Moose County is still on the map."

"I thought you were going to boycott us," Riker chided him. "What's the matter? Are you homesick?"

"Why aren't you out romancing the lovely Amanda? I thought this was national date night by act of Congress."

"None of your business."

The two men had been friends since boyhood, and their dialogue never needed to be polite or even sequential.

"How's your little cabin in the Potatoes?" the editor asked. "Does it meet your modest needs?"

"It's adequate. I have six bedrooms, and I can park ten cars and seat twelve for dinner. Right now the wind's roaring as if a locomotive is headed for the side of the building. But it was beautiful earlier in the day. I had lunch with the editor of the *Spudsboro Gazette*, and I'm sending you a copy of the paper. Note the column called 'Potato Peelings.' You might want to apply for syndication rights."

"Are you going to write anything for us?"

"I'm sending you my travel notes, and you can edit them if you think they're worth running. Also, I may write about the local conflict between the environmentalists and the proponents of economic growth. Moose County may get into the same kind of pitched battle before long."

"Good! There's nothing like a bloody controversy to bolster circulation. How do the cats like the mountains? Has Koko found any dead bodies yet?"

"No, but there was a murder here a year ago . . . OUCH!"

"What was that?" Riker asked in alarm.

"I thought I'd been shot! It was a clap of thunder right overhead. We're very close to the action up here on the mountaintop. Better hang up. There's a lot of lightning . . . Wow! There it goes again! Talk to you some other time."

Qwilleran felt better after chatting with his old friend, and he went upstairs to read. It had started to rain with ferocity, and between claps of thunder there was prolonged rumbling, echoing among the mountain peaks. With his feet on the new ottoman and with Yum Yum curled up on his lap, he was well into the second chapter before he realized that Koko was absent.

Any variance in the cats' usual behavior concerned him, and he rushed downstairs to investigate. As he reached the bottom stair he heard murmuring and mumbling in the living room; Koko was talking to himself as he always did when puzzled or frustrated.

Through the archway Qwilleran spotted the cat at the far end of the room, studying the secretary desk. It was a tall, narrow piece of furniture fully nine feet in height, with a serpentine base and a glass-doored bookcase above. Only a room with a ten-foot ceiling could accommodate such a lofty design. There were no books on the shelves to command the attention of the bibliocat. Instead, he was intent on examining the wall behind the desk, thrusting a paw in the narrow space and mumbling frustrated gutturals.

There was another crack of thunder and bolt of lightning directly overhead. "Come on upstairs, Koko," said Qwilleran. "We're having a read. Book! Book!"

The cat ignored the invitation and went on sniffing, pawing, and muttering.

That's when Qwilleran clapped a hand over his moustache. He was beginning to feel a disturbance on his upper lip. Koko never pursued a mission with such single-minded purpose unless there was good reason. The serpentine base of the desk was built down to the floor, so there could be nothing underneath it. That meant that Koko had found something behind it!

Confident that the furniture was in two sections, Qwilleran threw his arms around the bookcase deck and lifted it off, setting it down carefully on the floor. Immediately he realized the object of Koko's quest. The bookcase had concealed the upper half of a door in the wall.

"Of course!" he said aloud, slapping his forehead with the flat of his palm. "What a blockhead!" On his walks around the veranda he had been vaguely aware of a discrepancy in the fenestration on the south side of the building. There were eight windows. Yet, when one was in the living room, there were only six. With other matters on his mind he had failed to make a connection, but Koko knew there was another room back there!

A cat can't stand a closed door, Qwilleran thought; he always wants to be on the other side of it. There was no need to try the large key; he was sure it would fit the lock. But first he had to slide the desk away from the wall. Even after removing the drawers he found it remarkably heavy. It was solid walnut, built the way they built them a hundred years ago.

Koko was prancing back and forth in excitement, and Yum Yum was a bemused spectator.

"Okay, here goes!" Qwilleran told them as he turned the key and opened the door. Koko rushed into the secret room, and Yum Yum followed at her own queenly pace. It was dark, but the wall switch activated three lights: a desk lamp, a table lamp, and a floor lamp. This was J.J. Hawkinfield's office at home, furnished with a desk, bookshelves, filing cabinets, and other office equipment.

The Siamese had little interest in office equipment. They were both under the long library table, sniffing a mattress that had been stenciled with the letters L–U–C–Y.

"You devil!" Qwilleran said to Koko. "Is that what your performance was all about? Is that why I strained my back moving five hundred pounds of solid walnut?"

Nevertheless, he was standing in the private office of a murdered man. The open shelves were empty except for a single set of law books. An empty safe stood with its door open. There was a computer station with space for a keyboard, monitor, and printer, but its surfaces were bare. On the walls were framed diplomas, awards, and certificates of merit issued to J.J. Hawkinfield throughout the years, as well as family photos.

Having checked the scent on the mattress, Koko was now on the library table, industriously exercising his paws on a large scrapbook. Qwilleran pushed him aside and opened its cover. At that moment there was a thunderous crash overhead, followed by a flash of lightning, and the lights went out. Qwilleran stood in total blackness, darker than anything he had ever experienced.

CHAPTER 7

"Now what do we do?" Qwilleran asked his companions. He stood in the middle of a dead man's office in total darkness, listening to the rain driving against the house. The darkness made no difference to the Siamese, but Qwilleran was completely blind. Never had he experienced a blackout so absolute.

"We can't stay here and wait for the power lines to be repaired, that's obvious," he said as he started to feel his way out of the room. He stumbled over a leather lounge chair and bumped the computer station, and when he stepped on a tail, the resulting screech unnerved him. Sliding his feet across the floor cautiously and groping with hands outstretched, he kicked a piece of furniture that proved to be an ottoman. "Dammit, Koko! Why didn't you find this room before I bought one!" he scolded.

Eventually he located the door into the living room, but that large area was even more difficult to navigate. He had not yet learned the floor plan, although he knew it was booby-trapped with clusters of chairs and tables in mid-room. A flash of violet-blue lightning illuminated the scene for half a second, hardly enough time to focus one's eyes, and then it was darker than before. If one could find the wall, Qwilleran thought, it should be possible to follow it around to the archway leading to the foyer. It was a method that Lori Bamba's elderly cat had used after losing his sight. It may have worked well for old Tinkertom, who was only ten inches high and equipped with extrasensory whiskers, but Qwilleran cracked his knee or bruised his thigh against every chair, chest, and table placed against the wall.

Upon reaching the archway, he knew he had to cross the wide foyer, locate the entrance to the dining room, flounder through it to the kitchen, and then find the emergency candles. A flashlight would have solved the problem, but Qwilleran's was in the glove compartment of his car. He would have had a pocketful of wooden matches if Dr. Melinda Goodwinter had not convinced him to give up his pipe.

"This is absurd," he announced to anyone listening. "We might as well go to bed, if we can find it." The Siamese were abnormally quiet. Groping his way along the foyer wall, he reached the stairs, which he ascended on hands and knees. It seemed the safest course since there were two invisible cats prowling underfoot. Eventually he located his bedroom, pulled off his clothes, bumped his forehead on a bedpost, and crawled between the lace-trimmed sheets.

Lying there in the dark he felt as if he had been in the Potato Mountains for a week, rather than twenty-four hours. At this rate, his three months would be a year and a half, mountain time. By comparison, life in Pickax was slow, uncomplicated, and relaxing. Thinking nostalgically about Moose County and fondly about Polly Duncan and wistfully about the converted apple barn that he called home, Qwilleran dropped off to sleep.

It was about three in the morning that he became aware of a weight on his chest. He opened his eyes. The bedroom lights were glaring, and both cats were hunched on his chest, staring at him. He chased them into their own room, then shuffled sleepily through the house, turning off lights that had been on when the power failed. Three of them were in Hawkinfield's office, and once more he entered the secret room, wondering what it contained to make secrecy so necessary. Curious about the scrapbook that Koko had discovered, he found it to contain clippings from the *Spudsboro Gazette*—editorials signed with the initials J.J.H. Qwilleran assumed that Koko had been attracted to the adhesive with which they were mounted, probably rubber cement.

The cat might be addicted to glue, but Qwilleran was addicted to the printed word. At any hour of the day or night he was ready to read. Sitting down under a lamp and propping his feet on the editor's ottoman, he delved into the collection of columns headed "The Editor Draws a Bead."

It was an appropriate choice. Hawkinfield took potshots at Congress, artists, the IRS, the medical profession, drunk drivers, educators, Taters, unions, and the sheriff. The man had an infinite supply of targets. Was he really that sour about everything? Or did he know that inflammatory editorials sold papers? From his editorial throne he railed against Wall Street, welfare programs, Hollywood, insurance companies. He ridiculed environmentalists and advocates of women's rights. Obviously he was a tyrant that many persons would like to assassinate. Even his style was abusive:

"So-called artists and other parasites, holed up in their secret coves on Little Potato and performing God knows what unholy rites, are plotting to sabotage economic growth . . . Mountain squatters, uneducated and unwashed, are dragging their bare feet in mud while presuming to tell the civilized world how to approach the twenty-first century . . ."

The man was a monomaniac, Qwilleran decided. He stayed with the scrapbook, and another one like it, until dawn. By the time he was ready for sleep, however, the Siamese were ready for breakfast, Yum Yum howling her ear-splitting "N-n-NOW!" Only at mealtimes did she assume her matriarchal role as if she were the official breadwinner, and it was incredible that this dainty little female could utter such piercing shrieks.

"This is Father's Day," Qwilleran rebuked her as he opened a can of boned chicken. "I don't expect a present, but I deserve a little consideration."

Father's Day had more significance at Tiptop than he knew, as he discovered when he went to Potato Cove to pick up the four batwing capes.

The rain had stopped, and feeble rays of sun were glistening on trees and shrubs. When he stood on the veranda with his morning mug of coffee, he discovered that mountain air when freshly washed heightens the senses. He was seeing details he had not noticed the day before: wildflowers everywhere, blue jays in the evergreens, blossoming shrubs all over the mountains. On the way to Potato Cove he saw streams of water gushing from crevices in the roadside cliffs—impromptu waterfalls that made their own rainbows. More than once he stopped the car, backed up, and stared incredulously at the arched spectrum of color.

The rain had converted the Potato Cove road into a ribbon of mud, and Qwilleran drove slowly, swerving to avoid puddles like small ponds. As he passed a certain log cabin he saw the apple peeler on the porch again, rocking contentedly in her high-backed mountain rocker. Today she was wearing her Sunday best, evidently waiting for someone to drive her to church. An ancient straw hat, squashed but perky with flowers, perched flatly on her white hair. What caused Qwilleran to step on the brake was the sight of her entourage: a black cat on her lap, a calico curled at her feet, and a tiger stretched on the top step. Today the shotgun was not in evidence.

Slipping his camera into a pocket, he stepped out of his car and approached her with a friendly wave of the hand. She peered in his direction without responding.

"I beg your pardon, ma'am," he called out in his most engaging voice. "Is this the road to Potato Cove?"

She rocked back and forth a few times before replying. "Seems like y'oughta know," she said with a frown. "I see'd you go by yestiddy. Road on'y goes one place."

"Sorry, but I'm new here, and these mountain roads are confusing." He ventured closer in a shambling, non-threatening way. "You have some nice cats. What are their names?"

"This here one's Blackie. That there's Patches. Over yonder is Tiger." She recited the names in a businesslike way as if he were the census taker.

"I like cats. I have two of them. Would you mind if I take a picture of them?" He held up his small camera for her approval.

She rocked in silence for a while. "Iffen I git one," she finally decided.

"I'll see that you get prints as soon as they're developed." He snapped several pictures of the group in rapid succession. "That does it! . . . Thank you . . . This is a nice cabin. How long have you lived on Little Potato?"

"Born here. Fellers come by all the time pesterin' me to sell. You one o' them fellers? Ain't gonna sell."

"No, I'm just spending my vacation here, enjoying the good mountain air. My name's Jim Qwilleran. What's your name?" Although he was not prone to smile, he had an ingratiating manner composed of genuine interest and a caressing voice that was irresistible.

"Ev'body calls me Grammaw Lumpton, seein' as how I'm a great-grammaw four times."

"Lumpton, you say? It seems there are quite a few Lumptons in the Potatoes," Qwilleran said, enjoying his unintentional pun.

"Oughta be!" the woman said, rocking energetically. "Lumptons been here more'n a hun'erd year—raisin' young-uns, feedin' chickens, sellin' eggs, choppin' wood, growin' taters and nips, runnin' corn whiskey . . ."

A car pulled into the yard, the driver tooted the horn, and the vigorous old lady stood up, scattering cats, and marched to the car without saying goodbye. Now Qwilleran understood—or thought he understood—the reason for the shotgun on the porch the day before; it was intended to ward off land speculators if they became too persistent, and Grammaw Lumpton probably knew how to use it.

Despite the muddy conditions in Potato Cove, the artists and shopkeepers were opening for business. Chrysalis Beechum met him on the wooden sidewalk in front of her weaving studio. What she was wearing looked handwoven but as drab as before; her attitude had mellowed, however.

"I didn't expect you to drive up here in this mud," she said.

"It was worth it," Qwilleran said, "if only to see the miniature waterfalls making six-inch rainbows. What are the flowers all over the mountain?"

"Mountain laurel," she said. They entered the shop, stepping into the enveloping softness of wall-to-wall, floor-to-ceiling textiles.

"Was this place ever an old schoolhouse?" he asked.

"For many years. My great-grandmother learned the three Rs here. Until twenty years ago the Taters were taught in one-room schools—eight grades in a single room, with one teacher, and sometimes with one textbook. The Spuds got away with murder! . . . Here are your capes. I brought six so you'll have a color choice. What are you going to do with them, Mr. . . . ."

"Qwilleran. I'm taking them home to friends. Perhaps you could help me choose. One woman is a golden blond; one is a reddish blond; one is graying; and the other is a different color every month."

"You're not married?" she asked in her forthright way but without any sign of personal interest.

"Not any more . . . and never again! Did you have a power outage last night?"

"Everybody did. There's no discrimination when it comes to power lines. Taters and Spuds, we all black out together."

"Where's your mother today?"

"She doesn't work on Sundays."

With the weaver's help Qwilleran chose violet for Lori, green for Fran, royal blue for Mildred, and taupe for Hixie. He signed traveler's checks while Chrysalis packed the capes in a yarn box.

"I never saw this much money all at once," she said.

When the transaction was concluded, Qwilleran lingered, uncertain whether to broach a painful subject. Abruptly he said, "You didn't tell me that J.J. Hawkinfield was the man your brother was accused of murdering."

"Did you know him?" she asked sharply.

"No, but I'm renting his former home."

She gasped in repugnance. "Tiptop? That's where it happened— a year ago today! They called it the Father's Day murder. Wouldn't you know the press would have to give it a catchy label?"

"Why was your brother accused?"

"It's a long story," she said with an audible sigh.

"I want to hear it, if you don't mind."

"You'd better sit down," she said, kicking a wooden crate across the floor. She climbed onto the bench at the loom, where she sat with back straight and eyes flashing.

Qwilleran thought, She's not unattractive; she has good bones and the lean, strong look of a mountaineer and the lean, strong hands of a weaver; she needs a little makeup to be really good-looking.

"Forest went to college and studied earth sciences," she began boldly, as if she had recited this tale before. "When he came home he was terribly concerned about the environment, and he resented the people who were ruining our mountains. Hawkinfield was the instigator of it all. Look what he did to Big Potato! And he set up projects that will continue to rape the landscape."

"Exactly what did Hawkinfield plan?" Qwilleran asked in tones of concern. His profession had made him a sympathetic listener.

"After developing Tiptop Estates and making a pile of money, he sold parcels of land and then organized syndicates to promote condos, a motel, a mobile home park, even a ski lodge! Clear-cutting has already begun for the ski runs. Isn't it ironic that they're naming a *scenic drive* after that man?"

"What did your brother do about this situation?"

"Perhaps he was a little hotheaded, but he believed in militant action. He wasn't the only one who wanted to stop the desecration, but Hawkinfield was a very powerful figure in the valley. Owning the newspaper and radio station, you know, and having money and political influence, he had everybody up against the wall. Forest was the only one who dared to speak out."

"Did he have a forum for his opinions?"

"Well, hardly, under the circumstances. All he could do was organize meetings and outdoor rallies. He had to pass out handbills to get an audience. At first nobody would print them, but a friend of ours worked in the job-printing shop at the *Gazette* and vol-unteered to run off a few flyers between jobs. Unfortunately he got caught and was fired. We felt terrible about it, but he didn't hold it against us."

"What kind of response did you get to your announcements?" Qwilleran asked.

"Pretty good the first time, and there was a reporter in the crowd

from the *Gazette*, so we thought we were going to get publicity—
good or bad, it didn't matter. It would be exposure. But we were
so naive! There was not a word reported in the paper, but he
photographed everyone in the audience! Is that dirty or isn't it?
Just like secret police! People got the message, and only a few brave
ones with nothing to lose showed up for the next rally. This environmental issue has really separated the good guys from the bad
guys in this county."

"In what way?"

"Well, for one thing, the board of education wouldn't let us use
the school auditorium or playfield, and the city wouldn't let us use
the community house, but one of the pastors stuck his neck out
and let us use the church basement. I'll never forget him—the
Reverend Perry Lumpton."

"Is he the one with the contemporary-style building on the way
to the golf club?"

"No, he has the oldest church in town, sort of a historic building."

"And what was Hawkinfield's reaction?"

"He wrote an editorial about 'church interference in secular
affairs, in opposition to the economic welfare of the community
which it pretends to serve.' Those were the very words! But that
wasn't the end of it. The city immediately slapped some code vi-
olations on the old church building. Hawkinfield was a real
stinker."

"If your brother is innocent," Qwilleran asked, "do you have
any idea who's guilty?"

Chrysalis shook her head. "It could be anybody. That man had
a lot of secret enemies who didn't dare cross him. Even people
who played along with him to save their skins really hated his guts,
Forest said."

"Were there no witnesses to the crime?"

"No one actually saw it happen. The police said there was a
struggle and then he was pushed over the cliff. All the evidence
introduced at the trial was circumstantial, and the state's witnesses
committed perjury."

Qwilleran said, "I'd like to hear more about this. Would you have dinner with me some evening?" One of his favorite diversions was to take a woman to dinner. Beauty and glamor were no consideration, so long as he found her interesting, and he was aware that women were equally enthusiastic about his invitations. Chrysalis hesitated, however, avoiding his eyes. "How about tomorrow night?" he suggested. "I'll pick you up here at closing time."

"We're closed Mondays."

"Then I'll pick you up at home."

"You couldn't find the house," she said.

"I found it once," he retorted.

"Yes, but you weren't looking for it, and when you got there, you didn't know where you were. I'd better meet you at Tiptop."

Qwilleran, before returning home with his four batwing capes, decided to drive to the valley to have his Sunday dinner ahead of the Father's Day rush. After he parked he looked up at the mountains. Little Potato, though inhabited, looked lushly verdant, while Big Potato was blemished with construction sites, affluent estates carved out of the forest, and Hawk's Nest Drive zigzagging through the wooded slopes. He found himself being drawn into a controversy he preferred to avoid; he had come to the Potatoes to think about his own future, to make personal decisions.

At the Five Points Café the Father's Day Special was a turkey dinner with cornbread dressing, cranberry sauce, and nips. "Hold the nips," he said when he ordered, but the plate came to the table with a suspicious mound of something gray alongside the scoop of mashed potatoes. He was in Turnip Country, and it was impossible to avoid them. As he wolfed the food without actually tasting it, his mind went over the story Chrysalis had told him. He recalled Koko's initial reaction to the Queen Anne chair and the French door at the scene of the crime. How would Koko react to the veranda railing that the carpenter had been called in to repair? It overhung a hundred-foot drop, straight down except for projecting boulders on its craggy facade. Qwilleran could reconstruct the scene: a chair thrown through the glass door and a violent struggle on the veranda before Hawkinfield crashed through the railing and fell to his death.

Upon returning to Tiptop he conducted a test, buckling Koko

into his harness and walking him around the veranda on a leash. The cat pursued his usual order of business: indiscriminate tugging, balancing on the railing, examining infinitesimal specks on the painted floorboards. When they reached the rear of the house, however, he walked cautiously to the repaired railing, then froze with tail stiffened, back arched, and ears flattened. Qwilleran thought, He knows something happened here and exactly where it happened!

"Who did it, Koko?" Qwilleran asked. "Tater or Spud?"

The cat merely pranced in circles with distasteful stares at the edge of the veranda.

The experiment was interrupted by the telephone; answering it, Qwilleran heard a woman's sweet voice saying, "Good afternoon, Mr. Qwilleran. This is Vonda Dudley Wix, a columnist for the *Gazette*. Mr. Carmichael was good enough to give me your phone number. I do hope I'm not interrupting a blissful Sunday siesta."

"Not at all," he said in a monotone intended to be civil but not encouraging.

"Mr. Qwilleran, I would dearly love to write a profile of you and your exploits, which Mr. Carmichael tells me are positively prodigious, and I'm wondering if I might drive up your glorious mountain this afternoon for an impromptu interview."

"I'm afraid that would be impossible," he said. "I'm getting dressed to go out to a party."

"Of course! You're going to be tremendously popular! A journalistic lion! And that's why I do so terribly want to write about you before all the best people engulf you with invitations. I promise," she added with a coy giggle, "to spell your name right."

"To be perfectly frank, I don't plan to be social while I'm here. My purpose is to do some necessary work in quiet seclusion, and I'm afraid any mention in your popular column would defeat my purpose."

"Have no fear, Mr. Qwilleran. I would cover that aspect in my profile and even envelop you in a protective air of mystery. Perhaps I might run up to see you tomorrow."

As a columnist himself, Qwilleran knew his reaction when a subject declined to be interviewed; he considered it a personal affront. Yet, he had no intention of being peeled as one of Vonda

Dudley Wix's potatoes. He said, "I'm still in the process of getting settled, Ms. Wix, and tomorrow I have another appointment downtown, but I could meet you somewhere for a cup of coffee and talk for a few minutes. Just tell me where to meet you."

"Oh, please come to my house and have tea!" she cried. "I live on Center Street in a little Victorian gingerbread cottage. Tell me when it's convenient for you."

"How about ten-thirty? I have an appointment at eleven-fifteen, but I can give you half an hour."

"Delightful! Beyond my wildest dreams!" she said. "May I have a *Gazette* photographer here?"

"Please—no photos," Qwilleran said.

"Are you sure? You're such a handsome man! I saw you lunching at the club, and I adore your moustache! It's so romantic!"

"No pictures," Qwilleran said firmly. Why, he wondered, did strangers feel free to talk to him about his moustache? He never said, "I like the size of your nose . . . Your ears are remarkably flat . . . You have an unusual collarbone." But his moustache was considered in the public domain, to be discussed without permission or restraint.

When he concluded his conversation with the columnist, he found Koko sitting on Lord Fitzwallow's sideboard with ears askew, waiting for a recap.

"That was Vonda Tiddledy Winks," Qwilleran told him as he unbuckled his harness.

"Yow," said Koko, who never wasted words.

"And you're having an early dinner tonight because I'm going to a cocktail party. Maybe I'll bring you some caviar."

Shortly after five o'clock Qwilleran walked down Hawk's Nest Drive, past the Wilbank house, to Seven Levels. There were half a dozen cars parked there, and Dolly Lessmore greeted him at the door, carrying a double old-fashioned glass and wearing something too short, too tight, and too red, in Qwilleran's opinion.

"We were going to have it around the pool," she said, "but everything is so wet after last night's rain. Come into the family room, Jim, and meet your neighbors from Tiptop Estates. May I call you Jim? Please call me Dolly."

"My friends call me Qwill," he said.

"Oh, I like that! What will you have to drink?"

"What are you having?"

"My downfall—brandy and soda."

"I'll have the same—on ice—without the brandy."

"Qwill, you remember my husband, the golf nut."

"Hi there," said Robert with a handshake that was more athletic than cordial.

"Are you getting comfortably settled at Tiptop?" Dolly asked.

"Gradually. Sabrina Peel is coming tomorrow to throw a few things around and liven it up. Is it okay if I have a carpenter build a gazebo in the woods?"

"Sure! Anything you like . . . as long as you pay for it and don't take it with you when you leave," she added with a throaty laugh. She steered Qwilleran into a cluster of guests. "These are your nearest neighbors, Del and Ardis Wilbank. *Sheriff* Wilbank, you know . . . And this is Dr. John and Dr. Inez Wickes, veterinarians . . . Qwill has two cats," she explained to the Wickes couple. "John and Inez have a perfectly enchanting house over a waterfall, Qwill. It's called Hidden Falls. Perhaps you've seen the sign."

"We thought it was a good idea," said Inez with chagrin, "but honestly, it runs all the time, like faulty plumbing. There are nights when we'd give anything to shut it off, especially after all the rain we've had this spring."

"The water table is dangerously high," said her husband, whose sober mien was emphasized by owl-like eyeglasses. "We have unstable slope conditions here, and we have to worry about mudslides. I've never known the ground to be so saturated."

The hostess introduced several other couples living on Hawk's Nest Drive, and their conversation followed the usual formula: "When did you arrive? . . . How long are you staying? . . . How do you like our mountain? . . . Do you play golf?"

Qwilleran was glad that no one mentioned his moustache, although the women stared at it with a look of appreciation that he had come to recognize. There were two other moustaches there, but neither of them could equal his—in luxuriance or character.

It was a stand-up cocktail party, for which he was grateful. He liked to wander in and out of chatty groups or draw one guest aside for a moment of private conversation. He was curious by nature and an interrogator by profession. Catching Del Wilbank standing alone, nursing a drink and staring out at the pool, he went to him and said, "I've admired your house, Sheriff. It's an ingenious design."

"*We* like it," said Wilbank gruffly, "but it's not everybody's idea of a house. Look at those diagonal boards long enough and you start leaning to one side. Our property is three-point-two acres. Ardis wanted to see the sunsets, so we cleared out about fifty trees. The TV reception's not very good."

"I presume you knew Hawkinfield," Qwilleran said.

"Everyone knew J.J."

"It was an unfortunate end to what I understand was a distinguished career."

"But not totally unexpected," the sheriff said. "We knew something was going to erupt. J.J. was an independent cuss and didn't pull any punches. It was a crime waiting to happen."

"I hear he went over the cliff," Qwilleran ventured.

Wilbank nodded grimly. "That's a long way down! There was a violent altercation first."

"What time of day was it?"

"About two in the afternoon. Ardis and I were at home, waiting for our son to call from Colorado."

"Were there witnesses?"

"No. J.J. was home alone. His daughter was visiting from out of town for Father's Day, and she went down to Five Points for groceries. When she got back, she saw broken glass and a broken railing on the back porch. She screamed for her dad and couldn't find him. Then she heard their Doberman howling at the bottom of the cliff. She came running down the hill to our house, hysterical. That was a year ago today. I was just standing here, thinking about it."

"Were there many suspects?"

"All you need is one, if you've got the right guy. We traced him through his vehicle. When J.J.'s daughter went down the hill for groceries, she saw this old army vehicle coming up. When she got back, it was gone. Good observation on her part! It led us right to Beechum. He'd been a troublemaker all along."

"Did he have a record?"

"Nothing on the books, but he'd threatened J.J. He was appre-hended, charged with murder, brought to trial, and convicted—open-and-shut case. These Taters, you know . . . some of them have a murderous streak. You've heard of the Hatfields and Mc-Coys? Well, that crew didn't live in the Potatoes, but we have the same breed around here. Hot-tempered . . . prone to hold grudges . . . quick with the shotgun."

Qwilleran said, "That's odd. I've been to Potato Cove a couple of times, and I didn't get that impression at all. They come across as amiable people, totally involved with their handcrafts."

"Oh, sure! But don't look at one of them cross-eyed, or you might get the top of your head blown off."

CHAPTER 8

Qwilleran nursed his glass of soda, sampled the hors d'oeuvres, and listened to the other guests at the Lessmore party as they discussed the problems of mountain living: the inadequacy of fire protection, the high cost of blacktopping a circular drive, poor television reception, the threat of mudslides, the possibility of get-ting street lights and mail delivery on Hawk's Nest Drive.

When he thought it was time to go home, he asked the hostess for a taste of liver pâté for the Siamese—there was no caviar—and started the uphill walk to Tiptop. Hawk's Nest ascending, he dis-covered, was steeper than Hawk's Nest descending, and the calves of his legs, accustomed to the flatlands of Moose County, were already sore from Saturday's ramble in the woods. He trudged up the slope slowly and found himself repeatedly smoothing his mous-tache. It had a peculiar sensitivity to certain stimuli, and he felt a sensation in its roots whenever he encountered prevarication, de-ception, or any degree of improbity. And now it was sending him signals. Koko, with his twitching whiskers and inquisitive nose, had the same propensity. In a way they were brothers under the skin.

Qwilleran spent the rest of the evening reading *The Magic Mountain* and wishing he had some kind of muscle-rub. He read aloud to the Siamese, but the day's exercise, coupled with lack of sleep on the previous night, sent him to bed early. In spite of the offending lace on the bed linens, he slept well until seven-thirty, when a noisy engine and broken muffler told him that Dewey Beechum had arrived to start building the gazebo.

He pulled on some clothes hurriedly and went down to the parking lot to greet the carpenter. "Better build it over there," he suggested, pointing to a small clearing.

"T'other side o' them trees is better," said the man. "That's where I'm fixin' to put it."

"Well, I have to admit you were dead right about the rain, Mr. Beechum, so I'll take your word for it."

"Rain ain't over yit," the workman mumbled to himself.

Qwilleran watched him unload tools and materials from his truck and then helped carry them to the building site. To be sociable he remarked, dropping his subjective pronouns like a Tater, "Had a scare Saturday just before the rain. Went for a walk in the woods. Got lost."

"Ain't safe 'thout a shotgun," Beechum said. "See any bears?"

"Just a big black dog. Are there bears in these woods?"

"Not more'n two-hun'erd-pounders. Killed five-hun'erd-pounders when we was young-uns. Hard times then. Hadda kill our meat."

Qwilleran listened politely, then excused himself and returned to the house to feed the cats. Feeding the cats, he reflected, was the one constant in his unstructured life—the twice-daily ritual around which his other activities pivoted. A few years ago he would never have believed this to be possible. "Don't be alarmed if you hear hammering and sawing," he told them. "It's being done for your benefit. I'll be back around one o'clock, in case I get any phone calls."

After having breakfast downtown he bought four hot dogs, laid in a supply of flashlights, and opened a checking account at the First Potato National. He was on Center Street when a train rumbled through town on the ledge directly above the bank. The ground shuddered, and the roar of locomotive and freight cars re-verberated through the valley.

"Has there ever been a washout here?" he asked the young bank teller. "Did a locomotive ever come crashing down on the central business district?"

"Not that I know of," she said with the detachment of her profession. "Would you like plain checks or the ones with a moun-tain design? There's an extra charge for designer checks."

"Plain," he said.

At ten-thirty he reported for his appointment with Vonda Dud-ley Wix. Of all the Victorian houses in the residential section of Center Street, the Wix residence had the fanciest gingerbread trim on gables and porch, as well as the greatest number of hanging flower baskets. Before he could ring the bell, the door opened, and the buxom Ms. Wix greeted him in a blue satin hostess gown and pearls. Her hair, he was sure, was dyed.

"You're so delightfully punctual, Mr. Qwilleran," she cried. "Please come in and make yourself comfortable in the parlor while I brew the tea."

She swept away in ripples of satin that highlighted her rounded contours, while Qwilleran ventured into a room with red walls, rose-patterned carpet, and swagged windows. Reluctant to sit on any of the delicate carved-back chairs, he wandered about and looked at the framed photos on the marble-top tables and shawl-draped piano.

"Do you like Darjeelin'?" she asked when she returned with a silver tea service on a tea cart.

"When it comes to tea, my education has been sadly neglected," Qwilleran said. It was his courteous way of saying he never drank the stuff if he could avoid it. His hostess arranged her folds of blue satin on the black horsehair settee, and he lowered himself carefully to the seat of a dainty chair with a carved back. Then he opened a barrage of questions: "Are these all family heirlooms? . . . How long have you lived in Spudsboro? . . . Does the river ever flood your backyard?"

While giving conscientious answers Ms. Wix poured tea into finger-trap cups that were eggshell thin, using a pearl-handled silver tea strainer.

"An excellent brew," he remarked. "What is your secret?"

"Don't overboil the water!" she said in a confidential whisper. "My late husband adored my tea, but I never revealed my secret."

"How long has Mr. Wix been . . . gone?"

"Almost a year, and I miss him dreadfully. It was a late marriage. We had only eight years together, eight blissful years."

"My condolences," Qwilleran murmured, waiting a few respectful moments before resuming his interrogation: "Who painted the portrait of you? . . . Do you do your own decorating? . . . When was this house built?" He noticed a small recording device on the tea table, but she had forgotten to turn it on.

"Isn't it a charming house? It was built more than a hundred years ago by a Mr. Lumpton who owned the general store. Spudsboro was a sleepy old-fashioned town for decades until J.J. Hawkinfield took over the newspaper and brought the community to life."

"Was your husband a journalist?"

"Oh, no! Wilson was a highly successful building contractor. He had the contract to build all the houses on Hawk's Nest Drive. He was also on the city council. Wilson was responsible for introducing trash containers and parking meters on Center Street."

"I suppose you studied journalism in college?" he asked slyly.

"Oh, dear, no! I simply had a natural gift for writing, and J.J. elevated me from subscription clerk to columnist overnight! That was twenty-five years ago, and I've been 'peeling potatoes,' so to speak, ever since. I'm afraid I'm telling you my age," she added with coy girlishness.

"Then you knew J.J. very well. How would you describe him?"

"Let me see . . . He had black, black eyes that could bore right through a person . . . and a very *important* nose . . . and a stern expression that made everyone toe the line—employees, city officials, everyone! I believe that's how he achieved such great things for the city. Better schools, new sewers, a good library . . ."

"Did you feel intimidated?"

"Not really," she said with a small, guilty smile. "He was very nice to me. Before I married Wilson, J.J. used to invite me to swimming parties at Lake Batata and wonderful Christmas parties at Tiptop. It was very exciting."

"What happened to their three sons?" Qwilleran asked.

She set down her teacup and turned to him with a doleful face. "They were killed—all three of them! The two younger boys were buried in an avalanche while skiing, and the older boy was lost on the river. Their mother, poor soul, had a nervous breakdown and is still hospitalized somewhere in Pennsylvania . . . May I pour you some tea?"

Qwilleran allowed his cup to be refilled and then asked, "What was the local reaction to J.J.'s murder?"

"We were all simply ravaged with grief! He was the most important personage in the Potatoes! Of course, we all knew it was one of those awful mountain people, and it's a wonder he wasn't lynched before he came to trial."

Qwilleran glanced at his watch and rose abruptly. "I regret I must tear myself away. This has been a most enjoyable visit, but I have another appointment."

"I understand."

"Thank you for the delicious tea."

Vonda Dudley Wix escorted him to the door and said goodbye with effusive expressions of goodwill, and Qwilleran went on his way with smug satisfaction at his handling of the interview.

Returning to Tiptop, he prepared for the visit of Sabrina Peel with somewhat more enthusiasm, chilling wine glasses, re-hanging the mountain painting, placing the iron candelabrum alongside the Fitzwallow chest. He also took care to move the secretary desk back across the door to J.J.'s office; someone had a reason for wanting him to keep out, and he thought it wise to preserve appearances.

Promptly at one-thirty the designer arrived with a vanload of accessories and a young man named Jimmie to carry them up the twenty-five steps. There were wall hangings, toss pillows, a pair of eight-foot folding screens, accent rugs, lamps, and boxes of bric-a-brac.

She said, "You don't have to buy these things, you know. They were on the floor in our studio, and I'm renting them to you. The florist is on the way here with some rental plants. Do you intend to do much entertaining?"

"I might have one or two persons in for drinks, that's all," Qwilleran said.

"Then let's close the French doors to the dining room and bank
some large plants in the foyer . . . I never saw *that* before!" She
pointed to the seven-foot, eight-branch iron tree.

"I bought it from the blacksmith in Potato Cove."

"You have a good eye, Qwill. It shows some imagination, and
it's not overdone. Happily it distracts the eye from that hideous
Fitzwallow huntboard, which I hasten to say did not come from
our studio."

"You call it a huntboard? That's appropriate. My cat is always
hunting for something underneath it."

"You didn't tell me you have a cat."

"I have two Siamese, and they're up there on the stairs, watching
your every move."

"I hope they're not destructive," the designer said, and she called
up to them, "If you scratch it, kids, you've bought it!"

"Yow!" Koko retorted.

"He's a sassy brat, isn't he?" said Sabrina. "Now let's go to work
on the living room. We'll create a more intimate setting by stopping the eye with folding screens as room dividers."

Qwilleran watched her work with manifest enjoyment as she
whirled around the room, her pleated skirt swirling about her
knees and her silky mop of hair swirling around her shoulders.
With crisp authority she directed Jimmie in placing screens,
grouping chairs, skirting tables, setting up lamps, throwing
throw rugs, tossing toss pillows, and hanging wall hangings. She
herself arranged brass candlesticks, ceramic bowls, carved boxes,
and stacks of design magazines. When she had finished, the
room looked inhabited by a person of taste, although not necessarily Qwilleran's taste. Nevertheless, he was grateful for the
metamorphosis.

Then the florist arrived with indoor trees and large potted plants.

"Do I have to water these things?" Qwilleran inquired.

"No, sir," said the florist. "For rental plants we send a visiting
nurse once a week to test the soil for moisture."

As the room was transformed, Koko's curiosity overcame his

misgivings, and he watched from the archway. Yum Yum held back, poised for flight.

Qwilleran said to Sabrina, "Would you stay for a glass of chardonnay?"

"I'd love to," she said without hesitation. "Jimmie can go back downtown with the florist . . . Jimmie, tell Mr. Poole where I am, and if my four-o'clock client comes in, tell her I'm running late. Give her an old magazine to read." To Qwilleran she explained, "She's my doctor's wife, and revenge is sweet."

Sabrina with her chardonnay and Qwilleran with his apple juice sat in the portion of the living room that was now pleasantly secluded by screens and plants. It was made comfortable with chatty new furniture groupings and made lively with red and gold accents.

"My compliments to the designer," he said, raising his glass. "I hope the screens are sturdy; the cats are sometimes airborne when they're in a good mood."

"You'll find them quite stable," she assured him. "They were custom-made to do heavy duty in the studio. What are you building in the woods?"

"A screened gazebo, so the cats can take an airing if it ever dries up. No one told me it rains so much in the mountains. Also, no one told me that Hawkinfield had been murdered."

"Didn't you know?" Sabrina asked. "What's more, you have a painting done by the murderer." She waved a hand toward the foyer.

"Forest Beechum? Is that his work?" Qwilleran said in surprise. "That fellow really knows how to paint mountains!"

"He did several mountain studies for my clients. Too bad he got himself in such bad trouble."

"Were you satisfied with the verdict?"

"Frankly, I didn't follow the trial, but—from what I hear— there's no doubt that he was guilty." Her wineglass was empty.

"Will you have a touch?" Qwilleran asked, tilting the wine bottle. "How did you get along with Hawkinfield as a client?"

"Fortunately we had very little contact with him," the designer said. "We worked with Mrs. Hawkinfield, but after she was hospitalized we ran into trouble with J.J. He refused to pay a rather sizable bill for what his wife had ordered, saying she was incompetent and we had taken advantage of her disturbed condition. That's the kind of person he was." Sabrina tapped her fingers irritably on the arm of the chair.

"Were you able to collect?"

"Not until we took him to court, and—believe me!—it took a lot of nerve to sue a man as powerful as Hawkinfield. It infuriated him to lose the case, of course, and he relieved his spite by writing a scathing editorial about the moral turpitude (whatever that means) of artists in general and interior designers in particular. I don't think anyone really liked the man—except the woman who writes the 'Potato Peelings' column. He was not only opinionated but ruthless, and he had a completely wrong-headed attitude toward women. A man of his intelligence, living at this moment in history, should have known better." She tossed her head and flung her hair back gracefully, using both well-manicured hands in an appealing gesture. "We all knew he was psychologically abusive to his wife and daughter. He worshipped his sons, and after they were killed, he sent the girl away to boarding school—away from her mother, away from her friends, away from these mountains—everything she loved."

Qwilleran liked designers. They circulated; they knew everyone; they were in touch. He asked, "Why did she leave the mountain painting and take everything else of value?"

"She thought mountains would be too regional to sell in her shop. It's in Maryland, and she gets a sophisticated clientele from Washington and Virginia."

"What kind of shop does she have?"

"It's called Not New But Nice. Sort of an upscale, good-taste jumble shop."

"Clever name."

"Thank you," Sabrina said, patting her bangs. "It was my idea."

"Do you keep in touch with her?"

"Only to help her appraise things now and then. All J.J. left her was this house and contents, and she's trying to get all she can out of it. I suppose you can't blame her, but she's really turning out to be a greedy little monster." There was more finger-tapping on the chair arm. "She expects me to do appraisals gratis, and she's asking more than a million for this—this *white elephant*. I imagine she's charging you an arm and a leg for rent."

"I still have one of each left," Qwilleran replied. "What happened to the rest of J.J.'s assets?"

"They went into a trust for the care of his wife. You know, Qwill, you could buy this place for a lot less than she's asking. Why don't you make an offer and open a B-and-B? I could do wonders with it, inside and out." Sabrina construed his scowl. "Then how about a chic nursing home?" she suggested with a mischievous smile. "Or an illegal gambling casino? . . . No? . . . Well, I must get back to the valley. These mountain retreats lull one into a false sense of something or other. Thanks for the wine. I needed it. Where did I leave my shoulder bag?"

"On a chair in the foyer," he said. "May I take you to lunch at the golf club some day?"

"I know a better place. I'll take you to dinner," she countered.

As they left the living room, the designer stopped in the archway to view her handiwork. "We need one more splash of color over there between the windows," she said. "A couple of floor pillows perhaps."

Qwilleran had entered the foyer in time to see two furry bodies leaping from a chair. Sabrina's handbag was slouched on the chair seat, and it was unzipped. He then realized that the Siamese had been too quiet for the last half hour and too suspiciously absent. There was no way of guessing what larceny they might have committed.

"Thank you, Sabrina, for what you've accomplished this afternoon," he said. "And you make it look so easy! You're a real pro."

"You're entirely welcome. My bill will be in the mail," she laughed as she shouldered her handbag and zipped the closure.

He walked with her down the twenty-five steps, and when he returned to the house he said, "Okay, you scoundrels! What have you done? If you've stolen anything, she'll be back here with Sheriff Wilbank."

Koko, sitting on the stairs halfway up, crossed his eyes and scratched his ear. Yum Yum huddled nonchalantly on the flat top of the newel post while Qwilleran searched the foyer. He found nothing that might have come from a woman's handbag. Shrugging, he went out to check Beechum's progress with the gazebo. The carpenter had gone for the day, but the structure was taking shape—not the shape Qwilleran had requested, but it looked good. When he returned to the house he encountered a disturbing scene.

Koko was on the living room floor in a paroxysm of writhing, shaking, doubling in half, falling down, contorting his body.

Qwilleran approached him with alarm. Had he been poisoned by the plants? Was this a convulsion? "Koko! Take it easy, boy! What's wrong?"

Hearing his name, Koko rose to a half-sitting position and bit his paw viciously. Only then did Qwilleran realize that something virtually invisible was wrapped around the pad and caught between the spreading toes. Gently he helped release Koko from the entanglement. It was a long hair, decorator blond.

CHAPTER 9

Qwilleran gave the Siamese an early dinner. "Will you excuse me tonight?" he asked them. "I'm taking a guest to the golf club." He had some crackers and cheese himself, having gone hungry at the club on his last visit.

While he was dressing, the telephone rang, and he ran downstairs with lather on his face; there was no extension upstairs.

Sabrina Peel was on the line. She said, "Qwill, I lost a letter while I was at Tiptop. If you find it, just drop it in the mail; it's all stamped and addressed. It may have slipped out of my handbag when I was fishing out my car keys."

He said he had not seen the letter but promised to look on the veranda and in the parking lot. Hanging up, he gave an accusing scowl at Koko, who was sitting near the phone. Koko stretched his mouth in a yawn like an alligator.

At the appointed time a chugging motor alerted him to the arrival of Chrysalis Beechum in one of the family wrecks. The Beechums were the only two-wreck family he had ever known. He went down the steps to greet her as she climbed out of the army vehicle, looking almost attractive. Her long hair was drawn back and twisted in one long braid hanging down her back, and she wore a stiff-brimmed black hat like a toreador's. The sculptured planes of hollow cheeks and prominent cheekbones gave her face a severe but strikingly handsome aspect. Her clothes were much the same: jogging shoes, long skirt, and a top that was obviously handwoven.

"Good evening," he said. "I like your hat. You wear it well."

"Thank you," she said.

"Have you ever seen the interior of Tiptop?"

"No."

"Would you like to come in for a quick tour? The proportions are quite impressive, and there's some historic furniture."

"No, thanks," she said, her eyes flashing.

"Then let's take off. Your car or mine?" he quipped without getting any amused response. He opened the car door for her. "I've reserved a table at the golf club. I think you'll approve of the food. It's quite wholesome—almost too wholesome for my depraved taste." Still, his small talk with a light touch fell flat.

"Do you play golf?" she asked.

"No, but I have a membership at the club that permits me to use the dining room and bring guests."

As they started down Hawk's Nest Drive he pointed out the homes of the sheriff, the realty couple, and the veterinarians. His passenger looked at them without interest or comment.

"How was business in Potato Cove today?" he asked in an effort to involve her.

"We're closed Mondays," she said moodily.

"That's right. You told me so . . . Your father came this morning to start building my gazebo. He said it's going to rain some more."

"How do you like his hat?" she said.

"It looks as if it might have historic significance." That was Qwilleran's tactful way of saying that it was moldy with age and mildew.

With a revival of interest Chrysalis said, "It's a family heirloom. My grandfather chased some revenuers with a shotgun once, and they ran so fast that one of them lost his hat. Grampa kept it as a trophy. He was a hero in the mountains."

"Was your grandfather a moonshiner?"

"Everyone was running corn liquor in those days, if they wanted to support their families. It was the only way they could make any money to buy shoes, and flour for making bread, and seed for planting. Grampa went to jail once for operating a still, and he was proud of it."

"How long has your family lived in the mountains?"

"Since way back, when they could buy a piece of land in a hollow for a nickel an acre. They chopped down trees to build cabins and lived without roads—just blazed trails."

"One has to admire the pioneers, but how did they survive?"

"By hunting and fishing and raising turnips. They carried water from a mountain spring and made everything with their own hands: soap, medicines, tools, furniture, everything. My grandmother told me all this. The affluent ones, she said, had a mule and a cow and a few chickens and an apple tree."

"When did it change?"

"Actually, not until the 1930s, when road building started and electricity came up the mountain. Some of the Taters didn't want electricity or indoor plumbing. They thought it was unsanitary to have the outhouse indoors. We still resist the idea of paved roads on Little Potato. We don't want joyriders polluting our air and littering our roadsides. There are some older Taters who've never been off the mountain."

Qwilleran said, "I have a lot to learn about mountain culture. I hope you'll tell me more about it."

They arrived at the golf club and presented themselves at the door of the dining room—Qwilleran in his blue linen blazer with a tie, Chrysalis in her jogging shoes and toreador hat. The tables were dressed for dinner with white cloths, wineglasses, and small vases of fresh flowers. "Reservation for Qwilleran, table for two, nonsmoking," he told the hostess.

"Oh . . . yes . . ." she said in bewilderment as she glanced at her chart and then the roomful of empty tables.

"We're a little early," he said.

"Follow me." The hostess conducted them to a table for two at the rear of the dining room, adjoining the entrance to the Off-Links Lounge, where golfers were celebrating low scores or describing missed putts with raucous exuberance.

Chrysalis said, "It sounds like a Tater horse auction."

"May we have a table away from the noise?" Qwilleran asked the hostess.

She appeared uncertain and consulted her chart again before ushering them to a table between the kitchen door and the coffee station.

"We'd prefer one with a view," he said politely but firmly.

"Those tables are reserved for regular members," she said.

Chrysalis spoke up. "The other one is all right. I don't mind the noise."

They were conducted back to the entrance of the lounge. Dropping two menu cards on the table the hostess said, "Want something from the bar?"

"We'll make that decision after we're seated," Qwilleran replied as he held a chair for his guest. "Would you like a cocktail or a glass of wine, Ms. Beechum?"

"I wish you'd call me Chrysalis," she said. "Do you think I could have a beer?"

"Anything you wish . . . and please call me Qwill."

"I learned to like beer in college. Before that I'd just had a little taste of corn liquor, and I didn't care for it."

A waiter in his late teens was hovering over the table. "Something from the bar?"

"A beer for the lady—your best brand," Qwilleran ordered, "and I'll have a club soda with a twist." The drinks arrived promptly, and he said to his guest, "The service is always excellent when you're the only customers in the place."

"Want to order?" the young man asked. His nametag identified him as Vee Jay.

"After we study the menu," Qwilleran replied. "No hurry." To Chrysalis he said, "I see you're wearing something handwoven. There's a lot of artistry in your weaving."

"Thank you," she said with pleasure. "Not everyone really notices it. The women in my family have always been weavers. Originally they raised sheep and spun the wool and made clothes for their whole family. I was weaving placemats to sell when I was seven years old. Then, in college I learned that weaving can be a creative art."

"Do you ever do wall hangings? I like tapestries."

"I've done a few, but they don't sell—too expensive for the tourist trade."

Consulting the menu she decided she would like the breast of chicken in wine sauce with pecans and apple slices, explaining, "At home we only have chicken stewed with dumplings."

Qwilleran ordered the same and suggested corn chowder as the first course. He asked the waiter to hold the food back for a while and to serve the salad following the main course.

The chowder arrived immediately.

"Return it to the kitchen," Qwilleran said to Vee Jay. "We're not ready. We requested that you hold it back." Vee Jay shuffled away with the two bowls.

Chrysalis said, "You know, just because the Taters cling to some of the old ideas like stewed chicken and dirt roads and no telephones, it doesn't mean that they're backward. They maintain old values and old customs because they know something that the lowlanders don't know. Living close to the mountains for generations and struggling to be self-sufficient, they develop their minds in different ways."

"You're probably right. I'm beginning to believe there's something mystical about mountains," Qwilleran said.

When they were finally ready for the soup course, the waiter returned with the two bowls. By this time the chowder was cold.

Qwilleran addressed him stiffly. "Vee Jay—if that is really your name—we would have ordered vichyssoise or gazpacho if we had wanted cold soup. Take this away and see that it's properly heated." To his guest he said, "I apologize for this."

In due time the chowder returned, accompanied by two salads.

"We asked to have the salad served *after the entree*," Qwilleran complained, losing patience.

The sullen waiter whisked the salads away and, before the diners could raise their soup spoons, served two orders of chicken in wine sauce, maneuvering the table setting to find room for the large dinner plates.

Now angry, Qwilleran called the hostess to the table. "Please look at this vulgar presentation of food," he said. "Is it your quaint custom to serve the entree with the soup?"

"Sorry," she said. "Vee Jay, remove the soup."

"Madame! If you please! We have not yet started the soup course! Remove the chicken and *keep it hot* until we're ready." He explained to Chrysalis, "This is the first time I've had dinner here. We should have gone to Amy's Lunch Bucket. It would have been more congenial."

"Don't worry," she said. "I don't go out enough to know the difference."

After a few moments of silent sipping of chowder, Qwilleran asked, "Are the shops in Potato Cove considered successful?"

"I don't know what you mean by 'successful,' " she said, "but we were kind of surprised when some promoters in Spudsboro invited us to move down into the valley. They want to build an addition to the mall and call it Potato Cove."

"How do your people react to that offer?"

"Most of us want to stay where we are, although the promoters tell us there'd be publicity and we'd get more traffic. The rent would be low, because the mall management would consider us an attraction."

"Don't do it!" Qwilleran said. "Potato Cove is unique. It would lose its native charm in a mall. You'd have to stay open seven days a week, eleven hours a day, and the rent would go up as soon as you were installed. They're trying to exploit you."

"I'm glad to hear you say that. I don't trust the Spuds. They do everything for their own benefit with no consideration for us. They drive up our mountain and dump trash and used tires in our ravines instead of going to the Spudsboro landfill where they'd have to pay fifty cents."

"Have you protested?"

"Often! But Taters never get a square deal from the local government. You'd think we didn't pay taxes! And now they're trying to push us off our mountain."

"How can they do that?"

"Well, you know how it is. Old folks have to sell their land because they need money or can't pay their taxes. The Spuds buy the land for next to nothing and then turn around and sell it to developers for a lot of money. That's what Hawkinfield did on Big Potato, and that's what we're afraid will happen to us. The developers will come in; taxes will go up; and more and more Taters will have to sell out. When you live on land that's been in your family for generations, it's heartbreaking to lose it. Lowlanders who don't have roots like ours don't understand how we feel."

The meal progressed with a minimum of annoyance after that, although Qwilleran found the chicken unusually salty for a dining room that prided itself on flavoring with herbs. He did his best to maintain a pleasant attitude, however. He said, "I must ask you about something that baffled me the first night I was here. It was Friday, around midnight. The atmosphere was very clear, and I saw a circle of light on Little Potato. It was revolving."

Chrysalis rolled her eyes. "I don't know whether I should tell you about that. It's kind of far-out . . . You have to understand my mother. She's a positive thinker, you know. She believes that sheer willpower can make things happen. Do you buy that?"

"I'll buy anything," he said, thinking of Koko's supranormal antics.

"It's not just her own idea. My grandmother and great-grandmother believed the same way. They survived hard times and both lived to a ripe old age. I wish I had their conviction."

"How about your mother? Has she been able to make things happen?"

"Well . . . my father was in a terrible accident at the factory once, and the doctors said he couldn't possibly pull through. But my mother and grandmother willed him to live. That was twenty-five years ago, and you'd never know anything had happened to him, except for a slight limp."

"That's a convincing story."

"Some people call it witchcraft."

"Tell that to Norman Vincent Peale," Qwilleran said. Noticing that she was picking at her food, he inquired how she liked the chicken.

"It's rather salty. I'm not used to much salt."

"I agree the chef has a heavy hand with the saltshaker. Someone should set him straight . . . Are there any other examples of your mother's positive thinking?"

"She always used to arrange good weather for our family reunions," Chrysalis said with a whimsical laugh. "Seriously, though, she made up her mind that Forest and I would go to college, and you know what happened? The state started offering free tuition to mountain students!"

"With all that you've told me, how do you explain your mother's speech affliction?"

She stared at him with the hollow-cheeked sadness he had seen when she spoke of her brother's imprisonment. "She blames herself for the terrible thing that happened to Forest."

"I don't understand," Qwilleran said.

"She used all her mental powers to stop Hawkinfield from ruining the mountains. She didn't want him murdered; she just wanted him to have a change of heart!" Chrysalis stopped and stared into space until Qwilleran urged her to go on. "The horrible irony was that my brother was convicted of the murder—and he was innocent. She made a vow never to speak another word as long as he's in prison."

Qwilleran murmured sympathy and regrets and then said, "What about the circle of light on the mountain?"

She shook her head. "Some of our kinfolk go out on top of Little Potato at midnight, carrying lanterns. They walk in a silent circle and meditate, concentrating on getting Forest released— somehow." She shook her head.

"Do they think the moving circle increases their effectiveness?" he asked gently, although he had his doubts.

"It's supposed to concentrate the force of their collective will. That's what they say."

"You sound as if you're not entirely convinced."

"I don't know . . . I don't know what to think. When we picket the courthouse, we march in a circle, the same way."

"Now that you mention it," he said, "it seems to me that pickets always move in a circle."

"The picketing was Amy's idea," said Chrysalis. "She and Forest were getting ready to marry when he was arrested. They were going to be married at the waterfall at the cove, where the mist rises up like a veil. All the plans were made . . . and then this happened. He was held without bail and railroaded to prison. It's my brother's baby that Amy takes to the Lunch Bucket every day. His name is Ashley . . . I'm sorry. I've been talking too much, but it's good to have a considerate listener who's not a Tater. Lately, I've been getting to be like my mother, not wanting to speak."

"You must not let that happen, Chrysalis. Tell me about the trial. What did you think was wrong about it?"

"Well, first, the court-appointed attorney wasn't even there for the arraignment. He phoned to say he'd be late, but the court didn't want to wait around."

"That sounds like a violation of constitutional rights," Qwilleran said.

"How did we know? We were just Taters. Then Forest was held without bail, and the attorney said it was for his personal safety because the whole town was out to get him. *My brother!* I couldn't believe it!"

"If there was so much animosity, didn't he try for a change of venue?"

She nodded. "It was denied."

"What was the attorney's name?"

"Hugh Lumpton."

Qwilleran huffed into his moustache; another one of those ubiquitous Lumptons!

Chrysalis said, "He didn't put a single defense witness on the stand, and he let the state's witnesses get away with lies! The jury brought in a guilty verdict so fast, we hardly knew it was over!"

"I'm no lawyer," Qwilleran said, "but it seems to me you should be able to get a new trial. You'd need a different attorney—a good one."

"What would it cost? We tried to borrow money to hire one

when Forest was first accused, but the banks—being mixed up with
the land speculators, you know—refused to give us a mortgage.
They advised us to sell, but you wouldn't believe what the speculators offered for our choice piece of the mountain. But now it
doesn't matter; we'd sell our land for any amount of money if it
would get Forest out of prison."

"There might be another way," Qwilleran said, smoothing his
moustache. "Let me think about it. But your brother would still
have to convince a jury that he's innocent."

They finished the meal with sparse conversation. The salad
dressing also was salty. Chrysalis moodily declined dessert and simply sipped a cup of tea, silent behind her staring, hollow-cheeked
mask.

When they left the dining room, it was still only partially occupied, and there were plenty of empty tables with a view of the
golf course. Qwilleran told his guest to wait in the vestibule while
he had a few words with the hostess. Eight words were sufficient.
Speaking calmly he said, "Give this to the management with my
compliments," and he tore up his membership card.

It was still full daylight, and Chrysalis said, "Would you like to
drive up to Tiptop the back way? It's only a logging trail, but it
goes up the outside of Big Potato, and there's something I want
you to see." She directed him through a maze of winding roads in
true wilderness. "There!" she said when they reached the top of a
knob. "Stop the car! What does that look like?"

Qwilleran saw a vast area of wiped-out forest—a tangle of
stumps, fallen trees, and dead branches. "It looks like the aftermath
of a tornado or a bombing raid."

"That's slashing!" she said. "Everything is leveled, and then
they take the good straight hardwood and leave the rejects.
Maybe you've seen the logging trucks leaving the mountains.
This is what'll happen to the whole outside of Big Potato if we
don't stop them, and this is what speculators would like to do to
L'il Tater."

The logging trail narrowed to a mere wagon track twisting upward. She pointed the way, and Qwilleran clutched the wheel as
the car lurched through the rough terrain.

"Would you care to come in for a nightcap?" he asked when they finally reached the Tiptop parking lot.

"No, thank you, but I enjoyed the evening, and thank you for listening. It was very kind of you."

He walked her to the decrepit army vehicle. "I'm sincerely sorry about your brother's predicament. I hope something can be done."

She climbed into the driver's seat. "It would be easier to move a mountain," she said with a helpless shrug.

Qwilleran watched her leave before mounting the steps to the veranda. Koko was waiting for him in the foyer, prancing back and forth as if he had something urgent to report, but Qwilleran had other things on his mind. He went directly to the phone and called Moose County without waiting for the discount rates.

"Polly, this is Qwill!" he announced abruptly.

"Dearest! I'm so thankful you called. We have terrible news. Halifax Goodwinter has taken his own life!"

"NO!"

"He buried his wife last Friday, you know, and last night he overdosed."

"This is hard to believe! Did he leave an explanation?"

"Nothing. Nothing at all. But the rumor is circulating that his wife's death was a mercy killing. She'd been hopelessly ill for so long, and the poor man was going on eighty. There'll never be another country doctor like Dr. Hal. The whole county is grieving. Melinda is definitely moving back from Boston to take over his practice, but it won't be the same."

"I agree," said Qwilleran with a gulp. He was worrying less about Moose County's medical prospects than about his own personal relationships. Before Melinda moved to Boston, she had been hell-bent on marriage, and he had been equally determined to stay single, even though he found her disturbingly attractive.

"Now that you've heard the bad news, Qwill," Polly was saying, "how's everything in the mountains?"

"I'm spittin' mad," he said.

"That sounds like mountain vernacular, and you've been there only three days."

"I've just had an infuriating experience at a restaurant."

"What did they do wrong?"

"Everything! They gave me the worst table in the place. The service was abominable. The soup was cold. The food was too salty. It was the salty food that explained the whole conspiracy."

"Are you saying it was done purposely?"

"Damn right it was! I made the mistake of taking the wrong person to dinner. My guest was a mountaineer. They're called Taters around here."

"Really! Are they so undesirable?"

"They're an unpopular minority, although they were here first, and they get a rotten shake at every turn. In Moose County we have cliques but no prejudice like this, and I was unprepared. The whole dinner was an embarrassment."

"What are you going to do?" Polly knew Qwilleran was not one to turn the other cheek.

"I've got to think about it."

"I'm sorry you're so upset."

"Don't worry," he said, his anger subsiding. "I'm going to consult Koko. He'll come up with an idea. How's Bootsie?"

"He's fine. He weighs ten pounds."

"Ten pounds going on thirty! And how are you?"

"I'm fine. The library board is giving a formal dinner Friday, and I'm altering the neck of my long dress so I can wear my pearls. I miss you, dearest."

"I miss you, too." There was a breathy pause. Despite his facility with words, Qwilleran found terms of endearment difficult. "À bientôt," he said with feeling in his voice.

"À bientôt, dearest."

He went outdoors and walked briskly around the veranda a few times. The sun was dropping behind the West Potatoes, and the dragon clouds were waging a riotous battle—violent pink and purple against a turquoise sky. When a damp chill from the northeast chased him indoors, Koko was still prancing.

"What's on your mind?" he asked absently.

"Yow!" said Koko with urgency, running back and forth through the living room arch.

"Where's Yum Yum?" It occurred to Qwilleran that he had not

seen her since returning from dinner. Immediately he checked all
the comfortable chairs in the living room and all the beds upstairs.
Calling her name he rushed from room to room, opening closets,
cabinets, and even drawers. Then—back in the living room—he
saw Koko dive under the floor-length skirt that Sabrina had draped
on a round table.

"You devils!" he muttered as he fell on his hands and knees and
peered under the skirt. There they were, both of them, wearing
beatific expressions, and on the floor between them was a stamped,
addressed letter with perforations in two corners. "Who stole this?"
he demanded, although he knew Koko was the culprit, attracted
by the adhesive on the stamp and the envelope. Although Yum
Yum's famous paw pilfered Scrabble tiles and cigarette lighters,
Koko specialized in documents, leaving fang marks as evidence.
Qwilleran dropped the Peel & Poole letter in a drawer of the Fitzwallow huntboard for safekeeping until he could mail it, noting as
he did so that it was addressed to Sherry Hawkinfield in Maryland—probably a bill for Sabrina Peel's appraisal services.

Before going upstairs to finish the evening with a book, he gave
the Siamese their bedtime snack, a dry food concocted by a gourmet cook in Moose County. Qwilleran watched them gobble and
crunch, but his mind was elsewhere. He had no desire to take sides
in local politics and no intention of becoming a gullible confederate
in a Tater obsession. Yet, the shabby treatment at the golf club and
the emotional outpourings from his dinner guest were stirring his
blood.

The matter of a good attorney could be handled easily; he had
only to call Hasselrich, Bennett & Barter in Moose County, but
old Mr. Hasselrich—he of the fluttering eyelids and quivering
jowls—would expect a well-organized brief. Some kind of preliminary investigation of the Father's Day murder would be necessary,
something that could be done quietly without causing alarm in the
valley.

As Qwilleran absentmindedly watched the Siamese washing up
after their snack, he started patting his moustache; an idea was
formulating. For cover he would use a ploy that had worked on a
previous occasion. It would explain his presence in the Potatoes

and his need to see a transcript of the Beechum trial, and it would enable him to question a number of local residents, especially those victimized by Hawkinfield's damaging editorials. To spread the word and establish his credentials he would first break the news to Carmichael at the *Gazette.*

"Colin," he would say, "I want you to be the first to know. I plan to write a biography of J.J. Hawkinfield."

CHAPTER 10

Beechum had been right again. It rained all night, charging in like a herd of elephants, battering the trees, beating on the roof, soaking the earth. By Tuesday morning the downpour had abated leaving the trees dripping, the atmosphere soggy, and the ground muddy. Qwilleran doubted that the carpenter would show up to work on the gazebo.

While he was preparing his breakfast coffee and thawing a four-day-old doughnut, the telephone rang, and a man's voice said genially, "How are you, Qwill? Getting settled? I hear you had dinner at the club last night. This is Colin Carmichael."

"Let's say that I participated in a farce that masqueraded as dinner," Qwilleran retorted in a bad humor. "How did you hear about it?"

"They called me because I sponsored you."

"If they want to apologize, it's too late. I've torn up my card."

"It's not exactly an apology. It's an explanation," the editor said. "They thought I should explain the situation to you. To put it bluntly, you brought a Tater to the club as your guest, and the members don't care for that."

"That's what I suspected," Qwilleran said belligerently. "Tell the members they know what they can do. Editors excluded, of course."

"Honestly, I hated to call you, Qwill. Sorry it happened."

"So am I. It tells me something about Spudsboro that I didn't want to know."

"Don't hold it against me. How about lunch?"

"I think it would be better if I dropped into your office. There's something I want to discuss with you, and I'd like to see some back copies while I'm there."

"Sure. Any time after two will be okay. We're putting a special to bed at two, and it's quite important. I want to be on top of it."

"What kind of special?"

"Sixteen pages of June brides, heavy on advertising, of course."

"Of course," said Qwilleran. "See you after two."

To his surprise, the red pickup with one blue fender pulled into the lot, and he went to the building site to greet the carpenter.

"Morning, Mr. Beechum. That was quite some rain we had last night."

"Gonna git worse."

"Hmmm . . . well . . . but the job is shaping up nicely. I didn't know it was going to be hexagonal, though."

"Hex what?"

"It has six sides instead of four."

"Figgered to git you sumpin' special."

"I appreciate that." Qwilleran sauntered around with his hands in his pockets. "Nice view from here. You were right about that, too."

"Lotsa purty sights in the mount'ns." The carpenter straightened up and pointed with his handsaw. "They's a purty trail down that-away."

"Thanks, but I'm not taking any more chances on getting lost in the woods."

"Iffen you git lost, jes' keep on goin'. You bound to come out somewheres."

"I admire your philosophy, Mr. Beechum. What about the caves? I hear there are some interesting caves in the mountains. Do you know anything about the caves?"

"Fulla bats. You like bats? Know a feller was bit by a bat. Kicked the bucket."

"I gather you don't recommend the caves. How about the spectacular waterfall at the cove?"

"Purty sight! Lotsa pizen snakes back there, but it's a mighty purty sight!" The carpenter's eyes were twinkling roguishly.

Qwilleran thought, This is mountain humor—scaring lowlanders with tales of snakes, bears, and bats. Let him have his fun. "When do you think this job will be finished?" he asked.

"Like 'bout when I git it done. Gonna rain some more."

"The man on the radio said the rain is over for a while," Qwilleran assured him.

"Them fellers don't know nothin' on radio," said the weather expert.

Qwilleran returned indoors to dress for downtown, and while he was shaving he heard another vehicle pull into the parking lot. A peek out the front window of the upstairs hall revealed Dolly Lessmore in brilliant yellow stepping out of her white convertible. He toweled the lather off his face and rushed downstairs to admit her.

"Hope I'm not interrupting anything," she said gaily. "I just wanted to see what Sabrina did for you. The plants do a lot for the foyer, don't they? Where'd you get that gorgeous candleholder?"

"From Potato Cove," Qwilleran said. "Go into the living room and sit down. I'll bring some coffee."

"I was hoping you'd say that."

"Shall I add a surreptitious soupçon of brandy?"

"What I don't know won't hurt me," she said, "but not too much, please; I'm on my way to the office . . . Are these the cats?" The Siamese were walking regally into the room as if they expected to be the main attraction.

"Some persons call them that," he said. "I think of them as domestic software."

Dolly turned away. "I don't know anything about cats. We've always had dogs."

At that pronouncement Koko and Yum Yum turned around and walked out, their long, lithe bodies making U-turns in unison. Foreparts seemed to be leaving the room while hindparts were still coming in.

Qwilleran served coffee in the new mugs, explaining that they were handmade by Otto the Potter and remarking, "The cove's an interesting little business community. I hope no one convinces them to move into a mall."

"Don't worry! Those Taters don't have enough sense to grab a good offer when they get one. They'd rather play store all summer and go on welfare all winter. Don't get friendly with Taters, Qwill."

He huffed into his moustache. Now he knew the reason for her impromptu visit; the club had notified her of his *faux pas.* "Didn't you hire a Tater to make repairs to this house?" he challenged her.

"Well, you know, Mr. Beechum does very good work for not much money." Dolly surveyed the living room with approval. "Sabrina did a super job here. She's a Virgo. That's a good sign for a designer."

"What's your sign?" he asked. "Or is that a trade secret?"

"I'm a Leo."

"I assume that's a good sign for selling real estate."

"It's a good sign for selling anything," she said with a throaty laugh.

"How about Hawkinfield's sign? Does anyone know?"

"Oh, sure. He was a Capricorn, meaning he was tough and power-hungry and always seemed to win, but he had a sensitive side that not many people knew. When he lost his three sons, his life was wrecked. Did you know about that?"

"I knew there were a couple of fatal accidents."

"The thing that drove him half-mad," said Dolly, turning suddenly serious, "was the suspicion that the mountain people were responsible."

"How did he figure that?"

"You don't know the story. I'll tell you . . . There was an avalanche on a ski trail. A group from the Valley Boys' Club went cross-country skiing with an adult counselor. They always hired a Tater guide, of course, who knew the mountains. Well, the skiers were strung out along the trail, with the guide leading and the counselor bringing up the rear, and most of them had squeezed through this one narrow pass when the snow started to slide off the cliff above. The counselor yelled a warning, but the two young Hawkinfield boys panicked and got tangled up in their skis. Snow and ice came thundering down on top of them."

"How do you know all these details?" Qwilleran asked.

"The counselor told us; he plays golf at the club. He yelled for help, but the rest of them were too far ahead. The pass was blocked. He dug frantically with his hands at the mountain of snow, but it was hopeless. There were tons of it! It was two days before they found the bodies. J.J. wrote an editorial on the loss of his sons that would break your heart! Privately, though, he was furious. He imagined a Tater plot. The guide, he thought, had spaced the skiers out along the trail, and an accomplice on top of the cliff started the snowslide."

"That's a far-fetched scenario, Dolly. Having someone to blame may have been a safety valve for his emotions, but . . . do you believe Taters would be so malicious?"

"You haven't heard the whole story. The following summer his one remaining son went rafting on the river with a couple of high school buddies. It was after a heavy rain—a real mountain down-pour—and the river was turbulent. That's what the kids like, of course—risks! Their raft turned over, and the other two saved themselves, but the body of the Hawkinfield boy was never found. J.J. hired private detectives, thinking his son had been kidnapped by Taters; that's how crazed he was! Those were rough years for him. His wife ended up in a private mental hospital, and he lived alone in this big house."

"What about his daughter?"

"He thought it would be better for her if she went away to school."

Qwilleran said accusingly, "You didn't tell me he'd been mur-dered on the premises. As it happened, I found out from other sources."

"Oh, come on, Qwill. You're not spooked by anything like that, are you?" she asked teasingly.

"I myself don't object to a homicide or two," he retorted, "but a purchaser of the inn could sue you if you don't reveal the skel-etons in the closet."

"Well, now you know," Dolly said with a shrug. "J.J. had made enemies, but we never dreamed it would end the way it did, and now that his murderer turned out to be a Tater, we can't help wondering about the other incidents involving his sons."

"Did you attend the trial?"

"Yes, I was there with Sherry Hawkinfield. The poor girl had no one, you know."

"What convicted Forest Beechum?"

"The crucial testimony came from her. She was here for Father's Day, and on Saturday she went to Potato Cove to buy a gift for her dad. She bought a painting and asked the artist to deliver it on Sunday as a surprise. Robert and I were supposed to come up here for a drink on Sunday afternoon and then take J.J. and Sherry to dinner at the club. While we were dressing, we heard police cars and an ambulance going up the mountain. We phoned the Wilbank house, and Ardis told us there'd been a murder at Tiptop. We couldn't believe it!"

"What time was that?"

"We were due there at three. I think it was about two-thirty when we found out."

"Del Wilbank told me there were no witnesses to the actual incident. Where was Sherry?"

"She'd gone down to Five Points to buy cocktail snacks. The artist was coming up the mountain as she drove down, and he was gone when she returned . . . You seem quite interested in this, Qwill."

"I should be! I'm living at the scene of the crime, and I might hear chains rattling in the middle of the night," he said lightly. "Seriously, though, I've been searching for a writing project, and I've come to the conclusion that J.J. would be a good subject for a biography."

"That would be super! Absolutely super!" Dolly said. "It would put Spudsboro on the map, for sure. If there's anything Robert and I can do to help . . . Well, look, I've got to hie myself down to the office. Thanks for the coffee. The brandy didn't hurt it a bit!"

Qwilleran walked with her down the long flights of steps, and she said, "Are you sure you don't want to buy Tiptop and open a country inn? You'd make a charming host."

"Positively not!"

"It'll be a year-round operation when the ski runs are completed. This could be another Aspen!"

"If it doesn't stop raining, Tiptop could be another Ark," Qwilleran said.

Returning to the foyer he found Koko prowling aimlessly. "Any comment?" he asked the cat. Koko merely stretched out on the floor of the foyer, making himself a yard long, and he rolled over a few times in front of the Fitzwallow huntboard.

"Treat!" Qwilleran announced, striding toward the kitchen. Koko scrambled to his feet and raced him to the feeding station, but Yum Yum failed to report. For either of them to ignore the T-word was cause for alarm. Qwilleran went looking for her, starting with the new hiding place under the table skirt in the living room. There she was!

"Yum Yum! *What are you doing?*" he said in shock.

She was completely absorbed in an aggressive ritual, biting small clumps of fur from her flanks. Feathery tufts were scattered on the gray carpet. Briefly she stopped and gave him a deranged look with slightly crossed eyes, then went on biting.

"What's the matter, sweetheart?" Qwilleran asked tenderly as he drew her out from her retreat. She made no protest but cuddled in his arms as he walked back and forth in the foyer. She made no protest, but neither did she squeeze her eyes in bliss or extend a paw to touch his moustache. "Are you homesick?" he asked. "Is it stress?" She had been yanked away from familiar surroundings and subjected to four days on the road, after which she found herself in a strange house with an unhappy history. Furthermore, he had neglected her for three days while pursuing his own interests. Koko might be tough and self-reliant, but Yum Yum was sensitive and emotionally vulnerable, having been an abused kitten before Qwilleran rescued her.

With one hand he punched the phone number of Lori Bamba in Moose County, still cradling Yum Yum in his arm. Lori, his part-time secretary, was knowledgeable about cats.

"Qwill!" she cried. "I didn't expect to hear from you for three months! Is everything all right?"

"Yes and no," he said. "I'm concerned about Yum Yum. Suddenly she's started tearing her fur out."

"Where?"

"On her flanks."

"Mmmm . . . yes . . . that sometimes happens. It could be an allergy. Has it just started?"

"I noticed it for the first time today. She was hiding and doing this secret thing to herself, and it seemed, well, obscene! I know she's been under stress lately."

"The vet can give her a shot for that," Lori said, "but wait a day or two and see what develops. Give her some extra attention. It could be a hormonal thing, too. If it continues, take her to the doctor."

"Thanks, Lori. That relieves my mind. I thought I had a feline masochist on my hands. How's everything in Moose County? I heard about Dr. Halifax."

"Wasn't that a shame? I don't know what we'll do without that dear man. The whole county is upset. Otherwise, everything's okay. I've been able to handle your correspondence without bothering Mr. Hasselrich."

"And how's the family?"

"The family's fine. Nick is still looking for a different kind of work. We were thinking of starting a bed-and-breakfast."

"Don't move too quickly," Qwilleran cautioned. "Give it plenty of thought. Get some advice."

After talking with Lori, he willingly changed his plans for the morning. He had intended to spend time at the public library, have lunch somewhere, and call on Colin Carmichael after two o'clock. Instead, he spent the next few hours sweet-talking Yum Yum, scratching her chin, fondling her ears, stroking her fur, and doing lap service. Only when she fell into a deep, contented sleep did he steal out of the house and drive down the mountain.

Upon reaching Five Points he was undecided. He had seen a certain bowl at the woodcrafter's shop in Potato Cove, and it kept haunting him. About fifteen inches in diameter, it was cut from the burl of a cherry tree and turned on a lathe until the interior was satin-smooth. In contrast, the top edges and entire exterior were rough and gnarled. He liked it. There had been a time in his life when art objects held little appeal for him, but that had changed along with his circumstances and increased leisure. On a previous visit to the cove he had lingered over the bowl, and now he decided to go back and buy it. He could have lunch at Amy's, walk around for a while, and reach the *Gazette* office in Spudsboro around two o'clock.

"Sumpin' told me you'd be back to git it," said Wesley, the wood crafter, gleefully. Word had spread around the cove that a stranger with an oversized moustache, who claimed to be a journalist, was hanging around the shops and buying high-ticket items.

Qwilleran loaded the bowl in the trunk of his car—it was even heavier than it looked—and drove to the Village Smithy to tell Vance that his candelabrum was a great success. While there he also bought a hand-forged cowbell with a tone that reminded him of Switzerland.

The blacksmith said, "Somethin's screwy with your car. It don't sound right. You git it from bouncin' 'round these mount'n roads."

"Glad you mentioned it," Qwilleran said. "Where's a good repair shop?"

"I kin fix it. Are you gonna be around? Gimme your keys."

"That's very good of you, Vance. I'll have lunch at Amy's and see you later."

At the Lunch Bucket the plump and pretty proprietor was behind the high counter, smiling as usual, and the baby was burbling in his basket.

Qwilleran said, "I have to confess I've forgotten the baby's name."

"Ashley," she said proudly. "Two months, one week, and six days."

"I like your mountain names: Ashley, Wesley, Vance, Forest, Dewey. Names like that have dignity."

"It's always been that way in the mountains; I don't know why. Women have first names like Carson and Tully and Taylor and Greer. I think it's neat. With a name like Amy, wouldn't you know I'm from the prairie?" She made a comic grimace.

"What brought you to Little Potato?"

"I dated Forest in college and loved the way he painted mountains—so real and yet out of this world. He painted all the signs for Potato Cove, too. They wanted him to paint the signs for Tiptop Estates, but he refused because he didn't believe in what Hawkinfield was doing to Big Potato. Anyway . . . we were going to be married at the waterfall last June when all the wildflowers were out. Here's his picture." Amy opened the locket that she wore and showed Qwilleran the face of a lean, unsmiling young man with long, black hair. "Suddenly our whole life caved in. I'll never be able to think of Father's Day without getting sick . . . What can I get you to eat?"

Qwilleran ordered soup and a veggieburger, and while she was preparing it, he said, "There are conflicting reports on what happened at Tiptop on that day."

"I can tell you God's honest truth. Wait till I finish this burger." She ladled up a bowl of vegetable soup. "Here, you can start with this. It's especially good today. I hit it just right, but be careful— it's very hot."

"That's the way I like it," he said, thinking of the corn chowder at the golf club. It was thick with vegetables, including turnips, which he swallowed without complaint. "Excellent soup, Amy! A person could live on this stuff!"

"Sometimes we have to," she said as she carried the burger to his table and sat down.

Qwilleran was the only customer, and he wondered how this tiny, unpopular restaurant could survive. "Where do you buy your groceries?" he asked.

"We belong to a co-op where we can buy in bulk. Other things come from the Yellyhoo Market on the river. We buy right out of the crates and off the back of trucks. There's a big saving."

"You were going to tell me Forest's story, Amy."

"Hope it doesn't spoil your lunch, Mr. . . . ."

"Qwilleran."

"Well, here goes. It started the Saturday before Father's Day, when Sherry Hawkinfield came into the weaving studio. Forest was minding the store while Chrys did a few errands. He used to show his mountain paintings there—all sizes. The tourists bought the small ones, but Sherry wanted a large one as a Father's Day gift and tried to haggle over the price. Imagine! It was only $300. Forest told her the painting would be worth $3,000 in a big-city gallery, and if she wanted something cheap, she should go to Lumpton's Department Store. He was never very tactful."

"I can see that," Qwilleran said.

"So, anyway, she wrote a check for $300 and asked him to deliver the painting the next day as a surprise for her father. She wanted it exactly at one o'clock . . . Would you like coffee sub with your burger, Mr. . . . ."

"Qwilleran. No, thanks. I'll skip the beverage today."

"Well, he drove to Tiptop on Sunday, and Sherry told him where to hang the painting in the hallway. Just as he was pounding the nail in the wall, the Old Buzzard rushed in—that's what Forest called him. The Old Buzzard rushed in from somewhere and said to his daughter, 'By God! What's that damned rabble-rouser doing in my house? Get him out of here!' She didn't say anything, but Forest said, 'I'm delivering a painting of a mountain, sir, so you'll know what mountains used to look like before you started mutilating them, *sir*!' And the man said, 'Get out of my house and take that piece of junk with you, or I'll have you arrested for trespassing and littering!' And he grabbed a stick out of the umbrella stand and was threatening him. Forest won't stand for abuse, verbal or otherwise, so he said, 'Go ahead! Hit me, sir, and I'll have the publisher of the *Gazette* charged with assault and battery!' The Old Buzzard was getting as red as a beet, and Sherry told Forest he'd better leave."

"He left the painting there, I gather."

Amy nodded. "She'd paid for it, you know. Anyway, he stomped out of the house and drove back to the cove, madder than I've ever seen him."

"What time was that?"

"About one-thirty, I think. At three o'clock the police came, and Forest was charged with murder! We couldn't understand it! We didn't know what it was all about! We were all so confused. And then—when Sherry told such horrible lies at the trial—it was like a nightmare! . . . Excuse me."

Two tourists had walked into the restaurant, and Amy went

behind the counter, greeting them with her usual smile, her eyes glistening unnaturally. There was a happy squawk from Ashley.

"Goo goo goo," she said. "His name is Ashley," she told the customers. "He's two months, one week, and six days."

Qwilleran smoothed his sensitive moustache. He thought, If Amy's story is true, and if Forest didn't kill J.J., who did? And why is Sherry Hawkinfield protecting the murderer?

Chapter 11

As Qwilleran was leaving Amy's Lunch Bucket she said meekly, "If you want real coffee, you can get it at the bakery up the hill."

"Thanks, Amy. You're a real friend," he said.

"Have you ever seen the waterfall? It's very exciting. The trail starts behind the bakery."

"Are there poison snakes back there?"

"Of course not! There are no poison snakes in the Potatoes, Mr. . . ."

"Qwilleran."

He ambled up the gradual incline on the wooden sidewalk until he scented a yeasty aroma and came upon an isolated building with the remains of a steeple. The weaving studio occupied an abandoned schoolhouse; the bakery occupied an abandoned church. Hanging alongside the door was a barnwood sign shaped like a plump loaf of bread, but he read the lettering twice before he could believe what he saw: THE HALF-BAKED BAKERY. A screened door flapped loosely as he entered.

"Why the screened door?" he asked by way of introduction. "I thought you didn't have flying insects in the Potatoes."

"It's the damned health code," said a man in crumpled whites with a baker's hat sagging over one ear like a deflated balloon. "They make us wear these stupid hats, too."

The same uniform was worn by a woman taking a tray of crusty

Italian bread from an oven. Like all the equipment—grinders, mixers, dough tables, scales and whatnot—the oven looked second-hand if not actually antique. At the front of the shop were four wooden student chairs with writing arms, as well as a coffeemaker with instructions: "Help Yourself . . . Pay at Counter . . . Cream in Fridge." Separating the bakery from the snack area was a scarred glass case displaying cookies, muffins, Danish pastries, and pecan rolls, although very little of each. What elevated this humble establishment to the sublime was the heady fragrance of baking bread.

Qwilleran helped himself to coffee and bought an apple Danish from the baker. "If you don't mind my saying so," he said as he pulled out his bill clip, "you picked a helluva name for your bakery."

"Tell you why we did it," the man said. "Everybody told us we were half-baked to open a whole-grain bakery in Potato Cove, but we're doing all right. Overhead's low, and we wholesale to a food market and a couple of restaurants in the valley, so we have a little cash flow we can count on."

"Do you supply the golf club?" Qwilleran asked slyly.

"Hell no! But you see that tray of bread? It's going to an Italian restaurant. They pick it up every day at four o'clock." He looked at Qwilleran's moustache. "Are you the fella that bought Vance's big candlestick?"

"Yes, I'm the proud possessor of fifty pounds of iron." Qwilleran looked around the shop. The unifying note in the bakery was paint; everything paintable had been painted orchid: walls, ceiling, shelving, tables, student chairs, even the floorboards. "Unusual paint job you have here," was Qwilleran's comment.

"Thrift, man! Thrift! Lumpton Hardware advertised a sale of paint, and all those fakes had was pink and blue. It was my wife's idea to mix 'em."

Qwilleran carried his purchase to an orchid student chair and bit into a six-inch square of puffy, chewy pastry heaped with large apple slices in thick and spicy juices. It was still warm.

"I'm forced to tell you," he said, "that this is absolutely the best Danish I've ever eaten in half a century of pastry connoisseurship."

The baker turned to the woman. "Hear that, sugar? Take a

bow." To Qwilleran he said, "My wife does the gooey stuff. Wait till you taste the sticky buns! Everything we use is whole grain and fresh. Apples come from Tater orchards—no sprays, no chemicals. We stone-grind our flour right from the wheat berries. Bread's kneaded and shaped by hand. Crackers are rolled the same way."

"That's my job," said his wife. "I like handling dough."

"Bread untouched by human hands may be cheaper, but nobody says it's as good," the baker said. "You're new around here."

"I'm here for the summer. My name's Jim Qwilleran. What's your name?"

"Yates. Yates Penney. That's my wife, Kate. How do you like the Potatoes, Mr. . . . ?"

"Qwilleran. I'm not sure I like what's happening to Big Potato."

"You said it! The inside of Big Potato looks like a mangy cat, and the outside looks like a war zone. City people come up here because they like country living, and then they drag the city along with 'em. The Taters have the right idea; they build themselves a rustic shack and let everything grow wild, the way Nature intended. We're from Akron, but we know how to fit in. Right, sugar?"

Qwilleran said, "What is this waterfall I've heard about?"

"You mean Purgatory?"

"Is that what it's called? I'd like to see it."

The baker turned to his wife. "He wants to go to Purgatory." They communicated silently for a few moments until she nodded, and then he explained, "We don't encourage sightseers because they throw beer cans and food wrappers in the falls, but you don't look like the average tourist."

"I take that as a compliment. Is the trail well-marked? I'd like a quiet, leisurely walk without getting lost."

"It's quiet, all right," said Kate. "Nobody goes back there on a Tuesday afternoon. Only on weekends."

"You can't get lost either," Yates assured him. "Just follow the creek upstream. It's about half a mile, but all uphill."

"That's okay. I've been practicing. Where did Purgatory get its name?"

"Some old-time Taters named it, I think. It's not an Indian

name, I know that. Anyway, the water drops off a high cliff and down into a bottomless pit, and the mist rises like steam. Quite a sight!"

"Good! I'll take a little ramble. I have some time to kill while Vance works on my car."

"What's wrong with it?"

"Nothing serious. Mountain-itis, I guess you'd call it. While I'm standing here I'd like to pay for some Danish and sticky buns. I can pick them up when I finish with the falls."

"We close at four," Kate warned him.

"If it's only half a mile, I'll be back well before that," Qwilleran said.

"Take care!"

"Don't fall in," the baker said with a grin.

Behind the bakery Qwilleran could hear the creek before he could see it. Swollen by heavy rain, the waters were rushing tumultuously over boulders in the creek bed. An irregular path on the edge of the stream had been worn down by generations of Taters and perhaps by Indians before them, who made the pilgrimage without benefit of handrails, curbs, steps, or warning signs. This was raw nature, and the footing was muddy and treacherous. Sharp rocks and wayward roots protruded from the walkway, camouflaged by pine needles and oak leaves that were wet and slippery. Tufts of coarse wet grasses grew over the edge, dripping and ready to chute an unwary wanderer into the stream.

After a few stumbles Qwilleran realized the impossibility of ogling the rushing stream and walking at the same time. Only by alternating a few careful steps with a few motionless moments could he appreciate the wild beauty. Brilliant green ferns abounded, thriving in the damp shadows. Every cleft rock had its trickle of water trying to find the creek and soaking the ground en route. Then there were the wild flowers—clumps of them in yellow, white, pink, blue, and red, growing among the wild grasses or in the crevices of rotting logs or across the face of rock outcroppings. Hundred-foot pine trees rising like the vaulted ceiling of a cathedral filtered the sun's rays through their sparse upper branches. Moose County could never produce a show like this!

The course of the creek angled sharply and sometimes plunged out of sight, only to reappear with added force. Qwilleran was following it upstream, of course, and its exuberance increased—in noise and in turbulence. When the waters were not splashing wildly over boulders, they were cascading smoothly over rock ledges in a series of naturally terraced waterfalls. And Qwilleran, when not picking his way along the precarious path, was clicking his camera. Take it easy, he told himself, or you'll run out of film.

The higher he climbed, the more dramatic the views and the louder the thunder of water, until he groped his way around the last projecting cliff and found himself in a rock-walled atrium. There it was! Purgatory! An immense column of water, four times higher than its width, poured over a lofty cliff with unimaginable force and deafening roar—tons of water dropping straight down into a black hole in the rock from which rose clouds of vapor.

Qwilleran caught his breath. To be alone in the woods with this mighty dynamo gave him an eerie sensation, as if he were a supplicant consulting an oracle in a rock-walled temple, somewhere in the distant past. Perhaps Native Americans had worshipped their spirits here. Perhaps, he thought for one giddy moment, this was where he would find the answers. Overwhelmed by the experience, he had forgotten the questions.

Then the hypnotic moment passed, and he was a summer vacationer with a camera. Climbing carefully over the surrounding boulders he found numerous photogenic angles and clicked the shutter recklessly until he realized he had only one picture left. For the final shot he wanted to try a profile of the cascade entering the cauldron of billowing steam.

The path had ended, but he edged around the perimeter of the atrium until he found the right angle. Studying the view-finder critically for his final shot, he made one impulsive move—a step backward.

Immediately his feet shot out from under him and—sprawled on his back—he started to slide slowly but inexorably toward the abyss. Twisting his body in panic, he clutched at wet rocks and grabbed handfuls of shallow-rooted weeds. Nothing stopped his slide down the muddy slope. His bellowing shouts were drowned by the pounding waters . . . and now he was enveloped in fog . . . and now he was slipping into the black hole. He grabbed for the rim, but it crumbled. Grasping wildly at the nearly vertical walls of the chasm, he managed to slow his descent and find a ledge for his toe. It bore his weight. It was a wisp of hope.

He clung to his perch and tried to think. Spread-eagled against the face of the rock he ran bleeding hands over its surface in search of a projection. Behind him the shaft of water was thundering, and he was drenched like a drowning man. Something flashed into his mind then: mountain climbers in Switzerland . . . scaling the flat face of a peak . . . with infinite patience. Patience! he told himself. The mist stung his face and blinded him, but he fought his panic. Running his hands painstakingly over the flat surface in search of crevices, testing craggy ledges for strength, he inched upward. Time lost its meaning. He spent an eternity clinging and creeping, never knowing how much farther he had to climb. Patience! When the darkness lessened he knew he was approaching the rim, although he was still enveloped in mist.

Eventually one exploring hand felt level ground. It was the rim of the pit, but the trial by mud was not over. He had to hoist himself out of the hole, and one misstep or one miscalculation could send him plunging back into the depths. The terrain above him was slimy, but it was blessedly horizontal. After several tries he found something growing from a crevice, something tough and fibrous that he could grab as he clambered out. Facedown in the mud he crawled and squirmed out of the mist and away from the pit until he felt safe enough to collapse and hug the earth. No matter that he was muddied from head to foot, his clothing in shreds, his hands and knees bloodied, his watch smashed, his camera lost; he was on terra firma.

Only then did he pay attention to a shooting pain in his ankle. It had been torturing him throughout the ordeal, but the life-or-death struggle had superseded all else. When he turned over and tried to sit up, he yelped with pain and shock; his ankle was swollen as big as a grapefruit. Rashly he tried to stand up and fell back with a cry of anguish. For a moment he lay flat on the ground and considered the problem. A little rest, he thought, would reduce the swelling.

He was wrong. His ankle continued to throb relentlessly, responding to every move with agonizing spasms. How do I get out of here? he asked himself. At the bakery they had said no one went to the waterfall on a Tuesday afternoon. Having great lung power, he tried a shout for help, but it was drowned out by the roar of the falls. Suppose he had to stay in the woods all night! Beechum had predicted more rain. The nights turned cold in the mountains, and his lightweight clothing was wet and tattered.

With a burst of determination he proposed to drag himself along the trail, an inch at a time if necessary. Fortunately it was all downhill; unfortunately the path was studded with sharp rocks, and his hands, elbows, and knees were already lacerated. Even so, he squirmed downhill a few yards, trying to save his ankle, but the pain was non-stop and the swelling had reached the size of a melon. Defeated, he dragged himself to a boulder and leaned against it in a sitting position.

For a while he sat there thinking, or trying to think. Vance would wonder why he hadn't called for his car; Yates would wonder why he hadn't picked up his baked goods.

Now that he had inched his way out of the atrium, the crashing noise of Purgatory was somewhat muffled. "HELP!" he shouted, his voice echoing in the rocky ravine. There was no answering cry. The sky, glimpsed between the lofty treetops, was now overcast. The rain was coming. If he had to spend the night in the woods, wearing cold, wet clothing and lying on the drenched ground, covering himself with wet leaves like a woodland animal, he would be ready for an oxygen tent in the morning . . . that is, if anyone found him in the morning. They might not find him until the weekend.

"HELP!"

Then a chilling thought occurred to him. The Taters may have intended him to disappear in the Purgatory abyss. If so, they could have only one motive; they suspected his purpose in visiting their precious mountain. They may have mistaken him for a federal agent. What were they growing in the hidden coves and hollows? What was stockpiled in those caves? Beechum's banter about bears and bats and poisonous snakes may have been something more than mountain humor.

"HELP!"

Did he hear a reply, or was it an echo?

He tried again. "HELP!"

"Hallo," came a distant cry.

"HELP!"

"Coming! Coming!" The voices were getting closer. "Hold on!" Soon he could see movement in the woods, screened by the underbrush, then heads bobbing along the trail. Two men were coming up the slope, and they broke into a run when he waved an arm in a wide arc.

"For God's sake! What happened?" the baker shouted, seeing the tattered, mud-caked figure leaning against a boulder. "What happened to your ankle?"

"You look like you been through a *ce*-ment mixer!" the black-smith said.

"I sprained my ankle, and I was trying to drag myself back to the cove," Qwilleran said shortly. He was in no mood to describe his ordeal or confess to the careless misstep that sent him sliding ignominiously into the pit.

They hoisted him to a standing position, with his weight on his right foot, and made a human crutch, unmindful of the mud being smeared on their own clothes. Then slowly they started down the precarious slope to Potato Cove. Qwilleran was in too much pain to talk, and his rescuers were aware of it.

At the end of the trail a group of concerned Taters waited with comments and advice:

"Never see'd nobody in such a mess!" said one.

"Better hose him down, Yates." That was the baker's wife.

"Give 'im a slug o' corn, Vance. Looks like he needs it."

"Somebody send for Maw Beechum! She's got healin' hands."

Qwilleran's rescuers stripped off his rags behind the bakery and turned the hose on the caked blood and dirt, the icy water from a local well acting like a local anesthetic. Then, draped in a couple of bakery towels, he was assisted into a backroom and placed on a cot among cartons of wheatberries and yeast. Kate, serving hot coffee and another Danish, explained that Mrs. Beechum had gone home to get some of her homemade medicines.

When the silent woman arrived, she went to work with downcast eyes, making an icepack for the ankle and tearing up an old sheet for bandages. Then she poured antiseptic from a jelly jar onto the wounds and larded them with ointment.

Yates said, "With that stuff you'll never get an infection, that's for sure. When you feel up to it, we'll fix you up with pants and a coat and drive you home. You can say goodbye to those shoes, too. What size do you take? . . . Hey, Vance, get some sandals from the leather shop, size twelve." He appraised the bandaging. "Man, you look like a mummy!"

The wrappings on Qwilleran's hands, elbows, and knees restricted his movement considerably, but the ankle torture was somewhat relieved after the ice pack and tight bandaging. He wanted to thank Mrs. Beechum, but she had slipped away from the bakery without so much as a nod in his direction, leaving him a jar of liniment.

Kate said, "You should use ice again tonight and keep your foot up, Mr. . . . ."

"Qwilleran."

Yates buckled on the sandals, and Wesley brought him a carved walking stick, which looked more like a cudgel. "I don't know how to thank you people," he said.

"We aim to be good neighbors," said Kate.

The three men drove away, Yates driving Qwilleran in his newly repaired car, and Vance following in his pickup. Qwilleran was abnormally quiet, still dazed by his experience. He felt that his precipitous slide into the black hole had never happened. Yet, if it were true and if he had not survived, would anyone ever know his fate? What would have happened to Koko and Yum Yum, penned up in a house that no one had reason to visit?

The baker respected his silence for a while but threw curious glances at him repeatedly. Finally he said, "What really happened at Purgatory, man?"

Qwilleran was jolted out of his reverie. "What do you mean?"

"You don't wind up in that condition just by twisting your ankle."

"I told you I was trying to drag myself back to the cove. The path was muddy and full of sharp rocks."

"You were soaking wet from head to foot."

"There's a lot of mist at the falls. You should know that."

Yates grunted, and no more was said for a few minutes. When they reached Hawk's Nest Drive, he tried again. "See anybody in the woods?"

"No. It was just as your wife said: no one around on Tuesday. This is Tuesday, isn't it? I feel as if I've been on that trail a week!"

"Did you hear anything unusual?"

"Not with the water roaring! I couldn't hear myself think!"

"See anything strange?"

"What are you getting at?" Qwilleran said with slight annoyance. "I saw the creek, boulders, fallen trees, mud, large and small waterfalls, flowers, more mud . . ."

"Okay, okay, I'll shut up. You had a rough time."

"Sorry if I barked at you. I'm feeling edgy."

"You should be! You've been through hell!"

At Tiptop his rescuers helped him up the twenty-five steps, and the sight of Qwilleran dressed in baker's whites and supported by two strangers sent the Siamese flying upstairs, where they watched from a safe elevation. He offered the men a beer and was glad when they declined; he needed a period of rest in which to find himself again. There were moments when he was still in the abyss, clinging to a slippery wall of rock.

"I'll bring up your baked goods," Yates said. "Anything more we can do? Be glad to do it."

"There's a burl bowl in the trunk of my car that you could bring up. And again, I don't know how to thank you fellas."

When they had gone and Qwilleran had dropped on the gray velvet sofa with his ankle elevated on one of Sabrina's pillows, the Siamese walked questioningly into the room.

"You'll have to bear with me awhile," he told them. "You almost lost your chief cook."

They huddled close to his body, playing the nursing role instinctive with cats, and made no demands, although it was past their normal dinnertime. At intervals Koko ran his nose over the white uniform and grimaced as if he smelled something rotten.

When the telephone rang, Qwilleran was undecided whether to answer, but it persisted until he grabbed his walking staff and moved to the foyer with halting steps.

"I thought you were going to drop in this afternoon," said Colin Carmichael.

"I dropped into a waterfall instead," Qwilleran said, recovering some of his spirit.

"Where?"

"At Potato Cove. I'm lucky I got out alive."

"Are you all right?"

"Except for a sprained ankle. Do you happen to have an elastic bandage?"

"I could pick one up at the drug store easily enough and run it up the mountain in no time. Anything else you need?"

"Perhaps one of those cold compresses that can be chilled in the freezer."

"No problem. Be right there."

"The front door's unlocked, Colin. Just walk in."

Having maneuvered successfully to the foyer, Qwilleran hobbled to the kitchen to feed the cats. They were used to dodging his long strides and found his new slow-motion toddle with a stick perplexing. He was back on the sofa when the editor arrived.

Carmichael frowned at the ankle. "That's quite a balloon you've got there. Is it painful?"

"Not as bad as it was. Excuse my attire; the baker at the cove had to lend me some clean clothes. Go out to the kitchen, Colin. There's a bar in the pantry. Help yourself, and you can bring me a ginger ale from the fridge. You might also throw the compress in the freezer."

The editor lingered. "I hated to call you about the Tater thing, Qwill. Don't hold it against me."

"Forget it. I'm not here to get involved in local politics or prejudices."

"What happened to your hands?"

"I tried to save myself and grabbed some unfriendly rocks. The bandages make them look worse than they are."

When they settled down with their drinks, Carmichael glanced around the living room. "This is a lot of house for one guy."

"It was the only place that would rent to cats. I have two Siamese," Qwilleran said.

"Where are they?"

"In hiding. They avoid veterinarians and editors."

"Our star columnist is going around with a red face since her interview with you. It seems you asked all the questions, and she did all the talking. She's too embarrassed to call you again."

"Let's leave it that way, Colin. Tell her I'm on a secret mission and don't want her to blow my cover. Tell her anything. Tell her I'm opening a health spa for men only, with retired burlesque strippers as masseuses."

"There's some speculation anyway—as to your identity, and your reason for being here, and why you're willing to pay such high rent."

"I'm beginning to wonder about the rent myself."

"Well, tell me how you sprained your ankle, Qwill."

Qwilleran related the episode in cool, journalistic style without histrionics, underplaying his descent into the pit and his heroic struggle to climb to safety. In concluding he said, "Let me tell you one thing: I wouldn't be sitting here tonight if it weren't for some of those Taters . . . Your glass is empty, Colin. Go and help yourself."

"Not this time, thanks. My family's expecting me home for dinner. We're having a backyard barbecue for my little girl's birthday . . . But tell me what you wanted to discuss in my office."

"It's only a wild notion. How would you react to a biography of Hawkinfield? I've thought of writing one, but it would require a lot of research."

"That's a great idea!" said the editor. "You can count on our complete cooperation. We can line up interviews for you. Everyone will be glad to talk."

"It's only in the thinking stage," Qwilleran said. "I might open with the murder trial, then flashback to J.J.'s regime at the *Gazette*, his civic leadership, the loss of his family, and his violent end."

Carmichael was pounding the arm of his chair. "That would make a damn good movie, too, Qwill! You've got me all fired up! After this news a backyard barbecue is going to seem like small potatoes."

"I'll need to get a transcript of the trial, of course, and there are considerations I'll want to discuss with an attorney. Would you recommend Hugh Lumpton?"

"Well," said the editor, "he's a great golfer. Drives a $40,000 car. Always has a lot of women around him. But—"

"That doesn't tell me what I need to know, does it?"

"Just between you and me, Qwill, I wouldn't even hire him to write my will—not that I have any firsthand experience, you understand. It's just what I pick up at the club and at the chamber. You'd be better off going to one of the lawyers next door to the post office . . . Well, see here, is there anything I can do for you before I leave? Anything I can send you from the valley?"

"Not a thing, thanks. I appreciate the items from the drugstore. And tell your daughter that Koko and Yum Yum said happy birthday."

"Great! She'll flip! She loves cats, especially ones that talk."

After Carmichael had left, Qwilleran undertook a slow trek to the kitchen in search of food for himself, but he was intercepted by Koko, who was rolling and squirming on the floor in front of the Fitzwallow huntboard. Whatever his motive, the performance was a subtle reminder to Qwilleran that he had forgotten to mail Sabrina's letter to Sherry Hawkinfield. It was still in the drawer of the cabinet, fang marks and all. He looked at the address and then called directory assistance for a telephone number in Maryland: a shop called Not New But Nice. He had to repeat it twice to make himself understood.

When he punched the number, a recording device answered, but he was prepared; it was early evening, and he presumed the shop would be closed. In his most ingratiating voice he left a message that was purposely ambiguous:

"Ms. Hawkinfield, please call this number in Spudsboro regarding a valuable painting by Forest Beechum that belongs to you . . ."

Qwilleran turned to Koko. "Do you think that will get results? The key word is *valuable*."

"Yow!" said Koko, hopping on and off the huntboard in excitement.

CHAPTER 12

Qwilleran was sure that Sherry Hawkinfield would not return his call until morning. It was her place of business that he had phoned. He sat on a kitchen chair trying to eat soup with a bandaged hand that could hardly hold a spoon, while his left leg was propped on another chair with a cold compress wrapped around the ankle. Watching him from a respectful distance were two Siamese with anxious eyes, and their solicitude did nothing but make him jittery.

"I appreciate your concern," he said, "but there are times when I wish you would go away." They edged closer, looking doubly worried. Then suddenly they became agitated, running to and from the back door, Koko with his ears swept back and Yum Yum with her tail bushed. A moment later there was snuffling on the veranda and the click of claws.

"It's Lucy," Qwilleran said morosely. "Keep quiet and she'll go away." But the cats only increased their frenzy, and Lucy started to whine.

In no mood for domestic drama and muttering under his breath, Qwilleran kicked off the compress and limped to the refrigerator, where he found the four hot dogs he had bought for himself. He threw them to the overfed Doberman, and soon the commotion subsided, indoors and out.

His irritability was a delayed reaction to the unnerving experience at the waterfall. Why did I come to these damned mountains? he asked himself. Polly would blame it on his impulsiveness; she often questioned his precipitate actions, doing so with a polite sideways glance of mild reproach. So did Arch Riker but with blunt disapproval. How could they understand the messages telegraphed to Qwilleran through his sensitive moustache? How could he understand them himself?

He would have paced the floor if he'd had two good ankles. He would have enjoyed a pipeful of Scottish tobacco if he hadn't given it up. His books and radio were upstairs; so was his ottoman; so was his bed. Sooner or later he would have to tackle the ascent.

To reach the top he sat down on the second stair and went up backward, dragging his hand-carved walking staff and accompanied by the Siamese, who were always entertained by the eccentric behavior of humans and who had determined not to leave him alone in his travail.

As soon as he had sunk into his lounge chair and cushioned his left foot on the ottoman, the telephone rang.

"Yow!" Koko yowled in his ear.

"I'm not deaf!" he yelled back.

There was a slim chance that it might be the call from Maryland, so he hoisted himself out of the chair and—groaning and muttering—bumped down the stairs on his posterior. He reached the foyer and grabbed the handset after the ninth ring.

Qwilleran was taking a moment to adjust his attitude when a woman said impatiently, "Hello? Hello?"

"Good evening," he said with the silky charm and mellifluous voice that had thrilled women for three decades.

Then, rather pleasantly she said, "Are you the one who called me and left a message? I'm Sherry Hawkinfield." She had a young voice, a cultivated voice. She had gone to a good school.

"Yes, I'm the one," he replied. "My name is Jim Qwilleran."

"You sound . . . nice," she said archly. "Who are you? I don't recognize the name."

"I'm renting Tiptop for the summer. Dolly Lessmore made the arrangements."

"Oh . . . yes . . . of course. I just happened to come back to my shop after dinner, and I found your message."

"All work and no play makes . . . money," Qwilleran said.

"You're so right! What did you want to know about the painting?"

"It's a fantastic interpretation of mountains, and I understand it's quite valuable. Is it possibly for sale? If so, what are you asking for it? Also there's an antique English huntboard in the foyer that has a great deal of primitive appeal. Ms. Lessmore tells me you're disposing of some of the furnishings. Is that correct?" In the astonished pause that ensued he could visualize dollar signs dancing in her eyes.

"The whole house is for sale," she said eagerly, "completely furnished. It would make a neat country inn. Dolly says you're a prospect."

"I'm giving it some thought. There are certain details that should be discussed."

"Well, I might fly out there for the weekend to see some friends in the valley. We could talk about it then," she said with growing enthusiasm.

"I'd appreciate that. When would you arrive?"

"If I got a Friday morning flight, I'd rent a car at the airport and drive up to see you in the afternoon."

"Perhaps we could have lunch while you're here," he suggested cordially. "Or dinner."

"I'd love to."

"It would be my pleasure, I assure you, Ms. Hawkinfield."

"Then I'll see you Friday afternoon. What's your name again?"

"Jim Qwilleran, spelled with a QW."

"I'm glad you called, Mr. Qwilleran."

"Please call me Qwill."

"Oh, that's neat!"

"May I call you Sherry?"

"I wish you would. Where are you from?" She was beginning to sound chummy.

"Another planet, but a friendly one. The Beverly Hills of outer space."

This brought a giddy laugh. "I'll look forward to meeting you. Want me to call you from the airport and set a time?"

"Why don't you simply drive up to Tiptop? I'll be here . . . waiting," he said meaningfully. (With my ankle in a sling, he told himself.)

"All right. I'll do that."

"I don't need to tell you how to find Tiptop," he said, in what he knew was a weak jest.

"No," she giggled. "I think I remember where it is."

There were pauses, as if neither of them wanted to terminate the conversation.

"Bon voyage," he said.

"Thank you. *Au revoir.*"

"Au revoir." Qwilleran waited for the gentle replacing of the handset before he hung up. Turning to Koko, who was waiting for a report, he said, "I haven't had a phone conversation like that since I was nineteen."

Koko replied with a wink, or so it seemed; there was a cat hair in his eye.

Once more Qwilleran went upstairs the hard way. He shooed the Siamese into their room, and as he pulled down the window shades in his own bedroom, he saw the revolving circle of light on Little Potato. Forest's kinfolk were trudging with their lanterns in grim silence.

His sleep that night was reasonably comfortable except when he shifted position rashly, and in the morning the ankle showed noticeable improvement despite the heavy atmosphere that usually aggravates aches and pains. Rain had started to fall—not torrentially but with steady determination, and according to the meteorologist on the radio it would rain all day. There was a danger of flooding in some areas.

Qwilleran slid downstairs to feed the Siamese and make a breakfast of coffee and sticky buns. Also, in spite of his unwillingness to pay for extra telephone services, he called the company to request an extension. By exaggerating his predicament dramatically he wangled a promise of immediate installation.

Next he had a strong urge to confide in someone, and he called Arch Riker at the office of the *Moose County Something* even though the full rates were in effect.

"Don't tell Polly," he cautioned Riker when the editor answered, "but I'm sitting here with a sprained ankle, and I had a narrow escape yesterday."

"What fool thing have you been doing?" his old friend asked.

"Taking some pictures of a waterfall that cascades down for about forty feet and disappears into a black hole. I almost disappeared myself. I'm lucky to get out alive. I lost the camera that Polly gave me, and it was full of exposed film."

Riker said, "I knew you were making a mistake by going into those mountains. You should never stray from solid concrete. How bad is the ankle? Did you have it X-rayed?"

"You know I always avoid X rays if possible. I'm using ice packs and some homemade liniment from one of the mountain women."

"How's the weather?"

"Rotten. If it doesn't rain all day, it rains all night. They never told me I was moving to a rain forest."

"Glad to hear it! Now maybe you'll stay indoors and write a piece for us. We need something for Friday. Could you rip something off and get it faxed?"

"The most interesting possibility," Qwilleran said, "is a topic I'm not prepared to cover as yet—the murder that took place here a year ago."

"I hope you're not going to get sidetracked into some kind of unauthorized investigation, Qwill."

"That remains to be seen. The case involves power politics and possibly perjury on a grand scale. I have a hunch that the wrong man was convicted."

Riker groaned. He knew all about Qwilleran's hunches and found it futile to discourage him from following them up. Reluctant to take him seriously, however, he asked, "What does the Inspector General think about the case?"

"Koko is busy doing what cats do. Right now he's rolling on the floor in front of the telephone chest; somehow it turns him on. I'm worried about Yum Yum, though. I may have to take her to the doctor."

"I suppose you heard about Dr. Goodwinter. I saw Dr. Melinda yesterday, and she asked about you. She wanted to know how you are, and she batted her eyelashes a lot."

"What did you tell her?"

"Blood pressure normal; appetite good; weight down a few pounds—"

"How does she look?" Qwilleran interrupted. "Has she changed in three years?"

"No, except for that big-city veneer that's inescapable."

"Does she know about Polly?"

"The entire county knows about Polly," Riker said, "but all's fair in love and war, and I could tell by Melinda's expression that her interest isn't entirely clinical."

"Gotta hang up," Qwilleran said abruptly. "Doorbell's ringing. It's the telephone man. Okay, Arch, I'll send you some copy, but I don't know how good it'll be."

He limped to the door, leaning heavily on his cane and assuming an expression of grueling physical pain.

"Hey, this is some place!" said the installer when he was admitted. He was a wide-eyed, beardless young man not yet bored with his job. "I never saw the inside of Tiptop before. The boss said you live here alone and hurt your foot. What happened?"

"I sprained an ankle."

"You'd better get off of it."

Wincing appropriately, Qwilleran shuffled into the living room and sprawled on the sofa.

The installer followed him. "You buy this place?"

"No, I'm renting for the summer."

"This is where a guy was killed last year."

"So I've been told," Qwilleran said.

"Used to be a summer hotel for rich people. My grandmother was a cook here, and my grandfather drove a carriage and brought people up from the railroad station. The road wasn't paved then. He used to talk about drivin' people like Henry Ford, Thomas Edison, and Madame Schumann-Heink, whoever she was."

"Famous Austrian opera singer," Qwilleran said. "What did your grandparents do after the inn closed?"

"Moonshinin'!" the installer said with a grin. "Then they opened a diner in the valley and did all right. They served split-brandy in teacups—that's half brandy and half whiskey. The diner's torn down now, but lots of old people remember Lumpton's famous tea."

"Are you a Lumpton?" Qwilleran asked. He had counted forty-seven Goodwinters in the Moose County phone book but twice that many Lumptons in the Spudsboro directory.

"On my mother's side. My cousins own Lumpton's Pizza. Sheriff Lumpton is my godfather. You know him? He was sheriff twenty-four years. Everybody called him Uncle Josh. He always played Santa for the kids at Christmas, and he sure had the belly for it! Still does. But now they have some skinny guy playin' Santa . . . Well, I better get to work. Where d'you want the extension?"

"Upstairs on the desk in the back bedroom," Qwilleran said from his bed of pain. "Can you find it all right?"

"Sure. If you hear it ring, it's just me checkin' it out."

The phone rang a couple of times, and eventually the young man came downstairs. "Okay, you're all set. I left a phone book on the desk. Your big cat's sure a nosey one! Watched everythin' I did. The little one is bitin' herself like she has fleas."

"Thanks for the prompt service," Qwilleran said.

"Take it easy now."

As soon as Qwilleran heard the van drive away, he went upstairs to find Yum Yum. He could now climb one step at a time if he led with his right foot and leaned heavily on his staff. The telephone, he discovered, had been installed on the desk as requested, but in the wrong room. It was in the cats' bedroom, and Koko was being aggressively possessive about it. Yum Yum was on the bed, gnawing at her left flank, and there were small tufts of fur on the bedcover.

Qwilleran brushed Koko unceremoniously aside and called the Wickes Animal Clinic. Dr. John, according to the receptionist, was in surgery, but Dr. Inez had just finished a C-section and could come to the phone in a jiffy.

When Inez answered, he said, "This is Jim Qwilleran, your neighbor at Tiptop. Do you make house calls? Something's very wrong with my cat, and I'm grounded with a sprained ankle."

"What's wrong?" she asked, and when he described Yum Yum's behavior, she said, "I know it looks kinky, but it's not unusual for spayed females. We can give her a shot and dispense some pills. No need to worry. One of us will run up the hill with the little black bag around five o'clock. What happened to your ankle?"

"I slipped on some wet leaves," he explained.

"Will this rain ever stop?" she complained. "The waterfall under our house is running so high, it may wash out our sundeck. See you at five."

Qwilleran babied Yum Yum until she fell asleep and then went to work on copy for the *Moose County Something*: a thousand words on the feud between the environmentalists and the Spudsboro developers.

"What has happened," he asked his Moose County readers, "to give a negative connotation to a constructive word like 'develop'? It means, according to the dictionary, to perfect, to expand, to change from a lesser to a higher state, to mature, to ripen. Yet, a large segment of the population now uses it as a pejorative." He concluded the column by saying, "The civic leaders of Moose County who are campaigning for 'development' should take a hard look at the semantics of a word that sounds so commendable and can be so destructive."

"And now, old boy," he said to Koko, who had been sitting on the desk enjoying the vibrations of the typewriter, "I've got to figure out how to get this stuff faxed. May I use your phone?" He tottered into the cats' room and called the manager of the Five Points Market, saying, "This is Jim Qwilleran at Tiptop. Do you remember me?"

"Sure do!" said the energetic Bill Treacle. "Did you run out of lobster tails?"

"No, but I have a food-related problem. I sprained my ankle yesterday. Do you make deliveries?"

"Not as a rule. What do you need?"

"Some frozen dinners and half a pound of sliced turkey breast from the deli counter and four hot dogs."

"I'm off at six o'clock. I'll deliver them myself if you can wait that long," said Treacle. "I've never seen the inside of Tiptop."

"I can survive until then. If you wish, I'll show you around the premises and even offer you a drink."

"I'll take that! Make it a cold beer."

At that point some twinges in the left ankle reminded Qwilleran that he had been sitting at a desk too long. He sank into his lounge chair, propping both feet on the ottoman, and thought about Moose County . . . about the sunny June days up there . . . about the old doctor's suicide . . . and about Melinda Goodwinter's wicked green eyes and long lashes. Her return to Pickax after three years in Boston had crossed his mind oftener than he cared to admit. Her presence would definitely disturb his comfortable relationship with Polly, who was a loving woman of his own age. Melinda, for her part, had a youthful appeal that he had once found irresistible, and she had a way of asking for what she wanted. To be friends with both of them, to some degree or other, would be ideal, he reflected wistfully, but Pickax was a small town, and Polly was overpossessive. The whole problem would be tidily solved if he decided not to return to Moose County, and that was a distinct possibility, although he had not given it a moment's thought since arriving in the Potatoes.

Reaching for a pad of paper he jotted down some options, commenting on each to faithful Koko, who was loitering sociably. Yum Yum was on the bed, wretchedly nipping at her flanks and tearing out tufts of fur.

Move back to a large city. "Which one? And why? I'm beginning to prefer small towns. Must be getting old."

Buy a newspaper. "Now that I can afford one, I no longer want one. Too bad."

Travel. "Sounds good, but what would I do about you and Yum Yum?" he asked Koko, who blinked and scratched his ear.

Teach journalism. "That's what everyone says I should do, but I'd rather do it than teach it."

Try to get into acting. "I was pretty good when I was in college, and television has increased the opportunities since then."

Build a hotel in Pickax. "God knows it needs a new one! We could go six stories high and call it the Pickax Towers."

He had been so intent on planning the rest of his life that he failed to hear a car pulling into the parking lot, but Koko heard it and raced downstairs. Qwilleran followed, descending the stairs lamely. Through the glass of the French doors he could see the top of an umbrella, ploddingly ascending the twenty-five steps. It reached the veranda, and Qwilleran—sloppily attired, unshaven, and leaning on a cane—recognized the last person in the world he wanted to see.

CHAPTER 13

Qwilleran recognized the hat waiting outside the front door—a large one with a brim like a banking plane—and wished he could slink back upstairs, but it was too late. She had caught sight of him through the glass panes.

"A thousand pardons!" she cried when he opened the door in his grubby condition. "I'm Vonda Dudley Wix. I'm calling at an inopportune time. I should have telephoned first. Do you remember me?"

"Of course." He remembered not only the hat but also the young-old face beneath it and the scarf tied in a perky bow under her chin. "Come in," he said, exaggerating his limp and his facial expressions of agony.

"I won't stay," she said. "Colin told me about your misfortune, and I brought you some of my Chocolate Whoppers to boost your morale." She was holding a paper plate covered with foil.

"Thank you. I need a boost," he said, brightening at the mention of something chocolate. "Will you come in for a cup of coffee?"

"I don't drink coffee," she said as she parked her umbrella on the veranda. "It goes to my head and makes me quite tipsy."

"I don't have tea. How about a glass of apple juice?"

"Oh, feathers! I'll throw discretion to the winds and have coffee," she said airily, "if it isn't too much trouble."

"No trouble—that is, if you don't mind drinking it in the kitchen. My computerized coffeemaker does all the work."

Leaning on his carved walking staff he conducted her slowly to the rear of the house, while she chattered about her last visit to Tiptop, and how it had changed, and what delightful parties the Hawkinfields used to give in the old days.

Qwilleran pressed the button on the coffeemaker (the dial was set permanently at Extra Strong) and unwrapped the cookies: three inches in diameter, an inch thick, and loaded with morsels of chocolate and chunks of walnuts.

"They're a trifle excessive," said his guest, "but that's how my boss liked them. I used to bake them for J.J. once a week." Qwilleran thought, That's why he let her keep on writing that drivel. "This is the first time I've made them since he died," she added.

"I feel flattered." He poured mugs of the black brew.

"Are the rumors true, Mr. Qwilleran?"

"What rumors?"

"That you're going to buy Tiptop and open a bed-and-breakfast?"

"I'm a writer, Ms. Wix. Not an innkeeper. By the way, the cookies are delicious."

"Thank you . . . Oooooh!" Taking her first sip of coffee, she reacted as if it were turpentine. Then, composing herself, she said, "This is the kind of coffee I used to prepare for my late husband. Wilson never drank alcohol or smoked tobacco, but he *adored* strong coffee. The doctor warned him about drinking so much of it, but he wouldn't listen." She sighed deeply. "It was almost a year ago that he had his massive heart attack."

Qwilleran set down his mug and touched his moustache with misgivings. "Was your husband overweight?" he asked hopefully.

"Not at all! I have his picture right here." She rummaged in her handbag and produced a snapshot of a broad-shouldered, muscular man with close-cropped gray hair. "He worked out at the gym faithfully and was never sick a day in his life!" Mrs. Wix found a tissue in her handbag and touched her eyes carefully. "He died not long after J.J. They were business associates, you know."

Qwilleran thought, It would be interesting to know what kind of stress triggered the attack. Shock at the murder of his colleague? Fear for his own life? Anxiety about his financial future? Guilt of some kind? . . . Stalling for time while he formulated a pertinent

question, Qwilleran changed the subject. "You spell your name
W-i-x, but there's a street downtown spelled W-i-c-k-s and an
animal clinic spelled W-i-c-k-e-s. Any connection there?"

"Are you interested in genealogy?" she asked with sudden animation. "All three names go back to my husband's great-great-
grandfather, Hannibal W-i-x-o-m, who settled here in 1812 and
operated a grist mill. He had several daughters but only one son,
George, who married Abigail Lumpton and earned his living by
making furniture. He shortened the name to W-i-x, and some of
his descendents became W-i-c-k-s or W-i-c-k-e-s, because they
weren't careful about the spelling on county records in those days."

Qwilleran nodded, although his mind was elsewhere.

"Interestingly," she went on, "I've been able to trace families
by the name of W-i-x in Vermont, Indiana, and recently Utah.
Actually the name originated in England, the family being founded
by Gregory W-i-c-k-s-h-a-m, who fought in the War of the
Roses. Subsequent branches of the family altered it to W-i-c-k-s-
u-m or W-i-x-x-o-m, one of the latter being quite high up in the
English court. Don't you find this intriguing?" she asked.

Qwilleran blinked and said, "Yes, indeed. May I fill your cup?"

"Only halfway. It's very strong. But so good!" She adjusted her
hat primly.

"That's a handsome hat, Ms. Wix, and you wear it very well.
Not every woman could carry it off."

"Thank you. It's supposed to enhance my best profile." She
tilted her head coquettishly.

"How long was your husband associated with Hawkinfield?"

"Ever since the beginning of Tiptop Estates. J.J. thought highly
of Wilson as a builder and was instrumental in getting him elected
to the city council. Of course, my husband knew how to handle
him," she said with a sly, conspiratorial smile. "Wilson simply let
him have his own way!"

An ideal pair, Qwilleran thought. The quintessential yes man
and the quintessential apple polisher.

"May I remove my scarf?" she was asking. "It's a trifle warm."

"By all means. Make yourself comfortable. Are you sure you
won't have a cookie?"

She whipped off her scarf with evident relief. "No, I made them expressly for you."

Qwilleran asked casually, "I imagine you and your husband were shocked by Hawkinfield's murder. Where were you when you heard the news?"

"Let me see . . . It was Father's Day. I gave Wilson a present and took him to dinner at the golf club. As soon as we walked into the dining room, the hostess broke the news, and we were so distressed we turned around and went home. J.J. had been my employer and friend for twenty-five years, and he was *so good* to Wilson after we were married!" Ms. Wix removed her hat and mopped her brow with a tissue. "Wilson was one of the pallbearers, and he was supposed to be a state's witness at the trial, but before he could testify, he collapsed—right there in the courtroom—and died on the way to the hospital."

"Were you there?"

"No. It was all over by the time they notified me. A terrible shock! I was under a doctor's care for three days." She was now fanning herself with a brochure from her handbag.

"You say Wilson was supposed to testify for the prosecution. Do you know the nature of his testimony?"

"I think it was about death threats," she said, gasping a little. "I'm not sure. He didn't want to talk about it. It was all very upsetting to both of us."

"You mean threats that Forest Beechum had made?"

"I think so . . . yes . . . I didn't want to know about it."

"You don't know if they were verbal or written?"

"May I have a glass of water . . . cold?"

While Qwilleran was adding ice cubes to the glass, the Siamese, who had finished napping upstairs, sauntered into the kitchen in search of crumbs. Moving in a ballet of undulating bodies and inter- twining tails, they performed their complex choreography around chair legs and table legs.

"You have . . . three of them?" she asked between sips of water.

"Only two, Koko and Yum Yum."

"I believe . . . I'm seeing double," she said.

"Does the cold water help?" he asked anxiously.

THE CAT WHO MOVED A MOUNTAIN   143

"This coffee . . . I'd better go home." She stood up and quickly sat down again, her face alarmingly flushed. There were droplets of moisture on her brow and chin.

"Are you sure you're all right? Do you want to lie down? Try eating a cookie."

"Just let me . . . get a breath of fresh air," she said. "Where's my hat?" She clapped it on her head at a careless angle, and he assisted her from the kitchen to the veranda as well as he could, considering his own unstable condition. What could he do? To drive her home would be an impossibility. She might have to stay. He might have to call a doctor.

Slowly they moved around the long veranda, Qwilleran limping and leaning on his staff, Vonda walking unsteadily and leaning on Qwilleran. In the past he had served liquor to guests who had shown an adverse reaction, but this was the first time it had happened with coffee. He should have served her fruit juice.

By the time they arrived at the front of the house and at the top of the twenty-five steps, Ms. Wix was breathing normally. Her flush had faded, and she seemed to be in control, even to the extent of straightening her hat.

"I'm all right now," she said, inhaling deeply. "Forgive me for my little spell of nerves."

"No need to apologize," he said. "It was my fault for serving such strong coffee. Are you sure you can drive?" She was searching for car keys in her handbag.

"Oh, yes, I'm perfectly all right now, and I know this road very well."

He watched her drive away. It had stopped raining, and she had forgotten her umbrella—her scarf, too, he later discovered. Returning them would be a good opportunity to ask a few more questions, he thought as he massaged his moustache.

Qwilleran sequestered the cats in the kitchen in preparation for the doctor's visit. Otherwise they would sense the hospital connection and go flying to the farthest corner of the house. As he climbed upstairs awkwardly to shave and dress, he wondered which of the two doctors would respond. He rather hoped for Inez; a woman might have a more comforting way with the sensitive and high-strung Yum Yum. He also wondered if he should consider reducing his consumption of coffee. Polly had urged him to temper its potency, but the sudden demise of Wilson Wix brought the message home.

It was John Wickes who arrived at five-fifteen, a serious-looking man with large eyeglasses and a thoughtful way of speaking. "Having a little trouble?" he asked soothingly.

Qwilleran described Yum Yum's latest aberration.

"Where is she?"

"They're both locked up in the kitchen. Follow me."

They found the Siamese on the kitchen table, guarding the remains of the Chocolate Whoppers—a mound of nuts and chocolate bits. Everything else had been devoured. When the little black bag appeared, however, Yum Yum rose vertically in space and landed on top of a kitchen cabinet. Koko, knowing instinctively that the thermometer and needle were not for him, moved not a whisker.

"Leave her alone," Wickes said quietly. "She'll come down when she's ready."

"Then pull up a chair and let's have some five o'clock refreshment," Qwilleran suggested. "Whiskey? Wine?"

"A little scotch, I think. It's been a busy day: vacationers walking in with sick cats and dogs, the usual patients for vaccinations, ear crops, spaying, etc. . . . plus surgical emergencies. Inez did a caesarean on a pregnant cat today, and I had to do a sex change on a male because of blockage. So . . . yes, I'll have a little scotch— against the weather."

"Do you always have this much rain in the Potatoes?"

"No, it's very unusual and a little frightening," the doctor said, maintaining his unruffled tone of voice. "The river is running so high we've had to sandbag the clinic property, and here on the mountain I'm worried about Lake Batata. It was man-made by damming the Batata Falls, and if the heavy downpour continues, it could burst its bounds and flood the mountainside. Inez and I are ready to evacuate if necessary."

His matter-of-fact comment led Qwilleran to ask, "Are you serious about this, John?"

"Dead serious."

"Who converted the waterfall into a lake?"

"Hawkinfield, about ten or fifteen years ago."

"Did he get permission?"

"I doubt whether he thought it necessary."

"How well did you know him?"

"I bought my lot from him and took care of his dogs. Beyond that I didn't care to go."

Qwilleran said, "I suppose Lucy was one of them."

"The Doberman? She was the last of his dogs. Has she been hanging around?"

"Once she brought me home when I was lost in the woods, for which I was grateful, and another time she came begging for food, although she's as big as a barrel."

"Lucy was always obese. I tried to convince Hawkinfield that he was hurting his dog by overfeeding, but it was useless to try to tell him anything, and it was never wise to oppose him too strongly. He had ways of retaliating."

"Where were you and Inez when you heard about the murder?"

"Where were we?" he mused. "We were spending Father's Day in the valley with our sons and their families. Someone phoned us the news, and it wasn't greeted with much sorrow. John Jr. is the gadfly on the board of education, and my younger son runs the county animal shelter. Hawkinfield persecuted both of them in editorials because they wouldn't dance to his tune. The man was unhinged, but he had power. That's the worst kind."

"I assume you're a native Spud," Qwilleran said.

"I was born in the valley, but we were all Taters originally. My forebears drifted down out of the mountains and adapted to valley environment—and valley mentality." He drained his glass.

Since Yum Yum showed no intention of deserting her perch, Qwilleran poured again. "Vonda Wix gave me a brief rundown on the genealogy of your family."

"Yes, no matter how you spell it, we all stem from a prolific old stud in the fifteenth century. One of his descendents settled here in the early nineteenth and operated a grist mill, chiefly to grind corn for the moonshiners. Making homemade whiskey was traditional among the pioneers as part of family medicine, you know. There's still a little 'midnight farming' being done on Little Potato."

At that moment there were two soft thumps to be heard, and Yum Yum descended from her lofty perch. She walked slowly and sinuously past the kitchen table, each velvet paw touching the floor like a caress. The doctor picked her up gently and began a leisurely examination while crooning to her in some unknown tongue. She was completely under his spell and reacted not at all when her temperature was taken or when the injection went into her flank. "Here are some tablets," he said. "Follow the dosage on the label."

Qwilleran said, "Your bedside manner is admirable, John."

The doctor shrugged off the compliment with his eyebrows and a flicker of a smile. "How's your ankle, Qwill?"

"On the mend somewhat. I appreciate your coming up here, though."

"Glad to do it. Come down the hill and have a drink with us Sunday afternoon, if our house hasn't washed away."

The Siamese followed the doctor to the door as if reluctant to see him go.

"Our next visitor," Qwilleran told them, "comes bearing turkey, so treat him with diplomacy. But don't expect any dinner from me after stuffing yourselves with my Chocolate Whoppers!"

While they waited for Bill Treacle, Sabrina Peel called to say she had some floor pillows for the living room. Might she drop them off the next afternoon? She would like to arrive late and then take Qwilleran to dinner at the restaurant called Pasta Perfect.

"You'll have to drive," he said. "I've sprained my ankle."

"Hope you don't object to sharing a town wagon with drapery samples and wallpaper books."

Shortly after six o'clock a car pulled into the parking lot and a smiling Bill Treacle—still exuding pep after an eight-hour shift at the market—appeared at the door with two sacks of groceries. "Hey, you weren't lying!" he said when he saw Qwilleran hobbling with the aid of a stick. "Want me to put this stuff in the refrigerator? Some of it should go in the freezer right away. Okay?"

"First door on the left," Qwilleran instructed him, pointing down the foyer, "and while you're there, help yourself to a beer. You can bring me a ginger ale. We'll sit in the living room."

"This is some barn of a place," the young grocer observed as he started down the hall. When he returned with the drinks he was accompanied by the Siamese, walking beside him like an honor guard, their tails rigidly at attention.

"Friendly brutes, aren't they?" he said.

"Cats are instinctively attracted to a source of energy," Qwilleran explained. "Have a chair, and excuse me if I keep my foot elevated."

"What happened to it?"

"I slipped on some wet leaves."

"There's plenty of those around. I never saw so much rain in June. Let me know if there's anything I can do for you while you're laid up. Okay?"

Qwilleran seized his cue. "There's one thing you could do, Bill. I noticed that Lumpton's Hardware has fax service, and if you'll take some copy and shoot it through tomorrow, I'll be grateful. It's a column I write for my hometown newspaper, and they want to run it Friday."

"Is that your job? Everybody's been wondering who you are and why you're here."

That was another cue. "One reason I'm here is to write a biography of J.J. Hawkinfield."

"No kidding! I didn't know he was that important. I can tell you a few things about the Old Buzzard if you want to know. I used to work for him at the *Gazette*."

"How was he as a boss?"

"Unbelievable! If there was a mistake made, he'd come storming into the production department or newsroom and yell, 'Who's responsible for this stupid error?' And he'd fire somebody on the spot, or else rage around the department and sweep everything off the desks and dump files out on the floor. He was really nuts!"

"Do you know the Beechums?"

"Sure do! Do you know about Forest and the trial? Have you met Chrys? I used to date her before all this happened. Now Forest is locked up without being guilty; their mother has stopped talking;

and Chrys has turned off about everything. Bad news all the way around."

"Are you the one who printed handbills for Forest?"

"Maybe it wasn't the smartest thing to do—okay?—but nobody was cooperating, and I had to help somehow. He was a hundred percent right about what was happening to Big Potato. So, being in charge of job printing at the *Gazette*, I ran off a few flyers between orders. The Old Buzzard caught up with me and not only canned me but blackballed me wherever I applied for another job. But I got back at him!" Treacle said with a grin. "I knew the hospital spent a lot of money to print forms and booklets. They were giving the *Gazette* jobbing shop $20,000 of business a year. Okay? So I showed the hospital auxiliary how they could set up their own print shop and do the work with volunteers."

Qwilleran asked, "How did Hawkinfield react?"

"They say he nearly busted a blood vessel. It turned out to be a break for me, too. A guy on the hospital board of commissioners owns Five Points Market, and he was so impressed he gave me this job. So that was another kick in the head for the Old Buzzard . . . Hey, the cats kinda like me, don't they?"

Koko and Yum Yum were being sociable as cats do when they have an ulterior motive—sniffing shoelaces, rubbing ankles, purring throatily. They knew he was a grocer and not a printer. He also happened to be sitting in Yum Yum's favorite chair.

Qwilleran said, "If Forest is innocent, it means the real criminal is free and possibly walking around Spudsboro. Have you thought of that?"

"Yeah, but nobody's ever gonna do anything about it. The public wanted a quick conviction—okay? And they wanted to hang a Tater—okay? The judge and the prosecutor were both coming up for reelection, so what have you got? A beautiful frame-up."

"How do you explain this prejudice against Taters?"

"Don't ask me! When the first settlers came to the Potatoes, there were Indians here, and it was whites against redskins. Now it's valley whites against mountain whites."

"Did you attend the trial?"

"Sure did. I took time off from my job. I sat with the Beechums."

"Were you in the courtroom when Wilson Wix collapsed?"

"He dropped dead right in front of me! He was a Hawksman, you know. That's what they called the Old Buzzard's cronies on the council, zoning board, school board, and all that. Wix was a nice guy, but he was a Hawksman."

"Do you remember the day Hawkinfield was murdered?" Qwilleran asked.

"Sure do. My sister and I were taking our parents out to dinner for Father's Day—okay? First I drove them up to the top of Big Potato, like my dad used to do when we were kids, before the waterfall was dammed. When we got to the top there were a couple of cars in the Tiptop parking lot, and we heard a dog howling, so we turned around and drove down again."

"What time was it?"

"Two o'clock, I'm pretty sure, because we had a reservation at The Great Big Baked Potato for two-thirty. Later on, after we found out what happened, I remembered the dog was howling like the Old Buzzard was already dead. So what were those two cars doing in the parking lot? . . . Anyway, after Forest was arrested and charged, I went to his attorney with this information. I didn't have a description of the cars or license numbers. All I knew was that neither of them was the Beechum jalopy, and maybe I could testify to that. He told me I was a known accomplice of Forest and had been fired for dishonesty, so any testimony from me would do more harm than good. That's what he told me."

"You're referring to Hugh Lumpton?" Qwilleran asked. "Did he do a conscientious job of defending Forest in your opinion?"

"That guy? He did a lousy job! I could've done better myself. In the first place, the county doesn't pay much when they assign a lawyer. In the second place, he's a Spud and he plays golf with the prosecutor. The whole thing was a joke, only it wasn't funny. At the end, all Lumpton said to the jury was that the prosecution hadn't proved their case. The jury wasn't out long enough to get a cup of coffee, and when they came back with a guilty verdict, I was ready to commit murder myself!"

"I'm curious about the Lumptons. I see the name everywhere."

"Yeah, you can't spit without hitting a Lumpton. They're in pizza, furniture, hardware, everything. They've been here for generations. Some moved to the valley and made good, and some are still Taters. For a long time we had a popular sheriff who was a Lumpton. He was jolly and sort of easygoing. Who says cops have to go around looking fierce and rattling handcuffs? Josh Lumpton was too independent for the Old Buzzard, and he finally got him defeated. Now the sheriff is a guy named Wilbank."

"Did Wilbank take the stand at the trial?" Qwilleran asked.

"Yeah, he told how Sherry Hawkinfield came running down the hill to his house and said her dad was missing, and how they found the body at the foot of the cliff, and how the front hall was wrecked. The worst was Sherry's testimony—a bare-faced lie! How can they get away with that? It was her word against a Tater's, so you know who they believed. And then there were other trumped-up lies."

"I heard something about a death threat."

"Are you kidding? Forest wouldn't be stupid enough to send an anonymous threat through the mail!"

"Was it produced as evidence?"

"No, that was another fishy thing. It had disappeared, although Robert Lessmore testified he'd seen it."

"This is all very interesting," Qwilleran said. "How about another beer?"

"Thanks, but I'm bowling tonight. Just give me the papers you want faxed, and I hope your ankle gets better soon—okay?"

Bill Treacle left, and Qwilleran relented and gave the Siamese some turkey for their good behavior. For his own dinner he thawed some beef pepper steak. As he ate his meal at the kitchen table, Koko sat on a chair opposite with his chin barely clearing the edge of the table, his bright eyes watching every move intently.

"Don't just sit there looking omniscient," Qwilleran said to him. "Come up with an idea. What do we do next?"

With a grunt Koko jumped from the chair and ran from the kitchen. His exodus was so abrupt, so urgent, that Qwilleran limped after him, first taking care to cover his plate of beef. He found the cat rolling on the carpet at the foot of the telephone chest, stretching to his full length and muttering to himself.

Qwilleran placed his hand on the telephone. "Do you want me

to make a call?" he asked. "Are you on the phone company's payroll?"

Koko scrambled to his feet and raced wildly about the foyer while Qwilleran called Osmond Hasselrich at his home in Pickax. It was his first contact with the attorney since leaving Moose County, and they had a long conversation.

As later events indicated, that was probably not what Koko wanted at all.

CHAPTER 14

On Thursday morning the trees were still dripping, but the sun shone intermittently and Qwilleran's ankle was gradually responding to treatment. Drinking his breakfast coffee in the kitchen he recalled how his conversations with the friendly telephone installer, the saturnine veterinarian, the flaky *Gazette* columnist, and the overly energetic grocer had left him with no answers, only conjectures. He guessed that the "death threat" was not received by Hawkinfield in his lifetime but was forged following his murder and shown to Robert Lessmore (a golf buddy of the prosecutor), who thereby testified to seeing such a document, overlooking the discrepancy in timing. Meanwhile, it had been conveniently destroyed by the same hand or hands that forged it. If the instruments of law and order in Spudsboro were as corrupt as Treacle intimated, a veritable network of collaborators could be involved in the frame-up of a Tater, including Sherry Hawkinfield, and all of this was done to protect the actual perpetrators of the crime, there being more than one, Qwilleran surmised.

It occurred to him that Wilson Wix may have been enlisted against his better judgment, and the stress of committing what he knew to be perjury triggered his heart attack. One could not lay the whole blame on caffeine. Qwilleran poured a third cup.

He had a strong urge to visit the Old Buzzard's office once more in search of clues if not answers. The obstacle was the heavy desk concealing the door. Then Dewey Beechum arrived to work on the gazebo, and the problem was solved. The dampness of the season had caused his historic hat to grow moss, and his beard was curling and looking wilder than ever.

Qwilleran called to him from the veranda and beckoned him up the steps. "It's hard for me to leave the house," he explained to the carpenter. "I've hurt my ankle. How's the job progressing? It's impossible to see from here."

"Finish up today, like as not. Built the screens in my barn. Aimin' to save time."

"Good idea! I'll be around here all day. Just add up your bill, and I'll write you a check. Do you think we're going to have any flood damage?"

"Iffen it don't stop rainin'."

"We could use a few hours of sunshine and a little breeze to dry things up," said Qwilleran, who had learned the banal art of weatherspeak in Moose County.

Beechum gave a sour look upward, perhaps searching for a black snake in a tree. "Won't git it," he pronounced.

Having disposed of the amenities, Qwilleran explained his problem. The workman nodded and followed him into the house, trudged through the living room without looking to right or left, lifted the bookcase off the base with ease, pulled the desk away from the wall without asking any questions, and returned to his work on the gazebo.

Taters were strong, silent types, Qwilleran reflected. They worked hard, lived long lives, never worried about being overweight, and did a little midnight farming as a hobby.

Koko was delighted to see the office open again. He immediately went in to sniff Lucy's mattress. Yum Yum, on the other hand, was sleeping off her medication on a down-cushioned chair in the living room. It was the one chair that was more comfortable than all the rest, and with true feline instinct she had commandeered it.

There was something in Hawkinfield's office that Qwilleran expressly wished to examine: a family photograph hanging on the wall. Seated in the center of the group was J.J. with his lofty brow and "important" nose, obviously the master of the house. Standing behind him were three bright-looking boys of graduated heights, and on either side were seated a pretty woman with a shy smile and a teenage girl with a sullen pout. She had the Hawkinfield nose and an exaggerated overbite. Was this the Sherry Hawkinfield, Qwilleran wondered, that he had invited to dinner? He could only hope she had improved with age.

Sprawling in J.J.'s lounge chair and propping his ankle on J.J.'s ottoman, he delved into another of the editor's scrapbooks and read attacks on the county animal shelter, Mother's Day, and the high school football coach. It was prose written by a madman with a passion for exclamation points. In one tirade he aimed his barbs at a sheriff who was running for reelection. This candidate, Hawkinfield pointed out, was three months in arrears on his water bill, regularly had his wife's parking tickets voided, and at one time succeeded in hushing up his own felonious bad-check charge. No name was mentioned, but even a stranger in the Potatoes like Qwilleran could guess that it was Uncle Josh Lumpton, who forthwith lost his post to Del Wilbank.

Koko, tired of sniffing Lucy's mattress and the law books on the shelf, suddenly landed on the desktop with whiskers twitching and paws digging. He wanted desperately to get into the center drawer, the shallow one that is usually a catchall. Qwilleran obliged him, having an avid curiosity of his own. In the compartments at the front of the drawer there were pencils, pens, paper clips, rubber bands, a few pennies, three cigarettes in a squashed pack, two large screws, and one stray postage stamp. Koko pounced on the stamp and carried it away to sniff and lick in some dark corner. Now how did that cat know it was there? Qwilleran asked himself.

At the rear of the drawer the miscellaneous papers and file folders included a large yellow legal pad on which Hawkinfield apparently drafted his editorials in longhand, using a soft lead pencil. The one on the pad was datelined two days after Father's Day of the previous year. It had never been published and had never journeyed beyond the center drawer of Hawkinfield's desk, but before Qwilleran could read it, the doorbell rang.

Beechum had finished the gazebo and was coming to collect payment. Qwilleran knew it was rash to pay for the work without inspecting it, but he trusted the man and even added a bonus for prompt service. He then asked the carpenter to move the desk back against the office door—but not before he had retrieved the yellow legal pad. After that it was time to shave and dress for dinner with Sabrina Peel, and Qwilleran transferred the pad to his own desk upstairs.

When Sabrina arrived she brought two pillows in bright red and gold, each a yard square, to stack on the living room floor between two windows. "I think they make the statement we want," she said. "They balance the color accents and add some desirable weight at that end of the room . . . How's the ankle, Qwill?"

"The Pain-and-Anguish Scale went down sixteen points when you walked in," he said, admiring the misty green silk dress that complemented her decorator-blond hair. "Shall we have a drink before we leave?"

"Mmmm . . . no," she said. "I've requested a choice booth, and they won't hold a reservation more than fifteen minutes. I hope you don't object to the no-smoking section . . . Where did you find that fabulous burl bowl? At Potato Cove? . . . I see you need candles. I could have brought you some."

"I have plenty," he said. "The candle dipper sold me a lifetime supply, but I haven't found time to stick them in the candleholder . . . Let me check out the Siamese before we leave."

The two cats were exactly where he thought they would be—perched on top of the new floor pillows, looking haughty and possessive, their cold blue eyes challenging anyone to dethrone them.

With Qwilleran taking one experimental step at a time, he and Sabrina walked slowly down the long flight to the parking lot.

"Do you mind living alone?" she asked.

"I've tried it both ways," he replied, "and I know it can be a letdown to come home to an empty apartment, but now I have the Siamese to greet me at the door. They're good companions; they need me; they're always happy to see me come home. On the other hand, they're always glad to see me go out—one of the things that cats do to keep a person from feeling too important."

On the way down Hawk's Nest Drive she pointed out clients' houses. She had helped the Wilbanks select their wallpapers . . . Peel & Poole was redesigning the entire interior for the Lessmores . . . Her partner had done the windows and floors for the Wickes house.

"Are you the only design studio in town?" Qwilleran asked her slyly.

"The only good one," she retorted, flashing an arch smile at her passenger. "I'd give anything to get my hands on Tiptop and do it over, inside and out."

"Would you kill for it?"

He expected a flip reply, but Sabrina was concentrating on traffic at the foot of the drive and she ignored the remark.

They turned onto a road that roughly paralleled the overflowing banks of the Yellyhoo River and then led into the foothills where the restaurant called Pasta Perfect occupied a dimple in the landscape. It was a rustic roadhouse that appeared ready to collapse.

Qwilleran said, "In the flat country where I live, this place would look like a dump, but in the mountains even the dumps look picturesque."

"It was a challenge to blend its dumpishness with an appetizing interior," Sabrina admitted. "The owners wanted a shirt-sleeve ambiance that looked and felt *clean*, so I had the old wood floors refinished to look like old wood floors, left the posts and beams in their original dark stain, and painted the wall spaces white to emphasize all the cracks and knots and wormholes."

The restaurant was a rambling layout of small rooms that had been added throughout the years, and Sabrina and her guest were seated in the Chief Batata Room, where high-backed booths provided privacy as well as a mountain view through panels of plate glass. The focal point of the room was a painted portrait of an Indian chief smoking a peace pipe.

Sabrina said, "I want you to look at this staggering menu, Qwill.

The fifteen kinds of pasta and all the sauces are house-made, fresh daily." For an appetizer he ordered smoked salmon and avocado rolled in lasagna noodles, with a sauce of watercress, dill, and horseradish. Sabrina chose trout quenelles on a bed of black beans with Cajun hollandaise—and a bottle of Orvieto wine.

"How are you enjoying your vacation?" she asked.

"So far, it's been nothing but rain and minor calamities, but let's not talk about that. What do you know about the Fitzwallow huntboard?"

"J.J. bought it at an auction, claiming there was a Fitzwallow in his ancestry. It's a monstrous thing, and his wife hated it."

"My cat has taken a fancy to it," Qwilleran said. "If he isn't jumping on top of it, he's rolling on the floor at the base. I think he has some Fitzwallow blood himself. One thing I wouldn't mind owning, though, is Forest Beechum's painting. What is it worth?"

"It's definitely worth $3,000, Qwill. As an artist he's an unknown, but it's good, and it's big! He did this painting of Chief Batata, too. I thought it would be amusing in the no-smoking room, but I'm afraid no one gets the joke. I suppose you're an ex-smoker like the rest of us."

"I used to smoke a pipe, thinking I looked thoughtful and wise while puffing. Also, re-lighting it filled in lengthy pauses when I didn't know what to say. Now I have to sit and twiddle my thumbs and look empty-headed."

"Qwill, I can't imagine you ever looking empty-headed. What do you do, anyway? There's been a lot of speculation in the valley."

"I'm a wandering writer, searching for a subject, and I think I've found it. I want to write a biography of J.J. Hawkinfield. He was a large, power-mad frog in a small puddle, with a bombastic style of writing, a penchant for making enemies, and a succession of family sorrows ending in his own murder. It's the Greek tragedy of the Potato Mountains! It calls for a Greek chorus of Taters and Spuds!"

"Will it be a whitewash?" she asked. "Or are you going to paint him warts and all?"

"Being a journalist by profession, I'm especially interested in the warts."

"Do you think you can get people to talk?"

"The public," Qwilleran said, "is immensely fond of talking to authors—especially about someone who's dead and can't lash back. I may start with ex-sheriff Lumpton."

Sabrina laughed. "That freeloader! Don't believe a word you get from Uncle Josh."

"What do you know about him?"

"Well, he and J.J. were feuding for years. He's in the trucking business now, and he's building an enormously expensive house. We're doing the interior with a no-limit budget."

"Trucking logs out of the mountains must be lucrative," Qwilleran commented.

"According to conventional wisdom, Uncle Josh was stashing the money away in a coffee can buried in his backyard all the time he was sheriff."

The waiter brought the antipasto on very cold plates, followed by the entrees on very hot plates. Having ordered tagliatelle in a sauce of ricotta, leeks, and ham, Qwilleran twirled his fork in rapt appreciation for a while. Eventually he asked, "Who is this partner you're always mentioning?"

"Spencer Poole. He's an older man and a wonderful person. When I was in high school he gave me a summer job, folding samples and keeping the studio dusted. After I graduated from design school, he took me into the firm because he liked the sound of Peel & Poole."

Uh-huh, Qwilleran thought, grooming his moustache. It was more likely because she's a stunning young woman.

Sabrina said, "I told him it should be Poole & Peel, since he's the senior partner, but he pointed out the importance of vowel sounds in the name of a design studio. He said 'ee-oo' has more class than 'oo-ee,' which is associated with hog calling. Spencer is fussy about details, but that's what makes him a terrific designer. He's taught me a lot," she said, her eyes sparkling. They were green tonight; a few days ago they were blue.

"With a name like Peel, you must be Scottish," he remarked. "My mother was a Mackintosh."

"Say something in Scots," she said teasingly.

"Mony a mickle mak' a muckle," he recited.

"Many small things make a large thing," she guessed.

"That's its popular meaning, although the dictionary defines mickle and muckle as synonyms. George Washington used the expression in the popular sense, however, and if it's good enough for the Father of our Country, it's good enough for me."

"My partner would love the sound of it," she said.

Speaking seriously in a lower voice, Qwilleran said, "Your partner seems like an astute individual. Does he have any idea who really killed Hawkinfield? The man's enemies are easy to identify; the ones who arouse my suspicion are his so-called friends."

Sabrina put down her fork and stared at him. "Well," she said hesitantly, "when it first happened . . . Spencer thought it might be the husband of J.J.'s girlfriend. But now I guess there's no doubt it was Beechum."

Qwilleran stroked his moustache. "Hawkinfield had a girlfriend? Was it well-known?"

"This is a very small town, Qwill. It was well-known but not talked about. She worked at the *Gazette*—still does, in fact—and she thought J.J. walked on water. That's the kind of woman he liked. She used to bake cookies for him all the time, and he called her Cookie, even around the office. Everyone knows he paid for her face-lift."

"But she had a husband?"

"Not until a few years ago. She married a run-of-the-mill house builder who immediately landed the contract for all the houses on Big Potato, and he turned out to be a real Hawksman."

"Did he know about his wife's connection with Hawkinfield?"

"Who knows? He was a simple soul—sort of a male Pollyanna. We all liked him when we worked with him on interiors. He had a massive heart attack and died . . . Don't quote me on any of this."

When dessert was served—almond ravioli with raspberry sauce— Qwilleran returned to the subject of the biography. He said, "In doing my research I'd like to explore Hawkinfield's relationship with his children—just for background information, so that I feel comfortable with my subject."

"Yes, I can understand that," she said. "The three boys were the center of his universe, you know, and they were really bright kids, but J.J. neglected his daughter because she had the misfortune to be female. He gave the boys bikes, skis, golf lessons, even private tutoring. Sherry got piano lessons, which she hated."

"How did she feel about her father?"

"Not enthusiastic! She referred to him flippantly as her male parent and scorned her mother for being weak. When I was doing the interior of Tiptop, Sherry latched onto me as a sort of role model. That's how she acquired an interest in selling decorative accessories."

"Was she as smart as her brothers?"

"She was shrewd, rather than book smart—even devious," Sabrina said. "I think her second-class standing in the family slanted her that way; she had to look out for Sherry. And now that she's in business for herself, that's not a bad quality to have."

"I saw a family photograph," Qwilleran said, "and she looked like an unhappy girl—certainly unattractive."

"Yes, her teeth needed attention, and she desperately wanted a nose job, but J.J. considered that an extravagance. Fortunately, her maternal grandmother left her some money, so she was able to have orthodontal work and esthetic surgery. What a difference! Her personality blossomed, and she became quite popular. In fact . . ." Sabrina glanced around the room and dropped her voice, "her father sent her away to school because she was dating a Lumpton boy—a really good-looking kid. Two years later, after graduating from her school in Virginia, she sneaked off and married him."

"I'll bet there were fireworks on Big Potato when that happened," Qwilleran said.

"Were there ever! J.J. was sure the boy just wanted to marry an heiress and get into a 'good' family. You see, he was the son of the infamous Josh Lumpton! So Sherry was given a choice: annulment or disinheritance. She was no fool; she opted to stay in her father's will, thinking she'd inherit millions. Actually, all she got was Tiptop. The rest is in trust for her mother."

"What happened to Josh Lumpton's son?"

"He and Sherry are still close. They'll probably marry when she sells the inn and gets her million plus. He went on to law school and passed the bar, although he doesn't have much of a practice. He'd rather play golf . . . Are you interested in all this small-town gossip?" she asked.

"I live in a small town," he said, "where gossip is the staff of life. I live in a barn." He told her about his converted apple barn with its balconies and tapestries and contemporary furnishings.

"It sounds fabulous! I'd love to see it," she said.

There was no lingering over the espresso. Thunder storms were gathering, according to the local weathercast, and Sabrina wanted to be home before the deluge. "Driving in the mountains is spooky during an electrical storm," she told Qwilleran as she drove him home. "By the way, did you find the letter I lost?"

"Yes, I did," he replied without revealing that it was still languishing in a drawer of the huntboard. "It was in the house. I found it on the floor. If you'd lost it outdoors, it would have been rain-soaked, I'm afraid."

"I'm fed up with these storms," she said. "Basements are flooding on Center Street, and a bridge washed out downriver." She declined his offer of a nightcap. "Some other time. Meanwhile, if you decide to buy Tiptop—"

"You'll be the first to know, Sabrina," he promised. "Perhaps we can have dinner again soon—my treat."

"Perhaps," she said with a glance he was unable to interpret.

Qwilleran walked slowly and carefully up the twenty-five steps to Tiptop, thinking, She's a charming woman, interesting, very friendly . . . probably in her middle thirties . . . seems to live alone . . . an acquaintance worth cultivating. Then he thought, What could she do with Tiptop? It wouldn't hurt to ask for a design proposal and an estimate . . . Her eyes looked green tonight. I thought they were blue . . . What's her relationship with Spencer Poole? She has an enormously warm regard for him. Mentions him often . . .

He unlocked the door, expecting a greeting from two excited cats with tails held high. It was always dark in the foyer, day or night, and he switched on the lights, but no pale fur bodies emerged from the gloom. Nor were there any welcoming yowls. Instead, he heard human voices upstairs.

CHAPTER 15

When Qwilleran walked into the house and heard muffled voices upstairs, he instinctively looked around for a weapon before realizing he had a formidable one in his left hand. Brandishing the carved walking staff, which had the heft of a cudgel, and forgetting to limp, he started up the stairs two at a time. Halfway up he stopped.

He heard a man's voice saying, "Well, thanks for being with us, Bob; good luck at the tourney . . . and now a look at the weather . . ."

Qwilleran finished the flight of stairs at a slower pace and found the cats on his desk: Koko lounging sphinx-like on the yellow legal pad and Yum Yum lounging sphinx-like on the radio, the controls of which were unwisely located on top. Neither of them stirred; both regarded him with infuriating complacency.

"You rascals!" he said after counting to ten. "Why didn't you tune in some good music?"

Only then did he realize he was walking without pain. Filled with immediate ambition he busied himself with activities neglected in the last few days: putting candles in the eight-branch candelabrum, throwing the baker's white duck uniform into the washer, writing a thank-you note to Mrs. Beechum with a testimonial for her homemade liniment. The storm roared in on schedule—with crashing thunder, flashing lightning, and pounding rain, and the Siamese were glad to huddle in Qwilleran's bedroom and listen to a chapter of *The Magic Mountain*. He had to shout to be heard above the tumult outdoors. When he tuned in the eleven o'clock news, flood warnings were in effect.

The next morning he opened his eyes and rotated his left foot painlessly; his elation knew no bounds. He was ready to plunge into the bogus research for the biography he had no intention of writing! He was eager to drive again after being grounded for three days. When he raised the blinds in the bedroom, however, the view from the window suggested that Tiptop was flying through a cloudbank at an altitude of 35,000 feet. Furthermore, the meteorologist on the radio predicted dense fog on the mountains until late afternoon, with heavy humidity. The flood warning had been changed to flood watch after last night's rain.

Qwilleran stepped out onto the veranda and inhaled the moist smells of fog and drenched treebark, noting that only three of the twenty-five steps to the parking lot were visible; the rest were shrouded in mist. Sherry Hawkinfield's plane would never be able to land, he told himself.

Indoors he warmed a sticky bun in the oven, but his fingers faltered over the controls on the coffeemaker: Extra Strong or merely Strong? Three cups or two? Remembering the fate of Wilson Wix, he opted for moderation. Then he fed the cats and watched them gulp and gobble with jerking of heads and swaying of tails. In his earlier days he would have had neither the time nor the inclination to watch animals eat. In many ways Qwilleran had changed since Kao K'o Kung came to live with him.

After he had showered and shaved and dressed, he again checked the veranda; there were now four steps visible. He went upstairs and made a pretense of straightening his bed; housekeeping was not one of his strong points. Koko was back on the desk, sitting on the legal pad.

"Let me see that thing," Qwilleran said.

It was the editorial that Hawkinfield had written before he died, intending to run it the following week, and it brought a tremor to Qwilleran's upper lip. Rushing into the cats' room to use their phone, he called the editor of the *Gazette*.

He said, "Colin, I want to start my research on the Hawkinfield bio by interviewing Josh Lumpton. Can you break the ice for me and give me a good reference? Don't mention my book on crime."

"How soon do you want to see him?"

"This morning. Immediately."

"Sounds as if the ankle is okay and you're rarin' to go. How's the fog on the mountain? It's not too bad down here. The airport's still open. But the river's raging."

"The fog is dense, but I can get through. Where is Lumpton's place of business?"

"South of town on the Yellyhoo, half a mile beyond the city limits—that is, if he isn't flooded out. If I don't call you back in five minutes, it means he's still high and dry and willing to see you. He's an agreeable guy."

There was no return call. When Qwilleran ventured down the steps, the mist swirled about him. When he drove down Hawk's Nest with fog lights on, nothing was visible except a few feet of yellow line on the pavement. Houses had disappeared in the white-out, but he could tell their location by counting the hairpin turns. At the foot of the drive the visibility improved, however, and he dropped Sabrina's letter to Sherry Hawkinfield in a mailbox.

South of Spudsboro the flooding had almost reached the pavement, and the ramshackle Yellyhoo Market had virtually washed away. Truckloads of sandbags were traveling toward the downtown area where banks, stores, and offices could not afford to wash away. Lumpton Transport was located safely on higher ground—a fenced parking lot for truck cabs, trailers, flatbeds, refrigerated trucks, tankers, and moving vans. There was no name on the headquarters building, but an oversized sign painted on its concrete-block front shouted: YOU GOT IT? WE MOVE IT.

The receptionist conducted Qwilleran into the boss's private office, a plain room with a large girly-type wall calendar as the sole decoration. There, surrounded by a bank of computers, was a jolly mountain of flesh in khaki chinos, seated regally in a huge chair. His pudgy face was wreathed in smiling folds of fat.

"Come on in," he called out affably. "Sit you down. Colin said you were comin' over. What's the name again?"

"Qwilleran. Jim Qwilleran spelled with a QW." He leaned across the desk to shake hands.

"Want some coffee? . . . Susie, bring some coffee!" the booming voice shouted in the direction of the door. "How d'you like our weather? Colin says you're stayin' at Tiptop."

"It's much wetter than I expected. Did you ever see it as bad as this?"

"Only once. In 1963. The Yellyhoo looked like the Mississippi, and Batata Falls looked like Niagara. I don't worry about the river reachin' us here, but if the county has to close South Highway, we're out of business."

The coffee arrived in heavy china mugs decorated with dubious witticisms, the boss's mug bearing the good-natured message: "I'm Fat But You're Ugly." "How about a jigger of corn to liven it up?" he suggested with his great, hospitable smile.

"No, thanks. I like my coffee straight."

"So you're gonna write a book about my old buddy! Great fella! Smart as the dickens! Never be another like him! But he was jinxed—had one stroke of bad luck after another."

Qwilleran wondered, Was it bad luck or was it calculated retaliation? He asked, "Didn't Hawkinfield make a lot of enemies with his outspoken editorials?"

"Nah. Nobody took that stuff serious. He was okay. Did a whole lot of good for the community. Everybody liked him."

"How long were you sheriff?"

"Twenty-four years!" Lumpton patted his bulging stomach with pride.

"That's an illustrious record! Everyone talks about you."

"My constituents been bendin' your ear? Hope they didn't tattle too much." He wheezed a husky chuckle.

Genially Qwilleran asked, "Should I infer that you're covering up a few secrets?"

The trucker gave him a sharp look before chuckling again with the aplomb of a seasoned politician.

Qwilleran continued: "How did you feel about losing your last campaign for office, Mr. Lumpton?"

"Didn't waste no tears over that. Twenty-four years of bein' a public servant is long enough! It was time I got out—and started makin' some money." He gestured toward his computers.

"But wasn't J.J. responsible for your losing the election?"

"Hell, no! I just didn't feel like campaignin'."

"Do you think Wilbank's a worthy successor?"

"He's okay. He's doin' a good job. Got a lot to learn, but . . . sure, he's okay. Me, I know the county inside out. I know every man, woman, and child in the Potatoes."

"How many of them are Lumptons?"

"Plenty! And I did my part—four sons, three daughters, five grandkids." The trucker was leaning back in his big chair, swiveling, and enjoying the interview.

Qwilleran switched his approach from amiable to serious. "If Hawkinfield was so well liked, why was he murdered?"

"You don't know the story? There was this nutty young fella on Li'l Tater—a real troublemaker. He had some kind of crazy grudge against J.J.—even threatened to kill him. J.J. paid no attention. I guess editors get letters from cranks all the time. But . . . it finally happened. The kid just blew his stack."

"Wasn't it your son who represented him at the trial?"

Lumpton nodded. "Court-appointed. They all take a few cases like that."

"I hear the trial was remarkably brief."

"Sure was! Our judicial system at its best! Everybody doin' his job and doin' it well! That way, it didn't cost the county a whole lot of money. A long jury trial can wreck a county's budget for the year!"

"But wasn't there radically conflicting testimony?" Qwilleran asked.

"Sure, the defendant pleaded not guilty and told some cock-and-bull stories, but you can't believe them Taters."

"What do you know about Hawkinfield's daughter? She seems to be the last of the family."

"Don't know her. Knew the three boys that got killed. Don't know the daughter."

"I believe she's the one who was married to your son briefly."

Lumpton frowned. "Guess so. They weren't married long enough to notice."

"Also, she's the one who gave the incriminating testimony at the trial."

"Oh, her! She doesn't live around here."

Qwilleran gazed at his subject with a cool eye and paused before saying in a deeper voice, "Who really killed Hawkinfield, Mr. Lumpton?"

The big man's eyes popped. "Did I hear you right?"

"You certainly did! There are rumors in the valley that they convicted the wrong man."

"Somebody's crazy! If there's any rumors in this county, I start 'em. Whatcha gettin' at, anyway? You ask a lotta questions. Are you one of them investigative reporters?"

"I'm an author trying to get a handle on my subject matter," Qwilleran said, softening his approach. "No one can write a biography without asking questions. Since you were in law enforcement for twenty-four years—and know everyone in the county—I thought you might have a lurking suspicion as to the real motive for Hawkinfield's murder."

"Look here," said the trucker, standing up and losing his official smile. He was a mountain of a man, Qwilleran realized. "Look here, I'm busy. I don't have time to listen to this—"

"Sorry, Mr. Lumpton. I won't take any more of your time. Sherry Hawkinfield will be here this weekend, and I'll get her to fill in some of the blanks." He was on his feet and edging out of the office. "One more question: Exactly what is the Hot Potato Fund?"

"Never heard of it!" The trucker was lunging around the end of his desk in a manner that hastened Qwilleran's departure.

"Thank you, Mr. Lumpton," he called out from the hallway.

He drove directly to the office of the *Gazette*. Downtown Spudsboro was misty, but the mountains had disappeared in the fog. When he entered Colin Carmichael's office he was carrying a plastic sack from the Five Points Market.

"Qwill! You're walking like Homo sapiens instead of an arthritic bear," the editor greeted him.

"I see you're sandbagging the building," Qwilleran observed.

"We're also moving our microfilm out of the basement. Did you see Uncle Josh?"

"Yes, he was ready to talk, but he disliked some of my questions . . . May I close the door?" he asked before sitting down. "First, let me confess something, Colin. I have no intention of writing a biography of Hawkinfield—and never did. All I want is to find out who killed him . . . You look surprised!"

"Frankly, I am, Qwill. I thought that matter had been put to bed."

Qwilleran tamped his moustache. "I've had doubts about the case for several days, and last night I found something in Hawk-infield's study that leads me to suspect Josh Lumpton."

Carmichael stared at him incredulously. "On what grounds? I know Hawkinfield hounded him out of office, charging corruption, but that was a few years ago. Josh runs a clean business. His computerized operation is unique in these parts. We gave it a spread on our business page. He's treasurer of the chamber of commerce."

"Be that as it may," Qwilleran said, drawing the legal pad from the plastic sack. "I have here in my briefcase one of Hawkinfield's unpublished editorials, datelined for the Wednesday after his death. It's my theory that he was killed to forestall its publication. Some-one—and who could it be but his daughter?—knew it was going to be published and tipped off the murderer. Her false testimony at the trial—and I do mean false!—suggested that she was protecting someone. Was it her once-and-future father-in-law? No doubt she also collaborated in trapping Forest Beechum. In court he was defended *incompetently* by Josh's son, who is also her lover, if my information is correct."

"Let me see that," the editor said, reaching for the legal pad.

"I'll read it to you. You have to imagine anywhere from one to four exclamation points after each sentence. J.J. liked to yell in print." Qwilleran proceeded to read:

In our hysterical and ineffective war against drugs and drug lords around the world, we are tricked into forgetting those home-grown murderers who not only prey on the poor but rob the government of millions in lost revenue!! Bootleggers, some of you may be surprised to know, are still operating illegally and profitably!!! Perhaps you think the manufacture and sale of illegal whiskey died with the repeal of Prohibition. Not so! Cheap booze is still killing people!! And networks of respected citizens are involved in this heinous racket!!! Are we talking about some far-off sink of iniquity in crime-ridden New York or California? No, we are talking about this blessed valley of ours, this ideal community, this latter-day Eden, which is sinking into an abyss!

First, the local moonshiner produces the whiskey, running it in filthy stills hidden in mountain caves and using additives to fake quality, as well as dangerous short-cuts to make a cheaper product!! Then the hauler has a contract to transport it out of the mountains disguised as honest cargo—in a furniture van or under a load of logs!!! Finally the big-city bootlegger waters it down and sells it to the dregs of society! Everyone makes a profit except the consumer, who dies of lead poisoning!!

Now brace yourself for the most shocking fact!!! The distilling and hauling operations are financed by local investors who innocently or not so innocently buy shares in the illegal and aptly named Hot Potato Fund, which is purported to promote the local economy! Civic leaders, church deacons, and elderly widows are sinking their savings in this profitable, damnable underground venture!! They never question that their quarterly dividends are unreported and said to be nontaxable! Or do they?

Who is guilty? Look around you!! Your next-door neighbor is guilty! Your boss is guilty!! Your golf partner is guilty!!! Your good old uncle is guilty!!!!

When Qwilleran finished reading, he looked up at his listener and waited for a reaction. Carmichael was thinking, with lowered eyes and twirling thumbs.

"How about that?" Qwilleran demanded. "Have you heard of the Hot Potato Fund? Is this why Taters discourage outsiders from prowling around their mountain? Is this why Lumpton Transport is doing so well?"

"What are you going to do with that information?" the editor wanted to know.

"If I'm on the right track, it'll be used as evidence in court. There'll be a new trial."

"Give me that pad," Colin said, "and forget you ever saw it."

"Why?" Qwilleran asked mockingly. "Is the *Gazette* involved in this, too?"

"All right, I'll tell you something I'm not supposed to, but for God's sake, keep it under your hat. Okay?"

Qwilleran held up his right hand. "I swear," he said lightly.

"We received an anonymous tip about a week ago. I don't know why informers like to tip off the media, but they do. I spoke to Del Wilbank about it and learned that the feds have been investigating the Potatoes for months. They have undercover agents in the valley and the mountains. We can expect a major bust any day now. And believe me, it'll be a big story when it breaks, hitting all the wire services. So . . . until then, you don't know anything."

Qwilleran pushed the pad across the desk. "You can have it, but keep it in your safe. How do you suppose Hawkinfield knew about the operation?"

"From what I hear, he had everything but wire taps."

"I still want to find his killer, but I need evidence before I take the matter to the police . . . How would you like to break for lunch, Colin?"

"Not today. How about Monday?" the editor suggested.

Qwilleran went alone to The Great Big Baked Potato, after he had stopped at Five Points for some delicacies for the Siamese, including the white grape juice that was champagne to Koko. Just in case Sherry Hawkinfield's plane landed, he put in a supply of cashew nuts, crackers, and a chopped liver canape spread.

His enforced confinement had whetted his appetite for steak, and he ordered a twelve-ounce cut, medium rare. "But no potato," he specified to the waitress.

"No potato? Is that what you said?" she repeated in a whining voice.

"That's right. No potato."

"But that's our specialty."

"Be that as it may, *hold the potato!*"

She returned with the manager. "Sir, is this your first time here?" he asked. "We're famous for our baked potatoes."

"Where are they grown?" Qwilleran inquired, expecting to hear Idaho or Maine or Michigan.

"Right here in the foothills, sir, where the soil is ideal for growing potatoes with flavor."

Now Qwilleran knew why these were the Potato Mountains! As he pondered a decision, a young woman at the next table leaned over and said in a pleasant voice, "Take the potato. It's better than the steak." He noticed that she was eating only a potato with a variety of toppings. He noticed also that she had hair like black satin. He took her advice. She had left the restaurant when his meal was served; otherwise he would have thanked her. The steak tasted of tenderizer, but the potato was the best he had ever eaten.

By the time Qwilleran drove home, the fog had burned off in the valley, but halfway up Hawk's Nest Drive it closed in like a white blanket, and he reduced his speed. Although it was difficult to see anything but a small patch of pavement, he was aware of rivulets of water running diagonally across the road. Farther along, the asphalt was covered with mud, and he slowed even more, hugging the cliff on the right and watching for downbound foglights. He had just passed the spot where the Lessmore house should be, when something loomed up in front of him. He eased on the brakes, leaned on the horn, and veered across the yellow line, stopping his car just before crashing into the obstruction. It was another vehicle, skidded diagonally across the road and smashed against the roadside cliff. Backing into his own lane, he turned on the flashers and hurried to the wreck. The cause of the accident was obvious: a mudslide . . . fallen rocks . . . a tree across the road.

As he approached the driver's side of the wrecked car, a woman behind the wheel signaled frantically and shouted, "I can't open the door! I can't open the door!" It was the woman with black satin hair.

CHAPTER 16

The woman trapped in the wrecked car on the mountainside was in a panic. "I can't get out!" she screamed.

"Are you hurt?" Qwilleran shouted through the glass as he tried the door handle. It was jammed.

"No, but *I can't get out!*"

"Turn off the ignition!"

"I did! *What shall I do?*"

"Can you roll down the window?"

"Nothing works!"

It was a two-door model, and Qwilleran tried the opposite door, but the fenders were folded in, and the car was wedged between the wall of rock and the large tree that had tumbled down from the top of the cliff.

"I'll go for help!" he shouted at the driver.

"It might explode!" she cried hysterically.

"No chance! Stay cool! I'll be right back!"

Starting uphill at a jogtrot, he was amazed that his ankle would support the effort. Running downhill to the Lessmore house might have been easier, but he was sure the couple were both at work downtown. He knew how the road curved near the Wilbank residence, and he was sure Ardis would be at home on a day like this. If not, he was prepared to run all the way to Tiptop. Now he wished he had invested in a CB radio or cellular phone.

At the Wilbank driveway he shouted, "Hallo! Hallo!" while jogging toward the house. By the time the front door materialized through the mist, Ardis was standing on the deck.

"Trouble?" she called out.

"Accident down the hill! Call the police and a wrecker! A woman's trapped in the car but not hurt!"

"Del's home," she said . . . "Del, there's an accident!"

Qwilleran started back downhill and was picked up by the off-duty sheriff on the way to the scene. Together they set out flares. Already the sirens could be heard in the valley, amplified by the stillness of the atmosphere.

The trapped driver was pounding on the window glass. "Get me out! Get me out!"

"Help's on the way! The sheriff is here!" Qwilleran reassured her, shouting to be heard. He noticed the rental sticker in the rear window. "Are you Sherry? I'm Qwilleran from Tiptop! Didn't expect you in this fog! When did your plane land? I thought all flights would be canceled."

He was trying to divert her attention, but she was too frightened for small talk. *"Could it catch fire?"*

"No! Don't worry! You'll be out in a jiffy!"

She only glared at him and hammered on the window uselessly. So this was Sherry Hawkinfield! If she were not so terrified she would be quite attractive, he thought.

Police, fire and rescue vehicles arrived, and Qwilleran stepped back out of the way, talking with Ardis, who had walked down to see the wreck. One man with a chainsaw was working on the tree trunk that barricaded the road. The rescue crew was cutting open the car with the Jaws of Life.

When the woman was finally helped out of the wreckage, her first words were, "Hell! I didn't buy insurance! How stupid! Why didn't I take out insurance?"

"Hi, Sherry," said Wilbank. "What are you doing up here?"

"Going to Tiptop to discuss business . . . Where is he?"

"Here I am," said Qwilleran. "As soon as they clear the road I'll drive you up there . . . Hold on!" he shouted to the driver of the tow truck. "Let's get her luggage out of the trunk!"

"Howya!" said the man. It was Vance, the blacksmith. "Glad you're gittin' around ag'in."

The sheriff said to Qwilleran, "How's everything at Tiptop?"

"Wet outside, comfortable inside. Is this your day off? Why don't you and Ardis come up for drinks at five o'clock?"

On the drive to the mountaintop he said to Sherry, "Would you like something for your nerves when we arrive? A drink, or a nap, or a shower?" She was looking disheveled in her travel denims and rumpled hair.

"All three," she said peevishly, staring at the dashboard. "What rotten luck!"

He tried to relieve the leaden silence that followed by making such insipid remarks as, "This is the worst fog I've ever seen." . . . And then, "Well, at least we don't worry about flooding up here." . . . And as he carried her luggage up the stone steps, "Fog has an interesting smell, doesn't it?"

When at last they entered the foyer of Tiptop, she was composed enough to say, "I could use that drink. Can you mix a sherry manhattan?"

"Six-to-one? Lemon peel?" asked Qwilleran, who had worked his way through college tending bar.

"I want to freshen up first."

He gestured toward the stairway. "Make yourself at home. You have your choice of the four front rooms, and you know where the towels are kept. I'll take your luggage up."

"I can carry it," she said sharply. "First I need to make a phone call. Now that I have no car, my friend will have to pick me up here after work."

"Go ahead, and ask your friend to stay for a drink."

Soon he heard her on the phone saying, "Honey, you'll never guess what happened to me!"

After she had gone upstairs, Qwilleran quickly retrieved the old-fashioned key from the drawer of the huntboard and hung it on the picture hook behind the Beechum painting—just in case she might be nosy. Her offhand manners led him to expect anything. What had she learned at that school in Virginia?

A moment later he heard a scream on the second floor, and he dashed up the stairs three at a time. Sherry was standing in the upper hall looking wild-eyed and petrified. "Those cats!" she cried. "I'm deathly afraid of Siamese!"

Koko and Yum Yum, who had emerged languidly from their bedroom after their midday nap, were yawning widely and showing cavernous pink gullets and murderous fangs. Sherry screamed again.

"Take it easy," Qwilleran said. "They won't pay any attention to you. Didn't Dolly tell you I had two cats?"

"I didn't know they were *Siamese!*"

He settled the matter by announcing, "Treat!" and two furry bodies rippled down the stairs to the kitchen. He followed and gave them something crunchy to eat while he mixed a sherry manhattan for his guest. For himself he poured white grape juice and also gave Koko half a jigger in a saucer.

As he was carrying the tray into the living room, Sherry came downstairs slowly, looking at everything. "It's different. You've done something to it," she said.

"Sabrina brought in the plants and accessories to make it look more comfortable," he explained.

Sherry had changed into white pants and a white blouse with a red scarf—a striking complement to her pearly white skin and shiny black hair. It was a severe cut—shoulder-length like Sabrina's, with bangs like Sabrina's, and she tossed it back with a gesture he recognized.

Qwilleran served drinks in the living room, which Sherry studied minutely as if inventorying the accessories and estimating their retail price. After he proposed a toast, she said, "Thanks for getting me out of that scrape."

"One good turn deserves another," he replied. "You recommended the potato in the restaurant, and it was the best potato experience I've ever had. Why haven't I been served one before?"

"This is turnip country. Most of the commercial potato crop is shipped to gourmet centers in New York and California—"

"—where they're called Potato potatoes, no doubt," he said, hoping to get a smile, but she was still stiffly out of sorts.

Losing no time in getting down to business, she said, "So you're interested in the painting." She nodded toward the foyer.

"That's why I phoned you. Is it for sale?"

"Everything's for sale."

"What are you asking for it?" He recalled that Sabrina estimated it would bring $3,000.

"Well, it's been appraised at $5,000, but you can have it for $4,500."

"It's a good painting," Qwilleran said, "but isn't that a trifle steep for the work of an unrecognized artist?"

"Ordinarily it would be," she said, "but this is no ordinary situation. It was painted by a convicted murderer, and the painting has notoriety value. I suppose you know what happened."

Qwilleran nodded sympathetically, but he thought, My God! She not only sent an innocent man to prison, but she's profiteering from her treachery. Wasn't the original price $300, including delivery? To Sherry he said, "I'll give your offer some serious consideration."

"What about the Fitzwallow chest? You said you were interested. I'd let that go for $1,000."

"It's a unique example of folk art. The question is: What would I do with it—unless I bought the inn?"

"The way things are going in the Potatoes," she said, "Tiptop will be a good investment."

"It needs a lot of work, though, chiefly lightening and brightening. The veranda makes the rooms dark even in broad daylight, as you must know. Today's vacationers like sunlight."

"You could take off the veranda and build open decks all around the building," Sherry suggested, showing some animation. "That's what my mother always wanted to do."

"It would be a costly project," Qwilleran objected.

"The building's listed for $1.2 million, but if you want to buy from me direct, I'll let it go for a million. You can use the difference for remodeling."

"Is that ethical? Dolly Lessmore has the listing."

"She's had it for almost a year and hasn't done a damn thing. I'd like to unload it so I can concentrate on my retail business."

"Your shop has a clever name," Qwilleran remarked. "Did you think of it?"

"Yes," she said, looking pleased. "Glad you like it." She held out her glass. "Is there another one where this came from?"

"Forgive me. I'm being an imperfect host," Qwilleran apologized. "But only because I find our conversation so engaging."

When he carried the tray to the kitchen, both cats were in the foyer in their listening position—extremities tucked under compact bodies, ears pointed toward the living room. "You two behave yourselves," he said quietly as he passed.

Sherry was beginning to relax, and she accepted her second manhattan with more grace. "You mix a good cocktail, Mr. Qwilleran," she complimented him.

"Call me Qwill," he reminded her.

"What are you drinking?"

"Just the straight stuff. I never combine the grape and the grain." He clinked the ice cubes in his white grape juice. "Incidentally, white looks very good on you."

"Thank you," she said. "I wear it a lot. Well, tell me about you. What do you do?"

"I'm an author," he said with an appealing display of pride mixed with modesty and a hint of apology.

"What have you written? Your books must be selling pretty well, but I never saw your name."

"I write textbooks," he said, exercising his talent for instant falsehood. "They're rather dull stuff, but they pay well."

"What's your subject?"

"Crime."

"Oh," she said, and her eyes were momentarily downcast. "That must be fascinating. I'm afraid I don't have much time to read. What brought you to the Potatoes?"

"I was looking for a mountain retreat for the summer, where I could work without distractions, and the Potatoes were recommended by a friend who had camped here. I didn't expect to rent anything this large, but I wanted to be on the summit of the mountain." He decided it was unwise to mention the cats again.

"Are you accomplishing anything?"

"As a matter of fact, I've decided on a new project. I'm planning to write a biography of your father."

"No! Do you mean it?" Qwilleran thought her surprise was tempered by qualms rather than enthusiasm.

"Yes, he was a remarkable man. I don't need to tell you that. He made a great contribution to the growth and well-being of the community. He practiced an aggressive, adversarial style of journalism that is rare in these times, and his editorials were blockbusters. Yet, there was a warmly human side to him as well." Qwilleran thought, I can't believe I'm saying this! "I'm referring to his love of family, his deep sorrow at the loss of his sons; the pain he must have suffered over your mother's illness . . . I suppose you were a great source of support and comfort to him." Searching her face for reactions, he found her attempts to assume the right expression almost comical. "The city is planning to name a scenic drive after your father. Do you think he would approve?"

"I think he'd rather have the city named after him," she said in a burst of candor brought on by the second manhattan.

"Did you have a good father-daughter relationship?" he asked innocently.

"Well, to tell the truth, Qwill, I was one of those early mistakes that happen to young couples. My parents were still in college when I was born, and my father was not too happy about it. Besides, he preferred sons to daughters. But in recent years we developed a real friendship. That happens when you get older, I guess."

Or when the prospect of an inheritance looms on the horizon, Qwilleran thought.

"We'd reached the point," she continued, "where he'd confide in me and I felt free to discuss my problems with him. So his death was a terrible loss to me . . . *What's that?*" She stiffened with fright and looked toward the foyer, where sounds of thumping and muttering and whimpering could be heard.

Qwilleran said, "The cat's talking to himself. He's faced with some kind of problem. Excuse me a moment."

Koko was on the floor, writhing and biting his paw, and Qwilleran released him from the entanglement of a long hair, thinking as he did so, This is the second time! Most unusual!

"He had something caught in his toes," he explained to his guest when he returned.

She had been sitting on the sofa with her back to one of the folding screens, but now she was walking around to inspect the rented furnishings. It appeared to Qwilleran that she kept glancing at the secretary desk at the far end of the room.

He said, "How do you like Sabrina's idea for foreshortening the room with folding screens?"

"Neat," she said without enthusiasm. She sat down again and helped herself to cashews.

"Gray was apparently your mother's favorite color. Sabrina said she had beautiful gray eyes."

"Yes, she liked gray. She always wore it."

"You have your mother's eyes, Sherry."

"I guess I do," she replied vaguely as if preoccupied.

"Sorry to hear about her illness." Sherry was fidgeting, and Qwilleran was working hard to engage her attention. "I haven't been able to find Lake Batata. Is it a myth?"

"No, it's there. That's where my brothers used to go fishing."

"I assume that you don't care for fishing."

"I was never invited," she said with a half-hearted shrug.

"Do you remember when Lake Batata was a waterfall?"

"Uh . . . yes, I remember. In winter it was one big icicle as high as a ten-story building . . . Excuse me, Qwill, but I think I could use that nap now. The accident, you know . . . and the drinks . . ."

"Yes, of course. I understand."

"Uh . . . are they still out there?" she asked timidly.

"If you're apprehensive, I'll run interference for you," Qwilleran offered, "but the cats won't bother you."

Koko and Yum Yum were still in the foyer, listening, and he shooed them into the kitchen. Locking them up there might be the courteous thing to do, he was aware, but he was disinclined to do so. A hunch was making itself felt on his upper lip.

Sherry went upstairs, holding on to the handrail, and as soon as she was out of sight, he inspected the secretary desk in the living room. The obliging Mr. Beechum had replaced it as requested but without entirely covering the door to Hawkinfield's office. An inch of the door frame was visible on one side. If Sherry had noticed it—and he was sure she had—what thoughts would cross her mind? If he now positioned it properly, would she notice the change? He was sure she would. Her gray eyes always appeared to be observing, intently.

As he wrestled with this decision, an unusual noise in the foyer alarmed him. It was a soft thud accompanied by a gentle clatter and the tinkling of a bell. "Now what the devil is that?" he muttered.

It was the telephone, lying on the carpeted floor alongside the huntboard, and Koko was sitting there looking proud of his accomplishment.

"Bad cat!" Qwilleran scolded as he picked up the instrument and checked the dial tone.

Koko expressed his nonchalance by rolling on his back at the base of the cabinet, squirming and stretching as he had done many times before, but this time, one long elegant foreleg was stretched halfway under the piece of furniture. The pose, combined with the importunate telephone maneuver, was sufficient to arouse Qwilleran's curiosity. The cat was trying to communicate!

There was a flashlight in the drawer, and he beamed it under the chest, but all he could see was a collection of dustballs wafted in by drafts from the French doors. It was clear why Mrs. Hawk-infield disliked it; not only was it an ugly piece of furniture, but it was built too low for a vacuum cleaner, and to use the attachments would mean lying flat on one's face.

"Forget it," Qwilleran said to Koko.

"Yow!" the cat replied in a scolding tone, and he toppled over on his back and extended his forepaw under the huntboard again.

Qwilleran stroked his moustache and obeyed. From the um-brella stand he selected a slender bamboo cane with a crook handle. Then, getting down on his knees and touching his head to the floor, he took a few blind swipes under the chest. Out came several dustballs or "kittens," as his mother used to call them—fluffy balls of lint, dust, and hair that collected under furniture. Fuzz from the gray carpet made the Hawkinfield kittens predominantly gray. The cane also dredged up a short length of ribbon and a fragment of tissue from some long-forgotten gift.

"That's all," he said to Koko, who was prancing back and forth, obviously excited about the show, and he turned off the flashlight that was projecting its narrow beam of light under the huntboard.

"Yow!" Koko protested.

"There's nothing under there, and I don't enjoy standing on my head to entertain man or beast."

"Yow-ow-ow!" the cat insisted in a loud, clear voice, and Yum Yum appeared from nowhere to add her supportive "N-n-NOW!"

Qwilleran felt a creeping sensation on his upper lip, and he went down on his knees again, turned on the flashlight, pressed forehead to floor, and combed the space under the chest with the crook handle. Out came a rubber dogbone.

"Dammit! Is that all you wanted?" Qwilleran said in conster-nation, his face flushed.

"Ik ik ik," Koko chattered, ignoring the bone.

"I do this under duress, I want you to know." Once more he used the cane to explore the murky back corners. First he snagged another kitten . . . and then a hard rubber ball . . . and then a kitten so unusual, so significant, that Qwilleran dropped it in a drawer of the huntboard. After returning the cane to the umbrella stand and cleaning up the debris, he sat down to plan his course of action.

Chapter 17

When Sherry wandered downstairs after her nap, she had added gold jewelry and a whiff of perfume. She looked refreshed. In Qwilleran's opinion she also looked stunning. She had style, but it was style copied from her role model. Tossing her hair back with both hands, she asked, "How much did Sabrina charge you for decorating all this?"

He was glad to be able to say, honestly, that a bill had not yet arrived from Peel & Poole. "If I buy the inn, Sabrina will re-design it inside and out," he said, partly to needle Sherry for her tasteless query. "She has some clever ideas. Also a charming personality," he added to carry his taunt further.

"Have you met her husband?" Sherry asked, not without malice in her attitude. "He's a real charmer!"

"Husband?" Qwilleran repeated casually, feeling a mild disappointment.

"Spencer Poole. He taught her everything she knows. He's an older man with white hair, but he's a virile type and lots of fun."

"Would you care for coffee? Or other refreshment?" he asked absently. He was remembering the souvenir he had found under the huntboard—a dusty ball of hair. White hair.

"Other," she replied slyly. "Same thing. But I'll wait until my friend gets here. The wind's coming up. I hate it when it whips around the house and howls."

She watched Qwilleran light the eight candles in the dusky foyer and ran her hand over the smooth interior of the rough burl bowl, asking how much he had paid for the bowl and the candelabrum.

"What time do you expect your friend?" he asked.

"Right about now. He's Hugh Lumpton. Do you know him?"

"I've heard the name. Isn't he an attorney and a golfer?"

"Yes, but the other way around," she said with an impish grimace.

"How long have you known him?"

"Since high school. I think I hear his car." She ran to the front door. "Yes, here he is!"

The man she greeted had a gauntly handsome face with that look of concentration that Carmichael had mentioned, plus a golfer's suntan emphasized by a light blue club shirt and a shock of ash-blond hair. It was easy to understand why he had a female following.

Their meeting was reasonably ardent, with most of the ardor on Sherry's part. "Lucky you weren't hurt," he said to her.

"This is Jim Qwilleran, who came to my rescue . . . Qwill, this is Hugh Lumpton."

They shook hands. "What was the last name again?" the attorney asked.

"Qwilleran, spelled with a QW. But call me Qwill." He waved his guests into the living room. "What may I serve you to drink?"

"Qwill makes a super manhattan," Sherry said as she settled familiarly on the sofa.

"Go easy on those things," Lumpton warned her. "I'll have bourbon, thanks, with a little water."

As Qwilleran prepared the drinks, he was wondering, Has Josh talked to him? How much does Hugh know? Does he know how much I know?

"No!" he said to Koko, who was ready for another swig of grape juice. "You've had your quota."

When he carried the tray into the living room, Sherry and Hugh were sitting on the sofa with their handsome heads close together—a striking couple. They were whispering—not necessarily sweet-nothings, Qwilleran guessed; more likely they were comparing notes, such as: *He says he's a crime writer. He's asking a lot of questions. Someone's been in the office, or tried to get in . . . He's been talking to my dad. He knows I defended Beechum. He's questioning the trial.* They were only conjectures on Qwilleran's part. Nevertheless, the pair on the sofa pulled quickly apart and assumed sociable smiles as soon as he entered the room.

Lumpton proposed a toast. "Tip of the topper to Tiptop!"

Sherry said, "Qwill may buy it, honey."

"What would you do with it?" the attorney asked him.

"Open a country inn if I could find a competent manager. Hotel keeping is not exactly my forte."

"Qwill is an author. He writes textbooks on crime," Sherry said. "He's going to write a biography about my father." She recited it as if reading a script.

"Is that a fact?" Lumpton said without looking surprised.

Qwilleran said, "J.J. would make a challenging subject. You have a famous father yourself, Hugh. I met him this morning."

"Famous or infamous? He's always had a penchant for getting his name in the headlines, sometimes as a hero and sometimes as a villain, but that goes with the territory when you're sheriff. I'm glad to see him established in the private sector now."

Sherry said, "Hugh makes a lot of headlines himself. He's going to Michigan next week to play in an invitational."

"Bob Lessmore and I are competing," the golfer said. "Ironically, the course here is under water, while Michigan is in the throes of a drought."

It was not much after four o'clock, and Qwilleran had a bombshell of a topic that he wanted to drop a little later. Meanwhile, it was important to keep the conversation polite, and he steered it through the details of Sherry's accident . . . Lucy's rescue mission in the woods . . . the preponderance of Lumptons in the Potatoes.

Qwilleran was sitting in Yum Yum's favorite lounge chair facing his guests, who were on the sofa in front of a folding screen. After a while he became aware of movement above their heads, and glancing upward he perceived Koko balancing on the top edge of the screen, having risen to its eight-foot summit without effort and without sound. Qwilleran avoided staring at him, but in the periphery of his vision there was an acrobatic cat teetering precariously with all four feet bunched on a very narrow surface. He was looking down on the visitors with feline speculation like a tiger in a tree, waiting for a gazelle.

Don't do it! Qwilleran was thinking, hoping Koko would read his mind. Koko could read minds, but only when it suited him.

Somewhat worried about the impending catastrophe, Qwilleran asked questions about white-water rafting, the new electronics firm, and the history of Spudsboro. Soon another air-borne bundle of fur appeared on top of the screen; Yum Yum had chosen this vantage point to observe the chopped liver on the cocktail table. Nervously the host talked about book publishing, the weather in Moose County, and the peculiar spelling of his name.

Eventually it was time to serve a second round of drinks, and he rose slowly from his chair and moved quietly from the room, hoping not to provoke the Siamese into any precipitous action.

Despite the menacing sound of the wind, his guests seemed to be enjoying the occasion. Conversation flowed easily, with a modicum of pleasant wit.

Qwilleran decided it was the auspicious time to launch his wild shot. It was his only recourse, considering his lack of credentials as an investigator.

"If either of you can suggest sources of information on J.J.," he began, "I'll appreciate your help. For dramatic effect I propose to start the book with his murder. Sherry, I hope this subject is not too painful for you . . . Then I'll flash back to his career and family life throughout the years, ending with the trial. And that brings up a sensitive question. In doing my research, I find reason to believe that the wrong man may have been convicted. It seems some new evidence has been brought to light."

"I was the defense attorney," Lumpton said briskly, "and this is the first intimation I've had of any new evidence—or even a rumor of such. What is your source of information?"

"That's something I don't wish to divulge at this time, but I suspect that the murderer was not a hot-headed environmentalist! Why does this interest me? First of all, I don't like to see an innocent man sent to prison. Secondly, to be perfectly frank, the exposé of a crooked trial would make a damned good finale for my book. How do you react?"

Sherry was looking scared. Lumpton was moistening his lips. Both of them had set down their glasses on the cocktail table.

Lumpton said, "This is preposterous! I defended Beechum at the court's request, but there was no doubt from the very beginning that he was guilty."

Qwilleran said, "I'm reluctant to doubt your statement, but I'm led to suspect that more than one person was involved in the murder, and one or more persons may have committed the big P."

"What?" Sherry asked in a small voice.

"Perjury!"

What happened next may have been caused by the sudden gust of wind that slammed against the building. Whatever the cause, the cats' timing was perfect. Both of them flew down from the screen, narrowly missing the two heads on the sofa, and landed on the cocktail table, scattering drinks, nuts, coasters, and chopped liver.

"I knew it!" Sherry shrieked. "They're dangerous! Where are they? Where did they go?"

Qwilleran rushed to the kitchen for towels, while the guests dropped to their knees, sopping up wet spills with cocktail napkins, collecting cashews and ice cubes, and avoiding broken glass.

"I apologize," Qwilleran said. "They've never done that before. I think they were spooked by the wind. I hope you didn't cut yourselves. Let me get some fresh glasses, and we'll have another round."

"Not for me," said Sherry, noticeably shaken.

"No, thanks," said the attorney, "but I'd like to ask what you intend to do with your information."

"Naturally, I'd prefer to hold it for the publication of my book, but I feel morally obliged to report my findings to the police at once, namely, that J.J. wrote a blistering exposé of certain criminal activities in this area. *Someone* knew the editorial was about to be published. *Someone* found it necessary to stop its publication by eliminating the editor. *Someone* came to the house at a prearranged time and threw him over the cliff. *Someone* forged death threats purportedly from Beechum, which conveniently disappeared before they could be introduced by the prosecution, but *someone* testified to having seen them."

He stopped, and there was silence in the room as his listeners considered his threatening statements. Outdoors the wind was banging a loose shutter or downspout.

"My only contribution to the inevitable investigation," he went on, "is some material evidence found in the foyer here, where the assault is said to have occurred. It's been hidden under a piece of furniture for a year. Would anyone like to see it?"

As he strode to the Fitzwallow huntboard, Lumpton sprang to his feet and followed. With the only light coming from the eight candles in the iron candelabrum, he half-stumbled over two cats streaking toward the staircase.

Qwilleran opened the drawer slowly and produced a handful of ash-blond hair mixed with lint and dust. "This is it," he said calmly, keeping his eyes on the attorney.

It took Lumpton a split second to recognize it and reach for the Queen Anne chair. As he swung it over his head, ready to crash down on his accuser's head, a burst of loud music from the second floor broke the rhythm of his swing just enough to give Qwilleran the edge. Qwilleran seized the iron candelabrum and rammed it into his attacker's midriff like a flaming pitchfork. The chair fell and Lumpton bellowed and sank to his knees. Sherry screamed! Dropping the candelabrum, Qwilleran picked up the heavy burl bowl and overturned it on the attorney's head, rendering him a limp lump on the floor.

Candle flames were licking the carpet, and Sherry screamed again. "Fire!"

"Shut up and sit down!" Qwilleran ordered as he stamped his feet on the smoldering carpet. "Pick up that chair and sit in it!"

"Can I—"

"No! Sit there. Put your feet together. Fold your hands. You won't have long to wait."

In minutes a car could be heard pulling into the parking lot, and soon the Wilbanks were climbing the steps, struggling against gale-force winds.

"*Treat!*" Qwilleran yelled, and two cats came running down the stairs fast enough to resemble a continuous streak of pale fur. "Koko, you keep an eye on this woman. Don't let her move or open her mouth."

As if he understood his instructions, the cat assumed a belligerent stance, lashing his tail and staring at his captive in the Queen Anne chair. Yum Yum sniffed Lumpton's loafers but found no shoelaces to untie.

When Qwilleran admitted the Wilbanks, they stepped into the foyer with gasps of relief, Ardis saying, "Isn't this wind awful?"

"We can only stay for one drink," Del said. "We're moving to a motel in the valley."

"We're worried about mudslides," said his wife. "Why is it so dark in here? Did the power go off again?"

Qwilleran flicked a switch, lighting the six wall sconces and three chandeliers. They illuminated a grim tableau. He said, "Allow me to introduce our other guests. On the floor, under the wooden bowl, we have the attorney for the defense, actually J.J.'s murderer. In the chair, scared speechless, is the accomplice before and after the fact, guilty of perjury . . . There they are! Do your duty, Del. The telephone's over there."

As the sheriff was calling for an ambulance and a deputy, Ardis said, "What's wrong with Sherry? She looks as if she's in a trance."

"She's all right. Talk to her," Qwilleran said. Then he yelled, *"Treat!"* Both cats shot out of the foyer, and he followed them to the kitchen, where he gave them a crunchy snack.

Wilbank wandered into the kitchen, too. "I saw Colin this afternoon. He told me everything that you and he talked about. He said you suspected Josh Lumpton of killing J.J."

"I did, until I found some evidence incriminating Hugh. When I confronted him with it, he picked up the same chair that clobbered J.J. and would have pitched me over the cliff, too, I imagine, if I hadn't been ready for him. If my guesses are right, he killed J.J. to protect himself and his father. I see Hugh as the mastermind of the Hot Potato Fund, while Josh was the organizer of the bootleg operation. J.J.'s editorial would have exposed both of them. Hugh's future wife collaborated because she wanted to inherit her father's estate. They compounded their crime by conspiring to send an innocent man to prison. This time around, justice will be done. If it isn't, my attorneys are going to raise the roof of the courthouse, and I daresay the *Gazette* won't let the prosecutor get away with anything this time."

"The prosecutor was defeated in the last election," said Wilbank. "A woman holds the office now."

"She'll find some former witnesses guilty of perjury, including Sherry," Qwilleran predicted.

"Ardis and I know Sherry pretty well. It's hard to believe she'd be a party to it."

"Sherry was a would-be heiress who wanted to see her male parent underground, although she found it expedient to profess filial friendship. On the weekend of the murder, perhaps J.J. read his inflammatory editorial to her. Writers with any ego like to read their stuff to a friendly ear, you know. Did Colin show it to you?"

Wilbank nodded. "It's in his safe. He said he made the situation clear to you."

"Quite clear! What will happen to Sherry now?"

"We'll take her with us and work something out with the prosecutor . . . I think I hear the sirens."

As the paramedics maneuvered the stretcher down the twenty-five steps, the Wilbanks told Qwilleran they'd take a raincheck on the drink; they left with a silent young woman in tow, who tossed her hair back nervously.

He had a strong desire to call Polly Duncan and break the news of his successful investigation. Now that it was all over, he could tell her the whole story without alarming her. He felt free to boast to Polly; she listened with understanding. But first he had to wait for the discount phone rates to go into effect.

Tuning in the eleven o'clock news on the local radio station, he heard this brief announcement: "A police prisoner in Spudsboro General Hospital is a new suspect in the Father's Day murder of J.J. Hawkinfield last June, name withheld pending charges. A spokesperson for the sheriff's department refused to predict what effect the suspect's apprehension will have on the previous murder trial. Forest Beechum is currently serving a life term for the crime."

Before the announcer could conclude with dire predictions of damaging rain and severe flooding, Qwilleran's telephone rang, and an excited voice cried, "Did you hear the newscast? They have a new suspect! Forest may be coming home! Wouldn't it be wonderful?"

"I'm very happy for you, Chrysalis. I've recently talked to my attorneys in Pickax, and they expressed an interest in the case, so if you want legal advice, you can call on them."

"Are they high-priced?"

"You don't need to worry about that. The Klingenschoen Foundation makes funds available for worthy causes."

"I'm so happy! I could cry!"

Qwilleran himself was exhilarated by the events of the day, and when he called Polly he said, "G-o-ood e-e-evening!" in a musical and seductive voice. She knew it well.

"Dearest, I'm so glad to hear from you!" she cried. "I've had a most unnerving experience!"

"What happened?" he asked in a normal tone, thinking that Bootsie had swallowed a bottle cap or fallen down a heat register.

"I'm still trembling! I attended that formal dinner I told you about and arrived home after dark. Just as I approached my driveway, I saw a car in front of the main house, parked the wrong way, and someone was behind the wheel. It was standing there with the lights off. I thought it was strange, because no one's living in the main house, and curb parking isn't allowed on Goodwinter Boulevard, you know. When I turned into the side drive, the car started up and followed me—without lights! I was terrified! When I reached the carriage house, I parked near the door, left my headlights on, and had my doorkey ready. Then I jumped out, almost tripping on my long dress, and saw this man getting out of the car! I was able to get inside and slam the door before he reached me, and I sat down on the stairs and bawled like a baby!"

Qwilleran had been speechless as he listened to the chilling account. "This is terrible, Polly! Did you call the police?"

"As soon as I could collect my wits. Gib Campbell was on patrol duty, and he was there in three minutes. The prowler had gone, of course."

"You weren't able to see his face?"

"The outdoor lights weren't on, unfortunately."

"You should always leave them on when you go out in the evening."

"I thought I'd be home before dark; the days are so long in June."

A specific dread swept over Qwilleran. "I don't like the sound of this, Polly. I'd better get back to Pickax. I'll leave tomorrow morning."

"But your vacation has only just begun!"

"I'm canceling it. I can't have anything happening to you."

"It's a sweet thought, dear, but—"

"No buts! Can you stay home until I arrive?"

"I have to be at the library tomorrow and Monday."

"Well, don't go anywhere after work, and if you see anyone who looks the least bit suspect, ask for a police escort. I'll be home Tuesday and I'll call you every night while I'm on the road."

"Qwill, dear, you shouldn't do this."

"I'm doing it *because I love you, Polly*! Now hang up so I can call Brodie!"

Qwilleran called the Pickax police chief at his home. "Andy, I'm sorry to bother you. Do you know about the prowler on Goodwinter Boulevard tonight?"

"Just happened to pick it up on my radio on the way home from the lodge meeting, Campbell responded. No trace."

"The prowler was after Polly. He was waiting for her when she came home."

"Where are you?" Brodie asked.

"I'm still in the Potato Mountains, but I'm leaving for Pickax tomorrow. This worries me, Andy. Polly's connection with me is well known around the county—around Lockmaster County, too. I'm a prime prospect for a ransom demand."

"You're talking about . . . kidnapping? We've never had a kidnap case in a hundred years!"

"Things are changing. Outsiders are coming in, and you can expect more incidents. I'll be home Tuesday. What can you do about it in the meantime?"

"We'll step up the patrols on Goodwinter, and I'll talk to Polly tomorrow—see that she gets a ride to work. We don't want to lose a good librarian!"

After the two calls to Pickax, Qwilleran paced the floor anxiously, and the roaring of the wind added to his agitation. Soon the nightly downpour started, hitting the veranda roofs and the upstairs windows like hailstones. Before retiring, he packed for the journey and assembled his luggage in the foyer. The Siamese were nervous, and he allowed them to stay in his room. They promptly fell asleep, but the events of the day churned in his mind.

Sometime in the middle of the night, as he was tossing restlessly and listening to the wind and rain, a sudden, deafening roar drowned out all other sounds. It was like a locomotive crashing into the side of the house, like a jet shearing off the mountaintop, like an earthquake, a tornado, and a tidal wave! He turned the switch on his bedside lamp, but the power was off. Gradually the booming pandemonium receded into the distance, and he ventured downstairs with the bedside flashlight and even stepped out onto the veranda. Nothing seemed to be damaged, but there was an unearthly moaning on the mountain.

Somehow he made it through the night, trying the radio on batteries from time to time, but the local station never transmitted after midnight. When he finally managed to catch a few hours' sleep, he was aroused by the fitful behavior of the Siamese, pouncing on and off the bed. The sheriff's helicopter was circling the mountain.

Once more he tried the radio and found the station on emergency programming. Along with directives, warnings, and pleas for volunteers, there was this repeated announcement:

"Big Potato Mountain and parts of Spudsboro have been declared a disaster area, following the collapse of Lake Batata Dam early this morning. The dam burst at 3:45 A.M., dumping tons of water down the mountainside, washing out sections of Hawk's Nest Drive, and destroying homes on the drive as well as certain commercial buildings on Center Street and at Five Points. The Yellyhoo River, already overflowing its banks, has been swollen by the rush of water from the artificial lake, and it is now feared that debris carried down the mountainside will collect in the Yellyhoo south of town and dam the rampaging flood water from the north. Residents on both sides of the river are being evacuated. The power has failed in most of the county, and most subscribers are without telephone service. The hospital, municipal buildings,

and communications centers are operating on emergency genera-
tors. At this hour there is no report on casualties. The sheriff's
helicopter is searching for survivors. Stand by for further information."

CHAPTER 18

"We're trapped!" Qwilleran said to the cats after hearing the
news of the Batata washout. "It could be days before we get
out of here! And we don't have a phone, water, refrigeration, or
even a cup of coffee! Don't sit there blinking! What shall we do?"

Then he remembered the old logging trail down the outside of
the mountain. It emerged from the forest onto the highway north
of town, beyond the golf course and near the airport. "Okay, we're
going out the back way. Fasten your seat belts!"

There was no way of knowing what had happened to the Lessmores, or their house, or their place of business, but after reaching
Pickax there would be time enough to return the keys and explain
his sudden departure to Dolly, Sabrina, Colin, and Chrysalis. In his
hurry he abandoned most of his purchases, having lost interest in
the objects bought so impulsively at Potato Cove. Only the five
batwing capes went into his luggage. Even his box of secondhand
books was left behind with the exception of *The Magic Mountain*,
and there was no point in taking the expensive turkey roaster that
the cats had declined to use.

The Siamese were silent while Qwilleran packed the trunk of
the car and placed their carrier on the backseat. Soon he headed
for the trail that Chrysalis had shown him. In passing the gazebo
he stopped to admire Dewey Beechum's handiwork: a handsome
hexagonal structure that the cats would never use. It had a cedar
shake roof and a cupola and carved wood brackets supporting the
roof between the six screened panels. There was one puzzling detail, and Qwilleran left the car to walk over and confirm his sus-

picions. No door! There was no way to get into the thing! He could imagine Beechum removing his moldy green hat to scratch his head while saying, "Y'didn't let on as how y'wanted a door."

The logging trail was hardly more than a set of tire tracks between the trees, and as long as he stayed in the muddy ruts, Qwilleran thought, it would be navigable. The trail wound in and out, up and down, back and forth—always descending—but the lower the altitude, the muddier the tracks, enough so that he became alarmed. He gripped the steering wheel and hoped for the best. Despite the swerving and jolting, there was not a sound from the backseat; that in itself was ominous. The small car bounced in and out of ruts and wheeled successfully through large puddles until a misleading depression in the road swallowed the wheels, and the car sank axle-deep in the mire.

Qwilleran gunned the motor and spun the wheels; the second-hand, three-year-old, four-cylinder, two-tone green sedan would move neither forward nor backward. It only sank deeper. Stunned by this new misfortune, Qwilleran sat behind the steering wheel and felt his throat tightening and his face burning. Why? Why? Why, he asked himself, did I ever come to the Potatoes?

He considered leaving the car and slogging the two miles back to Tiptop through slimy clay that would be shin-deep—lugging the cat carrier, slipping and falling and dropping it. And if he stayed in the car, what would happen? No one in Spudsboro would know that he had left Tiptop. No one would miss him. No one would come searching for him. Worse yet, no one ever used this route! Occasionally he heard the chop-chop of the helicopter, but that was scant help; trees arching over the trail provided complete camouflage.

The Siamese had been mercifully silent during this crisis, and once more he considered struggling back to Tiptop, leaving them in the car until he could return with help, but the phones were out of order. How would he make his plight known? He leaned forward with his arms circling the steering wheel and his head on his arms, in an effort to think logically, yet nothing even remotely resembling a solution occurred to him.

"Yow!" said Koko, for the first time that day.

Qwilleran ignored him.

"YOW!" the cat repeated in a louder voice. It was not complaint nor rebuke nor expression of sympathy. It was a cry of excitement.

Qwilleran looked up and caught a glimpse of a moving vehicle approaching through the trees. It was lurching slowly up the hill—a rusty red pickup with one blue fender, the body of the truck riding high over the wheels. It stopped inches away from his front bumper, and Chrysalis leaned out of the driver's window.

"Where are you going?" she called out.

"Nowhere! I'm stuck!"

She jumped out of the truck cab, wading through the mud in rubber boots that reached above her knees. "I was going up to Tiptop to see if you were all right. I heard about the washout on the radio and thought you'd be marooned."

"I was, and I should have stayed that way," Qwilleran said, "but there's a serious emergency at home. I need to get there in a hurry. If you'll be good enough to drive me to the airport, I'll rent a car."

"Perhaps I could haul you out and tow you down," she suggested.

"Around these sharp turns? No thanks!" From where he sat in his stalled car he could see a thousand-foot drop down the mountain. "Let me put my luggage and the cats in your truck and leave the car here."

"Do you have boots? The mud's over a foot deep here."

"I'll take off my shoes and roll up my pants."

With his shoes hanging around his neck and his socks in his pocket, he transferred the baggage. The cat carrier went on the seat between them.

"Nice cats," Chrysalis said. "Siamese?"

"Yes. They're good companions and very smart."

"Yow!" said Koko.

"He knows we're talking about him," Qwilleran explained. "His vocabulary is limited, but he expresses himself well."

She said, "Don't worry about tracking mud into the cab; we've got enough dirt in this thing to grow strawberries. When we get to Bear Crossing, there's a stream where you can wash your feet and put on your shoes." She backed the truck down the trail and around two hairpin turns before crashing through underbrush to make a U-turn.

"You handle this swamp buggy like a stunt driver," he said with admiration.

"This old crate will go anywhere, and it's a lot more fun than the school bus!" She was a different person since hearing about the arrest of a suspect, and Qwilleran almost regretted that he was leaving. "When are you coming back to the Potatoes?" she asked.

"Probably never. I'm needed at home. I've checked out of Tiptop, and if you can haul my car out of the mud, you're welcome to keep it. I'll give you the keys and send you the title." Before Chrysalis could adequately splutter her surprise and thanks, he changed the subject. "Were you surprised to hear about the washout?"

"Not really. We always knew it would happen someday. Too bad, though. Damage is already estimated at ten million, according to the latest on the radio. I hope no one got hurt, but it'll be a miracle if they didn't. The air is so full of disaster news that they haven't mentioned any more about the suspect. I wonder who it is. I wonder how they found out. I wonder how soon Forest will be coming home."

"George Barter of Hasselrich, Bennett & Barter can probably expedite things for you. He planned to fly down here Monday."

"I hope he's bringing boots," she said.

"The disaster may delay his visit—I'm sure it's being reported on national news—but when he arrives, he'll have some good news. The Klingenschoen Foundation wants to establish a conservancy to save Little Potato. They'll buy any property that's for sale, to insure that it's never commercially developed. Some Taters may opt to sell and retain lifetime rights to live on the property. And the price paid will be fair. No gouging."

"I can't believe this!" Chrysalis said. "I've heard about the conservancy idea, but I never dreamed it would happen to Li'l Tater!

Was it your suggestion, Qwill? We're so lucky that you came to the Potatoes! How can we thank you?"

"In the mountains we aim to be good neighbors," he said.

"Yow!" was the affirmation from the carrier.

Later, driving away from the airport in a rental car, Qwilleran tried to organize his ambivalent feelings about the Potatoes. So much rain! So much corruption and prejudice! And yet he had never seen so many rainbows . . . witnessed such dramatic skies . . . felt such magic in the mountain air! Too much had happened in one week. One week? To Qwilleran it seemed like a year! Time became distorted in the mountains. Look what happened to Rip Van Winkle!

He and the Siamese again spent a night at the Mountain Charm Motel, famed for its uncomfortable beds and country-style fripperies. Despite its shortcomings, it was the only hostelry in the area that welcomed pets. After dinner he turned on the television, minus the sound, to keep Koko and Yum Yum entertained. It was a nature program, and they huddled together at the foot of one lumpy bed, staring at the screen, while Qwilleran lounged on the other lumpy bed, trying to read the newspaper. His mind could not focus on world news. Unanswered questions plagued him: What really triggered Wilson Wix's heart attack? Did Robert Lessmore's investment firm promote the Hot Potato Fund? Was Yates Penney a baker from Akron or a federal agent?

Then he reflected, If Koko had not found that key behind the painting and that door behind the secretary desk, Forest Beechum would be spending the rest of his life in prison. Did Koko know what he was doing? Or was he simply on the scent of a postage stamp and a dog's mattress? As for finding the key, was Koko pursuing his hobby of tilting pictures? Or did he know that something was not where it should be?

Though Qwilleran found it difficult to rationalize Koko's behavior, he could understand why Sherry had hidden the key as she did. Were not women prone to hide things in the sugar bowl, behind the clock, under the carpet, or in their underclothing?

Sherry wanted no unauthorized person in her male parent's office until she could find time to examine, and possibly burn, his personal papers.

Picking up *The Magic Mountain*, Qwilleran thought a good read would relax his mind, but he was unable to find his place. Yum Yum not only untied shoelaces; she stole bookmarks.

Either Koko lost interest in the mating rituals of Brazilian beetles, or he knew he was on Qwilleran's mind. With a stretch and a yawn he deserted the tube and hopped onto the other bed, saying a cheerful "Yow!"

"Yow indeed!" Qwilleran said. "Is that all you have to say? When you sniffed the label on the sherry bottle, were you getting high on the adhesive? Or were you trying to tell me something? And all the time you were wallowing on the floor in front of the Fitzwallow huntboard, you knew there was something of interest underneath it. Was it the dog's toys? Or the ash-blond hairball?"

Koko's large black eyes—black in the dim lamplight of the motel—were brimming with concentration, and Qwilleran told himself, He's trying to transmit a thought; I must relax; I must be receptive.

Koko was concentrating, however, on a spider crawling up the wall, and after springing at it and knocking it down, he ate it.

"Disgusting!" Qwilleran said and went back to his own thoughts, recalling his incredible week in the Potatoes: getting lost in the woods, the unpleasant episode at the golf club, the horrifying accident at the waterfall, the pain and incapacitation that resulted, the washout and the prospect of being marooned on Tiptop, the ordeal on the muddy trail . . .

"I don't know why I came to the damned Potatoes in the first place! Do you know, Koko?" Then he answered his own question. He remembered the party celebrating his inheritance . . . all those good friends . . . all that mediocre food . . . someone suggesting the Potato Mountains for a vacation . . . himself jumping at the idea and pursuing it like a fool, persevering against odds, agreeing to pay $1,000 a week for a white elephant. Why? What attracted him? How could he explain his stubborn resolve?

Koko was watching him with twitching whiskers, and Qwilleran put a hand to his own moustache. Slowly the cat rose from his lounging position on the bed. He arched his back and stiffened his tail and pranced, stiff-legged, around the mattress. Qwilleran watched the performance and wondered what it was supposed to convey, if anything.

Round and round Koko paraded until Qwilleran recalled the revolving circle on top of Little Potato—the silent marchers with lanterns, believing in the power of thought and fervently *willing* their kinsman to be returned to them.

No! he thought. How could their influence be felt in Pickax, many hundreds of miles away? "Impossible!" he said aloud, and yet he stroked his moustache with a heavy hand, and as he pondered the cosmic conundrum, Koko caught another spider.

THE CAT WHO
BLEW THE WHISTLE

CHAPTER 1

   The engineer clanged the bell. The whistle blew two shrill blasts, and the old steam locomotive—the celebrated Engine No. 9—huff-puff-puffed away from the station platform, pulling passenger cars. She was a black giant with six huge driving wheels propelled by the relentless thrust of piston rods. The engineer leaned from his cab with his left hand on the throttle and his eyes upon the rails; the fireman shoveled coal into the firebox; black cinders spewed from the funnel-shaped smoke stack. It was a scene from the past.

Yet, this was a Sunday afternoon in the high-tech present. Thirty-six prominent residents of Moose County had converged on the railway station in Sawdust City to pay $500 a ticket for a ride behind old No. 9. It was the first run of the historic engine since being salvaged and overhauled, and the ticket purchase included a champagne dinner in a restored dining car plus a generous tax-deductible donation to the scholarship fund of the new community college.

When the brass bell clanged, a stern-faced conductor with a bellowing voice paced the platform, announcing, "Train leaving for Kennebeck, Pickax, Little Hope, Black Creek Junction, Lockmaster, and all points south! All abo-o-oard!" A yellow stepbox was put down, and well-dressed passengers climbed aboard the dining car, where tables were set with white cloths and sparkling crystal. White-coated waiters were filling glasses with ice water from silverplated pitchers.

Among the passengers being seated were the mayors from surrounding towns and other civic functionaries who found it in their
hearts, or politics, to pay $500 a plate. Also aboard were the pub-
lisher of the county newspaper, the publication's leading columnist,
the owner of the department store in Pickax, a mysterious heiress
recently arrived from Chicago, and the head of the Pickax Public
Library.

The flagman signaled all clear, and No. 9 started to roll, the cars
following with a gentle lurch. As the clickety clack of the drive
wheels on the rails accelerated, someone shouted, "She's rolling!"
The passengers applauded, and the mayor of Sawdust City rose to
propose a toast to No. 9. Glasses of ice water were raised. (The
champagne would come later.)

Her black hulk and brass fittings gleamed in the sunlight as she
chugged across the landscape. Steel rumbled on steel, and the
mournful whistle sounded at every grade crossing.

It was the first run of the Lumbertown Party Train. . . . No one
had any idea it would also be almost its last.

Moose County, 400 miles north of everywhere, had a rich
history, and railroads had helped to make it the wealthiest county
in the state before World War I. Fortunes had been made in mining, lumbering, and transportation, and many of the old families
were still there, hanging on to their inherited money or lamenting
the loss of it. Only the Klingenschoen millions had escalated into
billions, and then—by an ironic quirk of fate—had passed into the
hands of an outsider, a middle-aged man with a luxuriant pepper-
and-salt moustache and a unique distaste for money.

The heir was Jim Qwilleran, and he had been a hardworking,
prizewinning journalist Down Below, as Moose County citizens
called the polluted and crime-ridden centers of overpopulation.
Instead of rejoicing in his good luck, however, Qwilleran considered a net worth of twelve digits to be a nuisance and an embarrassment. He promptly established the Klingenschoen Foundation
to dispose of the surplus in philanthropic ways. He himself lived
quietly in a converted barn and wrote the twice-weekly "Qwill

Pen" column for the local paper. Friends called him "Qwill," with affection; the rest of the county called him "Mr. Q," with respect.

If a cross-section of the populace were to be polled, the women would say:

"I love his column! He writes as if he's talking to me!"

"Why can't my boyfriend be tall and good-looking and rich like Mr. Q?"

"His moustache is so romantic! But there's something sad about his eyes, as if he has a terrible secret."

"He must be over fifty, you know, but he's in terrific shape. I see him walking and biking all over."

"Imagine! All that money, and he's still a bachelor!"

"He has a wonderful head of hair for his age. It's turning gray at the temples, but I like that!"

"I sat next to him at a Red Cross luncheon once, and he listened to everything I said and made me feel important. My husband says journalists are paid to listen. I don't care. Mr. Q is a charming man!"

"You know he must be a nice person by the way he writes about cats in his column."

And if the men of Moose County were polled, they would say:

"One thing I'll say about Mr. Q: He fits in with all kinds of people. You'd never guess he has all that dough."

"He's a very funny guy, if you ask me. He walks into the barber shop, looking as if he's lost his last friend, and pretty soon he's got everybody in stitches with his cracks."

"All the women like him. My wife goes around quoting his column like it was the Constitution of the United States."

"They say he lives with a couple of cats. Can you beat that?"

"You wonder why he doesn't get married. He's always with that woman from the library."

"People think it's strange that he lives in an apple barn, but what the heck! It's better'n a pig barn."

Qwilleran did indeed live in a converted apple barn, and he spent many hours in the company of Polly Duncan, head librarian. As for the cats, they were a pair of pampered Siamese with extraordinary intelligence and epicurean tastes in food.

The barn, octagonal in shape and a hundred years old, had a fieldstone foundation two feet thick and as high as Qwilleran's head. Framing of twelve-by-twelve timbers rose to a roof three stories overhead. Once upon a time a wagonload of apples could go through the barn door, and bushels of apples were stored in the lofts. Now the interior was a series of balconies connected by ramps, surrounding a central cube of pristine white. There were fireplaces on three sides, and three cylindrical white flues rose to the octagonal roof. It was a lofty perch for cats who enjoyed high places. As for the spiraling ramps, the Siamese considered them an indoor race track, and they could do the hundred-meter dash in half the time required by a human athlete.

One evening in early summer Qwilleran and his two friends had just returned from a brief vacation on Breakfast Island, and he was reading aloud to them when the telephone rang. He excused himself and went to the phone on the writing desk.

"I got it, Qwill!" shouted an excited voice. "I got the job!"

"Congratulations, Dwight! I want to hear about it. Where are you?"

"At the theatre. We've just had a board meeting."

"Come on over. The gate's open."

The home of the Pickax Theatre Club had been carved out of the former Klingenschoen mansion on the Park Circle. Behind the theatre a fenced parking lot had a gate leading to a patch of dense evergreen woods that Qwilleran called the Black Forest. It was a buffer between the traffic on the Park Circle and the apple barn. Within minutes Dwight's car had negotiated the rough track through the woods.

"Glad everything worked out so well," Qwilleran said in greeting. "How about a glass of wine to celebrate?"

"Just a soft drink," said the young man. "I'm so high on good news that anything stronger would launch me into space. How do you like my new facade?" He stroked his smooth chin. "My new bosses don't go for beards. I feel suddenly naked. How would you feel without your moustache?"

"Destitute," Qwilleran said truthfully. His moustache was more than a facial adornment, more than a trademark at the top of the "Qwill Pen" column.

As Qwilleran carried the tray of drinks and snacks into the lounge area, Dwight pointed to the top of the fireplace cube. "I see you've got your ducks all in a row."

"I haven't heard that expression since the Army. How do you like them? They're hand-painted, hand-carved decoys from Oregon. Polly brought them back from her vacation."

"What did she think about Oregon? I hear it's a beautiful state."

"I doubt that she saw much of the landscape," Qwilleran said. "She was visiting a former college roommate, who's now a residential architect, and it seems they spent the whole time designing a house for Polly. She's going to build on a couple of acres at the east end of my orchard."

"I thought she wanted to keep her apartment on Goodwinter Boulevard."

"That was her original idea when they started converting the boulevard into a college campus. She thought she'd enjoy living among students. But when they began paving gardens for parking lots, she changed her mind."

"They should've made one large parking lot at the entrance and kept a grassy look on campus," Dwight said.

"God forbid anyone would have to walk a block from his car, Dwight. Rural communities live on wheels. Only city types like you and me know how to use their legs. . . . But tell me about the new job."

Dwight Somers, a publicity man from Down Below, had come north to work for a prosperous Moose County developer. Unfortunately the job fizzled, and the community that had benefited from his creativity and vitality was in fear of losing him.

"Okay," he began. "I told you I was having an interview with a PR firm in Lockmaster, didn't I? They want me to open a branch for them in Pickax, and we have a highly promising client for starters. Do you know Floyd Trevelyan in Sawdust City?"

He referred to an industrial town that was considered unprogressive and undesirable by Pickax standards, although it had a larger population and a thriving economy.

"I'm not acquainted with anyone in Sawdust City," Qwilleran said, "but I know the phone book is full of Trevelyans. This barn was part of the Trevelyan Apple Orchard a hundred years ago."

"Well, this guy is president of the Lumbertown Credit Union in Sawdust City—good name, what?—and it's a really going institution. He and his family have a big house in West Middle Hummock with acreage. He also happens to be a railroad nut, and he has a model train layout that's worth half a mil. That's not all! Now he's into rolling stock—a steam locomotive and some old passenger cars. He intends to use them for charter excursions."

"What will he use for tracks?"

"The old SC&L Line still hauls slow freight up from Down Below. No problem there. Floyd's idea is to rent his train out for dinners, cocktail parties, business functions, weddings, tourist excursions—whatever. We're calling it the Lumbertown Party Train. The civic leaders in Sawdust City are hot for tourism, like everyone else around here, and they've given him a few perks—helped him get a liquor license, for one thing."

"Does he expect to make any money on this venture?" Qwilleran asked, remembering the dashed hopes of Dwight's previous employer.

"Well, in Floyd's case it's a hobby or maybe a calculated loss for tax purposes. He's spent a mint on equipment, but he seems to have it to spend, so why not? It all started when he stumbled across this SC&L engine in mothballs. Steam locomotives are almost impossible to find, he says, and here was one with local connections. A great find! He's spent hundreds of thousands to restore it, starting with the removal of pigeon droppings. After that he bought a dining car, and then an Art Deco club car, and then a private railcar that had belonged to a textile magnate. The PV had fabulous appointments, but everything was in bad shape, and he spent a fortune to renovate the three cars. Amanda's Studio of Design supervised the renovation. How's that for a plummy contract? Maybe Amanda will retire now, and Fran Brodie can take over."

"Is it old family money he's sinking into this project?" Qwilleran asked. "I know there are some well-heeled Trevelyans as well as some on public assistance."

"No way! Floyd came up from a working class branch of the Trevelyan clan, but he inherited upwardly mobile genes from his pioneer ancestors. He started out as a carpenter and parlayed his toolbox into the largest construction firm in the county. Luckily he got in on the ground floor of the Moose County revival when federal funds were pouring in."

"Do you mean to say that a builder in Sawdust City was doing more business than XYZ Enterprises?" Qwilleran asked in astonishment.

"Believe it or not, XYZ didn't even exist until Exbridge, Young and Zoller formed a syndicate and bought out Trevelyan Construction. Floyd took their millions and opened the Lumbertown Credit Union. He was tired of the blue-collar image, and this move made him a white-collar VIP in his hometown—sort of a local hero. For offices he built a building that looks like an old-fashioned depot. The interior is paneled with narrow boards, highly varnished, and he even got a couple of old, uncomfortable waiting-room benches. To cap it all, he has model trains running around the lobby. The depositors love it! They call it the ChooChoo Credit Union, and the president is affectionately called F.T. . . . How do you feel about model trains, Qwill?"

"At the risk of sounding un-American, I must say I never caught the fever. As a kid I received an oval track and four cars for Christmas. What I really wanted was a baseball mitt. After the cars went around the track six or eight times, I was a very bored first baseman. Let's assume that my whole life has been colored by that one disappointment. . . . Still, I wouldn't object to writing a column on toy trains, if your client will cooperate."

"We call them *model* trains," Dwight informed him. "The adult hobbyists outnumber the kids, if my statistics are accurate."

"I stand corrected," said Qwilleran, who had a journalist's respect for the right word.

"Do you realize, Qwill, that serious collectors will fight for vintage models? Floyd paid over a thousand dollars for a ten-inch locomotive in the original box."

"Would he be interested in an interview?"

"Well, he's not exactly comfortable with the media, but I'll coach him. Give me a couple of days, and then you can call him at the Lumbertown office. His home in West Middle Hummock is called The Roundhouse, and it's two miles beyond the fork, where Hummock Road splits off from Ittibittiwassee. You can't miss it. His mailbox is a locomotive. Don't use his address; he's antsy about theft. You should see his security system!"

"When does the Party Train make its debut?"

"In a couple of weeks. Three weeks max. What I'm planning is a blastoff that'll attract the best people in the county and get publicity around the state. How would you react to a trial run at $500 a ticket, with proceeds going to charity? Everything would be first-class: champagne dinner with Chateaubriand, fresh flowers, live music—"

Qwilleran interrupted. "Give the proceeds to the scholarship fund of the new college, and I'll buy two tickets. I'll also twist Arch's arm until he buys a couple . . . Refresh your drink, Dwight?"

"No, thanks. I'll coast along with what I have . . . Hey, these snacks are good! What are they? They look like dry dog food."

"A friend sent them from Down Below—her own invention. She calls them Kabibbles."

"She should package these and sell them."

As he spoke, two slinky fawn-colored bodies with brown extremities were creeping silently toward the coffee table and the bowl of Kabibbles. Eyes that were celestial blue in daytime glistened like jet in the artificial light. Their concentration on their goal was absolute.

"No!" Qwilleran thundered, and they rose vertically on legs like springs before running away to contemplate their next maneuver. Their names were Koko and Yum Yum. The male, whose real name was Kao K'o Kung, had a lean, strong body with musculature that rippled beneath his silky fur; he also had a determination that was invincible. Yum Yum was daintier in size and deportment, but she knew how to get what she wanted.

"How did the cats like Breakfast Island?" Dwight asked.

"They don't care where they are," Qwilleran replied, "as long as they get three squares a day and a soft place to sleep."

"What's going to be done about the mess on Breakfast Island?"

"It hasn't been officially announced, but XYZ Enterprises will forfeit their equity in the resort, and the Klingenschoen Foundation will restore the south end of the island to its natural state. That includes reforestation and beach nourishment. Mother Nature is expected to do the rest."

"A major undertaking, if you ask me," said Dwight.

"But worth it."

"What about the Domino Inn and the other bed-and-breakfasts?"

"The plan is to have them function as youth hostels, elder hostels, and a summer campus for the new college. The islanders will continue to live in their secluded village, and the exclusive summer estates will have their taxes raised. . . . Now tell me about the theatre club, Dwight. What happened at the board meeting tonight?"

"We decided to go out on a limb and do a summer production for the first time. I'm recording secretary and always tape the minutes. Want to hear it?"

Dwight took a small recorder from his pocket and placed it on the coffee table. After a few seconds of fast-forwarding, familiar voices could be heard. Though distorted by the limitations of the device, they were recognizable: Larry Lanspeak, owner of the department store . . . Fran Brodie, interior designer . . . Scott Gippel, car dealer, who served as treasurer of the club . . . Dwight's own voice . . . and Junior Goodwinter, young managing editor of the newspaper.

LARRY: Now for new business. Considering the influx of tourists, should we do a summer play?

JUNIOR: The campers and fishermen and boaters have no place to go in the evening, except bars. Not even a movie house.

GIPPEL: I'm for giving it a shot. Let's grab some of those tourist dollars. Let's do a Broadway comedy with lots of belly laughs.

JUNIOR: Or a good mystery.

DWIGHT: Or a campy melodrama, like *Billy the Kid,* that'll get the audience booing the villain.

LARRY: Or a musical with a small cast, like *The Fantasticks.*

FRAN: I'd like to see us do *Midsummer Night's Dream*.

GIPPEL: You're nuts! That's Shakespeare!

LARRY: Yes, but it has comedy, romantic love, glamorous court scenes, and magic. What more can you ask?

JUNIOR: You can have a lot of fun with *Dream*. I played Puck in college.

LARRY: All the costumes for *Henry VIII* are in the basement. We could use them for the court scenes.

DWIGHT: *Thrift, thrift, Horatio!*

FRAN: How about using students for extras, as we did in *Henry*?

GIPPEL: Now you're talkin' turkey! All their friends and relatives will buy tickets. I say: Go for it. How many kids can we use?

FRAN: There's no limit to walk-ons. High-schoolers can play the lords and ladies, and junior high kids can do the fairies.

GIPPEL: *Fairies?* Are you kidding? You'd better make them little green men. Kids don't go for fairies. I've got three at home, and I know.

DWIGHT: Three little green men? Or three kids?

(Laughter)

FRAN: I like the idea of little green men! Let's do it! I'd love to direct.

Dwight turned off the recorder. "What do you think of it, Qwill?"

"Sounds okay to me, but Polly will have a fit if you convert Shakespeare's fairies into extraterrestrials. She's a purist."

"That detail isn't finalized, but we're going ahead with auditions. Off the record, we're precasting Junior as Puck and the Lanspeaks as the duke and his bride. They'll also double as Oberon and Titania. They've done the roles before, and we've got to take a few shortcuts if we want the show on the boards before Labor Day."

It was eleven o'clock, and the Siamese had come stalking back into the room. They stared pointedly at the visitor.

Suddenly he said, "Well, I'd better head for the hills. Thanks for everything."

"Glad your career has taken a propitious turn, Dwight."

"And that's not the only good news. I had a date with Hixie last night, and everything's coming up roses."

"You're lucky! She's great fun." It was an appropriate match. Hixie Rice was another transplant from Down Below, and she was in charge of public relations for the newspaper. Qwilleran put on a yellow baseball cap hanging near the kitchen door and accompanied his guest to his car. "We have an owl in the woods," he explained, "and if he sees a good head of hair, he might think it's a rabbit. I'm quoting Polly, the ornithology expert."

"Well, I'm safe," Dwight said, passing a hand over his thinning hair. He cocked his head to listen. "I can hear him hooting. Sounds like Morse code—long and short hoots."

As the happy young man drove away, Qwilleran watched the taillights bouncing through the ruts of the Black Forest and wondered what had happened to Hixie's previous heartthrob. He was a doctor. He owned a cabin cruiser. He had a beard. Qwilleran walked around the barn a few times before going indoors; it was pleasantly warm, with a soft breeze. He listened and counted.

"Whoo-o-o hoo hoo . . . hoo hoo hoo . . . whoo-o-o."

Qwilleran decided to call him Marconi and write a "Qwill Pen" column about owls. Fresh topics were in short supply in the summer. Sometimes the newspaper had to rerun his more popular columns, like the one on baseball and the one on cats.

When he went indoors, all was quiet. That was not normal. The Siamese should have been parading and demanding their nightly treat with ear-piercing yowls. Instead, they were assiduously washing their paws, whiskers, and ears, and the bowl on the coffee table was empty. Stuffed with Kabibbles, they staggered up the ramp to their apartment on the top balcony. Qwilleran, before he called it a day, wrote a thank-you note to a woman named Celia Robinson.

CHAPTER 2

When Qwilleran wrote his thank-you note for the Kabibbles, he sat at his writing table in the library area—one side of the fireplace cube that was lined with bookshelves. For serious work there was a writing studio on the balcony, off-limits to the Siamese, but the bookish, friendly atmosphere of the library was more comfortable for writing notes and taking phone calls. For this brief letter to Celia Robinson he used a facetiously bombastic style that would send her into torrents of laughter. She laughed easily; it took very little to set the dear woman off.

> Dear Celia,
>
> I find it appropriate to pen an effusive expression of gratitude for the succulent delights that arrived today to tantalize my taste buds and heighten my spirit. Your Kabibbles are receiving rave reviews from connoisseurs in this northern bastion of gastronomy. I suggest you copyright the name and market them. You could become the Betty Crocker of the twenty-first century! Perhaps you would grant me the distribution franchise for Moose and Lockmaster counties. Let me know your new address so I can order Kabibbles in ten-pound sacks or twenty-gallon barrels.
>
> Gratefully,
> Q

No one in Pickax knew about Qwilleran's whimsical acquaintance with Celia Robinson, not even Polly Duncan—especially not Polly, who was inclined to resent the slightest intrusion on her territory. The crosscountry acquaintance had begun when Junior Goodwinter's grandmother died suddenly in Florida. Through long-distance conversations with her next-door neighbor, Qwilleran conducted an investigation into the death, and he and Celia developed a chummy rapport. He called her his secret agent, and she called him Chief. He sent her boxes of chocolate-covered cherries and the paperback spy novels that she liked; she sent him homemade brownies. They had never met.

The case was closed now, but Qwilleran had an ulterior motive for continuing the connection: She enjoyed cooking. Fondly he envisioned her relocating in Pickax and catering meals for himself and the cats. It was not an improbability; she wanted to leave the retirement village in Florida. "Too many old people" was her complaint. Celia was only sixty-nine.

Qwilleran posted the letter in his rural mailbox the next morning, walking down the orchard wagon trail to the highway, Trevelyan Road. The trail was the length of a city block. It ran past the skeletons of neglected apple trees, between other trees planted by squirrels and birds in the last hundred years, alongside the remains of the old Trevelyan farmhouse that had burned down, and past the two acres where Polly would build her new house. After raising the red flag on the oversized mailbox, he took a few minutes to consider the construction site. The fieldstone foundation of the old house was barely visible in a field of waist-high weeds. An abandoned lilac bush was doing nicely on its own, having grown to the size of a two-story, three-bedroom house, and it still bloomed in season. When the wind direction was right, its fragrance wafted as far as the apple barn.

Polly wanted to preserve the old stone foundation—for what purpose she had not decided. She kept asking, "Shall I build in front of it, or behind it, or beyond it? I can't build on top of it."

Qwilleran had tried to make suggestions, but her questions were merely rhetorical; she was an independent person and had to make her own decisions. As head librarian she had a brilliant reputation. She was efficient and briskly decisive. She charmed the members of the library board, improved the collection, controlled the budget, coped with the quirks of an old library building, staged events, and solved the personal problems of her young assistants with kindness and common sense. In facing her own dilemmas, however, she melted into a puddle of bewilderment.

Returning from the mailbox, Qwilleran became aware of two

pairs of blue eyes staring at him from an upper-level window of the barn. He waved to them and kept on walking—through the Black Forest to the Park Circle, with its important buildings and multi-lane traffic. The proximity of town and country was one of the attractions of living in a small city (population 3,000). On the perimeter of the Park Circle were two churches, the courthouse, the K Theatre, and a building resembling a Greek temple: the public library.

Qwilleran walked briskly up the stone steps of the library—steps rounded into gentle concavities by a century of feet. Now added to the feet of book-subscribers were the feet of video-borrowers, and Qwilleran doubted that the steps would last another half-century. In the main room he headed directly toward the stairs to the mezzanine, nodding pleasantly to the young clerks who greeted him as Mr. Q. They also glanced mischievously at each other, amused at the sight of the middle-aged friend of their middle-aged boss paying a call in broad daylight. The relationship between the head librarian and the richest man in the northeast-central United States was a subject of constant conjecture in Pickax.

Qwilleran bounced up the stairs, noting the familiar sight of Homer Tibbitt at one of the reading tables, surrounded by books and pamphlets. Although well up in his nineties, the county historian spent every morning at the library, pursuing some esoteric research project. Or perhaps he was avoiding his overly attentive wife, as the giggling clerks surmised. In her eighties, Rhoda Tibbitt could still drive, and she chauffeured her husband to and from his life's work.

Polly was seated in her glass-enclosed office in front of a deskful of paperwork. When she spoke, her serenely low-pitched voice gave Qwilleran a shudder of pleasure as it always did, no matter how often they met or how many hours they had spent together the evening before.

"Morning," he said with an intimate nuance. He never used terms of endearment, except to Yum Yum, but he could infuse a two-syllable greeting with warmth and affection. He slid into a hard, varnished oak chair, library-style circa 1910.

Polly said, "You look especially vibrant this morning, dear."

"I'm a veritable fountain of news," he announced as he launched into his report on Dwight's new job, the Party Train, and the theatre club's decision to do *A Midsummer Night's Dream*. He avoided mentioning that the fairies might be updated. He even revealed Dwight's date with Hixie Rice as a kind of romantic milestone on the social scene. Outsiders might call it gossip, but in Pickax this was legitimate sharing of information. Good news, rumors, bad news, scandal, and other data somehow reached the library first, and Polly's assistant, Virginia Alstock, was tuned in to the Moose County grapevine for its dissemination.

Today Polly's reactions were subdued. She seemed preoccupied, glancing frequently at the stack of manuals on home building that occupied a corner of her desk.

The title on top of the pile was *How to Build a Better House for Less Money,* and he asked, "Are you making any progress with your house plans?"

"I don't know," she said with a world-weary sigh. "It's all so confusing. In Oregon, Susan did sketches for a one-story house that would integrate with the terrain. No basement. Heating equipment in a utility room next to the laundry. . . . But these books say that a twostory house is more economical to build and to heat, and it would give Bootsie a chance to run up and down stairs for exercise."

"Build a one-story house with a basement and let him run up and down the basement stairs," Qwilleran suggested with simple logic. Bootsie was the other male in Polly's life, a husky Siamese. He was grossly pampered, in Qwilleran's opinion.

"I'm not fond of basements. I've seen too many that leak," she objected. "I was thinking of a crawl space with good insulation. What do you think, Qwill?"

"You're asking the wrong person. I'm only a journalist; I leave the house building to the house builders. Why not line up a professional firm like XYZ Enterprises?"

"But it's so large and commercial, and I've lost respect for them since the fiasco on Breakfast Island. It's my belief that a small builder gives more personal attention to one's needs and ideas. Mrs. Alstock's in-laws in Black Creek hired a young man. He finished on schedule and very close to the estimated cost. We should encourage young people in the trades, don't you think? He works out of Sawdust City."

"Hmmm," Qwilleran mused, having heard that the Sawdusters were all roughnecks who threw bottles through tavern windows on Saturday nights. "What is his name?"

"He's a Trevelyan—another of those 'hairy Welshmen,' as they're called, but I have no objection to long hair and a shaggy beard if he does a good job."

"Want me to check him out for you? The paper has a stringer in Sawdust City."

"Well . . . thank you, Qwill, but . . . Mrs. Alstock is taking me to see her in-laws' house tomorrow night, and Mr. Trevelyan will be there. I'll have my sketches with me, and if he impresses me favorably—"

"Find out if he eyeballs the construction from the sketches," Qwilleran suggested, remembering the underground builder he had encountered in Mooseville.

"Oh, no! In Pickax the plans and specifications must be drawn up by an architect in order to obtain a building permit."

Changing the subject abruptly, Qwilleran said, "I'm keeping you from your work. How about dinner tonight at the Old Stone Mill?"

"I'd love to, dear, but I've called a special meeting of the library board. We'll have dinner at the hotel, then come back here to discuss the paving of the parking lot. We've had it out for bids."

Teasingly he said, "I hope your literary ladies enjoy the inevitable chicken pot pie and lemon sherbet, spelled 'sherbert' on the menu."

Polly smiled, recognizing his genial thrust at the hotel's cuisine and the library's frugal allowance for boardmembers' meals. "You're welcome to join us," she said coyly.

"No thanks, but why don't you get the board to budget a few dollars for cushions for these chairs?"

"Go away," she said affectionately, waving him out of her office. She was wearing the ring he had given her for Christmas—a fiery black opal rimmed with tiny diamonds. He knew that she was wearing it to impress the "literary ladies."

Leaving Polly's office, Qwilleran stopped to say hello to Homer Tibbitt. The old man's eyes were glazed after poring over his books, and he blinked a few times before he could recognize the face.

"Tell me, Homer. How can you sit on these hard chairs for so many hours?" Qwilleran asked.

"I bring an inflated cushion," said the historian. "Also a thermos of decaf, but don't tell Polly. The sign says: No food or beverages. I take my brown bag into the restroom every hour or so and have a swig."

Qwilleran nodded with understanding, knowing there was a shot of brandy in Homer's decaffeinated coffee. "How are you feeling these days?" The old man was wheezing audibly.

"I suffer the usual tweaks and twinges of advancing age, plus a touch of bronchitis from these dusty, mildewed records." He slapped his chest. "My tubes whistle. You can hear me all over the building. I'm trying to do a paper *(whistle)* on Moose County mines, 1850 to 1915."

"What do you know about the Trevelyan family?"

"They go back six generations, all descended from two brothers who came from Wales *(whistle)* to supervise the mines. Second generation built sawmills and founded Sawdust City." Mr. Tibbitt stopped for a coughing spell, and Qwilleran rushed to the water cooler for a cup of water. "Sorry about that," the old man apologized when the coughing was relieved. "Now, where was I?"

"Sawdust City," Qwilleran reminded him. "The Trevelyans."

"Believe it or not, that ugly little town was the county seat originally, when Pickax was only a bump in the road. When they switched government functions to Pickax because of *(whistle)* its central location, the Sawdusters rose up in arms and tried to secede from Moose County. All they accomplished was an independent school system."

"Do you know a Floyd Trevelyan, Homer? He's president of the Lumbertown Credit Union in Sawdust City."

"Can't say that I do. We Pickaxians are unmitigated snobs, you know. Are you aware you're living *(whistle)* in the old Trevelyan orchard? No one would touch the property for generations until you came along—a greenhorn from Down Below, heh heh heh."

"Because of snobbery?" Qwilleran asked.

"Because of the Trevelyan curse," the historian corrected him. "The apple trees withered, the farmhouse was struck by lightning, and the farmer hanged himself."

"Who pronounced the curse?"

"Nobody knows."

"For your information, Homer, Polly is building a house where the farmhouse used to be."

"Well, don't tell her *(whistle)* what I said."

"That's all right. She's not superstitious."

"Just the same, don't tell her," the old man warned.

After leaving the library, Qwilleran continued his walk downtown, making a few unscheduled visits for the purpose of sharing information:

To Scottie's Men's Store to look at summer shirts. Nothing caught his fancy, but he chatted with the proprietor and told him about the Party Train.

To Edd's Editions, a shop specializing in pre-owned books from estate libraries. Eddington Smith was interested to hear about the Party Train because he had several books on railroads. Qwilleran bought one on the digging of the Panama Canal.

To the office of the newspaper which, for strange reasons, was named the *Moose County Something*. His longtime friend from Down Below, Arch Riker, was publisher and editor-in-chief and was pleased to hear about the Party Train.

To Toodle's Market to buy six ounces of sliced roast beef from the deli counter and two packages of macaroni and cheese from the frozen food chest. In the checkout line he stood behind Wally Toddwhistle's mother, who made costumes for the theatre club. She asked if he'd heard about *A Midsummer Night's Dream,* and he asked if she'd heard about the Party Train.

Returning to the barn, he found it good to be greeted by importunate yowls and waving tails, even though he knew the cats' real motive. He diced roast beef for them and heated both packages of macaroni and cheese for himself. Dicing, thawing, and pressing the button on the computerized coffeemaker were his only kitchen skills.

After dinner the three of them gravitated to the library area for a session of reading. Qwilleran's growing collection of old books was organized according to category: biography, classic fiction, drama, and so forth. He added his new purchase to the history shelf. Yum Yum waited patiently for him to sit down and make a lap; Koko was alert and awaiting his cue.

"Book! Book!" It was one of several words understood by Kao K'o Kung, among them: treat, brush, leash, and NO! The cat surveyed the expanse of shelving before jumping up and teetering on the edge of the classic fiction collection. He sniffed the bindings critically, then pawed *Swiss Family Robinson* with enthusiasm.

A curious choice, Qwilleran thought. He realized it was mere coincidence but a provocative one, Koko having a unique sense of association. Yet, the connection between an 1813 Swiss novel and the inventor of Kabibbles was too absurd even for a willing believer like Qwilleran.

He sprawled in his favorite lounge chair and propped his feet on the ottoman. Yum Yum hopped lightly into his lap and turned around three times counterclockwise before settling down. Koko took his usual position on the arm of the chair, sitting tall.

Qwilleran opened the book, which he had bought for its illustrations, and said, "This is a book primarily for young people but is suitable for cats of any age. There are chapters on . . . let's see . . . whales, turtles, ostriches, and bears. You'll like it. Chapter One: *Shipwrecked and Alone.*"

Yum Yum was the first one to sigh and close her eyes; then Koko started swaying drowsily; finally Qwilleran, mesmerized by the sound of his own voice, read himself to sleep.

One afternoon, before his appointment with the president of the Lumbertown Credit Union, Qwilleran drove to Sawdust City out of sheer curiosity. The town itself might be material for the "Qwill Pen" column. He knew only that it was the industrial hub of the county, straddling the mouth of the Ittibittiwassee River, where pollution was an ongoing problem. Although freight trains made regular runs to points Down Below, most manufactures were shipped by truck. Their tires constantly tracked mud from unpaved side streets onto the highway, giving the town the nickname of Mudville. Nevertheless, there was a healthy job market there, and Sawdust City was home to 5,000 working-class residents whose soccer team regularly trounced others in the county.

Outside the town limits Qwilleran noticed an athletic field with a running track, one softball diamond, and three soccer fields with goal nets—no tennis courts. There was also an extensive consolidated school complex with its own football stadium.

On Main Street there was plenty of downtown traffic as well as cafés, gas stations, churches, a storefront library, gun shops, pawnbrokers, apparel shops with racks of clothing on the sidewalk, taverns, and a video store. The Lumbertown Credit Union occupied a new version of an old depot, while the real railway station was a neglected relic on the outskirts of town, surrounded by tracks, boxcars, trucks, and warehouses. The residential neighborhoods were notable for their neat lawns, swarms of schoolchildren on summer vacation, basketball hoops, barbecues, and satellite saucers. In every sense it was a thriving town. Whether it would be material for the "Qwill Pen" was questionable. Qwilleran knew only that Sawdust City stood in sharp contrast to West Middle Hummock, where the Lumbertown president lived. This was the most fashionable of the Hummocks with the largest estates, owned by families like the Lanspeaks, the Wilmots, and—in happier days—the Fitches. When Qwilleran set out to interview Floyd Trevelyan his route lay out Ittibittiwassee Road between stony pastures and dark woods, past abandoned mines and ghostlike shafthouses. After passing the Buckshot Mine, where he had suffered a nasty tumble from his bike, he reached a fork in the road. Ahead was Indian Village, a more or less swanky complex of apartments and condominiums. Hummock Road branched off to the left, forming a triangular meadow where car-poolers left their vehicles. Share-the-ride had been a Moose County custom long before the first energy crisis; it was the neighborly thing to do and an opportunity to keep abreast of rumors. Beyond the meadow the road passed a blighted hamlet or two before emerging in a landscape of knobby hills, bucolic vistas, architect-designed farmhouses, and no utility poles. All cables were underground, and the road curved to avoid cutting down ancient trees.

Then there was a rural mailbox shaped like a locomotive and a sign hanging between railroad ties announcing "The Roundhouse." There was nothing round about the residence that perched on a hill at the end of the drive. It was a long, low contemporary building with wide overhangs and large chimneys—almost brutal in its boldness—and the rough cedar exterior was stained a gloomy brownish-green.

Qwilleran parked at the foot of a terraced walkway and climbed wide steps formed from railroad ties, then rang the doorbell and waited in the usual state of suspense: Would this interview make a great story? Or would it be a waste of his time?

The man who came to the door, wearing crumpled shorts and a tank top, was obviously one of the "hairy Welshmen" for whom Sawdust City was famous. Although seriously balding toward the brow, his head was rimmed with hair that was black and bushy, and although his jutting jaw was clean-shaven, his arms and legs were thickly furred. So also was his back, Qwilleran discovered upon following him into the foyer.

His initial greeting had been curt. "You from the paper?"

"Jim Qwilleran. Dwight Somers tells me you have a railroad empire on the premises."

"Downstairs. Want a shot or a beer?"

"Not right now, thanks. Let's have a look at the trains first. I'm completely ignorant about model railroading, so this visit will be an education." Following the collector toward a broad staircase to the lower level, Qwilleran quickly appraised the main floor: architecturally impressive, poorly furnished. On the way downstairs he tossed off a few warm-up questions: How long have you been collecting? How did you get started? Do you still have your first train?

The answers were as vapid as the queries: "Long time . . . Dunno . . . Yep."

The staircase opened into a large light room with glass walls overlooking a paved patio and grassy hillside. The opposite wall formed a background for a table-height diorama of landscape and cityscape. There were buildings, roadways, rivers, hills, and a complexity of train tracks running through towns, up grades, across bridges, and around curves. A passenger train waited at a depot; a freight train had been shunted to a siding; the nose of a locomotive could be seen in the mouth of a tunnel.

"How many trains do you have?" Qwilleran asked, producing a pocket tape recorder.

"Six trains. Thousand feet of track." The hobbyist started toying with a bank of controls at the front edge of the layout, and the scene was instantly illuminated: the headlight of the locomotive in the tunnel, the interior of the passenger coaches, and all street lights and railway signals. Then the trains began to move, slowly at first, and gradually picking up speed. One train stopped to let another pass. A locomotive chugged around a curve, with white smoke pouring from its smokestack. It blew its whistle as it approached a grade crossing and stopped at the station with a hiss of steam.

Qwilleran was impressed but said coolly, "Quite realistic!"

An engine pulled cars up a grade to cross a bridge while another passed underneath. Trains backed up as cars were coupled. A train of boxcars, tank cars, and gondolas stopped to give right-of-way to a diesel speeding through with passenger coaches and an observation car.

"Watch 'em take those curves," Trevelyan said proudly. He operated the remote controls with practiced skill, switching tracks, unloading coal from hopper cars, and dumping logs from a flatcar. In a freight yard with seven parallel tracks he had a switch engine shifting boxcars. "You hafta be quick to figure how fast they go, what route to take and which turnouts to switch. . . . Wanna try it?"

"And derail the whole railroad? No thanks," Qwilleran said. "Did you play with trains when you were a kid?"

"Me? Nah, my folks were too poor. But I had the real thing in the backyard. Our house, it was next to the track, and I knew every train schedule and all the crews. The engineers, they always clanged their bell and waved at me. Man! Did I feel like a big shot! Saturdays I'd go down to the yard and watch 'em switchin'. I wanted to stow away in a boxcar, but I knew my pop would lick the devil outa me."

"I suppose you wanted to grow up to be an engineer," Qwilleran said.

"Funny thing, I wanted to be a crossin' guard and sit in a little shack high up, lookin' down the tracks and workin' the gate. That's a kid for you!"

Above the confusion of mechanical noises in front of him, Qwilleran heard an elevator door open at the far end of the room and turned to see a frail woman in an electric wheelchair coming hesitantly in their direction. Although she was in Trevelyan's line of vision, he ignored her. He was saying, "There was four of us kids. Pop worked in the plastic plant till the chemicals killed 'im. I took Vocational in school. English and that kinda stuff, you could shove it! I could build things and tinker with motors, so who needed English? Summers I got jobs with builders. Finally got to be a contractor myself, licensed and all that."

The woman in the wheelchair was fixing her gaze eagerly on Qwilleran, and he mumbled a polite good afternoon.

In a faltering voice she said, "You're Mr. Q. I see your picture in the paper all the time."

It was the kind of ambiguous comment that beggared reply, but he bowed courteously.

Trevelyan went on talking. "Like I said, I went as far as I could go with model trains. I'm into somethin' bigger now. Did Dwight tell you we're gonna—"

The woman interrupted shrilly. "My pop was an engineer!"

The man scowled and waved her away with an impatient hand. Obediently she wheeled back to the elevator, leaving Qwilleran to wonder who she might be. Her age was difficult to guess, her face and figure being ravaged by some kind of disease.

The trains were still running and performing their automatic ballet, but Qwilleran had all the information he could use and had even learned some railroad terms:

Roundhouse: a round building where locomotives were serviced in the Steam Era
Hog: locomotive

Hoghead: engineer
Wildcat: a runaway locomotive
Consist: a train of cars (accent on first syllable)
Gandy dancer: member of a section gang repairing rails
Whittling: taking a curve at high speed and braking the wheels
Rule G: the SC&L rule against drinking

Trevelyan said, "We don't worry about Rule G around this man's railroad yard. How's about wettin' your whistle?" He opened the door to a well-stocked bar. "Whatever you want, we got it."

"What are you drinking?" Qwilleran asked.

"Whiskey and soda."

"I'll take the same without the whiskey."

His host gave him an incredulous glance, then shook his head as he poured plain soda. They carried their glasses outdoors and sat on the patio while the railroad buff talked about the Lumbertown Party Train and the $500 tickets.

"How many can you seat in the dining car?" Qwilleran asked.

"Thirty-six at a shot. We figure to have a double shift, two o'clock and six o'clock. We figure we can sell out."

"How long will the ride last?"

"We figure we can kill three hours on the rails, round trip, with a layover at Flapjack."

"How did you go about buying your rolling stock?"

"Went to train museums, read PV magazines, answered ads."

"PV meaning . . . ?"

"Private varnish—all about private railroads. But I found my hog in a scrapyard in Sawdust City. She was a mess! I almost cried. As soon as those SC&L sharpies saw I was hooked, they upped the price outasight. I didn't care. I hadda have that baby! Spent another bundle to fix 'er up. Diesels—you can have 'em. Steam is where it's at—for me anyway."

"What's the big attraction?"

The collector shrugged. "A hog's nothin' but a firebox and a big boiler on wheels, but what a sight when she rolls! Raw power! My Engine No. 9 is a 4-6-2."

"You'll have to explain that," Qwilleran said.

THE CAT WHO BLEW THE WHISTLE   225

Without a word Trevelyan went into the train room and re-turned with a framed photo of No. 9. "Four small wheels in front keep the engine on the rails. The six big babies with pis-ton rods are the drivin' wheels; they deliver the power. The two in back hold up the firebox and the engineer's cab. Dwight tells me you signed up for the first run. Tell him to show you through my PV; it's a palace on wheels! . . . How long did you know Dwight?"

"Ever since he arrived from Down Below. He's a real pro—knows his job—good personality."

"Yeah, nice fella . . . How come he isn't married?"

"I don't know. Why don't you ask him?" Qwilleran replied in a genial tone that masked his annoyance at the prying question. Then he changed the subject. "There's a town south of Pickax called Wildcat, and I often wondered why. Any railroad connec-tion?"

"Sure is! A runaway train was wrecked on the trestle bridge there in 1908—worst wreck ever! Old railroaders still talk about it."

"Are their recollections being recorded?" Qwilleran asked. "Is there a railroad library in Sawdust City? Are any old engi-neers still living?" He was feeling an old familiar urge. With a little research and some oral histories from retired railroad per-sonnel, plus stories handed down in their families, he could write a book! It would capture the horror of train wrecks as well as the nostalgia of the Steam Era when trains were the glamorous mode of transportation and locomotive engineers were the folk heroes. Homer Tibbitt, who had grown up on a farm, still remembered the haunting sound of a steam whistle in the middle of the night. He said it had filled him with loneli-ness and nameless desires. He doubted that it could be equaled today by the honking of a diesel, or the roar of a jet, or the whining tires of an eighteen-wheeler on a freeway.

"Ready for another drink?" the host asked. "I am."

Qwilleran declined, saying he had to meet a newspaper deadline, but on his way out of the house he asked casually, "Do you happen to know a Trevelyan who's a house builder?"

"My son," was the prompt reply. "Just starting out on his own."

"Does he know his stuff? A friend of mine is thinking of hiring him."

"Sure, he's a whizbang! Learned the trade from me. I taught him the whole works. I said to both my kids: The trick is to start early and work hard. That's what I did."

"You have another son?"

"A girl. She took bookkeepin' in high school. Works in my office now."

Strange family situation, Qwilleran thought as he drove away from The Roundhouse. There was the unkempt president of a successful family business. Then there was the undistinguished furniture in a pretentious house. And how about the shabbily treated woman in a state-of-the-art wheelchair? Who was she? She seemed too old to be his wife, too young to be his mother. Was she a poor relative or former housekeeper living on his charity? In any case, the man should have made some sort of introduction or at least acknowledged her presence. The financial success that had vaulted him from Sawdust City to West Middle Hummock had hardly polished his rough edges.

On the way home Qwilleran stopped at Toodles' Market for a frozen dinner and six ounces of sliced turkey breast. He was not surprised when Yum Yum met him at the kitchen door, slinking flirtatiously, one dainty forepaw in front of the other.

"There she is! Miss Cat America!" he said. "Where's your side-kick? Where's Koko?"

The other cat came running, and the two of them sang for their supper—a duet of baritone yowls and coloratura trills, the latter more like shrieks. After Qwilleran had diced their favorite treat and arranged it on their favorite plate, Koko made a dive for it, but Yum Yum looked at the plate sourly and veered away with lowered head.

Qwilleran was alarmed. Was she ill? Had she found a bug and eaten it? Was it a hair ball? Had she swallowed a rubber band? He picked her up gently and asked, "What's wrong with my little sweetheart?" She looked at him with large eyes filled with reproach.

Meanwhile, Koko had polished off two-thirds of the repast,

leaving the usual one-third for his partner. Qwilleran, with Yum Yum still in his arms, picked up the plate and placed it on the kitchen counter. Immediately she squirmed from his grasp, landed on the counter, and devoured the turkey.

"Cats!" he muttered. "They drive you crazy!"

CHAPTER 3

Qwilleran wrote a thousand words about Floyd Trevelyan's model trains and walked downtown to the office of the *Moose County Something* to file his copy. Junior Goodwinter had a managing editor's ability to read at the rate of fifty words a second, and he scanned the "Qwill Pen" copy in its entirety before Qwilleran could pour himself a cup of coffee.

"You seem pretty enthusiastic about this guy's trains," the editor said.

"The trick is to sound that way whether you are or not," Qwilleran retorted. "I like to increase the reader's pulse beat. . . . Actually, I was impressed by the train layout but not enthusiastic."

"How about putting some of your fake enthusiasm into an extra assignment?"

"Like what?"

"You know, of course," Junior began, "that the club is doing *Midsummer Night's Dream*. We want to run a short piece on each of the leads—about eight inches with a head shot. It's not supposed to be a blurb for the play or a bio of the actor; it's a miniature think-piece on the actor's perception of both the role and the theme of the play."

"All that in eight inches?"

"Only you can do it, Qwill. Your style is concise and pithy. What's more, your readers devour anything and everything you write, and you'll get a by-line on each piece—also free coffee for life."

Junior was wheedling him, and Qwilleran was succumbing to the flattery. "How many pieces would there be?"

"Nine or ten. Since you live behind the theatre, it'll be easy to drop in during rehearsal and catch the actors on their break. We'll alert them to start thinking about it. Someone like Derek Cuttle-brink does more thinking about his costume than about the essence of his role."

"How is he cast?"

"He's doing Nick Bottom, the weaver."

"That's a good one for him. He'll enjoy hee-hawing like a don-key."

"He'll be a howl! As soon as he walks on stage he'll bring down the house."

Derek, a resident of Wildcat, was a waiter at the Old Stone Mill. With his outgoing personality, engaging candor, and impressive height (six-feet-eight, going on nine) he was a favorite with restaurant diners, theatregoers, and impressionable young women.

"When do you want to start the series?" Qwilleran asked.

"Soonest. We're rehearsing five nights a week. . . . And say! Do you keep in touch with that Chicago heiress you brought over from Breakfast Island?"

"I didn't bring her over; she happened to be on the same boat," Qwilleran said tartly. "Why do you ask?"

"Well, she's joined the club, and she's helping with costumes. She has some good ideas."

That's appropriate, Qwilleran thought. Her own wardrobe was straight out of *Arabian Nights*.

"Also," Junior went on with relish, "she and Derek are hitting it off like Romeo and Juliet. If it's true that she has an annual income of $500,000, Derek's on the right track for once in his life."

Qwilleran huffed into his moustache. "Don't place any bets. In my opinion, she's a mighty flighty young woman. . . . See you at rehearsal."

"Before you leave the building," Junior called after him, "our esteemed editor-in-chief wants to see you."

Arch Riker had the florid complexion and paunchy figure of a veteran journalist who has been a deskman throughout his career and has attended too many press luncheons. When Qwilleran appeared in the doorway, he was sitting in his high-back executive chair and swiveling in deep thought. "Come in. Come in," he said, beckoning. "Help yourself to coffee."

"Thanks. I haven't had one for the last three minutes. What's up, Arch?"

"Good news! . . . Sit down . . . After we ran our editorial on the Lumbertown Party Train, all tickets for the kickoff sold out, for both sittings! At $500 a ticket, that's pretty good for a county in the boonies. It was a stroke of genius, of course, to earmark the proceeds for college scholarships."

"The charity angle was Dwight Somers's idea, not that of the train owner," Qwilleran said. "Trevelyan doesn't strike me as a great philanthropist."

"Dwight just called and suggested we run a profile on the guy," Riker said. "What say you?"

"I've just handed in a column on his personal collection of model trains, and I think that's enough for now."

"I agree. We can cover the actual event from the social angle. . . . So you met Floyd-boy! What's he like?"

"Not your average bank president. He's a rough-hewn, self-made man who started as a carpenter. He's sunk a fortune in his Party Train, and his model collection is incredible! What makes a guy want to own more, bigger, and better than anyone else? I've never understood the urge to collect. You never got bitten by the bug either, did you?"

"Once!" Riker admitted. "When I was married to an antique collector, I collected antique tin like a madman. It's strange how suddenly I lost interest when wife, house, and cats went down the drain, *k-chug!*"

Qwilleran nodded solemnly, remembering his own bitter past, when he himself almost went *k-chug!*

His friend was in a talkative mood. "Mildred wants me to start another collection of something, so it'll be easier to buy me Christmas presents. I tell her I don't need Christmas presents. Every day in my life is Christmas since we took the plunge. . . . Qwill, why don't you and Polly—"

Qwilleran interrupted. "Don't—start—that—again, Archibald!"

"Okay, okay. At least you two will be within whistling distance when she builds her house. How's it coming?"

"She's hired the son of Floyd Trevelyan to build it. He's based in Mudville. His father says he's good."

"What else do you expect a parent to say?" Riker remarked caustically. "Personally, I'd think twice before hiring a Sawduster to fix a leaky faucet!"

"Well . . . you know Polly . . . when she makes up her mind!"

About two weeks later, on a Sunday afternoon, Qwilleran and Polly drove to Sawdust City and met Arch and Mildred Riker on the railway platform. Well-dressed patrons were arriving from all parts of the county, and curious Sawdusters watched as the strangers' cars were whisked away and parked by young men in red jumpsuits. It was the first valet parking in the history of Mudville. The weather was warm enough for the women to wear sheer summer dresses and cool enough for the men to wear light blazers. The one exception was Whannell MacWhannell of Pickax, sweltering in his pleated all-wool kilt and full Scottish regalia.

Surprisingly, the Chicago heiress was there with the waiter from the Old Stone Mill, and Riker said, "Derek must have been getting some good tips lately."

Qwilleran said, "Last week I saw him buying her a hot dog at Lois's. This must be her turn to treat."

Today, as always, she was theatrically dressed—the only woman wearing a hat. The high-crowned straw wound with yards of veiling and accented with a cabbage rose was vintage Edwardian. Furthermore, she was incredibly thin by Moose County standards. Polly, who wore size sixteen, guessed her size to be a four, or even a two.

Also attracting attention was a young woman in a pantsuit. In Moose County the custom was skirts-on-Sunday, but this eye-catching beauty in a well-cut summer pantsuit made all the women in skirts look dowdy. She was with Floyd Trevelyan. He himself was well groomed and properly dressed for the occasion. Was she his wife? His daughter? They were not mingling with the crowd.

Newspaper photographers and a video cameraman added excitement, and a brass band was blaring numbers like "Chattanooga Choo Choo" and "Hot Time in the Old Town Tonight." Riker recognized the trombone player, who worked in the circulation department of the *Moose County Something*.

Polly said, "I do hope they're not going on the train with us."

Commemorative programs had been handed to the passengers waiting on the platform, and Mildred said, "Can you believe this? They brought the crew out of retirement for this historic run. The engineer is eighty-two; the brakeman is seventy-six; the fireman is sixty-nine—all veterans of SC&L."

Riker said, "I hope I can shovel coal when I'm sixty-nine."

"Dear, you couldn't even shovel snow last winter," his wife said sweetly.

"Do you suppose anyone had the foresight to check the engineer's vision and blood pressure? Has the fireman had an EKG recently? Will there be a doctor on the train?"

"Where's the hog?" Qwilleran asked, exhibiting his knowledge of railroad slang.

There had been no sign of the locomotive, except for puffs of steam rising from behind a warehouse. Then abruptly the music stopped, and the brasses sounded a fanfare. As the chatter on the platform faded away, No. 9 came puffing and whistling around a curve. The crowd cheered, and the band struck up "Casey Jones."

Old No. 9 was a magnificent piece of machinery, towering above the passengers on the platform. Its noble nose had a giant headlight; the black hulk and brass fittings glistened in the sunlight; the piston rods were marvels of mechanical magic as they stroked the huge driving wheels; even the cowcatcher was impressive. Leaning from the cab and waving at the waiting crowd was an aging engineer with tufts of white hair showing beneath his denim cap. He was beaming with pride.

Mildred, who had an artist's eye, called the locomotive a masterpiece of sensitive beauty and brute strength. "No wonder they called it the Great Iron Horse!"

When the freshly painted coaches came around the bend, her husband said, "They're still the same old moldy, muddy green."

"That's a perfectly acceptable color," Mildred said. "I can mix it on my palette with chrome oxide green and cadmium red deep, with a little burnt umber to muddy it."

Dwight Somers, overhearing the conversation, informed them that the traditional Pullman green was designed to hide mud and soot.

"What do you know about the engineer?" Polly asked.

"He was an SC&L hoghead for fifty years. Many times his skill and bravery saved lives, and he only jumped once. He'd tell his fireman to jump, but Ozzie Penn was like the skipper who stays with his ship, braving it out."

"That's comforting to know," Riker said. "I trust they gave him a gold watch when he retired."

Then the conductor swung down the steps of the first car and shouted "All abo-o-oard!"

Qwilleran had reserved a table for four in the center of the dining car, where woodwork gleamed with varnish, tablecloths were blindingly white, and wine glasses sparkled. There was a hubbub of delight as the diners were seated. Then came one of those long, unexplained waits inflicted on train passengers. The wags in the crowd made wild conjectures: "They ran out of coal. . . . The fireman slipped a disc. . . . The chef forgot his knives. . . . They're sending out for more ice cubes."

Eventually the bell clanged, the whistle screamed and, as the train started to move, an army of waiters in white coats surged down the aisle with bottles of champagne. Everyone applauded.

Qwilleran, riding backward, saw Floyd Trevelyan at an end table with his attractive companion, and their body language was not that of a husband and wife or father and daughter. Also in his line of vision were Carol and Larry Lanspeak with a fresh-faced young woman and the bearded doctor who had been Hixie Rice's escort for the last six months. All four seemed inordinately happy, leading Qwilleran to mumble a question to Polly. She replied that the young woman was Dr. Diane, the Lanspeaks' daughter, who had escaped the medical madness Down Below and had returned to Moose County to go into practice with Dr. Herbert.

Polly said, "I'm transferring my medical records to Dr. Diane. I didn't like the man who replaced Dr. Melinda."

The train was rolling along at a comfortable excursion clip through typical Moose County landscape: fields of potatoes and pastures dotted with boulders and sheep.

The waiters kept pouring champagne, and Qwilleran produced a bag of snacks to accompany the drinks. "I'd like you to taste these," he said. "A friend of mine made them."

"Who?" Polly asked too quickly.

"A woman I know in Florida." He was purposely taunting her with incomplete information.

"They're very good," Riker said. "I'll have another handful."

"They're rather salty," Polly murmured.

Mildred, who wrote the food column for the newspaper, said they were actually croutons toasted with parmesan cheese, garlic salt, red pepper, and Worcestershire sauce.

Qwilleran said, "Koko and Yum Yum think they're the cat's meow."

The food expert nodded. "They detect the anchovy in the Worcestershire."

In a far corner of the car, out of the path of the bustling waiters, a white-haired accordionist was playing show tunes with the blank demeanor of one who has played the same repertoire at thousands of banquets.

Polly said, "His lack of passion is refreshing. We attended a Mozart concert in Lockmaster where the string ensemble was so passionate, they almost fell off their chairs."

"I watched their antics," Qwilleran said, "and forgot to listen to the music."

"It's the same way in art," Mildred declared. "The artist is becoming more important than the art. I blame the media."

"We get blamed for everything," Riker said.

They discussed the curriculum at the Moose County Community College: No music. No art. Plenty of English, accounting, data processing, office systems, and business management. Introductory courses in psychology, economics, history, sociology, etc. No cosmetology. No real estate. No tennis.

Polly said, "They're making giant strides with the remodeling of the campus. The administration offices are staffed and operating, and I introduced myself to the president. Dr. Prelligate is a very interesting man."

"In what way?" Qwilleran asked bluntly.

"He combines a solid academic background with a most congenial personality. He's from Virginia and has that ingratiating Southern charm."

"I adore Southern men," Mildred said girlishly. "Is he married?"

"I don't believe so."

"But *you are!*" Riker informed his wife.

Polly had more to report. "Dr. Prelligate's staff has been feeding a dirty orange-and-white stray who looks exactly like Oh Jay. I phoned the Wilmots and learned that Oh Jay disappeared last November, right after they moved from Goodwinter Boulevard."

Riker said, "That's called 'psi trailing.' He's been on the road nine months, panhandling and living off the land! That's a fifteen-mile hike!"

"Well, the Wilmots said he can stay on campus," Polly said in conclusion, "and he's going to be the college mascot."

"And the school colors," Qwilleran guessed, "will be orange and dirty white."

The soup course was served: jellied beef consommé. It was rather salty, according to Polly. The Chateaubriand was an excellent cut of beef, and everyone agreed that neither the meat nor the chef could have come from Mudville.

Meanwhile, the cars rolled gently from side to side, the whistle blew at grade crossings, and the conversation in the dining room was animated. Eventually the landscape became craggy, and there were dramatic views never seen from the highway. The tracks ran through the town of Wildcat, then down a steep grade to the Black Creek gorge, and across a high bridge. Now they were in Lockmaster County with its rolling hills and lush woods. By the time the cheesecake and coffee had been served, the train pulled into

Flapjack, an early lumber camp converted into a public recreation park.

The TV crew from Minneapolis was waiting. They wanted to video the train owner with his handsome companion on the observation platform of the private car, but Trevelyan vetoed that. He preferred to put on a striped railroad cap and lean out of the engineer's cab. In addition, there were sound bites of the Chicago heiress in her soufflé of a hat and Whannell Mac-Whannell in his kilt, each describing the thrill of riding behind old No. 9.

Polly told the portly Scot that he cut a magnificent figure in his tartan, and she wished Qwilleran would buy a kilt.

"Your man has the right build," Big Mac assured her, "and his mother was a Mackintosh, so he's entitled."

Riker explained with the authority of an old friend, "It's the idea of wearing a skirt that bugs Qwill, and you'll never convince him otherwise."

Qwilleran was relieved when Dwight Somers put an end to the kilt claptrap by inviting them to see the private railcar. "The corporate jet of its day!" he said.

No one was prepared for its splendor: the richly upholstered wing chairs in the lounge, the dining table inlaid with exotic woods, the bedrooms with brass beds and marble lavatories. All of the woodwork was carved walnut, and the window transoms and light fixtures were Tiffany glass.

Dwight said, "The Lumbertown Party Train would be great for a wedding. Have the ceremony in the club car and the reception in the diner en route to Flapjack. Then uncouple the private car and leave the newlyweds on a siding for a week, with access to the golf course, riding stables, hiking trails, and so forth. At the end of the week the train returns with the wedding guests whooping it up in the club car, and they all huff-puff-puff back to Moose County and live happily ever after. . . . You should keep it in mind, Qwill," he added slyly.

Ignoring the remark, Qwilleran asked with mock innocence, "Is the woman with Floyd his bookkeeping daughter?"

"No, that's his knee-crossing secretary," Dwight said with a polite leer. "He met her in Texas while he was shopping for rolling stock."

"Was she a cheerleader?"

"Something like that" was the cryptic reply.

The brass bell of No. 9 clanged, and the commanding voice of the conductor swept the passengers back on board. As the train chugged north, waiters handed out souvenir whistles—long wooden tubes that duplicated the shrill scream of a steam loco-motive. For a while the dining car reverberated with ear-splitting noise. Then the accordionist started playing requests. Mildred asked for "The Second Time Around." Qwilleran requested "Time Af-ter Time" for Polly. She might not know the lyrics, but the melody was unmistakably affectionate.

By the time the train rumbled through the outskirts of Pickax, the excitement was winding down, and conversation reverted to the usual: "Are you going to the boat races? . . . Have you tried the new restaurant in Mooseville? . . . How are your cats, Qwill?"

"After a lifetime of sharing a dinner plate with Koko," he re-plied, "Yum Yum suddenly demands separate dishes. I don't know what's going on in that little head."

Mildred said, "She's had her catsciousness raised."

Qwilleran groaned, Polly shuddered, and Arch said, "There are good puns and bad puns, and that's the worst I've ever heard. . . . Conductor! Throw this lady off the train!"

Then he asked Polly about her house.

"They're supposed to pour the concrete this week. Once the trenches are dug for the footings, they don't lose any time because a rainstorm could cause an earthslide. It's all so exciting! I've always lived in small, rented units, but now I'll have a guest room and family room and two-car garage."

"Who's your builder?"

"The name on the contract is Edward P. Trevelyan. He's a big shaggy fellow with a full beard and a mop of black hair, and his grammar is atrocious! Incidentally, his father owns this train."

Finally No. 9 whistled at the grade crossings of Sawdust City, and the historic ride ended with a great hissing of steam. The valets in red jumpsuits ran for the parked cars, and the passengers drove back to Pickax, Mooseville, West Middle Hummock, and Purple

Point. Qwilleran drove Polly home to Goodwinter Boulevard, now cluttered with paving equipment, piles of lumber, and other signs of campus renovation.

Polly said, "This has been a delightful afternoon, dear."

"Glad you enjoyed it. You look particularly attractive today."

"Thank you. I'm feeling more relaxed now that work on the house has actually started. It bothers me, though, that I can't understand the architect's plans with their abbreviations and arcane symbols. I'd appreciate it if you'd come up and look at the blueprints."

When Qwilleran finally left Polly's apartment, it was eleven P.M. and time for the nightly news. He tuned in the car radio in time to hear the WPKX announcer say, ". . . paid $500 a ticket to ride behind the historic No. 9 steam locomotive on the SC&L Line, netting the Moose County Community College more than $16,000 for scholarships. Popular-priced excursions on the new Party Train will be announced, according to spokesperson Dwight Somers. . . . In local baseball, Lockmaster walloped Pickax nine to four, with the Safecrackers hitting two homers, one with bases loaded. . . . Next, the weather, after this late bulletin from Sawdust City: A surprise move by the state banking commission has padlocked the Lumbertown Credit Union, pending a state audit. No further details are available at this time."

CHAPTER 4

The morning after the train ride and the afterglow at Polly's apartment, nothing disturbed Qwilleran's deep sleep until the telephone rang at nine o'clock. He had slept through the yowling demands coming from the top balcony; he had slept through the rumble of the cement mixing truck down the lane. He thought it was predawn when he said his sleepy hello into the bedside phone.

"What's the matter? Aren't you up yet?" Arch Riker shouted at him. "All hell's breaking loose! Didn't you hear the news from Sawdust City?"

"Only on the radio last night," Qwilleran replied with a lack of energy or interest. "Any more news?"

"Only that Floyd Trevelyan can't be reached for clarification. It sounds like a bust! It must be a major case to warrant surprise action like this—on a Sunday, for Pete's sake!"

Always grouchy before his first cup of coffee, Qwilleran replied with irritable sarcasm, "I can imagine a SWAT team of bookkeepers in business suits and knit ties, armed with portable computers, parachuting down on the Lumbertown office and kicking in the doors."

"You're not taking this seriously," the publisher rebuked him. "Consider the timing! It happened while the evening excursion was in progress. The Capitol gang evidently knew the schedule of the Party Train."

"Thanks to Dwight Somers's hype, everyone in three states knew the schedule."

"Anyway, we'll soon find out what it's all about. Junior is contacting the state banking commission, and Roger's on his way to Sawdust City, via Trevelyan's home in West Middle Hummock. We'll have a story for the front page, and if my hunches are right, it'll bump the Party Train to page three. . . . Talk to you later."

Now that Qwilleran was awake, more or less, he pressed the Start button on the coffee maker and shuffled up the ramp to release the Siamese from their loft. As soon as he opened their door, they shot out of the room like feline cannonballs and streaked down to the kitchen. Qwilleran followed obediently.

"Yow-ow-ow!" Koko howled upon arriving at the feeding station and finding the plate empty.

"N-n-now!" echoed Yum Yum.

As Qwilleran opened a can of red salmon, crushed the bones with a fork, removed the black skin, and arranged it on *two plates,* he thought, Cats don't fight for their rights; they take them for granted. They have a right to be fed, watered, stroked on demand, and supplied with a lap and a clean commode . . . and if they don't

get their rights, they quietly commit certain acts of civil disobedience. . . . Tyrants!

The two gobbling heads were so intent on their salmon that
even the loud bell of the kitchen phone failed to disturb them.

This time the call was from Polly. "Qwill, did you hear
about the state audit in Sawdust City? What do you think of
the timing?"

"It looks fishy," he said, having gulped his first cup of coffee
and geared up his usual cynicism. "Any crank can call the hotline
to the state auditor's office and blow the whistle on a state-
regulated institution. One of the universities was investigated for
misuse of funds, you remember, and it was a false alarm—the work
of an anonymous tipster. In Trevelyan's case, the tip could be a
spiteful hoax perpetrated by a customer who was refused a loan."

"That's terrible!" she said.

"In a way," he said, "it's better to embarrass the management
than to barge into the office with a semiautomatic and wipe out
innocent depositors."

"Oh, Qwill! Things like that don't happen up here."

"Times are changing," he said ominously.

There was a pause on the line before she said softly, "I slept
beautifully last night. It was a wonderfully relaxing day and evening—just what I needed. I've been worrying too much about my
house."

"No need to worry, Polly. I'll keep an eye on the action at the
end of the trail—when I go down to the mailbox—and I'll keep
you informed."

"Thank you, dear. À bientôt!"

"À bientôt."

Qwilleran poured another mug of the blockbuster brew he
called coffee and sat down at the telephone desk to call a number
in Indian Village. "Dwight, this is Qwill," he said soberly.

"Oh, God! Oh, God!" the publicity man wailed. "What the
hell's going on? I didn't hear the news until this morning, on the
air. I called Floyd's number in West Middle Hummock, but he
wasn't home."

"Who answered?"

"His wife. She sounded as if she didn't know anything had happened, and I didn't want to be the messenger bringing bad news."

"I didn't meet his wife when I was there."

"She usually stays in her room, confined to a wheelchair. I don't know exactly what her problem is, but it's one of those new diseases with a multisyllabic name and no known cure. What a shame! All that money, and she can't enjoy it."

"Hmmm," Qwilleran murmured with a mixture of sympathy and curiosity. "So what happened? Could she tell you where he was or when he'd be back?"

"Well, she's quite frail and speaks in a weak voice that's hard to understand, but I gathered that he came home last night and went out again. Just between you and me, I think it's not unusual for him to stay out all night. Anyway, the nurse took the phone away from Mrs. T and told me not to upset her patient. So I asked to speak to the daughter, but she wasn't home either. The way it works: A nurse comes every morning, a companion every afternoon, and the daughter stays with her mother overnight."

"Sad situation," Qwilleran said. "Do you know anything about matters in Sawdust City?"

"No more than you do. You know, Qwill, I worked my tail off, getting that show on the road yesterday—"

"And you did a brilliant job, Dwight. Everything was perfectly coordinated."

"And then this bomb dropped! Talk about suspicious timing! It couldn't be purely coincidental."

"Is Floyd mixed up in politics?"

"Why do you ask?"

"Has he made any enemies in the state bureaucracy? Did he support the wrong candidate for the legislature?"

"Not that I know of. Maybe he distributed a little judicious graft here and there; he had no trouble getting a liquor license for the train, you know. But no. He's bored with politics. If it doesn't have steel wheels and run on steel tracks, he's not interested."

Qwilleran said, "I'm sorry about this for your sake, Dwight. Let's hope it's a false alarm."

"Yeah . . . well . . . it was a kick in the head for me, after I'd tried so hard to create a favorable image for Floyd *and* Lumbertown *and* Sawdust City.''

"One question: Was Floyd a passenger on the six o'clock train?"

"No, he had to go home and take care of his wife—*he said!* I went on both runs, and I've had enough accordion music to last my lifetime!''

"Arch has the staff digging for facts, so it'll be in the first edition if anything develops. If you hear any rumors, feel free to bounce them off a sympathetic ear. And good luck, whatever the outcome, Dwight.''

"Thanks for calling, Qwill. How about lunch later in the week when I've finished licking my wounds?"

When the *Moose County Something* appeared, the front page was not what Qwilleran had been led to expect. The Party Train had the banner headline:

JOY IN MUDVILLE

OLD NO. 9 ROLLS AGAIN!

The Lumbertown crisis was played down with only a stickful of type in a lower corner of the page: Sawdust C.U. Closed for Audit. Either there was no alarming development, or the editor had chosen not to throw the depositors into panic. That was small-town newspaper policy. Riker, with his background on large metropolitan dailies, preferred the eye-grabbing, heart-stopping, hair-raising headline; Junior Goodwinter, born and bred 400 miles north of everywhere, had other ideas, rooted in local custom. He always said, "Don't try to make bad news worse.''

Qwilleran was pondering this viewpoint over a ham sandwich at Lois's Luncheonette when Roger MacGillivray blustered into the restaurant and flung himself into the booth where Qwilleran was reading the paper.

"I suppose you're wondering why we didn't play it up," the young reporter said.

"You're right. I did . . . Why?"

"Because there was nothing to report! Junior was stonewalled when he called the commission, and no one in Mudville would talk to me. Two state vehicles were parked behind the Lumbertown building, and there was a notice plastered on the front door with some legal gobbledy-gook, but the doors were locked front and back, and the dirty dogs completely ignored my knocking. Also they refused to answer when I called from a phone booth. Before I left, I got a shot of the building exterior with some old geezers standing on the sidewalk in a huddle. I also got a close-up of the official notice on the door, and another one of the license plate on a state car. . . . How's that for brilliant photojournalism?" he finished with a bitter laugh.

"They didn't use any photos," Qwilleran said, tapping his newspaper.

"I know, but you have to hand in *something,* just so they know you've been there."

"Could you see through the window?"

"I could see auditors at work stations, that's all. But then I talked to the old geezers and got some man-on-the-street stuff, which I phoned in, and which they didn't print."

"Maybe later," Qwilleran said encouragingly. "What did the old geezers say?"

"Well! It was an eye-opener, I thought. First of all, they like Floyd. He's the local boy who was captain of the high school football team, started to work as a carpenter, and made millions! They like the interest he pays. They like the electric trains in the lobby. They think this underhanded action on the part of vipers in the state capitol is unfair and probably in violation of the Constitution. They don't trust government agencies."

"Did you try to reach Floyd's secretary?"

"Yeah, but no luck. When I asked the old geezers about her, they sniggered like schoolkids. Anyway, they told me she lives in Indian Village, so I phoned out there. No answer. I went to Floyd's house. He wasn't there, and no one would talk or even open the door more than an inch. It's been a frustrating day so far, Qwill. On days like this I'd like to be back in the school system, teaching history to kids who couldn't care less."

After his conversation with Roger, Qwilleran did a few errands before returning home. Whenever he walked about downtown, he was stopped by strangers who read the "Qwill Pen" or recognized him from the photo at the top of his column. They always complimented him on his writing and his moustache, not necessarily in that order. In the beginning he had welcomed reader comments, hoping to learn something of value, but his expectations were crushed by the nature of their remarks:

"I loved your column yesterday, Mr. Q. I forget what it was about, but it was very good."

"How do you think all that stuff up?"

"My cousin in Delaware writes for a paper. Would you like me to send you some of her clippings?"

"Why do you spell your name like that?"

Now, whenever he was complimented, he would express his thanks without making eye contact; it was eye contact that led to monologues about out-of-state relatives. Instead, he would say a pleased thank-you and turn his head aside as if modestly savoring the compliment. He had become a master at the gracious turnoff. Fifty percent of the time it worked.

On this day the situation was quite different. While he was waiting in line to cash a check at the Pickax People's Bank, a security guard hailed him. "Hi, Mr. Q."

Immediately the young woman ahead of him in the line turned and said, "You're Mr. Qwilleran! Reading your column is like listening to music! Whatever the subject, your style of writing makes me feel good." There was not a word about his moustache.

Surprised and pleased, he made eye contact with a plain young woman of serious mien, probably in her early twenties. "Thank you," he said graciously without turning away. "I write my column for readers like you. Apparently you know something about the craft. Are you a teacher?"

"No, just a constant reader. I have one of your columns pasted on my mirror. You gave three rules for would-be writers: write, write, and write. I'm a would-be, and I'm following your advice."

There was not a word about sending him a manuscript for evaluation and advice.

"Have you thought of enrolling at the new college?" he asked. "They're offering some writing courses . . . and there are scholarships available," he added, with a glance at her plain and well-worn shirt, her lack of makeup, her limp canvas shoulder bag.

"I'd like to do that, but I'm rather tied down right now."

"Then I wish you well, Ms. . . . . what is your name?"

Her hesitant reply was mumbled. It sounded like Letitia Pen.

"P-e-n-n, as in Pennsylvania?" he asked and added with humorous emphasis, "Is that a *pen name*?"

"It's my own name, unfortunately," she said with a grimace. "I hate 'Letitia.' "

"I know what you mean. My parents named me Merlin, and my best friend was Archibald. As Merlin and Archibald we suffered the slings and arrows of outrageous first-graders."

"It's not as terrible as Letitia and Lionella, though. That's the name of my best friend."

"At least you could do a nightclub act. Can you sing? Dance? Tell jokes?"

Letitia giggled. The two of them were the only ones in the bank line who were enjoying the wait. The man behind Qwilleran cleared his throat loudly. The bank teller rapped on the counter to get Letitia's attention and said, *"Next!"*

Ms. Penn turned and stepped quickly to the window, saying a soft "I'm sorry."

Qwilleran advanced a few steps also, shortening the long line behind them; the bank was always rushed on Mondays and Fridays. Ahead of him his constant reader seemed to be withdrawing a substantial sum. He could see over her shoulder. The teller counted the bills twice. "Fifty, a hundred, hundred-fifty, two hundred, two-fifty . . ."

"I'd like an envelope for that," said Ms. Penn.

"There you are," said the teller. "Have a nice day, Ms. Trevelyan."

"Constant reader" stuffed the money into her shoulder bag and left the bank hurriedly.

That, Qwilleran observed, was a curious development. Why would she choose not to give her right name? Before leaving the bank, he consulted the local telephone directory and found seventy-five Trevelyans but no Letitia. There were no Penns at all—not that it mattered; it was one of the pointless things he did to satisfy his idle curiosity. After that, he walked home with a lighter step, buoyed by the knowledge that his twice-weekly words were not totally forgotten and might even be doing some good. He walked via the back road to pick up his mail and check Polly's building site.

There were no trucks and no workmen, but concrete had been poured and smoothly troweled. She had decided on a crawl space instead of a basement, and on a poured foundation instead of concrete block—this after extensive reading on the subject. On one of their recent dinner dates she had explained, "A poured foundation gives a stronger wall with less danger of cracks and leaks. Did you know they are supposed to leave a groove in the footings to tie in a poured concrete wall?" And after dinner they had visited the building site to check the grooves.

Now the walls had been poured, and Qwilleran phoned Polly at the library to report.

"Thank you for letting me know," she said. "Now I feel the project is finally under way."

"Yes, you have something concrete to show for all your planning," he said lightly.

"I wonder how long it takes to dry before they can start the framing. Mr. Trevelyan uses platform framing construction. I must phone him tomorrow morning to see if he spaces the joists on twelve-, sixteen-, or twenty-four-inch centers."

"I'd go with twelve-inch, considering the way Bootsie goes around stamping his feet," Qwilleran said in another attempt to amuse her.

With worry in her voice she said, "Will I regret my decision to eliminate the fireplace? It makes a charming focal point, but it adds to the initial cost and then creates extra work if one burns wood, and I would never consider the gas-fired type."

"Be of good cheer," he said. "I have three fireplaces, and you're welcome to come and enjoy one or more at any hour of the day or night. I'll chop the wood, keep the logs burning, and haul the ashes. Reservations should be made an hour in advance." He was doing his best to divert her, without success, and the conversation ended with frustration on Qwilleran's part.

He turned from the telephone to his stack of mail. An envelope with an Illinois postmark caught his eye:

Dear Chief,

I got your letter about the Kabibbles and almost died laughing. Glad you like them. I'll send some more. You can see by the envelope I've left Florida. I'm back on my son's farm. Sorry to say, I don't get along too good with my daughter-in-law—she's such a sourpuss—and you may think I'm crazy, but I'm thinking of moving to Pickax. It sounds very nice. I know you get lots of snow, but I love to throw snowballs at the side of a barn. I'd need to somehow find a furnished room because I sold everything when I moved to Florida, and maybe I could find a part-time job—cleaning houses or waiting on tables. I'd like to sort of give it a try for a year anyway. What do you think?

Yours truly
Celia Robinson

She gave a phone number, and Qwilleran called immediately without waiting for the evening discount rates as he was prone to do. The phone rang and rang, and he let it ring while fragments of thought teased his brain: Celia could cook . . . Did he need a live-in housekeeper? . . . No, he liked his privacy . . . Some macaroni and cheese, though . . . Some meatloaf for the cats . . .

He was wondering about Celia's mashed potatoes when a woman's harassed voice shouted a breathless hello.

In a menacing monotone he said, "I'd like to speak to Mrs. Celia Robinson."

"She's out back, collecting eggs. Who's calling?"

"Tell her it's the Chief."

"Who?"

"Chief of the Florida Bureau of Investigation," Qwilleran said with his talent for impromptu fabrication.

The receiver was put down abruptly, and a woman's voice could be heard shouting, "Clay, go and get Grandma quick. Tell her to hurry!"

There was a long wait, and then he could hear Celia's laughter before she reached the phone. "Hello, Chief," she said happily. "You must've got my letter."

"I did indeed, and it's a splendid idea! Your grandson can spend Christmas with you, and you can have snowball fights. How is Clayton?"

"He's fine. Just got back from science camp. He won a scholarship."

"Good! Now to answer your questions: Yes, you'll have no trouble finding part-time work. Yes, you can find a furnished apartment. There's one close to downtown, if you don't mind walking up a flight of stairs."

"I don't want to pay too much rent."

"No problem. The owner will be only too happy to have the premises occupied."

"Could I bring my cat? You remember Wrigley, from Chicago."

"By all means. I'll look forward to meeting him." He waited for her merry laughter to subside before asking, "Do you have transportation?"

"Oh, you should see the cute little used car I bought, Chief! It's bright red! I bought it with your check. I didn't expect you to send so much. It was fun helping you."

"You performed a valuable service, Celia. And now . . . Don't waste any of our glorious summer weather. Plan on coming soon. I'll send you the directions."

"Oh, I'm all excited!" she crowed, and he could hear her happy laughter as she hung up.

The apartment he had in mind was a four-room suite in the carriage house behind the former Klingenschoen mansion, now the K Theatre. It was imposing in its own right, being constructed of glistening fieldstone with carriage lanterns at all four corners and four stalls for vehicles. Qwilleran had lived there while his barn was being remodeled, and it was still equipped with his basic bachelor-style furnishings in conservative colors.

After talking to Celia, he tore into action, his first call being to Fran Brodie at the design studio. She had selected the original furnishings and also those in the barn.

"Fran, drop everything—will you?—and do a quick facelift on my old apartment . . . No, I'm not moving back into it. A woman who was a friend of Euphonia Gage in Florida has been advised by her doctor to move up here for the salubrious climate."

"Well! I never heard anything like that!" Fran exclaimed. "Perhaps we should open a health spa. What kind of person is she?"

"A fun-loving grandmother, who has a cat and drives a red car. . . . Yes, I agree the place needs some color—and some feminine fripperies, if you'll pardon the political faux pas. The cats' old hangout should be made over into a guest room for her teenage grandson, and my Pullman kitchen should be replaced by a full-scale cooking facility, with an oven big enough to roast a turkey. How fast can you do this? She'll be here in ten days."

"Ten days!" Fran yelped into the phone. "You're a dreamer! Free-standing appliances are no problem, and we can get stock cabinets from Lockmaster, but there's the labor for installing countertops, flooring, lighting—"

"Offer the workmen a bonus," Qwilleran said impatiently. "Get them to work around the clock! Send me the bill." He knew Fran liked a challenge; she prided herself on doing the impossible.

Breaking the news to Polly required more finesse, however. He called her at home that evening. "How did everything go today?" he asked pleasantly. "I see they painted the yellow lines on the library parking lot."

"Yes, but that wasn't the main event of the day," she said. "Mr. Tibbitt's seat cushion developed a slow leak and whistled every time he moved. It could be heard on the main floor, and the clerks were in hysterics. It *was* rather amusing in a bawdy way." Polly trilled a little discreet laughter.

Finding her in a good mood, Qwilleran broached the real subject on his mind. "I know your assistant likes to moonlight on her day off. Would she be willing to act as mentor for a new resident of Pickax?"

"What would it entail?"

"Driving someone around town and pointing out the stores, churches, restaurants, civic buildings, medical center, and so forth. Information on local customs would be appreciated—also city ordinances, like 'No whistling in public.' And she might throw in some current gossip," he added slyly, knowing that Virginia Alstock was the main fuse in the Pickax gossip circuit.

"Who is this person?" Polly asked crisply.

Expecting the third degree, Qwilleran roguishly teased her with piecemeal replies. "A friend of Junior's grandmother in Florida."

"Why would anyone in his or her right mind leave the subtropics to live in the Snow Belt? Is this person male or female?"

"Female."

There was a brief pause. "Where is she going to live?"

"In my old apartment."

"Oh, really? I didn't know it was available for rent. How did she find out about it?"

"The subject of housing arose in a telephone conversation, and I offered it to her."

There was another pause. "You must know her quite well."

"As a matter of fact," he said, thinking the game had gone on long enough, "she was instrumental in solving the mystery surrounding Euphonia's death."

"I see. . . . How old is she?"

"Polly, I never ask a lady her age. You know that."

There was an audible sniff. "Approximately."

"Well . . . old enough to have a teenage grandson . . . and young enough to like snowball fights."

"What is this woman's name?"

"Celia Robinson, and I'll appreciate it, Polly, if you'll alert Mrs. Alstock. Mrs. Robinson will be here in about ten days."

Qwilleran chuckled to himself after hanging up the receiver. He could imagine the gabby Mrs. Robinson and the gossipy Mrs. Alstock having lunch at Lois's Luncheonette.

For the next few days he made discreet inquiries, wherever he went, about parttime work for a newcomer. One day he met Lisa Compton in the post office. She worked at the Senior Care Facility, and her husband was superintendent of schools; between them they could provide answers for most questions.

Qwilleran mentioned his quest, and Lisa asked, "Does this woman have a warm, outgoing personality?"

"She's got it in spades," he said.

"Do you know about our new outreach program? It's called Pals for Patients. We supply Pals to home-bound Patients; the Patients pay us, and we pay the Pals, minus a small commission for booking and collecting. Patients who can't afford to pay are subsidized by the Klingenschoen Foundation. You probably know all about that."

"That's what you think," Qwilleran said. "No one tells me these things. . . . Was the program your brainchild?"

"No, it was Irma Hasselrich's last great idea. I merely implemented it," said Lisa. "What's your friend's name?"

Qwilleran hesitated, knowing that a bulletin would flash across the Pickax grapevine: *Mr. Q has a new friend.* He explained his hesitation by saying glibly, "Her last name is Robinson. Her first name is Sadie or Celia—something like that. We've never met. She was a dear friend of Euphonia Gage in Florida, who said Celia—or Sadie—had an exceptionally warm and outgoing personality."

"Okay. Send her to me when she arrives. We'll put her name on the list."

"She'll appreciate it, I'm sure. How's your grouchy old husband, Lisa?"

"Believe it or not, he's happy as a lark. You know Lyle's perverse temperament. Well, he's tickled to see Floyd Trevelyan in trouble. They've been enemies ever since Floyd sued the school board for expelling his son."

As it turned out, Floyd was in more trouble than anyone imagined, and the *Moose County Something* could gloat over its first front-page coverage of a financial scandal.

The Lumbertown Credit Union was closed indefinitely and its

assets frozen, pending a hearing before the state banking commission on charges of fraud.

Millions of dollars belonging to depositors were allegedy missing.

Also missing were the president of the institution and his secretary.

CHAPTER 5

News of the Mudville scandal broke in mid-morning, enabling the *Moose County Something* to remake the front page. Arch Riker phoned Qwilleran for help with rewrites and phones. "And listen, Qwill: Stop at Toodles' and pick up a few bottles of champagne."

Suffused with a newsman's urge to disinter the story behind the story, Qwilleran left in a hurry, although not without waving good-bye to the Siamese. He told them where he was going and when he might return, as if they cared. After their breakfast they could be infuriatingly blasé. Yum Yum merely sat on her brisket and gave him a glassy stare; Koko walked away and was heard scratching in the commode.

At the newspaper office the mood was one of jubilation. Rarely did breaking news break on their deadline. Ordinarily the public heard it first from the electronic media—sketchily, but first. Not until the next day would the newspaper come in a poor second. True, they were able to publish photos, sidelights, background facts, quotes from individuals involved, and opinions from casual observers. After all, the *Moose County Something* claimed to be the north-country newspaper of record. "Read all about it" was their slogan, recalling the cry of the oldtime corner newshawker.

When the presses were finally rolling, the champagne corks popped in celebration. If Qwilleran remembered his own exuberant days of champagne-squirting Down Below, it was without any wishful pangs of yearning. He was simply glad to be where he was when he was—and who he was.

Eventually Riker's booming voice announced, "Enough hilarity! Back to reality!" The staff calmed down and went to work, and Qwilleran went on his way, leaving his car in the parking lot and walking around town to do his own snooping.

First he went to the police station to see his friend Andrew Brodie, but the chief was absent—probably meeting with state and county lawmen to organize a manhunt, and womanhunt.

Qwilleran's next stop was Amanda's Studio of Interior Design on Main Street. Amanda was not there, but Fran Brodie was holding the fort attractively, sitting at a French writing table with her long slender legs crossed and her double-hoop earrings dangling. She had been one of the seductive young women who pursued Qwilleran when he arrived in Pickax to claim his inheritance. Only Polly Duncan remained in the running; in this case, he had done the pursuing. Fran was still a friend and confidante, however. He admired her talent as a designer, her dedication to the theatre club, and her strawberry blond hair. Also, she was the daughter of the police chief and an occasional source of privileged information.

When he entered the shop, she saw him immediately and turned her face away, groaning loudly—a bit of theatre-club pantomime.

"Is it as bad as all that?" Qwilleran asked. He knew that the studio had handled the renovation of the Party Train.

"That rat owes us tens of thousands!" she wailed. "Amanda's at the attorney's office right now. Floyd had signed a contract for the work, and we never dreamed he'd run out on it."

"Were the rail coaches the only work you'd done for him?"

"No. The first was the Lumbertown office, and he liked it. Maybe you've seen how we duplicated the atmosphere of an old railway depot. He had just sold his construction firm to XYZ Enterprises and had tons of money. He paid the bill in thirty days."

"And what about his house in West Middle Hummock? I had a glimpse of it when I interviewed him about the model trains. The interior didn't look like you; it looked like Mudville thrift shop."

"Well, *he said* his wife didn't want any professional help with the house. That meant one of two things: Either he'd rather spend the money on model trains, or Mrs. T was too ill to care. We accepted that. Apparently Floyd himself didn't care how the house looked as long as the bar was well stocked. I don't know who drinks all that stuff. I think they never have company. Maybe Floyd has drinking buddies from Sawdust City. . . . But then, he commissioned us to do the interiors of the PV and the diner and the club car, and believe me, they needed a lot of doing!"

"You did a beautiful job, Fran."

"Well, why not? He was willing to spend a fortune . . ."

"And you thought you were on the gravy train," Qwilleran said sympathetically.

Fran groaned again. "I'm afraid Amanda will have a stroke. You know how excitable she is."

"Did you work directly with Floyd on the cars?"

"No. With his secretary—or assistant—or whatever she is. Nice person. Good to work with. Nella Hooper has fine taste. When Floyd wanted something flashy, she toned him down."

"I saw her on the Party Train. Very attractive. Know anything about her background?"

"Only that she's from Texas. She never wanted to talk about herself, and I know when not to ask questions. Floyd had me do her apartment in Indian Village and gave me carte blanche to spend money. She wanted a southwestern theme."

"How about your father, Fran? Has he had anything to say about the embezzlement?"

"It's too soon."

"Or the disappearance of the principals?"

"Too soon."

The way it worked: The police chief would come home from his shift and talk shop with his wife at the kitchen table; then, when Fran made her daily phone call to her mother, Mrs. Brodie would pass along some tidbit of information in strict confidence; later, if Qwilleran dropped into the studio looking genuinely concerned and utterly trustworthy, Fran would feel free to confide in him. She was aware that he had helped the police on several occasions, behind the scenes.

"It's too early for any scuttlebutt," Fran said, "although I haven't called home yet. Why don't you come to rehearsal tonight? By that time I might have heard something."

"Will Derek Cuttlebrink be there?" Qwilleran asked. "He's on my list of leads to interview."

"He'll be there. So will his latest girlfriend."

"You mean—Elizabeth Appelhardt?"

"She prefers to be called Elizabeth Hart now."

"I must say they're an odd couple."

"But they're good for each other," Fran said. "She's talked him into enrolling at the college, and Derek is gradually nudging her into the mainstream. When you first brought her from the island, she was in a world of her own."

"Please! I didn't bring her here," Qwilleran said gruffly. "She happened to be on the same boat."

"Whatever," the designer said with raised eyebrows. "She's started wearing natural makeup and patronizing my hairdresser, and now she looks less like a character in a horror movie."

"I hear she's joined the club. That'll be good for her."

"Good for us, too! She has some fresh ideas for costumes and staging, although I expect some opposition from our older members."

"Any other news?"

"I'm doing an apartment in Indian Village for Dr. Diane—country French, lots of blue. She seems to have replaced Hixie in Dr. Herbert's life, but here's an off-twist: When Hixie broke her foot, she stayed with Dr. Herbert's mother until she could walk, and now Dr. Diane is staying with his mother until her apartment is ready."

Qwilleran said, "I'm sure there's some underlying significance to that fact, but it escapes me. . . . I like that paperweight. What is it supposed to be?" He pointed to a fanciful chunk of tarnished brass on Fran's desk.

"That's Cerberus," Fran told him. "The three-headed dog that guarded the gates of Hades in ancient mythology. Amanda picked it up at an estate sale in Chicago. It belonged to a wealthy meat-packer."

The detail was meticulous, even to the snakes that formed the dog's mane and tail. Qwilleran often bought a small object in the design studio; it pleased Fran, and it was advantageous to please the daughter of the police chief.

"If you like it," she said, "I'll give you a price on it and shine it up for you."

"I like it," he said, "but I have some other stops to make. How about shining it up and bringing it to the rehearsal tonight?"

As Qwilleran left the studio, he was chuckling to himself in anticipation of the cats' reaction to the grotesque bauble. They were always aware of any new item that arrived in their territory.

His next stop was the office of MacWhannell & Shaw. There was a question he wanted to ask an accountant.

Big Mac, as he was called, met him with a welcoming hand. "Just thinking about you, Qwill. We're planning Scottish Night at the lodge, and we'd like you to be our guest again."

"Thank you. I enjoyed it last year—even the haggis."

"I was telling the committee that your mother was a Mackintosh, and Gordie Shaw said you ought to join the clan officially, as a tribute, you might say, to her memory. The Shaws had Mackintosh connections, you know."

The suggestion hit Qwilleran in a tender spot. He had grown up with a single parent, and now that he was maturing he realized how much she had done for him. He could forget the piano lessons, and drying the dishes, and two-handed games of dominoes; he owed her a great deal. "What would it entail?" he asked.

"According to Gordie, you apply for membership, pay your dues, and receive a periodic newsletter. After that you probably start attending Scottish Gatherings and Highland Games."

"Sounds okay," said the writer of the "Qwill Pen" column, sensing a source of material. "Ask Gordie to send me an application."

"But I've been doing all the talking," the accountant said. "Is there anything I can do for you?"

"Just answer a question, Mac. How do you react to the Lumbertown fraud—or alleged fraud?"

"Fortunately, I have no clients who would be affected, but I sympathize with the Sawdusters. When a white collar crime is committed in a blue-collar community, it seems particularly reprehensible—to me, that is. Don't ask me why."

"At the risk of sounding financially naive, may I ask how a guy like Trevelyan can abscond with millions belonging to his customers? I'm sure he doesn't carry it out in a suitcase."

"Basically, he has to be a crook," said MacWhannell, "but if you're talking about ways and means, well . . . there are such practices as juggling the books, forging documents, falsifying financial statements, and so forth."

"Floyd is, or was, a carpenter by trade," Qwilleran pointed out. "Would he have such educated tricks in his toolbox?"

"Sounds as if there was an accomplice, doesn't it? This will be an interesting case. With today's crime information networks, he'll be found soon enough."

Leaving the accountant's office, Qwilleran passed the department store and saw Carol Lanspeak on the sidewalk, waving her arms and shouting. She was directing the setup of a clothing display in the main window, giving terse but loud instructions to an assistant inside the glass, while the young woman mouthed replies.

Catching Qwilleran's reflection in the plate glass, Carol turned and explained, "The one inside the window can hear the one outside, but not vice versa." She waved to her helper and told her to take a break. "This is our last window before back-to-school, Qwill. How time flies! And oh! Weren't you shocked by the news from Sawdust City? Some of our employees live there, and they're Lumbertown depositors. What will happen? When this has occurred elsewhere in the country, it's been a real disaster."

Qwilleran said, "If the guy is a swindler and a fugitive, can't his assets be liquidated to cover debts and embezzled funds? He has a big house in the Hummocks near you, and a model train layout that's worth a mint, and the Party Train. That alone must be valued in the millions."

"But the justice system is so slow, Qwill! And the victims are families with children, and factory workers subject to layoffs, and retirees with nest eggs on deposit. What will they do when emergencies arise?"

"Well, let me tell you something surprising," Qwilleran said. "This morning I was helping to man the phones at the paper, when our reporters were calling in man-on-the-street opinions, and the victims, as you call them, weren't blaming Trevelyan; they were blaming the government for deception and injustice! They called it a plot, a conspiracy, a dirty trick! They refused to believe that Floyd would take their money and skip. They said he'd been a high school football hero and a good carpenter; his picture hung in the lobby of the credit union; he paid daily interest; he was crazy about trains."

Carol shook her head. "Everyone in Sawdust City must be nutty from exposure to industrial pollution."

Before leaving for the rehearsal that evening, Qwilleran started to read the first few scenes of *A Midsummer Night's Dream* aloud. Both cats enjoyed the sound of his voice, whether he was reading great literature or the baseball scores. On this occasion Koko was particularly attentive and even got into the act a few times.

The first scene opened with an indignant father hauling his disobedient daughter before the duke for reprimand. *Full of vexation am I, with complaint against my daughter, Hermia.*

"Yow!" said Koko.

"That's not in the script," Qwilleran objected.

After the father had raved and ranted, the duke argued with gentle reasonableness. *What say you, Hermia? Be advised, fair maid.*

"Yow!" Koko said again.

The young woman was being forced by law to marry a man of her father's choosing, or enter a convent, or die. *Therefore, Hermia, question your desires.*

"Yow!"

Qwilleran closed the book. He said, "This is getting monotonous, if you don't mind my saying so." Later, as he walked through the Black Forest to the theatre, he construed Koko's responses as infatuation with a certain sound. To a cat, "Hermia" might have a secret meaning. Then again, Koko might be playing practical jokes; he had a sense of humor.

The K Theatre, originally the Klingenschoen mansion, was a great three-story mass of fieldstone, transformed into a two-hundred-seat amphitheatre. From the lofty foyer a pair of staircases curved up to the lobby, from which the seating sloped down to the stage. When Qwilleran arrived, the cast was doing a run-through without the book, while the director watched from the third row and scribbled notes. Other cast members were scattered throughout the auditorium, waiting for their scenes. Quietly he took a seat behind Fran Brodie.

The "rude mechanicals" were onstage: tinker, tailor, joiner, bellowsmaker, carpenter, and the six-foot-eight weaver, who delivered the final line of the scene: *Enough: Hold, or cut bowstrings.*

"Break! Take five!" Fran called out.

Qwilleran tapped her on the shoulder. "That line about bowstrings—I've never quite understood it."

"I take it to mean 'cooperate—or else,' but I don't know its origin. Ask Polly. She'll know."

Actors wandered up the aisle to get a drink of water in the lobby or stopped to ask Fran a question. As soon as she and Qwilleran were alone, she said in a low voice, "They've picked up Floyd's car. It was in that meadow where car-poolers park. It had been there all week, and the sheriff was aware of it, but Floyd wasn't on the wanted list then."

"Do you suppose someone tipped him off about the audit? Who could it be?"

"It looks as if an accomplice drove in from Indian Village and picked him up—Nella, for example. They're both missing."

"But how would she know about the audit?"

"Interesting question."

"If they're headed for Mexico," he said, "they've had a headstart of three days. She'd know a lot about Mexico, being from Texas."

"Wherever they went, they'll be found easily enough." Fran looked at her watch. "Time for the next scene. Don't go. I have more to report. . . . And do you know what? I brought your paperweight and left it in my car."

"Why don't you drive down to the barn when you're through here. I'll pour. You can bring the paperweight."

"Elizabeth Hart will be with me. Do you mind? I'm her ride tonight."

"That's fine. She's never seen the barn. . . . Is it okay to interview Derek now?"

"Sure. He won't be called for fifteen minutes."

Before interviewing the young actor, Qwilleran checked his bio in the most recent playbill:

DEREK CUTTLEBRINK. Veteran of five productions. Best remembered roles: the porter in *Macbeth* and the villain in *The Drunkard*. Lifelong resident of Wildcat. Graduate of Pickax High School, where he played basketball. Currently employed as a waiter at the Old Stone Mill. Major interests: acting, camping, folk-singing, girls.

The last of these was only too true. At performances in the K Theatre there was always a claque of Derek's girlfriends and ex-girlfriends and would-be girlfriends, ready to applaud as soon as he walked on stage. Whatever the source of his magnetism, his turn-over in female companions was of more interest than the Dow Jones averages in Pickax. Tonight Derek was sitting with his latest, Elizabeth Hart, in the back row, where they could whisper without disturbing the proceedings on stage.

Qwilleran asked her if he might borrow Derek for a brief interview in the lobby.

"May I listen in?" she asked.

"Of course."

The eccentric young woman he had met on Breakfast Island had improved her grooming, but her taste for exotic clothing had not changed. While other club members were in grungy rehearsal togs, Elizabeth wore an embroidered vest and skullcap, possibly from Ecuador, with a balloon-sleeve white silk blouse and harem pants. Their bagginess camouflaged her thinness. The interview was taped:

QWILLERAN: You're playing the role of Nick Bottom, the weaver. How do you perceive Mr. Bottom?

DEREK: You mean, what's he like? He's a funny guy, always using the wrong words and doing some dumb thing, but nothing gets him down. People like him.

ELIZABETH: (interrupting) His malapropisms are quite endearing.

DEREK: Yeah. Took the words right outa my mouth.

QWILLERAN: How does Bottom fit into the plot?

DEREK: Well, there's a wedding at the palace, and for entertainment they've got a bunch of ordinary guys to put on a play. Bottom wants to direct and play all the roles himself.

ELIZABETH: His vanity would be insufferable, if it weren't so ingratiating.

DEREK: Yeah. You can quote me. The players rehearse in the woods, and one of the little green men turns me into a donkey from the neck up. The joke of it is: the queen of the greenies falls in love with me.

ELIZABETH: She's a bewitcher who is bewitched.

DEREK: That's pretty good. Put it in.

QWILLERAN: How do you feel about little green men in a Shakespeare play?

DEREK: No problem. He called 'em fairies; we call 'em greenies. They're all aliens, right?

QWILLERAN: What is your favorite line?

DEREK: I like it when I roar like a lion . . . *Arrrrgh! Arrrrgh!* And at the end I have a death scene that's fun. *Now die, die, die, die, die.* That always gets a laugh.

Qwilleran, having completed his mission, more or less, returned to the barn through the Black Forest, listening for Marconi. It was still daylight, however, and Marconi was a night owl.

Yum Yum was waiting at the kitchen door. He picked her up and whispered affectionate words while she caressed his hand with her waving tail. Koko was not there. Koko was in the foyer, looking out the window.

The formal entrance to the barn was a double door flanked by tall, narrow windows. These sidelights had sills about twenty inches from the floor, a convenient height for a cat who wanted to stand on his hind feet and peer through the glass. There was something out there that fascinated Koko. With his neck stretched and his ears pricked, he stared down the orchard trail. Surveyors had been there and lumberyard trucks and carpenters' pickups and a cement mixer, but that was daytime activity, and there was no action after four-thirty. Yet Koko watched and waited as if expecting something to happen. His prescience was sometimes unnerving. He could sense an approaching storm, and a telephone about to ring. He often knew what Qwilleran was going to do before Qwilleran knew.

Koko also had a sense of right and wrong. The decoys on the fireplace cube, for example, were lined up facing east. One day Mrs. Fulgrove came to clean and left them facing west. Koko threw a fit!

On this summer evening he watched and waited, while Qwilleran listened to the tape of Derek's interview; to make an eight-inch think-piece out of it would require all his fictive skills. Only once was Koko lured away from the window, and that was when Derek roared like a lion.

A run-through without the book was always a long rehearsal, and it was dark when Qwilleran's guests arrived. As soon as the car headlights came bobbing along the wooded road, he floodlighted the exterior of the barn to play up its striking features: a fieldstone foundation ten feet high, three stories of weathered shingle siding, and a series of odd-shaped windows cut in the wall of the octagonal building. Visitors were usually awed.

Qwilleran put on his yellow cap and went to meet the two women, and as he opened the passenger's door Elizabeth stepped out and looked around. "You have an owl," she said. "It sounds like a great horned owl. They hoot in clusters. We had one in our woods on the island, and we used to count the hoots. The pattern varies with the season and the owl's personal agenda."

"Shall we go indoors? I'm thirsty," Fran said impatiently.

The interior was aglow. Indirect lighting accented the balconies and the beams high overhead; downlights created mysterious puddles of light on the main floor; a spotlight focused on a huge tapestry hanging from a balcony railing. Appropriately, the design was an apple tree.

As Fran gazed around in admiration, Elizabeth went looking for the cats.

Fran said, "I've been here a hundred times, and I never cease to marvel at Dennis's genius. His death was a flagrant waste of talent. If he had lived, would he have stayed in the north?"

"I doubt it," Qwilleran said. "His family was in St. Louis."

"I can't find Koko and Yum Yum," Elizabeth complained.

"They're around here somewhere, but we have an abundance of somewhere in this place. Shall we go into the lounge area and have a glass of wine or fruit juice?"

Koko, having heard his name, suddenly appeared from nowhere, followed by Yum Yum, yawning and stretching her dainty hind-quarters.

"They remember me from the island!" Elizabeth said with delight, as she dropped to her knees and extended a finger for sniffing.

Fran followed Qwilleran into the kitchen to watch him prepare wine spritzers.

"What did you want to tell me?" he asked quietly.

In a low voice she said, "The police have been questioning Floyd's associates, and they've discovered something that I consider bizarre. Have you heard of the Lockmaster Indemnity Corporation? They were supposed to be private insurers of depositors' funds in the Lumbertown Credit Union, but they're broke! They can't cover the losses!"

"How can that be? Sounds to me as if they're part of the scam."

"I don't know, but they'd transferred their assets to their wives' names. They call it estate planning. Dad calls it dirty pool."

"I'd say your dad is right. If they get away with it," Qwilleran said, "there's something radically wrong in this state!"

As he carried the tray into the lounge area—two spritzers and one club soda—Elizabeth rose gracefully from the floor. "We've been having a significant dialogue," she said. "They're glad to see me."

All five of them sat around the large square coffee table, where

Qwilleran had placed three small bowls of Kabibbles. There was also a copy of that day's *Moose County Something*. Fran commented on the in-depth coverage of the scandal, and Qwilleran gloated over the journalistic feat, while Elizabeth listened politely. She was known to have a high I.Q. and an interest in esoteric subjects, as well as a sizable trust fund, but she had no idea what was happening in the world. She avoided reading newspapers, finding them too depressing.

After a few minutes the host steered the conversation to her realm of interest. He said, "I hear you're working on costumes for the play. What do you have in mind for the fairies?"

"We call them greenies," she replied, "and the assumption is that they come from outer space. We know, of course, that extra-terrestrials have been visiting our planet for thousands of years."

"I see," he said.

"For our production they'll wear green leotards and tights, green wigs, and green makeup. We have to get parental approval for the young people to wear green makeup. The effect will be surreal, and Fran is coaching them in body movements that will make them appear amiable and slightly comic."

"How about the king and queen of the . . . greenies? Oberon and Titania usually wear something regal."

"They'll have glitter: green foil jumpsuits with swirling capes of some gossamer material—and fantastic headdresses. I really love this play," she said with eyes dancing.

Qwilleran remembered how dull her eyes had been when he first met her on the island. Moose County—or Derek—had a salutary effect. "Do you have a favorite character? If you were to play a role, what would you choose?" He expected her to choose Titania in green foil.

Her reply was prompt. "Hermia."

"Yow!" said Koko, whose ears were receiving the conversation even while his nose was tracking the Kabibbles.

"I can relate to her parent problem," Elizabeth explained, "although in my case it was my mother who insisted on ordering my life."

Fran said, "We'd have the greenies arriving in a spacecraft, if it were feasible, but we don't have the stage machinery. Larry thinks they should appear in puffs of stage smoke. Pickax audiences love stage smoke. But I'd like to see something more high-tech. Elizabeth has an idea, but I can't figure out the logistics. Tell Qwill about your pyramids, Elizabeth."

She turned to Qwilleran. "Do you know about pyramid power?"

"I've read about it—quite a long time ago."

"It's nothing new. It dates back thousands of years, and my father really believed in it. He had little pyramids built for my brothers and me, and we were supposed to sit in them to make wonderful things happen. I thought it was magic, but my mother said it was subversive. She had them destroyed after Father died." Her voice drifted off in a mist of nostalgia and regret.

Fran said, "Wally Toddwhistle can build us a portable see-through pyramid out of poles. For a scene change we'd black out the house briefly, and when the stage lights came on, there'd be a pyramid in the forest. Wouldn't it be wonderful if the poles could be neon tubes?"

Qwilleran questioned whether the audience would understand the magical implications of such a pyramid, and Fran said it would be explained in the playbill.

"How many playgoers read the program notes?" he asked. "Most of them are more interested in the ads for Otto's Tasty Eats and Gippel's Garage. That's been my observation based on preshow chitchat. How does Larry feel about it?"

"He thinks it'll clutter the stage without contributing dramatically, but we haven't given up yet, have we, Elizabeth?"

Qwilleran offered to refresh their drinks, but Fran said it was time to leave. On the way out, she handed him a black felt-tip pen. "Where did you find this?" he asked.

"On the floor near the coffee table."

"Yum Yum's at it again! She's an incorrigible cat burglar." He returned the pen to a pewter mug on the telephone table and escorted the women to their car, first putting on his yellow cap. When they had driven away, he walked around the barn a few times, reluctant to go indoors on this perfect midsummer night.

With a little suspension of disbelief one could imagine Puck and the other greenies materializing from the woods in a puff of smoke . . . A high-pitched yowl from the kitchen window reminded him that he was neglecting his duty.

"Treat!" he announced as he opened the kitchen door.

Yum Yum responded immediately, but . . . where was Koko? When he failed to report for food, there was cause for alarm. Qwilleran went in search and found him on the large square coffee table—not eating the Kabibbles, not playing with the wooden train whistle, not sniffing the book on the Panama Canal. He was sitting on the *Moose County Something* with its front page treatment of the Mudville scandal and two-column photo of the president. It was the same as the portrait hanging in the lobby of the Lumbertown Credit Union.

Koko's attitude indicated something was wrong—and not just the embezzlement. Qwilleran felt a tingling sensation on his upper lip and tamped his moustache with a heavy hand. Koko was trying to communicate. Perhaps the tipoff had been a hoax. Perhaps the auditors were trying to cover up their own mistake. Perhaps Trevelyan was being, so to speak, railroaded.

As if reading the man's mind, Koko slowly rose on four long legs, his body arched, his tail bushed. With whiskers swept back and eyes slanted, he circled the newspaper in a stiff-legged dance that sent shivers up and down Qwilleran's spine. It was Koko's death dance.

CHAPTER 6

Following Koko's macabre dance on the coffee table, Qwilleran brooded about its significance. He had seen that performance before, and it meant only one thing: death. And it pointed to Floyd Trevelyan. To Qwilleran's mind it pointed to suicide. The arrogant, self-centered, self-made man would self-

destruct rather than suffer the humility of capture, trial, and imprisonment. He was too rich, too cocky, too vain, too autocratic
to return to his hometown in handcuffs.

Qwilleran made no mention of his theory to Polly when they
had dinner Saturday night. His fanciful suspicions were always politely dismissed by the head librarian, whose mind was as fact-
intensive as the *World Almanac*. He had never told her about Koko's
supra-normal intuition either, nor his unique ways of communicating. By comparison her beloved Bootsie was a Neanderthal cat!

They had dinner at Tipsy's restaurant in North Kennebeck without referring to the scandal that had electrified Moose County.
Polly had other concerns: Would her house be ready in time for
Thanksgiving? Would the fumes of paint and vinyl and treated
wood—the "new-house smell"—be injurious to Bootsie's sensitive
system? Qwilleran's attempts to change the subjec were only temporary distractions from the major issues: insulation and roofing.

"Have you met Eddie Trevelyan?" she asked.

"Not formally," he replied. "When I walk to my mailbox, he
looks up and waves, and I say 'Lookin' good' or something original
like that. He has a helper called Benno—short, stocky fellow with
a ponytail—and a beautiful chow dog who comes to work with
him everyday and sits in the bed of Eddie's pickup or in the shade
of a tree. I tell him he's a good dog, and he pants for joy with his
tongue hanging out. His name is Zak, I found out."

There were other details that he thought it wise to omit; Polly
would only worry. There were the cigarette butts all over the property. There was the "essence of barroom" that Eddie exuded much
of the time.

"At first the men—they're both young—seemed to be enjoying
their work, bantering back and forth," Qwilleran reported. "But
now there's an air of tension that's understandable. To see one's
parent, a leading citizen, suddenly branded as a thief must be hard
to take. Eddie keeps nagging Benno to 'get the lead out' and pound
more nails. It occurs to me that he's rushing the job in order to
collect his second payment. When is it due?"

"When the house is weathered-in. Oh, dear! I hope this doesn't
mean he'll be cutting corners."

"If his operating capital is tied up in the credit union, he may be strapped for cash to meet his payroll and pay bills. Has he dropped any hints?"

"No, he hasn't, and I talk to him on the phone every morning, early, before he gets away."

The next day, after Sunday brunch at Polly's apartment, they drove to the building site. Polly was appalled by the cigarette butts; she would tell Mr. Trevelyan to get a coffee can and pick them up. The future rooms were a maze of two-by-fours; she thought the rooms looked too small. Rain was predicted, and she worried that the roof boards would not be installed in time.

Polly's constant worrying about the house caused Qwilleran to worry about her. "Why don't we take a pleasant break," he suggested, "and drive to the Flats to see the wildfowl. They might be nidulating, or whatever they do in July." This was a noble concession on his part; she was an avid bird watcher, and he was not. "We might see a puffin bird," he added facetiously.

"Not likely in Moose County," she said with a bemused smile, "but I really should go home and study the blueprints, in order to figure out furniture arrangement."

After dropping her off, Qwilleran went home to the barn, grateful for the company of cats who never worried. Both were pursuing their hobbies. Yum Yum was batting a bottle cap around the floor, losing it, finding it, losing it again—until she flopped down on her side in utter exhaustion. Koko was standing on his hind legs in the foyer, gazing down the orchard trail. Did he know that a chow came to work with the builder every day? Had Zak ventured up the trail to the barn? In any case, it seemed abnormal for a four-legged animal to spend so much time on two legs.

"Come on, old boy! Let's go exploring," he suggested. "Leash! Leash!"

Yum Yum, recognizing the word, scampered up the ramp to hide. Koko trotted to the broom closet, where the harnesses were stored, and purred while the leather straps were being buckled. Then, dragging his leash, he walked purposefully to the front door. When it was opened, however, he stood on the threshold in a freeze of indecision. He savored the seventy-eight-degree temperature and the three-mile-an-hour breeze; he looked to right and left; he noted a bird in the sky and a squirrel in a tree.

"Okay, let's go. We don't have two days for this excursion," Qwilleran said, picking up the leash and shaking it like reins. "Forward march!"

Koko, an indoor cat in temperament and lifestyle, stepped cautiously to the small entrance deck and sniffed the boards, which were laid diagonally. He sniffed the spaces between the boards. He discovered an interesting knot in the wood and a row of nailheads. In exasperation Qwilleran grabbed him and swung him to his shoulder. Koko was quite amenable. He liked riding on a shoulder. He liked the elevation.

Everyone had advised Qwilleran to "do something" about the orchard, a tangle of weeds and vines choking neglected apple trees. Many had lost their limbs for firewood; others had fallen victim to storms.

"Why don't you clean out that eyesore?" Riker had said. "Plant vegetables," Polly suggested. "Have a swimming pool," Fran Brodie urged.

At the building site, Qwilleran allowed the excited cat to jump down but held a firm hand on the leash. It was not the skeleton of the house that interested Koko, nor the tire tracks where the builders parked their pickups, nor the spot under a tree where Zak liked to nap in the shade. Koko wanted only to roll on the floor of the future garage. He rolled ecstatically. Both cats had discovered this unexplainable thrill at their Mooseville cabin, where the screened porch was on a concrete slab. They rolled on their backs and squirmed voluptuously. Now Koko was inventing new contortions and enjoying it immensely.

"Let's not be excessive," Qwilleran said to him, jerking the leash. "If that's all you want to do, let's go home."

On the way back to the barn he had an idea: He would add a screened porch on a concrete slab for the Siamese, where they could have a sense of outdoor living and roll to their hearts' content. Eddie could build it after he finished Polly's house. It would not be attached to the barn; that would only destroy the symmetry of the octagonal structure. It would be a separate summer house—a pergola—like the one he had visited on Breakfast Island, and like the one he had built in the Potato Mountains.

Yum Yum met them at the door and sniffed Koko with disapproval; he had been out having fun, and she had been left at home.

"That's what happens," Qwilleran advised her, "when you elect to be asocial." At any rate, he hoped the jaunt had satisfied Koko's curiosity and there would be no more absurd trail gazing. It was a futile dream. Soon the cat was back in the foyer, standing on two legs at the window, watching and waiting.

Ordinarily Qwilleran would have shrugged off Koko's aberration, but he was feeling edgy. There was the itch of suspicion without the opportunity to scratch. There was the uneasy feeling that Koko knew more than he did. And there was frustration caused by too much of Polly's house and not enough of Polly.

He was still feeling cranky the next day when he walked downtown to hand in his thousand words on the aurora borealis. The colorful phenomenon in the midnight sky was a tourist attraction, although locals took it for granted, and some thought "Northern Lights" was simply the name of a hotel in Mooseville.

Looking more than usually morose, Qwilleran walked through the city room where staffers sat in front of video display terminals and stared blankly at the screens. In the managing editor's office, the slightly built Junior Goodwinter was further dwarfed by the electronic equipment surrounding him.

When Qwilleran threw his copy on Junior's desk, the young editor glanced at the triple-spaced typewritten sheets and said, "When are you getting yourself a word processor, Qwill?"

"I like my electric typewriter" was the belligerent reply, "and it likes me! Are you implying that a word processor would make me a better writer? And if so, how good do you want me to be?"

"Don't hit me!" said the younger man with an exaggerated cringe. "Forget I said it. Have a cup of coffee. Sit down. Take a load off your feet. Will you be at the softball game tonight?"

"I haven't decided" was the curt answer. Polly usually accompanied him to the annual event, but he doubted she could tear herself away from her blueprints.

Junior threw him a copy of Monday's paper. "Read the third bite," he said.

A new feature on the front page was a column of brief news items of twenty-five words or less, each preceded by a single word in caps: ARRESTED, or HONORED, or LEAVING, or PRO- MOTED. Other newspapers labeled such a column "Briefs" or "Shorts." Hixie Rice, who had been responsible for naming the paper the *Something,* wanted to call the new front-page column "Undies." The editorial committee decided, however, on "Bites."

Qwilleran read the third bite:

SHOT: Police are investigating the shooting of a watchdog in West Middle Hummock Sunday night. The animal was penned in a dog-run on Floyd Trevelyan's estate.

"What do you deduce from this?" he asked Junior.

"That victims of the embezzlement are finally transferring their hostility from the government to the embezzler. Roger's been hanging out in Mudville coffee shops, and he says the emotions range from gloomy self-pity to vengeful rage. Someone was trying to get back at Floyd by killing his dog."

"Stupid!" Qwilleran murmured.

"And now read the first letter on the ed page, Qwill."

To the Editor:

I am writing in behalf of the Sawdust City High School Summer Camp Fund, which enables seniors to spend a week in the woods, living with nature, studying ecology, and learn- ing to share. For twenty-four years this has been a tradition at our school.

This year forty-seven students have spent their junior year selling cookies, washing cars, chopping wood, and cleaning garages to earn money for the camping experience. They de- posited their earnings regularly in the Lumbertown Credit Union and watched them earn interest—a worthwhile lesson in thrift and financial management. Next week they were to shoulder their backpacks, hike into the woods, and pitch their tents.

How can we explain to them that there will be no campout for the new senior class? How can we explain that $2,234.43 of their own money is being withheld by order of the government?

Elda Mayfus-Jones
Faculty Sponsor
SCHSSCF

Qwilleran finished reading and said irritably, "Why doesn't Ms. Mayfus-Jones just tell them their uncle Floyd is a crook, and he spent their $2,234.43 on toy trains to run around his office lobby?"

"You're in a grouchy mood today," Junior said. "I thought the K Foundation could afford to stake these kids to the money until their deposits are released."

"The Foundation could afford to send all forty-seven brats on a round-the-world cruise!" Qwilleran snapped. "All they have to do is apply. It's in the telephone book under K. That's between J and L." He started to leave without finishing his coffee.

"Hey!" Junior called after him with a grin. "If the kids get their money, you can go camping with them for a week and write a 'Qwill Pen' series!"

Qwilleran stomped from the room. As he passed the publisher's office, Riker beckoned to him. "I've just been talking to Brodie. How come they haven't caught that guy? They nabbed the Florida crooks right away, and they were pros! Floyd is only a small-town conniver. Why haven't they found him?"

"They'll never find him."

"What makes you think so? Do you know something we don't know?"

Qwilleran shrugged. "Just a hunch." If he were to mention Koko's input, it would only lead to an argument. Riker thought he took the cat's abstract messages too seriously. "You seem to be giving the scandal a lot of space, Arch."

"We're trying to keep the public outrage alive, spur the manhunt, and goad the banking commission into action. Our stories are being picked up by major newspapers around the state. We've assigned Roger to the Mudville beat exclusively until something breaks, one way or the other . . . So! . . . Where are you going from here, Qwill?"

"Home."

"How's Polly's house progressing?"

"Slowly, and that's what concerns me, Arch. She worries about it too much. She worries unnecessarily. I'm afraid she's headed for a nervous collapse."

His friend nodded sympathetically.

"Polly's so desk-bound that she's not getting any exercise—not even fresh air. She didn't even want to go bird watching yesterday."

"Are you bringing her to the game tonight?" Riker asked.

"Are you kidding? That's the last thing in the world she'd want to do!"

Chatting with his old friend bolstered Qwilleran's flagging spirits somewhat, and walking a few miles helped dispel his gloom. He took the long way home and, in doing so, passed the photo studio of John Bushland. His van was in the parking lot, meaning that the photographer was shooting a subject in the studio or developing film in the darkroom.

Bushy, as the nearly bald young man liked to be called, was a recent transplant from Lockmaster, and it was evident that he was doing well. The van was new. The lobby, it was obvious, had been professionally designed. On the walls were framed photographs from Bushy's prize-winning Scottish series. There was even a receptionist in the lobby, and she was not bad-looking. True, she seemed to be doing invoices and correspondence as well as phones, but she was a pleasant addition to the lobby.

Qwilleran said to Bushy, "Your business seems to be thriving."

"Yeah, they keep me busy all right: studio portraits Wednesdays and Saturdays by appointment only; commercial work at my own pace; free-lance assignments for the newspaper."

"Your photo of Trevelyan on the front page—wasn't it the same one that hangs in the Lumbertown lobby? You made him look good!"

"I'll say I did! If the police use it for their Wanted poster, they'll never catch the guy! You see, I was shooting his train layout for a hobby magazine, and the editor wanted a head-shot of Floyd. I tried a candid, but it made him look like the wild man in a carnival. So I got him to put on a shirt and tie and do a formal sitting in the studio. His secretary came along. She's a knockout, but she drove me crazy, telling Floyd to turn his head, or raise his chin, or not look at the camera. Finally I asked her to wait in the lobby while I took the picture. That didn't make points with her boss, but I got a good portrait."

"Interesting sidelight," Qwilleran said. . . . "Are you going to the game tonight?"

"Should I?" asked the newcomer to Pickax.

"It's the sporting highlight of the year!" Qwilleran said seriously, as if it were true. "Take your receptionist."

Once a year there was a softball game between the Typos and the Tubes—two scrub teams composed of newspaper staffers and hospital personnel. Compared to the regular league games, their efforts were ludicrous, and the only spectators were family members and fellow employees, but everyone had a good time. On this occasion, Qwilleran was in no mood to attend the game alone, but he knew Roger MacGillivray would be on the sidelines, hurling scurrilous insults at the Tubes. Roger was the on-the-spot reporter in Mudville.

The softball field had been merely a bare spot in the landscape west of Pickax until the K Foundation added two more diamonds, a soccer field, bleacher seats, and a pavilion. Now it was named Goodwinter Field, after the founders of the city. A Goodwinter was playing shortstop this year—Junior, the managing editor. Others were recruited from the city room, sports department, and photo lab. Their bright red T-shirts and baseball caps made a lively scene when they were in the field. The hospital team, composed mostly of technicians, wore T-shirts in operating-room green and happened to win every year.

Most of the spectators sat in the second and third rows of the bleachers. Junior's wife was there with a baby in a car tote and a small boy who couldn't sit still. Bushy had brought his receptionist, who was more attractive than Qwilleran had previously thought. Arch and Mildred Riker were there, of course, wearing red baseball caps with the MCS logo.

"Where's Polly?" Mildred asked.

Hixie Rice and Dwight Somers were a chummy duo seated apart from the others, a development that was duly noted by the matchmakers at the game. She waved to Qwilleran and called out, "Where's Polly?"

When he saw Roger arriving and heading for the pavilion, he followed him. "Nice piece in the paper today, Roger."

"Thanks. I finally learned how to make no-news sound like news."

"The shooting of the dog was a bizarre twist."

"Right! The natives are restless. Someone threw a brick through the Lumbertown office window this afternoon, and when they talk about F.T., the initials stand for something else."

The cry of "Batter up" sent the two men scurrying to the bleachers with their soft drinks. At Qwilleran's suggestion they climbed to the top row. "Better view," he explained. More privacy, he thought.

The sun was still high in the sky, where it belonged on a summer evening in the north country. The play on the field was leisurely. The sports fans were appropriately rude.

During a lull in the game, Qwilleran asked, "How did you find out about the dog?"

"The family reported it to the police, and I went out to their house. They're not supposed to talk to the media, and the nurse wouldn't let me in, but then the daughter saw me and said it was all right. She was in my history class when I was teaching—an A-plus student. When I'd assign a chapter, she'd augment it with research in the library. . . . *Sock it to 'im, Dave! Break his bat!* . . . She should've gone on to college."

"Why didn't she?"

"They wanted her at home to take care of her invalid mother. I think she's a lonely and frustrated girl. I could tell she wanted to talk to me, lawyer or no lawyer. We went out on the patio and reminisced about high school—had a few laughs."

"Could you tell how she was reacting to the publicity and the pressure?"

"She was all broken up about the dog. He was a chow. His name was Zak, spelled Z-a-k. *Dead on second! Good mitt, Juny! . . .* Finally she told me, off the record, that the dog really belonged to her brother, but the lawyer wanted the public to think he was Floyd's."

"So all the dog lovers would feel sorry for his client," Qwilleran suggested.

"Right! Her brother lives in an apartment where they don't allow pets, so he kenneled Zak at his parents' house, nights. Served a double purpose. Everybody in the country has a watchdog. . . . *Make it three, Dave. You're hot!*"

Dave made it three, the green shirts trotted onto the field, and the red shirts took their turn at bat.

"Was Floyd's son in any of your classes?" Qwilleran asked.

"All I can say is: He occupied a seat. A student he was not! He and his buddy from Chipmunk were always in trouble."

"What kind of trouble?"

"Fighting . . . carrying knives . . . underage drinking . . ."

"Any drugs?"

"Alcohol was the chief problem then. That was a few years ago, you know. Eddie and the other kid were expelled. . . . *Okay, Typos! Murder those bedpan pushers!*"

From the third row Riker bellowed, *"Send those bloodsuckers to the morgue!"*

Nevertheless, at the end of the sixth, the score stood 12 to 5 in the Tubes' favor. Qwilleran watched with mild enthusiasm; he preferred hardball to softball. He liked the overhand or sidearm pitch, the crack of a real baseball, the long run to first, and *nine* innings. At the next lull he asked Roger, "Does Floyd's daughter think the shooting was connected with the charge against her father?"

"She didn't say, and I didn't ask. Sensitive subject."

"What time did the shooting take place?"

"About two in the morning. Her mother was awake and heard the shot. She rang for her daughter."

"Did anyone hear the dog bark at the prowler?"

"I guess not."

The game ended at 13 to 8, and Roger stood up, yelling. *"Good try, guys! Next year we'll anesthetize those tube jockeys!"*

When Qwilleran returned to the barn after the game, Yum Yum was curled up like a shrimp in his favorite lounge chair, asleep. Koko was in the foyer, looking out the window.

"If it's Zak you're waiting for, give up!" Qwilleran told him. "He won't be coming around anymore. . . . Let's have a read. Book! Book!"

After one last intense look down the trail, Koko tore himself away from the window and did some educated sniffing on the bookshelves. Finally he nosed *The Panama Canal: An Engineering Treatise.*

"Thank you for reminding me," said Qwilleran, who had forgotten to open the book since bringing it home.

It contained many statistics and black-and-white photos of World War I vintage, and although Qwilleran found it quite absorbing, Yum Yum quickly fell asleep, and Koko kept yawning conspicuously.

"To be continued," Qwilleran said as he replaced the book on the history shelf.

CHAPTER 7

After the ball game and the Panama Canal session, Qwilleran phoned Polly at her apartment. "Did you read the front page today?" he asked. "Did you see the item about the Trevelyan dog?"

"Wasn't that a senseless, uncivilized thing to do?" she replied vehemently. "What did they hope to accomplish? It won't bring the fugitive back! It won't compensate them for their financial losses!"

"And it wasn't even Floyd's dog," Qwilleran told her. "It belonged to his son, your builder."

"That's even worse!"

"He's the chow who came to work with the crew every day—a beautiful animal, friendly and well-behaved."

"Are there any suspects, have you heard?"

"Not as yet, I guess. Police are investigating."

"Oh, dear," Polly sighed. "One evil only leads to another." Qwilleran changed the tone of his voice from objective to warmly personal. "And how is everything with you and Bootsie?"

"We're well, thank you. And what did you do today, dear?"

"Well, this evening I watched the Tubes trounce the Typos in the annual ball game. I knew you'd be too busy to go, but everyone wanted to know where you were." This was stretching the truth; there had been only two inquiries, although everyone was probably wondering why the richest bachelor in the northeast central United States was alone. Hope sprang eternal in the breasts of several hundred single and soon-to-be-single women in Moose County.

"I'm sorry, dear," Polly said. "I know I haven't been good company recently. I've had so much on my mind."

"That's all right," he said and then added naughtily, "Celia Robinson arrives tomorrow, and I feel obliged to spend some time with her. She doesn't know anyone up here."

There was an eloquent pause before Polly said coolly, "That's very hospitable of you."

"You'll meet her sooner or later, although I think she's not your type. She splits infinitives."

"I'll look forward to meeting her." Polly's voice dripped icicles.

"Well, I'll let you get back to your blueprints."

"Thank you for calling . . . dear."

"I'll keep in touch. Don't let the house get you down, Polly."

Qwilleran hung up with a pang of misgiving. He had deliberately irked Polly by mentioning Celia, and he recognized it as an act of unkindness to vent his own frustration. It was like shooting the embezzler's dog, he realized.

Tomorrow, he told himself, he might call and apologize; then again, he might not.

The next day was sunny with little breeze and temperatures higher than usual. An Anvil Chorus of ringing hammers at the end of the trail indicated that the carpenters were working feverishly. After coffee and a roll, Qwilleran walked down to the building site. There were now three men on the job, all wearing sweatbands and no shirts. Their perspiring backs glistened in the sun.

Qwilleran called to them, "Could you guys use some cold drinks? I live at the end of the trail. Be glad to bring a cooler down here."

"Got any beer?" asked the helper with a ponytail.

"No beer!" Eddie ordered. "No drinkin' on the job when you work for me . . . *Benno!*" The way he spoke the man's name was a reprimand in itself.

Qwilleran went home and loaded a cooler with soft drinks, which he delivered by car. The trio of workers removed their nail aprons and dropped down under a tree—Zak's tree—and popped the cans gratefully.

After a couple of swallows, Eddie set down his drink and started sharpening a pencil with a pocketknife.

Qwilleran said, "I notice you sharpen that pencil a lot."

"Gotta have a sharp pencil when you measure a board," the carpenter said, "or you can be way off."

"Is that so? It never occurred to me. . . . Where's your dog? Is it too hot for him today?"

The two helpers looked at their boss questioningly, and Eddie said with a glum scowl, "He won't be comin' with me no more. Some dirty skunk shot him, night before last."

"You don't mean it!" Qwilleran said in feigned surprise. "Sorry to hear it. Was it a hunter, mistaking him for a wild animal?"

Furiously Eddie said, "Wasn't no accident! I could kill the guy what done it!"

Qwilleran commiserated with genuine feeling and then said he'd leave the cooler and pick it up later.

Eddie followed him to the car. "D'you live in the barn up there? Somebody in my family built it, way back. This was his orchard. I see you fixed up the barn pretty good. I poked around one day when there wasn't nobody home, 'cept a cat lookin' at me out the window. At first I thought it was a weasel."

"Would you like to see the inside of the barn when you've finished work today?" This was a rare invitation. Qwilleran discouraged ordinary sightseers.

"Would I! You bet!" the young man exclaimed. "We quit at four-thirty. I'll drive up and bring your cooler back."

"Good! We'll have a drink." Qwilleran knew how to play the genial host.

Before driving back up the trail, he picked up his mail and noticed with foreboding a bulky envelope from the accounting firm. It suggested tax complications with pages of obscure wordage in fine print. When he opened it, however, out fell a large swatch of plaid cloth in bright red—the Mackintosh tartan. He felt the quality. It was a fine wool, and the red was brilliant. An accompanying note from Gordie Shaw stated that custom made kilts could be ordered from Scottie's Men's Store. There was also an application for membership in the Clan Mackintosh of North America. It was simple enough; the dues were low; his mother's clan affiliation qualified him for membership. It was something he would have to think about seriously—the membership, not the kilt. He left the envelope on the telephone desk where it would catch his eye and jog his decision.

Qwilleran planned to stay home all day, waiting for an important phone call. Celia Robinson was driving up from Illinois and was instructed to telephone upon reaching Lockmaster.

Throughout the day there were frenzied sounds of building at the end of the trail: the clunk of two-by-fours, the buzz of a table saw, the syncopated rhythm of hammers. Qwilleran admired a carpenter's skill in sinking a nail with three powerful blows. His own attempts started with a series of uncertain taps, a smashed thumb, and a crooked nail, which he tried to flatten by beating it into the wood sideways.

At about two o'clock the phone rang, and Koko's uncanny sense knew it was important; he raced to the telephone and jumped on and off the desk. Qwilleran followed, saying, "I'll take it, if you don't mind."

A cheery voice said, "I'm in Lockmaster, Chief, and I'm reporting like you said. Permission requested to proceed." This little charade was followed by a trill of laughter.

"Good! You're thirty miles from Pickax, which is straight north," he said crisply. "When you reach the city limits, it's three more blocks to a traffic circle with a little park in the center. Look for the K Theatre on your right. It's a big fieldstone building. Turn into the driveway. I'll be watching for you. Red car, did you say?"

"Very red, Chief," she said with a hearty laugh.

Qwilleran immediately jogged through the woods to the carriage house to check its readiness. The windows were clean, the phone was connected, and the rooms had been brightened with framed flower prints, potted plants, and colorful pillows. He added a copy of the *Moose County Something* to the coffee table. The kitchen was miraculously complete, even to red-and-white checked dishtowels. In the bedroom there was a floral bedspread; in the guest room, a Navajo design. He thought, Nice going, Fran!

Qwilleran went downstairs, just in time to see a red car pulling into the theatre parking lot. The driver rolled down her window and gave him a wide, toothy smile. "We made it!"

"Welcome to Pickax," he said, reaching in to shake her hand.

She was a youthful-looking, gray-haired woman whose only wrinkles were laugh lines around the eyes and smile creases in the cheeks.

"You look just like your picture in the paper, Chief!"

He grunted acknowledgment. "How was the trip?"

"We took it easy, so as not to put a strain on Wrigley. Most of the way he was pretty good." In the backseat a black-and-white cat peered mutely through the barred door of a plastic carrier. "One motel in Wisconsin didn't take pets, but I told them he was related to the White House cat, so they let him stay."

"Quick thinking, Celia."

"That's something I learned from you, Chief—how to make up a neat little story. . . . Where shall I park?"

"At the doorway to the carriage house—over there. I'll carry your luggage upstairs, but first we'll show the apartment to Wrigley, to see if it meets with his approval."

Celia laughed merrily at this mild quip. "I'll carry his sandbox and water dish."

As they climbed the stairs, Qwilleran apologized for the narrowness of the flight and the shallowness of the treads. "This was built a hundred years ago when people had narrow shoulders and small feet." This brought another trill of laughter, and he thought, I've got to be careful what I say to this woman; she's jacked up.

Upstairs she gushed over the spaciousness and comfort of the rooms, while Wrigley methodically sniffed the premises that had once been home to two Siamese.

"Now, while I'm bringing up your luggage," Qwilleran instructed Celia, "you sit down and make a list of what groceries you need. Then I'll do your shopping while you take a rest."

"Oh, that's too much trouble for you, Chief!"

"Not at all. I have an ulterior motive. Did you bring your recipe for chocolate brownies?"

She laughed again. "I brought a whole shoebox of recipes!"

He had a reason for wanting to shop alone. Otherwise it would be all over town that Mr. Q was buying groceries in the company of a strange woman who laughed at everything he said and was not at all like Mrs. Duncan.

"This evening," he said in a businesslike way, "it will be my pleasure to take you to dinner, and tomorrow a pleasant woman by the name of Virginia Alstock will drive you around and give you a crash course in what Pickax is all about."

"Oh, Chief! I don't know what to say. You're so kind!"

"Don't say anything. Get to work on that list. I have a four-thirty appointment."

"Yes, sir!" she said with a stiff salute and torrents of laughter.

Qwilleran himself was a chuckler, not a laugher, and on the way to Toodles' Market he began to wonder how much of Celia's merriment he could stand. He pushed a cart up and down the aisles briskly, collecting the fifteen items on her list. At the check-out counter the cashier expressed surprise.

"Gonna do some cooking, Mr. Q?"

Ordinarily he checked out a few ounces of turkey or shrimp and a frozen dinner. Tonight he was buying unusual items like flour, potatoes, bananas, and canned cat food. "Just shopping for a sick friend," he explained.

He delivered the groceries to the carriage house and returned to the barn just as Eddie Trevelyan's pickup came bouncing up the trail. The young man, in jeans and a tank top, jumped out of the cab and gestured toward the decrepit orchard. "Y'oughta do somethin' about them weeds and rotted trees."

"What would you suggest?" Qwilleran asked amiably.

"I could clean 'em out with a bulldozer and backhoe, pave the road, and build a string of condos." He glanced toward the front window.

"There's the weasel again. You sure he's a cat?"

"Sometimes I'm not sure *what* he is" was the truthful answer. "Hey, this is some barn, ain't it?"

"Wait till you see the interior. Come in and have a drink." As soon as they went indoors, Koko came forward with mouth open and fangs bared, emitting a hostile hiss. His stiffened tail was straight as a fencer's sword.

"Does he bite?" the visitor asked, drawing back.

"No, he's overreacting because you think he's a weasel. Sit down and make yourself comfortable. Sit anywhere," he added, noting the young man's reluctance to step on the unbleached Moroccan rug or sit on the pale, mushroom-tinted furniture. "What's your drink?"

"Shot 'n' a beer's okay." He sank into a capacious lounge chair and stared in awe at the balconies, catwalks, ramps, and giant fireplace cube.

"How do you like it?" Qwilleran called from the bar.

"Piece o' work, man!"

"I heard about the house you built for the Alstocks in Black Creek. It's been highly praised."

"Yeah . . . well . . . ." Eddie was uncomfortable with the compliment.

At the barn the drinks were usually served on a tray, but on this occasion Qwilleran carried the beer can and shot glass by hand. "How are you getting along with Mrs. Duncan?" he asked.

"She's okay, but she worries too much. She's always on my back about somethin'." He downed the whiskey. "Hey, I don't know your name."

"Qwilleran. Jim Qwilleran."

"I think I heard it somewheres."

"Could be. . . . I noticed you had an extra helper today."

"The job'll go faster now."

"Who's your regular man? You two seem to work well as a team."

"Benno. He's from Chipmunk. I knew him in high school. We both took Vocational. What do you do?"

"I'm a writer. I write books . . . about . . . baseball." It was the whitest lie Qwilleran could devise on the spur of the moment. He could get away with it because Eddie obviously did not read the *Moose County Something*.

"I like soccer," Eddie said, and Qwilleran became an instant soccer enthusiast.

After the builder's second shot of whiskey, he seemed more relaxed. "Wotcha think of my dog?"

"Beautiful chow! Friendly personality! What was his name?"

"Zak."

"Good name. Who came up with that?"

"My sister."

"Did she get along with Zak, or was he strictly a man's dog?"

"Zak liked everybody. But him and me, we were like buddies. He was a joker, too. I'd take him out on a job, and he'd hang around all day till I started to pack up. Then he'd take off, and I'd hafta chase him. The louder I yelled, the faster he'd run, like he was laughin' at me. He liked to run, di'n't like to be chained. He had a long dog run at my folks' house. That's where they got 'im. Right between the eyes. Musta come outa the kennel to see who was prowlin' around."

"Did he bark? Shouldn't he have barked?"

"Di'n't nobody hear any barkin'."

"Where was his body found?"

"Right near the fence."

Qwilleran smoothed his moustache. "So he was evidently shot at close range, and he didn't bark. Sounds as if the shooter was someone he knew."

Eddie's delayed response and nervous eyeballs gave the impression that he knew more than he was telling. "Zak knew lotsa people."

Qwilleran was at his sympathetic best: the concern in his eyes, the kindly tilt of his head, the way he leaned toward his listener, the gentle tone of his voice. "How's your mother feeling these days?"

Eddie looked startled. "D'you know her?"

"We've met, and I feel very bad about her illness. Does she have good medical care?"

"Aw, the doctors don't know nothin'. There's one doctor that has a cure, but he's in Switzerland."

"Is that so? Have you thought of taking her there?"

"Yeah, my sister and me, we thought about it, but . . . we di'n't have the dough. The trip, y'know . . . the treatment . . . stayin' there a long time . . . outa sight! I dunno . . ."

"How about another drink?" Qwilleran suggested.

"Nah, I gotta hit the road."

"Some coffee? I could throw a burger in the microwave."

"Nah, I gotta meet a guy in Sawdust."

As the contractor drove away in his pickup, Koko ambled inquisitively into the room as if saying, Has he gone?

"That was impolite to hiss at a guest," Qwilleran reprimanded him, though realizing the cat had never before seen such a hairy human. He himself was pleased that he had concealed his connection with the media, while establishing a contact with the Trevelyan family that could be pursued without arousing suspicion. He made a mental list of procedures:

—Continue to take an insulated chest of cold drinks to the building site.

—Talk soccer with the crew during their break; read the soccer news in the daily paper.

—Attend a soccer game.

—Show interest in the house construction and ask dumb questions.

Qwilleran's ideas concerning the shooting of the dog were crystallizing. The perpetrator (a) had a grudge against Floyd and (b) knew where and how the dog was kenneled, although he (c) was unaware that he was shooting someone else's pet. One distasteful idea came to mind: The crime was purposely committed to encourage public sympathy for Floyd. The notion was not completely farfetched in this stronghold of dog owners.

In any case, since Zak had not barked and was shot at close range, the shooter was obviously someone he knew, and yet . . . that could be anyone. Zak was friendly to a fault.

Regarding the police investigation of the shooting, Qwilleran assumed that they knew all of the above but had more important matters to investigate, such as the whereabouts of the embezzler himself.

Something Eddie had said now started a new train of thought: Floyd might have stashed the stolen money in Swiss banks; he might now be in Switzerland and not Mexico as everyone assumed; he might be arranging to fly his wife there for treatment. This theory, Qwilleran realized, had its flaws, but if it were viable, why had Koko performed his death dance? Baffled, he decided to table the matter and take Celia Robinson to dinner.

First he had to feed the cats. He often reflected that he was retired from the workplace, had no family responsibilities, and was the richest man in the northeast central United States. Yet his entire life was structured around the humble routine of feeding the Siamese, brushing their coats, entertaining them, doing lap service, and policing their commode. Early in his life it would have been inconceivable!

The question now arose: Where to take the loudly gleeful Mrs. Robinson to dinner? The New Pickax Hotel was the usual choice for business dinners and social obligations; no one went there for fun. On this evening Polly would be dining there with the library board, a group of genteel older women whose voices never rose higher than a murmur. The dining room was small, furthermore, and other tables would be occupied by lone business travelers intent on their tough steak. Celia's shrieks of laughter would reverberate like a tropical bird in a mortuary.

Qwilleran's own favorite restaurant was the Old Stone Mill, but he was too well known there, and the entire staff kept tabs on his dining companions. The safest choice was a steakhouse in North Kennebeck named Tipsy's. It occupied a large log cabin; the atmosphere was informal; the patrons were noisy; and the restaurant had the distinction of being named after the owner's cat. That would please Celia.

When he called for her, she was obviously wearing her best dress, her best jewelry, and full makeup. She looked nice, although she would be conspicuous at Tipsy's.

"Where are we going?" she asked with excitement. "I saw ads in the paper for Otto's Tasty Eats and the Nasty Pasty. Such funny names! And *Moose County Something* is a crazy name for a newspaper! I also read about a town called Brrr; was that a misprint?"

"Brrr happens to be the coldest spot in the county," he informed her.

"That's a good one!" she exclaimed with hearty laughter. "Wait till I tell my grandson! I write to Clayton once a week, sometimes twice."

"You can plan on plenty of two-letter weeks while you're here," Qwilleran said. "People who live 400 miles north of everywhere tend to be *different*. It's called frontier individualism."

On the way to North Kennebeck Celia continued to be convulsed with merriment at signposts pointing to Chipmunk, West Middle Hummock, and Sawdust City. "I don't believe it!" she cried when Ittibittiwassee Road crossed the Ittibittiwassee River. "Are they for real?"

"Sawdust City is not only real but recently it's been the scene of a major financial scandal."

"I like scandals!" she cried happily.

"Virginia Alstock will fill in the details tomorrow, but briefly: The president of a financial institution has disappeared along with his secretary and millions of dollars belonging to depositors. Mrs. Alstock will also take you to meet Lisa Compton at the Senior Care Facility. Would you care for part-time work as a companion for elderly shut-ins?"

"Oh, yes! I'm good with old people and invalids. I cheer them up."

"I believe it!" he said sincerely.

Celia became serious. "Do you think I laugh too much, Chief?"

"How much is too much?"

"Well, my daughter-in-law says I do. My husband was just the opposite. He always expected the worst. I've always been an optimist, and I began laughing to make up for his bad humor, but the more I laughed, the worse he got, and the worse he got, the more I laughed. It was funny when you think about it. I noticed you never laugh, Chief, although you've got a terrific sense of humor."

"I'm a chuckler," he said. "My laughter is internal. I wrote a column once about the many kinds of laughter. People giggle, titter, guffaw, snicker, cackle, or roar. My friend Polly Duncan, whom you'll meet, has a musical laugh that's very pleasant. Laughter is an expression of mirth involving the facial muscles, throat, lungs, mouth, and eyes. It's usually involuntary, but one can control the volume and tone to suit the time and place. It's called fine-tuning. . . . My next lecture will be at 9 A.M. tomorrow."

"I never thought of that," she said. "I'm going to try fine-tuning."

"There's a hostess at the restaurant where we're going who greets customers with loud, cackling laughter. I always think, There goes another egg."

Celia tried to smother her screams of delight. "What's the name of the restaurant?"

"The Chicken Coop."

She exploded again but cut it short.

"No, it's really called Tipsy's." Then he explained how it was founded in the 1930s and named after a white-and-black cat whose markings made her look inebriated, and whose deformed foot made her stagger. "Her portrait in the main dining room was the subject of countywide controversy recently," he said, "resolved only when art fakery was revealed."

When they arrived at the restaurant and were greeted by the hostess with a cackling laugh, Celia struggled to keep a straight face as she mumbled to Qwilleran, "Another egg!"

The menu was limited. Qwilleran always ordered the steak. Celia asked if the fish had bones, because she wanted to take some home to Wrigley. During the meal she had many questions to ask.

"Who is your friend with the nice laugh?"

"The administrator of the public library. It's her assistant who will chauffeur you around town tomorrow."

"Where do you live?"

"No doubt you've noticed the evergreen forest behind the theatre parking lot. Beyond that is an old orchard with a hundred-year-old apple barn. That's where I live."

"You live in a *barn*?"

"I've fixed it up a little. You'll see it one of these days. After you're settled, we'll have a talk. I think . . . I may have another assignment for you, Celia."

After dropping his dinner guest at her apartment, Qwilleran hurried to the barn to make a phone call. Just inside the kitchen door he picked up a black felt-tip pen from the floor. "Drat that cat!" he muttered as he dropped it into the pewter mug on the desk. A pen lying on a desktop was fair game to Koko, but he never filched one from the mug. He suspected Yum Yum.

It was the Compton residence that he called, and Lisa answered. "Do you want to speak to my grouchy husband?"

"No, I want to speak with his charming wife. It's about Pals for Patients."

"Sure. What can I do for you?"

"Does the Trevelyan family in West Middle Hummock ever call you for help?"

"All the time! The Pals we send out there never keep the job very long. It's a long drive for only a few hours' work, and it's an unhappy family. No one's assigned to them at the moment—not since the credit union closed. Their daughter worked there, but now she's at home, taking care of her mother herself. Why do you ask?"

"I've met the son. He's building Polly's house. It was his dog who was shot. Did you read about it?"

"Nasty business!" Lisa said.

"I agree. I have no sympathy for Floyd, but I feel sorry for his family, especially his wife, and I have a suggestion. The Celia Robinson I mentioned to you has a cheerful disposition that would do wonders for Mrs. Trevelyan, I'm sure. Mrs. Robinson will call at your office tomorrow, and I wish you'd see what you can do."

"You don't think she'd mind the drive?"

"She's just driven for three days with a cat in the backseat, and there were no complaints—from either of them. She's an inspiration, I tell you! She could even make Lyle smile."

"Hands off my husband!" Lisa said. "He may be an old curmudgeon, but he's mine! . . . Okay, I'll see what I can do."

Qwilleran hung up slowly with a satisfied feeling of accomplishment. Already his logical mind was telling him how to brief Celia for her assignment. As he sat at the desk, making notes with a black felt-tip, he realized that neither cat had greeted him at the door. He glanced around casually, then with mounting concern. That's when he saw the blood-red splotch on a light-colored sofa.

Logic gave way to panic! He jumped up, knocking over the desk chair, and rushed toward the lounge area. "Koko! Yum Yum!" he shouted. There was no answer.

CHAPTER 8

Words can hardly express Qwilleran's panic when he glimpsed the blood-red splotch in the lounge area, nor his relief upon finding that it was the swatch of fabric in the Mackintosh tartan. The Siamese had stolen it! The envelope containing the application for membership in the clan was on the floor nearby. And where were the culprits? On top of the fireplace cube, observing Qwilleran's brief frenzy with wonder, as if thinking, *What fools these mortals be!*

"You devils!" he said, shaking his fist in their direction. Then he had second thoughts. It was not necessarily a two-cat caper. Which one of them was guilty? They both looked annoyingly innocent. Most likely Koko had heisted the envelope for some obscure reason of his own. Did he smell the red dye in the cloth?

At one time in his brief but stellar career he had chewed red neckties.

Then Qwilleran had a quirky thought. "If you're trying to get me into a kilt," he shouted at Koko, *"no dice!"*

Nevertheless, he read the application blank once more. By nature he was not a joiner of clubs, societies, or associations (apart from the press club). Yet, as Big Mac had said, it would be a tribute to his mother if he joined the clan; she had been so proud of her Scottish heritage. Having reached middle age, he now found himself thinking about her with appreciation and admiration. He remembered her precepts: Give more than you get. . . . Be yourself; don't imitate your peers. . . . Always serve beverages on a tray.

She had died when he was in college. If she had lived longer, she would have gloried in his success as a journalist, wept over the crisis that almost ruined his life, and finally delighted in his new prosperity, especially since it was her Klingenschoen connection that sowed the seed.

Qwilleran filled out the membership application. Polly would be happy. "But no kilt!" he muttered to himself.

"YOW!" came a comment from the top of the fireplace cube.

The day after his visit with Eddie Trevelyan, Qwilleran drove to the mailbox with another cooler of soft drinks in the trunk. This was Phase One in his plan to get into the Trevelyan household by the back door. For Phase Two he would need Celia's help and the cooperation of Lisa Compton.

There were five trucks at the building site; electrician and plumber were "roughing in," according to Eddie. Qwilleran dropped off the cooler and returned to the barn to read his mail. One letter piqued his curiosity. The stationery had character, and the envelope was hand written in a distinctive script. He read:

Dear Mr. Q,

Just a note to say I'm sending you a memento from my father's personal collection. Whenever you sit in it, your creativity will scintillate. I want you to have this souvenir because I shall never forget that you saved my life on the island and encouraged me to improve my lifestyle.

My brother will bring it over on his boat, and Derek will pick it up at the pier in Mooseville and deliver it in his truck.

Gratefully,
Liz

Qwilleran's first thought was: No! Not a pyramid! What will I do with it? Where can I put it? How large is it? Can I donate it to a school or museum without hurting Elizabeth's feelings? She had wanted him to call her Liz, a diminutive that only her father had used, but Qwilleran had no desire to be a surrogate parent.

He read the rest of his mail, throwing most of it into the waste-basket or red-inking it for handling by the secretarial service. A few letters he would answer himself, by postal card or phone call. Cards required fewer words than letters and were cheaper to mail. Despite his new wealth, there was an old frugality in his nature.

After that he went to work in his balcony studio, which was off-limits to the Siamese. The closed-door policy, he liked to explain, kept the cats out of his hair and the cat hairs out of his typewriter. Now he was trying to find something different to say about baseball for the "Qwill Pen" column.

He wrote, "Compared to a nervous, hyped up, violent, clock-watching game like football, baseball is a spectator sport that en-courages relaxation. The leisurely pace—punctuated by well-spaced spurts of running, sliding, and arguing—promotes a feeling of well-being, enhanced by the consumption of a hot dog or beverage of choice. The continual pauses—for bat-swinging, mitt-thumping, cap-tugging, belt-hitching, hand-spitting, and ho-meplate-dusting—produce a pleasant hypnosis."

Qwilleran's concentration was interrupted by the urgent ringing of the doorbell, as well as banging on the kitchen door. He ran down the ramp and found Derek Cuttlebrink towering on the doorstep. "Special delivery from Breakfast Island!" he announced. "Want me to carry it in?"

"Will it come through the doorway?" Qwilleran asked. A pyramid large enough to sit in, he reasoned, would have awkward dimensions.

"No problem," Derek yelled as he returned to his pickup and unloaded an item of furniture. "Where d'you want me to put it?" he asked as he maneuvered it through the kitchen door.

"Do I have to tell you?" Qwilleran responded tartly. "What is it supposed to be?"

"A rocking chair! Handmade! Antique! One size fits all! It belonged to Elizabeth's old man." Derek set the rocker down and sat in it. "Comfortable, too! Try it; you'll like it!"

It was made entirely of bent twigs, except for the rockers—and the bowl-shaped seat that appeared to be varnished treebark. Qwilleran thought, It's the ugliest chair I've ever seen! He slid into the seat cautiously and was immediately tilted back as if ready for dental surgery. It was, however, a remarkably comfortable sling.

"There's something I'm supposed to give you." Derek dashed out to his truck and returned with a snapshot. "This is her old man, posing with his chair. She thought you'd like to see what he looked like. Now I've gotta get to work. I'm on for the dinner hour, five to eight."

"What about your rehearsal?" Qwilleran called after him.

"The rude mechanicals aren't scheduled tonight."

After Derek had driven away, raising more dust than other visitors had done, Qwilleran grabbed the phone and called Amanda's Studio of Design, hoping Fran Brodie would be in-house. She answered.

"Stay there! I'll be right over!" he shouted. He hung up while she was still sputtering, "What . . . What . . . ?"

He usually chose to walk downtown, but this time he drove. At the design studio he barged through the front door and threw a snapshot on Fran's desk. "Know anything about this? The chair, not the man."

The designer's eyes grew wide. "Where did you get this picture? Who is he? Is he selling the chair?"

"The man's dead. The chair is in my barn. It's supposed to be a thank-you from Elizabeth for saving her life on the island.

If I'd known I was getting this, I'd have thrown her back in the swamp."

"Very funny," Fran said, "but you don't know what you're talking about. This is a twistletwig rocker, a hundred years old, at least. It was the poor man's bentwood, made of willow."

"Well, the poor man can have it! Even Whistler's Mother would think it was ugly. Koko sniffed it and made a face. Yum Yum won't go anywhere near it; that should tell you something!"

"I don't consider Yum Yum an arbiter of taste!" The two females had feuded briefly at one time, and Yum Yum won. "As a matter of fact, it's a beautiful piece of folk art, and a dealer on the East Coast recently advertised one for $2,000."

"You're pulling my leg!"

"I'm not! This is a choice collectible! Do you want to sell? Amanda will give you a thousand without blinking. Is it comfortable?"

"Very, but I still think it's a nightmare masquerading as furniture."

"Go back! You're not ready!" Fran said impatiently. "The chair is linear sculpture! It'll be a dynamic accent for your light, contemporary furniture. Live with it for a while, and you'll be writing a treatise for the "Qwill Pen" on the charms of twistletwig. I'll help you do some research."

She had said the magic word; whenever anyone mentioned material for his column, Qwilleran went on red alert. To save face he pointed to a wooden box on her desk. "What's that? Is that another high-priced collectible?" It was slightly crude, in the size and shape of a two-pound loaf of bread.

"That's an English pencil box," Fran said. "A country piece, rather old. I believe it's walnut. It came from the Witherspoon estate in Lockmaster."

The wood was a mellow brown enhanced by the distress marks of age. The lid was rimmed with a fine line of brass, and there was a small brass key in the lock. Qwilleran lifted the lid and found a shallow compartment.

"You could use it for cufflinks," she suggested.

"I don't use cufflinks. No one in Pickax uses cufflinks! What I need is a place to lock up my pens. One of our resident cat burglars has been swiping them, and I suspect Koko."

"This would be perfect, and you could use the drawer at the bottom for paper clips."

"Yum Yum opens drawers and collects paper clips." He tugged at the drawer. "It's jammed."

"No, it isn't. There's a secret latch."

"I'll take it," he said. "Also my snapshot."

Carrying the pencil box under his arm, Qwilleran walked to his car two blocks away; parking was a major problem in downtown Pickax. He could never set foot in the center of town without meeting a dozen acquaintances, and today he threw greetings to his barber, an off-duty patrolman, the cashier from Toodles' Market, and the proprietor of Scottie's Men's Store, who said, "Aye, there's the Laird hi'self! When will you be comin' in to be measured for a kilt?"

"Not until you hear from my undertaker," Qwilleran retorted.

Then Larry Lanspeak, on the way to the bank, stopped him to ask, "What's that you're carrying? Your lunch bucket?"

"No, a pistol case. I'm on my way to a duel. . . . How's the play coming, Larry?"

"We've had problems. Fran and the new girl from Chicago wanted to incorporate a pyramid in the forest scenes. Imagine cluttering the stage, complicating the blocking, and confusing the audience with such a senseless gimmick! Carol, Junior, and I had to threaten to drop out before Fran would listen to reason. That girl is a good client of hers and also made a sizable donation to the club's operating budget. Politics! Politics!"

Arriving home with his English pencil box, Qwilleran filled the top compartment with felt-tip pens. One of the black ones was missing again, and he found it in the foyer. The drawer he filled with jumbo paper clips. The Siamese watched, their inquisitive tails curved like scimitars.

"Foiled, you villains!" he said as he locked the lid. He left the key in the lock, since neither cat had learned how to turn keys. It would be only a matter of time, he surmised.

He and Polly dined early at the Old Stone Mill, as she was attending a dessert-and-coffee wedding shower for one of the library clerks. "Would you care to join us?" she asked teasingly. "Men often attend showers now, you know."

"This man doesn't," he said, putting a brusque end to the subject. "The electrician and plumber were working on your house this morning. It's beginning to look less like a lumberyard and more like a habitation."

"What am I going to do with all those mounds of soil they excavated for the foundation?" she asked with a worried frown.

"I suppose they'll use some of it for fill and then grade the lot. They'll move the dirt anywhere you say, with two swipes of the bulldozer."

"I'd love to have a berm between the house and the highway. With plantings it would give a sense of privacy, but I don't want it to look landscaped. I want it to look completely natural. How does one do that?"

Rather too sharply Qwilleran said, "One calls Kevin Doone. He attended horticultural college for four years to learn how to do that."

"Do I bore you with my concerns about the house, dear?" Polly asked with a frank gaze.

"You never bore me! You know that. But—for your own sake—I wish you'd delegate your problems to the professionals instead of trying to make all the decisions yourself."

"It'll be the only house I'll ever build, and I want it to express *me*," she said meekly. "I've always lived in places where I've had to compromise and make do."

"I understand, and I apologize for being flip. What else is preying on your mind? I want to hear."

"Well . . . the interior. I'd love to have white plastered walls and Williamsburg blue woodwork. I saw it in a magazine—with country antiques—but one needs good furniture with such a stark background. My things aren't good, but they're family heirlooms, and I couldn't part with them. I know wallpaper backgrounds are more flattering to a hodgepodge of furniture, but . . . I'm absolutely smitten with the idea of white walls and blue woodwork. Last night I couldn't sleep for thinking about it."

The solution would be so easy, he thought, if she would let him bankroll a houseful of pedigreed country antiques. She could have the twistletwig rocker for starters. But Polly would never approve of such largess. He said, "Suppose one of your clerks came to you with such a problem. How would you advise her?"

After a pause, she said with an abashed half-smile, "I'd tell her to keep the things she loves and use wallpaper."

"And I believe you'd be right."

Polly breathed a large sigh. "I've been doing all the talking. How thoughtless of me! What have you been doing?"

"Well, I had a chat with your builder, and he's not a bad fellow, in spite of his raggle-taggle appearance and double negatives. I've come to the conclusion that Moose County is bilingual. Half of us speak standard English, and the other half speak Moose."

"What did you talk about?"

"Soccer, and the fact that one of his ancestors built the barn. Neither of us mentioned his father, of course, but I inquired about his mother's health. He seems to think that a Swiss doctor has a cure for her rare disease. One wonders how true it is, and how effective, and how safe."

"It's not to be dismissed out-of-hand," Polly asserted. "Alternative medicine has always been practiced in other countries, and now by maverick physicians here."

Then it was time for her to leave for the wedding shower. Qwilleran drove her back to the library, where her car was parked, and then went home to phone Celia.

She was waiting eagerly for his call. "I had a ball!" she cried. "Virginia is a lot of fun. She's contralto soloist at the Little Stone Church. She told me I could sing in the choir. And do you want to hear something funny? There's a cat that attends services every Sunday! They leave the front door ajar, and she walks in, picks out a lap, and sleeps all through the sermon. . . . Besides working at the library, Virginia has three teenagers, a dog, two cats, a hutch of rabbits, and some chickens."

"Where did you have lunch?"

"Lois's Luncheonette, and Lois sent two free desserts to our table—bread pudding. It wasn't as good as mine. I use egg whites to make it fluffy and whole wheat flour to make it chewy, plus nuts and raisins, and vanilla sauce."

"How do I place an order?" Qwilleran asked. "Do you accept credit cards?" There was laughter on the line before he could ask, "Did you meet Lisa Compton?"

"Yes, I did, and she's very nice. She told me about a sad case in West Middle Hummock where she can send me to—"

"Celia," he interrupted, "why don't you jump into your little red car and drive down here? You can see the apple barn, meet the cats, and tell me about the sad case."

Moments later she stepped out of her car in the barnyard and gasped at the sight. "I grew up on a farm and never saw anything like this!" She was equally enthralled by the interior but shocked at the condition of the orchard.

"According to legend," Qwilleran explained, "a curse was placed on the orchard a hundred years ago. I thought the curse had exceeded the statute of limitations, but lately the property's been under surveillance by the FBI."

"Really?"

"Yes, we have our own Feline Bureau of Investigation."

Celia laughed at his quip, but it was controlled laughter. She was fine-tuning.

The Siamese were listening to the conversation from a safe distance, sitting alertly and ready for flight if the visitor's laughter should hit the wrong note. Meanwhile they were sensing that she came from a poultry farm, lived with a black-and-white cat named Wrigley, and manufactured Kabibbles in her kitchen.

"Seriously," he said, "I'm glad you've enlisted in the Pals for Patients program. You're perfect for the job. What do you know about your first assignment?"

"Only that the patient is the wife of the man who disappeared with a lot of money that doesn't belong to him. It must be terrible for the poor woman, to be ill and have that happen. A practical nurse comes in five mornings a week, and I work afternoons. The rest of the time her daughter is there."

Qwilleran said, "I've heard that they're two lonely and unhappy women. With your cheerful personality you'll be very good for them. And you can do more than that! There's an element of mystery surrounding the scandal. I believe there's more to the story than people think." Then he added with heavy implication, "The police investigators may be on the wrong track."

Excitedly she asked, "Are you investigating it yourself, Chief?"

"I have no authority to do so, and the Trevelyans' lawyer has instructed them not to talk to the media."

"But you're not really media," she protested. "You just write a column, don't you?"

Qwilleran took a moment to enjoy an internal chuckle. "Be that as it may, it would be inadvisable for me to involve myself personally in the case."

Celia was sitting on the edge of her chair. "Could I help you, Chief?"

"I'm sure you could. When do you start?"

"Tomorrow afternoon."

"Suppose you get the lay of the land, and we'll talk again tomorrow evening. By that time I'll have planned our strategy."

"Is there anything special I should do tomorrow?"

"Just be friendly and sympathetic. They may welcome the chance to talk to someone. Don't ask too many questions; keep it conversational. And never . . . *never* let them know you're associated with me!"

"I'll write it down," she said. "I always write everything down." Her large handbag was on the floor near her chair, and she fumbled in it for a notepad, whereupon two quiet slinky Siamese approached in slow motion to explore its contents.

"No!" Qwilleran said firmly, and they withdrew backward at the same slow pace. "It's never a good idea to leave your handbag open while they're around," he explained. "Koko is an investigator, and Yum Yum is a kleptomaniac."

CHAPTER 9

With unusual anticipation Qwilleran awaited Celia Robinson's report on her first day in West Middle Hummock. He
patted his moustache frequently as he assured himself he was finally
on-line with the investigation.

Copy was due for his Friday column, but his profound treatise
on baseball was not quite finished, so he dashed off a thousand
words on "the sweet corn of August," one of Moose County's
much-vaunted crops. Like vintners with certain wines that don't
travel well, farmers produced only enough sweet corn for local
consumption—a rare delicacy that had never been exported.

He delivered the copy by bicycle, then took a long ride, hoping
the monotony of pedaling would crystallize his thoughts about the
Trevelyan case. It was an inspiration, he believed, to use Celia as
a secret agent. In Florida she had proved herself to be entirely
trustworthy: she used common sense; she followed instructions; she
read spy novels. They would call this investigation Operation
Whistle.

As Qwilleran approached the Park Circle, he was wondering
whether to make an illegal left turn into the theatre driveway, or
cut through the park where biking was prohibited, or circle the
park and make an illegal U-turn. Before he could make up his
mind, a police car pulled him to the curb, and Andrew Brodie
stepped out.

"See your license?" the chief barked. "Attempting to elude an
officer. Biking without a helmet. Exceeding the speed limit. Failure
to provide a reflector on the rear fender."

"Write me a ticket," Qwilleran shot back, "and I'll see you in
court on your day off."

Brodie was an imposing figure on the Pickax landscape, always
growling and scowling and snapping commands—except when he

was playing the bagpipe at weddings and funerals. He did both very well. Qwilleran considered him one of his best friends, and the two friends rarely missed an opportunity to exchange gibes. After the usual banter, the chief dropped his official brusqueness and said in a voice brimming with innuendo, "I've noticed some activity behind the theatre."

The eagle-eyed cop had apparently seen the red car, but Qwilleran ignored the oblique reference and launched a long explanation that had nothing to do with the question. One of his many skills was his seemingly innocent failure "to get it."

"Yes, the parking lot's busy these days," he began. "They're in the throes of producing a new play, and you know what that means: actors rehearsing every night, set builders and costume makers on the job every day. It's quite an ambitious project: *A Midsummer Night's Dream* with a cast of hundreds. Your daughter's directing it. Shakespeare wrote it. Junior Goodwinter is playing Puck. Carol and Larry are doubling as—"

"Knock it off!" Brodie interrupted. "You've rented your carriage house to somebody—older woman—drives a red car—Florida plates."

Qwilleran's aimless babbling about the play had given him time to formulate a defense. "The real estate division of the K Foundation handles rentals. I don't get involved with that."

"But you know who she is," the chief said accusingly.

"Of course! Everyone knows who she is: a friend of Euphonia Gage in Florida."

"What's she doing up here?"

"I'm not entirely clear about this, but I believe it had to do with doctor's orders. She was in a deep depression following the death of her favorite grandson—or something like that—and Euphonia had praised Moose County as a good place to start a new life."

Brodie was unconvinced. "What kind of new life does she expect to start at her age?"

"Again: Don't quote me! But I've heard that she's a good cook, and the rumors are that she intends to start a small catering business. And you have to admit this town could stand some improved food service. The catering department at the hotel is an abomination. In fact, I wouldn't be surprised if the economic development division of the K Foundation had been instrumental in bringing this woman up from Down Below."

"So what was she doing in West Middle Hummock today? She was seen driving into Floyd Trevelyan's property."

"What time was it?"

"Around noon."

Qwilleran had to think fast. "She was probably delivering a hot lunch to a shut-in. Mrs. Trevelyan is said to be—"

"So why didn't she come out until after five o'clock?"

"Andy, how many spies do the state police have stationed in Floyd's trees? And why haven't they found the guy yet? Maybe they're looking in the wrong place."

"Go home! You're wasting my time." Brodie jerked his thumb over his shoulder and headed back to his official vehicle.

"It was your idea to stop and chat," Qwilleran called after him.

"Go home and get that two-wheeled suicide contraption off the street."

"Okay, tell me how to get out of this traffic without breaking the law!"

"Follow me!" The police car led the way to the head of the circle with light flashing and stopped the flow of traffic in both directions while the richest man in the northeast central United States made his illegal U-turn.

Arriving at the barn he said to Yum Yum, "I had a touch-and-go session with your boyfriend a minute ago." She was in love with Brodie's badge.

Polly was dining with the Hasselriches that evening, an obligation she usually dreaded, so he thawed a frozen dinner for himself and opened a can of crabmeat for the Siamese. Then, at a suitable hour, he telephoned Celia and invited her to the barn "for a cold drink on this warm evening."

She arrived with a joyful, toothy smile and, while Qwilleran reconstituted limeade concentrate, wandered about the barn in search of the Siamese. They were nested together in the bowl-shaped seat of the twistletwig rocking chair.

"We used to have a rocker like yours at the farm," she said when they were seated with their cold drinks. "It was handed down in my husband's family. He burnt it when we got television."

"What was the connection?" Qwilleran asked with genuine curiosity.

"Well, for TV he had to have a recliner, and we didn't have room for both. You've got lots of room here. Where are your TV sets?"

"We have only one. It's in the cats' loft apartment. They enjoy nature programs or commercials without the audio."

Celia laughed with delight. "I wish my husband was alive, so I could tell him that! We had barn cats, and they weren't allowed in the house. They certainly didn't have TV in the hayloft!"

After a few minutes of polite small talk, Qwilleran broached the subject. "How did you fare at West Middle Hummock today?"

"Well! It was very interesting! It's a nice drive out there, and I didn't mind it at all. They have a cute mailbox like an old railroad engine, and they call the house The Roundhouse on the sign, but it isn't round at all!"

He explained that railroad yards used to have round buildings for servicing locomotives in the days of steam, and there was a turntable in the center to shunt the engines into different stalls.

"Learn something every day!" she said with an airy wave of the hand.

"How well were you received?"

"Well, first I met the nurse, who was in a hurry to go off duty. She impressed me as being kind of a cool cucumber. I'll bet she lives in Brrr." Celia stopped to enjoy a laugh at her own humor. "She showed me the medicines and told me not to get off schedule or the patient might wind up in the hospital. Then she left, and I met the patient's daughter. She could be quite pretty if she was happy, but I'm afraid she's a very bitter young lady—in her early twenties."

"What's her name?"

"When I asked, she didn't answer right away, but then she said it was Tish. Later, though, her mother called her Lettie. She hates Lettie. I know how she feels. I always hated Celia."

As his informer rambled on, Qwilleran was doing some quick

arithmetic: Lettie plus Tish equals the young woman he met in the bank; she claimed her last name was Penn, although the teller called her Trevelyan. He said, "Her name is probably Letitia—a bad choice, any way you look at it. Letitia Trevelyan sounds like 'thank you' in a foreign language."

Celia giggled. "I must remember to tell that one to my grandson." She dug in her large handbag for her notebook and wrote it down, then went on: "Tish was polite but not what you'd call friendly. That's all right; I didn't expect an afternoon social. She said she was going out and would be back at five o'clock—my quitting time—but first she took me into her mother's room. Oh, my! That poor woman! She can't be more than fifty, but her body is so frail, and her face is so white! The way her eyes looked, they were searching for something. I don't think she gets enough *attention,* although she's never left alone."

"That could be true," Qwilleran said. "Attendance is not attention."

"She told me to call her Florrie. I fixed her a nice little lunch but had to coax her to eat. She wanted to talk. Her voice is thin and whiney."

"What did she talk about?"

"Well, she skipped around a lot. She doesn't like vegetables. Someone killed their dog. The nurse is mean to her. No one comes to see her. She hates what's on TV. Lettie goes out and never says where she's going." Celia stopped for breath. "I listened and sympathized with her until she got tired and wanted to lie down. I asked if she'd like me to sing to her."

"Don't tell me you sang *Mrs. Robinson!*" Qwilleran said teasingly.

"Oh, you remembered!" That was cause for more laughter. "No, I sang hymns, and she fell asleep and had a peaceful nap. That gave me time to poke around the house. It's big and has an elevator, but it doesn't look as if anybody loves it, if you know what I mean. And those electric trains in the basement! Never saw anything like it! Do you suppose they let schoolkids come and see them at Christmastime?"

"Probably not."

"There was a family album in Florrie's sitting room, and when she woke up I asked if we could look at it together. I took her down on the elevator and wheeled her out on the stone patio, and we had a good time looking at snapshots."

"Did you learn anything?"

"Oh, I learned a lot! She grew up in a railroad family. Her father was a famous engineer. They lived in Sawdust City near the tracks. Railroad people liked to live near the tracks, Florrie said. Watching the trains was big entertainment, I guess. They knew everybody. Everybody waved."

Qwilleran said, "You have a good ear for detail and apparently an excellent memory."

Celia waved her small notebook. "I wrote everything down. Her grandfather, uncles, and brothers all worked on the railroad. They were firemen, brakemen, engineers, flagmen, crossing guards, and hostlers, whatever they are."

"Did Florrie wonder why you were writing things down?" he asked with a note of concern.

"I know what you're thinking, Chief, but I was careful to explain that I wrote long letters to my grandson twice a week and jotted down things to tell him."

"Smart thinking! Perhaps we should put Clayton on the payroll."

She laughed, of course, before continuing. "Let me tell you about Florrie's wedding pictures! She married a carpenter who was crazy about trains, and he married her because her father was an engineer. That's what she said! And here's where it gets good: The marriage ceremony was in the cab of a steam locomotive, with everyone wearing coveralls and railroad caps—even the bride and the preacher! Her flowers were tied on a shiny brass oilcan, and when the couple was pronounced man and wife, the preacher pulled the handle that blows the whistle. That meant the best man had to fire the boiler, too, and it got very hot in the cab, and there was coal dust on her flowers." In recounting it, Celia rocked back and forth with mirth.

"Did Florrie think this was funny?"

"No, she didn't laugh or smile or anything. It was just something she thought Clayton would be interested to hear about. They had the reception in the depot. Her mother-in-law made the wedding cake like a train of cars coming around a curve. It was all done with loaf cakes and chocolate icing. For music they had a man with a guitar singing songs about train wrecks."

"No wonder her husband turned out the way he did," Qwilleran said. "He was a nut even then."

"Now comes the sad part. After a few pictures of the young couple and their two young children, the pages of the photo album were blank. I wanted to know why no more snapshots, and Florrie said, 'My husband got too rich. I never wanted to be the wife of a rich man. I liked it when he'd come home tired and dirty from digging a basement or shingling a roof, and we'd sit at the kitchen table and drink a beer and talk before we ate supper. . . . ' Isn't that sad, Chief?"

"It is indeed. Did she say anything else about her husband?"

"Not a word, and I didn't think I should ask."

"You're right. The questions will come later."

"When Tish came home, I said good-bye to Florrie, and she held out her arms for a hug." Celia blinked her eyes at the recollection. "On the way out I had a few words with Tish. She'd brought home an armful of library books, and we talked a bit about our favorite authors. She said she'd like to be a writer herself. I asked if she'd studied it in college, and she said, 'My father didn't think college was necessary, because I could go right into the family business.' "

"How did she say it? Regretfully? Apologetically? Matter-of-factly? Bitterly?"

"Kind of stiffly, I thought. So then I looked innocent and said, 'What business is your family in?' She looked surprised, so I explained that I'd just moved to town a couple of days ago and didn't know anything about anything. She said they were in the financial business, but she was on vacation."

"I'm proud of you, Celia," Qwilleran said. "You've done very well for starters."

"Thank you. I really enjoyed every minute. And before I left, I told Tish I was sorry to hear their dog had been shot. Tish felt sick about it. He was a beautiful chow. And that gave me an idea! Pets are supposed to be good for elderly patients—for their morale, you know—so I suggested bringing Wrigley to visit her mother. He's a lovable cat, very clean, very quiet. Tish thought it would be wonderful, so that's what I'm going to do. Do you have any other suggestions, Chief?"

"Yes. Continue to do your Pals for Patients job. Take Wrigley, by all means. Both of those lonely women need your cheery presence, and Tish may prove to be your best source of information. Continue to play the uninformed newcomer. At the same time, acquaint yourself with all the published facts on the scandal to date. I have a file of clippings for you to take home and read. Good luck! I'll call you tomorrow night."

"Oh, I'm so excited!" she exclaimed. She reached for a long wooden object on the coffee table. "Is this what I think it is?" She blew one end and produced the high pitched whistle of a steam locomotive. Yum Yum vanished; Koko stood his ground and swiveled his ears wildly.

Qwilleran could do his best thinking with his feet elevated, a legal pad in his left hand and a black felt-tip in his right, and this is how he settled down in the library area after Celia had driven away. Yum Yum immediately came trotting down the ramp. Whenever he sat down, her built-in antenna signaled his whereabouts and flashed green. There she was, ready to curl up on his lap, and who could deny that appealing little creature? He had known her when she was a trembling, mistreated kitten. Now she was a self-assured young lady who wanted her own plate at dinnertime and who had once tried to steal the police chief's badge off his chest. Qwilleran propped his writing pad against the furry body on his lap and started an off-the-cuff list of questions that needed to be explored. The writing surface rose and fell as she inhaled and exhaled:

Does Tish have any life of her own, apart from job and family responsibilities? Did she, or does she, resent her father's interference in her career possibilities?

When he was gallivanting around the country in pursuit of his personal pleasures, how did Tish feel about being a live-in Cinderella? How did she react to his all-night absences and travels with his secretary, while Florrie wasted away at The Roundhouse?

How much, if anything, does Tish know about the embezzlement? Was she a collaborator in juggling the books? Was that Floyd's reason for wanting her in his office instead of in college? Did she collaborate willingly, or was Floyd a tyrant who gave orders and insisted on being obeyed?

Does she know where he is? Does she have any guesses where he is?

It was about eleven o'clock when headlights came bobbing through the Black Forest. Koko announced the fact, having seen them first. Qwilleran switched on the exterior lights and went out to investigate. There were two sets of headlights. He stood with his fists on his hips and listened to the owl hooting until the vehicles came into full view.

The first was a pickup truck, and Derek Cuttlebrink unfolded his long frame from the driver's seat. "Brought you a load of wood," he announced flippantly.

Two women from the second vehicle walked forward. "Hi, Qwill," said Fran Brodie. "We're delivering a surprise!"

Elizabeth was with her. "You can sit in it, Mr. Q, and wonderful things will happen! I have it on good authority."

"Not another rocking chair!" he said, trying not to sound ungrateful, yet leaving himself leeway to refuse it.

What Derek was unloading from the truck was an armload of five-foot poles. "Where shall I set 'em up?" he asked, pausing on the threshold.

Fran, who had led the way into the barn, pointed toward the lounge area. "Over there, Derek. There's plenty of space between the fireplace and the sofa." Having been the interior designer for the barn, she retained a proprietary interest in it. Whenever she visited, she went about straightening pictures, moving furniture,

and giving unsolicited advice. Her sincere, good-natured aggres-
siveness usually amused Qwilleran, but he drew the line at five-
foot poles.

"What the devil are those things supposed to be?" he demanded
in a cranky voice.

"It's a portable pyramid," Elizabeth announced with the air of
a generous benefactor. "Wally Toddwhistle designed it; Derek will
put it together for you."

"Only takes a jiffy," Derek said. "All you need is a screwdriver.
Got a screwdriver?"

"There's a toolkit in the broom closet." Qwilleran threw himself
on the sofa and watched with a dour expression as five-foot poles
were joined to become ten-foot poles, which fitted together to
make a ten-foot square; then four other ten-foot poles were attached to the corners and joined at the apex.

"Voilà! A pyramid!" cried Elizabeth.

Derek crawled into the cagelike structure and sat crosslegged.
"Wow! I'm getting vibrations! I'm getting ideas! How about selling
Elizabeth the barn, Mr. Q, and I'll open a restaurant?"

"How about telling me what this damn fool thing is all about?"
Qwilleran retorted.

Fran spoke up. "Larry and Junior ganged up on us and wouldn't
let us use it in our stage set. I thought you'd enjoy experimenting
with it. Then you could write a column about pyramid power. It
has something to do with the electromagnetic field."

"Hmmm," he murmured, mellowing a trifle.

Derek, still in the pyramid, said, "Somebody get my guitar!"

Elizabeth ran out to his truck, returning with the instrument,
and he sang a ballad titled "The Blizzard of 1912." Everyone said
he'd never done it better. Derek said he'd felt inspired. Qwilleran
suggested some refreshments.

With their drinks and bowls of Kabibbles, they sat around the
big coffee table, facing the pyramid. Fran and Derek were in the
usual rehearsal clothes, straight from the ragbag, but Elizabeth was
striking in a baggy red jumpsuit tied about the middle with a long
sash of many colors. The Siamese sat a safe distance from both
guests and pyramid.

"How are the rehearsals progressing?" Qwilleran asked.

"Situation normal," said the director. "Larry is allergic to green makeup . . . The prop girl has eloped, and we can't find any of the props . . . The stage manager broke his thumb. And the donkey head hasn't arrived from Down Below."

"Hee-haw! Hee-haw!" Derek put in for dramatic effect.

Yum Yum scooted up the ramp and looked down from the second balcony, but Koko merely wiggled his ears.

"When is the first dress rehearsal?"

"Monday. The tickets are selling very well. We may not have a show, but we'll have an audience."

"How many intermissions?"

"One. We're cutting after Bottom and Titania are bewitched. It sends the audience out smiling and brings them back ready for more."

"Hey! What are those ducks up there?" Derek asked, pointing to the top of the fireplace cube.

Qwilleran said, "From left to right: Quack, Whistle, and Squawk. They're hand-carved decoys that Polly brought from Oregon. Actually, left to right, they're a merganser, a pintail, and a lesser scaup."

Derek tried quacking, whistling, and squawking like a duck before the conversation returned to community theatre: its problems, calamities, and embarrassments.

"Like the time we were doing a romantic costume play," Fran recalled. "Hoop skirts, powdered wigs, and satin breeches! The female lead was in a car crash on opening night, and Larry had to do her whole part, reading from the book, wearing a beard and tattered jeans. Talk about embarrassing! To the audience it was high comedy. They loved it!"

Then Qwilleran remembered, "In my first stage experience, I played the butler and dropped a silver tray with a whole tea service—*crash!* I felt like cutting my throat with the butter knife."

"The worst thing," Derek said, "is when somebody forgets his lines—freezes—goes blank! For some reason the audience stares at *you!* And you're standing there with egg on your face."

At that moment, Qwilleran, who was keeping an eye on Koko

and the cheese, saw the cat approach the pyramid and cautiously step into the so-called electromagnetic field. When he reached the exact center, the hair on his back stood on end! His tail puffed up like a porcupine! Then the lights went out.

"Don't move," Qwilleran warned his guests. "Stay where you are till I find the flashlights." He groped his way to the kitchen, while the others said, "What happened? . . . There's no storm . . . Transformer blew, somewhere in the neighborhood, maybe . . ."

Qwilleran announced that everything was out: refrigerator, electric clock, everything. He distributed flashlights and asked Derek to go to the top balcony and check for lights on Main Street. "If we're the only ones affected, I'll call the power company."

Soon Derek shouted down to the main floor, "The whole county's without power! It's blacked out in every direction."

"We'd better go home," Fran said.

Qwilleran accompanied them to their vehicles and collected the flashlights after they had turned on their headlights. On the way to the parking area, Fran grabbed his arm and said in a low voice, "They found the girl."

"What girl?"

"Trevelyan's secretary, but not him."

"How do you know?"

"My mother got it from Dad when he came off his shift. The girl was in Texas, but not hiding out—just driving around to the mall and the hair-dresser as if nothing had happened."

"Did they pick her up?"

"Not yet. They're checking out her story—that she was fired two weeks before the surprise audit, which she claims to know nothing about."

Qwilleran said, "That sounds like a well-rehearsed explanation. She was on the Party Train with her boss on the day of the audit."

"Well, according to her story, the management had fired her with two weeks' notice. The train ride was her farewell party. After that, she drove to her home state, alone. One thing she volunteered: Her boss always talked about Alaska and might have gone there."

Or Switzerland, Qwilleran thought. Floyd must have known an audit would be inevitable, but how would he know the timing?

And then he thought, The person who tipped him off to leave town may have been the one who blew the whistle. It was improbable, but not impossible.

When Qwilleran returned to the barn, he made a cursory search for the Siamese, flashing his battery-operated lantern to left and right. To his surprise, Koko was still in the pyramid, sitting in dead center, looking as large as a raccoon.

"Koko! Get out of that thing!"

There was no response.

He likes it, Qwilleran decided. He's getting a treatment. Then he yelled the word that always got results: "Treat!" Yum Yum's paws could be heard pelting down the ramp. As for Koko, he stepped calmly out of the pyramid and shook himself until he returned to his normal size and shape. One thing disturbed Qwilleran: the instant that Koko left the center of the pyramid, the lights came on, and the refrigerator started humming. There was a glow above the trees to the west: the lights of Main Street.

Whether his suspicions were right or wrong, Qwilleran immediately went to work with the screwdriver, disassembling the pyramid. He carried the poles gingerly from the barn and pitched them into the jungly remains of the orchard.

"Whoo-hoo-hoo . . . hoo-hoo," flashed a message from Marconi.

"Same to you!" Qwilleran shouted.

CHAPTER 10

The morning after the blackout, Qwilleran regretted his impulsive dumping of the pyramid poles. Was the power failure a coincidence or not? With some experimentation he might be able to write a column about it, if Koko would cooperate. The cat never liked to do anything unless it was his own idea, and any attempt to deposit him bodily in the cagelike contraption would be thwarted by a whirlwind of squirming, kicking, spitting, and snarling. Then . . . the morning newscast on WPKX affected Qwilleran's decision:

"Police are investigating last night's homicide at the Trackside Tavern in Sawdust City. James Henry Ducker, twenty-four, of Chipmunk Township, was the victim of a knifing during a power failure, while soccer fans held a post-game celebration. The Moose County Electric Cooperative is unable to explain the power outage that blacked out the entire county between eleven thirty and eleven forty-five. There was no equipment failure, according to a spokesman for the co-op. No storm conditions or high winds were recorded by the WPKX meteorology department. An inquiry is continuing."

The murder changed Qwilleran's thinking entirely. If he even hinted at his conjecture in print, the national media—always hungry for bizarre news from the boondocks—would pounce on it. TV crews and news teams from Down Below would descend on Moose County, and the family of James Henry Ducker would sue Koko for three billion. Forget it! he told himself.

As for the victim, residents of Chipmunk were subject to mayhem, and post-game soccer celebrations were notoriously violent, especially in Mudville, which was known for its roister-doister taverns. Qwilleran could imagine the yelling, table banging, brawling, and bottle smashing prompted by the total darkness. In the resulting bedlam someone could empty a semiautomatic without being heard.

Bedlam was the order of the day as he prepared breakfast for the Siamese. "Feeding time at the zoo!" he shouted above the cacophany of yowls and shrieks. "Let's hear it for Alaska smoked salmon!" he exhorted in his Carnegie Hall voice. "Smoked over alderwood fires! Age-old process!" He was reading from the can, and the louder he projected, the louder they howled. All three of them enjoyed exercising their lungs. On such a day, when the atmosphere was clear and the windows were open, the din could be heard as far as the theatre parking lot.

For his own breakfast Qwilleran walked downtown to Lois's

Luncheonette and stopped at the library on the way back, to visit with Polly in her fishbowl of an office on the mezzanine.

"Where were you and Bootsie when the lights went out?" he inquired.

"We both retired early and missed it completely," she said with a weariness unusual so early in the morning. "I felt some discomfort after dining with the Hasselriches. It was rather stressful, and my digestion is below par these days."

"I've reiterated, Polly, that you're worrying too much about your house."

"I suppose so, but it's such a tremendous responsibility. I'm working on my color schemes now. One has to bear in mind the exposure of each room, the choice of advancing or receding hues, tints that are flattering to complexions, and so forth."

"Fran Brodie could do that for you, one-two-three."

"But I want to do it myself, Qwill! I've told you that!" she said curtly. "If I make mistakes, I'm prepared to live with them." Then, with a slight inquiring lift of eyebrows, she asked, "How did Mrs. Robinson enjoy dinner at Tipsy's?"

Ah! The women have been talking, Qwilleran thought: Robinson to Alstock to Duncan. He replied, "She seemed favorably impressed. It would have been more enjoyable if you were there. What did your literary ladies have for dinner? Was it chicken pot pie again?"

"Turkey chow mein," Polly said stiffly.

The mention of food was his cue to invite her to dinner. Instead, he asked where he would find dog books. He said he planned to write a column on chows. Dinner dates with Polly were becoming more of an obligation than a pleasure.

On the way out, Qwilleran stopped to check on Homer Tibbitt's current project.

"Railroads!" the old man said. "The SC&L Line was the lifeblood of the county in mining and lumbering days, and it was all done with steam. I grew up on a farm outside Little Hope and knew the language of the whistles before I knew the alphabet. When I was five years old, my brothers and I would go into town on Saturdays to watch the trains go by. I remember the station platform: wood boards put together with nailheads as big as dimes. Little Hope was only a flagstop, and most trains went straight through. I could hear them coming, getting louder and louder, until the big wheels went roaring past. It was frightening, I tell you! Seventy-five tons of iron, breathing fire!"

"Were there many wrecks?"

"Yes, a lot of blood was spilled, most of it for the sake of being on time. Being on time made money for the SC&L and meant a bonus for the engineer, so he'd go too fast, trying to get his lading to a cargo ship that was ready to sail. . . . One of these days I'll write a book."

When Qwilleran picked up his mail and daily paper, he usually walked down the trail, but now he drove in order to deliver a cooler of beverages. The morning after the blackout, Eddie's only helper was one of the Herculean young blond men indigenous to Moose County.

"Where's Benno?" Qwilleran asked.

Eddie walked over to him and started sharpening a pencil. "I dunno.

Prob'ly hung over."

"Where were you when the lights went out last night?"

"Over at a friend's place. It di'n't last long." Eddie looked red-eyed and minus pep, and Qwilleran was in no mood to linger. He wanted to go home and read what the *Something* had to say about the murder.

The headline read: BLACKOUT SPAWNS KILLING IN BAR.

When the lights went on again at the Trackside Tavern in Sawdust City, following last night's brief power outage, one customer was found dead, the victim of a knifing. The body of James Henry Ducker, 24, of Chipmunk Township, was slumped in a booth, bleeding profusely from wounds apparently inflicted by a hunting knife or similar weapon. He was pronounced dead at the scene.

The table in the booth had been swept clean of beer bottles

and shot glasses in the scuffle that preceded the assault, according to barkeeper Stan Western.

"We always have a noisy demonstration when the lights go out," he said, "but last night was a blinger! Never heard such rowdy carrying-on. Soccer fans, mostly."

The rowdy outburst followed an Intercounty League game between Sawdust City and Lockmaster, which the visiting team won by the close score of 5 to 3.

Police questioned patrons, but no one in the dimly lighted bar had noticed the deceased or his drinking partner in the corner booth.

Western said Ducker was not a regular customer. Barmaid Shirley Dublay had noticed a ponytail on the man who was later killed, but she was unable to describe the second individual in the booth where the crime was committed. "I was too busy," she said. "The other barmaid called in sick, and I was working the floor all alone."

No arrests have been made. Sawdust City police and state troopers are investigating.

The reason for the 15-minute blackout remains a mystery, according to a spokesperson for the Moose County Electric Cooperative.

Also on page one was a sidebar with Roger MacGillivray's byline, describing the scene of the crime:

On a normal night the Trackside Tavern on East Main Street in Sawdust City is a quiet neighborhood bar, where folks drop in for a nip, a friendly chat, and maybe a game of pool. When the TV set isn't covering sports, the radio is tuned into country western and the new rock station, but there are no video games.

Factory workers, downtown businessmen, truckers, railroad personnel, and retirees mingle at the long bar, or in the handful of booths, or at the small scarred tables. It's strictly a male hangout, following an incident ten years ago that made it unpopular with women.

Otherwise, its hundred-year-old history includes some swashbuckling fights when it was Sully's Saloon before Prohibition, a period as a blind pig, and a series of different owners as the Trackside Tavern.

The typical old north-country atmosphere of the tavern has remained unchanged, however: Knotty pine walls hung with mounted deer heads, wide pine floorboards rippled with a century of workboots and scraping chairs, and a wood-burning stove that heats the barnlike interior in winter. On the rare summer occasions when air conditioning is needed, the front and back doors are opened to funnel lake breezes through the barroom.

The mood is easy-going, relaxing—except on Thursday nights if the local soccer team is playing a home game. "Strangers come in and whoop it up," said barkeeper Stan Western. "They're always welcome. Good crowd, mostly. Never had anything like this happen before. I think that fights between fans that started on the field after the game carried over into the bar."

Roger was honing his craft as a newswriter, Qwilleran thought, but he should have explained the incident that kept women away from the Trackside.

As for the soccer-brawl theory as a motive for murder, Qwilleran had a different idea, and he wanted to run it past his friend at the police station. He phoned first, to be sure Brodie was there, then drove downtown in a hurry. The sergeant waved him into the inner office.

"Too late for coffee, if you came for a handout," the chief said.

"That's all right," Qwilleran said lightly. "Your constabulary brew leaves something to be desired. Nothing personal, of course."

Brodie grunted a constabulary reply.

"What did you think of the mysterious blackout, Andy?"

"Hard to figure. A woman called the station this morning and wanted us to investigate. She thought it was done purposely by UFOs. We told her it was only a large fish going over the dam near the hydro plant."

"Did she buy that?"

"I don't know. The sergeant hung up."

"Whatever the cause," Qwilleran said, "it was a convenient cover-up for murder. Did you like the coverage in the paper?"

"Not bad. Most of it was accurate. It wasn't a hunting knife, though. That was a reporter's guesswork. It was some other kind, but that's classified. It could affect the investigation."

"Are you in on the case, Andy?"

"We cooperate with the Sawdust PD and the state troopers."

"Do you find it strange that none of the customers noticed the person who was with Ducker?"

Brodie gave him a sharp glance. "Don't believe everything you read in the paper."

"Are you implying that you have a description of the suspect?"

"Are you just here to ask questions?" the chief growled.

"No, as a matter of fact, I have a theory to bounce off your official skull. As you know, Polly is building a house at the corner of the orchard trail and Trevelyan Road."

"How's she comin' with it?"

"That's a long story, but my point is that one of the carpenters is a young Chipmunk fellow with a ponytail—"

"A lot of guys have 'em if they jog or do sweaty work outdoors," Brodie interrupted.

"Hear me out, Andy. This guy failed to show up for work today. His peers call him Benno. I have a wild hunch—" Qwilleran stroked his moustache. "I have a hunch that Benno is James Henry Ducker, and that the murder was not soccer-related but drug-related. I know you don't have a big drug problem up here . . ."

"But it's starting, and Chipmunk is where it's at."

"That being the case, he could have been dealing in bennies."

"Who does he work for?"

"Polly's contractor is Eddie Trevelyan, Floyd's son."

"Sure, I knew him when he was in high school and I was with the sheriff's department. Eddie got into trouble and would have had a juvenile record, only his father pulled strings to get it off the books. He was good at that! Even so, Eddie was expelled from Pickax High, and—wouldn't you know?—Floyd-boy sued the school board."

Qwilleran said, "Eddie seems to be doing all right now. He works hard and does a good job, as far as I can see. Drinks heavily, I suspect, but not during work hours. Smokes a lot—only the legal stuff. Keeps a sharp pencil, so he can't be all bad."

"Yeah, all he needs is a shave and a haircut."

"Eddie told me that Benno had been his buddy since high school."

"Then your hunch is right. Benno is James Henry Ducker, and Eddie has lost a carpenter as well as a father who can pull strings."

"Any news on the manhunt, Andy?"

"Nothing for publication."

"I wonder what happened to the Lumbertown Party Train."

"It's on a siding in Mudville."

"One more question, and then I'm leaving," Qwilleran said. "What happened at the Trackside Tavern ten years ago that scared women away?"

"Who knows? That's not my beat. Look it up in your newspaper files."

"The *Something* wasn't publishing ten years ago, and the *Pickax Picayune* was never more than a chicken-dinner newspaper. But there's some hushed-up reason why women don't patronize that bar."

Brodie waved the subject away, saying impatiently, "Maybe they didn't like the cigars and four-letter words. Maybe the bartender wouldn't mix pink drinks. Who cares? It was ten years ago. Why don't you ask your smart cat? Lieutenant Hames was asking about him the other day. He was up here for a few days."

"What was he doing here?" Qwilleran asked. He had known the detective Down Below while working for the *Daily Fluxion,* and now he wondered why a metropolitan lawman would be involved in an investigation 400 miles north of everywhere, unless—

"He was up here with his family, doing some camping and fishing. They caught some big ones. I met him at a drug seminar Down Below a while back and gave him a big selling on Moose County. His kids were crazy about it."

As Qwilleran was leaving the police station, he saw Dwight Somers coming out of city hall. "Dwight, you old buzzard! Where've you been?"

"Buzzin' around the county, picking up clients," the publicity man said. "How about an early dinner at the Mill?"

"Suits me. I'll meet you there after I go home and feed the cats."

Dinner at the Old Stone Mill was brief. Dwight had another appointment, and Qwilleran was anticipating another report from Celia.

The younger man was elated. He had lined up the Moose County Community College as a client and was working on a great project with the K Foundation. "That's the good news," he said. "On the down side, I'm being hounded by Floyd-boy's creditors. Just because I promoted his party train, they think I'm going to pay his outstanding bills. It's strange they haven't found him, isn't it?"

"Are you in touch with the family?" Qwilleran asked.

"Only with their attorney. He doesn't allow them to talk to anybody, including me."

"Didn't you tell me that Floyd's secretary had an apartment in your building in Indian Village?"

"Yeah, but I never got an invitation to drop in for a neighborly visit. Perhaps I'm too neat and clean. I've seen some scruffy types knocking on her door, and Floyd himself was a little on the wild side, sartorially."

It was a one-drink, small-steak, no-dessert dinner, and the publicity man apologized for having to rush away. As they walked to the parking lot, Qwilleran asked, "Do you happen to remember the name of the engineer who drove the locomotive when we took our historic ride?"

"Historic in more ways than one," Dwight said bitingly. "There'll never be another. The government will be sure to get their hands on Floyd's rolling stock. . . . But to answer your question: Sure, his name is Ozzie Penn. He's Floyd's father-in-law."

"If he could tell me some good railroad stories, I'd interview

him—not for the 'Qwill Pen.' I want to write a book on the Steam
Age of railroading."

"Well, he's in his eighties, but in good shape and mentally sharp.
We got a doctor's okay before letting him drive No. 9. He lives at
the Railroad Retirement Center in Mudville," Dwight said as he
stepped into his car. There was a packet on the seat, which he
handed to Qwilleran. "Here's the video of our train ride. Run it
and see if you think we could sell copies to benefit the college."

"Thanks. I'll do that," Qwilleran said, "and . . . uh . . . keep it
under your hat, Dwight, about the railroad book. I'll be using a
pseudonym, and I haven't told anyone but you."

The two men went their separate ways.

At home Qwilleran looked up the phone number of the Railroad Retirement Center; the address was on Main Street. Then he
checked the Trackside Tavern. First, out of curiosity, he called the
bar.

"Not open!" the man's harried voice shouted into the phone
before slamming the receiver.

At the Retirement Center the male switchboard operator paged
Ozzie Penn and tracked him down in the TV room.

"Hello? Who is it?" said a reedy voice with the surprise and
apprehension of one who never receives a phone call.

"Good evening, Mr. Penn," Qwilleran said slowly and dis-
tinctly. "I was one of the passengers on the Party Train when you
drove old No. 9. We all had a good time. That engine's a wonderful piece of machinery."

"Yep, she be a beaut!"

"My name is James Mackintosh, and I'm writing a book on the
old days of railroading. Would you be willing to talk to me? You've
had a long and honorable career, and I'm sure you know plenty of
stories."

"That I do," said the old man. "Plenty!"

"May I visit you at the Center? Is there a quiet place where we
can talk? You'll receive payment for your time, of course. I'd like
to drive out there tomorrow."

"Tomorrow?"

"Saturday."

"What be yer name again?"

"Mackintosh. James Mackintosh. How about one o'clock?"

"I ain't goin' no place."

As Qwilleran replaced the receiver, he thought, This old man speaks a fascinating kind of substandard English that will fade out in another generation. Eddie Trevelyan's speech was simply the bad grammar common in Moose County. Ozzie Penn spoke Old Moose.

"May I use your TV?" Qwilleran asked the Siamese, who had been watching him talk into the inanimate instrument. The telephone was something even Koko had never understood.

The three of them trooped to the highest balcony, furnished to feline taste with soft carpet, cushioned baskets, empty boxes, a ladder, scratching pads and posts, and a small TV with VCR. There was one chair which the cats commandeered, while Qwilleran sat on the floor to watch the video.

It was a festive collage of important people arriving at the depot and milling about on the platform, with the camera lingering on certain subjects: woman with large hat, man with oversized moustache, woman in expensive-looking pantsuit, man in Scottish tartan. (Koko yowled at certain images for no apparent reason.) The car valets jumped around like red devils. The brass band tootled. Then the great No. 9 came puffing around a curve, blowing its whistle. The elderly engineer leaned from his cab; two firemen posed in the gangway with their shovels. Then the conductor bawled the destinations, and feet mounted the yellow stepstool. When the diners drank a toast in ice water, Qwilleran thought, It was symbolic!

Although the camera occasionally panned picturesque stretches of countryside, the emphasis was on the passengers, who might be induced to buy the video to benefit the college. Qwilleran rewound the tape, thanked the Siamese for the use of their facilities, and went down the ramp to greet Celia Robinson.

Her face was lively with smiles, and her large handbag produced a box of chocolate chip cookies. "We can have a party. They're good with milk. Do you have any milk, Chief?"

"No, only a milk substitute called black coffee," he apologized, "but I'm a master at its preparation." With a grand flourish he pressed a button on the computerized coffeemaker, which started the grinding, gurgling, and dripping. The brew that resulted was good, Celia said, but awfully strong. As they sat down with their coffee and cookies, Qwilleran said to her in an ominous tone of voice, "Celia, you're being tailed by the police."

"What!" she cried. "What have I done?"

"Only kidding; don't be alarmed. The police chief has seen your red car in the parking lot and knows you're living in the carriage house, and the detectives staking out the Trevelyan property know you've visited The Roundhouse. Next, they'll see you driving through the Black Forest for these meetings."

"Should I get my car painted?"

"That won't be necessary, but it emphasizes the need to keep Operation Whistle under wraps. Here's what I suggest for your cover: You're planning to start a specialized catering service: hot meals for shut-ins . . . refreshments for kids' birthday parties . . . gourmet delicacies for cats and dogs. We might run an ad in the paper to that effect."

"Do you mean it?" she asked in astonishment.

"Only to fool the cops. You might take a casserole to Florrie, just in case you're stopped. . . . And now, what happened today? Did you take Wrigley?"

"Oh, he was a big hit! He sat on Florrie's lap, and she stroked him and looked so happy! Tish didn't want to miss the fun, so she fixed lunch for us and gave Wrigley a bit of tuna. After a while I asked the name of the bank that they own, so I could open an account. Tish said it was a credit union especially for railroad workers, and she began to get very fidgety. Pretty soon she said she had to go and buy groceries. Then I thought of a sneaky question to ask Florrie . . . It would be nice if I could tape these conversations, Chief."

"It would arouse suspicion," he said.

"I mean, with a hidden tape recorder. My grandson had one that he used in Florida. I could phone him, and he'd send it by overnight mail."

"It's illegal, Celia, to tape someone's conversation without permission. Thousands of persons do it and get away with it, but if it came to light in this case, you'd be in trouble, and Operation Whistle would be involved. It's a bright idea, but please forget it. You're doing very well with your little notebook. Did you do your homework?"

"Yes, I read all the clippings about the scandal and figured out some ways to get the women to talk. After Tish left, I asked Florrie what time her husband usually came home to supper. She looked at me funny—all bright-eyed and excited—and said, 'If he comes home, they'll put him in jail, and they'll take all his trains away. He stole a lot of money.' She finished with a wild laugh that frightened Wrigley. I tried to calm her down, but she wanted to go down on the elevator and show me the trains. Have you ever seen them, Chief?"

"I have indeed—a fantastic display! I wrote a column about Floyd's model railroad a couple of months ago, before he absconded."

"Well! Wait till you hear this! Florrie told me to press the button and start the trains running, but I was afraid of pressing the wrong one and wrecking the whole shebang. So Florrie wheeled herself to the switchboard and started pushing buttons and turning knobs. All the trains started to move at the same time—faster and faster until they crashed into each other and into bridges and buildings! I screamed for her to turn it off, but she was enjoying it and laughing like crazy. Then a fuse blew, I guess, because all the lights went out, but it was too late. The whole thing was wrecked! I was a wreck myself, believe me! When Tish came back from the store, I was still as limp as a rag, and I couldn't find Wrigley."

"How did she react to the disaster?"

"Quite cool. She disconnected something and said it was all right—no danger. But after we tucked Florrie in for her afternoon nap, Tish put her face in her hands and started to bawl. She really sobbed and wailed! I said, 'I'm terribly sorry about the trains, but there was nothing I could do.' She shook her head from side to side and said it wasn't the trains she cared about; it was other things. I put my arm around her and said, 'Have a good cry, dear. It'll do you good. Don't be afraid to tell me your troubles. I'm your friend.' That started another gush of tears."

Qwilleran said, "You tell this story very well, Celia."

"Do you think so? I used to tell stories to Clayton when he was little . . . So after a while Tish dabbed her eyes and sniffled and suddenly said in a bitter voice, *'I despise my . . . mother's husband!'* I tried to get her to talk about it and unburden herself."

Qwilleran nodded, but his thoughts were elsewhere. If Tish despised her father—for whatever reason—could she have been the one who blew the whistle? Or could her show of hostility be camouflage for her own involvement in the fraud?

"Yow!" came a warning from Koko, who was looking out the kitchen window.

"Someone's coming!" Qwilleran jumped to his feet. "He heard a car coming through the woods!"

"Police? Where shall I go?" Celia asked in alarm, grabbing her handbag.

"Stay where you are."

It was only Mr. O'Dell, the maintenance man, wanting to pick up his check for services rendered.

"So . . . go on, Celia. Did Tish talk?"

"Yes, she told me about F.T. That's what she calls her father. He terrorized her and her brother Eddie when they were growing up. Today she resents the fact that he made her take business courses in high school and go to work in his office instead of going to college. But mostly she hates the way he ruined Florrie's life— with his neglect, and his stingy way with money, and his girl-friends."

Qwilleran checked the notes he had been taking. "It's not true, you know, that the Lumbertown Credit Union is only for railroad employees. Tish was trying to steer you away from the subject."

"I believe it. She's very cagey about certain things. Just before I left, I said to her, 'Florrie told me something I didn't understand. She said her husband stole some money and might go to jail. Was she out of her head?' When I said that, Tish got terribly flustered, saying there are some complications at his office, and no one knows for sure what it's all about. Then she froze up, so I didn't ask any more questions. We searched for Wrigley and found him crouched in his sandbox, as if it was the only safe place in the house. They want me to take him again on Monday, but . . . Oh! Look at the parade!" she squealed, pointing to the top of the fireplace cube.

Soberly Qwilleran said, "Left to right, their names are Quack, Whistle, Squawk, Yum Yum, and Koko."

The two cats were in perfect alignment with the decoys, folded into compact bundles that made them look like sitting ducks.

"You can't tell me," he said, "that cats don't have a sense of humor!"

Celia's explosive laughter disturbed the masquerade, and the two "live" ducks jumped to the floor. "I'm sorry, kitties," she apologized. "I've always heard that cats don't like to be laughed at. . . . Well, that's all I have to report. I'd better go home and see if Wrigley is recovering from his scare."

As Qwilleran escorted her to the parking area, he said, "I may devise a new strategy this weekend. Shall we get together for a briefing Sunday evening?"

"Okay with me, Chief," she said blithely.

Back at the barn, another pantomime was in progress. Koko was on the telephone desk, pushing the English pencil box with his nose, pushing it toward the edge of the desk.

"NO!" Qwilleran thundered. Rushing to the spot, he caught the antique treasure before it landed on the clay tile floor. "Bad cat!"

Koko flew up the ramp in a blur of fur.

CHAPTER 11

For his interview with Ozzie Penn, Qwilleran went equipped with his usual tape recorder plus some snapshots of No. 9 making her comeback on Audit Sunday, as the newspaper called it. Before leaving, he trimmed his moustache somewhat and hoped he would look more like James Mackintosh, author, than Jim Qwilleran, columnist.

The Railroad Retirement Center was directly across Main Street from the Trackside Tavern, still closed. Two police vehicles were parked at the curb, one obviously from the forensic lab. The Cen-

ter, formerly a railroad hotel, was a three-story brick building without such unnecessary details as porches, shutters, or ornamental roof
brackets.

When Qwilleran walked into the lobby, it was vacant except
for a young male telephone operator at the switchboard. Behind
him was a bank of pigeonholes for mail and messages, with a room
number on each; all were empty. The lobby was clean, one could
say that for it. Brown walls, brown floors, and brown wood furniture gleamed with high-gloss varnish, reminding Qwilleran of a
press club Down Below that occupied a former jail. Through double glass doors he could see a television screen, lively with colorful
commercials. Several elderly men sat around it, staring or dozing.
A few others were playing cards.

"Are you Mr. Mackintosh?" the operator asked. "Ozzie's waiting for you. Room 203. Elevator down the hall; stairs at the back."

Qwilleran trusted his knees more than he trusted the grim-
looking elevator with folding metal gate. He chose to walk up the
brown varnished stairwell to a brown hallway, where he knocked
on the brown door of 203. It opened immediately, and there stood
the old engineer he remembered from Audit Sunday—a big, husky
man, though slightly stooped. He had changed, however, since the
debut of No. 9. The ruddy face that had beamed with pride in the
window of the engineer's cab was now gray and weary.

"Good afternoon, Mr. Penn. I'm the one who's writing a book
on railroading in the Age of Steam. Mackintosh is the name."

"Come in. I been waitin'. Where ye from?"

"Chicago."

"Set ye down. Call me Ozzie." His welcome was cordial, although he seemed too tired to smile. He slapped his denim chest
and said, "Wore my over-halls for the pitcher."

"Sorry I didn't bring a camera, Ozzie, but I have some good
photos of you in the cab of No. 9, and they're yours to keep."

The old man accepted the snapshots gratefully. "By Crikey, she
be a purty hog, no mistake."

They sat with a small lamp table between them, and Qwilleran
set up his tape recorder. "Mind if I record this? Did you drive
No. 9 in the old days?"

"Yep. I were a young-un then. Them diesels, they be okay, but ain't nothin' like steam!" The man spoke pure Old Moose.

Qwilleran's practiced eye roved over the shabby furnishings without staring or criticizing. "That's a beautiful oil can," he said, nodding toward a shiny brass receptacle with a thin, elongated spout. "How was it used?"

"That were for oilin' piston rods and drivers. Kep' the wheels on the rails for nigh onto fifty year, it did. They give it me when I retired. Better'n the gold watch, it were."

"I believe it! You were a master of your craft, I'm told. What does it take to make a good engineer?"

Ozzie had to think before answering. "L'arnin' to start up slow and stop smooth . . . L'arnin' to keep yer head when it be hell on the rails . . . Prayin' to God fer a good fireman . . . And abidin' by Rule G," he finished with a weak chuckle.

"What's the fireman's job on a steam locomotive?"

"He be the one stokes the firebox an' keeps the boiler steamin'. Takes a good crew to make a good run and come in on time. Spent my whole life comin' in on time. Eleventh commandment, it were called. Now, here I be, an' time don't mean nothin'."

Qwilleran asked, "Why was it so important to be on time?"

"Made money for the comp'ny. Made wrecks, too . . . takin' chances, takin' shortcuts."

"Were you in many wrecks?"

"Yep, an' on'y jumped once. I were a young-un, deadheadin' to meet a crew in Flapjack. Highballin' round a curve, we run into a rockslide. Engineer yelled 'Jump!' an' I jumped. Fireman jumped, too. Engineer were killed."

"What do you know about the famous wreck at Wildcat, Ozzie?"

"That were afore my time, but I heerd plenty o' tales in the SC&L switchyard. In them days the yard had eighteen tracks and a roundhouse for twenty hogs." His voice faded away and his eyes glazed as his mind drifted into the past.

Qwilleran persisted with his question.

"It weren't called Wildcat in them days. It were South Fork. Trains from up north slowed down to twenty at South Fork afore goin' down a steep grade to a mighty bad curve and a wood trestle bridge. The rails, they be a hun'erd feet over the water. One day a train come roarin' through South Fork, full steam, whistle screechin'. It were a wildcat—a runaway train—headed for the gorge. At the bottom—crash!—bang! Then hissin' steam. Then dead quiet. Then the screamin' started. Fergit how many killed, but it were the worst ever!"

Both men were silent for a moment. Qwilleran could hear the gold watch ticking. Finally he asked, "Did they ever find out what caused the wreck?"

"Musta been the brakes went blooey, but the railroad, they laid it on the engineer—said he were drinkin'. Saved the comp'ny money, it did, to lay it on the engineer. Poor feller! Steam boiler exploded, an' he were scalded to death."

"Horrible!" Qwilleran murmured.

'Yep. It were bad, 'cause he weren't a drinkin' man."

"So that's why they changed the name of the town to Wildcat! You're a very lucky man, Ozzie, to have survived so many dangers! If you had your life to live over again, would you be a hoghead?"

"Yep." After the excitement of telling the story, the old man was running out of steam.

Qwilleran said, "Too bad the Trackside is closed. We could get some food and drink."

"There be another place down the street," said Ozzie, reviving somewhat. "Better'n the Trackside."

As the two men walked down Main Street, slowly, Qwilleran asked if any women lived in the Retirement Center.

"Nope."

"I hear women never go into the Trackside. Do you know why?"

"Nope."

"Railroads are hiring women as engineers now," Qwilleran said.

"Not up here! Not the SC&L!"

The old man was breathing hard when they arrived at the bar and grill called The Jump-Off. A middle-aged woman with a bouncer's build and a rollicking personality greeted them heartily. Four young women in baseball jerseys were talking loudly about their recent win. A few elderly men were scattered about the room. The hearty greeter took their order: rye whiskey straight for Ozzie, ginger ale for Qwilleran.

When Ozzie had downed his drink, Qwilleran asked, "How did you feel about driving old No. 9 and hauling the Party Train?"

"Purty good" was the answer.

"It hasn't made any more runs since then."

"Nope."

"Too bad the credit union had to close. Sawdusters must be feeling the pinch. Were you affected?"

"Nope. Had m'money in a bank."

Hmm, Qwilleran mused; why not in his son-in-law's corporation? "Can you stand another rye, Ozzie? And a burger?"

"Doc says one won't do no harm, so I figger two'll do some good."

Qwilleran signaled for refills. "Did someone tell me Floyd Trevelyan is your son-in-law?"

"Yep."

"How do you like the model trains at his house?"

"Never see'd 'em," Ozzie said, staring into space. There was an awkward silence, which Qwilleran filled with questions about the quality of the burgers, the degree of doneness, the availability of condiments, and the kind of fries. The bar served railroad fries: thick, with skins on. Finally he said, "I met your daughter once. Do you have other children?"

Ozzie's reply was bluntly factual: "One son killed on the rails. One killed in Vietnam. One somewheres out west."

"Sorry to hear that. Do you see your daughter often?"

"Nope. Don't get around much."

Qwilleran coughed and took a bold step. "Did you know she's seriously ill? You ought to make an effort to visit her. She may not have long to live."

Ozzie blinked his eyes. Was it emotion or the rheuminess of old age?

Suddenly he said angrily, "Ain't see'd 'er since she married that feller! Way back then I said he weren't no good. They wasn't even married in church! Guess she l'arned a lesson."

In a voice oozing with sympathy, Qwilleran said, "She tells people she's very proud of you, Ozzie—proud to have a father who's a famous engineer. No matter what happened, you were always her hero."

"Then why di'n't she listen to me? She were a good girl till she met that crook. I knowed he'd turn out bad."

"Yet you agreed to drive No. 9 for him."

"That publicity feller wanted me to do it. Paid good money. It were an honor. All those people cheerin' and the band playin'! Nobody knowed No. 9 were owned by a crook!"

"Have you never seen your grandchildren?"

"Nope."

"The boy is a house builder, and the girl is an accountant, I believe. Is your wife living?"

"Nope. Been gone nine year."

"How did she feel about being estranged from your daughter?"

"Never talked about it. Wouldn't let her say Florrie's name in the house. . . . You say the boy's buildin' houses? Like father, like son. Prob'ly turn out to be another crook!"

Qwilleran thought of their physical resemblance; Eddie had the black Trevelyan hairiness. He said, "Ozzie, a reunion with your daughter might prolong her life. It would mean so much to her. You might find it painful, but it could be the finest thing you've ever done. How long since you've seen her?"

"Twenty-five year. She were on'y nineteen when they had that sham weddin' in an engine cab. In over-halls! Not even a white dress! I di'n't go. Wouldn't let m'wife go neither."

Ozzie hung his head and said no more, and Qwilleran thought, He'd be shocked if he saw her!

After a silence during which they munched their burgers, Qwilleran said, "The woman who takes care of Florrie could pick you up some afternoon and bring you back. Her name is Mrs. Robinson."

There was no response from Ozzie.

"Mrs. Robinson has a video of you driving No. 9 for the Party Train. She'd be glad to show it to you."

"Like t'see that! Fred and Billy, they'd like t'see it, too."

"Who are they?"

"Fred Ooterhans, fireman, and Billy Poole, brakeman. We worked together since I-don't-know-when. We was the best crew on the SC&L. Still together at the Center, playin' cards, shootin' the breeze."

Qwilleran paid the tab and said, "It's been a pleasure meeting you, Ozzie. Thank you for the interview."

"Gonna print it in the book?"

"That's my intention. And don't be surprised if you get a call from Mrs. Robinson."

Shared weekends had always been important to Qwilleran and Polly, ever since he lost his way in a blizzard and stumbled into her country cottage looking like a snowman with a moustache. And yet, weekends were losing their savor, and he blamed it on Polly's house. In an effort to restore some of the magic, however, he proposed Saturday night dinner at the Palomino Paddock in Lockmaster, a five-star, five-thousand-calorie restaurant.

Polly was surprised and pleased. "What is the occasion?"

"You don't know it, but we're exchanging our vows tonight," he said. "You're vowing to stop worrying about your house, and I'm vowing to end the Cold War with Bootsie."

"I'll wear my opals," she said, entering into the spirit of the occasion.

The Paddock was a mix of sophistication and hayseed informality, decorated with bales of straw and photographs of Thoroughbreds. The servers were young equestrians, fresh from a day of riding, eventing, jumping, or hunting. The chef-owner lived on a two-hundred-acre horsefarm.

Seated in a stall, Polly and Qwilleran drank to their new resolve—she with a glass of sherry and he with a glass of Squunk water.

He said, "Don't forget, the play opens Thursday evening, and I have four tickets. We can have dinner with the Rikers."

"Who's playing my namesake?" Polly had been named Hippolyta by a parent who was a Shakespeare scholar.

"Carol Lanspeak. Who else?"

"She's not very Amazonian."

"She doesn't look like a fairy queen, either, but she's doubling as Titania." He pronounced Titania to rhyme with Britannia.

"According to my father, Qwill, Shakespeare took Titania from Ovid and undoubtedly used the Elizabethan pronunciation of the Latin, which would be Tie-tain-ia."

"Try that on Moose County for size," Qwilleran quipped. "Did your father ever explain *Hold, or cut bowstrings?*"

"He said that etymologists have been debating its source for two centuries. I could look it up for you."

"No thanks. Sometimes it's more fun not to know. . . . By the way, I've uncovered another Hermia case: a father who forbade his daughter to marry the man of her choice, disowning her when she disobeyed, and forbidding his wife ever to mention their daughter's name."

"Shakespeare at least had a happy ending. Is there more to your story?"

"There may be. Meanwhile, I've been reading the play aloud, and Koko gets excited whenever I mention Hermia. He also knocked *Androcles and the Lion* off the shelf—not one of Shaw's best, but I enjoyed reading it again. I played the lion when I was in college. It was a good role; no lines to learn."

"What else have you been reading?"

"A mind-boggling book on the engineering of the Panama Canal. Do you realize the Big Ditch took ten years to complete? It's forty miles long, and they dug out 240 million cubic yards of earth!"

She listened in a daze, and Qwilleran knew she was wondering how many cubic yards of earth would be necessary to build a berm on her property.

He rattled on, doubting that she was really listening. "The book was written by Colonel Goethals, the engineer in charge. It was published in 1916. The flyleaf of my copy was inscribed by Euphonia Gage to her father-in-law. It was a Christmas present. He would be Junior Goodwinter's great-grandfather. I'll give the book to Junior when I've finished reading it."

"That will be nice," Polly mused.

When it was time to order from the menu, Qwilleran had no problem in making a choice: she-crab soup, an appetizer of mushrooms stuffed with spinach and goat cheese, a Caesar salad, and sea scallops with sun-dried tomatoes, basil, and saffron cream on angel hair pasta. Polly ordered grouper with no soup, no appetizer, and no salad.

"Are you feeling all right?" he asked anxiously. She tended to keep her ailments a secret.

"Well, I've been plagued with indigestion lately," she confessed, as if it were a character flaw. "I have an appointment with Dr. Diane this week."

He thought, She's getting ulcers over that damned house!

Polly seemed to enjoy her spartan dinner and seemed to be having a good time. And yet, Qwilleran sensed a curtain between them. She was really thinking about her house, and he, to tell the truth, was really thinking about the briefing of his secret agent.

Celia arrived at the barn Sunday evening in a flurry of smiles and youthful exuberance. "I had a wonderful weekend!" she cried. "I attended service at the Little Stone Church and met the pastor during the coffee hour in the basement. The choirleader said she could use another voice, and everyone was so friendly! Then Virginia took me to Black Creek to meet her folks, and we had a lovely brunch. I know I'm going to like it here, Chief."

"Good!" he said. "Make yourself comfortable while I concoct an exotic drink."

While he opened cans of pineapple juice and grapefruit juice, Celia found the wooden whistle on the coffee table and blew a few toots. "This takes me back!" she said. "When I was little and living on a farm, I could hear train whistles blowing all the time. That was to warn people to get off the tracks. Anybody who didn't have a car or a truck used to walk the rails to get to the next town." She sipped her drink. "My! This is good! What did you put in it?"

"I never reveal my culinary secrets," Qwilleran replied pompously.

"In the newspaper the police say they're investigating the scandal. Aren't they getting anywhere?"

"They do things their way, Celia, and we do things our way. We're searching for answers to questions, not hard evidence, which is what they have to have. That's why any scraps of information you pick up at The Roundhouse will help solve the puzzle."

"Something's bothering me, Chief. I feel guilty because I'm sort of . . . *spying* on Tish and Florrie."

"No need to feel that way. You're giving them something they desperately need: friendship, warmth, and sympathy, and at the same time helping to bring a criminal to justice. Just remember not to sound like an interrogator; keep the conversation chatty. Talk about your grandson, and ask Tish about her grandparents. Talk about your brothers, and inquire about hers."

Celia laughed at this. "I'll never go to heaven, Chief, after telling so many lies for you. I only had sisters."

"St. Peter will understand this ignoble means to a noble end. You must also bear in mind, Celia, that Tish may be lying to you; she may be part of the scam."

"Oh, my! That's hard to believe!"

"Nevertheless, keep your wits about you. It would be interesting to know what they're doing for money. Tish is laid off; all credit union deposits are frozen; her father has disappeared; that house must be costly to maintain, to say nothing of the cost of nursing care and medication. Did Floyd provide for the family before decamping? Did he keep a safe in the house? Is that where he kept his ill-gotten gains? Or did he have millions stashed in a suitcase under the bed?"

Celia laughed uproariously. "Now you're really kidding, Chief. How could I find out stuff like that?"

"They're merely questions to keep in the back of your head. How did Tish feel about the secretary who absconded with Floyd? The attorney has instructed them not to talk about the case, but if you can get her to break down, find out what kind of work she did at the Lumbertown office. Did she suspect tampering with the books? If so, did fear of her father prevent her from reporting it?

Perhaps . . . Tish was the one who blew the whistle. This is all long-range probing, of course."

"It's going to be so much fun!" Celia said in great glee.

"Then let's confer again tomorrow evening."

"Do you mind if it's later than usual? Choir practice is Monday nights at seven."

"Not at all. Call me at your convenience," Qwilleran said as he escorted her to the parking area. "How's your little car running?"

"Just fine! It gets good mileage, and I love the color!"

After the red car had driven away, Qwilleran walked the floor to collect his thoughts—through the much-used library area, the seldom-used dining area, the spacious foyer, the comfortable lounge, and back to the library. Twenty-eight laps equaled one mile, Derek Cuttlebrink had computed in one of his goofy moments. Whenever Qwilleran traversed this inside track, both cats would fall into line behind him, marching with tails at twelve o'clock.

Around and around the fireplace cube the three of them traipsed, the man feeling like a Pied Piper without pipes. On the sixth lap he noticed the twistletwig rocker in front of the fireplace cube, its intricately bent willow twigs silhouetted against the white wall. According to Elizabeth Hart, one could sit in the grotesque piece of furniture and expect to think profound thoughts. What Qwilleran needed at the moment was a little profundity, and he undertook to test her theory.

He slid into the rocker's inviting contours gingerly, not quite trusting it to bear his weight. When there was no sign of collapse, he relaxed and began to rock, slowly at first, and then more vigorously. The action attracted Koko, who circled him three times and then leaped lightly into his lap. This was surprising; Koko was not a lap-sitter.

"Well, young man, what's this all about?" Qwilleran asked.

"Yow!" Koko replied as he started to dig in the crook of Qwilleran's elbow. Yum Yum sometimes gave a few casual digs before settling down, but Koko was excavating with zeal. His claws were retracted, but his paws were powerful. Could this be blamed on the twistletwig mystique?

"Who do you think you are?" Qwilleran demanded. "Digger O'Dell? Colonel Goethals? This is not the Panama Canal!"

The cat stopped for a few moments, then resumed his chore with increased energy. The game was not only ridiculous; it verged on the painful.

"Ouch! *Enough!*" Qwilleran protested. *"Hold or cut bowstrings!"*

CHAPTER 12

Qwilleran started the week by grinding out a thousand pseudo-serious words on the history of sunburn. It was inspired by an oil painting in Polly's apartment depicting a beach scene at the turn of the century; the women wore bathing suits with sleeves, knee-length skirts, matching hats, and long stockings. The ninety miles of beaches bordering Moose County were now frequented by summer vacationers without stockings, hats, sleeves, or skirts—and sometimes without tops. He titled his column "From Parasols and Gloves . . . to Sunscreen with SPF-30." For his readers who had never seen a parasol, he described it as a light, portable sunshade carried like an umbrella, its name derived from French, Italian, and Latin words meaning "to ward off the sun."

He had to work hard to stretch the subject into a thousand words, and he was not particularly proud of the result when he delivered the copy to Junior Goodwinter. "Consider it a summer space filler," he said as he threw it on the editor's desk.

After scanning the pages, Junior said, "It's topical, but I've seen better from the Qwill Pen. Want us to run it without a by-line and say you're on vacation?"

"It's not *that* bad," Qwilleran protested. "Any more news from Mudville?"

"There's a rumor they've located Floyd-boy's secretary in Texas, but nobody will confirm it."

"How about the murder in the tavern?"

"The police are being cagey, which means (a) they're onto something big or (b) they're not onto anything at all and hate to admit it. What's really odd is that the power company can't explain the outage. Being countywide, it couldn't be part of a local murder plot—or could it? I'm beginning to agree with the UFO buffs. Do you have a theory, Qwill? You usually come up with a wild one."

Qwilleran smoothed his moustache. "If I told you my theory, you'd have me committed."

Leaving the managing editor's office, he stopped in the city room and put a note in Roger MacGillivray's mailbox: "While you're scratching for stories in Mudville, find out what happened at the Trackside Tavern ten years ago. Your reference to it was provocative. Perhaps you know what happened. Perhaps it's too horrendous to mention in a family newspaper. Whisper in your uncle Qwill's ear."

On the way out of the building, Qwilleran passed Hixie Rice's office. The vice president in charge of advertising and promotion hailed him. "Qwill, I loved your column about the sweet corn of August—and about this being the corniest county in the state! I sent Wilfred out to buy several dozen ears. We're sending them to advertisers as a promo."

He grunted a lukewarm acknowledgment of the compliment. "Not to change the subject," he said, "but was Floyd Trevelyan a customer of yours?"

"Yes and no. He was tight-fisted with advertising dollars."

"His son lives in Indian Village. Do you know him?"

"I see him in the parking lot. I thought Gary Pratt looked like a black bear, but Floyd's son is *too much*!"

"Is he in your building?"

"No, I think he's in Dwight's building. Why? Is it important?"

"No, I'm just addressing my Christmas cards early," Qwilleran said with a nonchalant shrug.

Hixie looked at him with suspicion. "You've got something up your sleeve, Qwill! What is it?"

"Are you still chummy with the manager at Indian Village?"

"Not exactly chummy, but she's on my Christmas list in a big way, and she's extremely cooperative. What can I do for you?"

"Floyd Trevelyan's secretary had an apartment in G building. Tell the manager you have a friend Down Below who's being transferred to Pickax and wants to rent an upscale apartment. Ask if Nella Hooper's is vacant—or will it be vacant soon."

"Would you like to tell me what this is all about?"

"Only my journalistic curiosity," he said. "If the apartment is not available, someone must be paying the rent, and it would be interesting to know who—or why."

"I smell intrigue," Hixie said. "Anything else?"

"Find out when Eddie Trevelyan moved in. That's all. Get back to work! Sell ads! Make money for the paper!"

"How's Polly? I haven't seen her lately."

"She's fine—excited about her new house, of course. By the way, she's due for a physical and wants to switch doctors. She doesn't care for the man who bought Melinda's practice. Have you heard any good reports about the Lanspeaks' daughter?"

Hixie waggled an accusing finger at him. "Qwill, you old rogue! Is that your underhanded way of finding out what happened to my late lamented romance? Well, I'll tell you. He was a wonderful, sincere, thoughtful, attentive *bore*! But I still see his mother once a week for French lessons."

"Pardonnez-moi," he said with a stiff bow.

Qwilleran next stopped at Amanda's Studio of Design to see Fran Brodie. She was in-house three days a week, sketching floor plans, working on color schemes, and greeting customers.

"Cup of coffee? Cold drink?" she asked.

He chose coffee. "Have you started dress rehearsals?"

"Tonight's the first. We test our system for handling extras. A busload of lords and ladies will come from the high school in time for the first act—complete with sweeping robes and elaborate headdresses. After the first scene they're not needed until the end of the play. What do we do with them in the meantime? There's no room backstage. Do we put them on the school bus to wait? Do we send them back to school for an hour? You know how giddy kids can get if they're having to wait."

Qwilleran thought for a moment. "Would the Old Stone Church let you use one of their social rooms? Bus the kids across the park, give them a horror video, and pick them up an hour later."

"Super!" Fran exclaimed. "Why didn't we think of that? The Lanspeaks are pillars of the church; they can swing it for us. . . . More coffee?"

While she poured, he asked, "What's the latest from your confidential source? The last thing you told me, the police were checking the secretary's story."

"It turned out to be true, Qwill. Nella Hooper was really fired two weeks before Audit Sunday. She collected severance pay and filed for unemployment benefits."

"How long ago did you do her apartment in Indian Village?"

"More than a year."

"I suppose Floyd paid for the furnishings."

"No, the credit union paid the bill; they could take it as a business expense. Did I tell you the FBI went in with a search warrant? Nella hadn't left anything but the furniture and a tube of toothpaste."

"What brand?"

Fran smirked at his humor. "How do you like my flowers?" A magnificent bouquet of white roses stood on her desk.

"You must have acquired a well-heeled admirer," Qwilleran said. "How come I can't smell them? How come I'm not sneezing?"

"They're silk! Aren't they fabulous? Amanda found this new source in Chicago. My grandmother used to make crepe paper flowers during the Depression and sell them for a dollar a dozen. These are twenty-five dollars *each!* Why don't you buy a big bunch for Polly?"

"She'd rather have fresh daisies," he said truthfully.

"Qwill, why doesn't Polly let me help her with her house?" Fran said earnestly. "I don't mean to belittle your beloved, but she's a color-fusser. I showed her some fabrics, and she fussed over the colors, trying to get a perfect match. I could teach her something if she'd listen."

"I don't know the answer, Fran. I'm even more concerned than you are." He started to leave.

"Wait a minute! I have something for you to read." She handed him the working script of a play. "See if you think we should do this for our winter production. The action takes place at Christmastime. I'd love to play Eleanor of Aquitaine. . . . You could grow a beard and play Henry," she added slyly.

"No thanks, but I'll give it a read."

🐾 On the way home Qwilleran took a detour into the public library to see Polly, but she was out of the building, the clerks informed him. They always considered it appropriate to tell their boss's friend where she had gone and why: to Dr. Zoller's office to have her teeth cleaned, or to Gippel's Garage to have her brakes adjusted. Today she had an appointment with the vet; Bootsie had been vomiting, and there was blood in his urine.

"If she returns, ask her to call me," he said in a businesslike tone, but he was thinking, That's all she needs to push her over the edge! A sick cat!

At the barn he loaded a cooler of soft drinks into his car and drove down the trail for his mail. Eddie was bending over a whining table saw, lopping off boards as if slicing bread, while two new helpers climbed about the framed building, hammering nails with syncopated blows.

"Comin' right along!" he called out encouragingly.

"Yeah," said Eddie, walking in his direction and sharpening a pencil. "If it don't rain tonight, I'll do some gradin'. I'll do all that fill and start on that hill she wants next to the road."

"That'll make a long day for you," Qwilleran said.

"Yeah . . . well . . . a guy in Kennebeck'll rent me a skim-loader cheaper at night."

"How do you transport it all that distance?"

"Flatbed trailer."

Qwilleran asked, "Do you live in Kennebeck? That's where they have that good steakhouse."

"Nah, I live in . . . uh . . . out in the country."

"Where's Benno? Still hung over?"

"Di'n't you hear? He got his!"

"You mean, he was killed? In an accident?"

"Nah. A fight in a bar."

"That's too bad," Qwilleran said. "You'd known him a long time, hadn't you?"

"Yeah . . . well . . . gotta get back to work."

Driving back to the barn, Qwilleran wondered why Eddie considered it necessary to conceal his Indian Village address. The development on the Ittibittiwassee River was swanky by Moose County standards, catering to young professionals with briefcases and styled hair: Fran Brodie, Dwight Somers, Hixie Rice, and Elizabeth Hart had apartments there. Eddie hardly fitted the picture, with his rough appearance and rusty pickup.

Qwilleran arrived at the barn in time to hear the phone ringing and see Koko hopping up and down as if on springs. It was Polly, calling in a state of anxiety. Bootsie was in the hospital. He had feline urological syndrome. They were giving him tests. He might need surgery.

Listening to her anguished report, his reaction was: I told you so! Many times he had warned Polly that she was overfeeding Bootsie; he was gorging on food to compensate for loneliness; what he needed was a cat friend.

Now Qwilleran tried to comfort her by mumbling words of encouragement: She had caught it in time; Bootsie was in good hands; the vet was highly skilled; Bootsie was still a young cat and would bounce back; would she like to talk about it over dinner at the Old Stone Mill?

No, she said. Unfortunately the library was open until nine o'clock, and it was her turn to work.

It was raining slightly when Celia arrived for her briefing—not really raining, just misting. "Good for the complexion," they liked to say in Moose County.

She was wearing a plastic hat tied under her chin. "Did anyone expect this rain?" she asked.

"In Moose County we always expect the unexpected. Come in and tell me about the day's excitement at The Roundhouse. Did Wrigley steal the show? Did Tish break down and tell all? Did Florrie plant a bomb in the elevator? This is better than a soap opera."

"I decided not to take him," she said. "That train wreck really scared him! So I told them his little tummy was upset from eating a rubber band. I'm getting good at inventing stories, Chief."

"I'm proud of you, Celia."

"Well, wait till you hear! When I arrived, they both hugged me—Tish and Florrie—and said they'd been lonely over the weekend, and they wanted to know if I'd come and live with them! I and Wrigley! I almost fell over! I had to think quick, and I said my grandson was coming up from Illinois to live with me so he could go to school in Pickax, starting in September. They said Clayton could move in, too! I told them I was really touched by the kind invitation and would have to think about it. Whew!"

"Nice going," Qwilleran commented.

"So we had lunch and talked about this and that. Tish reads your column, Chief, and she raved about the one on sweet corn. I was dying to tell her I know you, but I didn't. They asked about Clayton, and I asked if they had many relatives. Tish has one brother—no sisters—grandmother dead, aunts and uncles moved away, grandfather a retired railroad engineer in Sawdust City. And here's the sad part: He lives twenty miles away and has never been to visit them! Her grandmother never even sent a birthday card! Tish hasn't met either of them. This family is very strange, Chief."

"Was anything more said about the dog?"

"I asked if they were going to get another watchdog. I said my son had a German shepherd. Tish got all teary eyed and talked about Zak and how sweet and cuddly he was. She said he might have been killed by her brother's best friend; they'd been having some violent arguments. Isn't that terrible!"

Qwilleran agreed but was not surprised. The pieces of the puzzle were beginning to fit together. "Could you get her to talk about the credit union?"

"Not yet, but I'm getting there! After Florrie went to have her nap, I told Tish she was a wonderful person to give up college and stay home to take care of her mother. I said office work must be boring for someone with her talent. Then she showed me a clipping of a book review she wrote for your paper, and they paid her for it! She was so thrilled to see her name in print! She signed it Letitia Penn. That's Florrie's maiden name. . . . I asked what kind of work she did at the office, and she said a little bit of everything. She seems afraid to talk about it."

"You're doing very well, Celia. Now I think it's time for that strange family to have a reunion. The grandfather has reached an age when many persons look back on their lives with remorse and a desire to make amends for past mistakes. I mentioned it to Mr. Penn when I interviewed him, and you might sound out the women tomorrow."

"I know they'll love it!"

"Do you mind picking up the old gentleman in Sawdust City?"

"Be glad to."

"When the family is together, you can show a video of the Party Train, with Mr. Penn in the engineer's cab," he said, and then thought, Unfortunately, it includes shots of F.T. in the engineer's cab and F.T. with his secretary.

"Oh, we'll have a ball!" Celia squealed. "I'll make some cookies." She stood up. "I should drive home now. When the sky's overcast, it get dark early, and the woods are kind of scary at night."

Qwilleran accompanied her to her car and asked if she had noticed a lot of cars in the theatre parking lot. "It's a dress rehearsal for *Midsummer Night's Dream,* and I have a pair of tickets for you for opening night, if you'd like to see the show."

"I'd love it! Thank you so much! I'll take Virginia; she's been so good to me . . . What's that rumbling noise?"

"Only a bulldozer working overtime at the end of the orchard." He opened the car door for her. "Fasten your seatbelt. Observe the speed limit. And don't pick up any hitchhikers."

The irrepressible Mrs. Robinson was laughing merrily as she started through the block-long patch of woods at a bumpy ten miles per hour.

———

🐾 To Qwilleran the rumbling of the tractor was a welcome sound. It meant that Polly could cross off one item on her worry list. The man-made hill between house and highway would give her a sense of privacy, though there was little traffic on Trevelyan Road. Paving it had been a political boondoggle; no one used it except locals living on scattered farms.

So Qwilleran listened to the comforting grunting and groaning of Eddie's skim-loader. Lounging in his big chair, he asked himself: What have we learned to date? Benno *may* have killed Zak. Yet, even if he were a vengeful victim of the embezzlement, he would have known that the dog was not Floyd's. Tish had said the two young men had been arguing violently. Over what? A soccer bet? A woman? Drugs? Eddie *may* have killed his friend in a fit of drunken passion. The tension between boss and helper had been evident on the job—ever since Audit Sunday. When Eddie visited the barn, Koko hissed at him.

"Yow!" said Koko, sitting on the telephone desk, perilously close to the English pencil box. His comment gave Qwilleran another lead: The police were being evasive about the murder weapon at the Trackside Tavern. "Not a hunting knife" was all Andy Brodie would say. Could it have been a well-sharpened pencil?

With a growl and an abrupt change of mood, Koko sprang from the desk and launched a mad rush around the main floor—across the coffee table, up over the fireplace cube, around the kitchen. Objects not nailed down were scattered: books, magazines, the wooden train whistle, one of the carved decoys, the brass paperweight. Qwilleran grabbed the wooden pencil box from the path of the crazed animal.

"Koko!" he yelled. "Stop! Stop!"

Another decoy went flying. There was the sound of breaking glass in the kitchen. Then the cat flung himself at the front door. He bounced off, picked himself up, gave his left shoulder two brief licks, and stormed the door again like a battering ram.

"Stop! You'll kill yourself!" Qwilleran had never interfered in a catfit; it usually stopped as suddenly as it had started. But he honestly feared for Koko's safety. He rushed to the foyer and threw a scatter rug over the writhing body and pinned him down. After a few seconds the lump under the rug was surprisingly quiet. Cautiously he lifted one corner, then another. Koko was lying there, stretched out, exhausted.

It was then that the growl of the bulldozer floated up the trail on the damp night air. So that was it! The constant stop-and-go noise was driving Koko crazy. Or was that the only reason for the demonstration? Qwilleran felt an urgent tingling on his upper lip. He pounded his moustache, put on his yellow cap, and started out with a flashlight.

CHAPTER 13

Following Koko's significant catfit, Qwilleran jogged to the building site, where the skim-loader was making its nervous racket—starting and stopping, advancing and retreating, climbing and plunging. He could see bouncing flashes of light as the vehicle's headlights turned this way and that. While he was still a hundred yards away from the earth-moving operation, the noise stopped and the headlight was turned off. Time for a cigarette, Qwilleran thought; he'd better not leave any butts around.

At that moment there was a gut-wrenching scream—a man's scream—and then an earth-shaking thud—and then silence.

"Hey! Hey, down there!" Qwilleran shouted, running forward and ducking as something large and black flew over his head.

His flashlight showed the tractor lying on its side, half in the ditch. The operator was not in sight. Thrown clear, Qwilleran thought as he combed the area with a beam of light. Then he heard a tortured groan from the ditch. The operator was pinned underneath.

Futilely he threw his shoulder against the machine. Desperately

he looked up and down the lonely highway. A single pair of headlights was approaching from the north, and he waved his flashlight
in frantic arcs until it stopped.

"Gotta CB? Gotta phone?" he yelled at the driver. "Call 911!
Tractor rollover! Man trapped underneath! Trevelyan Road, quarter mile north of Base Line!" Before he could finish, the motorist
was talking on his car phone. He was Scott Gippel, the car dealer,
who lived nearby.

Almost immediately, police sirens pierced the silence of the
night. Seconds later, red and blue revolving lights converged from
north and south, accompanied by the wailing and honking of
emergency vehicles.

While Gippel turned his car to beam its headlights on the scene,
Qwilleran climbed down into the ditch, searching with his flashlight. First he saw an arm, grotesquely twisted . . . next a mop of
black hair . . . and then a bearded face raked with bleeding claw-
marks.

A police car was first to arrive, followed by the ambulance from
the hospital and the volunteer rescue squad from the firehall. Seven
men and a woman responded. They had rescue equipment and
knew what to do. They jacked the tractor and extricated the unconscious body from the mud.

Qwilleran identified him for the police officer: Edward Trevelyan of Indian Village; next of kin, Letitia Trevelyan in West Middle
Hummock. The door closed on the stretcher, and the ambulance
sped away.

The others stood around, somewhat stunned, despite their composure during the rescue.

"I heard the tractor," Qwilleran said, "and was on my way here
to watch the action, when I heard a scream and the machine top-
pling over and a huge bird flying away. I think it was a great horned
owl. There's one living in the woods."

"When they're after prey at night, they can mistake anything
for an animal," the officer said. "You're smart to wear that yellow
cap."

Gippel said, "That guy'll never make it. His bones are crushed.
Do you realize how much that tractor weighs?"

"The soil is wet, though," Qwilleran pointed out. "He was partially cushioned by the mud."

"Don't bet on it!" Gippel was notorious for his pessimism, being the only businessman in town who refused to join the Pickax Boosters Club.

As Qwilleran walked back to the barn, he dreaded the task of notifying Polly. The thought of a serious accident on her property would blight her attitude toward the house and add to her worries.

By the time he arrived, his phone was ringing. It was Celia. "Bad news!" she said breathlessly. "Tish just called. Her brother's been in a terrible accident. He's in Pickax Hospital, and she asked me to go there, because she can't leave Florrie."

"Call me if there's anything I can do, no matter how late," he said. "Call and tell me his condition."

He turned on all the lights in the barn in an effort to dispel the gloom that hung over him. The Siamese felt it, too. They forgot to ask for their bedtime treat and were in no mood for sleep. They followed him when he circled the main floor. After several laps, he considered the twistletwig rocker, wondering if its efficacy included the therapeutic. When he gave it a try, both cats piled into his lap, Koko digging industriously in the crook of his elbow. Qwilleran endured the discomfort, remembering that it was Koko's catfit that had sent him down to the building site—before the accident happened!

Eventually Celia called back. "He's unconscious, and only a relative is allowed to see him. I said I was his grandmother. He looks more dead than alive. The nurse wouldn't tell me anything, except that he's critical . . . *What's that?*" she cried, hearing a crash.

"Koko knocked something down," he said calmly.

"The hospital will call me if there's a turn for the worse. Tomorrow morning, after Florrie's nurse reports, Tish will drive to town, and we'll go to the hospital together."

"That's good. She'll need moral support. Keep me informed, but right now you'd better get some rest. Tomorrow could be a hectic day for you." Qwilleran spoke softly and considerately; he returned the receiver to its cradle gently. Then he turned around and yelled, "Bad cat! Look what you've done!"

Koko gave him a defiant stare, while Yum Yum scampered away guiltily. The epithet could refer to either male or female, but it was Koko who had been nosing the pencil box for several days. Now it lay on the clay tile floor in two pieces. The tiny hinges had pulled out of the old wood, and the box had burst open. The drawer with the secret latch held firm, and the paper clips were secure, but pens, pencils, a letter-opener, and whatnot were scattered all over the floor. As Qwilleran gathered them up, he saw Koko walking away, impudently carrying a black-barreled felt-tip in his mouth.

"Bad cat!" he bellowed again. *"Bad cat!"* It may have vented his anger, but it did nothing to dent the cat's equanimity.

Qwilleran set his alarm clock for six forty-five, an unprecedented hour for a late-riser of his distinction. He wanted to break the news to Polly before she heard it on the radio.

At seven A.M. the WPKX announcer said, "A bulldozer rolled over late last night on the outskirts of Pickax, injuring Edward P. Trevelyan, twenty-four, of Indian Village. He was grading a building site in a secluded area when he was attacked by a large bird, thought to be an owl. He lost control of the tractor, which rolled into a ditch, pinning him underneath. The accident victim was taken to Pickax Hospital by the emergency medical service, after being freed by the volunteer rescue squad. His condition is critical."

Qwilleran called Polly shortly after her wake-up hour of seven-thirty and heard her say sleepily, "So early, Qwill! Is something wrong?"

"I have an early appointment and want to inquire about Bootsie before leaving."

"I phoned the hospital last night," Polly said, "and Bootsie was resting comfortably after the initial treatment. It was nice of you to call."

"One other thing . . . I'm sorry to report that Eddie Trevelyan is in the hospital."

"How do you know?" she asked anxiously.

"It was on the air this morning. He was in an accident last night."

"Oh, dear! I hope it wasn't drunk driving."

"They called it a tractor rollover. It looks as if he won't be able to supervise his crew for a while."

In the pause that followed, Qwilleran could imagine the questions racing through Polly's mind: How bad is it? How long will he be incapacitated? Can his helpers proceed without him? Will it delay my construction?

"Oh, no!" she cried. "Was he working on my property?"

"I'm afraid so. He was doing a little midnight grading while he had the use of a rented skim-loader."

"I feel terribly guilty about this, Qwill. I've been nagging him about the grading," Polly said in anguish. "It's so discouraging. Everything seems to be happening at once. First Bootsie, and now this!"

"One thing I can assure you, Polly. You have no reason to worry about the house. If any problem arises, it'll be solved. Just leave everything to me."

Qwilleran hung up with a sense of defeat, knowing his advice would be ignored; she would worry more than ever. It was nearly eight o'clock, and he walked briskly down the trail in the hope of finding workmen on the job. The site was deserted. The tractor lay on its side in the ditch; across the highway its flatbed trailer was parked on the shoulder; the pavement was a maze of muddy tracks. Soon a pickup pulled onto the property, and one of Eddie's workmen jumped out.

Qwilleran went to meet him. "Do you know your boss is in the hospital?"

"Yeah. He's hurt bad."

"Can you continue to work on the house?"

The man shrugged. "No boss, no pay. I come to pick up my tools."

"Do you know where Eddie rented this machine?"

"Truck-n-Track in Kennebeck."

At that moment a late-model car stopped on the shoulder, driven by Scott Gippel on his way to work. "Did you hear the newscast, Scott?" Qwilleran asked.

"Sure did! That guy's gonna cash it in, take it from me. It's the Trevelyan curse, all over again. Same place. Same family. Look! You can see the foundation where their farmhouse burned down."

"Well, don't be too worried about Eddie. He's young, and he's strong—"

"And he drinks like a sponge," the car dealer said. "He's probably got alcohol instead of blood in his veins."

Qwilleran let that comment pass. There had been a time when he fitted the same description, more or less. He said, "Could your tow truck get this thing out of the ditch and deliver it to Kennebeck?"

"Who pays?"

"I do, but I want it done fast . . . immediately . . . now!"

Without answering, Gippel picked up his car phone and gave orders.

Qwilleran waited until the carpenter had picked up his tools— and nothing belonging to Eddie. He waited until the tractor had been towed away. Only then did he go home and feed the cats. They were unusually quiet; they knew when he was involved in serious business.

He himself breakfasted on coffee and a two-day-old doughnut while pondering Koko's bizarre behavior in recent weeks: the interminable vigils at the front window . . . his perching on the fireplace cube with the decoys . . . his vociferous and absurd reaction to the name Hermia . . . his digging in the crook of Qwilleran's elbow, ad nauseam.

As the man ruminated, the cat was investigating the bookshelf devoted to nineteenth-century fiction.

"You'd better shape up, young man," Qwilleran scolded him, "or we'll send you to live with Amanda Goodwinter."

"Ik ik ik!" said Koko irritably as he shoved a book off the shelf. It was a fine book with a leather binding, gold tooling, India paper, and gilt edges. With resignation and the realization that one can never win an argument with a Siamese, Qwilleran picked up the book and read the title. It was Dostoyevsky's *The Idiot*.

"Thanks a lot," he said crossly.

Qwilleran's telephone was in constant use that morning. He called Kennebeck and instructed Truck-n-Track to send him Eddie's rental bill, not forgetting to credit the deposit. He instructed Mr. O'Dell to pick up Eddie's table saw and other tools and store them in a stall of the carriage house.

At one point he telephoned the Lanspeaks, who called their daughter at the medical clinic, who spoke to the chief of staff at the hospital, who revealed that the patient was in and out of consciousness, having sustained massive internal injuries and multiple fractures. The next twenty-four hours would be decisive.

Soon after, Celia called again. She had been to the hospital with Tish. Eddie was conscious but didn't recognize his sister. "I think they had him all doped up," she said. "We were wondering how to break the news to Florrie and how she'd take it, and we decided that the reunion with Grandpa Penn might soften the blow. What do you think, Chief?"

Qwilleran thought, It'll either soften the blow or deliver the coup de grâce. He said, however, "Good idea!"

"So I'll phone him and ask if I can pick him up this afternoon. I hope it isn't too short notice."

"It won't be. The social schedule at the Retirement Center seems to be flexible.

"Also, I have something to report right now, Chief, if you can see me for a few minutes before I leave for The Roundhouse."

When she arrived, she was flushed with excitement.

"Coffee?" he asked.

"I haven't time." Sinking into the cushions of the sofa, she rummaged in her handbag for her notebook and then dropped the roomy carryall on the floor, where its gaping interior immediately attracted the Siamese. It was used to transport such items as cookies, paperback novels, house slippers, drugstore remedies, and more. "What do you think they're looking for?" she asked, as the two blackish-brown noses sniffed the handbag's mysteries.

"Wrigley," Qwilleran said. "They think you've got Wrigley in there, and they want to let the cat out of the bag."

Celia howled with more glee than the quip warranted, Qwilleran felt, but he realized she was overexcited by the day's happenings. He waited patiently until she calmed down, then asked, "Where's Tish now?"

"Still at the hospital. They have a comfy waiting room for relatives in the intensive care wing, and that's where we had a heart-to-heart talk this morning—Tish and I. I asked if Eddie had friends we should notify, but she doesn't know any of his friends . . . I told you they're a strange family, Chief . . . Then she said Nella Hooper liked Eddie a lot and would be sorry to hear what happened, but she didn't leave a forwarding address. Nella, I found out, is the secretary at the credit union who was fired a couple of weeks before it closed. She and Eddie lived in the same apartment building. She wasn't a secretary, Tish said, but more like an assistant to the president. She had a degree in accounting and knew computers and made a big impression on Tish. They used to go to lunch together."

"First question," Qwilleran said. "What was this highly qualified woman doing in a tank town like Sawdust City? Besides everything you mention, she has smashing good looks! I've seen her."

"She loved trains! That's all. It was a dream job, traveling around the country with the president, looking at trains and—"

She was interrupted by the phone. Hixie was calling to say that Nella Hooper's apartment would not be available until October first—and maybe not then if she decided to come back. The credit union always paid her rent—quarterly—in advance. Eddie Trevelyan had moved to Indian Village four months before Audit Sunday. Hixie concluded, "Is he the one who was in that bad accident last night?"

"He's the one. Floyd's son. Thanks, Hixie. Talk to you later."

As Qwilleran returned to the lounge area, he was thinking, If they were going to fire Nella in July, why would they pay her rent until October? To Celia he said, "Did Tish mention why Nella was fired?"

"She wasn't fired, really. Nella's father in Texas has Alzheimer's disease, and her mother needed her at home, so Nella had to quit her job. But the office made it look like she was fired, so she could collect benefits. She left without saying good-bye, which really hurt Tish's feelings, although she realizes Nella had family troubles on her mind."

"Hmmm, makes one wonder" was Qwilleran's comment. "As I recall, Tish said she hated her father for cheating on Florrie. How does she react to Nella's relationship with her father?"

"Strictly business, she said. Her father's real girlfriend owns a bar in Sawdust City. Tish told Nella how she felt about F.T. and how he wouldn't spend the money to send Florrie to Switzerland. Nella was very sympathetic and said it would be easy to switch $100,000 into a slush fund for Florrie, and F.T. would be none the wiser. Also, it would be legal because it was all in the family. . . . Do you understand how this works, Chief?"

"I don't even understand why seven times nine always equals sixty-three."

"Me too! Glad I'm not the only dumbbell. . . . Well, anyway, the next thing was that Tish introduced Eddie to Nella, because he wanted money to build condos. If he could buy the land, he could borrow against it to start building, but F.T. wouldn't back him. Nella told him not to worry; she could work the same kind of switch because it was all in the family. But before anything happened, Nella had to quit, and the credit union went bust. Tish was lucky to have her savings in a Pickax bank. She didn't trust F.T." Celia had been talking fast. She looked at her watch. "I've gotta dash. If I'm late, the nurse gets snippy."

As Qwilleran walked with Celia to the parking area, she said, "Someone backed a truck up to the carriage house today and started unloading stuff. I went downstairs to see what it was all about, and I met the nicest man! He said he works for you."

"That's Mr. O'Dell. You'll see him around frequently. He's the one who cleaned your windows before you moved in."

"They may need cleaning again soon," she replied with a wink, and she drove away laughing.

Indoors Qwilleran found something on the floor that belonged on the telephone desk: the paperback playscript that Fran wanted him to read. Koko was under the desk, sitting on his brisket and looking pleased with himself. Qwilleran smoothed his moustache with a dawning awareness: There was a leonine theme in Koko's recent antics, starting with the lion in *A Midsummer Night's Dream* . . . then *Androcles and the Lion* . . . and now *The Lion in Winter.* Did he identify with the king of beasts? For a ten-pound house cat he had a lion-sized ego.

Or, Qwilleran thought, he's trying to tell me something, and I'm not getting it!

CHAPTER 14

When Qwilleran's secret agent reported to Operation Whistle HQ on Tuesday evening, she was in a state of exhaustion. "I'm absolutely whacked!" she said. "First, the hospital this morning . . . then the family reunion . . . and then some flabbergasting news!"

"Sit down before you fall down," Qwilleran said. "Relax. Have a swig of fruit punch. Say hello to Koko and Yum Yum."

The Siamese came forth, looking for her handbag. When plumped on the floor it looked like a treasure-filled wastebasket. "Have you been good kitties?" she asked them.

"No," Qwilleran replied. "Koko is still in the doghouse for malicious destruction of property. . . . Now go on with your story. In the last episode of *The Trials of the Trevelyans,* you were having a heart-to-heart talk with Tish, and Nella had just left without saying good-bye."

"Yes, that was the Sunday they had that train ride at $500 a ticket. After the train ride, Floyd came home, got a mysterious phone call, and said he had to go and see a man about a train. He left, and they never saw him again."

"When did Tish tell you this?"

"This morning at the hospital. I couldn't tell you because I had to rush off to The Roundhouse. . . . So then I called Grandpa Penn and said I'd pick him up at two o'clock. He sounded as if it was the video he was really excited about. I didn't mention Eddie's accident."

"Did Florrie know he was coming?"

"Oh, yes! She was thrilled at the idea of seeing 'Pop' after so many years. She wanted to get all dressed up. At two o'clock, like I promised, I drove out to Sawdust City. That retirement home is a depressing building. Have you seen it?"

"I have, and I think the residents spend most of their waking hours at the Trackside Tavern and the Jump-Off Bar. Who can blame them?"

Celia told how she walked into the lobby and found three old fellows sitting in a row—all shaved and combed and respectable in white summer shirts. "They all stood up, and I asked which one was the famous engineer. The tallest one said, 'I'm the hoghead.' I told him my car was at the curb, and he said, 'Full steam ahead.' But when I led the way to my car, all three men followed me! Before I knew it, three husky old men were squeezing into my little car. I was worried about my springs, but what could I do? I said, 'I didn't know you were bringing your bodyguards, Mr. Penn.' They all laughed."

"Well put," Qwilleran said.

"It turned out they were his fireman and brakeman, who'd always worked as a crew and still stuck together. Their names were Fred and Billy, and they were all excited about seeing the video. On the way to The Roundhouse they talked a mile a minute!"

"NO!" Qwilleran shouted, and Yum Yum—caught pilfering a pocketpack of tissues from the wonderful hand bag—dropped it and ran. "Sorry, he said. "Go on with your story."

"Well, when we got to the house, Tish ran down the steps and threw her arms around her grandpa. Florrie was in her wheelchair on the porch, wearing a pretty dress. Her old dad stumbled up the steps, crying 'My little Florrie!' And he dropped down on his knees and hugged her, and they both cried. When she asked, 'Where's Mom?' I cried, too."

"A touching scene," Qwilleran said.

"I took Fred and Billy out to the patio, so the others could have a private talk. The men remembered Florrie when she was a pretty young girl, waving at them as the train went by. They also knew about her wedding and didn't like it one bit! Then they started cursing F.T. to high heaven for stealing their life savings. They hoped he'd be caught and get prison for life. When I showed them the trains Florrie had wrecked, they laughed and cheered."

"Did you show the video?"

"Twice! Tish refused to look at it, and Florrie had to go to bed because the excitement had knocked her out, but the three men thought the video was wonderful. After that, I drove them back to Sawdust City."

"I'd say you handled everything nobly, Celia."

"Thanks, Chief, but that's not the end. When I got back to The Roundhouse, I got the shock of my life! Are you ready for it?"

"Fire away."

"It's something the lawyer had just told Tish. He said Floyd had put the Party Train in Florrie's name to protect himself from creditors and lawsuits!"

"Well! That puts a new complexion on the matter, doesn't it?" Qwilleran said. "The train can be sold and the proceeds used to send Florrie to Switzerland."

"But you haven't heard the whole story, Chief. *Grandpa Penn is buying the train!*"

"Wait a minute! Does he have that kind of money?"

"That's what I wondered," Celia said, "but Tish says he's had a good railroad job for fifty years and always believed in saving for a rainy day. What's more, his money is in banks and government bonds, so it's not tied up. He's turning everything over to Florrie. They've called the lawyer already."

"Will the old man have enough left to live on?" Qwilleran inquired.

"She says he has his railroad pension and social security and good medical insurance. He doesn't need much else. . . . What do you think of it, Chief?"

"Sounds like the ending of a B-movie made in the 1930s, but I'm happy for everyone. You didn't say how much he's turning over to Florrie, but he can sell the train for well over a million. More likely, two million. I heard that Floyd had put $600,000 in the locomotive alone. Just imagine! An old engineer's dream! To own the celebrated No. 9!"

Celia looked puzzled. "But if he wants to sell the train, who would buy it? That's an awful lot of money to spend on a thing like that."

"Train collecting is a growing hobby. More people than you think are pursuing it." It also occurred to Qwilleran that the economic development division of the K Foundation, currently promoting tourism, might take over the Party Train and operate it as Floyd intended.

"Well, it's time for me to go home and see what Wrigley's doing," she said.

Qwilleran handed her an envelope. "Here are your tickets for the play Thursday night, plus a little something extra in appreciation of your work."

"Oh, thank you!" she said. "I'm enjoying this assignment so much, I don't expect a reward."

"You deserve one. And the next time you talk to Tish, see if she has any idea who tipped off the auditors to the Lumbertown fraud . . . and why they haven't been able to find Floyd . . . and who made the mysterious phone call on the night of his disappearance. She's a smart young woman. She might be able to make some guesses."

"Yes, but I don't know how much longer she and Florrie will be here. Tish has already phoned the airline. They'll probably leave this weekend."

After Celia had driven away, Qwilleran walked around the barn exterior several times and pondered a few more questions: Does Tish want to leave the country in a hurry for reasons other than those stated? Is there really a doctor in Switzerland who has a miracle cure? Is Florrie actually as ill as she appears to be?

After the shocks, successes, and surprises of the last twenty-four hours, the next forty-eight were consistently disappointing. Operation Whistle came to a sudden standstill; Polly upset the plans for opening night at the theatre; and Qwilleran's imaginings about lurid secrets at the Trackside Tavern were squelched.

Wednesday morning: He ran into Roger MacGillivray at Lois's Luncheonette, and the reporter said, "Hey, Arch told me to check out what happened at the Trackside Tavern ten years ago. Women boycotted it because they weren't allowed to use the pool tables."

"Is that all?"

"That's all. They picketed the bar for a couple of weeks and then got a better idea. They opened the Jump-Off Bar and went into competition with the Trackside. The food's better, and the owner is a buxom, fun-loving gal that everyone likes. Floyd lent her the dough to get started and helped her to get a license."

"I've been to the Jump-Off establishment," Qwilleran said, "and I don't remember seeing any billiard tables."

"Right! I asked the boss lady, and she said the women didn't want to shoot pool when no one told them they couldn't. She considers that a big laugh."

Qwilleran huffed into his moustache. "Well, I suppose I'll see you at the play tomorrow night."

"I'm afraid not. We'd have to hire a baby-sitter, and that costs more than the tickets. Besides, Sharon's the Shakespeare nut, not me."

Wednesday afternoon: Celia phoned. "I won't have anything to report tonight, Chief. They didn't need me at The Roundhouse. Tish is there with Florrie. They're getting ready for their trip. I went to the hospital, and they've got Eddie trussed up like a mummy and hooked up to tubes and bottles. He doesn't look like anything human."

Wednesday evening: Qwilleran telephoned Polly to inquire about Bootsie.

"I'm bringing him home tomorrow," she said. "If you don't mind, I'll stay with him instead of going to the theatre. You can go and concentrate on your review. I'll look forward to reading what you think of the production."

With a hint of annoyance he replied, "What I think about it and what I say about it in print aren't necessarily the same. I don't need to remind you this is a small town."

Thursday morning: Celia called again, saying somberly, "Eddie isn't expected to last the morning. The hospital notified Tish to come right away. I'll meet her there and let you know what happens."

Thursday afternoon: "Chief, I have sad news. Eddie passed away at ten thirty-seven. Tish is in Pickax, and I'm looking after Florrie, but I'll be back in time for the play."

A gala crowd attended the opening of *A Midsummer Night's Dream*. There was excitement in the hum of voices in front of the theatre, in the foyer, and in the upstairs lobby. Half of the playgoers were friends, relatives, or classmates of the young extras. The rest were people Qwilleran knew. Among them:

The Comptons. "Where's Polly?" they asked him.

Hixie Rice and Dwight Somers. They too wanted to know why Polly was absent.

Dr. Diane Lanspeak with Dr. Herbert, Hixie's former attachment. As luck would have it, both couples had tickets in the same row.

Celia Robinson with her new friend, Virginia Alstock. Celia and Qwilleran exchanged discreet nods.

Dr. Prelligate of the Moose County Community College with a few faculty members.

Scott Gippel, the worried treasurer of the club. "Looks like we'll end up in the black, but you never know."

Three generations of the Olsen family. Jennifer Olsen was playing Hermia.

Amanda Goodwinter, alone. "I hate this play, but Fran's directing it, and she gave me a ticket."

Qwilleran met his guests in the upstairs lobby: Arch and Mildred Riker and Mildred's daughter, Sharon, who had driven in from Mooseville to use Polly's ticket. "What's with Polly?" Riker asked.

Qwilleran described the situation.

"Look here, Qwill! We've got to do something about your most favored friend. She's not herself these days. I realize how she feels about Bootsie, but her house is driving her batty. A sister of mine once had a nervous breakdown over the remodeling of her kitchen. What can we do about Polly?"

"I wish I knew. To make matters worse, her builder died this morning."

The lobby lights blinked, and they took their seats in the fifth row.

The play was wildly acclaimed. The audience applauded the students dressed as lords and ladies, as they made their entrance down the central aisle. Derek Cuttlebrink and the crew of rude mechanicals brought down the house, as expected. The greenies with their weird makeup and robotic movements stole the show, however. Meanwhile, the Shakespeare buffs waited for their favorite lines: *I am amazed and know not what to say . . . The course of true love never did run smooth . . . What fools these mortals be!*

As the king of the greenies delivered his line, *I am invisible,* and disappeared in a puff of smoke, Qwilleran heard the wail of a siren passing the theatre. It always alarmed him; he thought of fire. Then it faded away in the distance beyond the city limits. Moments later, he heard the honking of the rescue squad's vehicle. Then, just before intermission, Riker's beeper sounded, and the publisher, sitting on the aisle, made a quick exit to the lobby.

As soon as the first act ended, Qwilleran hurried up the aisle and found Riker in front of the telephone booth.

"Qwill, there's been a bad train wreck—south of Wildcat. The city desk is sending a man, but I think I should go, too. Want to come along? Sharon can take Mildred home."

The two men missed the second act. As they pulled out of the theatre parking lot, Riker said, "I'm taking you away from the play, and you have to write a review for tomorrow's paper."

"That's all right," Qwilleran said. "I know what I'm going to say about the first act, and I'll wing it for the second."

Outside the city limits Riker drove fast, and conversation was terse. "Roger's baby-sitting. He'll be sorry to miss a hot story."

"Yeah . . . well . . ."

"Who's on tonight?"

"Donald. The new guy."

"He's getting his baptism by train wreck. Wonder what kind of train it is."

"Freight is all they pull on SC&L."

"Northbound or southbound?"

"They didn't say."

Reaching the town of Wildcat, they noticed unusual activity. The hamlet consisted of a general store, bar, gas station, and antique shop, with railroad tracks running parallel to the main street. People were milling around the intersection or standing on the tracks and staring to the south. Riker had to sound the horn to get through. "It's supposed to be a half-mile south of town."

"If you remember the Party Train," Qwilleran said, "the tracks veer away from the highway south of Wildcat. We saw views from the train that we'd never seen before."

It was still daylight but overcast, and a strange glow lighted up the gloom ahead of them. As they rounded a curve, they found the highway blocked with police vehicles, ambulances, and fire trucks. A few private cars were parked on the shoulder, their occupants gawking at the emergency equipment. Riker found a space, and they walked toward the center of activity. As soon as an ambulance was loaded, it took off for Lockmaster or Black Creek, and another took its place. All surrounding towns had responded. Medics running into the woods and stretcher bearers come back from the wreck had to push through underbrush, although rescue personnel with axes and chain saws were frantically trying to clear a path.

Riker showed his press card to a state trooper. "Can we reach the scene of the accident?"

"Follow those guys, but stay out of their way," the officer said. "Take flashlights. It'll be dark soon."

The newsmen plunged into the woods, Riker grumbling that it was going to ruin his new shoes.

Voices could be heard shouting orders that bounced off the cliffs on both sides of the creek. The whining of chain saws and hacking of axes added to the feeling of urgency. When they emerged from the brush, they were on a railroad right-of-way with a single track and a string of old telegraph poles. A team of paramedics, carrying a victim strapped to a stretcher, came running up the track, hopping awkwardly from tie to tie.

As the newsmen hobbled toward the wreck, they could see a flatcar with a huge floodlight that illuminated the trestle bridge. On the opposite bank of the creek was another flatcar with a railroad wrecking crane. Then a surreal scene came into view: a row of dazed victims sitting or lying on the embankment, while white-coated doctors moved among them. No train was in sight.

"There's our guy!" Riker said. "Hey, Donald! Getting anything?" They ran to meet him.

"Not much," said the young reporter. "Only pictures. Nobody knows anything for sure."

"Keep on shooting," said the boss. "We'll hang around and try for quotes."

"They think the train was stolen from a siding in Mudville."

"My God!" Qwilleran shouted as he ran toward the gulch. "It's No. 9!"

Three jack-knifed cars were piled on top of a locomotive lying on its side in the mud—a grotesque monster still breathing smoke and steam.

CHAPTER 15

The Friday edition of the *Moose County Something* came off the presses two hours early, following the episode at Wildcat. The banner headline read:

TRAIN WRECKED IN BLACK CREEK
No. 9 and Party Train Crash
After Whittling Joyride

The fabled engine No. 9 roared at top speed through the village of Wildcat Thursday night before plunging down a steep grade and around a treacherous curve. It derailed and crashed into the muddy water of Black Creek. One person was killed. Forty were injured, some seriously.

The ill-fated run, unscheduled and allegedly unauthorized, left the switchyard at Sawdust City about 9:15, according to witnesses. It raced south with whistle blowing through Kennebeck, Pickax, and Little Hope, narrowly missing a consist of 20 freight cars being shunted at Black Creek Junction.

Residents of Wildcat heard the continuous screaming whistle that signified a runaway train and rushed to the crossroads in time to see the last car hurtling down the grade. Signals to slow down are clearly posted on the approach to Wildcat. An investigation is under way to determine whether the accident was due to mechanical failure or human error.

In either case the SC&L disclaims responsibility, a spokesman for the railroad said, since the Party Train was privately owned and berthed on a private siding.

At presstime, the reason for the unexpected run had not been ascertained. A spokesman for the Lockmaster County sheriff's department called the ill-fated run "a joyride for railroad nuts who knew how to shovel coal."

The Party Train is known to be the property of Floyd Trevelyan, who is wanted on charges of fraud in connection with the Lumbertown Credit Union. The crew and passengers were all residents of the Railroad Retirement Center in Sawdust City. The only fatality was the engineer, Oswald Penn, 84, retired after 50 years with SC&L. He had an outstanding safety record. He was Trevelyan's father-in-law.

Passengers and other crew members jumped to save their lives before the crash. Eighteen sustained injuries requiring hospitalization; 22 were treated and released. They were being questioned by investigators. Conspiracy has not been ruled out.

A paramedic on the scene said, "All these old fellows are long past retirement age. Looks like they wanted to make one last jump. They didn't know their bones are getting brittle. We've got a lot of fracture cases here."

Emergency medical teams, volunteer rescue squads, and volunteer firefighters from Lockmaster, Black Creek Junction, Flapjack, and Little Hope responded. The sheriffs of two counties were assisted by state police. SC&L wrecking equipment was brought from Flapjack to clear the right-of-way for northbound and southbound freight consists.

The Black Creek trestle bridge itself was not damaged, but

tracks and ties are being replaced. A repair foreman on the scene said, "The train was traveling so fast, it tore off the curved tracks and made them straight as a telephone pole. Man, that's real whittlin'."

Twelve hours before the headlines hit the street, Riker and Qwilleran drove away from the wreckage with divided reactions. One was exhilarated; the other was troubled.

Riker conjectured that the train was stolen by depositors defrauded by Trevelyan, who were indulging in a senseless act of revenge. It was ironic, he said, that the embezzler's father-in-law lost his life, trapped in the cab and scalded to death by the steam. Why didn't he jump, like the others? The alleged thieves knew what they were doing; the engine was fueled with plenty of coal and water for a short high-speed run.

Qwilleran, on the other hand, had privileged information that he could not divulge without exposing Operation Whistle. His professional instincts required him to tell Riker what he knew, but it would all be revealed in the end. Meanwhile, he had to protect his private mission—and Celia's part in it, for that matter. He had no doubt that Ozzie had intended to "go out whittlin' " and never intended to jump. He wondered if the old man had consciously wanted to re-enact the famous 1908 wreck at Wildcat, hoping to go down in railroad history.

While Riker had been flashing his press credentials on the embankment, Qwilleran had been talking quietly with the survivors. They balked at talking to the press, but Qwilleran introduced himself as a friend of Ozzie's. There were no secrets at the Retirement Center. They had heard all about this "Mackintosh feller from Chicago," who had interviewed Ozzie for a book he was writing and who had bought him two shots and a burger at the Jump-Off Bar. Now they all related the same story: The idea had come up suddenly, the day before, during a huddle at the bar. Ozzie Penn had said it would be a helluva joke to steal the train and wreck it. He would drive the hog, and he'd need a crew of three to keep up a good head of steam for a fast run. Anyone else could go along for the ride, unless he was too old to jump. Everyone would be expected to jump before the hog hit the curve north of the bridge.

They all knew how to jump. Now—waiting on the embankment, fortified by a good dose of pain-killer—they had no regrets. It was the most excitement they'd had in years!

They had known instinctively that Ozzie would not jump. He'd keep his hand on the throttle no matter what, and to hell with the reverse bar. He was a brave man. He'd proved it in countless emergencies. He always said he didn't want to die in bed; he wanted to go out whittlin'.

It gave Qwilleran a queasy feeling to realize that his own suggestion of a Penn family reunion had resulted in Ozzie's purchase of the train, Florrie's possible cure in Switzerland, the train's destruction, and Ozzie's death. Call it heroic or not, being scalded to death by steam was blood-chilling. Could it have been an old man's penance for abandoning his daughter so cruelly?

The next morning Qwilleran wrote his review of the play in time for the noon deadline and also dashed off the lyrics for a folksong, titled *The Wreck of Old No. 9*. These he took to the Old Stone Mill when he went there for lunch. He asked to be seated in Derek's station.

"Good show last night," he told the tall waiter. "Best role you've ever done."

"Yeah, I was really up," the actor acknowledged.

"Did you hear about the train wreck on the radio this morning?"

"Nah. I slept in, but they're talking about it in the kitchen."

Qwilleran handed him an envelope. "Here's a new folksong to add to your collection. You can sing it to the tune of the *Blizzard* ballad."

"Gee, thanks! Who wrote it?"

"Author unknown," said Qwilleran. He had done his bit to launch Ozzie Penn into the annals of local folk history. He knew Derek would sing it all over the county.

Another news item—one that would never be memorialized in song—appeared in the paper that day:

Edward Penn Trevelyan, 24, son of Floyd and Florence Trevelyan, died yesterday as a result of injuries suffered in a tractor accident. He had been on the critical list in Pickax Hospital since Monday.

Trevelyan was a resident of Indian Village and had recently started his own construction firm. He attended Pickax High School, where he played on the soccer team. He is survived by his parents and a sister, Letitia, at home. Funeral arrangements have not been announced.

It was Polly's day off, and Qwilleran phoned her at home. He assumed she would have read the obituary and the account of the train wreck. She had read both, yet she seemed unperturbed by either.

"How's Bootsie?" he asked.

"He's glad to be home."

"You missed a good play last night."

"Perhaps I can go next weekend."

Something's wrong with her, Qwilleran thought; she's in another world. "Would you like to drive up to Mooseville and have dinner on the porch at the Northern Lights?" he asked.

"Thank you, Qwill, but I'm really not hungry."

"But you have to eat something, Polly."

"I'll just warm a bowl of soup."

"Want me to bring you a take-out from Lois's? Her chicken soup is the real thing!"

"I know, but I have plenty of soup in my freezer."

"Polly, aren't you feeling well? You sound rather down. Is it indigestion again? Did you tell Dr. Diane about your condition?"

"Yes, and she gave me a digestant, but she wants me to take some tests, and I dread that!"

"I think I should drive over there to cheer you up. You need some fresh daisies and a friendly shoulder."

"No, I just want to go to bed early. I'll be all right by morning; we have a big day at the library tomorrow. But thanks, dear."

Following that disturbing conversation, Qwilleran stayed in his desk chair, staring into space and wondering what to do, whom to call. Koko was on the desk, rubbing his jaw against Cerberus, the three-headed dog, and he said to him quietly, "That's a paperweight, friend—not a fang scraper."

Koko went on rubbing industriously. One never knew when he was trying to communicate and when he was just being a cat. There was the matter of the felt-tip pens he had been stealing recently—not red ones, not yellow, only black. Was it a coincidence that Polly had hired the black-haired, black-bearded Edward Penn Trevelyan? Penn was Florrie's maiden name. Tish's pen name was Letitia Penn. Koko's attempts to convey information—if that's what they were—failed to get through to Qwilleran. He went for a long bike ride to clear his head. It was good exercise, and he filled his lungs with fresh air, but no questions were answered.

When Celia arrived that evening, she flopped on the sofa, dropped her shapeless handbag on the floor, and said, "Could you put a little something in the lemonade tonight, Chief? I need it!"

"I mix a tolerable Tom Collins," he said. "I take it you've had a hectic day."

"We've had two deaths in the family on the same day! Both funerals are on Saturday. The women leave for Switzerland on Sunday. Tish is upset! Florrie is hysterical!"

"Drink this and relax awhile," he said, presenting the tray. "Tell me what you thought of the play."

"I liked it! We both did. I had to read it in high school, but I'd never seen it on the stage. The greenies were fun—better than fairies. And I loved that young man who's so tall. Derek Cuttle-brink was the name in the program."

Qwilleran assured her that there was a whole village full of Cut-tlebrinks. "They're all characters!" he said.

"That nice Mr. O'Dell was there with his daughter. He talked to us in the lobby. Charming Irish accent!" She looked around the barn. "This would make a good theatre—with people on the balconies and the stage on the main floor."

Qwilleran said, "Everyone wants to convert it into a theatre or a restaurant or a poor man's Guggenheim. You've never seen the view from up above. Let's take a walk. Bring your drink."

They climbed the ramps, and he showed her his studio, the guestroom, the cats' loft apartment, and the exposed beams where the Siamese did their acrobatics.

368 LILIAN JACKSON BRAUN

When they returned to ground level, Celia dug into her handbag for her notebook. "Well! Are you ready for this, Chief? Tish told me some terrible things after Eddie died. Do you think a dying man comes back to life just before his last breath?"

"Sometimes there's a moment of lucidity before death," he said. "Great men utter memorable last words, according to their biographers, and others reveal lifelong secrets."

"Well, here's what happened yesterday morning. It's lucky the nurse was at the house when the hospital called. Tish drove into town in a hurry. Eddie was slipping away, but she talked to him, and all of a sudden his eyes moved, and he struggled to speak—just snatches of this and that."

"Were you there?" Qwilleran asked.

"I was waiting outside the room. Tish told me about it after. We came back to my apartment for a cup of tea, and she began to cry. Eddie had been mixed up in more dreadful things than anyone guessed."

At that moment the telephone rang. "Excuse me," he said and took the call in the library.

A shaking voice said, "Qwill, take me to the hospital. I don't feel well."

"I'll be right there!" he said firmly. "Hang up! Hang up!" As soon as he heard the dial tone, he punched 911. Then he dashed to the back door, calling to Celia, "Emergency! Gotta leave! Let yourself out!"

He drove recklessly to Goodwinter Boulevard and arrived just ahead of the ambulance. Using his own key, he let the EMS team into the apartment and ran up the stairs ahead of them.

Polly was sitting in a straight chair, looking pale and frightened. "Chest pains," she said weakly. "My arms feel heavy."

While the paramedics put a pill under her tongue and attached the oxygen tube with nose clips, Qwilleran made a brief phone call.

She was being strapped onto the stretcher when she turned a pathetic face to him and said, "Bootsie—"

"Don't worry. I've called your sister-in-law. She'll take care of him. I'll follow the ambulance." He squeezed her hand. "Everything will be all right . . . sweetheart."

She gave him a grateful glance.

He was there at the hospital when Polly was admitted and when Lynette Duncan arrived shortly afterward. The two of them sat in a special waiting room and talked about Polly's recent worries.

"You know," Lynette confided, "before she visited that friend in Oregon and got hooked on the idea of building a house, I wanted her to come and share the old Duncan homestead. I just inherited it from my brother. He'd had it ever since our parents died. Polly was married to my younger brother. He was a volunteer firefighter and lost his life in a barn fire. Tragic! They were newlyweds. Maybe she told you. Anyway, now I own this big house, over a hundred years old, with large rooms and high ceilings. Really nice! But too big for me. I think Polly would love it, and Bootsie could run up and down stairs."

It was the kind of nervous, rambling chatter heard in hospital waiting rooms when relatives wait for the doctor's verdict.

Finally a young woman in a white coat appeared. Qwilleran held his breath.

"Mrs. Duncan is doing very well. Would you like to see her? I'm Diane Lanspeak; I happened to be a few blocks away when they brought her in."

Qwilleran said, "I know your parents. We're all glad to have you back in Pickax."

"Thank you. I've heard a lot about you. One question: the cardiologist may recommend a catheterization. It's well to take pictures and determine exactly what the situation is. A mild heart attack is a warning. If Mrs. Duncan needs help in making a decision, who will—?"

"I'm her nearest relative," Lynette said, "but Mr. Qwilleran is—" She turned to look at him. No more needed to be said.

In the hospital room they found Polly looking peaceful for the first time in weeks, despite the clinical atmosphere and the tubes. They exchanged a few words, Polly speaking only about the capable paramedics, the kind nurses, the wonderful Dr. Diane.

When Qwilleran returned to the barn, Celia had gone, leaving a note: "Hope everything is okay. Call me if I can help."

The Siamese, unnaturally quiet, walked about in bewilderment; they knew when Qwilleran was deeply concerned, but not why. As soon as Qwilleran sat in the twistletwig rocker to calm his anxiety, Yum Yum hopped into his lap and comforted him with small, catly gestures: an extended paw, a sympathetic purr. Koko looked on with fellow-feeling, and when Qwilleran spoke to him, he squeezed his eyes.

The gentle rocking produced some constructive ideas: Polly would recover, move into the Duncan homestead, and forget about building a house. The K Foundation would reimburse Polly for her investment and complete the building as an art center. The Pickax Arts Council had been campaigning to get the carriage house for that purpose before Celia arrived.

As Qwilleran rocked and gazed idly about the lounge area, he caught sight of a small dark object on the light tile floor. His first thought: a dead mouse! Yet it was too geometric for that, more nearly resembling a large domino. Unwilling to leave the comforting embrace of the bent willow twigs, he tried to guess what the foreign object might be, but eventually he succumbed to curiosity.

"You'll have to excuse me for a minute, sweetheart," he said to Yum Yum as he hoisted himself out of the underslung rocker.

The unidentified object was the smallest of tape recorders, and the truth struck Qwilleran with suddenness: Celia's grandson had mailed it from Illinois; the cats had stolen it from her handbag; she had been secretly recording her meetings with Tish, in spite of his admonition. That explained her graphic reports and remarkable memory for details. She had transcribed the taped dialogue into her notebook, which she then consulted so innocently at their briefings.

While admiring her initiative, he frowned at her noncompliance.

Nevertheless, he lost no time in playing the tape.

CHAPTER 16

Before playing Celia's secret tape, Qwilleran asked himself, Shall I embarrass her by returning it . . . or let her think she lost it? He set it up on the telephone desk and prepared to take notes. The first sounds were nothing but sobs and whimpers, with sympathetic murmurs and questions from Celia. Then he heard a wracked voice say:

"I can't believe it, Celia! I thought she was my friend—my best friend! But she used me! She used all of us!"

"What do you mean, Tish?"

"She was going to divert funds for Mother's treatment in Switzerland! She was going to divert money for Eddie's condos, too. We believed her, because she was so knowledgeable and so *nice!* (Burst of sobs.) I even cheated so it would look as if she'd been fired. She's the one who suggested it. . . . Oh-h-h! She was so clever! Why didn't I see through her scheme?"

"What was her scheme, Tish? What did she do that was so bad?"

"It's what Eddie tried to tell me before he died. She wanted someone to do a special job for her, and he took Benno to see her."

"What kind of job? Didn't Eddie ask questions?"

"I guess not. My poor brother wasn't smart. He only went to tenth grade. And he drank too much. He ended up being an accomplice in a terrible crime." (Choking sobs.)

"Oh, dear! What kind of crime?"

(Long pause.) "Murder! When F.T. disappeared, they said he'd skipped with millions of dollars that didn't belong to him, but it was Nella who skipped. Floyd was dead!"

"Was Eddie able to tell you all this?"

"In snatches. He was gasping for breath. I had to put my ear close to his lips to hear him."

"Are you sure it's true?"

"People don't lie when they're dying, do they?"

"Maybe you're right, Tish. But how was Eddie an accomplice?"

"He helped Benno bury the body. But Nella was gone, and Benno didn't get his blood money. He wanted Eddie to pay off."

"How much? Do you know?"

"No, but it must have been a lot. Eddie's money was tied up. They argued. Benno shot his dog for spite. Then, one night in a bar, the lights went out. Benno pulled a knife. Eddie tried to get it away from him. He didn't mean to kill him—"

"Oh, Tish, I feel so sorry for you! I wish I could do something to help. What can I do?"

"Nothing. It just helps to have someone to talk to. You've been so good to us, Celia."

"Are you going to do anything about Eddie's confession?"

"I don't know. I can't think straight."

"But Nella should be arrested, if she plotted the murder and stole the money. Where did they bury the body?"

"Eddie tried to tell me, but he couldn't get it out. His eyes rolled up in his head, and he was gone." (Convulsive crying.)

"There must be something I can do to help you, dear."

"I don't know. I just want to get on that plane and never come back."

"Could I handle the funeral arrangements for you?"

"Would you? I'd be so thankful."

"Do you need me at the house this afternoon?"

"No, I'll be there, getting Mother ready for the trip. She's never been on a plane. I haven't either. Wouldn't it be ironic if it crashed in the Atlantic?"

"Oh, Tish! Don't say that!"

"The Trevelyan curse!" (Wild laughter.)

As the tape ended, Qwilleran realized the meaning of Koko's eccentric behavior in recent weeks. The first hint of something wrong was the cat's unusual vigil at the front window; he sensed impending evil!

The day after Audit Sunday, Qwilleran recalled, Koko performed his ominous death dance on the coffee table—specifically circling the scandal headline on the front page of the paper. After that, he became a cat possessed. While Yum Yum pursued wads of crumpled paper and collected paper clips, Koko was infatuated with black pens, duck decoys, the wooden whistle, the brass paperweight, and other significant items. The three-headed dog may have been symbolic of the three felons involved in the Lumbertown fraud and its bloody aftermath. (On the other hand, Koko may have found the sharp edges of the paperweight useful, Qwilleran had to admit.)

Then the question arose: Were Eddie's deathbed accusations only hallucinations? Did Nella really mastermind the plot? Dwight Somers had seen "scruffy characters" knocking on her door; both Eddie and Benno fitted that description. Did Nella urge Eddie to move to Indian Village and into her own building for devious reasons? She was nothing less than gorgeous, everyone agreed, and the unkempt high school dropout from Sawdust City could easily have fallen under her spell.

Qwilleran's eye fell on the wooden whistle that someone had knocked off the coffee table for the twentieth time. Perhaps Nella herself tipped off the auditors; that would account for the neat timing of the scheme. She juggled the books; she plotted the murder; she blew the whistle and collaborated with the auditors; she made the phone call that lured Floyd to the fork in the road, where he parked his car and met a pickup truck with two carpenters, one with a hammer and one with a shovel. His disappearance was intended to confirm his guilt, and it fooled everyone—except Koko.

Qwilleran looked at his watch. It was late, but not too late to call the police chief at home. "What are you doing tomorrow morning, Andy?" he asked, after some teasing about late-night X-rated TV movies.

"Taking the wife shopping," was the gruff reply.

"How about driving over to the apple barn first, for half an hour?"

"Business or social?"

"Business, but I'll have coffee waiting for you."

"Oh, no, you won't! I'm not ready to have my hair fall out. I'll bring a nontoxic take-out from Lois's."

"What time?"

"Nine o'clock."

On Saturday morning Koko knew something was afoot. While eating his breakfast, he kept looking over his shoulder and listening. When Brodie arrived, he was not in uniform, and Yum Yum kept staring at him.

"What's the matter with her?" Brodie asked.

"She's looking for your badge."

Qwilleran had been wondering how to report his information to the police chief without naming his collaborators: a pleasant gray-haired grandmother and an intuitive cat. He began by enlisting Andy's sympathy. "Polly's in the hospital," he said morosely. "Heart attack."

"How bad?"

"I phoned this morning, and she's out of danger. It was a shock, although I should have seen it coming. Too much stress and not enough exercise."

"You've gotta look after that lady, Qwill. She's an asset to the community. Why don't you and Polly—"

"Never mind," Qwilleran said. "You can go and play your bagpipe at someone else's wedding."

The two men sat at the breakfast bar with their coffee and some doughnuts from Lois's.

"How's the Lumbertown investigation coming along?" Qwilleran asked.

"To tell the truth, I think they've run out of places to look for that guy."

"It's my opinion that he's right here in Moose County—underground."

"You mean—hiding out?"

"No. Buried."

Brodie swallowed a gulp of coffee too fast and coughed. "What makes you think so? Have you been conversing with your psychic cat?"

"I have an informant."

"Who?"

"I'd be crazy to reveal my source."

"Why did he come to you? Why not the police?"

"Well, it's like this, Andy. A lot of people out there don't like the media, but they like the media better than they like the cops. Tipsters, you know, are whispering in our ears all the time."

Brodie grunted. "D'you pay for the information?"

"Why would we pay for it? We didn't ask for it; we didn't want it; we can't use it."

"So what did you find out?"

"Floyd was no financial wizard, but he hired someone who was. That person juggled the books to defraud the depositors, and Floyd wasn't savvy enough to realize it, or he was too involved with his trains to care. Then the true embezzler threw suspicion on Floyd by having him disappear, when actually she had plotted his murder."

"She?" Brodie said with unprofessional astonishment. "You mean—his secretary?"

"She posed as his secretary, although she was second in command, hired to introduce new accounting methods—and she sure did! Not only did she abscond with the loot, but she didn't even pay off her hitman. The investigators questioned her in Texas but let her slip through their fingers."

"She told them she was fired for accusing the Lumbertown president of sexual harassment," Brodie explained.

"Okay, now I want to show you a video of the Lumbertown Party Train on Audit Sunday, if the cats will allow us to use their TV. The suspect appears in several frames."

"Why don't you get a TV of your own?" the chief grumbled as they climbed the ramp to the highest balcony. The Siamese followed them, then bounded ahead to claim the only available chair.

"Sorry, we have standing room only," Qwilleran apologized.

"Now watch the crowd scenes for a gorgeous woman in trousers—also in the dining car with Floyd."

The video played. Brodie watched. Koko yowled at intervals.

"So where's the body?" he asked when the tape was rewinding.

"No one knows; that's for you guys to find out. The hitman himself was killed in that fracas at the Trackside Tavern, and his accomplice has since died in an accident. If you ever find the body, I believe your forensic experts will say he was killed by a blow, or blows, to the head, inflicted by a carpenter's hammer."

"You expect me to believe all this? Well . . . thanks for the entertainment. It was better than the play I saw Thursday night." They started down the ramp, and in passing one of the large windows Brodie said, "You should clear out that jungle and build a motel."

"The far end of the jungle," Qwilleran told him, "is where Floyd's son, Eddie, was fatally injured in the tractor rollover."

"Must be true what they say about the Trevelyan curse." After walking with his guest to the parking area, Qwilleran made a few turns around the barn before letting himself in the front door. As he opened it, something slammed into his legs, throwing him off balance. It was Koko, shooting out of the door like a cannonball!

"Koko! Come back here!" Qwilleran yelled, but the cat was headed lickety-split down the orchard trail. The man charged after him, shouting. Koko kept on going. It was a hundred yards to Trevelyan Road, and he was covering it with the speed of a gazelle. There was the danger that he might dash across the highway in front of a car.

"Koko! Stop!" Qwilleran yelled with all the breath he could muster during the chase.

The cat stopped, but not until he had reached the building site. He ignored the framework of the new building. He went directly to the concrete slab of the garage and started his digging act. His hindquarters were elevated, and his brisket was close to the slab as he scraped the rough surface. Then he flopped on his side and rolled luxuriously on the concrete, twisting this way and that in apparent ecstasy.

The demonstration chilled Qwilleran's blood. He remembered that Eddie had poured the slab early in the morning after Audit Sunday, although the cement work had been scheduled for later in the week. It was on that Monday, also, that Koko had commenced his vigil at the foyer window. Had he witnessed something unusual during the night? From his window on the top balcony he had a view of the orchard trail. With his feline nightsight he might have seen a truck without headlights pulling onto the property. Perhaps he heard the clink of shovels in the rocky soil. Later came Koko's resolute digging in the crook of Qwilleran's elbow, not to mention his interest in the Panama Canal.

Qwilleran grabbed Koko and carried him back to the barn. Now what? he asked himself. If he confided his suspicions to Brodie, the jackhammers would move in, digging up Polly's garage floor, and she'd have another heart attack.

Carrying a bunch of fresh daisies, Qwilleran went to the hospital and found Polly sitting in a chair, looking remarkably serene. She was feeling fine, she said. She was looking forward to the catheterization; it might be an adventure. The hospital food was better than she expected. Dr. Diane was a dear young woman. The cardiologist from Lockmaster was most encouraging.

There was a sparkle in Polly's eyes that Qwilleran had not seen for several weeks, and finally she said, "I have a subject to broach to you, dear. I hope you won't be offended."

"You know I'm offense-proof where you're concerned, Polly."

"Well, I believe that this little setback of mine is a message from the fates that I should not build a house; Bootsie and I should move into the Duncan homestead with Lynette. That is, if you think I can dispose of my two acres and a half-finished house."

"No problem," he said with a sigh of relief.

CHAPTER 17

It was mid–September, and in Moose County the vicissitudes of summer were simmering down. Most vacationers had left; children were back in school; and the new college reported excellent enrollment for its first semester.

Polly Duncan, who had been flown to Minneapolis for coronary bypass surgery, was convalescing at the Duncan homestead. She claimed to feel better than she had in years! Bootsie was enjoying his new diet, running up and down stairs, and losing weight.

The Pickax Arts Council hoped to move into its new gallery and studios by Thanksgiving. Thanks to the generosity of the Klingenschoen Foundation, they had taken over the unfinished house on Trevelyan Road. References to the legendary curse were avoided.

Celia Robinson received a postcard from Switzerland: Florrie was improving, and Tish had met an interesting ski instructor.

Word was circulating on the Pickax grapevine that Mr. Q had been seen in Scottie's Men's Store, being measured for a kilt.

As for the Lumbertown scandal, the body of Floyd Trevelyan, buried under concrete, had been disinterred, and Nella Hooper replaced him on the wanted list. It seemed odd to Qwilleran that the law enforcement agencies, with all their technology and expertise, had failed to find this spectacularly good-looking woman. Earlier they had found her and let her go after questioning. Now they had the video of the Party Train, in which she appeared several times. And yet . . . It was Arch Riker's theory that the lawmen weren't trying hard enough, and he wrote an editorial to that effect. Anything that happens 400 miles north of everywhere, he argued, is of lesser importance to the establishment Down Below.

Then, quite by accident, Qwilleran uncovered a new clue. Following the final matinee of *A Midsummer Night's Dream,* theatre club members were invited to an afterglow at the apple barn. Among those present were Fran Brodie, the Lanspeaks, Junior Goodwinter, Derek Cuttlebrink, Elizabeth Hart, and Jennifer Olsen, who was becoming the club's leading ingenue. The Lanspeaks inquired about Polly's health. Derek demonstrated his exuberance by climbing the loft ladder straight up to the third balcony. Fran reminded Qwilleran that he had promised to read her playscript and give an opinion. He apologized for overlooking it.

Derek, having brought his guitar, also volunteered to sing a new folksong, titled *The Wreck of Old No. 9:*

There was once a famous hoghead
On the old SC&L.
His name was Ozzie Penn,
And he could drive a hog through hell!
But he had to give up drivin'
'Cause they said he was too old.
They retired him with a dinner
And a watch of solid gold.
"You've survived your share of train wrecks
"In fifty years," they said.
"Now go home and join the lucky ones
"That get to die in bed."

Chorus:
"No, I want to go out whittlin',"
Said good old Ozzie Penn.
But they said his dreams were over,
And he'd never drive again.

He hung around the switchyard
And told hair-raisin' tales:
How he made the fastest runs
And kept the hog upon the rails.
Then one day he saw a vision
That made his old eyes shine.
On a siding east of Mudville
Sat old Engine No. 9!

The great steam locomotive,
A mighty 4-6-2,
Had a tender full o' coal
And—by Crikey!—looked like new.

Chorus:
"I want to go out whittlin',"
Said the famous engineer.
There was nobody to see him
Wipe away an old man's tear.

He rounded up his buddies
And said, "Let's have some fun!
"Let's take the whole dang consist
"For one last whittlin' run!
"You fellas gotta jump
"Before we hit the final curve.
"So don't sign on with Ozzie
"If you haven't got the nerve."
With a crew of three old-timers
And fifty deadheads, too,
They left the yard at Mudville
To make Ozzie's dream come true.

Chorus:
"I want to go out whittlin',"
They'd often heard him say,
And he'd earned his chance to do it
Now that he was old and gray.

With the whistle screamin' "wildcat!"
They whittled down the line,
All knowin' what would happen
To engine No. 9.
As the fiery, sweatin' monster
Plunged down the steepest grade,
The final order came to jump
And every man obeyed.
But Ozzie at the throttle

Said he'd go down with the hog
As it sank with hissin', scaldin' steam
In the muck o' Black Creek bog.

Chorus:
"I want to go out whittlin',"
Said good old Ozzie Penn,
And the hoghead got his wish
Because he'll never drive again.

Derek's listeners applauded and wanted to know if he'd written it himself. He glanced at Qwilleran, who nodded.

"Yep," said the folksinger in an offhand way.

Elizabeth said, with her eyes shining, "He's so talented!" Meanwhile, Yum Yum watched the festivities from the balcony, tantalized by the aroma of pizza drifting up from the main floor. Koko, always more adventurous, mingled with the guests, accepting compliments and slices of pepperoni. He was within earshot when Qwilleran commended Jennifer for her portrayal of Hermia.

"Yow!" he said.

"See? Koko agrees with me. I believe his favorite character in all of Shakespeare is Hermia."

"Yow!" Koko repeated with added emphasis.

Qwilleran pondered the incident when the guests had left. The Siamese were enjoying a private afterglow-of-the-afterglow under the kitchen table, nibbling sausage and cheese and fastidiously avoiding the bits of mushroom and green pepper. Qwilleran, watching them, suddenly said, "Hermia!"

Koko looked up from his plate and made the usual comment.

Qwilleran thought, There's more to Hermia than meets the ear! During the summer the cat had exhibited many quirks, which were now abandoned. As soon as the mystery of Floyd's disappearance was solved, Koko stopped staring out the foyer window in the direction of the two-car garage slab. At the same time he stopped his everlasting digging in Qwilleran's elbow and lost interest in the Panama Canal. After the crimes of Edward Penn Trevelyan and

James Henry Ducker were exposed, he no longer stole black pens or sat on the fireplace cube with the decoys.

Was it coincidence that he had pursued these activities so assiduously? Was it ordinary feline fickleness when he stopped? Qwilleran knew otherwise. Koko had a gift of intuition and prescience that was not given to mere humans—or even to the average cat—and he had an unconventional way of communicating. It amused Qwilleran to paraphrase Shakespeare: *There are more things in Koko's head, Horatio, than are dreamt of in your philosophy.*

When the Siamese had finished their gourmet treat and washed up, the three of them ambled into the library for a read.

"What'll it be?" Qwilleran asked. He had asked that question several weeks before, and Koko's choice was *Swiss Family Robinson*. And what happened? Celia Robinson moved to Pickax, and the Trevelyan women flew to Switzerland. Coincidence? "Sure," Qwilleran said with derision.

Now Koko sniffed the bookshelf devoted to drama and nudged the copy of *Androcles and the Lion*.

"We had that book a few weeks ago," Qwilleran reminded him. "Try again."

This time the cat's choice was a slender paperback, Fran Brodie's playscript of *The Lion in Winter*.

In a flash of revelation Qwilleran remembered the young woman in the Pickax People's Bank: Letitia Penn, who turned out to be Letitia Trevelyan . . . and who had a friend named Lionella. Later it developed that the one name was shortened to Tish and the other to Nella.

That was the answer! That remarkable cat knew from the beginning that the Lumbertown fraud was masterminded by Nella a.k.a. Lionella! Now Qwilleran understood Koko and the lions, but what about Hermia? There was something about this H word that triggered Koko's brain cells and was supposed to trigger Qwilleran's. Yet, he was stymied—until he thought about the dictionary. His unabridged dictionary always stimulated the associative process.

As he climbed the ramp to consult its erudite pages, the Siamese followed with vertical tails. On this occasion he had a reason for allowing them into his sanctum. One of them immediately inspected the typewriter and left a few cat hairs among the typebars; the other lost no time in knocking a gold pen off the desk.

Looking up the definition of Hermia, Qwilleran found what he already knew: Hermia was a lady in love with Lysander in *A Midsummer Night's Dream*. There were other proper nouns, however, that might have a similar sound to a cat's ear, and he read them aloud: "Hermo . . . Hermione . . . Hermitage . . . Hermes." Nothing attracted Koko's attention until he reached "Hermaphrodite."

The sound of the word brought an alarming response that started as an ear-splitting falsetto and ended in a menacing growl.

Qwilleran checked the definitions of hermaphrodite. It referred to a two-masted vessel, square-rigged forward, and schooner-rigged aft. It also referred to a vertebrate or invertebrate having male and female organs.

He read no further. He grabbed the telephone and called the police chief at home. "Andy! I've got a far-out idea!"

"Let's hear it—fast. My favorite program's just beginning."

"It's only a hunch, but it might help your colleagues in their womanhunt. First, it's a fact that Nella Hooper's name was shortened from Lionella. It's my guess that this person's name was really Lionel. The bloodhounds are hunting for a suspect of the wrong sex! Impersonating a woman was part of the scam. Now that Nella Hooper is on the wanted list, Lionel Hooper is probably growing a beard. . . . Now hang up and go back to the tube."

Qwilleran returned to the lounge area and sprawled on the sofa. The Siamese took up positions on the coffee table, where the day's last shaft of sunlight slanted in from a high window to warm their fur and make each guard-hair look like spun gold. It turned their whiskers into platinum. Yum Yum sat comfortably on her brisket like a regular cat. Koko sat tall like an ancient Egyptian deity.

"You've done it again, young man!" Qwilleran said with admiration. "You blew the whistle on the whole crew!"

Koko gazed at the man with a superior cast in his blue eyes, as if he were thinking, *What fools these mortals be!*

THE CAT WHO SAID CHEESE

CHAPTER 1

Autumn, in that year of surprises, was particularly delicious in Moose County, 400 miles north of everywhere. Not only had most of the summer vacationers gone home, but civic-awareness groups and enthusiastic *foodies* were cooking up a savory kettle of stew called the Great Food Explo. Then, to add spice to the season, a mystery woman registered at the hotel in Pickax City, the county seat. She was not beautiful. She was not exactly young. She avoided people. And she always wore black.

The townfolk of Pickax (population 3,000) were fascinated by her enigmatic presence. "Have you seen her?" they asked each other. "She's been here over a week. Who do you think she is?"

The hotel desk clerk refused to divulge her name even to his best friends, saying it was prohibited by law. That convinced everyone that the mystery woman had bribed him for nefarious reasons of her own, since Lenny Inchpot was not the town's most law-abiding citizen.

So they went on commenting about her olive complexion, sultry brown eyes, and lush mop of dark hair that half covered the left side of her face. Yet, the burning question remained: "Why is she staying at that firetrap of a flophouse?" That attitude was unfair. The New Pickax Hotel, though gloomy, was respectable and painfully clean, and there was a fire escape in the rear. There was even a presidential suite, although no president had ever stayed there—not even a candidate for the state legislature on an unpopular ticket. Nevertheless, no one had been known to lodge there for more than a single night, or two at the most, and travel agents around the country were influenced by an entry in their directory of lodgings:

NEW PICKAX HOTEL, 18 miles from Moose County Airport; 20 rooms, some with private bath; presidential suite with telephone and TV; bridal suite with round bed. Three-story building with one elevator, frequently out of order. Prisonlike exterior and bleak interior, circa 1935. Public areas unusually quiet, with Depression Era furnishings. Cramped lobby and dining room; no bar; small, unattractive ballroom in basement. Sleeping rooms plain but clean; mattresses fairly new; lighting dim. Metal fire escape in rear; rooms with windows have coils of rope for emergency use. Dining room offers breakfast buffet, luncheon specials, undistinguished dinner menu, beer and wine. No liquor. No room service. No desk clerk on duty after 11 P.M. Rates: low to moderate. Hospital nearby.

Business travelers checked into the New Pickax Hotel for a single overnight because no other lodgings were available in town. Out-of-towners arriving to attend a funeral might be forced by awkward plane schedules to spend two nights. In the hushed dining room the business travelers sat alone, reading technical manuals while waiting for the chopped sirloin and boiled carrots. Forks could be heard clicking against plates as the out-of-town mourners silently counted the peas in the chicken pot pie. And now, in addition, there was a woman in black who sat in a far corner, toying with a glass of wine and an overcooked vegetable plate.

One resident of Pickax who wondered about her was a journalist—a tall, good-looking man with romantically graying hair, brooding eyes, and a luxuriant pepper-and-salt moustache. His name was Jim Qwilleran; friends called him Qwill, and townfolk called him Mr. Q with affection and respect. He wrote a twice-weekly column for the *Moose County Something,* but he had been a prize-winning crime reporter Down Below—local parlance for metropolitan areas to the south. An unexpected inheritance had brought him north and introduced him to small-town life—a unique experience for a native of Chicago.

Qwilleran was admired by young and old, male and female—not only because he had turned his billion-dollar inheritance over to charity. His admirers appreciated his down-to-earth style: He drove a small car, pumped his own gas, cleaned his own windshield; he walked around town; he pedaled a bike in the country. As a journalist, he showed a sincere interest in the subjects he interviewed. He responded courteously to strangers when they recognized his moustache and hailed him on the street or in the supermarket. Understandably he had made many friends in the county, and the fact that he lived alone—in a barn, with two cats—was a foible they had learned to accept.

Qwilleran's housemates were no ordinary cats, and his residence was no ordinary barn. Octagonal in shape, it was a hundred-year-old apple storage facility four stories high, perched on an impressive fieldstone foundation and topped with a cupola. To make the barn habitable, certain architectural changes had been made. Triangular windows had been cut in the walls. The interior, open to the roof, had three balconies connected by a spiraling ramp. And on the ground floor the main living areas surrounded a giant white fireplace cube with great white stacks rising to the roof. The barn would have been a showplace if the owner had not preferred privacy.

As for the cats, they were a pair of elegant Siamese whose seal-brown points were in striking contrast to their pale fawn bodies. The male, Kao K'o Kung, answered to the name of Koko; he was long, lithe, and muscular, and his fathomless blue eyes brimmed with intelligence. His female companion, Yum Yum, was small and delicate, with violet-blue eyes that could be large and heart-melting when she wanted to sit on a lap, yet that dainty creature could utter a piercing shriek when dinner was behind schedule.

One Thursday morning in September, Qwilleran was closeted in his private suite on the first balcony, the only area in the barn that was totally off-limits to cats. He was trying to write

a thousand words for his Friday column, "Straight from the
Qwill Pen."

Emily Dickinson, we need you!
"I'm nobody. Who are you?" said this prolific American
poet.
I say, "God give us nobodies! What this country needs is
fewer celebrities and more nobodies who live ordinary lives,
cope bravely, do a little good in the world, enjoy a few pleasures, and never, *never* get their names in the newspaper or
their faces on TV."

"Yow!" came a baritone complaint outside the door. It was
followed by a soprano shriek. "N-n-now!"
Qwilleran consulted his watch. It was twelve noon and time for
their midday treat. In fact, it was three minutes past twelve, and
they resented the delay.
He yanked open his studio door to face two determined petition-
ers. "I wouldn't say you guys were spoiled," he rebuked them.
"You're only tyrannical monomaniacs about food." As they high-
tailed it down the ramp to the kitchen, he took the shortcut via a spi-
ral metal staircase. Nevertheless, they reached the food station first.
He dropped some crunchy morsels on two plates; separate plates had
been Yum Yum's latest feline-rights demand, and he always indulged her. He stood with fists on hips to watch their enjoyment.
Today she had changed her mind, however. She helped Koko
gobble his plateful; then the two of them worked on her share.
"Cats!" Qwilleran muttered in exasperation. "Is it okay with
you two autocrats if I go back to work now?"
Satisfied with their repast, they ignored him completely and busied themselves with washing masks and ears. He went up to his
studio and wrote another paragraph:

We crave heroes to admire and emulate, and what do we
get? A parade of errant politicians, mad exhibitionists, wicked
heiresses, temperamental artists, silly risk-takers, overpaid ath-
letes, untalented entertainers, non-authors of non-books . . .

The telephone interrupted, and he grabbed it on the first ring. The caller was Junior Goodwinter, young managing editor of the *Moose County Something*. "Hey, Qwill, are you handing in your Friday copy this afternoon?"

"Only if the interruptions permit me to write a simple declarative sentence in its entirety," he snapped. "Why?"

"We'd like you to attend a meeting."

Qwilleran avoided editorial meetings whenever possible. "What's it about?"

"Dwight Somers is going to brief us on the Great Food Explo. He's spent a few days in Chicago with the masterminds of the K Fund, and he'll be flying in on the three-fifteen shuttle."

Qwilleran's petulance mellowed somewhat. The K Fund was the local nickname for the Klingenschoen Foundation that he had established to dispense his inherited billion. Dwight Somers was one of his friends, a local public relations man with credentials Down Below. "Okay. I'll be there."

"By the way, how's Polly?"

"She's improving every day. She's now allowed to walk up and down stairs—a thrill she equates with winning the Nobel Prize." Polly Duncan was a charming woman of his own age, currently on medical leave from the Pickax Public Library, where she was chief administrator.

"Tell her Jody and I were asking about her. Tell her Jody's mother had a bypass last year, and she feels great!"

"Thanks. She'll be happy to hear that."

Qwilleran returned to his typewriter and pounded out another few sentences:

> Collecting nobodies makes a satisfying hobby. Unlike diamonds, they cost nothing and are never counterfeited. Unlike first editions of Dickens, they are in plentiful supply. Unlike Chippendale antiques, they occupy no room in the house.

The telephone rang again. It was a call from the law firm of Hasselrich Bennett & Barter, and Qwilleran groaned. Calls from attorneys were always bad news.

The quavering voice of the senior partner said, "I beg forgiveness, Mr. Qwilleran, for interrupting your work. No doubt the Qwill pen is penning another quotable column."

"No apology needed," Qwilleran said courteously.

"I trust you are enjoying these fine autumn days."

"There's no better season in Moose County. And you, Mr. Hasselrich?"

"I savor every moment and dread the onslaught of winter. And how, pray, is Mrs. Duncan?"

"Progressing well, thank you. I hope Mrs. Hasselrich is feeling better."

"She recovers slowly, one day at a time. Grief is a stubborn infection of the spirit." Eventually the attorney cleared his throat and said, "I called to remind you that the annual meeting of the Klingenschoen Foundation will be held in Chicago at the end of the month. Mr. Barter will represent you as usual, but it occurred to me that you might like to accompany him, since you have never appeared at one of these functions. You would be warmly welcomed, I assure you."

To Qwilleran, corporate meetings were worse than editorial meetings. "I appreciate the suggestion, Mr. Hasselrich. Unfortunately, commitments in Pickax will prevent me from leaving town at that time."

"I understand," said the attorney, "but I would be remiss if I were to allow the invitation to go untendered."

There were a few more polite words, and then Qwilleran hung up the receiver with smug satisfaction; he had avoided one more boring meeting with the financial bigwigs. Upon first inheriting the Klingenschoen fortune, his financial savvy was so scant that he needed to consult the dictionary for the number of zeroes in a billion. Wealth had never interested him; he enjoyed working for a living, cashing a weekly paycheck, and practicing economies. When the billion descended on him, he considered it a burden, a nuisance and an embarrassment. Turning the vast holdings over to a foundation was a stroke of genius on his part, leaving him happily unencumbered. He returned to the typewriter:

How do you recognize a nobody? You see a stranger performing an anonymous act of kindness and disappearing without a thank-you. You hear spontaneous words of wit or wisdom from an unlikely source. I remember an elderly man walking with a cane in downtown Pickax when the wind velocity was forty miles an hour, gusting to sixty. We sheltered in a doorway, and he said, "The wind knocked me down in front of the courthouse, but I don't mind because it's part of nature."

When the telephone rang for the third time, Qwilleran answered gruffly but changed his tune when he heard the musical voice of Polly Duncan. "How are you?" he asked anxiously. "I phoned earlier, but there was no answer."

"Lynette drove me to the cardiac clinic in Lockmaster," she said with animation, "and the doctor is astonished at my speedy recovery. He says it's because I've always lived right, except for insufficient exercise. I must start walking every day."

"Good! We'll walk together," he said, but he thought, That's what I've been telling her for years; she wouldn't take my advice. "I'll see you tonight at the usual time, Polly. Anything you need from the store?"

"All I need is some good conversation—just the two of us. Lynette is going out. À bientôt, dear."

"À bientôt."

Before returning to his treatise on nobodies, Qwilleran took a moment to relish Polly's good news. He still remembered her late-night call for help, her frightened eyes as the paramedics strapped her onto a stretcher, his own uneasy moments outside the Intensive Care Unit, and his long wait in the surgery wing of a Minneapolis hospital. Now she was convalescing at the home of her sister-in-law but yearning for her own apartment. After preparing a cup of coffee, he wrote:

I began my own collection of nobodies Down Below, my first being a thirteen-year-old boy who did all the cooking for a family of eight. The next was a woman bus driver who

set her brakes, flagged down another bus, and escorted a bewildered passenger onto the right one.

The next interruption was a call from John Bushland, the commercial photographer. "Say, Qwill, do you remember the time I
tried to shoot your cats in my studio? We couldn't even get them
out of their carrying coop."

"How could I forget?" Qwilleran replied. "It was the battle of
the century—between two grown men and two determined cats.
We lost."

"Well, I'd like to take another crack at it—at your house, if you
don't mind. There's another competition for a cat calendar. They'd
feel more comfortable on their own territory, and I could try for
candids."

"Sure. When do you want to try it? In daylight or after dark?"

"Natural light works better for eye color. How about tomorrow
morning?"

"Make it around nine o'clock," Qwilleran suggested. "Their
bellies will be full, and they'll be at peace with the universe."

Eventually he was able to stretch his thesis to a thousand words,
ending with:

> One word of caution to the novice collector of nobodies:
> Avoid mentioning your choice collectibles to the media. If
> you do, your best examples will become celebrities overnight,
> and there's no such thing as a prominent nobody.

Having worked against odds, the writer of the "Qwill Pen"
finished in time for the meeting at the newspaper office. He said
goodbye to the Siamese as he usually did, telling them where he
was going and when he would return. The more one talks to cats,
he believed, the smarter they become. His two Mensa candidates
responded, however, by raising groggy heads from their afternoon
nap and giving him a brief glassy stare before falling asleep again.

He walked downtown. No one in Pickax walked, except to a
vehicle in the parking lot. Qwilleran's habit of using his legs instead
of his wheels was considered a quaint eccentricity—the kind of

thing one could expect of a transplant from Down Below. He walked first to Lois's Luncheonette for a piece of apple pie.

The proprietor—a buxom, bossy woman with a host of devoted customers—was taking a mid-afternoon break and chattering to coffee-drinking loiterers. She talked about her son, Lenny, who worked the evening shift on the desk at the hotel and also attended classes at the new college. She talked about his girlfriend, Anna Marie, who was enrolled in the nursing program at MCCC and also worked part-time at the hotel. Students, she said, were glad to work short hours, even though the skinflint who owned the hotel paid minimum wage without benefits.

Qwilleran, always entertained by Lois's discourses, arrived at the newspaper conference in good humor.

The *Moose County Something* was a broadsheet published five days a week. Originally subsidized by the K Fund, it was now operating in the black. The office building was new. The printing plant was state-of-the-art. The staff always seemed to be having a good time.

The meeting was held in the conference room. Its plain wood-paneled walls were decorated with framed tearsheets of memorable front pages in the history of American journalism: *Titanic Meets a Mightier . . . War in Europe . . . Kennedy Assassinated*. Staffers sat around the large teakwood conference table, drinking coffee from mugs imprinted with newspaper wit: "If you can't eat it, don't print it" . . . "Deadlines are made to be missed" . . . "A little malice aforethought is fun."

"Come on in, Qwill," the managing editor said. "Dwight isn't here yet. Since we hate to waste time, we're inventing rumors about the mystery woman."

There were six staffers around the table:

Arch Riker, the paunchy publisher and editor in chief, had been Qwilleran's lifelong friend and fellow journalist Down Below. Now he was realizing his dream of running a small-town newspaper.

Junior Goodwinter's boyish countenance and slight build belied his importance; he was not only the managing editor but a direct descendent of the founders of Pickax City. In a community 400 miles north of everywhere, that mattered a great deal.

Hixie Rice, in charge of advertising and promotion, was another refugee from Down Below, and after several years in the outback she still had a certain urbane verve and chic.

Mildred Hanstable Riker, food writer and wife of the publisher, was a plump, good-hearted native of Moose County, recently retired from teaching fine and domestic arts in the public schools.

Jill Handley, the new feature editor, was pretty and eager but not yet comfortable with her fellow staffers. She came from the *Lockmaster Ledger* in the neighboring county, where the inhabitants of Moose County were considered barbarians.

Wilfred Sugbury, secretary to the publisher, was a thin, wiry, sober-faced young man, intensely serious about his job. He jumped up and filled a coffee mug for Qwilleran. It was inscribed: "First we kill all the editors."

Also present, watching from the top of a file cabinet, was William Allen, a large white cat formerly associated with the *Pickax Picayune*.

Qwilleran nodded pleasantly to each one in turn and took a chair next to the newcomer. Jill Handley turned to him adoringly. "Oh, Mr. Qwilleran, I love your column! You're a fantastic writer!"

Sternly he replied, "You're not allowed to work for the *Something* unless you drink coffee, like cats, and call me Qwill."

"You have Siamese, don't you . . . Qwill?"

"Loosely speaking. It's more accurate to say that they have me. What prompted you to leave civilization for life in the wilderness?"

"Well, my kids wanted to go to Pickax High because you have a larger swimming pool, and my husband found a good business opportunity up here, and I wanted to write for a paper that carries columns like the "Qwill Pen." That's the honest truth!"

"Enough!" said the boss at the head of the table. "Any more of this and he'll be asking for a raise . . . Let's hear it for our gold-medal winner!"

Everyone applauded, and Wilfred flushed. He had come in first in the seventy-mile Labor Day Bike Race, yet no one at the newspaper knew that he even owned a bike—such was his modesty and concentration on his work.

Qwilleran said, "Congratulations! We're all proud of you. Your pedaling is on a par with your office efficiency."

"Thanks," said Wilfred. "I didn't expect to win. I just signed up for the fun of it, but I decided to give it my best shot, so I trained hard all summer. I was confident I could go the entire route, even if I came in last, but everything turned out right for me, and after the first sixty miles I suddenly thought, Hey, chump, you can win this crazy race! That was between Mudville and Kennebeck, with only a few riders ahead of me, so I gave it an extra push to the finish line. Nine bikers finished, and they all deserve credit for a great try. They were as good as I was, only I had something going for me—luck, I guess. I'm hoping to compete again next year."

This was more than the quiet young man had said in his two years of employment, and all heads turned to listen in astonishment. Only Qwilleran could think of something to say: "We admire your spirit and determination, Wilfred."

Riker cleared his throat. "While we're waiting for the late Mr. Somers, let us resume our deliberations." Then he added in a loud, sharp voice, *"Who is the mystery woman and what is she doing here?"*

Mildred said, "She always wears black and is inclined to be reclusive. I think she's in mourning, having suffered a great loss. She's come to this quiet town to deal with her grief. We should respect her need for privacy."

Qwilleran stroked his moustache, a sign of purposeful interest. "Does she ever venture out of the hotel?"

"Sure," Junior said. "Our reporters in the field have seen her driving around in a rental car with an airport sticker, a dark blue two-door."

"And," Hixie added, signaling news of importance, "one day when I was getting an ad contract signed at the Black Bear Café, I saw her in the hotel lobby with a man! He was wearing a business suit and tie, and he was carrying a briefcase."

"The plot thickens," Riker said. "Was he checking out or checking in?"

Qwilleran said, "I haven't seen her. Is she good-looking? Is she young? Is she glamorous?"

"Why don't you have dinner at the hotel, Qwill, and see for yourself?"

"No thanks. The last time I went there, a chicken breast squirted butter all over my new sports coat. I considered it a hostile attack on the media."

Wilfred said shyly, "Lenny Inchpot told me she looks foreign."

"Very interesting," said Junior. "We have a foreign agent in our midst, a scout for some international cartel planning to come up here and pollute our environment."

"Or she's a government undercover operator, casing the area as a possible site for a toxic waste dump," Riker suggested.

The new woman on the staff listened in bewilderment, uncertain how to react to the straight-faced conjectures.

"Or she's a visitor from outer space," Mildred said merrily. "We had a lot of UFO sightings this summer."

"You're all off-base," Hixie declared. "I say the man with a briefcase is her attorney, and she's Gustav Limburger's secret girl friend, now suing him for patrimony."

Laughter exploded from all except Qwilleran and the new editor. She asked, "What's so funny?"

"Gustav Limburger," Mildred explained, "is a short, bent-over, mean-spirited, eighty-year-old Scrooge, living in seclusion in Black Creek. He owns the New Pickax Hotel."

"Well, what's wrong with my theory?" Hixie demanded. "He's rich. He's got one foot in the grave. He has no family. It wouldn't be the first time a dirty old man made a deal with a young woman."

There was more laughter and then a knock on the door, and Dwight Somers walked into the conference room, saying, "Let me in on the joke." The PR man had looked better before he shaved off his beard, but what he lacked in handsome features he made up in enthusiasm and personality. He nodded to each one at the table and nodded twice to Hixie. "Sorry to be late, gang. The plane lost its left wing somewhere over Lockmaster. Enemy fire is suspected."

"No problem," Riker said, motioning him to a chair. "The K Fund will buy the airline a new wing."

"Welcome to the *Moose County Dumbthing!*" Junior said, while Wilfred scurried to fill a coffee mug imprinted: "First we kill all the PR people."

The publisher asked, "Was this your first visit to Klingenschoen headquarters, Dwight? I hear it's impressive."

"Man! It's staggering! You're talking about an operation that occupies four floors of an office building in the Loop. They have a think tank of specialists in investments, real estate, economic development, and philanthropy. Their thrust is to make Moose County a great place to live and work without turning it into a megalopolis. They're for saving the beaches and forests, keeping the air and water clean, creating businesses that do more good than harm, and zoning that discourages high-density development."

"Sounds Utopian. Will it work?"

"If it works, it'll be a prototype for rural communities throughout the country—that is, if they want to thrive and still maintain their quality of life."

"What about tourism?" Junior asked.

"The K Fund soft-pedals the kind of tourism that alters the character of the community. They're bankrolling country inns that operate on a small scale, serve fine food, appeal to discriminating travelers, and get high class publicity. For tourists on a budget they're promoting small campgrounds that don't clear-cut the woods."

Someone asked about business opportunities.

"Now we come to the point," Dwight said. "If there's one industry that's clean, indispensable, and positive in image, it's food! The county's already known for fisheries, sheep ranches, and potato farms. Now the K Fund is backing enterprises such as a turkey farm and a cherry orchard, ethnic restaurants, and food specialty shops. The Great Food Explo will be a festival of all kinds of happenings related to food." He opened his briefcase and handed out fact sheets. "The Explo opens with a bang a week from tomorrow. Any questions?"

Someone said, "It sounds like it could be fun."

"The trend is to food as entertainment," Dwight said. "There are a lot of foodies out there! People are dining out more often, talking about food, buying cookbooks, taking culinary classes, watching food videos, joining gourmet clubs. Some of the new perfumes on the market smell like vanilla, raspberry, chocolate, nutmeg, cinnamon . . ."

Riker said, "I wouldn't mind having a Scotch aftershave."

"Don't worry! They'll get around to that."

"Starting next week," Junior said, "we're expanding our food coverage to a full page."

Qwilleran asked, "I suspect the mystery woman is part of a publicity stunt for the Explo."

"No! I swear it on a stack of cookbooks," Dwight said. He closed his briefcase. "I want to thank you, gang, for this opportunity to cue you in. I hope you'll jump on the bandwagon and call me if I can help."

"It's an appetizing prospect," Riker said. "Let's send Wilfred out for burgers and malts!"

CHAPTER 2

Qwilleran was a congenital foodie who needed no coaxing to participate in the Great Food Explo. He hoped it would open up new sources of material for his "Qwill Pen" column. Finding topics for the twice-weekly space was not easy, considering the boundaries of the county and the number of years he had been Qwill-penning.

From the newspaper he walked to Toodle's Market to buy food for his fussy felines. Toodle was an old respected food name, dating back to the days when grocers butchered their own hogs and sold a penny's worth of tea. Now the market had the size and parking space of a big-city supermarket, but not the hypnotic glare of overhead fluorescents. Incandescent spotlights and floodlights illuminated the meats and produce without changing their color or giving Mrs. Toodle a headache. It was she who ran the business, with the assistance of sons, daughters, in-laws, and grandchildren. Qwilleran bought a few cans of red salmon, crabmeat, cocktail shrimp, and minced clams.

His next stop was Edd's Editions, the used-book store. Here

there were thousands of volumes accumulated from estate sales in surrounding counties. Colorless books cluttered the shelves, tables, and floor, and Eddington Smith had a dusty, elderly appearance to match his stock. Also blending into the background was a portly longhair named Winston who dusted the premises with sweeps of his plumed tail. There was always an odor in the store, compounded of mildewed books from damp basements, the sardines that constituted Winston's diet, and the liver and onions that Eddington frequently prepared for himself in the back room. On this day the aroma was unusually strong, and Qwilleran made his visit brief.

"I want something for Mrs. Duncan, Edd. She likes to read old cookbooks. She finds them amusing."

"I hope she's feeling better?"

"She's recovered her sense of humor, so that's a good sign," Qwilleran said as he examined, hastily, three shelves of pre-owned recipe books. One was a yellowed 1899 paperback titled *Delicious Dishes for Dainty Entertaining,* compiled by the Pickax Ladies' Cultural Society. Leafing through it, he noted recipes for Bangers and Beans, Wimpy-diddles, and Mrs. Duncan's Famous Pasties. "I'll take it," he said, thinking, She may have been Polly's great-grandmother-in-law.

Meanwhile Eddington was unpacking a newly arrived carton of old books from a family of dairy farmers and cheesemakers.

Qwilleran spotted *Great Cheeses of the Western World—A Compendium.* "I'll take this, too," he said. "How much do I owe you? Don't bother to wrap them." He left in a hurry as the store odors became overwhelming.

Memories of the bookstore lingered in his nostrils as he walked home along Main Street, around Park Circle, through the theatre parking lot, then along a wooded trail to the apple barn. The theatre, a magnificent fieldstone building, had once been the Klingenschoen mansion, and the fine carriage house at the rear was now a four-car garage with an apartment upstairs. The tenant was unloading groceries from her car as Qwilleran crossed the parking lot.

"Need any help?" he called out.

"No thanks. Need any macaroni and cheese?" she replied with a hearty laugh. Her name was Celia Robinson, and she was a jolly gray-haired grandmother who supplied him with home-cooked dishes that he could keep in the freezer.

"I never say no to macaroni and cheese," he said.

"I've been meaning to ask you, Mr. Q. What do you think about the mystery woman at the hotel? I think you should investigate." Mrs. Robinson was an avid reader of spy fiction, and twice she had acted as his confidential assistant when he was snooping into situations that he considered suspicious.

"Not this time, Celia. No crime has been committed, and the gossip about the woman is absurd. We should all mind our own business . . . And how about you? Are you still in the Pals for Patients program?"

"Still doing my bit! They've started a Junior Pal Brigade now, and it's my job to train them—college students who want to earn a little money. Nice kids. They're very good at cheering up housebound patients." She stopped and sniffed inquiringly. "Did you just buy some rat cheese?"

"No. Only a book on the subject. It belonged to a cheesemaker and acquired a certain redolence by osmosis."

"Oh, Mr. Q! What you mean is—it stinks!" She laughed at her own forthrightness.

"If you say so, madame," he said with a stiff bow that sent her into further gales of laughter.

From there he tramped through the dense evergreen woods that screened the apple barn from the heavy traffic of Park Circle. As he approached the barn, he was aware of two pairs of eyes watching him from an upper window. As soon as he unlocked the door, they were there to meet him, hopping on their hind legs and pawing his clothing. He knew it was neither his magnetic personality nor the canned seafood that attracted them. It was the cheese book! Their noses wrinkled. They opened their mouths and showed their fangs. It was what the veterinarian called the Flehman response. Whatever it was called, it was not a flattering reaction.

Qwilleran gave the cheese book an analytical sniff himself. Celia was right; it had a definite overripe stink—like Limburger cheese.

It had been many years since his introduction to Limburger in Germany, but it was memorable. *Ripe* was their word for it. *Rank* would be more descriptive.

Limburger, he recalled, was the name of the old man so uncharitably described at the editorial meeting. He sounded like a genuine character. Like most journalists, Qwilleran appreciated characters; they made good copy. He remembered his interviews with Adam Dingleberry, Euphonia Gage, and Ozzie Penn, to name a few. He went into action.

First he relegated the cheese compendium to the tool shed, hoping it would lose its scent in a few days. Next he consulted the Black Creek section of the phone book and called a number. There were many rings before anyone answered.

A crotchety, cracked voice shouted, "Who's this?"

"Are you Mr. Limburger?"

"If that's who you called, that's who you got. Whaddaya want?"

"I'm Jim Qwilleran from the *Moose County Something.*"

"Don't wanna take the paper. Costs too much."

"That's not why I'm calling, sir. Are you the owner of the New Pickax Hotel?"

"None o' yer business."

"I'd like to write a history of the famous hotel, Mr. Limburger," Qwilleran persisted in a genial voice.

"What fer?"

"It's been a landmark for over a hundred years, and our readers would be interested in—"

"So whaddaya wanna know?"

"I'd like to visit you and ask some questions."

"*When?*" the old man demanded in a hostile tone.

"How about tomorrow morning around eleven o'clock?"

"Iffen I'm here. I'm eighty-two. I could kick the bucket any ol' time."

"I'll take a chance," Qwilleran said pleasantly. "You sound healthy."

"N-n-now!" came a cry not far from the mouthpiece of the phone.

"*Whazzat?*"

"Just a low-flying plane. See you tomorrow, Mr. Limburger."
He heard the old man slam down the receiver, and he chuckled.

Before going to see Polly, Qwilleran read the fact sheet about
the Great Food Explo. The opening festivities would center about
a complex called Stables Row. It occupied a block-long stone
building on a back street in downtown Pickax. In horse-and-buggy
days it had been a ten-cent barn: all-day stabling and a bucket of
oats for a dime. Later it was adapted for contemporary use, housing
stores, repair shops, and offices in ever-changing variety. Now it
was embarking on a bright new life. Large and small spaces had
been remodeled to accommodate a pasty parlor, soup bar, bakery,
wine and cheese shop, kitchen boutique, old-fashioned soda fountain, and health food store.

Special events during the Explo would include a pasty bake-off,
a celebrity dinner-date auction, and a series of cooking classes for
men only. Qwilleran knew his friends would coax him into enrolling, but he knew all he wanted to know about cooking: he
could thaw a frozen dinner to perfection. He opened a can of
minced clams for the Siamese and said, "Okay, you guys. Try to
stay out of trouble while I'm gone. I'm going to visit your cousin
Bootsie."

Qwilleran drove his car to Pleasant Street, a neighborhood of
Victorian frame houses built by affluent Pickaxians in an era when
carpenters had just discovered the jigsaw. Porches, eaves, bay windows, and gables had been lavished with fancy wood trim, to the
extent that Pleasant Street had been nicknamed Gingerbread Alley.
Here Polly's unmarried sister-in-law, the last Duncan-by-blood,
had inherited the ancestral home, and here Polly was recuperating.

On arrival, Qwilleran went slowly up the front walk, gazing up
at the architectural excesses with amazement. He was unaware that
Bootsie, Polly's adored Siamese, was watching him from a front
window. The two males—competitors for Polly's affection—had
never been friendly but managed to observe an uneasy detente.
Qwilleran turned a knob in the front door, which jangled a bell in
the entrance hall, and Polly arrived in a flurry of filmy blue. She

was wearing a voluminous caftan that he had given her as a get-well gift.

"Polly! You're looking wonderful!" he exclaimed. It had been painful to see her pale and listless. Now her eyes were sparkling, and her winning smile had returned.

"All it takes is a good medical report plus some blusher and eye shadow," she said gaily. "Brenda came over today to do my hair."

They clung together in a voluptuous embrace until Bootsie protested.

"Lynette has gone to her bridge club tonight, so we can have a tête-à-tête with tea and cookies. The hospital dietician gave me a cookie recipe with no sugar, no butter, no eggs, and no salt."

"They sound delectable," he said dryly.

They went into the parlor, which several generations of Duncans had maintained in the spirit of the nineteenth century, with velvet draperies, fringed lamp shades, pictures in ornate frames, and rugs on top of rugs. A round lamp table was skirted down to the floor, and as Qwilleran entered the room to take a chair, a fifteen-pound missile shout out from under the skirt and crashed into his legs.

"Naughty, naughty!" Polly scolded with more love than rebuke. To Qwilleran she explained, "He was only playing games."

Oh, sure, he thought.

"Lynette wants me to move in permanently, and I'm tempted, because Bootsie loves the house. So many places to hide!"

"So I've noticed. Does he ambush all your visitors? It's a good thing I have a strong heart and nerves of steel."

Polly laughed softly. "How do you like the cookies?"

"Not bad. Not bad. All they need is a little sugar, butter, egg, and salt."

"Now you're teasing! But that's all right. I'm happy to be alive and well and teasable . . . Guess who visited me today and brought some gourmet mushroom soup! Elaine Fetter!"

"Do I know her?"

"You should. She's a zealous volunteer who works hard at working for nothing. She volunteers at the hospital, the historical museum, and the library. I find her very good on phones and cataloguing, but she's not well liked, being somewhat of a snob. She lives in West Middle Hummock, and we all know that's a status address, and her late husband was an attorney with Hasselrich Bennett & Barter."

"How was the soup?"

"Delicious, but too rich for my diet. Gourmet cooks have a heavy hand with butter and cream. Incidentally, she grows her own mushrooms—shiitake, no less."

Qwilleran's interest was alerted. Here was a subject for the "Qwill Pen." There was something mysterious about mushrooms, and even more so about shiitake. "Would she agree to an interview?"

"Would she! Elaine loves having her name in the paper."

"When will you feel like restaurant dining again, Polly? I've missed you." Dining out was one of his chief pleasures, and he was a gracious host.

"Soon, dear, but I must be careful to order wisely. The dietician gave me a list of recommended substitutes, and she stressed small portions."

"I'll speak to the chef at the Old Stone Mill," Qwilleran said. "For you he'll be glad to prepare a three-ounce broiled substitute with a light substitute sauce."

She trilled her musical laugh. It was good to hear her laughter again. He realized now that her physical condition had affected her disposition, long before she felt chest pains.

"Did you have any other visitors today?" he asked, thinking about Dr. Prelligate. The president of the new college was being much too attentive to Polly, in Qwilleran's estimation, and the man's motives were open to question.

"The only one was my assistant," she said. "Mrs. Alstock brought some papers from the library for me to sign. She's doing an excellent job in my absence."

"I hope she filled you in on the latest gossip."

"Well—you probably know this—Derek Cuttlebrink is enrolled in Restaurant Management at the college. No doubt it was Elizabeth Hart's influence."

"Yes, a girlfriend with an income of a half-million can be subtly influential. Let's hope that Derek has finally found a career direction . . . What else did you hear from the library grapevine?"

"That Pickax is going to have a pickle factory. Is that good or bad?"

"Not good. We'll have to choose a Pickle Queen as well as a Potato Queen and a Trout Queen. The whole town will smell of dill and garlic from July to October."

"I thought you liked garlic, dear." She was goading him gently.

"Not as a substitute for fresh air. Can you imagine the TV commercials for Pickax Pickles? They'd be done in animation, of course—a row of pickles wearing tutus and dancing to the Pickax Polka, with pickle voices screaming, 'Perk up with Pickax Pickles.' . . . No, tell Mrs. Alstock there's no pickle factory on the K Fund agenda for economic development. The rumormongers will have to go back to the drawing board."

"Well, are you ready for some gossip that's absolutely true?" Polly asked. "The mystery woman came into the library and checked out books on a temporary card!"

"Hmff! If she's a reader, she can't be all bad, can she? What kind of book? How to build a bomb? How to poison the water supply?"

"Book withdrawals are privileged information," she said with a superior smile.

"So the library knows her name and address."

"No doubt it's in the files."

Qwilleran smoothed his moustache in contemplation and looked at her conspiratorially under hooded eyelids.

She recognized the humor in his melodramatic performance and retorted sweetly, "You're plotting a Dirty Trick! The Pickax Plumbers will break into the library after hours and burglarize the files, and we'll have a Bibliogate scandal."

Before he could think of a witty comeback, the front door slammed. There were footsteps in the entrance hall. Lynette had come home early.

"I didn't stay for refreshments," she explained. "I decided I'd rather visit with you two."

"We're flattered. Sit down and have a cookie," Qwilleran said in a monotone. He was reflecting that Lynette was a decent person—pleasant, helpful, generous, well-meaning, and smart enough to play bridge and handle health insurance in a doctor's office, but . . . she didn't get it! It never occurred to her that he and Polly might like a little privacy—once in a while.

Polly said to her sister-in-law, "We were just talking about the mystery woman."

Pontifically Qwilleran announced, "I have it on good authority that she's a fugitive from a crime syndicate or a terrorist group. She knows too much. She's a threat to the mob. Her life is in danger."

Lynette's eyes grew wide until Polly assured her he was only kidding. Then Lynette asked, "Does anyone mind if I turn on the radio for the weather report? Wetherby Goode says the cutest things!"

Qwilleran listened politely to the meteorologist's inanities: "Rain, rain, go away; come again another day." Then he made an excuse to leave. Polly understood; she gave him apologetic glances. Bootsie always escorted him to the front door, as if to speed the parting guest. This evening Qwilleran was escorted by a committee of three, and there was no opportunity for a private and lingering goodnight. Polly, he decided, had to get out of that house!

Arriving at the apple barn, Qwilleran stepped from his car and was virtually bowled over by a putrid stench coming from the tool shed, a hundred feet away. He was a man who made quick decisions. The cheese book had cost him six dollars, but he knew when to cut his losses. He turned his headlights on the shed, found a spade, and dug a sizable hole in the ground. Without any obsequies he buried *Great Cheeses of the Western World*. He hoped it would not contaminate the water table.

The Siamese were glad to see him. They had been neglected most of the day. They had had no quality time with him.

"Okay, we'll have a read," he announced. "Book! Book!"

One side of the fireplace cube was covered with shelves for Qwilleran's collection of pre-owned books from Eddington's shop. They were grouped according to category: fiction, biography, drama, history, and so forth, with spaces between that were large enough for Koko to curl up and sleep. He seemed to derive comfort from the proximity of old bindings. He also liked to knock a volume off a shelf occasionally and peer over the edge to see where it landed. In fact, whenever Qwilleran shouted "Book! Book!" that was Koko's cue to dislodge a title. It was a game. Whatever the cat chose, the man was obliged to read aloud.

On this occasion the selection was *Stalking the Wild Asparagus.* Qwilleran often read about nature, and he had enjoyed Euell Gibbons's book, even though he had no desire to eat roasted acorns or boiled milkweed shoots. The chapter he now chose to read was all about wild honeybees, and he entertained his listeners with sound effects: *Bzzzzzzz.* The Siamese were fascinated. Yum Yum lounged on his lap, and Koko sat on the arm of the chair, watching the reader's moustache.

Halfway through the chapter, just as the wild bees were swarming from a hollow tree, Koko's rapt attention faltered, his ears pricked, and his tail stiffened. He looked toward the back door. It was late, Qwilleran thought, for a car to be coming through the woods without invitation. He went to investigate. Standing on the threshold he saw no headlights, heard no motor noise, but unnatural sounds came from behind the toolshed. He snapped on the exterior lights and ventured toward the woods with a high-powered flashlight and a baseball bat.

As he approached the shed, there was scrambling in the underbrush, followed by dead silence, but the putrid odor told the story. A raccoon had dug up the cheese book and left it there, muddy and disheveled. The question now arose: How to get rid of it? Using the flashlight, he scoured the toolshed for containers with airtight lids and consigned the cheese book to a plastic mop pail. O'Dell's janitorial service would know what to do with it.

There was also a metal tackle box, empty and slightly rusted— the kind a mass murderer Down Below had used to send dynamite through the mails. For one brief giddy moment, Qwilleran considered mailing the cheese book to his former in-laws in New Jersey.

CHAPTER 3

Friday started with a whisper and ended with a bang! First, Qwilleran fed the cats. He watched in fascination as they groomed themselves from whisker to tailtip. They seemed to sense, Qwilleran thought, that a prize-winning professional photographer was coming and that they might become famous calendar cats. The female was dainty in her movements; the male brisk and business-like. He had extremely long, bold whiskers, and Qwilleran wondered if they accounted for his remarkable intuition. Koko was also a master of one-upmanship, and he had proved more than once that he had John Bushland's number.

Bushy, as the balding young man liked to be called, arrived without noticeable photo equipment—just a small, inconspicuous black box dangling around his neck.

Qwilleran met him at the door. "Come in quietly and make yourself at home. Avoid any sudden movements. Don't touch your camera. I'm making coffee, and we'll sit around and talk as if nothing is going to happen."

Bushy wandered into the library area and looked at titles on the shelves. "Wow!" he said softly. "You have a lot of plays. Were you ever an actor?"

"I was headed in that direction before I discovered journalism. A little acting experience, in my opinion, is good preparation for almost any career."

"Shakespeare . . . Aristophanes . . . Chekhov! Do you read this heavy stuff?"

"Heavy or light, I like to read them aloud and play all the roles myself."

"Do you realize how many plays have food in the title? *The Wild Duck, The Cherry Orchard, The Corn Is Green, Raisin in the Sun, Chicken on Sunday, A Taste of Honey* . . ."

Qwilleran brought a tray to the coffee table. "Sit down, Bushy, and have some coffee and shortbread from the new bakery on Stables Row. It'll remind you of our trip to Scotland. Ignore the cats."

They were warming themselves in a triangle of sunlight on the pale Moroccan rug. Koko had struck his leonine pose, with lower body lying down and upper body sitting up, like the fore and aft halves of two different animals.

Bushy said, "Junior wants me to pull a paparazzi stunt and get some candids of the mystery woman. He thinks they'll be useful to the paper and/or the police if she turns out to be a spy or a fugitive from the FBI or whatever. What do you think about her wig? I think it's a man in drag."

"I think everyone's overreacting," Qwilleran said. "Tell me about the Celebrity Auction. I hear you're on the committee."

"Yeah . . . well . . . the Boosters Club is raising money to aid needy families at Christmastime. People will bid against each other to have a dinner date with a celebrity, such as the mayor. I volunteered to take someone out on my cabin cruiser for a picnic supper. I'm no celebrity, but I'll throw in a portrait sitting in my studio."

Roguishly Qwilleran asked, "Is this outing going to be chaperoned?"

"Well, now that you mention it, we expect some flak from the conservative element, but what the heck! If they can stage an auction Down Below with a few million strangers, we can have one up here, where everybody is always watching everybody."

Meanwhile the Siamese were rehearsing every pose known to calendar cats. Yum Yum lounged seductively, extending one long, elegant foreleg. Koko sat regally with his tail curled just-so and turned his head in a photogenic profile. The intense rays of the sun heightened the blue of their eyes and highlighted their fur, making every guard hair glisten.

Bushy said under his breath, "Don't speak. They're lulled into a false sense of security. It's the moment of truth . . . Say cheese, you guys." He stood up in slow motion, moved stealthily to the right vantage point, lowered himself gradually to one knee, and furtively raised his camera. Immediately Koko rolled over and started grooming the base of his tail, with one hind leg raised like a flagpole. Yum Yum rocked back on her spine and scratched her right ear, with eyes crossed and fangs showing.

The photographer groaned and stood up. "What did I do wrong?"

"It's not your fault," Qwilleran said. "Cats have a sly sense of humor. They like to make us look like fools, which we are, I guess. Sit down and have another cuppa."

Now the cats turned their backs, Yum Yum in a contented bundle of fur, while Koko crouched behind her. He was staring at her backbone and lashing his tail in slow motion. Then, with body close to the floor, he moved closer, wriggling his hindquarters. She seemed quite oblivious of his curious pantomime. "What's that all about?" Bushy asked.

"They're just playing. It's a boy-girl thing."

"I thought they were fixed."

"It doesn't make any difference."

Suddenly, with a single swift leap, Koko pounced, but before he landed, she was gone, whizzing up the ramp with Koko in pursuit.

"Well, I've got to get back to the studio," Bushy said. "Thanks for coffee. Tell the cats I haven't given up!"

Before going to Black Creek for his interview with Gustav Limburger, Qwilleran had breakfast at Lois's Luncheonette. At that hour she was hostess, waitress, cook and cashier. "The same?" she mumbled in his direction. In a few minutes she banged down a plate of pancakes and sausages and sat down across the table with a cup of coffee.

"I hear your son won the silver in the bike race," he said.

"It ain't real silver," she said, jerking her head toward the bulletin board behind the cash register. It displayed the silverish medal, a green and white helmet, and a green and white jersey with a large "19" on the back. "You know what? He's in college now, and he's tellin' me all the things I been doin' wrong for the last thirty years. I bet those professors don't teach 'em about all the headaches in the hash-slingin' business. I should be teachin' at the college!"

"Does he plan to take over this place when he finishes his course?"

"Nah. His ambition is to be manager of the New Pickax Hotel! My God! That fleabag! He's outa his bleepin' mind."

"Do you know the old gentleman who owns it?" Qwilleran asked.

"Gentleman? Hah!" Lois made a spitting gesture. "He'd come in here for breakfast when you could get four pancakes, three sausages, and five cups o' coffee for ninety-five cents, and he'd leave a nine-cent tip! Talk about cheap! One day he had the nerve to ask if I'd like to marry him and run his mansion like a boarding house! Did I ever tell him off! I said he was too old and too tight and too smelly. All my customers heard me. He stomped out without payin' for his breakfast and never come back. I di'n't care. Who needed his nine cents?"

"I was under the impression he was well off," Qwilleran said.

"If he ain't, he should be! They built the state prison on his land! He made out like Rockefeller on that deal!"

The town of Black Creek, not far inland from Mooseville, had been a boomtown when the river was the lifeline of the county, and it flourished again when the railroad was king. After that, the mines closed and the forests were lumbered out, and it became a ghost town.

When Qwilleran drove there on Friday, it still looked like a no-man's-land. All that remained of downtown was a bar, an auto graveyard, and a weekend flea market in the old railroad depot. In the former residential area, all the frame houses had burned down or been stripped for firewood, leaving only the Limburger mansion rising grotesquely from acres of weeds. Victorian in style, with tall, narrow windows, a veranda and a turret, it had been a landmark in its day, being constructed of red brick. Local building materials were wood or stone; brick had to be shipped in by schooner and hauled overland by oxcart. The Limburgers had spared no expense, even importing Old-World craftsmen to lay the brick in artful patterns. Now one of the stately windows was boarded up; paint was peeling from the wood trim and carved entrance door; the lawn had succumbed to weeds; and the ornamental iron fence with spiked top was minus an eight-foot section.

When Qwilleran drove up, an old man was sitting on the veranda in a weathered rocking chair, smoking a cigar and rocking vigorously.

"Are you Mr. Limburger?" Qwilleran called out as he mounted the six crumbling brick steps.

"Yah," said the old man without losing a beat in his rocking. His clothes were gray with age, and his face was gray with untrimmed whiskers. He wore a shapeless gray cap.

"I'm Jim Qwilleran from the *Moose County Something*. This is an impressive house you have here."

"Wanna buy it?" the man asked in a cracked voice. "Make an offer."

Always ready to play along with a joker, Qwilleran said, "How many rooms does it have?"

"Never counted."

"How many fireplaces?"

"Don't matter. They don't work. Chimney blocked up."

"How many bathrooms?"

"How many you need?"

"Good question," Qwilleran said. "May I sit down?" He lowered himself cautiously into a splintery rocking chair with a woven seat that was partly unwoven. A dozen stones as big as baseballs were lined up on the railing. "Do you know what year this house was built, Mr. Limburger?"

The old man shook his head and rubbed his nose with a fist as if to relieve an itch. "My grandfader built it. My fader was born here, and I was born here. My grandfader come from the Old Country."

"Is he the one who built the original Pickax Hotel?"

"Yah."

"Then it's been in the family for generations. How long have you been the sole owner?"

"Long time."

"How large a family do you have now?"

"All kicked the bucket, 'cept me. I'm still here."

"Did you ever marry?"

"None o' yer business."

A blue pickup drove onto the property and disappeared around the back of the house. A truck door slammed, but no one made an appearance. Thinking of the uncounted bedrooms, Qwilleran asked, "Do you take roomers?"

"You wanna room?"

"Not for myself, but I might have friends coming from out of town—"

"Send 'em to the hotel."

"It's an interesting hotel, no doubt about it," Qwilleran said diplomatically. "Lately I've noticed a fine-looking woman there, dressed in black. Is she your new manager?"

"Don't know 'er." Limburger rubbed his nose again.

Qwilleran had an underhanded way of asking questions that were seemingly innocent but actually designed to goad an un-cooperative interviewee. "Do you dine at the hotel frequently? The food is said to be very good, especially since you brought in that chef from Fall River. Everyone talks about his chicken pot pie."

The old man was rocking furiously, as he lost patience with the nosy interviewer. He replied curtly, "Cook my own dinner."

"You do?" Qwilleran exclaimed with feigned admiration. "I envy any man who can cook. What sort of thing—"

"Wurst . . . schnitzel . . . suppe . . ."

"Do you mind if I ask a personal question, Mr. Limburger? Who will get the hotel and this splendid house when you . . . kick the bucket, as you say?"

"None o' yer business."

Qwilleran had trouble concealing his amusement. The whole interview resembled a comic routine from vaudeville days. As he turned away to compose his facial expression and consider another question, he saw a large reddish-brown dog coming up the brick walk. "Is that your dog?" he asked.

For answer the old man shouted in his cracked voice, "Get outa here!" At the same time he reached for a stone on the railing and hurled it at the animal. It missed. The dog looked at the stone with curiosity. Seeing that it was inedible, he came closer. "Mis'rable mutt!" Limburger seized a stick that lay ready at his feet and struggled to stand up. Brandishing the stick in one hand and clutching a stone with the other, he started down the brick steps.

"Careful!" Qwilleran called out, jumping to his feet.

The angry householder went down the steps one at a time, left leg first, all the while yelling, "Arrrrgh! Get outa here! Filthy beast!" Halfway down the steps he stumbled and fell to the brick sidewalk.

Qwilleran rushed to his side. "Mr. Limburger! Mr. Limburger! Are you hurt? I'll call for help. Where's your phone?"

The man was groaning and flailing his arms. "Get the man! Get the man!" He was waving feebly toward the front door.

Qwilleran bounded to the veranda in two leaps, shouting "Help! Help!"

Almost immediately the door was opened by a big man in work clothes, looking surprised but not concerned.

"Call 911! He's hurt! Call 911!" Qwilleran shouted at him as if he were deaf.

The emergency medical crew responded promptly and proceeded efficiently, taking the old man away in an ambulance. Qwilleran turned to the big man. "Are you a relative?"

The answer came in a high-pitched, somewhat squeaky voice that seemed incongruous in a man of that size. He could have been a wrestler or football lineman. Also incongruous was his hair: long and prematurely white. The journalist's eye registered other details: age, about thirty . . . soft, pudgy face . . . slow-moving . . . unnaturally calm as if living in a daze. Here was a character as eccentric as Limburger.

The caretaker was saying, "I'm not a relative. I just live around here. I kinda look after the old man. He's gettin' on in years, so I keep an eye on him. Nobody else does. I go to the store and buy things he wants. He don't drive no more. They don't let him drive. That's bad, when you live way out here like this. He's got a bad temper, but he don't get mad at me. He gets mad at the dog that comes around and dirties the sidewalk. I told him he'd fall down them steps if they wasn't fixed. I could fix 'em if he'd spend some money on mortar and a few bricks. All it would take is about ten new bricks."

With rapt attention, Qwilleran listened to the rush of words that answered his simple question.

The caretaker went on. "Last Halloween some kids come around beggin' like they do, and he chased 'em away with a stick, like he does the dog. Same night, a brick come through the front window. Somebody took a brick outa the front steps and threw it right through the window. I'm not sayin' it was the kids, but . . ." He shrugged his big shoulders.

Since they were on the subject of damaged property, Qwilleran asked, "What happened to the section of fence that's missing? Did someone drive a truck through it?"

The bland face turned to the gaping space. "Some lady wanted to buy a piece of it, so the old man sold it. I dunno what she wanted it for. I hadda deliver it in my truck, and she give me five dollars. She di'n't have to do that, but it was nice. D'you think it was nice? I thought it was nice, but the old man said she shoulda give me ten." Limburger's helper never referred to his boss by name.

"By the way, I'm Jim Qwilleran from the *Moose County Something*." He held out his hand. "I was interviewing Mr. Limburger about the hotel."

The fellow wiped his hand on his pants before shaking Qwilleran's. His eyes were riveted on the famous moustache. "I seen your picture in the paper. The old man don't take the paper, but I read it at Lois's. I go there for breakfast. It's yesterday's paper, but that don't matter. I like to read it. Do you eat at Lois's? Her flapjacks are almost as good as my mom's. D'you know my mom?"

Genially Qwilleran said, "I don't even know you. What's your name?"

"Aubrey Scotten. You know the Scotten Fisheries? My granddad started the business, and then my dad and uncles ran it. My dad died five years ago. My brothers run it now. I got four brothers. D'you know my brothers? My mom still lives on the Scotten farm on Sandpit Road. She grows flowers to sell."

"Aubrey is a good Scottish name."

"I don't like it. My brothers got pretty good names—Ross, Skye, Douglas, and Blair. I asked my mom why she give me such a dumb name, and she di'n't know. She likes it. I think it's a dumb name. People don't even spell it right. It's A-u-b-r-e-y. In school the kids called me Big Boy. That's not so bad."

"It's appropriate," Qwilleran said. "Do you work with your brothers?"

"Nah, I don't like that kinda work no more. I got me some honeybees, and I sell honey. I'm startin' a real job next week. Blair got me a job at the new turkey farm. Maintenance engineer. That's what they call it. I don't hafta be there all the time. I can take care of my bees. The hives are down by the river. D'you like bees? They're very friendly if you treat 'em right. I talk to 'em, and they give me a lot of honey. It was a good summer for honey flow. Now they're workin' on goldenrod and asters, and they're still brooding. I re-queened the hives this summer."

"I'm sure the bees appreciated that." It was a flip remark intended to conceal ignorance. Qwilleran had no idea what the man was talking about. He recognized possibilities for the "Qwill Pen," however. "This is all very interesting, and I'd like to hear more about your friendly bees. Not today, though; I have another appointment. How about tomorrow? I'd like to write about it in the paper."

The garrulous beekeeper was stunned into silence.

On the way back to Pickax, Qwilleran rejoiced in his discoveries: two more "characters" for the book he would someday find time to write. Both were worthy of further acquaintance. The good-hearted fellow who didn't like his name had the compulsive loquacity of a lonely person who yearns for a sympathetic audience. It was easy to imagine a comic dialogue between the talkative young man and the grumpy oldster who was stingy with words as well as money. It was less easy, however, to imagine Aubrey Scotten as a maintenance engineer.

Qwilleran knew about the turkey farm, underwritten by the K Fund. His friend, Nick Bamba, had been hired as manager—with option to buy in two years. They had sent him to a farm in Wisconsin to learn the ropes. At last Nick could quit his unrewarding job at the state prison near Mooseville. While the original Hanstable turkey farm would continue to supply fresh turkeys to the prison and to local markets, the new "Cold Turkey Farm" would raise birds, fast-freeze them, and ship to markets Down Below.

Meanwhile, Nick's wife, Lori, had submitted an idea to the K Fund which was accepted, and she would open a small restaurant in Stables Row. Details had not been announced.

Qwilleran admired the energy and ambition of the young couple, who were rearing a family of three as well as tackling new challenges. He questioned the wisdom, however, of hiring Aubrey Scotten as maintenance engineer of the Cold Turkey Farm. As soon as he returned to the barn, he called directory assistance for the number of the new enterprise and phoned the manager.

After a few pleasantries, Qwilleran said, "Nick, I just met a man who says he's been hired as your maintenance engineer."

"Aubrey Scotten? Yeah, aren't we lucky?"

"What do you mean?"

"He's a genius at repairing things—anything! Refrigeration, automated machinery, automotive equipment—anything! He has a God-given talent, that's all."

"Well!" Qwilleran said, "I'm surprised, to say the least."

"It's a long story. I'll tell you when I see you," Nick said. "And what do you think about Lori's venture?"

"I haven't heard any details."

"Call her! Call her at home. She'll be tickled to fill you in."

The golden-haired Lori Bamba had been Mooseville postmaster when Qwilleran first met her. Since then she had started a secretarial service and, later, a bed-and-breakfast inn on Breakfast Island, all the while parenting three children and five cats. Now she was opening a restaurant!

"How's it going?" he asked her on the phone. "Super! We'll be ready to open next Friday."

"What's the name of your restaurant?"

"First, I have to ask you a question. What does spoon-feeding mean to you, Qwill?"

"Being sick in bed when I was a kid."

"Well, smarty, the dictionary says it means pampering and cod-dling. My family loves any kind of food that can be eaten with a spoon, so I'm opening a high-class soup kitchen called the Spoo-nery."

"You mean you'll serve nothing but soup?"

"Soups and stews—whatever can be eaten with a spoon. Eat in or take out. How does it sound?"

"Daring! But if it's good enough for the K Fund, it's good enough for me."

"You'll like it! I've got dozens of exciting recipes."

"Well, I wish you luck, and I'll be your first customer. Just don't serve turnip chowder or parsnip bisque!"

Koko was antsy that afternoon. First, he walked away from the feeding station when the midday treat was served; he drove Yum Yum crazy by pouncing on her and chasing her up to the rafters; he pushed several books off the library shelves. When he started rattling the handle of the broom closet, Qwilleran got the message. As soon as the door was opened, Koko bounded into the closet and sat on top of the cat-carrier.

"You rascal!" Qwilleran said. "You want to roll on the con-crete!"

During the summer he had taken the Siamese to the cabin at the beach on several occasions, where their chief pleasure was roll-ing on the concrete floor of the screened porch. They writhed and squirmed and flipped from side to side in catly bliss that Qwilleran failed to understand. Yet, he indulged their whims. Soon they were driving to the log cabin he had inherited from the Klingenschoen estate.

It was a thirty-mile jaunt to the lake. In cat-miles it was probably perceived as a hundred and thirty, although the Siamese rode in privacy and cushioned comfort in a deluxe carrier on the backseat. Thoughtfully, Qwilleran used the Sandpit Road route to avoid heavy truck traffic; eighteen-wheelers disturbed Yum Yum's del-icate digestive system. Both cats raised inquisitive noses when they passed the Cold Turkey Farm and again when they reached the lakeshore with its mingled aromas of fish, seagulls, and aquatic weeds.

At the sign of a letter K on a post, a relic of the Klingenschoen era, they turned into a narrow dirt lane that wound through several acres of woods, up and down ancient sand dunes, and between oaks and pines and wild cherry trees. That was when Koko became excited, bumping around in the confines of the carrier and rumbling internal noises that alarmed his partner.

Qwilleran recognized the performance; the cat was sensitive to abnormal situations; something unusual lay ahead. He himself noticed recent tire tracks and was annoyed when he found another car parked in the clearing adjoining the cabin. He imagined insolent trespassers, surf-fishing and building illegal fires on the beach and throwing beer cans in the beach grass. When he parked behind the unauthorized vehicle, however, he noted a local license plate and a rental car sticker in the back window of a dark blue two-door.

His reaction was a gradual buildup of dumb disbelief, then amazement, then challenge and triumph! What a coup! He was about to come face-to-face with *that woman!* And he had her trapped!

CHAPTER 4

There was no doubt in Qwilleran's mind: the dark blue two-door with airport sticker in the window had been rented to the stranger who was mystifying Pickax. He had an exclusive news break! His colleagues would be green with envy.

The doors of the cabin were still locked; she would be walking on the beach, he assumed. The cabin perched on the crest of a high sand dune overlooking the lake, and he walked to the edge. At the foot of the weathered wooden steps leading down to the beach, he saw a large straw hat. Under it, with back turned to him,

was a figure dressed in black, sitting in a folding aluminum chair—
the kind perennially on sale at the hardware store.

He needed only a moment to decide on a course of action. He
would avoid frightening her or embarrassing her; he had everything
to gain by being pleasant—even hospitable. There were comfortable chairs on the porch; there were cold drinks in the car, as well
as two goodwill ambassadors who had winning ways—when they
felt like it.

As he started down the steps, his thudding footsteps were
drowned out by the splashing waves below and the screaming seagulls above. Halfway down, he coughed loudly and called out in
a comradely voice, "Hello, down there!"

The straw hat flew off, and a dark-haired woman turned to look
up at him.

"Good afternoon! Beautiful day, isn't it?" he said in the mellifluous voice he used in crucial situations.

She jumped to her feet, clutching a book. "My apology! I not
know someone live here."

English was not her native tongue; her accent had an other-
whereness that he considered charming. "That's all right. I live in
Pickax and just stopped to check for storm damage. There was a
severe wind storm a few days ago. What are you reading?" That
was always a disarming question, he had learned.

"Cookbook." She held it up for proof. "I go away now." Flustered, she started to fold her chair.

"You don't need to rush off. Perhaps you'd enjoy a glass of cider
on the porch. It has a magnificent view of the lake. By the way,
I'm Jim Qwilleran of the *Moose County Something.*"

"Ah!" she said joyfully, focusing on his moustache. "I see your
picture in the paper . . . But you are too kind."

"Not at all. Let me carry your chair." He ran down the few
remaining steps. "And what is your name?"

She hesitated . . . "Call me Onoosh."

"In that case, call me Qwill," he said jovially.

She smiled for the first time, and although she was not a beauty
by Hollywood standards, her olive complexion glowed and her
face was radiant. At the same time, a gust of wind blew her dark

hair away from her left cheek, revealing a long scar in front of her ear. She stuffed books and other belongings into a tote bag, and Qwilleran reached for it.

"Allow me."

As they reached the top of the dune, she exclaimed about the log cabin and the stone chimney. "Beautiful! Is very old?" She pronounced it *be-yoo-tiful*.

"Probably seventy or eighty years old." He ushered her into the screened porch. "Have a chair and enjoy the view, and excuse me for a moment while I unload the car and bring in my two companions. Do you like cats?"

"All animals, I adore!" Her face again glowed with happiness.

She could be in her thirties, he guessed as he went to the car. She could be from the Middle East. She may have lived in France. Her black pantsuit, far from being mourning garb, had a Parisian smartness.

He served the cider and asked casually, "Are you vacationing up here?"

"Yes, but no," she replied cryptically. "I look for place to live. I like to cook in restaurant."

"Where are you staying?"

"Hotel in Pickax."

"Have you been there long?"

"Two weeks. People very nice. Desk clerk give me big room in front. Very good. I talk to chef. I tell him how to cook vegetables. He try, but . . . not good."

"Yes, we do have friendly people here. How did you happen to find Moose County? It's off the beaten path, and few people know it exists."

Shyly she explained, "My honeymoon I spend here—long time ago. Was nice."

"Honeymoons are always nice," Qwilleran said. "So your husband is no longer with you?" He considered that a good way of putting a prying question.

She shook her head, and her face clouded, but it soon brightened. The Siamese, who had been rolling and squirming on the concrete of the back porch, now arrived to inspect the stranger and leave their seal of approval on her ankles. "Be-yoo-ti-ful!" she said.

"They're especially fond of people who read cookbooks."

"Ah! Cooking I learn very young, but something more is always to learn."

"What do you think of the food in our local restaurants?"

She looked at him askance, from behind her curtain of hair. "Is not too good."

"I agree with you, but we're trying to improve the situation."

Brightening, she said, "Mediterranean restaurant—very good here, I think."

"You mean, stuffed grape leaves and tabouleh and all that? When I lived Down Below I haunted Middle Eastern restaurants. We used to ask for meatballs in little green kimonos."

"Very good," she said. "I make meatballs in little green kimonos." She waved a hand toward a tangle of foliage on the dune. "Wild grapevines you have in woods. Very good fresh. In jars, not so good." She paused uncertainly. "You have kitchen? I stuff some for you."

Qwilleran's tastebuds were alerted. "I have kitchen, and I have salt and pepper, and I drive into town to buy whatever you need." Without any intention of mocking, he was imitating her cavalier way with pronouns, verbs, prepositions, and adverbs.

"Is too much trouble," she protested.

"Not so! Tell me what to buy."

She recited a list: ground lamb, rice, onion, lemon, fresh mint. "I pick small young leaves—boil five minutes—ready when you come back."

Before leaving, Qwilleran checked out the Siamese. They were asleep on the guest bed. If Koko had wanted so badly to drive to the cabin, why had he spent five minutes rolling on the concrete and the rest of the afternoon in sleep? Cats were unpredictable, unfathomable, and impossible not to like. Koko raised his head and opened one eye. "Mind the house," Qwilleran instructed him. "I'm running into town."

There were stores in Mooseville, but he would hesitate to trust their meat. Fish, yes. Lamb, no. He drove to Pickax. At Toodle's Market, where he was a regular customer for lunchmeat, the butch-

ers knew him and gladly ground some lamb, fresh. Onoosh had
not specified quantity, so he asked for two pounds, to be on the
safe side. At the produce counter, a Toodle daughter-in-law helped
him choose a lemon and three onions but said they never had fresh
mint. "Everybody has it in the backyard," she said. "It grows like
wild."

At the rice shelf he was puzzled. There was long grain, short
grain, white, brown, precooked, preseasoned.

Another customer, better-groomed and better-dressed than the
other women shoppers, said, "Having a problem, Mr. Q? Perhaps
I can help you. I'm Elaine Fetter. We've met at the library, where
I volunteer."

"Yes, of course," he said emphatically, as if it were true. She
was a statuesque woman with an air of authority and surely some
opinions about rice. "What kind of rice would you suggest for . . .
uh . . . meatballs?"

"I believe you'd be safe with white short-grain. Do you have a
good recipe for meatballs?" she asked. "I'm compiling a community cookbook for the Friends of the Library, and we'd be honored
if you would let us print one of your favorite recipes. I know—"

At that moment they were both startled by a loud BOOM!

"Oh, heavens!" she exclaimed. "What was that? It sounded so
close!"

"I'd better go and check it out," he said. "Excuse me. Thanks
for the advice." He snatched a package of white short-grain and
took his purchases to the checkout counter.

"Did you hear that sonic boom?" the cashier asked. "It was loud
enough to curdle the milk."

"Sounded like an explosion on Pine Street," Qwilleran said.
"They're doing construction work on Stables Row and could have
hit a gas main."

As he pulled out of the parking lot, scout cars were speeding
toward downtown, and the flashing lights of emergency vehicles
could be seen coming from the hospital and the firehall. The trouble was not on Pine Street, however. Main Street traffic was being
detoured. He parked where he could and ran toward the center of
town.

One irrelvant and irreverent thought crossed his mind: Whatever the blast might be, it was *not* happening on the newspaper's deadline, and Arch Riker would have a fit! It would be Monday before the *Something* could report it, while WPKX would be broadcasting it all weekend. That was the way it always seemed to happen in Pickax. Like the Friday night toothache after the dentist's office closed for the weekend, disasters always happened after the Friday newspaper had gone to press.

A procession of pedestrians was hurrying to the scene, and the shout went up: *"It's the hotel! The hotel blew up!"*

A cordon of yellow crime-scene tape kept onlookers away from the shattered glass and debris that covered the sidewalk and pavement in front of the New Pickax Hotel. There were business folk standing in front of their stores and offices . . . farmers in town on business . . . shoppers carrying bundles . . . teens wearing high school athletic jackets. Many were horrified; others were there for the excitement; a few grinned and said it was about time they bombed it. Stretcher bearers hurried up the front steps. The medical examiner arrived with his ominous black bag and was escorted into the building by the police.

"Somebody's killed," the watchers said.

On the far side of the yellow tape was a gathering of persons Qwilleran knew. To reach them he ran around the block and into the back door of Amanda's Design Studio. The shop was empty. He zigzagged through the furniture displays and found everyone on the sidewalk, watching and waiting: Amanda Goodwinter herself, her assistant, the installation man, and two customers. One of the studio's large plate glass windows was cracked. No one noticed Qwilleran's arrival; they were all looking up at the second floor of the hotel.

Like all the buildings on downtown Main Street, it was solidly built of stone that had survived fire, tornado, and even a minor earthquake. The windows of all three floors were shattered, however. On the second floor, wood sash had been blown out. Fragments of draperies and clothing hung from projections on the outside of the building. The arm of an upholstered chair lay on the sidewalk.

"Lucky it's only the arm of a chair," the installer said with a sly leer.

Amanda, cranky as usual, said, "Old Gus probably bombed it himself to collect the insurance, or had that creepy helper of his do the dirty work."

"He ain't creepy! He's an all-right guy!" the installer said belligerently. He was one of the big young blond men indigenous to Moose County, and he contradicted his employer with the confidence of an indispensable muscleman in a furniture business run by two women.

"Shut up and get some tape on that cracked glass!" Amanda shouted.

"Hi, Qwill!" said Fran Brodie, her assistant. "Are you covering this for the paper, or just nosing around?" She was not only a good designer and one of the most attractive young women in town; she was the daughter of the police chief and, as such, had semiofficial status. She said, "Dad always complains that nothing big ever happens on his turf, but this should keep him quiet for a while."

The chief was swaggering about the scene, towering over the other officers, giving orders, running the show. The state police were assisting.

"I was buying groceries and heard the blast," Qwilleran said. "Does anyone know what happened?"

In a confidential tone, Fran said, "They think it was a homemade bomb. They say room 203 is really trashed. Everyone's wondering about the mystery woman."

Qwilleran thought of Onoosh; hadn't the desk clerk given her a big room at the front? "Any injuries?" he asked. "Your dad was wearing his doomsday expression when he took the coroner into the building."

"Oh, he always looks like that when he's on duty. So far, it doesn't look serious. Larry Inchpot came out with a bandage on his head, and he and some others were hustled away in a police car—to the hospital, no doubt. Someone said a chandelier fell on his head."

Outside the yellow-tape bystanders were making guesses; a reporter was maneuvering to get camera shots; a WPKX newswoman was thrusting a microphone in front of officials and eyewitnesses. Inside the tape, an ambulance with open doors had backed up to the front steps. Then the coroner came out, and silence fell on the crowd. He was followed by medics carrying a body bag on a stretcher. A sorrowful moan arose from onlookers, and the question was repeated: Who was it? Guest or employee? No one knew.

"I can't hang around," Qwilleran told the designer. "I'm due back in Mooseville. I'll tune in my car radio to hear the rest."

He wanted to break the news to Onoosh, gently, and he wanted to observe her reaction. It would reveal whether she was really a cook looking for a job in a restaurant, or the intended victim of a murderous plot.

As he drove back to the cabin, he heard the *bleat-bleat-bleat* of a helicopter. That would be the bomb squad from the SBI—the State Bureau of Investigation. His radio was tuned in, with the volume turned down to muffle the country music favored by the locals. He turned it up when an announcer broke in with a news bulletin:

"An explosion in downtown Pickax at four-twenty this afternoon claimed the life of one victim, injured others, and caused extensive property damage. Thought to be caused by a homemade bomb, the blast wrecked several front rooms of the New Pickax Hotel. A member of the staff was killed instantly. Others were thrown to the floor and injured by falling debris. All windows facing Main Street were shattered, and those in nearby buildings were cracked. The hotel has been evacuated, and Main Street is closed to traffic between Church and Depot Streets. Police have not released the name of the victim, pending notification of relatives, nor the name of the guest registered in the room that received the brunt of the blast. Police chief Andrew Brodie said, 'There aren't many guests around on Friday afternoon, or the casualties would have been greater.' Stay tuned for further details."

Qwilleran stepped on the accelerator. A quarter-mile from the letter K on a post, he rounded the last curve in the road in time to see a car leaving the K driveway in a cloud of dust. It turned onto the highway without stopping, heading west. As he approached from the east, it picked up speed.

All his previous surmises were thrown into confusion as he covered the winding trail to the cabin faster than usual. Her car was gone. He thought, She sent me to buy lamb so she could escape;

she was headed for the airport. Then he thought, Maybe she wasn't the target of the bomb; maybe she was involved in the bombing. He tried to make sense of the disparate elements: the eccentric owner of the hotel . . . the mystery woman . . . property insurance . . . the old man's tumble down the stairs . . . the mechanical genius who worked for him . . . the possibility of a homemade bomb . . . and all the rumors he had heard in the last two weeks. Qwilleran felt his face flushing. Having fallen for her ruse, he was too embarrassed to think straight. That woman could have ransacked the cabin! She could have taken the cats!

He jumped from his car when he reached the clearing and rushed indoors, going first to the guestroom. The cats were still asleep, drugged by the lake air. Then he checked the lake porch. She had left her beach hat, the folding chair, and three books from the public library. They were all cookbooks.

In the kitchen a paper towel was spread with damp grape leaves, and the saucepan in which they had been boiled was draining in the sink; the salt and pepper shakers were standing ready; the chopping board and knife were waiting for the onion; and the countertop radio was blaring country music. He turned it off irritably.

Only then did he realize that Onoosh had been working in the kitchen and listening to the radio when the bulletin was broadcast. She had dropped everything, grabbed her tote bag, and headed for the airport. She knew the bomb was intended for her. He searched the cabin, hoping she might have left a note, but all he could find was a number on the telephone pad. It looked familiar. He called it and was connected with the airport terminal. "Did the five-thirty shuttle leave on schedule?" he asked.

"Yes, sir."

"A woman was racing to catch it. Do you remember a woman in a black pantsuit boarding the plane?"

"Yes, sir," said the attendant, who sold tickets, rented cars, and even carried luggage in the small terminal. "She turned in a rental and ran to the plane. Didn't even have any luggage. Lucky we had a seat for her. On Friday nights we're usually sold out."

Now Qwilleran thought he understood. Whether or not she was a cook, she was a fugitive—in hiding—fearing for her life.

With all due respect to the PPD and SBI, he believed they would never apprehend the bomber who killed the wrong person. The Pickax mystery woman, like the Piltdown man, would remain forever the subject of debate.

CHAPTER 5

Qwilleran sat glumly on the porch overlooking the lake without seeing the infinity of the blue sky, the turquoise expanse of water, and the white ruffles of surf at the shoreline. He was organizing his reactions. He grieved over the senseless death of a hotel employee; in a small town everyone was a friend or a neighbor or a nodding acquaintance or the friend of a friend. Further, he regretted the wanton destruction of the building, no matter how substandard its rating or how disliked its owner. And personally he was disappointed by the sudden departure of the fascinating woman who had said, "Call me Onoosh." An exclusive news story had slipped through his fingers; his vision of a Mediterranean restaurant on local soil had faded away; and he had lost a potential purveyor of meatballs in little green kimonos. All of these considerations added up to a determination to solve the who and why of the bombing. It was none of his business; it was police business. Yet, his curiosity began a slow boil.

Meanwhile, he had unwanted souvenirs of the afternoon's adventure: two pounds of ground lamb, a package of rice, and three large onions. The lemon he could use in Squunk water, an innocuous beverage from a local mineral spring. The rice could be returned to the store; Mrs. Toodle would be glad to give him a refund. As for the onions, he could hurl them into the adjoining woods—to spice the diet of a wandering raccoon.

The problem was . . . the lamb. When the Siamese staggered out of the guest room, he offered them a taste; they declined even to sniff it. "You ungrateful snobs!" he scolded. "There are disadvantaged cats out there who don't know where their next mouse is coming from!" He had pointed out that fact frequently, without effecting any change in their attitude. They liked Scottish smoked salmon, oysters, lobster out of the shell, caviar (fresh, not tinned), and escargots.

His next thought—to give the lamb to Polly as a treat for Bootsie—would lead to embarrassing inquiries and awkward explanations. His friend, though a wonderful woman in every way, was inclined to be overpossessive and unnecessarily jealous. That eliminated another solution.

To donate the lamb to Lois for her ever-bubbling soup pot would create a countywide stir. There were no secrets at the Luncheonette, and two pounds of ground lamb from the richest bachelor in northeast central United States would be good for two months of delectable gossip.

There remained Celia Robinson. As his so-called secret agent, she had proved an ability to follow instructions without asking questions, and she was probably the only individual in Moose County who could keep a secret. He telephoned her from the cabin, and there was no answer. He decided to put the problematic meat in the freezer. He knew Onoosh would never return, but if she did . . .

Qwilleran and the Siamese returned to the apple barn. There was no storm damage at the cabin; in fact, there had been no storm. The county was enjoying an exceptionally pleasant September.

He fed the cats a can of red salmon and then went to Lois's for the Friday dinner special, fish and chips. One of the part-time cooks was manning the deep-fryer, and Lois was waiting on tables, taking customers' money, and venting her rage about the bombing. Only a public figure with Lois's thirty years of experience could rave, rant, and rail so histrionically while pouring coffee and making change. Qwilleran's arrival launched another tirade:

"Oh! . . . Oh! . . . Did you hear the six o'clock news? D'you know who was killed? Anna Marie! Lenny's girlfriend! Sweet girl—never hurt a soul. Why her? Why her? . . . *Sit anywhere, Mr. Q. Fish and chips special tonight* . . . Only twenty years old! She was gonna be a nurse! Lenny and her were childhood sweethearts.

They were goin' to college together. She worked part-time as a housekeeper at the hotel . . . *How many pieces, hon? Two or three? Coleslaw or reg'lar? . . .* They say the cops are investigatin'. Ha! What the hell good is that? A beautiful girl with her whole life snuffed out! Somebody should sue! . . . *Are you guys through with the ketchup bottle? . . .* Lenny just called me from home. He was lyin' down and heard it on the radio. He's bein' very brave, that kid, but he's hurtin' inside—hurtin' bad. He was the one who got her the job. That makes it twice as bad . . . *Coffee, anybody? New pot.* . . . The blast dumped a light fixture on Lenny's head, but it ain't serious. They stitched him up and sent him home, but he's out of a job till they fix the damage. That'll take forever if they leave it to the ol' coot who owns the place . . . *More bread? Got enough butter? It's the real thing—not that low-cholesterol stuff.''*

Qwilleran's next destination was Gingerbread Alley. Even as he reached for the doorbell at the Duncan homestead, Polly yanked the door open. She was looking painfully grieved. Lynette, sober-faced, hovered in the background. In unison they said, "Did you hear the latest?"

"Yes," he said. "It's Anna Marie Toms. Did you know her?"

"She worked as a page at the library while she was in high school," Polly said. "Lovely girl—so conscientious."

"Her family lives in Chipmunk," Lynette added, "but they're good people. They go to our church."

"It's unfair to judge one by one's address," Polly protested. "Well, let's go into the parlor."

Qwilleran kept an eye on the skirted table as he seated himself. Lynette served instant decaf and pound cake from the new bakery.

"There's a rumor," she said, "that someone in Lockmaster wanted to buy the hotel, and old Scrooge wanted too much money, so they blew it up in revenge."

Stupid rumor, Qwilleran thought, and yet it was the kind of tale that flourished in scandal-hungry Pickax. He said, "Gustav Limburger is in the hospital. He fell down his front steps this morning. I was interviewing him about the history of the hotel. I'd like to know his condition, but the hospital won't give any information on the phone."

"I can find out," Lynette said. She worked for a clinic and had connections. When she returned, she recited a litany of bad news: multiple fractures, advanced osteoporosis, hypertension, cardiac arrhythmia, and more.

"Oh, dear! I should feel sorry for him," Polly said, "and yet . . ."

"He's a character," Qwilleran said. "Did you ever meet him?"

"My only contact was by mail. Every year when the library appealed for funds, he returned our envelope with two one-dollar bills. In spite of inflation, it never changed."

"Better than nothing," Lynette said. "By the way, the Toms family are patients at our clinic, and I suppose I shouldn't tell you this—I know you won't either of you repeat it—but Anna Marie was enrolled in prenatal care."

"Oh, dear!" said Polly.

Qwilleran huffed into his moustache as possibilities invaded his mind.

Then she said with an effort to be cheerful, "Well, what did you do this afternoon? Anything interesting?"

"I took the cats for a ride. Koko has been tormenting Yum Yum lately, and that means he's restless."

"Elaine Fetter phoned a while ago and said she saw you at Toodle's, buying ingredients for meatballs, and you're going to contribute your meatball recipe to the community cookbook! Have you been keeping secrets from me, dear?" she concluded with a mischievously oblique glance.

"Mrs. Fetter is confused. You know and I know, Polly, that I'm a culinary illiterate. The day I take up cooking will be the day the sky falls."

"But you *were* buying ingredients for meatballs!" she continued with the persistence of a prosecuting attorney. She enjoyed putting him in the hot seat, knowing his ability to wiggle out of any uncomfortable situation.

Qwilleran had to think fast; he did that well, too. "I was picking up groceries for Mrs. Robinson. She makes a special meatball for her cat, and I asked her to make a batch for my two gourmands."

"What makes it so special?"

"I don't know. I had to buy lamb, rice, onion, and lemon."

"That sounds Middle Eastern," Polly said. "I'd love to have her recipe. Could you get it for me?"

The situation was becoming sticky. "I'm afraid she doesn't share recipes. She's . . . uh . . . going into catering and wants to have a repertory of exclusive dishes." He congratulated himself on that ingenious fabrication but found it advisable to cover his tracks. He left early. He said he had some writing to do. Within minutes he was phoning Celia Robinson, and there was urgency in his voice.

"What's up, Chief?" she asked eagerly.

"I have a favor to ask, Celia—nothing to do with a criminal investigation."

"Aw shucks!" she said with a merry laugh.

"First, a question: Do you ever make meatballs with rice?"

"No, I use bread crumbs."

"If you were to make meatballs with rice, would Wrigley eat them?"

"Oh, sure, but he'd throw up. Rice is something he can't seem to digest."

"I see," Qwilleran said. "Well . . . if anyone asks you, would you be good enough to say that you make meatballs with rice for Wrigley? And if anyone requests your recipe . . . *just say no!*"

"Okay, Chief. It won't be the first fib I've told for you, and I haven't been struck by lightning yet!"

He hung up with a sense of relief. He was covered. He knew that Polly would mention the meatballs to her assistant, Mrs. Alstock, who would mention them to her dear friend, Celia Robinson. It was one of the complexities of living in a small town. In a way, life Down Below was simpler, despite traffic jams, air pollution, and street crime. There was a comfortable anonymity in a city of millions.

His next call was to the police chief at home. "Anything good on the tube tonight, Andy?"

"Nah, I turned it off, and I'm reading your column on Nobodies in today's paper. The trouble is, all the Nobodies in Pickax think they're Somebodies and exempt from paying traffic fines . . . What's on your mind?"

"The explosion. Was it pretty bad?"

"Everything in a certain radius was blown to bits. That poor girl never knew what hit her."

Qwilleran asked, "Am I correct in thinking room 203 was registered to the mystery woman?"

"Right, and she hasn't been seen since."

Qwilleran paused dramatically before saying, "I spent the afternoon with her."

"What! How come? How did you meet her? What do you know?"

"Why don't you put on your shoes, Andy, and come over for a Scotch?"

In five minutes the police chief drove into the barnyard. He was a tall, husky, impressive figure, even out of uniform, and he was especially impressive when he wore a full Scottish kit and played the bagpipe at weddings and funerals. He walked into the barn with a piper's swagger.

Qwilleran had a tray ready with Scotch and cheese, and Squunk water for himself. As the two men settled into big chairs in the lounge area, the Siamese walked into view with a swagger of their own. Coming close to the coffee table, they sat down with noses on a level with the cheese platter. As the guest raised his glass in a Gaelic toast, the two noses edged closer.

"No!" Qwilleran thundered. Both cats backed off a quarter of an inch and continued to contemplate the forbidden food with half-shut eyes.

"Cocky little devils," Brodie said. "Bet you spoil them rotten."

"Try this cheese, Andy. It's a kind of Swiss from the new Sip 'n' Nibble shop in Stables Row. It's run by two guys from Down Below. They like to be called Jerry Sip and Jack Nibble. Jerry's the wine expert, and Jack knows everything about cheese."

"Gimme a slice. Then tell me how you met that woman."

"It was a weird coincidence. I'd never seen her, but they were talking about her at the paper yesterday and mentioned that she drove a dark blue rental car. So, this afternoon I drove to the cabin on a routine inspection, and there was a dark blue two-door in my parking lot! My car almost reared up on its hind wheels! The woman was sitting on my beach at the foot of the dune, reading a cookbook, so I figured she wasn't dangerous."

Brodie grunted at intervals as Qwilleran told the whole story. "So she offered to make some stuffed grape leaves if I'd buy the ingredients, and that's what I was doing when the bomb went off."

The chief chuckled. "She wanted to get your car out of the drive so she could make a getaway."

"That was my first thought. For a few minutes I felt like an absolute dunce. Then I realized—correctly, I believe—that she'd heard the bulletin on the air and had to get out of town fast. Somehow she knew the bomb was intended for her. I called the airport, and they said she'd turned in the car and boarded the shuttle."

Brodie said, "She might have decamped in a hurry because she was a conspirator in the bomb plot. She was conveniently out of the building—and hiding out on your property—when the bomb exploded."

Qwilleran drew a heavy hand over his moustache, as he always did when he was getting a major hunch. A tingle on his upper lip was a signal that he was on the right track. "I maintain, Andy, that she's a fugitive trying to go underground. This neck of the woods is ordinarily as underground as you can get, but there's another clue to consider. When the wind blew her hair away from her face, I saw a long vertical scar in front of her left ear."

"Could be the result of an auto accident," Brodie suggested. "What name did she give you?"

"Only her first name: Onoosh."

"Onoosh? What kind of name is that? On the hotel register she signed Ona Dolman."

A dark brown paw stole slowly over the edge of the coffee table.

"No!" Qwilleran bellowed, and the paw was quickly withdrawn.

"I didn't know cats liked cheese," said the chief, who thought they lived on rodents and fish-heads.

"Since the new store opened, both cats are turning into cheese junkies," Qwilleran said.

"Well, I guess we'll never see Ona Dolman again, but it's no big loss. The hell of it is the murder of that innocent girl—Anna Marie Toms. I know the family—good people! Not everybody living in Chipmunk gets into trouble with the law. She was kind of engaged to Lenny Inchpot, Lois's son. I'll play the bagpipe at her funeral service, if they want me to."

"Do you know exactly how it happened, Andy?"

"It'll come out later, but I'll fill you in now—off the record." Brodie had gradually accepted this journalist from Down Below as trustworthy and useful. Qwilleran's experience as a crime reporter in major cities around the country had given him insights into investigative processes, and his natural instinct for snooping often unearthed facts of value to official investigators. In pursuing his private passion, Qwilleran was quite satisfied to remain in the background, tip off the authorities, and take no public credit. Brodie, for his part, appreciated his cooperation and occasionally leaked confidential information—through his daughter, the designer. It was a casual arrangement, unknown to other local law enforcement agencies.

"Anything you see fit to tell me is always off the record, Andy. That goes without saying."

"Okay. About four o'clock this afternoon an unidentified white male—about forty, medium build, clean-shaven—came in the front door of the hotel with a gift package and some flowers for Ona Dolman. Lenny, on duty at the desk, said she wasn't in but he'd send them up to her room as soon as the porter returned from his break. The suspect said the gift was hand-blown glass, very fragile, and he'd feel more comfortable taking it upstairs himself and putting it in a safe place. He asked for a piece of paper and wrote: OPEN WITH CARE, HONEY. So Lenny told him to ask the housekeeper on the second floor to let him into 203. When the suspect came back down, he yelled thank-you and went out the back door. The porter was having a cigarette in the parking lot and saw a blue pickup drive slowly down the back street and pick up a man in a blue jacket. So what? Blue pickups and blue jackets are a dime a dozen around here."

Qwilleran asked about witnesses on the second floor.

"The manager's office is up there. She didn't see the suspect, but the housekeeper asked where to get a vase for some flowers and later took the vacuum cleaner into 203, saying the flowers had made a mess on the rug. When she plugged in the cord or pushed the machine around, she probably tripped the bomb. Lenny feels he's responsible for her death. That boy's gonna need counseling."

"Bad scene," Qwilleran said somberly. "Can he describe the suspect?"

"Two witnesses got a close look at him—Lenny and the florist who sold him the flowers. The SBI computer is making a composite sketch from their descriptions, but I don't know how they'll find any clues in the rubble. A bomb blows up a lot of evidence."

"Yes, but the forensic people work miracles. Every year there seems to be new technology." Qwilleran poured another Scotch for Brodie and asked how he liked the cheese.

"Good stuff! I've gotta tell the wife about it. What d'you call it?"

"Gruyère. It's from Switzerland."

"Yow!" came a loud demand from the floor, and Qwilleran gave each cat a tiny crumb of it, which they gobbled and masticated and savored at great length as if it were a whole wedge.

Brodie asked, "Did Ona Dolman say anything at all that might finger the bomber?"

"No, I'm afraid I missed the boat. I intended to ask some leading questions while we were eating our grape leaves. I even picked up a bottle of good wine for her!" Qwilleran said with annoyance.

"Well, anyway, now that we know she left on a plane, we can start a search. If she was in hiding, she falsified information but there'll be prints on the car, if they haven't cleaned it." He went to the phone and called the airport; the car had been thoroughly cleaned when it was returned. Qwilleran said there would be prints on the kitchen sink at the cabin, and he turned over the key to Brodie, along with the folding chair, cookbooks, and straw hat that she had left behind.

"We'll need your prints, too, Qwill. Stop at the station tomorrow."

"I don't envy you, Andy. You don't know who she really is, where she really lives, why she's being pursued, where she went, who planted the bomb, where he lives, what's his motive, how he found her, and who drove the getaway vehicle."

"Well, we should be able to lift her prints, and just about every man, woman, and child in Pickax can describe her . . . What did you call that cheese?"

"Gruyère."

"Yow!" said Koko.

Qwilleran said, "I asked the guy at the cheese store why a cat would prefer this to Emmenthaler, which is also Swiss. He said it's creamier and saltier."

"Is it expensive?"

"It costs more than processed cheese at Toodle's, but Mildred says we should buy better food and eat less of it."

Brodie stood up. "Better be goin' home, or the wife'll call the police."

Just then a low rumble caught the attention of the two men. It came from under the coffee table. As they turned to look, Koko came slinking out, making a gutteral noise, waving his tail in low gear, sneaking up behind Yum Yum.

"Watch this!" Qwilleran whispered.

POW! Koko pounced! WHOOSH! Yum Yum got away, and they were off on a wild chase up the ramp.

"They're just showing off," Qwilleran said. "They do it to attract attention."

The chief went home carrying a wedge of Gruyère.

CHAPTER 6

On Saturday morning Qwilleran fed the cats, policed their commode, brushed their coats, and combed airborne cat hair out of his moustache and eyebrows. Koko had pushed a book off the library shelf. "Not now. Later," he said. "I have a lot of calls to make. Expect me when you see me." He replaced the playscript of *A Taste of Honey* on the shelf. Then he thought, Wait a minute!

Does that cat sense that I'm going to interview a beekeeper? And if he does, how can he associate my intentions with the word "honey" on a book cover? And yet, he had to admit, Koko sometimes used oblique avenues of communication.

He went to the police station to be fingerprinted and then to the library for a book on beekeeping. Rather than appear to be a complete dolt, he looked up the definitions of brooders, supers, and smokers, also swarming, hiving, and clustering. While there he heard the clerks greeting Homer Tibbitt, who arrived each day with a briefcase and brown paper bag. Although the sign on the front door specified NO FOOD OR BEVERAGES, everyone knew what was in the paper bag. He was in his late nineties, however, and allowances were made for age. With a jerky but sprightly gait, he walked to the elevator and rode to the mezzanine, where he would do research in the reading room.

Qwilleran followed, using the stairs. "Morning, Homer. What's the subject for today?"

"I'm still on the Goodwinter clan. Amanda found some family papers in an old trunk and gave them to the library—racy stuff, some of it."

"Do you know anything about the Limburger family?" Qwilleran dropped into a hard oak chair across the table; the historian always brought his own inflated seat cushion.

"Yes, indeed! I wrote a monograph on them a few years ago. As I recall, the first Limburger came over from Austria in the mid-nineteenth century to avoid conscription. He was a carpenter, and the mining companies hired him to build cottages for the workers. But he was a go-getter and ended up building his own rooming houses and travelers' inns. Exploiting the workers was considered smart business practice in those days, and he got rich."

"What happened to his housing empire?"

"One by one the buildings burned down. Some were pulled down for firewood in the Great Depression. The Hotel Booze is the only building still standing. The family itself—second generation—was wiped out in the flu epidemic of 1918. There was only one survivor, and he's still living."

"You mean Gustav?" Qwilleran asked. "He has a reputation for being quite eccentric."

"Haven't seen him for years, but I remember him as a young boy, recently orphaned. Pardon me while I refresh my memory." The old gentleman struggled to his feet and went to the restroom, carrying his paper bag. It was no secret that it contained a thermos of decaffeinated coffee laced with brandy. When he returned, he had recalled everything.

"Yes, I remember young Gustav. I was a fledgling teacher in a one-room school, and I felt sorry for him. He'd lost his folks and was sent to live with a German-speaking family. His English was poor, and to make matters worse, there was a lot of anti-German sentiment after World War One. It's no wonder he was a poor student. He played truant frequently, ran away from home a couple of times, and finally dropped out."

"Didn't he inherit the family fortune?"

"That's another story. Some said his legal guardians mismanaged his money. Some said he went to Germany to sow his wild oats and lost it all. I know he sold the Hotel Booze to the Pratts and kept the New Pickax hotel. I hear it was wrecked by a bomb yesterday."

"Apparently Gustav never married," Qwilleran remarked.

"Not to anyone's knowledge. But who knows what he did in Germany? When I was writing the Limburger history, I tried to get him to talk, but he shut up like a clam."

"He's in the hospital now, in serious condition."

"Well, he's up in years," Homer said of the man who was fifteen years his junior.

Driving north to the Limburger house, Qwilleran passed the decrepit Dimsdale Diner at the corner of Ittibittiwassee Road and noted half a dozen farm vehicles in the weedy parking lot. That meant the Men's Dimsdale Coffee and Current Events Smoker was in session. That was Qwilleran's name for the boisterous group of laughing, gossiping, cigarette-smoking coffee hounds who gathered informally in-between farm chores. He parked and joined them and was greeted by cheers.

"Here's Mr. Q! . . . Move over and make room for a big cheese from downtown! . . . Pull up a chair, man!"

Qwilleran helped himself to a mug of bad coffee and a stale doughnut and sat with the five men in feed caps and farm jackets. They went on with their quips, rumors, and prejudices:

"That explosion was an inside job. You can bet on it!"

"They should've dynamited the whole inside and then started over."

"Looks like that foreign babe was in on it."

"Old Gus was taken to the hospital when he heard the news."

"What'll happen to the hotel when he cashes in?"

"He'll leave it to that fella that does his chores."

"That's a laugh! Gus is too stingy to give a penny away—even after he's dead!"

"He won't die unless he can figger out how to take it with 'im."

"I'll bet he's got a coupla million buried in his backyard. What d'you think, Mr. Q?"

"If you believe everything you hear, there's enough money buried in Moose County backyards to pay the national debt."

With that, they all laughed, pushed back their chairs, and trooped out to their blue pickup trucks.

En route to Black Creek, Qwilleran detoured through the town of Brrr, so named because it was the coldest spot in the county. He wanted to chat with Gary Pratt, owner of the Hotel Booze and chummy host at the Black Bear Café. Gary was a big bear of a man himself, having a shaggy black beard and a lumbering gait. He was behind the bar when Qwilleran slipped onto a bar stool.

"The usual?" he asked, plunking a mug on the bar and reaching for the coffee server.

"And a bearburger—with everything," Qwilleran said.

The noon rush had not yet started, and Gary had time to lean on the bar in front of his customer. "What are they jawboning about in Pickax today?"

"The bombing. What else?"

"Same here."

"Any brilliant theories as to motive?"

"Well, folks around Brrr think it has to do with that foreign woman. They've seen her sitting on the beach and doing the tourist shops on the boardwalk. That hair of hers is what makes them leery. She'd come in here for lunch, and I'd try to get her into conversation. No dice. Then last Saturday she had dinner with one of our registered guests—a man."

"What kind of guy?"

"Looked like a businessman—clean-cut and about her age—wore a suit and tie. In Brrr, a suit and tie look suspiciously like the FBI or IRS, so he made folks nervous. He checked into the hotel about five-thirty, which looks like he came up on the shuttle flight and she picked him up at the airport. She drives a rental; we've seen it on our parking lot. So, anyway, they had dinner together—sat in a corner booth and talked like long-lost whatever."

"Intimately?" Qwilleran asked.

"No."

"Furtively?"

"Not that either—more like a serious business deal, but every time I took them another glass of wine or walked by with the coffee server, they were talking about the weather. The thing of it is, how much can you say about the weather? One guy around here has it figured out that the bombing was an insurance scam, and she was a plant; it was set up to look like the bomb was meant for her."

"Gary, can you honestly see that old geezer in Black Creek plotting a sophisticated insurance scam?"

"Not him. They suspect the property management sharpies in Lockmaster. They run the hotel for him. I have a theory myself. It's common knowledge at the Chamber of Commerce that Lockmaster has been trying to get him to sell. He won't. You know how the Germans are about property. Well! Now that the building is damaged, he'll be willing to sell—at their price."

Qwilleran huffed into his moustache as he reflected that everyone in Moose County considered everyone in Lockmaster to be a crook. Likewise, Lockmaster denizens thought Moose County was populated with hayseeds. Race, color, and creed had nothing to do with this absurd bigotry; it was purely a matter of geography.

He said to Gary, "This man wearing a suit and tie—was he swarthy like her?"

"No, he had light skin, reddish hair. They were together the next day, too, and then I think she drove him to catch the Sunday-night shuttle. He checked out around four-thirty—paid his bill with cash. Makes you wonder what he had in his briefcase."

The bearburger arrived with all the trimmings, and Gary changed the subject to the Labor Day Bike Race. "I didn't finish—didn't expect to—but it was fun. Have you heard what's next? The Pedal Club's sponsoring a bike-a-thon called Wheels for Meals. It'll benefit the hot-meal program for shut-ins—our contribution to Explo. Sponsors can pledge anywhere from a dime to a dollar per mile. I figure I'm good for thirty miles. After that, they'll have to cart me away in the sag wagon."

"What's the sag wagon?" Qwilleran asked.

"Just kidding. It's not an ambulance. It's a support vehicle with water, energy drinks, first aid, and racks for disabled bikes. No food. No hitchhiking."

"Okay, I'll sponsor you." Qwilleran signed a green pledge card for a dollar a mile. Then he said, "Do you happen to know Aubrey Scotten?"

"Sure. I knew him in high school. I know all the Scotten brothers. They belong to the Outdoor Club. Aubrey comes in for a burger once in a while. Have you met him?"

"Briefly. I'm supposed to interview him about beekeeping this afternoon. Do you think he'll make a good subject?"

"Oh, he'll spout off, all right. Most of the time he's laid back, but if he likes you, he won't stop yakking. I don't know how much of it you'll be able to use."

"Can you fill me in on a few things?"

"Such as . . . ?"

"Is he a reliable authority on beekeeping? Is his honey considered good? Was his hair always snow-white?"

Gary looked uncertain and then decided it was all right to talk to this particular newsman. "Well . . . about the hair: It happened while he was in the Navy. He had an accident, and his hair turned white overnight."

"What kind of accident?"

"Some kind of foul-up aboard ship, never really explained. Aubrey got clunked on the head and dumped in the ocean and nearly drowned. In fact, he was a goner when they hauled him out, but he came back to life. Those Scottens are a tough breed. It changed his personality, though."

"In what way?"

"For one thing, he'd been a bully in high school, and now he's a kind-hearted guy who won't swat a fly! For another thing, he used to work in the Scotten fishing fleet; now he's terrified of boats, and the sight of a large body of water gives him the screaming-meemies. The Navy gave him an honorable medical discharge and sent him home . . . Don't let anyone know I told you all this stuff." Gary poured another cup of coffee for Qwilleran. "But there was a plus! Aubrey turned into some kind of genius. He can repair anything—*anything!* He was never that way before. He fixed the big refrigerator here and my stereo at home."

Qwilleran's blood pressure was rising; a near-death experience would be more newsworthy than the honeybee business.

Then Gary said, "Aubrey won't talk about his accident, and neither will his family—especially not to the media. Some scientists wanted to come up here and study his brain, but his brothers put the kibosh on that scheme in a hurry."

For the second time in two days, Qwilleran had seen a good lead turn out to be no-story, so . . . back to the honeybees!

Surrounded by the devastation of Black Creek, the Limburger mansion loomed like a haunted house. Still, Qwilleran thought as he parked at the curb, it could be renovated to make a striking country inn, given a little imagination and a few million dollars. The exterior brickwork—horizontal, vertical, diagonal and herringbone—was unique. The tall, stately windows, with the exception of the Halloween casualty, had stained-glass transoms or inserts of etched and beveled glass.

On the railing of the veranda the row of stones waited for the patient's return, and the reddish-brown mongrel that had provoked the old man's accident was still hanging around.

Qwilleran mounted the crumbling brick steps with caution and rang the doorbell. When there was no answer, he walked around the side of the house, saying, "Good dog! Good dog!" The animal nuzzled and whimpered and looked forlorn; Qwilleran wished he had brought some stale doughnuts from the Dimsdale Diner.

"Hello! Hello? Is anyone here?" he shouted in the direction of the weathered shed. The door stood open, and a bulky white-haired figure materialized from the interior gloom. Aubrey seemed bewildered.

Qwilleran said, "I was here yesterday, when Mr. Limburger fell down the steps. I'm Jim Qwilleran, remember? I told you I'd return to ask you all about beekeeping."

"I di'n't think you'd come back," the young man said. "Folks say they'll come back, and they never show up. A man ordered twelve jars of honey, and I had 'em all packed up in a box. He never showed up. I don't understand it. It's not friendly. D'you think it's a friendly thing to do?" The plaint was recited in a high whining voice.

"Some people don't have consideration for others," Qwilleran said with sympathy. "How is Mr. Limburger? Do you know?"

"I just come from the hospital. He was in bed and yellin' his head off about the food. He likes rabbit stew and pigs' feet and stuff like that. He likes lotsa fat. I seen him eat a pound of butter, once, like candy. It made me sick."

Qwilleran pointed to the shed. "Is that part of your honey operation?"

"That's where I draw the honey off."

"Do you have any for sale? I'd like to buy a couple of jars."

"Pints or quarts? I don't have no quarts. I sold 'em all to Toodle's Market. Mrs. Toodle is very friendly. She knows my mom." He disappeared into the dark shed and returned with two oval jars containing a clear, thick amber fluid.

"Why are honey jars always flat?" Qwilleran asked. Cynically he thought, Makes them look like more for the money; makes them tip over easily.

"Flat makes the honey look lighter. Most people want light honey. I don't know why. I like the dark. It has lotsa taste. This is wildflower honey. I took some to Lois, and she give me a big breakfast. Di'n't have to pay a penny. She give me prunes, turkey hash, two eggs, toast, and coffee.''

Aubrey rambled on until Qwilleran suggested that they sit on the porch and turn on the tape recorder. First, Aubrey had to find something for Pete to eat. Pete was the reddish-brown dog. Qwilleran waited in Limburger's creaking rocker, which was situated on a squeaking floorboard. He rocked noisily as he thought about the poor old dog, coming every day to be fed at the back door and stoned at the front door—not that the old man ever struck his target. Still, the treatment must have confused Pete, and it was not surprising that he dirtied the brick walk.

When Aubrey appeared, he had walked through the house and come out the front door, carrying a large book which he handed to Qwilleran. It was a very old, leather-bound, gold-tooled Bible with text printed in Old German. The beekeeper explained, ''It came from Austria more'n a hunerd years ago. The old man's gonna leave it to me when he kicks the bucket. The cuckoo clock, too. It di'n't work, but I fixed it. Wanna see the cuckoo clock? It's on the wall.''

''Later,'' Qwilleran said firmly. ''Sit down and let's talk about bees. Do you ever get stung?''

Aubrey shook his head gravely. ''My bees ain't never stung me. They trust me. I talk to 'em. I give 'em sugar water in winter.''

''Would they sting me?''

''If you frighten 'em or act unfriendly or wear a wool cap. They don't like wool. I don't know why. Bees never sting me. I seen a swarm of wild honeybees go inside an old tree, once. I went to look, and they swarmed all over me. I think they liked me. They was all over my face and in my ears and down my neck. It was a crazy feeling.''

''I'll bet!'' Qwilleran said grimly.

''I went home and come back with an empty hive. I hived the whole swarm. I think they was glad to get a good home. Bees are smart. If there's an apple tree and a pear tree, they go to the apple tree. It's got more sugar. The old man don't like honey. He likes white sugar. I seen him eat a whole bowl of sugar with a spoon, once. It made me sick. Would it make you sick?''

Piecemeal, with numerous digressions, the interview filled the reel of tape: A bee hive was like a little honey factory. Every bee had a job. The workers built honeycombs. The queen laid eggs. The field workers collected nectar and pollen from flowers. They brought it back to the hive to make honey. The door keepers guarded the hives against robbers. The drones didn't make honey; they just took care of the queen. If the hive got crowded, the drones were thrown out to die.

Qwilleran asked, "How do they get the nectar back to the hive?"

"In their bellies. They carry pollen in little bags on their legs."

Skeptically Qwilleran asked, "Are you telling me the truth, Aubrey?"

"Cross my heart," said the big man solemnly. "Wanna see the hives?"

"Only if you lend me a bee veil. They might think my moustache is made of wool."

"If a worker stings you, he dies."

"That's small comfort. Give me a bee veil and some gloves."

They walked down a rutted trail to the river, where all was quiet except for the rushing of the rapids and the cawing of crows. On the bank stood a shabby cabin with a paltry chimney and a hand pump on a wooden platform at the door. A lonely outhouse stood in a nearby field.

Aubrey said, "My family had six cabins they rented to bass fishermen. Two burned down. Three blew away in a storm. I live in this one. The walls were fulla wild bees, and I hadda smoke 'em out and take off the siding, and underneath the walls were fulla honey."

As they neared the cabin, Qwilleran became aware of a faint buzzing; he put on the gloves and the hat with a veil. On the south side of the building, exposed to the sun and protected from the north wind, was a row of wooden boxes elevated on platforms— not as picturesque as the old dome-shaped hives pictured on honey labels. The boxes were Langstroth hives, Qwilleran later learned, designed in 1851.

Aubrey said, "The bees do all the work. I take the trays of

honeycomb up to the shed and draw the honey off and put it in jars. Those trays get pretty heavy."

"Sounds like sticky business," Qwilleran said.

"I hadda crazy accident, once. I di'n't put the jar right under the spout, and the honey ran all over the floor."

The busy bees paid no attention to the journalist. He spoke quietly and made no sudden moves. "What do they do in winter?"

"They cluster together in the hives and keep each other warm. I wrap the hives in straw and stuff. They can get out if they want, but the mice can't get in."

"What about snow?"

"It don't matter if the hives are buried in snow, but ice—that's bad. My whole colony was smothered by ice, once."

It was a fantastic story, if true, Qwilleran thought. He would check it against the bee book at the library. "And now I'd like to see the cuckoo clock," he said. Truthfully, it was the interior of the mansion that interested him: the carved woodwork, the staghorn chandelier, the stained glass. The furnishings were sparse. The old man had sold almost everything, Aubrey said. Only one room looked inhabited. There were two overstuffed chairs in front of a TV, a large wardrobe carved with figures of wild game, and a gun cabinet with glass doors. The pendulum of the carved clock wagged on the wall.

"Who's the hunter?" Qwilleran asked.

"The old man shoots rabbits and makes hasenpfeffer. He shoots crows, too. I used to do lotsa hunt'n' with my brothers. I was a good shot." He looked away. "I don't wanna hunt any more."

The clock sounded *cuckoo cuckoo cuckoo,* and Qwilleran said it was time to leave. He paid for his honey and left with a new respect for the thick amber fluid. How many bellyfuls of nectar would it take, he wondered, to make a pint of honey?

He propped his purchases in a safe place in his car, where they would not tip or spill. Then he drove to Toodle's Market to buy something fresh for the Siamese and something frozen for himself. On the way he thought about the industrious workers and the hapless drones . . . about nature's way of converting flowers into food without chemicals or preservatives . . . and about the mild-mannered beekeeper who talked to his bees. Not a word had been said about the hotel bombing, an incident that was on everyone's tongue.

Arriving at the market, Qwilleran opened his car door and heard a sickening sound as glass broke on concrete pavement in a puddle of amber goo. He looked down at the disaster, then up at the sky and counted to ten.

CHAPTER 7

A jar of honey spilled on a parking lot is not as bad as a jar of spilled honey mixed with broken glass. Qwilleran, having made this profound observation, notified Mrs. Toodle, and she summoned one of her grandsons. The three of them marched single file to the scene of the accident, Qwilleran apologizing profusely and Mrs. Toodle thanking him for reporting it. The situation tickled the funny bone of the young Toodle; it was almost as funny as the time he dropped a crate of eggs.

"You'll have to get every last bit of glass," his grandmother admonished. "If a dog comes along and licks the spot, he could cut his tongue." When her back was turned, Qwilleran slipped the young man a generous tip. "That's not necessary," she said, having developed eyes in the back of her head after years of running a supermarket.

He bought some corned beef at the deli counter—enough for the cats' dinner and a late-night snack for himself, then drove downtown to buy flowers for Polly. At five o'clock she would be venturing out of doors for her first walk since having surgery. He parked in the municipal lot and walked to the florist shop.

Downtown Pickax was a three-block stretch of heterogeneous stone buildings: large, small, impressive, quaint, ornate, and primitive. All were relics of the era when the county was famous for its quarries. Together with the stone paving, they gave the town its title: City of Stone. A Cotswold cottage, the Bastille, Stonehenge, and a Scottish castle did business side by side. To Qwilleran, Main Street was Information Highway; friends and acquaintances stopped him to report the latest scandal, rumor, or joke.

Today he bumped into Whannell MacWhannell, the accountant. Big Mac, a burly Scot, greeted Qwilleran with "Aye! There's a rumor the 'braw laird of Mackintosh' has ordered a kilt, tailor-made! You can wear it to Scottish Night at the lodge and the Highland Games in Lockmaster."

"That is, if I'm ' 'braw' enough to wear it at all. It's supposed to be a surprise for Polly, so don't spread the rumor." Even though his mother was a Mackintosh, and even though he had joined the clan as a tribute to her memory, Qwilleran had reservations about appearing in public in a kilt.

The two men stood on the sidewalk and gazed with dismay at the boarded windows of the hotel across the street. "A crying shame!" said the accountant. "It wasn't a good hotel, but it was all we had, and who knows what'll happen to it now? The owner's in the hospital, and the management agency will be dragging its feet. They're based in Lockmaster, you know, and couldn't care less about a little creeping blight in downtown Pickax."

Qwilleran said, "I met the owner just before he had his accident, and he's eccentric, to say the least. I hope his affairs are in order—legal and financial. I hope he has an attorney, and an estate-planner, and a will."

"The problem is that no one wants to work with the scoundrel," Big Mac said. "Our office used to do his tax work, but he was impossible. Didn't keep records. Wouldn't take advice. What does one do with a client like that? I've forgotten whether we fired him or he fired us. His local attorney bowed out in desperation, too. The Lockmaster agency probably handles all his affairs now. They have my sympathy!"

Main Street was crowded with Saturday shoppers, since there was no mall to lure them from downtown, and they were joined by quite a few sightseers, gawking at the scene of the explosion. Among them was Mitch Ogilvie, dressed more like a farmer than a museum manager.

Qwilleran grabbed him roughly by the arm. "Mitch, you dirty dog! What happened to you? I hear you left the museum. You look as if you're going to a costume party!" He was wearing grubby denims, field boots, and a feed cap. He had also grown a beard.

"Yeah, I'm working my way up the ladder," the young man said. "From hotel clerk . . . to museum manager . . . to goat farmer! I'm glad I wasn't working here when the hotel blew up."

"Yes, but what's this about goat farming?"

"Kristi started a new herd, and I helped her sell her mother's antiques. She realized enough to make some big improvements in the house and the farm, so I hired on."

"Have you learned how to milk goats?"

"Believe it or not, I'm the cheese-maker. I went to a farm in Wisconsin and took a course. The new cheese shop on Stables Row is handling our product. Maybe you've seen our label: Split Rail Farm. We got rid of the old white fence, and I built one myself out of split rails."

"I've not only seen your label, I've bought your cheese," Qwilleran said. "I've tried the feta and the pepper cheese. Great eating! I'd like to see the cheese operation; I might be able to write about it."

"Sure! Great! Anytime!"

Qwilleran suggested the next afternoon. "That is, if you don't mind working on Sunday."

"There are no days off in the goat business, Qwill." Mitch glanced at the hotel. "But it's safer than working at the Pickax Hotel . . . See ya!"

Qwilleran continued on his way to the shop called Franklin's Flowers. It was across from the hotel and next door to Exbridge & Cobb, Fine Antiques. Susan Exbridge was a handsome match for her upscale establishment. She collected Georgian silver, won bridge tournaments at the country club, received alimony from a wealthy developer, and bought her clothes in Chicago. When Qwilleran happened along, she was standing on the sidewalk, critiquing a display she had just arranged in the window.

Stealing up behind her and disguising his voice, he said, "There's a wrinkle in the rug, and the lamp shade is crooked."

She saw his reflection in the glass and turned quickly. "Darling! Where have you been all summer? The town has been desolate without you!" As one of the more flamboyant members of the theatre club, she overdramatized.

"It's been a hectic summer in many ways," he explained.

"I know. How's Polly?" The two women were not warm friends, but they observed the civilities, as one is required to do in a small town.

"Improving daily. We have to find her a place to live. Her apartment is being swallowed up by the college campus. Temporarily she's staying with her sister-in-law."

"Why don't you and Polly—" she began.

"Our cats are incompatible," he interrupted, knowing what she was about to suggest.

They discussed the possibilities of Indian Village, a complex of apartments and condominiums on the Ittibittiwassee River. There were nature trails; the river was full of ducks; the woods were full of birds.

"The quacking and chirping sometimes drive me up the wall," Susan said, "but Polly would love it." There was a tinge of snobbery in her comment. In Indian Village, the bridge-players never went birding, and the bird-watchers never played bridge. Some day, Qwilleran thought, he would write a column on cliques in Moose County. He might lose a few friends, but it was a columnist's duty to stir things up occasionally.

Susan opened the front door. "Come in and see my new annex."

The premises always gleamed with polished mahogany and shining brass, but now an archway opened into a new space filled with antiques of a dusty, weathered, folksy sort.

"Do you recognize any of those primitives?" she asked. "They were in Iris Cobb's personal collection, and I never had a place to display them until the store next door was vacated. I rented half of it, and Franklin Pickett took the other half. Honestly, he's such a pill! He always wants to borrow antique objects for his window display, but he never offers a few flowers for my shop."

In the archway a rustic sign on an easel announced: THE IRIS COBB COLLECTION. Qwilleran noted a pine cupboard, several milking stools, benches with seats made from half-logs, wrought-iron utensils for fireplace cooking, an old school desk, some whirligigs, and a faded hand-hooked rug with goofy-looking farm animals around the border. He picked up a basket with an open-work weave that left large hexagonal holes. It had straight sides and was about a foot in diameter. He questioned the size of the holes.

"That's a cheese basket," Susan explained. "They'd line it with cheesecloth, fill it with curds, and let it drip. It belonged to a French-Canadian family near Trawnto Beach. They were ship-wrecked there in 1870 and decided to stay. They raised dairy cattle and made their own cheese until the farmhouse was destroyed by fire in 1911. The daughter was able to save the cheese basket and that hooked rug. She still had them when she died at the age of ninety-five."

Qwilleran gave her a stony stare. "You should be writing fiction, Susan."

"Every word is true! Iris recorded the provenance on the cata-logue card."

Qwilleran shrugged a wordless apology to the memory of the late Iris Cobb. She had been an expert on antiques and a wonderful cook and a warm-hearted friend, but he had always suspected her of inventing a provenance for everything she sold. "And what is that?" he asked, pointing to a weathered wood chest with iron hardware.

"An old sea chest," Susan recited glibly, "found in an attic in Brrr. It had been washed up on the beach following an 1892 ship-wreck and was thought to belong to a Scottish sailor."

"Uh huh," Qwilleran said skeptically, "and there was a wooden leg in the chest thought to belong to Long John Silver. How much are you asking for the cheese basket and the chest? And are they cheaper without the provenance?"

"Spoken like an experienced junker," she said. "Because you're an old friend of dear Iris, I'll give you a clergyman's discount, ten percent. She'd want you to have it."

Qwilleran grunted his thanks as he wrote the check, thinking that dear Iris would have given him twenty percent. He said, "I don't suppose her personal cookbook turned up, did it?"

"I wish it had! Some of my customers would mortgage their homes to buy it! The book was a mess, but the recipes she had developed were priceless. She kept it in that old schooldesk, but by the time I was appointed to appraise the estate, it was gone."

"It was left to me in her will, you may recall—a joke, I presume, because she knew I was no cook and never would be."

"I hate to say this," Susan said, "but I think it was taken by one of the museum volunteers. There were seventy-five of them—on maintenance, security, hosting, cataloguing, etc. Mitch Ogilvie was the manager then, and he put a notice in the volunteers' newsletter, pleading for its return—no questions asked. No one responded. . . . I'll have my man put a coat of oil on the sea chest for you, Qwill, and deliver it to the barn."

Qwilleran left with his cheese basket and visited the florist next door, pushing through a maze of greeting cards, stuffed animals, balloons, chocolates, and decorated mugs to reach the fresh-cut flowers.

"Hello, Mr. Q," said a young clerk with long silky hair and large blue eyes. "Daisies again? Or would you like mums for a change?"

"Mrs. Duncan has an overriding passion for daisies and unmitigated scorn for mums," he said sternly. "Why are you pushing mums? Did your boss buy too many? Or does he get a bigger markup on mums?"

She giggled. "Oh, Mr. Q, you're so funny. "Most people like mums because they last longer, and we have a new color." She showed him a bouquet of dark red. "It's called vintage burgundy."

"It looks like dried blood," he said. "Just give me a bunch of yellow daisies without that wispy stuff that sheds all over the floor."

"You don't want any statice?" she asked in disbelief.

"No statice, no ribbon bows, no balloons." Then, having asserted himself successfully, he relented and said in a genial tone, "You had some excitement across the street yesterday."

She rolled her expressive blue eyes. "I was paralyzed with fright! I thought it was an earthquake. My boss was in the back room working on a funeral, and he was as scared as I was." She added in a whisper, although there was no one else in the shop, "The police have been here, asking questions. The man that planted the bomb bought some flowers from us."

"Did you see him?"

"No. I was in the back room working on a wedding. Mr. Pickett waited on him. He bought mums in that new color."

"Well, tell your boss to stock up on vintage burgundy. There'll be a run on it when the public discovers it was the bomber's choice. Don't ask me why. It's some kind of wacky mass hysteria."

Somewhat behind schedule—because of the spilled honey and the unplanned meetings on Main Street and the purchase of the antiques—Qwilleran hastily chopped corned beef for the Siamese. The salty meat seemed to give them a special thrill. Then they inspected the cheese basket on the coffee table, its open weave making a crisp lineal pattern on the white surface.

"We will not chew this basket!" Qwilleran warned them. "It belonged to Mrs. Cobb. You remember Mrs. Cobb. She used to make meatloaf for you. Her basket deserves your respect."

Koko sniffed it and walked away with the bored attitude of a cat who has sniffed better baskets in his time. Yum Yum tried it on for size, however, and found it a perfect fit. She curled into it with her chin resting on the rim, a picture of contentment.

Qwilleran drove to Gingerbread Alley and found Polly dressed for her first walk but apprehensive. "I know it's silly to feel this way, but I do," she said apologetically.

"One turn around the block, and you'll be ready for another," he predicted. He gave her the flowers.

"Daisies!" she cried. "They're the smiley faces of nature! Looking at them always makes me happy. Thank you, dear." She deposited them casually into a square, squat vase of thick green glass that showed off the crisscrossed stems. "Daisies arrange themselves. One should never fuss with them."

Qwilleran noted a large pot of mums in the entrance hall. "Unusual color," he remarked.

"It's called vintage burgundy. Dr. Prelligate sent them. Wasn't that a thoughtful gesture?"

He huffed into his moustache. Previously, Polly had thought the man good-looking, charming, and intellectual; now he was thoughtful as well. Obviously he was trying to keep Polly from moving out of her on-campus apartment—all the more reason why she should relocate in Indian Village.

They walked down the street slowly, hand-in-hand. She said, "You know the neighbors will be watching and circulating rumors. In Pickax hand-holding in public is tantamount to announcing one's engagement."

"Good!" Qwilleran said. "That'll give them something else to think about besides the hotel bombing." He did most of the talking as she concentrated on her breathing and posture. He described his interview with Aubrey and the mysteries of honey production. "The poet hit the nail on the head when he wrote about *the murmuring of innumerable bees*."

"That was Tennyson," Polly said. "Perfect example of onomatopoeia."

"I won a fourth-grade spelling bee with that word once," he said. "They gave me a dictionary as a prize. I would have preferred a book about baseball."

"How are Koko and Yum Yum?"

"They're fine. I'm reading Greek drama to them—Aristophanes right now. They like *The Birds* . . . For sport Koko and I play Blink. We stare at each other, and the first one to blink pays a forfeit. He always wins, and I give him a toothful of cheese."

"Bootsie won't look me in the eye," Polly said. "He's very loving, but eye contact disturbs him."

The excursion was more therapeutic than social, and Polly was glad to return to her chair in the Victorian parlor. Lynette was busy in the kitchen, preparing a spaghetti dinner for the new assistant pastor of their church. Qwilleran was invited to make a fourth, but he was meeting Dwight Somers at Tipsy's Tavern.

Meanwhile, he went home and read some more Aristophanes to the Siamese. "Do you realize," he said to them, "that you're two of the few cats in the Western world who are getting a classical education?" They liked the part about Cloud-Cuckoo-Land, where the birds built a city in the sky. He embellished the text

with birdcalls as he read about thirty thousand whooping cranes
flying from Africa with the stones; curlews shaping the stones with
their beaks; mud-larks mixing the mortar; ducks with feet like little
trowels doing the masonry; and woodpeckers doing the carpentry.
Yum Yum purred, and Koko became quite excited.

Tipsy's Tavern in North Kennebeck was a roadhouse in a
sprawling log cabin—with rustic furnishings, bustling middle-aged
waitresses, noisy customers, and a reputation for good steaks.
Dwight ordered a glass of red wine, while Qwilleran had his usual
Squunk water from a local mineral spring.

"Do you really like that stuff?" Dwight asked. "I've never tasted
it."

"It's an acquired taste." Qwilleran raised his glass to the light,
then sniffed it. "The color should be crystal clear; the bouquet, a
delicate suggestion of fresh earth." He sipped it. "The taste: a har-
monious blend of shale and clay with overtones of quartz and an
aftertaste of . . . mud."

"You're losing it!" his dinner companion said.

Chiefly they talked about the plans for the Explo. The bombing
had hurt morale downtown, but Dwight had jacked up the hype,
and merchants were rallying around. That was the commercial aspect of Explo. There was more. He said:

"The K Fund, frankly, is afraid of being perceived as a year-
round Santa Claus. That's why they're encouraging community
fund-raising for charity. They're matching, dollar for dollar, all the
money raised by the celebrity auction, bike-a-thon, pasty bake-off,
etc. All proceeds will go to feed the needy this winter. There'll be
more hardship than usual because of the financial scandal in Sawdust City."

"Who are the celebrities to be auctioned?" Qwilleran asked.

"The idea is to have five bachelors and five single women. In
some cases, the dinner-date package will include a gift. Everything
is being donated by restaurants, merchants, and other business
firms. The public will pay an admission fee—high enough to discourage idle sightseers—and that'll add a couple of thousand to the
take."

"Who's the auctioneer?"

"Foxy Fred. Who else? He's donating his services, and you know how good he is! People will have lots of fun . . . Here's a list of the packages being offered." He handed Qwilleran a printout.

1. Dinner and dancing at the Purple Point Boat Club with Gregory Blythe, investment counselor and mayor of Pickax.
2. Transportation by limousine to Lockmaster for a gourmet dinner at the five-star Palomino Paddock with interior designer Fran Brodie.
3. Portrait-sitting at John Bushland's photo studio and a picnic supper on his cabin cruiser, catered by the Nasty Pasty.
4. A cocktail dress from Aurora's Boutique and dinner at the Northern Lights Hotel with Wetherby Goode, WPKX meteorologist.
5. A boat ride around the off-shore islands and dinner at the exclusive Grand Island Club with Elizabeth Hart, newcomer from Chicago.
6. An afternoon of horseback riding on private bridle paths and dinner at Tipsy's with Dr. Diane Lanspeak, M.D.
7. A motorbike tour of the county and a cook-out at the State Park with Derek Cuttlebrink, former chef at the Old Stone Mill.
8. A poolside afternoon at the Country Club and dinner in the club gazebo with Hixie Rice, vice president of the *Moose County Something*.
9. An all-you-can-eat feast and acoustic rock concert at the Hot Spot with Jennifer Olsen, the theatre club's youngest leading lady.

Qwilleran read the list, nodding at the choices and chuckling a couple of times.

Dwight asked, "How does it strike you? Have we covered the bases? We included Derek and Jennifer to get the young crowd. Derek's groupies will attend en masse, screaming."

"He's not a former chef at the Old Stone Mill," Qwilleran said. "He's a former busboy, who spent two months in the kitchen mixing coleslaw. Girls like him because he's six-feet-eight—and an actor."

Dwight was making notes. "Got it! Any other comments?"

"Everything else looks good. It's well known that Elizabeth Hart has a trust fund worth millions; that'll up the bidding . . . Greg Blythe will go over big. Bidders will expect to get some hot investment tips as well as the Boat Club's famous Cajun Supreme, which is really carp."

"How does Dr. Diane's package hit you, Qwill?"

"She's a personable and intelligent young woman, and everyone likes Tipsy's steaks, but not everyone cares for riding. Are substitutions allowed?"

"You mean, like a complete set of blood tests and an EKG? I doubt it. But we're advertising the auction in Lockmaster, and their horsy crowd will be up here, bidding."

Then Qwilleran said, "Wait a minute! You have only nine packages on this list."

"Precisely why I'm buying your dinner tonight," Dwight said slyly. "Check this out for number ten: A complete makeup and hair styling at Brenda's Salon, prior to dinner at the Old Stone Mill with popular newspaper columnist, Qwill Qwilleran."

The popular columnist hemmed and hawed.

"You're an icon in these parts, Qwill—what with your talent, money, and moustache. Women will bid high to get you! Bidders would fight even to eat tuna casserole at the bombed-out hotel with the richest bachelor in northeast central United States. Fran Brodie will attract high-rollers, too. She's a professional charmer; the Paddock is self-consciously expensive; and the limousine will be driven by the president of the department store in a chauffeur's cap."

Qwilleran nodded with amusement. "That's Larry's favorite shtick. Where are you getting the limousine?"

"From the Dingleberry Brothers, provided they don't have an out-of-town funeral."

When the steaks arrived, Qwilleran had time to consider. Actually the adventure would be material for the "Qwill Pen." The twice-a-week stint was ceaselessly demanding, and readers were clamoring for three a week. Down Below, in a city of millions, it would be easy, but Moose County was a very small beat. Finally he said, "I hope we don't have to stand up in front of the audience like suspects in a police lineup."

"Nothing like that," Dwight assured him. "We've booked the high school auditorium, and there's a Green Room where the celebrities can sit and hear the proceedings on the PA. Onstage there'll be an enlarged photo of each celebrity, courtesy of Bushy. After each package is knocked down, the winner and celebrity will meet onstage and shake hands—amid applause, cheers, and screams, probably."

"I'm glad you explained all this, Dwight. It gives me time to disappear in the Peruvian mountains before auction night." He was merely goading his friend. Finally he said, "Let me congratulate you, Dwight, on your handling of Explo—and not just because you're buying my steak."

"Well, thanks, Qwill. It was a big job. Only one thing worries me. The timing of the explosion at the hotel could not have been worse; it gives 'Explo' a bad connotation. I can't help wondering if there's an element in the county that opposes our celebration of food. Nowadays we have anti-everything factions, but can you imagine anyone being anti-food?"

"The cranks are always with us," Qwilleran said, "hiding behind trees, peeking around corners, going about in disguise, and plotting their selfish little schemes."

When Qwilleran arrived home, it was dark, and the headlights of his car picked up a frantic cat in the kitchen window—leaping about wildly, clawing at the sash—his howls unheard through the glass. Qwilleran jumped from his car, rushed to the back door, and fumbled anxiously with the lock. In the kitchen, a single flick of the switch illuminated the main floor, and Koko flew to the lounge area. Qwilleran followed. There, on the carpet, Yum Yum appeared to be in convulsions, lashing out with all four legs, trying to turn herself inside out. Her tiny head was caught in one of the holes of the cheese basket. The more she fought the wicker noose, the greater her panic.

Qwilleran was in near-panic himself. He shouted her name and tried to grab her, but she was a slippery handful. Going down on his knees, he seized the basket with one hand and held it steady, at the risk of hurting her. With the other hand he captured her squirming flanks and squeezed her body between his knees. How could he withdraw her head without tearing her silky ears? It was impossible. Incredibly, she realized he was trying to help, and her body went limp. Murmuring words of assurance, he broke the strands of dry wicker with his free hand, one after the other, until her head could be freed from the trap.

She gulped a few times as he clutched her to his chest, massaged her ears, and called her his little sweetheart. "You gave us a scare," he said. After a few moments, Yum Yum wriggled out of his arms, licked a patch of fur on her breast, gave one tremendous shudder, and went to the kitchen for a drink of water.

CHAPTER 8

On Sunday morning the church bells rang on Park Circle— the sonorous chimes of the Old Stone Church and the metallic echo of the Little Stone Church.

Earlier in the morning, Qwilleran had received a phone call from Carol Lanspeak, who lived in fashionable West Middle Hummock. She and Larry drove into town every Sunday with garden flowers for the larger, older, grander of the two places of worship. This time they were bringing a new couple to church, recently arrived from Down Below: J. Willard Carmichael and his wife, Danielle.

"He's the new president of Pickax People's Bank, a distin-guished-looking man and a real live wire," Carol said. "His wife is much younger and a trifle—well—flashy. But she's nice. It's a second marriage for him. I think you'd like to meet Willard, Qwill, and they're both dying to see your barn."

Qwilleran listened patiently, waiting for her to come to the point.

"Would you mind if we stopped at the barn after the service—for just a few minutes?"

Qwilleran could never say no to the Lanspeaks. They were a likable pair—not only owners of the department store but enthusiastic supporters of every civic endeavor. "I'll have coffee waiting for you," he said.

"Then we'll skip the coffee hour at the church and see you about twelve-fifteen. Your coffee is better, anyway. Strong, but better."

It was to her credit that she liked his coffee. Some of his best friends made uncomplimentary remarks about its potency. It was, as Carol said, *strong!*

To the Siamese, Qwilleran said, "I want you guys to be on your best behavior. Some city dudes are coming to visit. Try not to act like country bumpkins. No picking of pockets! No untying of shoelaces! No cat fights!" Both of them listened soberly, Koko looking elegantly aristocratic and Yum Yum looking sweetly incapable of crime.

When the Lanspeaks' car eventually pulled into the parking area, Qwilleran pressed the button on the automated coffeemaker and gave the visitors a few minutes to admire the barn's exterior before going out to greet them. They were introduced as Willard and Danielle from Detroit.

"Grosse Point, really," she said.

They had an urban veneer, Qwilleran noticed. It was evident in the suavity of their manner, the sophistication of their dress and grooming, and the glib edge to their speech. He invited them indoors.

Carol said, "We've brought you some flowers from our garden. . . . Larry, would you bring them from the trunk?"

It was a pot of mums, blooming profusely.

"Thank you," Qwilleran said. "Unusual color."

"Vintage burgundy," Larry said.

Indoors there were the usual gasps and exclamations as the newcomers viewed the balconies, ramps, lofty rafters, and giant white fireplace cube. The Siamese were sitting on top of it, looking down on the visitors with bemused whiskers.

"Handsome creatures," said Willard. "When we're settled, I'd like to get a couple of Siamese. Is there a local source?"

"There's a breeder in Lockmaster," Qwilleran said with a lack of endorsement, referring to the friend of Polly's who had introduced the belligerent Bootsie into his peaceful life.

Danielle, who had been silently staring at the famous moustache, spoke up, "I'd rather have a kinkajou. They have sexy eyes and yummy fur." Her rather tinny voice reminded Qwilleran of the sound track of early talkies. The other members of the party looked at her wordlessly.

"Shall we have coffee in the lounge?" he suggested. As he served, he was thinking that Danielle was hardly Moose County's idea of a banker's wife—or even a Sunday churchgoer; her dress was too short, her heels too high. Everything about her was studiously seductive: her style, her glances, her semidrawl, her flirtatious earrings. Dangling discs twisted and flashed when she moved. "And what brings you people to the north woods?" he asked.

The husband, who seemed to be in mid-life, said, "I've reached the stage of maturity where one appreciates the values of country living. Danielle is still looking back, like Lot's wife, but she'll adapt . . . Won't you, sweetheart?"

Sweetheart was pointedly silent, and Qwilleran filled the void by asking her for her first impression of Pickax.

"Well, it's *different!*" she said. "All those farmers! All those pickup trucks! And no malls! Where do people go to shop?"

He glanced at the Lanspeaks, who wore sickly smiles. "We have an excellent department store downtown," he said, "and quite an assortment of specialty shops. We're old-fashioned. We like the idea of shopping downtown."

The banker said, "I'm surprised that mall developers Down Below haven't latched on to this county. There's a lot of undeveloped land between here and the lakeshore."

Qwilleran thought, This guy's dangerous. He said, "That land was owned by the wealthy Klingenschoen family and is now held in trust by the Klingenschoen Foundation—with a mandate to preserve its natural state in perpetuity."

"I don't care. I like malls," Danielle announced. "I lived in Baltimore before I married Willard."

"Ah! Home of the Orioles! Are you a baseball fan?"

"No. Football is more exciting."

Carol said, "Danielle has stage experience, and we're hoping to get her into the theatre club."

Sure, Qwilleran thought; she could play Lola in *Damn Yankees*. "Where are you living?"

"In Indian Village until our house is ready. We bought the Fitch house in West Middle Hummock—the modern one. I really love the neat modern stuff in this barn. It's exciting."

"Thank you, but all the credit goes to Fran Brodie, a designer at Amanda's Studio on Main Street."

"I'll have to go and see her. Our house needs a lot of doing-over. Nobody lived there for three years. It's funny, but it was built for another banker—but he died."

Qwilleran thought, For your information, sweetheart, he was murdered.

The sharp edge of her voice was disturbing the Siamese on the fireplace cube; they were getting restless. Carol too may have re-acted to the tension in the air and Danielle's sultry glances beamed in Qwilleran's direction. She said, "Qwill, I've been meaning to ask you: How's Polly?" She turned to the Carmichaels. "Polly Duncan is a very charming woman whom you'll meet eventually—head of the Pickax Public Library. Right now she's recovering from surgery. . . . How soon will she be back in circulation, Qwill?"

"Very soon. I'm taking her for a walk every day."

"Take her to the Scottish Bakery for afternoon tea. She'll love the scones and cucumber sandwiches."

There was increased activity on top of the fireplace cube. Koko stood up and stretched in a tall hairpin curve, then swooped down onto the Moroccan rug that defined the lounge area. Yum Yum followed, and while she checked the banker's feet for shoelaces, Koko walked slowly toward Danielle with subtle intent. She was sitting with her attractive knees crossed, and Koko started sniffing her high-heeled pumps as if she had a nasty foot disease or had stepped in something unpleasant. He wrinkled his nose and bared his fangs.

"Excuse me a moment," Qwilleran said, and grabbed both cats, banishing them to the broom closet, the only suitable detention center on the main floor.

When he returned to the group, Larry said, "We have something we'd like to discuss with you, Qwill. The recent financial disaster in Sawdust City is going to leave hundreds of families and retirees with no hope of a Christmas, and the Country Club is undertaking to buy food, toys, and clothing for them. We're planning a benefit cheese-tasting; you've probably heard about it. Sip 'n' Nibble will supply the cheese and punch at cost, and Jerry and Jack will sort of cater the affair."

A yowl came from the broom closet as Koko heard a familiar word.

"We were wondering how much to charge for tickets, when our new financial wizard came up with an idea. You explain it, Willard."

"It doesn't take a wizard to figure it out," the banker said. "The lower the ticket price, the more tickets you sell—and the more cheese the purchasers consume. You're better off to charge a higher price and attract fewer people. Your revenue remains the same, but your costs are lower. After all, you're doing this to raise money for charity—not to serve a lot of cheese."

Another round of yowls came from the broom closet.

Larry said, "We were planning to hold the event at the community hall until my dear wife came up with another idea. Tell him, Carol."

"Okay, it's like this. We could charge even more for tickets if we had the cheese-tasting in a really glamorous place. There are people in Moose County who'd give an arm and a leg to see this barn—especially in the evening when the lights are on. It's enchanting."

"You could ask one hundred dollars a ticket," the banker suggested.

It crossed Qwilleran's mind that the K Fund could write a check to finance all the Christmas charities, but it was healthier for the community to be involved. He said, "Why not charge two hundred dollars and limit the number of guests? The higher the price and the smaller the guest list, the more exclusive the event becomes." And, he mused, the less wear and tear on the white rugs.

"In that case," said Willard, "why not make it black tie and increase the price to three hundred?"

"And in that case," Larry said, "we would have two punch bowls, one of them spiked."

There were sounds of thumping and banging in the broom closet and an attention-getting crash.

"We'd better say goodbye," Carol said, "so the delinquents can get out of jail."

Qwilleran was heartily thanked for his hospitality and his generosity in offering the use of the barn. "My pleasure," he mumbled.

Larry pulled him aside as they walked to the parking area and said, "The Chamber of Commerce has formed an ad hoc committee to inquire into the future of the hotel. We can't afford to have a major downtown building looking like a slum. Not only that, but the city needs decent lodging. The owner is in the hospital, possibly on his death bed. His management firm in Lockmaster is suspect—as to capability and, let's face it, honesty. The committee will go to Chicago to petition the K Fund to buy the hotel, either from the owner or from his estate. I hope you approve."

"Excellent idea!" Qwilleran said. "But when it comes to renovating the interior, we don't want any Chicago decorators coming up here and telling us what to do."

All his guests had parting words. Carol whispered, "Koko's shoe-sniffing act was a riot!" . . . The banker said, "Let's have lunch, Qwill." . . . The banker's wife said, "I love your moustache!"

They drove away, and Qwilleran released two poised animals from a closet cluttered with plastic bottles, brushes, and other cleaning equipment knocked off hooks and shelves. Cats, he reflected, had a simple and efficient way of communicating; they were the inventors of civil disobedience. As for Koko's impudent charade with Danielle's shoe, it might be one of his practical jokes, or it might be a sign of a personality clash.

———————

As Qwilleran drove to the goat farm later that afternoon, he remembered only its shabbiness. Now it was registered as a historic place.

The Victorian frame building was freshly painted in two tones of mustard, set off by a neat lawn and a split rail fence. A bronze plaque gave the history of the farm built by Captain Fugtree, a Civil War hero. New barns had been added, goats browsed in the pastures, and a new pickup truck stood in the side drive.

The former hotel clerk and museum manager came out to greet him, looking like a man of the soil. "Kristi will be sorry to miss you. She's in Kansas, showing one of her prize does."

Qwilleran complimented him on the condition of the farm and asked about some shaggy dogs in the pasture with the goats.

"A Hungarian breed of guardian dog," Mitch said. "Do you notice a difference in the new herd? We're specializing in breeds that give the best milk for making the best cheese—two hundred of them now."

"Does Kristi still give them individual names?"

"Absolutely—names like Blackberry, Moonlight, Ruby, and so on, and they answer to their names. Goats are intelligent—also very social."

They were walking toward a large, sprawling barn—new, but with a weathered rusticity that suited the landscape. One side was open like a pavilion, its floor spongy with a thick covering of straw. Several does of various breeds and colors were lounging, mingling sociably, and amusing themselves as if it were a vacation spa. Hens strutted and pecked around a patient Great Dane, and a calico cat napped on a ledge. Qwilleran took some pictures. Two members of the sisterhood nuzzled his hand and leaned against his legs; a half-grown kid tried to nibble his notebook. This was the holding pen; from here the does would go into the milking parlor, fourteen at a time.

The rest of the barn had white walls, concrete floors hosed down twice a day, stainless-steel vats and tanks, and computerized thermometers. Here the milk was cooled, then pasteurized, then inoculated with culture and enzymes; later the curds would be hand-dipped into molds. This was the French farmstead tradition of cheese-making, using milk produced on the site.

"Sounds like a lot of work," Qwilleran observed.

"It's labor-intensive, that's for sure," Mitch said. "I mean, feeding and breeding the goats, milking two hundred twice a day, plus making the cheese. But there's a lot of joy in goat-farming, and I'll tell you one thing: The does are easier to get along with than some of the volunteers at the museum. The old-timers resented a young guy with new ideas . . . Want to go to the house and taste some cheese?"

They sat in the kitchen and sampled the farm's chèvre—a white, semisoft, unripened cheese. Mitch said, "It's great for cooking, too. I make a sauce for fettucine that beats Alfredo's by a mile!"

"You sound like an experienced cook," Qwilleran said.

"You could say so. It's always been my hobby. I was collecting cookbooks before I owned my first saucepan. I do more cooking than Kristi does."

"Does she still have ghostly visitors during thunderstorms?"

"No, the house isn't so spooky now that the clutter's gone and the walls are painted. We're thinking of getting married, Qwill."

"Good for you!" That was Qwilleran's ambiguous response to all such announcements. "By the way, do you remember the furor over the disappearance of Iris Cobb's cookbook?"

"I sure do. I thought it was quietly lifted by one of the volunteers, and I had an idea who she was, but it would have been embarrassing to accuse her, and I didn't have proof."

Qwilleran went home with a variety of cheeses: dill, garlic, peppercorn, herb, and feta. On the way back to the barn he pondered the fate of the Cobb recipe book. If it could be recovered, he would have the K Fund publish it for sale, the proceeds going to an Iris Cobb memorial. He could envision a chef's school in conjunction with the college, drawing students from all parts of the country and sending graduates to five-star restaurants. What a tribute it would be to that modest and deserving woman! The Iris Cobb Culinary Institute!

It was pie in the sky, of course. Whoever swiped it probably destroyed it after cannibalizing the best recipes. Everyone thought the culprit was a museum volunteer; no one ever suggested that the culprit may have been the museum manager.

CHAPTER 9

The electronic chimes of the Little Stone Church clanged their somber summons on Monday morning as hundreds of mourners flocked to the memorial service for Anna Marie Toms. Many were strangers. It was Moose County custom to attend funerals, for whatever reason: sympathy for the survivors, neighborly compassion, curiosity, grim sociability, or just something to talk about all week. Qwilleran walked to the Park Circle to see what was happening. The traffic jam was more than the local police could handle, and state troopers were assisting.

The crowd overflowed the church. Onlookers clustered on adjoining lawns and filled the circular park that divided Main Street into northbound and southbound lanes. Among them were persons that Qwilleran thought he identified as plainclothes detectives from the SBI. He also noticed a misplaced apostrophe in signs carried by Anna Marie's fellow students from Moose County Community College.

ANNA MARIE WE LUV YA

LENNY WER'E WITH YA

He had his camera and took snapshots to show Polly. A detective asked for his identification. Photographers from the *Moose County Something* and the *Lockmaster Ledger* were busy. The afternoon papers would carry their first coverage of the Friday bombing, and they would go all out.

From there Qwilleran walked downtown to the newspaper office and handed in his Tuesday copy. He said to Junior Goodwinter, "I saw Roger and Bushy at the memorial service. The *Ledger* was covering it, too."

"Yeah, we're giving it the works. But, do you know what? You'll never believe this, Qwill. Franklin Pickett, the florist, was in here an hour ago, trying to make a deal. He's the one who sold the flowers to the bombing suspect, and he wanted us to *buy his story!* I told him no thanks and suggested he try the *Ledger!*" The young managing editor exploded with laughter. "I even gave him the address. I told him to ask for the editor in charge of checkbook journalism. He wrote it all down."

"You have a wicked sense of humor," Qwilleran said.

"Well, the *Ledger* is always dumping their rejects on us, you know. They sent us the guy with the talking pig—right after we'd carpeted the city room! Everyone knows how pigs are!"

Qwilleran chuckled at the recollection. "So . . . what are you doing on the front page, Junior?"

"Police releases are minimal, as usual, but we've got man-on-the-street stuff, photos, and a computer sketch of the suspect based on witnesses' descriptions and supplied by the SBI. He's a white, fortyish, clean-shaven male, Qwill, so that lets you off the hook."

"Thanks. I was worried."

"Then we've got a sidebar on the history of the hotel, courtesy of good old Homer. Jill is at the memorial service right now, trying to get a sappy feature story. Roger went to the hospital, hoping to get an interview with Gustav Limburger, but the old crab threw a bedpan at him. Roger also contacted the realty firm in Lockmaster that manages the hotel, but they weren't talking to the media."

"What about the mystery woman? Wasn't her room the target?"

"Yeah. Ona Dolman, her name is. At least, that's the way she registered. She's skipped, though. Left without checking out. Didn't have any luggage to come back for, that's for sure. Owes for five nights. Ona Dolman is also the name she used at the car rental and the library and on traveler's checks. There's no evidence that she used a credit card or personal checks anywhere . . . So we've been busy! How did you spend your weekend?"

"Just scrounging material for my column. Did you talk to any hotel employees?"

"We buttonholed Lenny at the scene, but the police wouldn't

let him talk. The chef was chummy with Ona Dolman, according to one of the waitresses. After the blast he picked himself up off the floor, grabbed his knives, and took off! Probably went back to Fall River, Massachusetts. Sounds as if he knows something about Dolman that the rest of us don't know. Anyway, the police will be checking him out. Frankly, I hope he stays in Fall River."

After talking with Junior, Qwilleran made the rounds of the newspaper offices, where his twice-weekly visits were always welcomed as if he were handing out ten-dollar bills. He wanted to have words with Arch Riker, but the publisher was still at lunch. His secretary, Wilfred, said, "He's been gone a couple of hours, so he should be back soon. Are you sponsoring anybody in the bike-a-thon, Mr. Q?"

"If you're riding, I'm sponsoring. I always back a winner," Qwilleran said as he signed a green pledge card for a dollar a mile.

Next he picked up his fan mail from the office manager, who delighted in handing it to him personally. He knew her only as Sarah, a small woman with steel-gray hair and thick glasses, who had never married. Junior called her "Qwill's number one fan." She memorized chunks of the "Qwill Pen" and quoted them in the office; she knew the names of his cats; she crocheted catnip toys for them. For his part, Qwilleran treated Sarah with exaggerated courtesy and suffered good-natured ribbing in the city room about his "office romance."

"Would you like me to slit the envelopes for you, Mr. Q? There are quite a few today." She kept a record of his columns according to topic, plus a tally of the letters generated by each one. She was able to say that cats and baseball were his most popular topics.

"Sarah," he said sternly, "if you don't stop calling me Mr. Q, you'll lose your job. It's a condition of employment here that you call me Qwill."

"I'll try," she said with a happy smile.

"And yes, I'd appreciate it if you'd slit the envelopes."

Next, Hixie Rice beckoned to him from the promotion department. "Sit down," she said. "We have a problem to discuss. Did you see the teasers on the Food Forum in last week's editions? We haven't been getting any results—not one!"

"I remember seeing them," he said. "Show me a copy to refresh my memory." The announcement, which looked more like an ad than a news item, read:

ATTENTION! FOODIES!

Do you have questions about food, cooking, or nutrition? Are you hunting for a particular recipe? Would you like to share one of your own? Do you have any pet peeves about food, or food stores, or restaurants?

THE FOOD FORUM IS FOR YOU!

Send us your queries, quips, beefs, and suggestions. We want to hear from you. They'll be printed in the Food Forum on the food page every Thursday.

Hixie said, "Is there something wrong with our readers? Or is there something wrong with us?"

Qwilleran considered the questions briefly. "Well, first of all, our readers may not know what a foodie is. Second, they may not want to be called foodies. Third, you don't state whether their names will be used. Mostly, I would say, they don't quite get the idea, or they're waiting for someone else to start it. This is not Down Below; this is four hundred miles north of everywhere."

"What are you saying, Qwill? That we should run a dummy column on the first food page?"

"Something like that—to prime the pump . . . Why are you looking at me like that, Hixie? I see a sudden happy expression of premeditated buck-passing."

"Would you do it, Qwill? Would you write some fake letters with fake signatures? You'd be good at it."

"Are you implying that fakery is my forte? I've always left that to the advertising profession."

"Ouch! I don't care. Hit me again. Just do this one favor for me, and I'll be forever grateful. The Food Forum was my idea, and I'd hate to have a complete flop."

At that point Wilfred interrupted; the boss had returned.

"Okay, Hixie, I'll see what I can do," Qwilleran said.

"And don't let anyone on the staff know," she cautioned him.

"No problem. I'll hand in my copy disguised as a box of chocolates."

He was still in a bantering mood when he went into the publisher's office. "Were you having another power lunch?" he asked. "Or was it a three-Scotch goof-off?"

Riker rebuked him with a frown. "I was having an important luncheon with the editor in chief of the *Lockmaster Ledger.*"

"At the Palomino Paddock? Who paid?"

There was another scowl. "The *Ledger* is giving full coverage to the bombing, and we both think it's a two county story. We're sharing sources. We also discussed the hostility and prejudice that exists between the two counties. We should be working for the same goals instead of sniping at each other at every opportunity."

"Let's not get too brotherly," Qwilleran said. "Sniping is the spice of life."

"Since you're feeling so good," Riker said, "how'd you like to take on an extra assignment—in a pinch?"

Qwilleran's flippancy switched to wariness. "Like what?"

"Wednesday night's the opening session of Mildred's series of cooking classes for men only, and the course is a sellout. We should have a reporter there."

"What's the matter with Roger? He's on nights this week." Roger MacGillivray was a general assignment reporter married to Sharon Hanstable, Mildred's daughter.

"Sharon is assistant demonstrator for the course, so Roger has to stay home and baby-sit Wednesday night," Riker explained. Then his usually bland expression changed to a roguish one. "However, Roger could cover the story, and you could baby-sit. Or Sharon could stay home with the kids, and you could help Mildred with the demonstration."

Gruffly Qwilleran said, "Tell Roger to stay home. What time does the class start? Where's it being held?"

"Seven-thirty at the high school, in the home ec department. Take a camera."

"What's the deadline?"

"Thursday noon, firm. Earlier if possible."

"What is Mildred going to teach these guys? How to make grilled cheese sandwiches?"

Riker ignored the remark. "Most men who signed up want to master one or two specialties, like barbecued spare ribs or Italian spaghetti. If I do say so myself, I make a memorable stuffed cabbage, but nothing else."

"How come I've known you since kindergarten and never tasted your memorable stuffed cabbage?"

Shrugging off the question, Riker went on. "Some of the requests made by the class are meatloaf, Oriental stir fry, pan-fried trout, Swiss steak, and so on."

"Okay, Arch. If I do this for you," Qwilleran said, "you owe me one."

"Any time you say, friend."

On the way out of the building, Qwilleran picked up a paper from a bundle that had just come from the printing plant. The headline read: SEARCH TWO COUNTIES FOR BOMB MURDERER. He planned to read it with his lunch at Lois's.

Lois herself was waiting on table. "Is that today's paper?" she asked. "Is Lenny's picture in it?"

Qwilleran scanned the front page, the carry-over on three, and the photo spread on the back page. "Doesn't look like it," he said, "but Lenny had his picture in the paper when he won the silver, and I imagine he looks better in a helmet than a bandage. How's he doing?"

"Not good. He's down in the dumps. Him and Anna Marie were gonna get married, you know . . . What'll it be for you today, besides three cups of coffee?"

He ordered a Reuben sandwich and reserved a piece of apple pie, one of Lois's specialties that sold out fast. While waiting for the sandwich, he perused the paper. There were photos of the shattered interior of room 203; the fallen chandelier lying on the reservation desk; the hotel exterior, windowless and draped with debris. There was also a photo of Anna Marie copied from her driver's license, found in her handbag in the employees' locker room.

Of unusual interest was the computer-composite of the suspect's probable likeness, this being the first time such a technical advance had appeared in the local paper. It would also be running in the *Lockmaster Ledger,* and the good folk of two counties would carry it around and peer suspiciously into every passing face.

The lead story was set in large type, giving it importance and concealing the embarrassing truth that there was little to report that was not already generally known:

> Law enforcement agencies are combing two counties in their search for the suspect who allegedly planted a bomb in the New Pickax Hotel, killing one employee, injuring two others, and causing extensive property damage. The explosion occurred Friday at 4:20 P.M. No guests were on the premises at that time.
>
> Pronounced dead at the scene was Anna Marie Toms, 20, of Chipmunk, a part-time housekeeping aide at the hotel and nursing student at Moose County Community College.
>
> Desk clerk Leonard Inchpot, 23, of Kennebeck sustained a head injury when a chandelier dropped from a ceiling above the registration desk. Manager Isabelle Croy of Lockmaster was thrown to the floor in her second-floor office. Both were treated at the Pickax Hospital and released.
>
> "Several members of the staff were shaken up," said Croy. "Because it was late Friday afternoon, all the commercial travelers had checked out, and the dinner hour hadn't started yet. We feel terribly upset about Anna Marie. She was new and trying so hard to do a good job."
>
> Major damage occurred at the front of the building on the second floor, with the bomb allegedy planted in room 203. A police spokesperson said that a white, middle aged, clean-shaven man entered the hotel at approximately four o'clock

to deliver what he said was a birthday gift and also a bouquet of flowers for the occupant of 203. Shortly after, Toms was seen entering the room with a vacuum cleaner "because the flowers had made a mess on the rug," Croy said. The explosion occurred within minutes.

PPD chief Andrew Brodie said, "A couple of thousand bombings are reported in the U.S. every year. Dynamite and blasting caps and other components of homemade bombs are easy to buy, and too many nuts out there have the know-how. You can even make a bomb with fertilizer."

Room 203 had been occupied for the last two weeks by a woman registered as Ona Dolman of Columbus, OH. She has not been seen since the bombing. A spokesperson at the airport reported that a woman using that name returned a rental car at 5:20 P.M. Friday and boarded the shuttle flight to Minneapolis. The *Moose County Something* has not been able to locate anyone of that name in Columbus, OH.

Local police are being assisted in the investigation by detectives, bomb experts, and forensic technicians of the SBI, as well as the sheriff departments of Moose and Lockmaster counties.

The photo of room 203 was a scene of incredible destruction: walls gouged, doors ripped off, ceiling panels hanging down, and furnishings shredded and flung about the room like confetti. Qwilleran read the lead story twice; there was no mention that the desk clerk allowed the stranger to take the gift upstairs himself. Then Qwilleran wondered, If the "clean-shaven" stranger had worn a shaggy beard and long hair, and if he had been carrying a six-pack of beer instead of flowers, would he have been allowed to go up to 203? He also wondered about the manager's remark that commercial travelers checked out Friday afternoon. Did that fact have anything to do with the timing of the explosion? If the Lockmaster management firm had indeed plotted the incident, as some believed, did the in-house manager (from Lockmaster) suggest the best time to pull it off?

There was more on the front page. A bulletin stated: "Do not

open gifts or other unexpected packages delivered to your home
or place of business—if the sender is unknown. Play it safe! Contact
the police!"

A human interest anecdote with an ironic twist was included as
a sidebar:

> After the "birthday gift" had been delivered to room 203,
> the desk clerk notified the kitchen that it was Dolman's birth-
> day, and the chef, Karl Oskar, prepared to bake her a birthday
> cake. He was mixing the batter when the bomb exploded,
> and both he and the batter ended up on the floor.

Qwilleran finished his lunch and went to Amanda's Design Studio to speak with Fran Brodie. The designer was cloistered in a
consultation booth with an indecisive client and a hundred samples
of blue fabric. Fran saw him and made a grimace of desperation,
but he signaled no-hurry and ambled about the shop. He liked to
buy small decorative objects once in a while, partly to please the
daughter of the police chief.

When Fran finally appeared at his elbow, he was examining a
pair of carved wooden masks painted in garish colors. "That
woman!" she muttered. "She's a sweet little lady, but she can never
make up her mind. She'll come back tomorrow with her mother-
in-law and again on Saturday with her husband, who couldn't care
less. He'll point to a sample at random and say it's the best, and
she'll place the order. . . . What do you think of my Sri Lanka
masks?"

"Is that what they are? I'd hate to meet one of them in a dark
alley." They were mythical demons with wicked fangs, bulging
eyes, rapacious beaks, and bristling headdresses.

"By the way," Fran said, "you made a big hit with the new
banker's wife. She came in this morning, and all she could talk
about was you and your barn. She thinks you're charming. She
loves your voice. She loves your moustache. Don't let Polly hear
about Danielle; she'll have a relapse. But thanks for giving me credit
for the barn, Qwill. She'll be a good customer. She hates blue."

"Did you sign her up for the theatre club? I hear she's had stage
experience."

"Well . . . yes. She was a night-club entertainer in Baltimore. Her stage name was Danielle Devoe . . . Is that today's paper you're carrying?"

"Take it. I've read it. There's nothing new," he said. "You probably know more than the newspaper."

"I know they've run a check on Ona Dolman. Her driver's license is valid, but there's no such address as the one she gave the hotel. The suspect was described as wearing a blue nylon jacket and a black baseball cap with a 'fancy' letter D on the front. He got into a blue pickup behind the hotel."

Qwilleran thought, Nine out of ten males in Moose County drive blue pickups and wear blue jackets; they also wear high-crowned farm caps advertising fertilizer or tractors. Baseball caps are worn chiefly by sport fishermen from Down Below. The suspect's black one sounds like a Detroit Tigers cap; the letter D is in Old English script.

To Fran he said, "I think I'll take these hideous masks. Would you gift-wrap them and deliver them to Polly on Gingerbread Alley? I'll write a gift card."

Dubiously the designer said, "Will she like them? They don't represent her taste in decorative objects."

"Don't worry. It's a joke." On the card he wrote: "A pair of diet deities to bless your kitchen: Lo Phat and Lo Psalt."

CHAPTER 10

As Qwilleran fed the cats on Tuesday morning, a hundred questions unreeled in front of his brain's eye:

Who had bombed the hotel—and why? Would he strike again?

What would happen to the hotel now? Would it ever be restored? Was this the beginning of the end for downtown Pickax?

Were mall developers from Down Below implicated in the bombing? Did they want to see the demise of downtown shopping?

What was J. Willard Carmichael's true reason for moving to

Moose County? Did Pickax People's Bank have an interest in promoting mall development?

And what about Iris Cobb's cookbook? Would it ever be found?

And what about the Food Forum? Was it just another of Hixie's harebrained ideas? Why should he waste his time dummying a column for her when he had problems of his own?

Feeding words and thoughts into the bottomless maw of the "Qwill Pen" was one problem. Feeding two fussy felines was another, more immediate, more exasperating problem. They had been on a seafood binge, and he had stocked up on canned clams, tuna, crabmeat, and cocktail shrimp. Today they were turning up their wet black noses at a delicious serving of top-quality red sockeye salmon with the black skin removed.

"Cats!" he muttered. Koko was the chief problem, having spent his formative years in the household of a gourmet cook. That cat wanted to order from a menu every day! Yum Yum merely tagged along with her male companion. She was the type of cat who could live on love: stroking, hugging, sweet words, a ready lap.

Qwilleran found himself yearning for other times, other places—when Iris Cobb was his housekeeper, when he lived in Robert Maus's high-class boarding house, when Hixie was managing the Old Stone Mill and sending the busboy over with cat-sized servings of the daily specials. He was aware of the conventional wisdom: If they get hungry enough, they'll eat it. But he, unfortunately, was the humble servant of two sovereign rulers, and he knew it. He admitted it. What was worse, they knew it.

Qwilleran left the two plates of untouched salmon on the kitchen floor in the feeding station and went to breakfast at Lois's, knowing she often had interesting leftovers in the refrigerator, waiting to go into the soup pot. It was raining, so he drove his car.

He sat in his favorite booth and ordered pancakes. Lois's son was serving. The rather large adhesive bandage on his forehead indicated that he had looked up when the bomb exploded and the chandelier dropped.

"Will you be able to ride in the bike-a-thon Sunday?" Qwilleran asked him.

"I don't much feel like it, but everybody tells me I should." Lenny Inchpot had the lean and hungry look of a bike racer, the neatly groomed look of a hotel clerk, and the stunned look of a young man facing tragedy for the first time.

"If you bike, I'll sponsor you at a dollar a mile."

"Take it!" Lois shouted from the cash register. "Give him a green card!" It was not really a shout; it was Lois's usual commanding voice.

Qwilleran asked Lenny, "What's the best place to get some good pictures?"

"About a mile south of Kennebeck, where the road runs between two patches of woods. Know where I mean? We're just starting out—no drop-outs—no stragglers. It's some sight! You see a hundred bikers come over the hill! The paper's gonna print a map of the route on Friday, and everybody knows that's the best place to shoot, so get there early. Take a lotta film. There's a prize, you know, for the best shot."

As they talked, Qwilleran felt someone staring at them from a nearby table. It proved to be a husky man with a pudgy face and long white hair. He was eating pancakes.

"Good morning," Qwilleran said. "How are the flapjacks today?"

"They're good! Almost as good as my mom's. Lois always gives me a double stack and extra butter. I bring my own honey. D'you like honey on flapjacks? Try it. It's good." The beekeeper leaned across the aisle, offering Qwilleran a plastic squeeze bottle shaped like a bear cub.

"Thank you. Thank you very much . . . How is Mr. Limburger? Do you know?"

"Yeah. I took him a jar of honey yesterday, and he threw it at the window, so I guess he's feeling pretty good. Coulda broke the glass. He wants to come home. The doctor says: No way!"

Qwilleran dribbled honey on his pancakes and staged a lip-smacking demonstration of enjoyment. "Delicious! Best I've ever tasted!" Then he noticed the front page of Monday's newspaper on Aubrey's table. "What did you think of the hotel bombing?"

"Somebody got killed!" the beekeeper said with a look of horror on his face. He stared at his plate briefly, then jumped up and went to the cash register.

"Aubrey, don't forget your honey!" Qwilleran waved the squeeze bottle.

The man rushed back to the table, snatched it, and left the lunchroom in a hurry.

Lenny ran after him in the rain. "Hey, you forgot your change!"

Lois said, "What's the matter with him? He didn't even finish his double stack."

"He's wacko from too many bee stings," her son said.

"Well, you wash his table—good! It's all sticky . . . How'd you like the flapjacks, Mr. Q?"

"Great! Especially with honey. You should make it available to your customers."

"Costs too much."

"Charge extra."

"They wouldn't pay."

"By the way, Lois, could I scrounge a little something for the cats? Tack it on to my check."

"Don't be silly, Mr. Q. I always have a handout for those two spoiled brats. No charge. Is ham okay?"

With a foil-wrapped package in the trunk of his car, Qwilleran drove to the public library for a conference with Homer Tibbitt, but the aged historian was not to be found in his usual chair. Nor was he in the restroom, taking a nip from his thermos bottle. One of the clerks explained that rainy weather made his bones ache, and he stayed home.

A phone call to the retirement village where the nonagenarian lived with his octogenarian wife produced an invitation. "Come on over and bring some books on lake shipwrecks. Also the file on the Plensdorf family." At ninety-five-plus, Homer Tibbitt had no intention of wasting a morning.

The historian was sitting in a cocoon of cushions for his back, knees, and elbows when Qwilleran arrived. "I need all this padding because I'm skin and bones," he complained. "Rhoda's trying to starve me to death with her low-fat-this and no-fat-that. I'd give my last tooth for a piece of whale blubber."

"Homer, dear," his wife said sweetly, "you've always been as thin as a string bean, but you're healthy and productive, and all your contemporaries are in their graves." She served Qwilleran herb tea and some cookies that reminded him of Polly's dietetic delight.

He said to Homer, "Under these circumstances, my mission today may prove painful. I want to know what food was like in the old days, before tenderizers and flavor enhancers."

"I'll tell you what it was like! It tasted like *food!* We lived on a farm outside Little Hope when I was a boy. We had our own chicken and eggs, homemade bread made with real flour, milk from our own cow, homegrown fruit and vegetables, and maple syrup from our own trees. I never even saw an orange or banana until I went away to normal school. That's what they called teacher training colleges in those days. I never found out why. Rhoda thinks it's a derivation from the French . . . What was I talking about?"

"The food you ate on the farm."

"Our fish came from Black Creek or the lake, and sometimes we butchered a hog. Anything we didn't eat we took to Little Hope and exchanged for flour, sugar, and coffee at the general store."

"And calico to make dresses for your womenfolk," Rhoda added.

Qwilleran asked, "What happened when the mines closed and the economy collapsed?"

"With no jobs, there was no money for food, and no market for our farm produce. We all tightened our belts."

Rhoda said, "Tell him about the rationing in World War One."

"Oh, that! Well, you see, sugar was in short supply, and in order to buy a pound of it, we had to buy five pounds of oatmeal. We ate oatmeal every day for breakfast and sometimes dinner and supper. I haven't eaten the stuff since! After the war I went away to school and discovered fancy eating, like creamed chicken and peas, and prune whip. I thought that was real living! Then I came home to teach, and it was back to boiled dinners, squirrel pie, fried smelt, and bread pudding. What a letdown! Then came the Great Depression, and we majored in beans and peanut butter sandwiches."

Qwilleran said, "You haven't mentioned the foremost regional specialty."

The Tibbitts said in unison, "Pasties!"

"If you write about them," Homer said, "tell the greenhorns from Down Below that they rhyme with *nasty,* not *hasty.* You probably know that Cornish miners came here from Britain in the mid-nineteenth century. Their wives made big meat-and-potato turnovers for their lunch, and they carried them down the mine shaft in their pockets. They're very filling. Takes two hands to eat one."

Rhoda said, "There's disagreement about the recipe, but the real pasty dough is made with lard and suet. I don't approve of animal fat, but that's the secret! The authentic filling is diced or cubed beef or pork. *Ground meat is a no-no!* It's mixed with diced potatoes and rutabagas, chopped onion, salt and pepper, and a big lump of butter. You put the filling on a circle of dough and fold it over. Some cooks omit the rutabagas."

Qwilleran said, "There's a Pasty Parlor opening in downtown Pickax on Stables Row."

"Unfortunately," she said, "pasties are no longer in our diet. Homer and I haven't had one for years . . . Have we, dear?"

They turned to look at the historian. His chin had sunk on his chest, and he was sound asleep.

Having been briefed in Pasty Correctness by the knowledgeable Tibbitts, Qwilleran went to Stables Row to check out the Pasty Parlor, not yet open for business. Behind locked doors there were signs of frantic preparation, but he knocked, identified himself, and was admitted. A bright young couple in paint-spattered grubbies introduced themselves as the proprietors.

"Are you natives of Moose County?" he asked, although he noted something brittle about their appearance and attitude that indicated otherwise.

"No, but we've traveled up here on vacations and eaten a lot of pasties, and we decided you people need to expand your horizons," the young man said. "We made a proposal to the K Fund in Chicago and were accepted."

"What was your proposal?"

"A designer pasty! Great-tasting! Very unique! Choice of four crusts: plain, cheese, herb, or cornmeal. Choice of four fillings: ground beef, ham, turkey, or sausage meat. Choice of four veggies: green pepper, broccoli, mushroom, or carrot—besides the traditional potato and onion, of course. Plus your choice of tomato, olive, or hot chili garnish—or all three—at no extra charge."

"It boggles the mind," Qwilleran said with a straight face. "I'll be back when you're open for business. Good luck!"

From there he hurried through the rain to Lori Bamba's brainchild: The Spoonery. It was not yet open for business, but the energetic entrepreneur was lettering signs and hanging posters. He asked her, "Are you serious about serving only spoon-food?"

"Absolutely! I have dozens of recipes for wonderful soups: Mulligatawny, Scotch broth, Portuguese black bean, eggplant and garlic, and lots more. Soup doesn't have to be boring, although I'll have one boring soup each day for the fuddy-duddies."

"What does your family think about it?"

"Nick's very supportive, although he's working hard at the turkey farm. My kids are taste-testing the soups. My in-laws are helping set up the kitchen . . . How are Koko and Yum Yum? I haven't seen them since Breakfast Island.

"They're busy as usual, inventing new ways to complicate my life."

Lori said with her usual exuberance, "Do you know what I read in a magazine? Cats have twenty-four whiskers, which may account for their ESP."

"Does that include the eyebrows?"

"I don't know. They didn't specify."

"Are there twenty-four whiskers on each side, or is that the total?" he asked.

"I don't know. You journalists are such fuss pots!"

"Well, I'll go home and count," Qwilleran said. "And good luck, Lori! I'll drop in for lunch someday."

🐾 It was still raining. He went home to give the Siamese the ham he had begged from Lois, and he found Koko doing his grasshopper act. The cat jumped in exaggerated arcs from floor to desktop to chair to bookshelf. It meant that there was a message on the answering machine. The faster he jumped, it appeared, the more urgent the call. How did the cat know the content of the message? Perhaps Lori was right, Qwilleran thought; cats have ESP whiskers.

The message was from Sarah, the office manager, who had never phoned him at the barn before. "Sorry to bother you at home," said the deferential voice, "but an express letter came for you. I thought I should let you know."

He got her on the phone immediately. "Sarah, this is Qwill. About the express letter, what's the return address?"

"It's just hotel stationery. No one's name. It's from Salt Lake City."

"I'll pick it up right away. Thanks." Qwilleran felt a tingling on his upper lip; he had a hunch who was writing to him. He drove to the newspaper via the back road, to make better time.

Sarah handed him the letter. "Shall I slit the envelope for you?" she offered.

"Not this time, thanks."

He carried it to an empty desk in the city room and tore it open, looking first at the signature: Onoosh Dolmathakia. The handwriting was hard to decipher, and she spoke English better than she wrote it. She had trouble with verbs, and she was nervous, frightened. The brief note dripped with emotion:

Dear Mr. Qwill—

I sorry I leave and not say thank you—I hear it on radio about hotel bomb—I panick—he is threttan me many time— he want to kill me—I think it good I go away—long way away—so he not find me—how he find me in Pickacks is not to know—now I afraid again—I not feel safe if he alive—always I run away where he not find me—I leave this hotel now—I sign my right name—

Onoosh Dolmathakia

When Qwilleran finished reading the letter for the second time, he felt his neck flush and beads of perspiration drench his forehead—not at the thought of Onoosh being terrorized by a stalker, but at the realization that Koko had been feeding him this information ever since the bombing, and even before. Koko had been stalking Yum Yum boldly and repeatedly, in a way that looked like a purposeful campaign.

Qwilleran telephoned the police station. "Stay there!" he barked at Brodie. "I have some curious information." A few minutes later, he walked into the chief's office.

"What've you got?" Brodie demanded gruffly.

"A letter from Onoosh Dolmathakia, a.k.a. Ona Dolman. Don't ask any questions till you read it. She addressed it to me at the paper."

Brodie grunted several times as he read it, then threw it down on the desk. "Why the hell didn't she tell us his name—and how to find him? Stupid!"

"Not stupid," Qwilleran protested. "She's in panic. She's not thinking straight."

"We can assume he lives Down Below. That means he transported explosives across a state line—a federal offense. The FBI will get into the act now. My God! Did the guy fly up here on the shuttle with a homemade bomb on his lap—in fancy wrappings? Crazy woman! Why didn't she give us more information? She's left Salt Lake City by now."

Qwilleran said, "Dolman is obviously an Americanization of Dolmathakia and not the name of her ex-husband. All we know about him is that he might be a fan of the Detroit Tigers, judging by the description of his cap."

"There's gotta be a local connection. How would he know she

was here? Who drove the getaway vehicle? Did the same blue truck pick him up at the airport?"

"Well, the ball's in your court, Andy. I have unfinished business at home. Give me Onoosh's letter."

"I'll keep the original," the chief said. "You can have a copy."

Qwilleran went home and counted whiskers. He counted Koko's first and then Yum Yum's. It was just as he had surmised. He telephoned Polly immediately.

At the sound of his voice, Polly was convulsed with merriment. She said, "Lo Phat and Lo Psalt have just arrived, and I laughed so hard I almost ruptured my thoracic incision! When I saw the gift box, I thought it was a bomb, but it came from Amanda's, so I felt safe in opening it. I'm going to hang them in my kitchen. Qwill, you're so clever!"

"Yes, I know," he said tartly. "I should get a job in advertising."

"You sound rushed. Is something on your mind?"

"I want you to count Bootsie's whiskers and call me back," he said. "Include the eyebrows."

"Is this another joke?"

"Not at all. It's a scientific study. I plan to introduce it in the 'Qwill Pen' after the Food Explo. Cats all over the county will be having their whiskers counted."

"I still think you're being facetious," she said, "but I'll do it and call you back."

In a few minutes she phoned. "Bootsie has twenty-four on each side. Is that good or bad? Some are long and bold; others are shorter and quite fine."

"That means he's normal," Qwilleran said. "Yum Yum has twenty-four also. Koko has thirty!"

CHAPTER 11

The Great Food Explo was about to blast off, with Mildred Riker's cooking class lighting the fuse: Wednesday evening: First in a series of cooking classes for men only, sponsored by the *Moose County Something*.

Thursday: Introduction of the *Something*'s weekly food page, featuring a Food Forum for readers.

Friday noon: Official opening of Stables Row with ribbon cutting, band music, and balloons.

Friday evening: Open-house hospitality on Main Street, with all stores remaining open until 9:00 P.M. and offering refreshments and entertainment . . . to be followed by fireworks and a street dance in front of Stables Row.

Saturday: Food Fair and Pasty Bake-off at the county fairgrounds, sponsored by the Pickax Chamber of Commerce.

Saturday evening: Celebrity Auction sponsored by the Boosters Club to benefit the community Christmas fund.

Sunday: Wheels for Meals bike-a-thon staged by the Pedal Club to benefit the home-bound.

Qwilleran was involved in many of the week's activities, not entirely by choice. Reluctantly he had consented to cover the opening session of the cooking class. Without much enthusiasm he would join Mildred Riker and the chef of the Old Stone Mill in judging the Pasty Bake-off. With serious misgivings he would go on the auction block as a potential dinner date for who-knows-whom. In addition, he was committed to writing the "Qwill Pen" with a food slant for the duration of Explo.

Qwilleran's life seldom proceeded according to plan, however. On Wednesday he went to Lois's for lunch. Her Wednesday luncheon special was always turkey, and he always took home a doggie bag. Lois's Luncheonette was on Pine Street not far from

Stables Row, and as he approached he saw a crowd gathered on the sidewalk—not a friendly crowd. He quickened his step.

Milling about, waving arms and expounding vehemently, were men in work clothes and business suits. A few women office workers and shoppers wore anxious expressions and raised shrill voices.

Qwilleran asked loudly, "What goes on here? What's happened?" No one answered, but there was a general hubbub of indignation and complaint. Then he saw the hastily crayoned sign in the window: CLOSED FOR GOOD. The protesters were yelling:

"Where'll we get ham and eggs? There's no place for breakfast!"

"Where'll we get lunch?"

"There's the new soup kitchen, but who wants soup every day?"

"There's the new pasty place, but I get pasties at home."

"Who'll have apple pie that's any good?"

Qwilleran asked some of the quieter protesters, "Why did she close? Does anyone know?"

"Could be she's afraid of the new competition," a City Hall clerk suggested.

"If you ask me," said a salesman from the men's store, "she's tee'd off because Stables Row got all slicked up by the K Fund. If she wanted to fix up her place, her customers had to pitch in and do it."

An elderly man said, "Some people in town want her to quit so they can get the building and tear it down."

It was indeed a sad old structure. Qwilleran had often dropped a twenty into a pickle jar near the cash register to help defray the cost of shingles or paint. The labor was willingly donated on weekends by a confraternity of loyal customers. They enjoyed doing it. To work on Lois's beloved lunchroom was the Pickax equivalent of knighthood in the court of King Arthur. There was, in fact, a large round table where the in-group met for coffee and conversation. And now she was leaving the food business after thirty years of feeding Pickaxians. It was a calamity! First the hotel bombing—and now this!

Qwilleran went to the Old Stone Mill for lunch. He said to the excessively tall young man who was his waiter, "I hear you've enrolled in the Restaurant Management course, Derek."

"Yeah, Liz talked me into going to MCCC," said the scion of the Cuttlebrinks. "In two years I can get an associate degree. I'm carrying a full load. The boss here gives me flexible hours."

"I'm glad you've decided to stay in the food business."

"Yeah, Liz thinks I have a talent for it. Acting is something I can do as a hobby, she says."

"What's today's special, Derek?"

"Curried lamb stew."

"Is it good?" Qwilleran was aware that this was a senseless question; what waiter would denigrate the chef's daily special? Yet, restaurant-goers everywhere had been heard to ask it, and now Qwilleran repeated it. "Do you recommend it?"

"Well, I tried it in the kitchen before I came on duty," Derek said, "and I thought it bombed. You'd be better off to take the beef Stroganoff."

The cooking class at the high school was scheduled for 7:30 P.M., but Qwilleran arrived early, hoping to glean some quotable comments from the participants. Eleven men were present, some of whom he knew; all of them knew Qwilleran, or recognized his moustache. They included the new banker, a commercial fisherman, and even the tall waiter from the Old Stone Mill. They had an assortment of reasons for attending:

Mechanic from Gippel's Garage: "My wife went back to work, teaching school, and she says I've gotta do some of the housework. I like to eat, so maybe I'll learn how to cook."

J. Willard Carmichael: "Cooking has replaced jogging as the thing to do! Besides, Danielle is no bombshell in the kitchen, and it behooves me to set a good example."

Hardware salesman: "I'm a single parent with two kids, and I want to impress them."

Derek Cuttlebrink: "Liz gave me the course for a birthday present."

Commercial fisherman: "My wife sent me to find out how to cook fish without so much grease. She just got out of the hospital, and she's on a diet."

Qwilleran was tempted to say, I've got a good cookie recipe for you. Instead he said, "You must be Aubrey's brother. His honey farm was the subject of my column yesterday."

"Yeah! Yeah! We all read it. The family was glad to see him get some attention. He's kinda shy, you know. Stays by himself, mostly. But he's got a lot on the ball, in some ways."

There was an unmistakable aroma of Thanksgiving dinner in the classroom. Qwilleran decided it was Mildred's crafty psychology to put the class in a good food mood. Promptly at 7:30 she appeared, her ample figure filling out an oversized white bib-apron. A floppy white hat topped her graying hair, and the insouciance of its floppiness made her audience warm up to her immediately.

After a few words of welcome, she began: "Thanksgiving is not far off, and some of you checked turkey on your list of requests, so tonight we'll take the mystery out of roasting the big bird and make you all instant turkey experts. This will be a two-bird demonstration, because roasting takes several hours. Bird Number One has been in the oven since four o'clock and will be ready for carving and sampling at the end of the session."

Qwilleran's interest in the class increased as he visualized a take-home for the Siamese. He clicked his camera as Sharon Hanstable entered the arena with Bird Number Two on a tray—plucked, headless, raw, and sickly pale. In bib-apron and floppy hat, she was a younger, thinner version of her mother, with the same wholesome prettiness and outgoing personality. Smiling happily and bantering with the audience, she handed out notepads, pencils, and brochures containing roasting charts and stuffing recipes.

Mildred said, "This handsome gobbler, which weighs a modest twelve pounds, arrived in a frozen state from the new Cold Turkey Farm and has been defrosting for two days in the refrigerator. Please repeat after me: *I will never . . . thaw a frozen turkey . . . at room temperature.*"

A chorus of assorted male voices obediently took the oath.

"Now for Step One: Preset the oven at three hundred twenty-five degrees. Step Two: Release the legs that are tucked under a strip of skin, but do not cut the skin."

Eleven pencils and Qwilleran's ball point were busily taking notes.

"Step Three: Explore the breast and body cavities and remove the plastic bags containing neck and giblets. These are to be used in making gravy. Step Four: Rinse the bird and drain it thoroughly."

Qwilleran thought, This is easy; I could do it; what's the big deal?

"Meanwhile, Sharon has been mixing the stuffing. It's called 'Rice-and-Nice' in your brochure. It consists of cooked brown rice, mushrooms, water chestnuts, and other flavorful veggies. So . . . Ready for Step Five: Stuff the cavities lightly with the rice mixture."

Mildred tucked in the legs, placed the bird breast-up on a rack in the roasting pan, brushed it with oil, inserted a thermometer, and explained the basting process. By the time Bird Two was ready to go into the oven, Bird One was ready to come out—plump-breasted, glossy, and golden brown. She demonstrated the carving and the making of giblet gravy. Then the men were invited to help themselves.

"Good show!" Qwilleran said to Mildred as he filled his paper plate for the second time.

"Stick around," she said in a whisper. "You can have the leftovers for Koko and Yum Yum."

The day after the cooking class, Qwilleran's rave review appeared on the newspaper's new food page, along with a feature on fall barbecues, an interview with the chef of the new Boulder House Inn, and the Food Forum. The comments and questions submitted to the Forum were signed with initials only, and they were interesting enough to have readers guessing: Who was B.L.T. in Pickax? Who was E.S.P. in Mooseville?

Does anyone know a good way to cook muskrat? My grandmother used to bake hers with molasses. It sure was good!
—E.S.P., in Mooseville.

If they reopen the dining room at the Pickax Hotel, I hope they do something about those ghastly street lights on Main

Street. They shine in the windows and turn the food green or purple.

—B.L.T., in Pickax.

I once ate a delicious coconut cream cake with apricot filling that a dear lady made for a church bazaar. She has since passed away. Her name was Iris Cobb. Does anyone know the recipe?

—A.K.A., in Brrr.

I don't have time to cook anything with more than three ingredients, and here's a casserole that my kids are crazy about. A can of spaghetti in tomato sauce, a can of lima beans, and six boiled hot dogs cut in chunks.

—A.T.T., in Sawdust City.

My pet peeve—those restaurants so dark you can't read the menu without a flashlight. I won't mention any names, but you know who I mean.

—I.R.S., in Pickax.

Help! Does anyone know the secret of the wonderful meatloaf that Iris Cobb used to bring to potluck suppers at the museum? My husband still raves about it. Help save our marriage!

—B.S.A., in Kennebeck.

I think that I shall never see
A better cheese than one called Brie.
My brother goes for Danish blue;
My boss is nuts for Port du Salut.
Some folks in Pickax all declare
The tops in cheese is Camembert.
To each his own, but as for me,
I cast my vote for creamy Brie.

—J.M.Q., in Pickax.

The *Something* celebrated the debut of the food page with an in-house party in the city room. Staffers drank champagne and ate turkey sandwiches, thriftily made from the meat of Bird Number Two. They praised Mildred for her barbecue story, Jill for her interview with the chef, and Hixie for her brilliant idea of reader participation. Everyone was surprised that the Food Forum was such a success in the first issue. The identity of J.M.Q was guessed, of course, and Qwilleran explained Jack Nibble's theory: If people can't pronounce it, they won't eat it, and Pickaxians have a problem with the French cheeses. What Qwilleran did not explain was his complicity in ghostwriting the entire Food Forum. No one noticed the frequent dead-pan glances that passed between him and Hixie.

Friday was the big day in Pickax. A yellow ribbon, a block long, was tied across the front of Stables Row. At 11:00 A.M. the public started to gather for the noon ribbon-cutting. There were loafers, retirees, young people who looked as if they should be in school, mothers with small children, and a middle-aged newsman with a large moustache, who was there to see what he could see and hear what he could hear.

What he saw was a row of seven new business enterprises, encouraged and subsidized by the K Fund, intended to enrich life in the community and dedicated to clean windows and tasteful displays. Reading from south to north, they were:

The Pasty Parlor, with its exclusive, all-new, great-tasting designer pasties.

The Scottish Bakery, featuring scones, shortbread, meat-filled bridies, and a death-defying triple-chocolate confection called Queen Mum's cake.

Olde Tyme Soda Fountain, offering college ices (sundaes), phosphates (sodas) and banana splits at an antique marble soda bar with twisted wire stools and a peppy soda jerk pulling the taps.

Handle on Health, selling vitamins, safe snacks, organically grown fruits and vegetables, and diet-deli sandwiches.

The Kitchen Boutique, with displays of salad-spinners, wine racks, espresso-makers, cookbooks, woks, exotic mustards, and chef's aprons.

Sip 'n' Nibble, with assortments of wine and cheese hitherto unknown to many in Moose County.

The Spoonery, dedicated to fast-feeding with a spoon, either at a sit-down counter or a stand-up bar. Opening-day specials: sausage gumbo, butternut squash soup with garlic and cashews, borscht, and tomato-rice.

For the festivities, the entire block was closed to traffic, and as noon approached, it began to be crowded with downtown workers, shoppers, mothers with preschoolers in tow, and members of the Chamber of Commerce. Voices bounced between the stone facade of the old stables and the rear of the stone buildings facing Main Street. Not all was excitement and anticipation; there were cynical observations and dire predictions:

"They'll never make a go of it—not in this tank town! It's too fancy."

"I hear the prices are jacked up outasight."

"The mayor'll get his ugly mug in the paper again. Did you vote for him? I didn't."

"He's gonna be in that auction. I wouldn't let my wife bid a nickel to have dinner with that four-flusher!"

"Who needs a Pasty Parlor? What we need is a hot dog stand."

"Who's runnin' the soup kitchen? They must be nuts! Whadda they think this is—a hobo camp?"

"Why'd they string up all that ribbon? A coupla yards would be enough. They better not charge it to the taxpayers!"

If the sour comments were heard by Dwight Somers, they failed to dent his professional exuberance. He dashed around and talked on his cellular phone. "The school bus just arrived with the band. Alert the mayor to leave City Hall in five minutes." Then, seeing Qwilleran, he said, "How about this, Qwill? We're halfway through the Explo—and no more bombs, no homicides, no civil disturbance!"

"The game ain't over till it's over," Qwilleran quoted wryly. "The judges at the Pasty Bake-off could get food poisoning."

Larry Lanspeak pushed through the crowd to speak to the newsman. "The Celebrity Auction's a sellout! Carol is gonna bid on all the guys—just to inflate the bidding."

"Tell her to exercise caution," Qwilleran advised. "She might win Wetherby Goode. Are you staying open till nine tonight?"

"Sure! All the merchants are cooperating. Susan Exbridge didn't like the idea of idle browsers in her uppity-scale shop, but we talked her into it."

"Do you have any trouble with shoplifting, Larry?"

"Only in tourist season. One nice thing about a small town: Everybody is watching everybody."

The high school band was tuning up. A police siren could be heard, and the mayor's car approached. No one cheered; rather, the crowd became grimly silent. Then the band crashed into "The Washington Post March" with the confidence of young musicians who know most of the notes, and a police officer cleared the way for the mayor. Gregory Blythe was a middle-aged, well-dressed stockbroker, handsome in a dissipated way and insufferably conceited. Yet, he was always reelected; after all, his mother was a Goodwinter.

Dwight Somers led the applause as Blythe mounted a small podium and spoke into the microphone. "On this festive occasion I want to say a few words about the future of Pickax."

"Make it short!" someone yelled from the crowd.

"Excellent advice!" Blythe replied with a smile in the heckler's direction. Then he proceeded to speak too long, despite murmurs in the audience and the lack of attention.

Finally a child's shrill voice cried out, "Where's the balloons?"

"Let there be balloons!" the mayor decreed.

Two photographers rushed forward. Scissors were produced. The ribbon was snipped. Then, as the band struck up "Stars and Stripes Forever," multicolor balloons rose from behind Stables Row, and the crowd converged on the new shops, which had promised souvenirs and food-tasting.

Qwilleran caught sight of a husky, heavily bearded young man lumbering about like a bear. "Gary!" he shouted. "What brings you to town? Souvenirs, refreshments or balloons?"

"Just checking on my competition," said the proprietor of the

Black Bear Café. "I think I'll add pasties to my menu, but only the traditional kind. I know a woman who makes the crust with suet."

"What do you think of the Stables?"

"The building's neat. The Spoonery's a good idea. But the Pasty Parlor is off the wall. It's run by a couple from Down Below— nice kids—but they don't know a pasty from a pizza . . . Well, so long! Don't forget the bike-a-thon Sunday."

Qwilleran observed the crowds for a while and then went into the shop that was attracting the fewest visitors. The Kitchen Boutique was being managed by Sharon Hanstable.

"I loved your report on the turkey roast!" she greeted him. "Does it mean you're going to start cooking?"

"Only if hell freezes over. I attended the class under duress." He glanced around at the gadgets so foreign to his lifestyle: garlic presses, nutmeg grinders, pastry brushes. "What are those knives with odd blades?"

"Cheese knives," Sharon said. "The wide blade is for crumbly cheese; the pointed one for hard varieties; the narrow squarish one is for soft and semisoft."

"I'll take a set. Since Sip 'n' Nibble opened, I'm becoming a cheese connoisseur. So are the cats! . . . What are those round things?" He pointed to some circles of floppy rubber imprinted with the name of the shop.

"Take one to Polly," she said. "They're for unscrewing hard-to-open jars and bottles. They really work!"

Both of them looked suddenly toward the entrance. The band had stopped playing, and there was a roar of voices, including some angry shouting.

"Sounds like a riot!" Qwilleran said, dashing for the door just in time to hear glass shattering. A siren sounded. People were flocking to the south end of the block; others were running away. Witnesses were yelling to the police and pointing fingers. And the young couple who had opened the Pasty Parlor were looking in dismay at their smashed window.

As Qwilleran looked on, Lori Bamba came up behind him. "What happened, Qwill?"

"An anti-pasty demonstration," he said. "Militant right-wingers protesting against subversive ingredients in the filling."

He left Pine Street with an uneasy feeling that things were changing in Pickax—too fast. The locals were not ready for "designer pasties." The economic development division of the K Fund was partly to blame. Their theories sounded good, but they failed to understand a community 400 miles north of everywhere. Their ideas needed to be screened by a local commission. There was no one with whom he could discuss his apprehension. His friends in the business community were afire with optimism, and he hesitated to be a wet blanket. His closest confidante was recuperating from major surgery, and it would be unwise to trouble her. He did, however, take Polly the jar opener, and he praised the soup at the Spoonery.

She said, "We're going to watch the fireworks from our upstairs porch tonight. Would you like to join us, Qwill? Lynette has invited her bridge club, and there'll be refreshments."

"Thank you," he said, "but when one has seen fireworks over New York harbor, it's hard to get excited about a shower of sparks over the Pickax municipal parking lot."

When he returned to the barn, he found a mess in the lounge area. Someone had destroyed the Lanspeaks' potted mums that had been standing on the hearth. Someone had uprooted the vintage burgundy blooms and scattered them all over the white Moroccan rug.

Koko was sitting on the fireplace cube, waiting for Qwilleran's reaction.

"You, sir, are a *bad cat!*" was the stern rebuke.

Koko flicked a long pink tongue over his black nose.

Then Qwilleran relented. "I didn't think much of them myself. They look like dried blood . . . Sorry, old boy."

He stayed home for the rest of the day. When his antique sea chest arrived from Exbridge & Cobb, he had it placed outside the back door to receive packages. Finding a weathered wood shingle in the toolshed, he made a crude sign for it: DELIVERIES HERE. For dinner he hacked enough meat for two cats and one man from the carcass of Bird Number One. Later he read to the Siamese. Koko chose *Poor Richard's Almanack,* which provided such pithy tidbits as *A cat in gloves catches no mice.*

As the evening wore on, however, Qwilleran frequently tamped his moustache and consulted his watch. Koko was nervous, too. He prowled incessantly after the reading. Did he sense the forthcoming fireworks as he did the approach of a storm? The merchants on Main Street would serve their cookies and punch until nine o'clock; then the crowd would move to the Stables block for the sky show.

Promptly at nine the fireworks began, and Yum Yum hid under the sofa, but Koko was agitated. He growled; he raced around erratically. Qwilleran could hear, faintly, the crackling, thudding, and whining of the rockets; no doubt the cats could feel more than they could hear. At one juncture Koko howled as if in protest.

The radio was tuned in to WPKX, broadcasting live from their van parked on the Stables block. Later, they would jockey the discs for the street dance. When the dance music started, Qwilleran stayed tuned, waiting for the ten o'clock newscast. He was in the kitchen scooping up a dish of ice cream when an announcer broke in with a bulletin:

"The Food Explo festivities in Pickax tonight were marred by the killing of a downtown merchant in the course of an armed robbery. Police have not released the victim's name, pending notification of family. The shooting took place while Explo crowds were watching the fireworks. Further information will be broadcast when available."

CHAPTER 12

The WPKX bulletin reporting a homicide in downtown Pickax struck Qwilleran like the bomb that wrecked the hotel. In horror his mind raced through a roster of his friends who were merchants on Main Street: the Lanspeaks, Fran Brodie, Susan Exbridge, Bruce Scott, and more. He knew virtually everyone in the central business district.

First he called the newspaper, and the night editor said, "Roger is camping out at police headquarters, waiting for them to release the victim's name. An entire block of Main Street is taped off, between Elm and Maple, if that's a clue."

"It isn't," Qwilleran said. "That block has the highest concentration of retail stores." As a wild shot he then phoned the police chief's home.

"Andy isn't here," Mrs. Brodie said. "He got a phone call and took right off. There's been a murder. Isn't that terrible?"

"Did he say who was killed?"

"Only that it wasn't our daughter, thank the Lord. I don't know when he'll be back. He told me not to wait up. If he calls, I'll tell him you phoned."

Qwilleran tried to read, but the radio was blaring soccer scores, weather reports, and country music; the murder had put an abrupt end to the street dance. Hoping for another news bulletin, he was afraid to turn it off. Even the eleven o'clock newscast had no further information on the crime. That meant the police were having trouble locating next of kin. The Siamese sensed that he was upset and knew not to bother him; they merely comforted him with their calm presence. Around midnight the telephone rang, and he sprang to lift the receiver.

"Brodie here," the chief barked. "Did you hear the news? They took out one of our witnesses."

"No! Which one?"

"I'll stop by the barn on my way home, if you're gonna be up. I could use a drink, and that's no lie!"

Within a few minutes, Koko's ears swiveled, and he ran to the kitchen to look out the window. Seconds later, headlights could be seen bobbing through the woods. Qwilleran turned on the exterior lights and went out to meet his friend.

"They got Franklin Pickett," were Brodie's first words. "Poor guy died with flowers clutched in his hand."

Qwilleran poured a Scotch and a glass of Squunk water, and they sat at the bar within reach of a cheese platter.

"The cash drawer was rifled," Brodie went on, "but the robbery was a red herring. The real motive was obviously to silence a witness. Notice the timing! Nobody was looking or listening. The fireworks were shooting off, and everybody was gawking at the sky. You could shoot a cannon down Main Street. They were all at Stables Row or the big parking lot. The SBI detectives flew up again, second time in a week."

"Who discovered the crime?"

"Danny was on patrol, cruising Main Street. The stores were supposed to be locked up and lights out, except for security night-lights. Pickett's lights were on full blast. Danny checked and found the door unlocked—nobody in sight—no answer to his shout. Then he saw the cash register open and found Pickett in the back-room, face down in front of the flower cooler. The cooler door was open."

Qwilleran said, "If the killer had bought flowers on the day of the bombing, shouldn't Pickett have recognized him?"

"He could've worn a disguise, or it could have been his local accomplice on a mopping-up mission. We already decided there was a local connection. That would account for the timing. Some-body around here would know the schedule of events and when to hit. Might even be somebody Pickett knew. He could mingle with the crowd until nine o'clock, then go into the flower shop and take a long time making up his mind. Might even have bought a fifty-cent birthday card. That would take time, too, and Pickett wasn't one to pass up a fifty-cent sale, even if he had to stay open all night."

"What kind of flowers was the victim clutching?" Qwilleran asked with grim curiosity.

"Something dark red."

"Have some cheese, Andy."

"Is it the good stuff you gave me last time? I forget what you called it."

"It's a kind of Swiss cheese called Gruyère."

"YOW!" came a startlingly loud comment from under the bar. Koko knew by experience where to wait for crumbs.

Qwilleran said to Brodie, "If it's witnesses they're after, what about Lenny Inchpot? He's riding in the bike-a-thon Sunday. The three medalists are riding. The paper printed their names and shirt numbers in today's paper—also the route."

"We're trying to find him. He was seen at the street dance tonight but didn't go home, apparently. His mother's visiting her sister in Duluth, and you can bet Lenny's crashing with his bike buddies. We may have to nab him at the starting gate Sunday and ship him off to Duluth. He won't like being grounded. I hear he's got a lot of sponsors."

"Has the SBI come up with any leads on the bombing suspect?"

"Well, with no name and no car license and no fingerprints, they're working against odds, you might say, but . . . if you hang in there long enough, something usually happens to bust the case wide open. The homicide tonight may be the thin edge of the wedge." Brodie downed one more quick Scotch and said it was time to go home, adding, "Why doesn't your smart cat come up with some clues?" It was half in jest and half in wonder at Koko's past performances.

"He's working on it, Andy." Qwilleran was thinking about the cat's frenzy during the fireworks . . . his trashing of the dark red mums . . . his ominous howl at one particular moment. Were his psychic senses registering a gunshot on Main Street?

Now Lenny Inchpot was in danger. He was Lois's youngest. She'd crack up if anything happened to him.

Qwilleran checked his green pledge cards for the bike-a-thon and found only two. There had been three of them—for Gary, Wilfred and Lenny—on the telephone desk under the brass paperweight. The missing card was Lenny's. A search turned it up in the foyer—on the floor—well chewed. Neither cat was in sight.

Saturday was the day of the Pasty Bake-off. As Qwilleran fed the cats that morning, he said, "You guys have it made. You don't have to judge contests, go on the auction block, or write a thousand words twice a week when there's nothing to write about!"

At one-thirty he reported to the exhibit hall at the fairgrounds, the site of the Food Fair and Pasty Bake-off. At the door, he identified himself as a judge and was directed to a room at the rear; the directions could hardly be heard above the din of amplified music and reverberating voices in the great hall. Local cooks were exhibiting and selling homemade baked goods, preserves, and canned garden produce. Some of the items had already been honored with blue ribbons. Fairgoers wandered through the maze of edibles, stunned into silence by the ear-piercing music.

The judges' chamber was a bleak, ill-furnished cubicle, but Mildred Riker's greetings and light-hearted banter warmed the environment. She welcomed Qwilleran with a hug and a judge's badge. "Qwill, it's good of you to donate so much of your valuable time to Explo!" she shouted above the recorded noise.

"Think nothing of it," he said loudly. "I'm a food freak. But couldn't we turn down the volume, or disconnect the speaker, or shoot the disc jockey?"

Without another word, Mildred hurried from the room; the music faded to a whimper; and she returned with a triumphant smile.

"Now," Qwilleran began, "tell me how many hundred pasties I have to sample today."

"I hate to disappoint you," she said cheerfully, "but the preliminaries have narrowed the field down to fifteen. First the crust judges eliminated about a third of the entries. I feel sorry for the cooks who got up at four o'clock this morning to bake, and were scratched in the first heat. The next group of judges checked ingredients and correct prep of the filling. No ground meat! No disallowed vegetables! We'll do the final testing for flavor and texture."

"How many judges have been nibbling at the fifteen pasties before we get them?" he asked.

Before she could reply, a tall, gangling youth shuffled into the room. He threw his arms wide and announced, "Guess what! You got me instead of chef-baby."

"Derek! What happened to Sigmund?" Mildred cried in disappointment and some annoyance. Derek, after all, was only a waiter.

"He slipped on a sun-dried tomato and sprained his ankle. The sous-chef had to take over lunch, and the prep cooks are working on dinner already, so you're stuck with everybody's favorite wait-person."

"Well, I'm sure you're a connoisseur of anything edible," she said dryly. "Let's all sit down at the table and discuss the procedure. First I'll read some guidelines. The purpose of the competition is to preserve and encourage a cultural tradition, thus forging a spiritual link with the past and celebrating an eating experience that is unique to this region of the United States."

"Who wrote that?" Derek asked. "I don't even know what it means."

"Never mind. Just taste the pasties," she said sharply. She went on: "Entries are limited to twelve inches in length, with traditional crust and ingredients."

"What about turnips?" Qwilleran asked. "I hear the anti-turnip activists are quite vocal."

"We're awarding two blue ribbons—for pasties with and without."

"I must confess: I hate turnips" he said. "And parsnips. Always have."

"Taste objectively," Mildred advised. "A great pasty transcends its ingredients. It's an art, requiring not only culinary skill but an act of will!"

"Okay, let's get this show on the road," Derek said impatiently. "I'm starved, and I've got a four-o'clock shift."

Mildred opened the door and gave the signal, whereupon the no-turnip pasties were brought into the room. Reduced by the preliminaries to half their size, they were cut into bite-sized chunks and served to the judges, whose comments were brief and emphatic: "Too much onion . . . Rather dry . . . Good balance . . . Flat; needs seasoning . . . Too much potato . . . Excellent flavor." After some retasting, Number 87 was named winner in the no-turnip category.

Next came a tray of pasties identified with a T for turnip. One in particular was praised by the two male judges, but Mildred tasted it and said indignantly, "This is turkey! Dark meat of turkey! It's disqualified. How did it slip past the other judges?"

Qwilleran said, "But it deserves some kind of recognition. I detect a superior act of will in its fabrication. I wonder who baked it."

"I bet it was a guy," Derek said.

"Well, we can't accept it," Mildred said firmly. "Rules are rules when you're judging a contest. Emphasis is on tradition, and tradition calls for beef or pork."

"You can't convince me," Qwilleran said, "that the early settlers didn't make pasties with wild turkey—or venison or rabbit or muskrat or anything else they could shoot or trap."

"That may be true, but if we break the rules, all future competitions will lose significance. And do you realize what a controversy we'll have on our hands?"

Derek said, "Take a chance. Start a war."

Qwilleran had a suggestion. "Throw the superpasty out of the running, but find out who baked it and do a special feature on him or her on some future food page."

Mildred agreed. The crisis was past, but another crisis was yet to develop. When they emerged from the judges' chamber and handed the two winning numbers to the chairperson of the bake-off, he stepped to the microphone.

"Attention, please," he announced on the public address system. "Two blue ribbon winners in the Pasty Bake-off have been selected by our esteemed judges, and each will receive a prize of one hundred dollars, but we have a slight foul-up here. In order to preserve the anonymity of contestants during the judging, their names were deposited in the safe at our accountant's office, MacWhannell & Shaw, and since their office is closed until Monday, we regret we cannot identify the winners at this time. They will be notified, however, on Monday morning, and the winning names will be announced on WPKX and in the *Moose County Something.*"

As the judges left the exhibit building, Mildred said to Qwilleran, "Weren't you shocked by last night's murder? It was a case of armed robbery, they said. We've never had anything like that in Moose County!"

Qwilleran knew more than he wanted to disclose to the publisher's wife. He said, "The SBI is on the case, and we can assume it's a criminal element from Down Below that's responsible—not some bad boy from Chipmunk . . . By the way, the cats want to express their gratitude for Bird One. The carcass is getting thinner, and Koko and Yum Yum are getting fatter." That was not quite true, but it sounded good. Actually, Qwilleran monitored their intake, believing that Siamese were intended to be sleek. Even when he gave them a crumb of cheese for a treat, it was no larger than a grape seed. Yet, they chomped and bobbed their heads and washed their whiskers and ears for ten minutes, as if it had been a Delmonico steak.

For Qwilleran, one more Explo commitment remained: the Celebrity Auction. He dressed for the event with care. In his days as a hard-working journalist Down Below, there had been neither time nor money to waste on sartorial splendor. His new lifestyle supplied both, and the owner of Scottie's Men's Store was his mentor. For the auction, Scottie recommended a bronze, silk-blend sports coat, olive green trousers, and a silk shirt in olive, to be worn open-neck.

On the way to the high school auditorium, Qwilleran drove to Gingerbread Alley to obtain Polly's okay on his outfit. She said he looked distinguished and romantic. "Call me when it's over, no matter how late," she requested. "I won't sleep until I know who gets you."

The crowd that gathered for the auction had paid plenty for their tickets and were convinced they were going to have a good time. The auctioneer, Foxy Fred, circulated in his western hat and red jacket, whipping up their enthusiasm. His spotters, also in red jackets, handed out numbered flash cards to those intending to bid. Poster-sized photographs of the celebrities were displayed onstage, either hanging on the back wall or displayed on easels.

The celebrities themselves were assembled in the Green Room backstage, where they would be able to hear the proceedings on the PA system. Besides Qwilleran, there were the mayor, the WPKX weatherman, the town's leading photographer, and the ubiquitous Derek Cuttlebrink, plus five attractive women: the heiress from Chicago, the personable young doctor, the glamorous interior designer, the theatre club's popular ingenue, and the chic vice president of the *Moose County Something*.

Qwilleran said to them, "I expect Foxy Fred to hawk me as 'a gen-u-wine old news-hound in fair condition, with the patina of age and interesting distress marks.' Then the bidding will start at five dollars."

The balding John Bushland said, "You're bananas! They'll hock their teeth to bid on you, Qwill. You have more hair than all the rest of us put together."

Hixie Rice assured them all, "Dwight has some shills in the audience to liven up the action if it's too slow, or if the bids are too low."

Fran Brodie muttered to Qwilleran, "Wouldn't you know the mayor would have the chutzpa to wear a dinner jacket and paisley cummerbund? You're dressed just right, Qwill! If I were in the audience, I'd bid a month's commissions on you. Danielle Carmichael was in the studio yesterday, looking at wallpaper. They're both here tonight. Willard is going to bid on me, and she's going to bid on you, although he won't let her go over a thousand."

"Have you heard any more about the shooting?"

"Only that they know what kind of handgun was used, but it happened less than twenty-four hours ago. Give them a break!"

At that point, Pender Wilmot of the Boosters Club arrived in the Green Room to brief the somewhat nervous celebrities. "Packages will be auctioned in the order that appears in the printed program. Foxy Fred will open the bidding with a suggested starting price. If the bids start low, don't worry; he's a master at milking the audience. When your package is knocked down, the winner will come to the platform, and you'll walk out to meet your dinner date. Relax and have fun. It's all for a good cause."

Foxy Fred banged the gavel, and the bidding commenced. The mayor's package—dinner at the Purple Point Boat Club—was knocked down for $750, and the woman he went onstage to meet was Elaine Fetter—widow, champion volunteer, gourmet cook, and grower of mushrooms.

Fran whispered to Qwilleran, "She's been running after the mayor ever since she lost her husband. She lives in West Middle Hummock. I did her house. She has a fabulous kitchen."

Her own package—dinner at the Palomino Paddock—brought

$1,000 from Dr. Prelligate. After meeting him onstage, she said breathlessly to Qwilleran, "He's not at all like a college president; he's quite sexy! I wonder what I should wear for the dinner."

"Maybe you can get a decorating job out of it," he suggested. "Find out if he likes blue."

After Derek Cuttlebrink's motorcycle cook-out brought $325 amid screams from his young adherents in the audience, Jennifer Olsen was heard to complain in the Green Room, "That's unfair! Those girls pooled their money and drew straws. A hairdresser won, and she had hundreds of dollars to bid. Nobody will have nearly that much to bid on me."

The pretty young actress stopped pouting, however, when her all-you-can-eat package brought $400. She went onstage in a state of shock to meet her dinner date, and the others in the Green room heard her shriek "Dad!"

"That's parental love!" declared Dr. Diane backstage. "Poor Mr. Olsen will have to eat the Hot Spot's ghastly food and sit through two hours of ear-blasting rock. He'll be at the clinic Monday morning, complaining of deafness and heartburn."

Qwilleran's package—a complete makeup and hair styling, followed by dinner at the Old Stone Mill—was the last to go on the block. While other packages had been greeted with murmurs of interest and a few youthful shrieks, this one brought a storm of clapping, cheering, and stamping of feet.

Foxy Fred shouted, "Who wants to have dinner with a famous journalist?" He had been instructed not to mention money or moustache. "Shall we start with five hundred? Who'll give me five hundred? . . . Five hundred do I see? . . . I hear four hundred. No money! Go back to the hills . . . Who'll make it four-fifty?"

"Hep!" shouted a spotter, pointing at a flashcard.

"Four-fifty I've got. Make it five-fifty. Do I see five-fifty?"

"Hep!"

"That's the ticket! Now we're rollin'. Who'll bid six-fifty? Waddala waddala bidda waddala . . . Six-fifty I've got. Make it seven! Seven hundred for a thousand-dollar dinner date! . . . Who'll make it seven?"

"Hep!"

"Make it eight! Chance of a lifetime, folks! . . . I see eight in the back row. Do I see nine? Waddala waddala bidda waddala bidda bidda . . . Nine I've got over there at the left. Make it a thou! Let's hear from the heavy artillery! Dinner date you'll never forget! . . . A thousand I've got! Who'll bid twelve hundred? . . . Twelve I've got from the lady in the back row! Make it fifteen! Fifteen? Fourteen is bid. Make it fifteen! Where's that card in the back row?"

Qwilleran and Fran exchanged anxious glances. Had Danielle exceeded her thousand-dollar cap? He passed a hand ruefully over his warm face.

"Do I hear fifteen? Shoot the works! Don't lose him now! Make it fifteen!"

"Hep!"

"Fifteen is bid! Who'll go sixteen? Sixteen? Sixteen? . . . Fifteen once, fifteen twice!" The gavel banged down. "Sold for fifteen hundred to the lady back there with number 134. Don't faint, ma'am! The red jackets will escort you to the stage."

Qwilleran said, "Oh, God! Who can it be?" A list flashed into his mind: women who had been pestering him for the last five years . . . women who could afford fifteen hundred dollars . . . women he liked . . . women he didn't like. If only Polly could have been in the audience! They could have rigged it: She'd bid; he'd pay.

His colleagues in the Green Room were applauding; the crowd in the auditorium was going wild! Derek and Bushy pulled him to his feet and pushed him toward the stage.

Foxy Fred shouted, "Come on out, Mr. Q. Don't be bashful!"

Theatrically, Qwilleran's timing was perfect; suspense was building. The auctioneer was bawling, "Here's the lucky lady! Come right up, sister. Feeling a little weak in the knees?"

Qwilleran tidied his moustache, took a deep breath, and squared his shoulder. Walking onstage, he bowed modestly toward the bright lights and the hundreds of upturned faces, and the sight of the famous moustache increased the uproar. He looked across the stage to see a red-jacketed spotter assisting a little gray-haired woman up the steps.

"Sarah!" he shouted in astonishment.

CHAPTER 13

At the newspaper everyone called her Sarah. Now she was giving her name as Sarah Plensdorf. Qwilleran walked across the stage toward the nervous little woman, extending two reassuring hands. Tears of excitement or triumph were streaming down her face. His own reaction was: How could she—or why would she—spend that kind of money on a dinner date with *anyone?* It must be a practical joke, he decided, financed by the unholy three: Riker, Hixie, and Junior. It was the kind of trick they would play—an expensive joke, but tax-deductible . . . Well! He would spoil their fun; he would put on a good show! He grasped Ms. Plensdorf's two trembling hands, bowing over them courteously, and mumbling his pleasure that she had won. Then he brought down the house by giving her a bear hug.

The red-jacketed attendant ushered the two of them to a table in the wings, where Pender Wilmot invited them to set a date for their dinner.

"Would Monday evening be too soon?" Ms. Plensdorf asked shyly. "I'm so thrilled, I can hardly wait."

"Monday will be perfect," Qwilleran said. "I'll reserve the best table at the Mill and pick you up at seven o'clock." She lived, he now learned, in Indian Village, a good address, where many singles had upscale apartments.

Returning to the Green Room he reasoned that he could have done worse. At the office Sarah always dressed tastefully and spoke in a cultivated voice. Furthermore, she regularly commented intelligently on his current column and never mentioned his moustache. With the complete makeup and hair styling included in the package, she would be a presentable dinner date. Besides, it was all for a charitable cause. He was, in fact, glad that Sarah Plensdorf had edged Danielle Carmichael out of the running.

Back at the barn he wasted no time in phoning Polly to report the news.

"Sarah Plensdorf! What a surprise!" she exclaimed. "Well, I'm glad she won you, Qwill. She's a very sweet person."

"I know her only as office manager at the paper, and she seems to bring efficiency and a pleasant manner to the job. What I wonder is: Can she afford fifteen hundred dollars?"

"I'm sure she can. She donates generously to the library. The Plensdorfs made their fortune in lumbering in the early days, and I imagine she inherited a handsome amount."

"I see," Qwilleran said. "Do you know anything about her personal interests?"

"Only that she collects buttons."

"Buttons!" he repeated in disbelief. "Did I hear right?"

"Well, yes. Didn't you see her collection in the library display case last year? It was featured in your paper, too."

"I didn't see the display, and I didn't read the feature!" he declared defiantly.

"When are you taking her to dinner?"

"Monday night."

"If you want to bone up on buttons before then, you'll find one or two books on the subject at the library."

"Thank you for the suggestion, but . . . no thanks. I'll wing it."

Early rising was not a Qwilleran habit, but on Sunday morning he left the barn at seven-thirty and drove toward Kennebeck. The wooded hill south of the town was lined with cars, vans, and pickups on both shoulders. Those who had arrived early for a good vantage point were having tailgate breakfasts. By eight-thirty their cameras were at the ready.

First, a sheriff's car came slowly over the crest of the hill and started down the long gentle slope, followed by more than a hundred elegantly lightweight cycles with helmeted riders crouched over the handlebars. Qwilleran hoped he would not see Lenny's green jersey with number 19 on the back. There was a burst of applause for the gold and bronze medalists when they passed, but the silver medalist was nowhere in sight. The PPD had successfully grounded him; he might even be on his way to Duluth.

The ride was a joyful sight—until a rifle shot rang out. The crowd became suddenly silent. A second shot was heard, and parents pushed their children into their vehicles. "Just a rabbit hunter," someone yelled. Still, the motorcycle escort talked into a cellular phone, and the sheriff's car returned.

Qwilleran thought, Everyone's edgy. All their lives they've been used to hearing hunters' rifle shots. What a difference a homicide makes!

When he returned to the barn, he took a quick look into the sea chest before unlocking the back door. To his surprise, there was a carton labeled: "Product of Cold Turkey Farm. Weight, 12 pounds. Keep frozen until ready to use, then defrost in refrigerator."

Payola, Qwilleran thought, but then he remembered that payola was a big-city breach of ethics. In the country, 400 miles north of everywhere, neighbors helped neighbors and received neighborly expressions of gratitude, which they accepted with good grace. The question was: What to do with the bird? Actually, as he remembered Mildred's demonstration, prepping a turkey was not a staggering problem, and the oven did the rest. If one followed the instructions, it could be no harder than changing a tire—easier, perhaps. He would need a large pan with a rack. There were two turkey roasters in the apple barn, but they were being used for other purposes. Meanwhile, the cats were yowling in five octaves, and he banished them to the broom closet until he could open the carton and put the plastic-wrapped turkey into the refrigerator.

On the hour he tuned in WPKX, expecting to hear a report on the bike-a-thon: how many riders had started, how many had dropped out, and what milepost the leaders had reached. Instead, he heard a startling news bulletin:

"A fisherman was found dead this morning, as a result of multiple bee stings. According to the medical examiner, the insects had attacked in such numbers that the victim was virtually smothered. The body was found in a rental cabin belonging to Scotten Fisheries on the bank of Black Creek. No further details are available at this time, but police say . . . he was not . . . a resident of Moose County."

That last statement, spoken with significant emphasis, was typical of WPKX. It meant: Relax; he was not one of us.

Qwilleran had a sudden urge to visit Aubrey Scotten.

As usual, he liked to take the public pulse whenever an unusual happening occurred, so he stopped at the Dimsdale Diner. On a Sunday morning there were no pickups in the rutted parking lot and no farmers smoking and laughing around the big table. He sat at the counter on the only stool that still had a seat on its pedestal; the others stood like a row of grim stakes in a tank trap. To the half-awake counterman he said, "I'll have a cup of your famous bitter coffee and one of your special three-day-old doughnuts." The man shambled away to fill the order. A cheap radio spluttered in the background.

Qwilleran asked, "Where did you buy that radio? It has excellent tone."

"Found it," said the counterman.

"Did you hear about the guy who was stung to death by bees?"

"Yep."

"Who was he? Do you know?"

"Fisherman."

"Has that ever happened around here, to your knowledge?"

"Nope."

"Apparently he was allergic to bee venom."

"Guess so."

Someday Qwilleran would write a column about the laconic subculture in Moose County. Engaging them in conversation was a hobby of his. "Best coffee I ever drank! Great taste!" he declared. "What's your name?"

"Al."

"Thanks, Al. Have a nice day."

It was indeed a nice day, Moose County style: sunny—just cool enough for a sweater. On such a day Gustav Limburger's red brick mansion rose out of its green weeds with a forlorn grandeur. He drove into the side yard and tooted the horn. The door of the honey shed was open, and after a second blast of the horn, a dejected figure appeared in the doorway. He was not the big, fleshy man who had enthused about his bees, Lois's flapjacks, and the German Bible he would inherit. His whole frame drooped, and his pudgy face sagged.

Qwilleran jumped out of his car and went toward him, saying, "Remember me? Jim Qwilleran. I came to buy a couple of jars of honey."

Without a word Aubrey disappeared into the shade of the shed and returned with two of the flattened jars. The transaction was made in silence.

"Beautiful day, isn't it?" Qwilleran asked.

Aubrey looked around to see what kind of day it was, and then nodded absently.

"How's Mr. Limburger?"

"Same, I guess," he said in his squeaky voice. "Did you hear Lois has closed her restaurant?" The beekeeper nodded in a daze.

"How do you like your new job at the turkey farm?"

The man shrugged. "It's . . . okay."

"Look here, Aubrey! Are you all right? Is something worrying you?" Qwilleran asked out of curiosity and concern.

Two tears ran down the soft face and were wiped away with a sleeve.

Qwilleran slipped into his big-brother role. "Come on, Big Boy, let's sit down and talk about this. It'll do you good." He took the young man by the elbow and steered him to a weather-beaten bench outside the honey shed. They sat in silence for a few moments. "I was sorry to hear about the accident at your cabin. Did you know the man?"

Aubrey's breathing was a series of heavy sighs. "He was my friend."

"Is that so? How long had you known him?"

"Long time."

"Had he ever been up here before?"

There was more weary nodding.

"And the bees had never bothered him?"

There was no response.

"Where were you when it happened?"

"In the house." He jerked his head toward the brick mansion.

"He evidently did something that frightened or upset the bees."

Aubrey shrugged shoulders that seemed weighted by a heavy burden.

"I wish I could think of something to say or do that would help you, Aubrey. You must keep up your spirit. Go to see the old man in the hospital; do your job at the turkey farm; take care of your bees. It takes time to recover from the shock of a tragedy like this. Keep busy. Face one day at a time." While he was babbling platitudes, he was thinking about a recent morning at Lois's when the bombing was mentioned, and the sensitive young man said, "Somebody was killed." Then he rushed from the restaurant without finishing his pancakes. Now a longtime friend had been killed—and by his own bees, compounding the anguish. If bees died after stinging, did it mean that Aubrey had lost much of his swarm? He was a lonely person who seemed to yearn for a friend. He liked Lois because she was friendly; Gary at the Black Bear was friendly; his bees were his friends. Taking that thought as a cue, Qwilleran said, "At a time like this, it helps to talk to a friend, Aubrey. I want you to think of me as a friend and call me if I can help . . . Here's my phone number." The sincerity of Qwilleran's attitude said as much as his words.

Aubrey took the card and nodded, while drawing his sleeve across his face again. Then he surprised Qwilleran by following him to his car. "The police were here," he said anxiously.

"That's standard procedure in the case of accidental death. The police and the ambulance crew and the medical examiner are required to respond. What did the police say?"

"They kept asking about the bees. Could they arrest me for what my bees did?"

"Of course not! Cops always ask a lot of questions. They may come back and ask some more. Just answer them truthfully without going into a long-winded explanation. If they give you a hard time, let me know."

On the way home, Qwilleran frequently tamped his moustache with his fist. Instinct, and a sensation on his upper lip, told him there was more to this story than appeared on the surface. Furthermore, Koko had been agitated all weekend, a sure sign that he was trying to communicate. For one thing, he kept knocking *A Taste of Honey* off the bookshelf.

From the desolation of blighted Black Creek, Qwilleran drove to West Middle Hummock, where fine estates nestled among rolling hills and winding roads. The Lanspeaks lived there. So did the Wilmots. Elaine Fetter had suggested Sunday afternoon for the mushroom interview because her weekdays were consumed by volunteer work.

In preparation he had consulted the encyclopedia and had learned that the edible fungus is a sporophore consisting largely of water and having a curious reproductive system—what they called the sexuality of the mushroom. Although he was no gardener, he knew that one could plant a radish and get a radish, but there was something murkily mysterious about the propagation of mushrooms.

Mrs. Fetter specialized in shiitake, which she pronounced *shee-tock-ee*. The Japanese word with a double-i would confuse the proofreaders at the *Something*. After several years they were still uncomfortable with the QW in his name.

The Fetter residence was an old farmhouse on which money had been lavished, with open decks and ramps, giving it a contemporary look. The woman who greeted him was the same statuesque, self-assured, well-groomed shopper who had suggested short-grain rice at Toodle's Market.

"Do come in and let us start with a cup of tea in the keeping room," she said. She led the way through spacious rooms furnished with antique pine and cherry—to a large kitchen with a six-burner range, a bank of ovens, and shelves filled with cookbooks. Separated from the cooking center by an iron railing was an area with a fireplace and Windsor chairs around a trestle table. The railing looked like the missing section of the Limburger fence.

Qwilleran said, "This would make a spectacular feature for our new food page. John Bushland could take photos, if you'd permit it. Did you have a professional designer?"

"No, this is all my own idea, although Amanda's studio ordered a few things for me. I call this the nerve center of the house. I spend my mornings here, testing recipes and experimenting with new dishes. I'm writing a cookbook, you see, in addition to supervising the one for the Friends of the Library."

He set up his tape recorder, with her consent, and then asked, "Could you describe briefly the procedure in growing shiitake?"

"Of course! First you find a young healthy oak tree and cut it down after the leaves begin to fall and before it leafs out in spring. It should be four to six inches in diameter, with just the right thickness of bark."

"How thick is the right thickness? Already this sounds somewhat esoteric."

"Ah! This is a matter of study and experience. After cutting your logs in four-foot lengths, you buy commercial spawn; drill holes in these bed-logs, as they're called; then inoculate them with the spawn and seal the holes, after which they incubate for three months."

"Do you ignore them during the incubation?"

"Not at all! You must maintain the humidity by occasional deep-soaking or frequent watering with a gentle spray. An electric gauge measures the interior moisture of the logs." She explained the process glibly and concisely, like a lesson memorized from a textbook. "After inoculation you can expect fruiting in six to nine months."

"And what do you do with your crop?"

"Sell them to restaurants and the better markets in Lockmaster. Local grocers consider them too expensive, although shiitake are considered more delicious and nutritious than ordinary mushrooms. After we've visited the growing arbor, I'll sauté some for you—with parsley, garlic, and freshly ground black pepper."

From the kitchen they stepped through sliding glass doors to a patio, then down a ramp and along an asphalt-paved path to a wooded area on the bank of a stream. In the partial shade the bed-logs were stacked in a crisscross pattern; others stood on end around a central pole. Some were sprouting little buttons. "Just beginning to fruit," she said. "And over there is a flush ready to crop." She pointed to logs ringed with ruffles of large mushrooms, the caps as big as saucers and furrowed in a pattern of brown and white.

Qwilleran thought, By comparison, ordinary mushrooms look naked. "Are mushrooms still considered aphrodisiacs?" he asked, remembering a reference in the encyclopedia.

"There have been all sorts of superstitions in the past, and always will be," she replied. "There was a time when women weren't allowed in mushroom-growing establishments; it was thought the presence of a female would ruin the crop."

"When was that? In the Dark Ages?"

"Surprisingly, the superstition continued into the beginning of the twentieth century. And did you know that scientists used to battle over the question of whether the mushroom was a plant or an animal?"

On the way back to the kitchen, he said, "This shiitake project sounds like a lot of work, considering all your other activities."

"Oh, I have a little help," she said nonchalantly.

While she sautéed shiitake, Qwilleran perused her large collection of food-related books: Larousse, Escoffier, and Brillat-Savarin, as well as ethnic cookbooks of all kinds and the recipe collections of famous chefs. He wondered how original her own cookbook would be, and how much plagiarism occurred among food writers. Before he had a chance to examine the books, she called him to the table, and he tasted the best mushrooms he'd ever eaten.

Later, he reported the entire incident to Polly as they took their walk. "After five minutes with the encyclopedia and an hour with Elaine Fetter, I am now a mycological expert. I know that a mushroom cap is called the *pileus;* the gills underneath are *lamellae;* and the stem is the *stipe.* Also, there are three strains of shiitake, one of which is called *Koko.*"

"You overwhelm me with your erudition," Polly said. "What did you think of Elaine?"

"Well, I'm impressed by her vitality and expertise and collection of cookbooks, but . . ." He patted his moustache. "I have a sneaky feeling she wasn't telling the whole story. During my career I've interviewed about forty thousand individuals, and I get certain vibrations when they're holding something back—or lying."

"Did she mention her son?"

"No, the conversation was all about mushrooms and her personal activities. She didn't even mention the auction, and she's the one who snagged the mayor. What about her son?"

"Donald lives with her. He was driving the car when it crashed and killed her husband, and he's quite incapacitated. He's confined to a wheelchair, but growing shiitake is his therapy, and it gives him a reason for living."

"Hmmm . . . that puts a different slant on the story," Qwilleran said. "And actually it's a better story—one that could be rather inspirational. Also, it explains the ramps and asphalt pathways and the spaciousness of the house . . . Now what to do?"

"Perhaps I shouldn't have mentioned it."

"I'm glad you did—very glad! The question is: Why did she withhold that aspect of the mushroom enterprise? Does Donald avoid publicity because of his physical condition? Or does his mother keep him under wraps? Does she want the publicity for herself?"

"An astute observation," Polly said. "She's a very proud woman, and she has a powerful ego. It makes it hard for her to get along with other volunteers. She's always taking credit for what the others do . . . What *will* you do about it?"

"Put the column on hold until I can get to the bottom of the problem."

"I hope you'll handle it tactfully."

"Don't worry, and I won't involve you in any way. But it puts me in a bind. I'd scheduled it for this week, and now I'll have to find another topic in a hurry."

He declined an invitation to have tea with Polly and Lynette. He said he had to make some phone calls. He didn't mention it, but there was more than the shiitake situation that bothered him.

CHAPTER 14

Following his interview with Elaine and his enlightening conversation with Polly, Qwilleran hurried home to the barn. He waved at Celia Robinson, getting out of her red car in front of the carriage house. He looked into the sea chest at the back door—empty! He let himself in and went directly to the telephone without even speaking to the welcoming cats. He called Celia.

"Hi, Chief!" she hailed him in her usual cheerful manner. "Were you trying to reach me earlier? I've been out all day. I sang in the choir and then served at the coffee hour. Then Virginia Alstock took me to dinner with her folks, and we took them for a ride. It was a beautiful day! Did you do something special?"

"No, I'm just a working stiff," he said. "I did an interview out in West Middle Hummock. That's why I'm calling. Do you happen to know a Donald Fetter?"

"Sure! I know Donald very well. He's a subscriber to Pals for Patients. He's confined to a wheelchair, you know. It was an auto accident. His father was killed, and he'll never walk again. His mother says he was driving too fast on those winding roads and hit a tree. He's quite young . . . Why did you ask?"

"It's a long story—too long for the phone. Why don't you hop into your car and drive down here before dark? I have some new cheese for you to try—"

"Isn't that funny?" she interrupted. "I was just thinking about you when you called. Virginia gave me a new recipe for macaroni and cheese, and—"

"If you need a guinea pig, I'm willing to volunteer. Meanwhile, I may have a new assignment for you."

"Whoops!" she cried in her youthful way. "Give me ten minutes to feed Wrigley, and I'll be right there."

Qwilleran hung up and turned to the Siamese, who had heard the word "cheese" and were waiting in anticipation. "Our neighbor is coming for a conference, and I want you two heathens to behave like civilized human beings. Or, at least, civilized beings," he corrected himself. He arranged a cheese board for his guest and gave the cats a crumble or two: Havarti for Yum Yum, feta for Koko.

While waiting for Celia, he played the tape of his interview with the Mushroom Queen, as he now thought of her, uncharitably. She gave evasive answers to some questions and textbook answers to others, never striking a personal note. She never said, "I maintain the humidity" or "We inoculate the logs."

Postponing the mushroom column in light of the new information would be an inconvenience, but, for the moment, there was another matter on his mind.

Celia arrived in a flush of smiles. "What's that box outside the door? Where are those good kitties?"

Qwilleran replied, "The kitties, as you call them, are guarding the cheese. The box is a historic sea chest to be used for deliveries of macaroni and cheese if I'm not home."

As she went to the lounge area and dropped her large handbag on the floor at her feet, the Siamese followed her. They knew that handbag! Sometimes it contained a treat. "The autumn color is terrific this year," she said. "Especially on Ittibittiwassee Road. Virginia said it's because of the sharp frost we had . . . What's the new cheese?"

"Goat cheese from the Split Rail Farm. I wrote about it in my column Friday. This one has garlic . . . this one is flavored with dill . . . and that one is feta, quite salty."

"Yow!" said Koko.

"When my husband was alive," she said, "we kept a few goats and sold milk to folks in town who had trouble with cow's milk. I loved our she-goats. They're so sweet, the way they look at you with sleepy eyes! I called them April, May, June, and Holiday. The buck was March. My! He was a smelly critter." Celia gazed into space with a bemused expression. "Seems a long time ago." Then she snapped back to the present. "How was the autumn color in West Middle Hummock?"

"Spectacular! I went out there to interview Elaine Fetter about her mushrooms."

"Her mushrooms? Is that what she told you? The whole thing was Donald's idea! He was very depressed until he heard about growing—what do you call them?"

"Shee-tock-ee. They're a Japanese mushroom."

"Well, it gave him something to live for. We send Junior Pals out there, and they help with the heavy work—those big logs, you know. Did you taste the mushrooms? Did you see the kitchen? I wouldn't know how to act in such a big one. What's his mother like? I only met her once. Donald doesn't get along with her too good."

"She's a prominent club woman and volunteer—accustomed to running the show—somewhat conceited, they say—a gourmet cook—and she's writing a cookbook."

"Did you see the cookbooks she has in her kitchen? I never saw so many!"

"That, madame, is precisely why you are here," Qwilleran said in the declamatory style that always made her laugh.

"Okay. Shoot!" she said merrily.

"First, a little background information: Have you heard of Iris Cobb? She died before you moved up here."

"Virginia talks about her. She made wonderful cookies."

"She contributed greatly to the community, but she's chiefly remembered for her cooking. Her collection of personal cooking secrets was left to me in her will, but it disappeared before I could put my hands on it."

"You don't cook, Chief! What good would it do?"

"She also left me that pine wardrobe over there, a Pennsylvania German *schrank*. The cookbook, I think, was supposed to be a joke, but I planned to publish it and donate the proceeds to charity, in her name."

"That's pretty nice. Yes, I like that!" Celia said. "Any notion what happened to it?"

"There are three possibilities: It was in a piece of furniture that was sold to an out-of-state dealer when her apartment was liqui-dated. Or it was thrown out as junk, being a greasy, spotted, scuffed notebook with a broken spine and loose pages. Or it was simply stolen. A request for its return, with no questions asked, produced no results."

"Sounds like something I wouldn't mind reading myself," Celia said.

"You may get a chance. When I was in Mrs. Fetter's kitchen this afternoon, I noticed a battered black book among all the colorful jackets of slick new cookbooks. I didn't think too much of it at the time; I was concentrating on how to handle all the technical stuff on spawn and inoculation and incubation without boring my readers. Later, though, I remembered that the spine of the black book had been repaired with transparent tape. That's when my suspicions arose." He touched his moustache tentatively. "The next time you go to see Donald—if you do go, that is—you might sneak a peek. Could you manage that?"

"Could I! You know me, Chief! I'll go there with one of the junior trainees. Is there anything special I should look for, besides grease spots?"

"I don't imagine Iris ever put her name on it. If she did, no doubt it's been obliterated. But first you should look for almost illegible handwriting. Next you might look for certain recipes that made her a legend in her time, like butter pecan gingersnaps and lemon coconut squares. She also had a secret way with meatloaf and macaroni and cheese."

"Oh, this will be fun!" She rummaged in her large handbag for a notepad and made a few jottings. "If it turns out to be Mrs. Cobb's book, how will you go about getting it?"

"That's the difficulty. In a small town you don't send a cop with a search warrant and a court order to seize stolen property—especially when the suspect is a prominent woman who has a dinner date with the mayor . . . Although—off the record, Celia—the mayor himself has a few shadows falling across his illustrious past."

"Oh, this town is a hoot!" Celia squealed with laughter. "Somebody should write a book! . . . But look! It's getting dusk. I should get home before it's dark in the woods." She gathered up her large handbag and struggled to rise from the deep cushions of the sofa.

"Better check your handbag for stowaways," Qwilleran suggested, noticing that one cat was missing from the top of the fireplace cube. He escorted her to her car and then returned to check out the Siamese. Yum Yum had jumped down from the cube and was doing extravagant stretching exercises. Koko was sitting in front of the refrigerator, staring at the door handle. Inside, the frozen turkey was still hard as a rock.

The next morning a delegation arrived at the barn on official business. They were there to discuss arrangements for the cheese-tasting party: the two men from Sip 'n' Nibble, who were catering the event; Hixie Rice as volunteer publicist; Carol Lanspeak and Susan Exbridge, representing the Country Club. The male-dominated service organization had recently voted to allow women members to serve on committees.

"Not because they were suddenly conscious of women's rights," Susan explained dryly, "but because they need help with their projects."

"So true!" Carol said.

Jerry Sip and Jack Nibble, who had never seen the barn before, were overwhelmed by its size and rustic contemporary magnificence. The main floor was a hundred feet across, minus the space occupied by the fireplace cube, and living areas on all sides of the cube were roomy, to say the least.

"This is some place!" Jack said, "We can handle a hundred people here without a hitch. We'll have the punch bowls on the dining table and set up two eight-foot folding tables on either side—for the cheese service. With white tablecloths, of course."

"And flowers," Susan added. "For the dining table I'm bringing two very tall silver candelabra and a silver bowl for a low arrangement of fall flowers. They're coming from a florist in Lockmaster. I ordered several arrangements from Franklin a week ago, but now . . . his shop is full of police, and all his plants and flowers are dying, and no one knows exactly what's going on."

Carol said, "I hear the body is being shipped to his home town in Ohio. It's all too dreadful!"

There was a moment of respectful silence. Then Qwilleran asked about parking. "With a hundred guests there could be as many as fifty cars."

"Guests will park in the theatre lot," Carol explained, "and jitneys from County Transport will deliver them to the party. We purposely scheduled it for after-dark, because the exterior of the barn looks so spectacular under the floodlights, and the interior looks magical. The whole evening is going to be gala! I've special-ordered several evening dresses for my customers, and if the merchandise doesn't come in today's delivery, I'm in deep trouble!"

"Do you think I should lock up the cats?" Qwilleran asked.

"No, let them mingle with the guests. They're a delightful addition to a party—so elegant, so well behaved."

He uttered a grunt of doubt. "Who'll be guarding the sixteen running feet of cheese table? We're talking about cheese bandits here."

"No problem," said Jack Nibble, the cheese maven. "A bunch of students will be coming from the college to help serve, pick up empties, and all that."

"And what kind of punch are you serving?"

"None of your sissy-pink punches," said Jerry Sip. "The non-alky bowl will have three kinds of fruit juices plus a slug of strong cold tea and a dash of bitters. With the tea and the cranberry juice, it'll have a good color. The wine punch is amber-colored, like Fish House punch but nowhere near as potent."

"Smoking prohibited, I assume?"

"Definitely!" said Hixie, who had become militantly anti-tobacco since giving up cigarettes herself. Carol said, "The hosts who greet people and hand out programs will also circulate and be sure no one lights up. The programs list the cheeses being served."

"Yow!" came a loud comment from the kitchen. Jack and Jerry, startled, turned their heads quickly in that direction.

"That's only Koko," said Qwilleran. "He always has to put in his nickel's worth, no matter what the conversation . . . Well, it looks as if you've covered all the bases."

"Everything will run smoothly," said Jack. "Trust me."

And Carol added, "Everyone will have a perfectly fabulous time." Then, as the delegation was leaving, she said to Qwilleran, "Your dinner date was at the store as soon as we opened the doors this morning. Sarah wanted something special to wear. She bought a rust-colored silk with a Chanel jacket piped in black, and we're doing rush alterations for her."

Hixie also had a private comment to make to him as she handed him an advance copy of the program. "This should remind you of a cheese-tasting you and I went to Down Below. You were covering it for the *Daily Fluxion,* and you invited me."

He nodded. "It was held at the Hotel Stilton, and you wore a hat with vegetables on it."

"My God!" she said, rolling her eyes. "The things I wore when I was young and foolish! We've both come a long way since then, baby!"

Having said goodbye to the group, Qwilleran found Koko sitting in front of the refrigerator in rapt concentration, as if willing the door to fly open and the turkey to fly out. "Sorry, old boy," he said. "You'll have to wait a couple of days. How about a read instead?" He waved the program for the cheese-tasting.

With mumbles of appreciation, the Siamese ran to their positions: Koko jumping on the arm of Qwilleran's favorite chair and Yum Yum waiting patiently for his lap to become available. First he read the preface aloud. It said that cheese is mentioned in the Bible and in Shakespeare's plays, and that there are hundreds of different cheeses in the world today. It said that tonight's event would feature imports from nine countries. It said that those selected could be considered the Bach, Beethoven, and Brahms of the cheese world.

At each mention of cheese, Koko responded with an emphatic yowl.

"What is this? The Anvil Chorus?" Qwilleran complained. "I appreciate your interest, but your comments get boring after a while." It occurred to him that Koko might confuse "cheese" with "treat," or even "read." He wondered if a cat's ear is tuned to vowels and not consonants. As a test he tried using the French word for cheese:

"If Roquefort is considered the king of *fromages,* Cheddar must surely be the Houses of Parliament. The centerpiece on each *fromage* table tonight is a large wheel of Cheddar, one from Great

Britain and one from Canada. Even so, be sure to sample all twenty *fromages* in this unique adventure in tasting."

Koko yowled at every mention of *fromage,* leading Qwilleran to conclude that the cat was not comprehending words; he was reading minds, and the extra whiskers were probably responsible.

The program then listed the twenty cheeses with country of origin and kernels of information:

FROM FRANCE:

Roquefort, the king of cheeses—blue-veined, patented five centuries ago.

Brie, the queen of cheeses—soft, buttery, salty, and capricious— once an influence in French politics.

Camembert, invented by a woman—a soft, elegant dessert cheese associated with affluence.

Port du Salut, first made by Trappist monks—nothing monastic about its rich, ripe flavor.

Neufchâtel—small, white, creamy, mild-flavored—becomes pungent with age.

FROM GERMANY:

Tilsiter—full-bodied ripe flavor, pleasant to the nose and palate. More respectable than Limburger.

FROM ITALY:

Bel Paese—pearly white, sweetly mild, and agreeably rubbery in texture.

Fontina—yellowish and sometimes slightly smoky. A table cheese that also melts well for cooking.

Gorgonzola—blue-veined like Roquefort but less salty and more creamy than crumbly.

FROM SWITZERLAND:

Emmenthaler—the big cheese with big holes. Wheels weigh up to 160 pounds. Flavor: Swiss.

Gruyère—a smaller, saltier, creamier, more delicious Swiss with smaller holes (called "eyes").

Raclette—a rich cheese made for fondue and the melt-and-
scrape ritual called "raclette."

FROM DENMARK:
Havarti—mild, clean, slightly acid flavor that becomes sharper
with age.
Samsoe—similar to Cheddar in flavor with a slightly sweet, nutty
flavor.

FROM THE NETHERLANDS:
Edam—popular low-fat cheese with cushiony shape and red rind.
Texture: like soap but pleasant.
Gouda—yellow, fairly hard, and blessed with a strong flavor
minus bite. Smoked version is great!

FROM CANADA:
Cheddar—with the famous flavor and famous black rind. Need
we say more.

FROM GREECE:
Feta—soft, white, heavily salted. Crumble it on salads, pizza, and
other dishes.

FROM GREAT BRITAIN:
Cheddar—from the country where it all began. Complicated to
make, easy to love.
Stilton—a magnificent blue-veined cheese that slices well. A
classic with port wine.

As Qwilleran read this list aloud, Yum Yum fell asleep on his
lap with a foreleg over her ears, but Koko listened attentively.
Three times he yowled—at Brie, Gruyère, and feta. Because
they're salty, Qwilleran reasoned, but so is Roquefort . . . Yet,
Koko was unimpressed by the king of cheeses.

At midday he walked to the newspaper office and handed in his
copy on eating in the good old days. It began, "Where are the
foods of yesteryear?"

He also picked up his fan mail, but Sarah was not there to slit the envelopes for him. The office boy said with a grin, "She took the day off to get her hair and face done. Whoo-ee!" Officially the speaker was a "systems aide," but to Qwilleran he was still an office boy.

For lunch he went to the Spoonery, where the day's soup specials were New Orleans gumbo, Viennese goulash, oxtail, and turkey-barley. He had a bowl of the oxtail and pronounced it sensational. He also asked Lori if the turkey-barley soup really had any turkey in it.

"It's loaded! Big chunks! Want a bowl? The second bowl is twenty percent off," she said.

"No thanks, but I'd like a quart to take out." He planned to fish out a few chunks of turkey for the Siamese, avoiding the barley. That should satisfy them until the bird in the refrigerator was ready to fly.

Before he left the Spoonery, several copies of the Monday paper were delivered for customers to read with their soup, and Qwilleran grabbed one. The weekend had been an editor's delight, with the Celebrity Auction, the Pasty Bake-off and the bike-a-thon. Qwilleran chuckled as he read about the pasty winners' names being locked in a safe overnight—accidentally. More likely, he thought, Hixie had engineered the trick to delay the newsbreak until the *Something*'s deadline. The news story read:

PASTY WINNERS HERALDED

Two local cooks were elected to the new Pasty Hall of Fame Saturday after their contest entries survived three batteries of judges.

Lenore Bassett of Trawnto Beach placed first among the turnipless entries. George Stendhup of Sawdust City won in the turnip category. Each will receive a blue ribbon and a $100 prize.

After the process of blind judging—with entrants identified only by number—the suspense was prolonged by an accidental misunderstanding. Entrants' names were locked in a safe in the office of MacWhannell & Shaw. The bakers of the winning pasties were not known until this morning.

Stendhup, a toolmaker, was one of an unexpected number of male entrants. "I always knew the guys made better pasties than the gals," he said when contacted with the good news. Pork was his meat of choice. "I always add turnip for more guts."

Bassett could not be reached for comment, but her husband, Robert, said, "She's out of town on family business, but I'm gonna phone her the good news after five o'clock. Me and the kids always said Mom makes the best gol-danged pasties anywhere."

Mildred Riker, food editor of the *Something* and one of the final judges, said, "The response to this celebration of a cultural legend exceeded our wildest expectations, with more than a hundred entries. The overall quality was excellent, and the final judges were hard-put to name winners."

The sponsors of the Food Fair and Pasty Bake-off was the Chamber of Commerce.

Another headline caught Qwilleran's attention, although it was buried on page four. Notable for its brevity, it covered the who, what, when, and where of the newspaper rulebook, but not the why.

BIZARRE INCIDENT IN BLACK CREEK

The body of a tourist from Glassville, OH, was found in a riverbank cabin Sunday morning. Victor Greer, 39, renting the cabin for a weekend of fishing, had been stung to death by bees, according to the medical examiner. The incident was reported by the beekeeper, Aubrey Scotten. The cabin is owned by Scotten Fisheries.

The item, Qwilleran knew, was played down for two reasons: The victim was not a local man, and the county disliked adverse publicity. It was commonly believed that the metropolitan media, bored with ordinary shootings and beatings, watched the small-town newspapers like vultures, hoping to spot a bizarre country crime. Most country crimes reported Down Below were "bizarre," and the use of the word in the *Something* headline was a mistake, in Qwilleran's opinion. He wondered who had written it. The wire services would pick it up, and the TV networks would fly crews to the "grim ghost town" with nothing but a "haunted house" and a "death cottage" where "killer bees" attacked an innocent fisherman from Down Below. They would fluster the poor beekeeper and trick him into saying something stupid that would sound suspicious to a coast-to-coast audience, and the cameras would zoom in on the buzzing bees and make them look like monsters. Qwilleran hoped the intruders would be stung; it would serve them right!

Further, he sensed the need to steer the nervous, distraught Aubrey out of harm's way. His motive was not entirely altruistic; as a journalist he was drawn to a newsworthy character with an exclusive story to tell.

He walked home briskly to pick up his car keys. The quart of turkey soup he put in the refrigerator, closing the door as quietly as possible. Then he left the barn without disturbing the sleeping cats.

Arriving at the Limburger house, he parked in the side yard. For the first time the door of the honey shed was closed. First he went to the front door and clanged the old-fashioned doorbell; there was no response. He banged on the door without results. Yet, Aubrey's blue pickup was parked in the yard. He might be down at the creek with his bees.

Qwilleran rang the bell again and peered through the etched glass. A shadowy figure was shambling toward the front door. "Aubrey! It's your friend from Pickax!" Qwilleran yelled. "I need some more honey!" Purposely he used two buzz words: "friend" and "honey."

The door opened slowly and Aubrey said in his squeaky voice, "Threw it all out. I'm gonna let my bees go wild."

"Have the police been talking to you again?"

Aubrey shook his mop of long white hair. "They come back, but I hid in the cellar."

"Well, let me give you some friendly advice. You should get away from here. Strangers will be coming up from Down Below, and they're worse than the police. Go and stay with your family for a while. Where do your brothers live?"

"Up the road."

"Okay, I'll drive you there. Do you want to pack a bag—or anything?"

"I don't need nothin'." Then, as Qwilleran steered him toward his car, Aubrey added, "I wanna go to my mom's."

"That's fine. That's even better. Tell me where to go."

On the way Aubrey mumbled brief, half-hearted answers to questions intended to fill the awkward silence: Does your mother live alone? Do you see her often? How long has your father been gone? Have you talked to her since the accident?

A large old farmhouse between Black Creek and Mooseville was the Scotten homestead. It had a well-kept lawn and what seemed like acres of mums in bloom, some of them the color of dried blood. It looked like a commercial flower business. A woman was digging up clumps of mums and transferring them to pots. When the car pulled into the long driveway, she stuck the pointed spade in the ground and came forward—a tall woman like her sons, but her weathered face was gaunt under a large straw hat. She wore denims, with knee pads buckled on her legs.

"You poor boy!" she said, throwing her arms around her big son. "You look terrible! You need something to eat!" She looked at Qwilleran's moustache. "Do I know you? You must be the man from the paper. You wrote about the bees."

"I'm also a customer of Aubrey's. I stopped at the house to buy honey and thought he looked in need of some home cooking."

"Poor boy! Come in the house and I'll make you a big stack of flapjacks," she said. "I'd better give you a haircut, too. How long since you went to the barber, son?"

Qwilleran caught her eye and mumbled, "I want to speak to you."

"Aubrey, go in and wash up. I'll get rid of these muddy boots and be right there."

Qwilleran said, "Don't let anyone know he's here, not even your sons. All sorts of people will be pestering him—for various reasons. Wait till it blows over. Can you keep him for a few days?"

CHAPTER 15

Convinced that he was doing the right thing, Qwilleran left Aubrey with his mother and went home to dress for his dinner date with Sarah Plensdorf. First he fed the cats, scooping turkey chunks from the Spoonery carton and warming them in some of the broth, minus barley and carrots. "This will have to do," he told them, "till the real bird comes along."

Then he showered, shaved, trimmed his moustache, and dressed in his navy blue suit with white shirt and red paisley tie. He thought it was an appropriate getup for an evening with a button collector; whimsically, he chose a button-down collar.

On the way to Indian Village to pick her up, he reflected that she had donated $1,500 to charity for the privilege of a few hours in his company, and it was his responsibility to make the evening enjoyable, if not memorable. Making conversation with strangers or virtual strangers was no problem; it was one of his professional skills. In fact, asking questions and listening to the answers had made him a popular companion in Moose County. He hoped only that the cosmetician would not make the modest Sarah look like a china doll, or worse.

When he arrived at her apartment, she was ready and waiting—somewhat breathlessly, he thought. In her new rust-colored dress with Chanel jacket, she looked quite smart, and Brenda's Salon had given her a flattering hairdo and natural makeup that gave her a certain glow.

Gallantly he said, "I've been looking forward to this evening, Sarah."

"So have I, Mr. Q," she said excitedly. "Would you care for an apéritif before we leave?"

"I'd like that, but we have a reservation for seven-thirty, and I think we should be on our way." Then he added sternly, "And if you don't start calling me Qwill, I'll cancel the reservation!"

Amused and pleased, she concurred. She wondered if she would need a wrap. He said it might turn chilly later in the evening, and it would be wise to take one.

While she went to pick up her handbag and, presumably, have a last look in the mirror, Qwilleran appraised the interior: large rooms, evidently two apartments made into one . . . heavy on blue . . . antique furniture, old oil paintings, good Orientals. He was surprised, however, to see a dog. Dogs were not permitted in apartments in the Village. This one was a Bassett hound. Strangely, it was standing on hind legs with forepaws on a library table. He stared at the dog, and the dog stared at him.

Sarah returned. "That's Sir Cedric," she said. "A Victorian piece, carved wood. Realistic, isn't it?"

"I must say it's unique," Qwilleran said. The table was dark pine with ordinary carved legs at one end, while the other end was supported by the dog. "Clever! Very clever!"

As they drove away he asked his passenger, "Do you like living in Indian Village?" It was not the most intelligent question he had ever asked, but it was a start.

"I do indeed," she replied. "Every season of the year has its delights. Right now it's the autumn color, especially beautiful this year."

"Polly Duncan, whom you must know, would take an apartment out here, if it weren't for the long drive into town."

"You tell her," Sarah said emphatically, "that it's no trouble at all, after one does it for a week or so."

"How do you like working at the newspaper?"

"It's most enjoyable! Everyone seems to be having so much fun, and yet they manage to put the paper out on time. It was Junior Goodwinter who suggested me for the job. It's the first one I've ever had."

"Is that so?" he asked in surprise. "You handle it with great aplomb."

"Thank you. I attended an Eastern college and could have had a fine position in Boston, but my parents wanted me at home. I was an only child, you see, and we had a lovely family relationship. I went to Europe with my mother and on business trips with my father. Then there was community service, which is both social and rewarding. So I've had a busy life. My one regret is . . . that I never had a career. I think I would have been quite successful."

"I'm sure of that!" he said. Then, to introduce a light note to the conversation, he added, "My only regret is . . . that I was born too late to see Babe Ruth at bat or Ty Cobb in centerfield."

"That's right! You're a baseball fan! I clip and save all your columns on baseball—for old time's sake. My father never missed a World Series, and he started taking me along when I was seven. My mother didn't care for spectator sports, so he and I flew all over the country, and I learned to keep a detailed scorecard and figure batting averages. I believe it gave me a knack for math and a taste for minutiae."

Qwilleran glanced at her with admiration. "Minutiae" was a word he had never heard on a blind date. He said, "Do you remember the historic game in 1969 when the Mets took the series from the Orioles?"

"I do! I do! In 1968 the Mets had ended in ninth place, and since Father and I always rooted for the underdog, we were strong Met supporters. When they won—after that last exciting game—I remember the Met fans running out on the field and digging up the grass . . . Do you have any particular ball club allegiances, Mr. Q? . . . I mean, Qwill?"

"Well, I was a Chicago Cubs fan before I could walk, but I seldom see a big league game these days. Do you still follow the sport?"

"No," she said sadly. "Not since Father died. It was baseball that killed him. The 1975 Series between Cincinnati and Boston was unbearably suspenseful. It ran seven games. There were delays because of rain. Scores teetered back and forth. Incredible performances! Surprises and twists of fate! It was too exciting for Father. He had a heart attack." She sighed, and Qwilleran mumbled consolations.

When the two baseball fans arrived at the Old Stone Mill, they were shown to the best table—one with a bouquet of fresh flowers—and there was applause from other diners; everyone in Pickax knew about the $1,500 dinner date. Sarah blushed, and Qwilleran bowed to the smiling faces at other tables.

The waiter served them one dry vermouth and one Squunk water, and Sarah said, "When you write about Koko and Yum Yum in your column, Qwill, you show a wonderful understanding of cats. Have you always been a cat fancier?"

"No, I was quite ignorant of feline culture when I adopted them, but they soon taught me everything I needed to know. Now I'd find it difficult to live without them. What attracts me is their secret energy. It makes a cat a forceful presence at all times."

He was interrupted by the forceful presence of Derek Cuttlebrink, presenting the menus and reciting the specials: "Chicken breast in curried sauce with stir-fried veggies . . . roast rack of lamb with green peppercorn sauce . . . and shrimp in a saffron cream with sun-dried tomatoes and basil, served on spinach fettucine."

Sarah said, "I developed a taste for curry when we traveled in India, so that would be my immediate choice."

Derek asked Qwilleran, "You want a sixteen-ounce steak and a doggie bag?"

"You don't happen to have any turkey, do you?"

"Come back on Thanksgiving day. The soup du jour is oxtail."

"I had oxtail for lunch at the Spoonery. Who stole the recipe from whom?"

"You wanna know the truth," Derek confided, "our chef got the recipe from *Joy of Cooking*."

When the waiter had left the table, Sarah said, "He's rather outspoken, isn't he? But he's refreshing."

Qwilleran agreed. "He gets away with it because he's six-feet-eight. If he were five-feet-six, he'd be fired . . . Now, where were we? Speaking of cats, I assume you like animals."

"Very much. I volunteer my services at the animal shelter every Saturday."

"What do you do?"

"I wash dogs."

"Small ones, I hope," Qwilleran said.

"All sizes. Every dog gets a bath when he arrives at the shelter, and not one has ever given me any trouble. They seem to know we're doing something nice for them. Last Saturday I bathed a Great Dane. He jumped right into the tub. I put cotton in his ears and salve in his eyes, then wetted him down with the hose, applied shampoo, talked to him, hosed him off, and dried him. He loved it!"

"Apparently you're accustomed to dogs."

"Yes, we always had them at home. Now all I have is Sir Cedric. When I go home at the end of the day, he greets me, and we have some conversation, rather one-sided, I'm afraid . . . I wouldn't tell this to anyone else, Qwill."

"I understand exactly how you feel," he said with sincerity.

When the entrées were served, he took a deep breath and asked, "Didn't you have a display of buttons at the library a while ago?"

"You remembered! How nice!" she exclaimed.

"How, why, and when did you start collecting?"

"My father had a valuable collection of historic military buttons, and when we went to large cities for ballgames, he would search for Civil War buttons in the antique shops, and I would look for pretty glass ones. Now I have over a thousand—all kinds. My miniature paintings on porcelain are small works of art that I can hold in my hand. I also specialize in animal designs on ivory, silver, brass, copper, and even Wedgwood. I have a shell cameo of a dog's head carved from the Cassis Tuberca from the West Indies. You may remember it in my exhibit."

"Yes," he murmured vaguely.

Then she said, "If it isn't too presumptious, Qwill, I'd like to give you a memento of this occasion." She reached into her handbag and gave him a carved wood button depicting a cat's head.

"Well, thank you. That's a charming thought," he murmured.

"You might like to attend a meeting of the tri-county button club, too. Quite a few men belong."

"That's something to keep in mind . . . Shall we have dessert?"

The meal ended with crème brûlée for her and apple pie with cheese for him, and she declared it the most delightful dining experience of her entire life. As he drove her home, the conversation turned to shoptalk: the newspaper's fast-growing circulation, Wilfred's glory as a biker, and Mildred's new Thursday food page.

Sarah asked, "Did you notice the references to Iris Cobb in the Food Forum? She's greatly missed."

"Did you know her?"

"Very well! When I was a volunteer at the museum, she'd invite me to have lunch with her, knowing how I loved her pasties. I have an educated palate, you know—another of Father's legacies." She sighed and went on. "Did you know I was one of the preliminary judges for the pasty contest Saturday?"

"No. Filling or crust?"

"Filling. And now I must confide in you: There was one pasty that was extraordinary! To me it tasted as good as Iris Cobb's! It was made with turkey, which was disallowed, but the other judges and I were mischievous enough to pass it through to the finals." They were turning into the gates of Indian Village. Shyly, Sarah said, "Would you care to come in for a while and see my collection of buttons?"

"Thank you, but I have some scheduled phone calls to make. Another time, perhaps," he said, "but I'll see you safely indoors and say goodnight to Sir Cedric."

The animal holding up the library table, who had been standing on his hind legs for a hundred years, looked eerily alive. There was the shading of the brown coat, with the delineation of every hair, and there was the sad hound-dog expression in the eyes. Qwilleran patted his head. "Good dog! Good dog!"

On the way home he reflected that the evening would have been quite different if his auction package had been knocked down to Danielle Carmichael for her mandated cap of a thousand dollars. The conversation would have been about malls, football, and kinkajous instead of buttons, baseball, and carved wooden dogs, and she would never have referred to minutiae. Instead of a simple dress with Chanel jacket, she would have worn a sequinned cocktail sheath, thigh-high, and the other diners would not have applauded. Rather, they would have gasped, and some would have snickered. (This was Pickax, not Baltimore.) And the Christmas fund would have been five hundred dollars poorer. And he would not have heard the comment on the extraordinary pasty in the bake-off. By raising the ghost of Iris Cobb, Sarah might well be supporting his growing suspicions.

As soon as he arrived home, he made some phone calls. It was late but not too late for certain night owls of his acquaintance.

At the Riker residence, Mildred answered. "How was your fifteen-hundred-dollar dinner date?"

"Never mind that. Read about it in the 'Qwill Pen,'" he replied briskly. "Right now I'm interested in what the accountants' safe divulged. I read the winners' names in the paper today. Who baked the superpasty?"

"If I tell you, will you promise not to leak it? We're planning a feature, you know—the way you suggested."

He promised.

"Promise you won't even tell Polly?"

He promised again.

"Why are you so interested?"

"I'm writing a book on the origin and evolution of the pasty, from miner's lunch to gourmet treat."

"At this time of night? Come on, Qwill! You're keeping secrets."

"You're the one who's keeping secrets. I'm telling you flat-out that I'm writing a book." He was always on the verge of writing a book, but not about pasties. "Okay. It was Elaine Fetter of West Middle Hummock."

"I suspected as much."

"Do you know her?"

"Everybody knows her. And if I were you, I'd put that super-pasty feature on hold."

"What's the matter? What's this all about?"

"Tell you tomorrow. I'm in a hurry. Thanks for the information. Wake up your husband and tell him I said goodnight."

He hung up the phone without further civilities and called Celia Robinson. There had been lights in the carriage house when he drove in, and he knew she would be sitting up, reading the latest espionage thriller. In an undercover voice he asked, "Any luck?"

"You were right. I found what you wanted." She spoke in a hushed voice with abstract references. "There wasn't any name on it, but I checked what you mentioned. It's the real McCoy, all right."

"Good going!" he said. "Talk to you later."

And now, he wondered, how do we get our hands on it without embarrassing anyone? He sprawled in a lounge chair with his feet on an ottoman and cudgeled his brain. The Siamese sat quietly nearby, sensing that he was doing some concentrated thinking.

Suddenly, in one impulsive move, he swung his feet off the ottoman and went to the telephone desk. He called Hixie Rice at her apartment. There was no answer. He left a message on the machine.

Two minutes later she called back. "Sorry, Qwill. I've been avoiding someone. What's on your mind? How was your dinner date? What did you two talk about?"

"We talked about cats, dogs, baseball, buttons, pasties, and Iris Cobb, and that's why I'm calling you. I need to enlist your cooperation in a small, private, legal, innocuous intrigue."

"That's my specialty," she said.

"I want to run an ad in tomorrow's paper, if it isn't too late, but I must not be identified with it in any way. Can you handle that?"

"How big an ad?"

"Whatever it takes to be seen across the room: bold headline, sparse copy, plenty of white space."

"What's the message? Can you give it to me on the phone? I don't think I'm bugged."

He dictated about twenty words.

"Hmmm . . . interesting!" she said. "Do you expect results?"

"I don't need results," he told her. "This is a bluff. Stay tuned."

CHAPTER 16

The cheese-tasting was scheduled for Tuesday evening, and Qwilleran spent much of the day hanging out downtown. The reason was simple. The redoubtable Mrs. Fulgrove was coming to clean the main floor. The amiable Mr. O'Dell would do the floors and vacuum the furniture, but she would dust, scrub, polish, and complain—about public morals, politicians, the younger generation, popular music, and the cat hair, which she considered a Siamese conspiracy to make her work harder. The white-haired Pat O'Dell, on the other hand, usually had something constructive to say in his pleasing Irish brogue.

"Faith, an' it's a foine woman livin' upstairs o'er the garage," he said on this occasion.

"Yes, Mrs. Robinson is a cheerful and energetic soul," Qwilleran agreed.

"Her windows are in need of washin', I'm thinkin', what with so many cars in the parkin' lot and the exhaust leavin' a scum on the glass."

"Make arrangements with her to clean them, Mr. O'Dell, and send the bill to me." Celia had already remarked about the considerate and good-natured maintenance man; she thought she might invite him to dinner some evening and give him a good Irish stew.

So Qwilleran locked the Siamese in their loft apartment and made his getaway before Mrs. Fulgrove loomed on the scene. First, he stopped at the library to see if they had any books on button collecting, in case he should want to write a column on the hobby at some future date. They did. He leafed through one of them and was pleased to find his cat-button pictured and described as a valuable collectible.

Then he went to breakfast at the Scottish Bakery: scones, clotted cream, and currant jam served by a bonnie lassie wearing a plaid apron. The coffee was not bad, either.

Next he visited the health food store, whose bearded proprietor was the husband of the *Something*'s new feature editor. "Welcome to Pickax!" Qwilleran said. "We're always glad to give asylum to defectors from Lockmaster."

"Thank you. We like it here, although the bombing and the murder shook us up, I don't mind telling you."

"It's not a local crime wave, I assure you. It's a spillover from Down Below." Qwilleran patted his moustache with confidence. "Okay if I just browse around?"

He wandered among the vitamin bottles with strange names, trays of muffins with unusual ingredients, meatless sandwiches, and fruit and vegetables without the waxed finish that made them look so good at Toodle's Market. Then there were the snacks. What looked like a chocolate chip cookie had no butter, no sugar, and no chocolate. What looked like a potato chip was made without fat, salt, or potato.

Qwilleran said, "I have a friend who'll be a good customer of yours. Tell me honestly, do your kids eat this stuff?"

"Oh, sure! Our family goes in for alternatives. Our kids were brought up that way, and they think junk food is weird."

From there Qwilleran walked to the police station to inquire about Lenny Inchpot. The witness to the bombing had been found and put on a plane to Duluth, where he would stay with his aunt for a while.

At the Chamber of Commerce across the street, he found them making plans for a Lois Inchpot Day in Pickax, in an effort to lure her back to town and reopen her lunchroom. The mayor would issue a proclamation to that effect, and loyal customers were painting the walls and ceiling, water-stained from the last roof leak.

Then it was time for a bowl of soup at the Spoonery. The day's specials were bouillabaisse, roasted peanut with garlic, sausage and white bean, and chicken with rice and dill. Qwilleran played safe with the bean soup.

After that he visited the Kitchen Boutique to buy a thermometer, basting syringe, and roaster with rack. He was going to roast that blasted bird if it was the last thing he ever did in his life.

Triumphantly, Sharon said, "Mother and I knew you'd break down and start cooking—someday."

"Don't bet on it," he said. "I'm just picking these up for a friend." It was one of the impromptu prevarications that he had developed into an art.

By that time the Tuesday edition of the paper was on the street, and he read his ad. Within a few hours the entire county would be talking about it:

$10,000 REWARD

for information leading to the recovery of the late Iris Cobb's personal recipe book, missing since her death. Confidentiality guaranteed. Write to P.O. Box 1362, Pickax City.

When Qwilleran returned to the barn, the cleaning crew had gone and there was not a cat hair or mite of dust to be seen. He climbed the ramp to the top level and opened the door to the loft apartment. "Okay, you can come out and start shedding," he said.

In the kitchen he tested the progress of the thawing turkey, and before he could close the door, Koko executed a *grand jeté* over the bar and landed in the refrigerator with the bird.

"Out!" Qwilleran yelled, dragging him from the refrigerator and slamming it shut. The cat howled as if his tail had been caught in the door. "Don't overreact, you slyboots! Cats are supposed to be known for their patience."

Koko went slinking away, licking his wounded feline ego.

Qwilleran dressed for the cheese-tasting in dinner jacket and black tie, with a rare set of black studs in his shirt-front. They were from India, inlaid with silver and gold—a gift from Polly. Appraising himself in the full-length mirror, he had to admit that he looked good in evening clothes.

It was dark when the jitneys started delivering the well-dressed guests, and the exterior lights transformed the barn into an enchanted castle. Indoors, mysterious illumination from hidden sources dramatized the balconies and overhead beams, the white fireplace cube and its soaring white stacks, the contemporary tapestries, and the clean-cut modern furniture. Add to that the glamor of beaded dinner dresses, the courtliness of men in evening wear, and the bonhomie of such on occasion; it had all the ingredients of a magical evening, one never to be forgotten in Pickax, for more reasons than one.

John Bushland was on hand with a camcorder, the idea being to sell videos of the festivities and raise an extra thousand or two for a good cause. Although distinguished guests received ample coverage, the Siamese received more than their share of footage. They sat on the fireplace cube, watching in an attitude of wonder. Later they would sail to the floor like flying squirrels, Koko on the trail of cheese crumbs and Yum Yum on the lookout for shoelaces. As the proliferating number of feet endangered her tail, she fled to the first balcony and watched from the railing.

Among those present were the Rikers, Lanspeaks, and Wilmots; the mayor in his red paisley cummerbund; Don Exbridge with his new wife and his former wife; and the new banker with the flashy Danielle. If one wanted to count, there were three attorneys, four doctors, two accountants, one judge, and five public officials coming up for re-election. One of them was the cranky but popular Amanda Goodwinter, running again for city council and wearing a dinner dress she had worn for thirty years.

The focus of attention was the dinner table, with its silver punch bowls and lighted candles. Flanking it were the two white-skirted buffets, each with eight cheese platters and a large wheel of Cheddar. Jerry Sip and Jack Nibble presided at the buffets, assisted by college students looking professional in white duck coats.

Jack Nibble was heard to say, "We have three blues on the cheese table. Try all three and compare; it's the only way to learn. The one from France is crumbly; the Italian is spreadable; the one from England slices well."

And Dr. Prelligate replied, "Do I detect nuances in your observation?"

"Anyway you eat it," said Amanda Goodwinter, "it's still moldy cheese."

Then Jerry Sip said, "If you like a rich, creamy cheese with superb flavor, try the double-cream Brie."

"Yow!" came an endorsement from the floor.

Amanda said, "That cat and yours truly are the only ones here who tell it like it is!"

Pender Wilmot, who had cats of his own, said, "They all know the word 'cream' when they hear it."

"I have it on good authority," said Big Mac, "that Qwill feeds his on caviar and escargots. Too bad he can't take them as dependents."

"They're so elegant!" Dr. Diane enthused. "We have to dress up for special occasions, but Siamese always look formally attired." She gazed up at Yum Yum on the balcony railing, and the little female turned her head this way and that to show off her left and right profiles. "They're also vain!"

Not all the conversation was about cats and cheese. There were speculations about the bombing, the murder, and the $10,000 reward. Riker pulled Qwilleran aside and demanded, "Did you run that ad? You're crazy! Who's going to pay off?"

"Don't worry, Arch. No one will claim it, but it's large enough to put a lot of sleuths on the trail. I'm betting that the guilty person will mail the cookbook anonymously to the P.O. box, rather than be exposed."

Qwilleran circulated, listening and looking for ideas. He was always the columnist, always on duty, always hoping for material to fill the space on page two above the fold. What he heard was mostly small talk:

Don Exbridge: "It's never safe to recommend a restaurant. If you do, the chef quits the next day, the management replaces him with a hash-slinger, and your friends think you have a tin palate."

Larry Lanspeak: "Has anyone been to the Boulder House Inn? The chef grows his own herbs and knows how to cook vegetables—with a bone in them."

Carol Lanspeak: "Qwill, there's a fuchsia silk blouse at the store that Polly would love—scarf neck, drop shoulder. In fact, I've laid one aside in her size. If you want me to, I'll gift-wrap it and drop it off here."

Pender Wilmot: "Who's interested in starting a gourmet club? I'm taking applications."

Arch Riker: "Deal us in—but not if it's just another dinner club where you talk about the national deficit while you're eating. I want to learn something about food and wine."

Mildred Riker: "Someone has said that food worth eating is worth talking about."

Qwilleran: "Would this be a club for gourmands, gourmets, or gastronomes?"

Don Exbridge: "Get the dictionary, somebody!"

Dr. Diane: "How would it work? Would we flock around to restaurants? Or would we have to cook?"

Willard Carmichael: "In Detroit we belonged to a hands-on group. The host planned the menu and prepared the entrée. Other members were assigned to bring the other courses. Recipes were provided—all unusual, but not freaky. No fried grasshoppers."

Danielle Carmichael: "You had to follow the recipe exactly or pay a forfeit—like running the dishwasher or paying for the wine."

Qwilleran: "I'll join if I can be permanent dishwasher."

Amanda Goodwinter: "Don't put my name on the list. The last time I attended a gourmet dinner, I had indigestion for a month!"

The evening wore on, with much consumption of cheese and the amber-colored punch. Voices grew louder. A few couples started to leave. Suddenly there was a commotion in the kitchen—a thumping and growling, followed by a shattering crash! Conversation stopped abruptly, and Qwilleran rushed to the scene. Koko was having a cat fit. He raced around the kitchen in a frenzy, flinging himself at the refrigerator.

When Qwilleran tried to intervene, the cat leaped over the bar and crashed into a lamp, sending the shade and the base flying in opposite directions. Women screamed and men yelled as he zipped around the fireplace cube and headed for the cheese tables.

"Stop him!" Qwilleran shouted as the cat skidded through the cheese platters and scattered crumbs of Roquefort, cubes of Cheddar, slices of Gouda, and gobs of runny Brie, before leaping to the punch table and knocking over the lighted candles.

"Fire!" someone shouted.

Qwilleran dashed to a closet for a fire extinguisher, at the same time bellowing, "Grab him! Grab him!"

Three men tore after the mad cat as he streaked around the fireplace cube with fur flying. Pender, Larry, and Big Mac tore after him, bumping into the furniture and each other. Around and around they went.

"Somebody go the other way!"

Somebody did, but the trapped animal only sailed to the top of the cube and looked down on his pursuers.

"We've got him!"

A moment later Koko swooped over their heads and pelted up the ramp, not stopping until he reached the roof, where he perched on a beam and licked his fur.

Qwilleran was embarrassed. "My apologies! The cat went berserk! I don't know why."

"He drank some of Jerry's amber punch," Big Mac suggested.

Truthfully, Koko wanted everyone to go home, Qwilleran suspected, leaving him unlimited access to the cheese tables.

The guests were understanding but decided it was time to think about leaving. The dinner jackets on Larry, Pender, and Big Mac looked more like gray fur than black wool. A few cat hairs might have been an annoyance, but a million cat hairs—thanks to the amber punch—made it a joke. It was a merry crowd that boarded the jitneys, twelve at a time, for the ride back to the parking lot, and the students cleaning up the mess grinned to each other; it was the best thing that would happen all semester.

The Sip 'n' Nibble partners were philosophical. Jerry said, "Don't feel bad about it, Qwill. There's nothing like a minor catastrophe to make a party a success. They'll talk about this for the rest of the century."

"That's what I'm afraid of."

"I just hope they mention the name of our store," Jack added, "including the address and telephone number."

Carol said, "It was really funny to see three adult males chasing a little cat in a cloud of flying fur! I wonder if Koko has any left. It was better than a car chase! Aren't we lucky that Bushy got it on tape? We'll sell loads of videos."

Jack Nibble summed it up. "I'd say we achieved our goals: to show everyone a good time and educate a few palates. And it doesn't have to be double-cream to be good; the feta we brought is low-fat."

"Yow!" came a loud affirmative from somewhere overhead.

When everyone had gone, with promises to send a clean-up crew the next day, Qwilleran changed into a jumpsuit and went into the kitchen. Koko was ahead of him, trying to claw his way into the refrigerator. "You rascal!" Qwilleran said. "So that's why you wanted everyone to go home! If you'll just cool it, we'll prep the turkey tonight and throw it in the oven first thing in the morning. Stand back!" He opened the refrigerator door cautiously, expecting a flank attack, but Koko knew when the battle was won. He watched calmly as the prepping began.

Qwilleran remembered Mildred's instructions: Remove the plastic wrap; release the legs without cutting the skin; explore the two cavities. He put his hand gingerly into the breast cavity and withdrew a plastic bag containing the neck. Then he turned the bird around and, with more confidence, explored the body cavity. It was cold but not frosty. Koko was watching with ears back and whiskers bristled. Qwilleran groped for the plastic bag. Instead, he found something hard and very, very cold. His first thought was: a block of ice. His second was: a practical joke! He threw everything back into the tray and shoved the naked bird into the refrigerator. Then he called Nick Bamba at home.

"Hope I'm not calling too late, Nick. Just wanted to thank you for the *cold* turkey. I'm getting it ready to roast tomorrow . . . Yes, thanks to Mildred, I know how. But I have one question: Was there supposed to be anything *special* about the bird you delivered to me? . . . No, there's nothing wrong with it. I just had a . . . *special feeling* about it." He tamped his moustache. "Thanks again, Nick. I'll let you know how it turns out."

Hanging up the phone, Qwilleran kept his hand on the receiver. Should he, or should he not, call the police chief at home again?

He punched the number that he knew by heart, and when the gruff voice answered, he said, "We had the cheese-tasting here tonight, you know, and Jerry and Jack left a variety of cheeses. Why don't you run over for a nibble—and a sip? Also . . . I have something peculiar to report—very peculiar!"

"I'll be there in two shakes," Brodie said. He arrived in a matter of minutes, and his first comment was: "You've got a big box at your back door."

"That's an antique sea chest. It's for package deliveries."

"And you've moved the furniture around."

"That was to accommodate the crowd. We had a hundred guests. The committee is coming tomorrow to put everything back the way it was."

They sat at the bar, where Qwilleran had ready a Scotch and a plate of leftover party cheeses. He pointed out Cheddar, Gouda, Bel Paese, Emmenthaler, Stilton, and Port du Salut.

"Where's the one I like so much?"

"Try the Emmenthaler, Andy. There wasn't any Gruyère left. Everyone liked the Gruyère."

"Yow!"

"Including our smart cat."

When Brodie had finished his first Scotch, Qwilleran said, "Before I top your glass, Andy, I'd like you to look at a gift I received Sunday." Keeping one eye on Koko, he brought the turkey from the refrigerator and pushed the tray toward the chief. "What would you say this is?"

"Are you pullin' my leg? It's a turkey!"

"Do you know how to stuff a bird?"

Brodie scowled. "That's my wife's job."

"Well, let me explain. This is the head-end, and that's the tail-end. There are two cavities. Put your hand in the breast cavity and see what you find."

Reluctantly and suspiciously, the chief did as instructed and drew out a plastic bag. "That's the neck! Are you playin' games?"

"Now put your hand in the body cavity. That's where they always store the sack of giblets."

With a glowering glance at his friend, Brodie thrust his hand into the bird. Immediately, a strange expression spread across his craggy face. It was a mixture of shock and disbelief. "What the hell!" he blurted as he drew forth a small handgun. "Who gave you this bird?"

"Nick Bamba. It was frozen solid when it arrived—probably part of a shipment going Down Below. It's been thawing in the fridge for two days, and Koko's been going crazy. Do you want a plastic bag for the evidence?"

"Gimme a trash bag," Andy said. "I'm taking the whole bird."

"There goes your turkey," Qwilleran said to Koko. To his surprise, the cat seemed unconcerned, sitting on his haunches in his kangaroo pose and grooming a small patch of fur on his chest. Could it be that Koko sensed there was something not quite right about that turkey? Qwilleran himself sensed there was something not quite right at the Cold Turkey Farm. Nick Bamba, he knew, needed a large work force, since young turkeys required much attention. Supervisory and technical posts were held by full-time workers with special skills, but there were jobs for college students and others needing part time employment or a second source of income. Nick's contingency payroll included off-duty police officers, clerks from the public library, the beefy installer from the design studio, an alterations apprentice from the men's store, and two of Mrs. Toodle's grandchildren. Lenny Inchpot wanted to sign on, after his job at the hotel blew up, but his mother vetoed it for reasons of her own.

Did one of these employees shoot the florist and hide the gun in a turkey to be shipped Down Below? Was it assumed that the bird would be lost in a labyrinth of human chaos in some distant metropolis? That was hardly smart thinking; the plastic wrapper clearly identified its source. On the other hand, the lucky recipient might consider it a wonderful Crackerjack prize—something to keep handy for the next prowler, attacker, mugger, burglar, carjacker, or other urban menace.

So . . . who was guilty of the homicide, and was he the accomplice of the original bomber? Certainly it was not the fresh-faced

Toodle grandchildren . . . nor the fun-loving bumpkin who installed wall-to-wall carpet for Amanda . . . nor the honeybees' best friend, who was too humane to hook a fish or swat a fly.

It was after midnight. Qwilleran wondered if Aubrey Scotten had recovered enough to report to his midnight shift at the Cold Turkey Farm. Or had his mother stuffed him with homemade food and sent him to bed early?

CHAPTER 17

The morning after the cheese-tasting and Koko's calamitous catfit, the Country Club sent a crew to remove the folding tables and silver punch bowls and return the furniture to its normal arrangement. Meanwhile, Qwilleran spent the morning in his balcony studio, writing a thousand words about cheese. In two weeks he had learned a great deal from Jack Nibble and quoted him at length: "Never grate cheese in advance . . . To get your money's worth from cheese, serve it at room temperature . . . Cheese belongs with a good meal and makes a bad one better."

In the afternoon, Qwilleran went for a long bike ride, hoping to clarify his thinking on various matters; too much had been happening too fast. He walked through the woods to the carriage house, where his bike was parked in one of the stalls, and waved to Celia Robinson. She was having a jolly conversation with Mr. O'Dell, who was there to blow fallen leaves into huge piles for the city's vacuum truck.

"Nice man," she commented to Qwilleran as he tested the air in his tires. "Isn't this a wonderful day for a bike ride? Where are you going?"

"Out Ittibittiwassee Road to the stone bridge and back the same way."

"Oh, my! That's quite a ways! How long will it take?"

"Couple of hours."

"Well, be careful. Get back before dark!"

Ittibittiwassee Road, part of the route for the Labor Day Race, still had the orange-and-white markers planted on the shoulder by the Pedal Club. They would remain in place until November, at which time the county snowplows would send them flying through the air like toothpicks. When Qwilleran turned onto the highway at the Dimsdale Diner, the first milepost he encountered was number 15. From there he ticked off his thoughts by the mile:

Milepost 16: What to write for Tuesday's paper? Should be about food. The dictionary says turnips are edible. How about a thousand derogatory words about turnips? People live on them in times of famine or war; that's why they're such a depressing vegetable. We call a bad play or movie a turkey; in France they call it a turnip. The *Larousse Encyclopedia* says that turnips can be boiled, scalloped, glazed, stuffed, creamed, molded, puréed, or souffléd. I say: Any way you mash it, it's still a turnip. Has it ever been used as fertilizer? Brodie says you can make a bomb out of fertilizer. Is there such a thing as a turnip bomb?

Milepost 18: Too bad about the shiitake. It would make a good column, but not until the family situation is straightened out. Are the mushrooms his or hers? Where was Donald during the interview? She never even mentioned him. Is she hiding something? If so, what? Celia says mother and son don't get along well.

Milepost 19: How to handle it tactfully? Down Below they'd try to probe family secrets and make a scandal out of it.

Milepost 20: The shiitake had a great taste. Butter, garlic, parsley, and freshly ground pepper, she said. Polly will be interested, except for the butter.

Milepost 22: First, shiitake; and now Iris's cookbook. What's going on in Madame Fetter's kitchen? Did she pilfer the book from the museum? Or is she a receiver of stolen goods? She must have known it was hot. The museum had appealed for its return, no questions asked.

Milepost 25: Everyone's talking about the reward and P.O. Box 1362. How will Madame Fetter react? Will she have any qualms about an exposé? Will she take some sort of action? If she takes the book to the post office to be weighed for postage, those savvy postal clerks will notice that it's local—going to Box 1362—with no return address. They'll recognize her. They know everyone who's ever bought a stamp.

Milepost 26: Even if she mails it from Lockmaster, it's risky. The *Ledger* picked up the story of the reward. So maybe she won't try to mail it at all. She could burn it—after copying a few of the recipes. She could plant it in someone else's kitchen and claim the reward herself. Just a thought; she can't be that low. Or someone who's seen the book in her kitchen could squeal, and I'd have to fork over money for information I already have.

Milepost 29: Too bad I didn't take the book myself when I was there. I was lawfully on the premises, and the book is lawfully mine. No crime! And she couldn't accuse me without incriminating herself. I could have Celia sneak it out of the kitchen, but that's burglary; it's not her own property. I can't involve Celia in anything that might blow her cover. She's too valuable to me.

At that point, Qwilleran reached the stone bridge, took a breather, and biked home, arriving just before dusk. After stabling his bike in the carriage house, he walked to the barn on bicycle legs—with bent knees and bouncing gait. In the sea chest he found two deliveries: a Lanspeak Department Store bag and a foil-wrapped brick, slightly warm. The Siamese knew what it was and gave him a clamoring welcome.

"Okay! Okay! Later!" he said, tossing the brick into the refrigerator for security reasons. Then he turned his attention to the Lanspeak bag. Before opening it, he said to himself, Hey, wait a minute; it's too heavy for a silk blouse! It was indeed heavy. It was a thick, black, scuffed, greasy notebook with loose pages.

"Ye gods!" he said aloud. "It's Iris's cookbook!" He rushed to the phone, followed by two demanding cats. "Later! Later!" he shouted at them.

After two rings he heard Celia's voice saying playfully, "Carriage House Inn-on-the-Park. May I help you?"

"I'd like to reserve a table for six for dinner," he said.

"Oh, I'm sorry, Chief. I thought it was—someone else. Did you find my meatloaf?"

"Yes, and we all thank you profusely, but that's not all I found!"

"Were you surprised?"

"That's putting it mildly. I didn't expect you to . . . help yourself to the evidence."

"I didn't!" she cried defensively. "It was given to me!"

"Well! That's a surprise. Did Mrs. Fetter explain its illegal presence on her bookshelf?"

"No! No! Donald gave it to me! He saw me reading it and said, 'Why don't you take that *something-something* piece of *something* home and keep it? Mom's not supposed to have it anyway. But don't tell her I gave it to you.' Those aren't his exact words, but that's the idea."

"Well! What can I say? Was that on Monday?"

"Yes, when I went out there with the junior trainee. Sorry I didn't deliver it to you right away. I wanted to copy a few of the recipes. I hope you don't mind."

"Celia, not only do I not object; I'm promoting you to Senior Executive Assistant in charge of Sensitive Investigations."

Her laughter rang out as he said good night. For a while he stared at the phone. He was thinking, If Donald had waited another twenty-four hours, he could have turned in his own mother and collected the reward . . . although he might have had to split it with her.

He examined the cookbook, oblivious of the caterwauling around him. The black cover was gray with decades of spilled flour; Iris had always boasted of being a sloppy cook. It bulged with loose pages and yellowed newspaper clippings, liberally spotted and smeared. Qwilleran thought he could identify bacon grease, tomato juice, olive oil, chocolate, coffee, and blood. Splashes of liquid had blotted some of the handwriting, which was virtually indecipherable even at its best. He went to his studio and typed a release for the *Moose County Something* and *Lockmaster Ledger*.

A missing cookbook, originally owned by Iris Cobb, has been anonymously returned to its rightful owners, the Klingenschoen Foundation, which intends to publish it. The announcement of a $10,000 reward for information leading to its recovery produced no tips or clues, according to a spokesperson for the K Fund. The return of the book was voluntary, and no inquiries will be made.

It was while he was giving the Siamese a couple of slices of meatloaf that the phone rang. His hello brought only labored breathing. "Hello?" he repeated with a questioning inflection.

Then he heard a high-pitched voice say, "I'm gonna kill myself." The words were spoken in a monotone, but desperation made them almost falsetto.

"What? What did you say? Is this Aubrey?"

"I'm gonna kill myself."

"Where are you? Are you at your mother's house?"

"I come home. I come home to get a gun. I'm gonna shoot myself."

Qwilleran had heard suicide threats before. Aubrey needed to talk to someone.

"What did your mother think about your leaving?"

"Di'n't tell her."

"How did you get home?"

"Walked."

"Where was she when you left?"

"Diggin' in the yard."

"Don't you think you should have told her?"

"She don't need me. She's got her grandkids. I'm gonna shoot myself."

"But who would take care of your bees? They need you! You told me yourself, they're your friends."

"They're gone. I smoked 'em out."

"Did you blame them for what happened? They didn't know what they were doing."

There was a breathy pause. "I'm goin' crazy. Can't eat. Can't sleep. I'm gonna shoot myself."

"Now, wait a minute, Big Boy. We have to talk about this. I'm your friend. I want to know what's troubling you."

"I got the old man's gun. I'm gonna put it under my chin and pull the trigger."

"Okay, but don't do anything until I get there! I'm leaving right away—do you hear? I'll be there in ten minutes. Turn the outside lights on."

Qwilleran grabbed his jacket and car keys and had the presence of mind to throw the remainder of the meatloaf in the refrigerator. Without saying goodbye, he rushed out the door to his car. Gunning the motor, he bumped through the darkening woods and made a tire-screeching turn onto Park Circle, heading for Sandpit Road. Traffic was light at that hour, and he could speed. Reaching Black Creek, he looked across the forlorn landscape and saw the yard lights of the Limburger house in the distance. It meant that Aubrey had been listening; he was obeying orders.

Qwilleran parked at the curb and hurried to the lighted veranda. As he climbed the crumbling brick steps, the front door opened, and a ghost of a man stood there, his shoulders drooping, his face almost as white as his hair, and his eyes unfocused.

"Thanks for turning on the lights," Qwilleran said, following the shuffling feet into the front hall. A single dim lightbulb burned in the branched chandelier. The door to the gun cabinet was open. "Look here, Big Boy," he said. "Let's go somewhere and have a good talk, friend-to-friend. Let's get away from this gloomy place. Everything will turn out all right. Don't worry. You need to talk to someone who understands, when you're feeling down. Come on. Let's go. Turn out the lights. Lock the door."

Aubrey needed someone to take charge. He did as he was told, moving slowly as if in a trance. Then Qwilleran took him by the elbow and piloted him down the steps and into the car.

He could write a thousand words for his column with the greatest of ease, but he had to work hard to fill the silence that amplified the rumble of the motor as they drove to Pickax. "It's a nice night. Crisp but not chilly. Just what you expect in early October. Soon it will be Halloween—then Thanksgiving, before we know it. We haven't had Indian summer as yet, though. After that, anything can happen. Dark, isn't it? No moon tonight. You can see the glow on the horizon from the Pickax streetlights. Not much traffic tonight. No one goes out on Wednesday night . . . There's the Dimsdale Diner. They stay open all night. You never see any trucks in the parking lot, though. I think the cook sleeps behind the counter. His pancakes are the worst I've ever eaten. I wonder what he does to them. They say Lois is going to open her lunchroom again."

While he talked about everything and nothing, his passenger slumped in a stupor. Qwilleran hoped that his planned shock treatment would work. They turned off Park Circle, crossed the theatre parking lot, and plunged into the woods. As they emerged from the dark stand of evergreens, Qwilleran reached for the remote control, and instantaneous floodlights turned the towering barn into something unreal. Aubrey sat up and stared.

"An old apple barn," Qwilleran told him. "Built more than a hundred years ago. Wait till you see the inside."

As they walked through the kitchen door, he pressed a single switch that illuminated balconies, ramps, beams, and the giant fireplace cube. Two cats who had been sleeping on the sofa rose, arched their backs, stretched, and jumped down to inspect the visitor. They circled him inquisitively, sniffing his field boots and finding them quite fascinating.

"What are they?" Aubrey asked.

"Siamese cats. Very friendly. You can see they're attracted to you. They know you like animals. The little female is Yum Yum; the male is Koko. Talk to them. Tell them your name."

"Aubrey," the man said hesitantly.

"Yow!" Koko replied in his piercing Siamese baritone.

Qwilleran said, "See? He's pleased to meet you. Take off your jacket and sit down in that comfortable chair. Would you like some cheese and crackers? What do you drink? Coffee? Beer? Wine? Ginger ale?"

"Beer," Aubrey said in a daze as he sank into the deep cushioned chair. He could not take his eyes from the cats, who were milling about gracefully, striking poses, gazing at him, doing all the right things, as if they had been assigned to patient therapy.

Yum Yum made a half-hearted pass at the laces of the field boots before jumping into Aubrey's lap and kneading in the crook of his elbow, purring loudly. Then she looked up at him with soulful eyes.

Qwilleran thought, She's a witch!

"Big eyes," Aubrey said. "Why's she lookin' at me like that?"

"She wants to play Blink. She stares at you, you stare at her, and the first one who blinks loses the game." He put a can of beer and a plate of cheese at Aubrey's elbow.

Then it was Koko's turn to do his mesmerizing act. He jumped to the arm of the big chair and sniffed Aubrey's sleeve. Then the cold wet nose traveled up his sleeve and sniffed his ear.

"It tickles," he said, almost smiling.

"Do you know that cats have twenty-four whiskers on each side? They're all guaranteed to tickle. Count them and see if I'm right."

Aubrey turned his head and met the hypnotic gaze, eyeball to eyeball.

Qwilleran thought, They know he's troubled. Cats have a natural aptitude for care-giving. He said, "Give Koko a taste of cheese, and he'll be your friend for life."

The man followed orders and was pleased when both cats took crumbs of cheese from his fingers. "Just like a dog I used to have," he said. "His name was Spot—black and white—mixed breed. On'y way he'd eat was from my hand. I never saw cats like these . . . You let 'em in the house!" he added in surprise.

"This is where they live. They never go outdoors."

Aubrey stroked their silky fur constantly while he talked.

Qwilleran thought, It's a miracle; he's talking!

Aubrey went on, as though some healing flow of energy was passing from the cats to the man. "When Spot was killed, I di'n't want another dog. I joined the Navy. I was gonna learn electronics. I like that stuff. But I had an accident. I hadda come home."

Cautiously and with all the kindliness he could muster, Qwilleran asked, "What kind of accident?"

"I come near drownin'. When I come to, I thought I was dead. I felt different. But I wasn't dead. I was in sick bay. The medics said I owed my life to my buddy. Vic, his name was. He jumped in after me. They said there was sharks all around."

"Frightening experience."

"When somebody saves your life, you owe 'im one. That's what they say."

"Do you still keep in touch with . . . Vic?"

Aubrey turned a horrified face to Qwilleran. "That was him in the cabin!" He broke down in a fit of sobbing, covering his large face with his hands.

"That's all right," Qwilleran said soothingly. "It's good to let go. Get it off your chest."

The Siamese were alarmed but stayed nearby—each a silent but sympathetic presence. When the sobbing finally subsided and Aubrey started wiping his face on his sleeve, Qwilleran offered handfuls of tissues. The man clutched at them.

"Now you'll feel better," Qwilleran said.

He was right. Aubrey relaxed into dazed tranquility.

"Perhaps you're ready for something to eat now—a meatloaf sandwich?"

"Yeah. I'm hungry."

"Let's go and sit at the bar. We'll take the cheese with us, so the cats don't get it."

Aubrey hunched over the bar and devoured cheese and crackers and drank beer while Qwilleran threw together sandwiches with Celia's meatloaf, mustard, and dill pickle. Then, after two sandwiches and three cans of beer, Aubrey wanted to talk. Words poured forth in a torrent of disconnected thoughts and naive remarks.

Qwilleran listened attentively. Suddenly he said, "Excuse me a moment. I'll be right back." He spiraled up the circular staircase that led from the kitchen to his studio and made a phone call. At the first gruff hello, he thundered, "Where's Koko's turkey? He wants his turkey!"

"It's at the lab," Brodie said, sounding grumpy. "Buy him another one. You can afford it. Is that all you called about?"

"Not by a long shot. Seriously, Andy, I hate to bother you again, but I think you should haul your bagpipe over here on the double. It's important. I want you to meet someone."

"What the hell kind of invitation is that?" the chief demanded. He sounded as if his favorite TV program had been interrupted.

"Trust me. You won't be sorry."

"Business or pleasure?"

"Tonight it's just a friendly get-together. You're off-duty. You just happen to drop in for a drink . . . But tomorrow it may be police business. Tonight it's off-the record, off-the-cuff, and off-the-wall."

"Get out the Scotch," Brodie said. "I'll be right there."

CHAPTER 18

Qwilleran and his guest had finished eating their sandwiches at the bar and were back in the lounge area with mugs of coffee. The Siamese were still hanging around, having been fed crumbs of cheese and crumbles of meatloaf by their new friend. Without warning, Koko's body stiffened and his head jerked toward the back door. Then he scampered to the kitchen to look through the window.

"Koko can see headlights and hear motors when they're half a mile away," Qwilleran explained.

Minutes later, a weird noise came from the parking lot, and he jumped up to investigate. Andrew Brodie was approaching the kitchen door, his bagpipe skirling a Scottish tune.

"Is this the place where they give free drinks to pipers?" he called out as Qwilleran went to meet him.

"Depends how good you are. As a matter of fact, I've always wanted to hear bagpipe music in the barn. The acoustics are phenomenal."

Brodie dropped his bagpipe in the kitchen and swaggered into the lounge area, where a hefty young man with white hair was sitting with one cat on his lap and another on his shoulder. "Aubrey! What are you doing here, for Pete's sake?" he barked. "Playing St. Francis?"

"Hi, Andy. I had a big sandwich and a coupla beers, and now I'm talkin' to the cats. They're friendly. We play Blink. D'you know how to play Blink?"

Qwilleran said, "You guys seem to know each other."

"Cripes, I've known Aubrey ever since he was in high school and I was with the sheriff. I know all his brothers, too. And his mother grows the best flowers in the county! How's she doin', Aubrey?"

"Mom's got some arthritis, but she's doin' all right. She still makes flapjacks better'n Lois's. D'you know Lois's lunchroom is closed?"

"Don't worry. She'll be back in business again. She's always threatening to close . . . Who are your two friends?"

"This one's Yum Yum, and this one's Koko. He wants to tickle my ears with his whiskers."

Qwilleran said to Brodie, "Make yourself comfortable. Have some cheese. Aubrey was telling me an interesting story. As an old friend of the family, you ought to hear it."

Turning to the young man, the off-duty chief said, "Aren't you the one that reported the body down by the river?"

"Yeah. I found him in my cabin. That's where I live. The family used to have five cabins for rent. Now there's only one left, and I live there with my bees. The hives are on the side that gets the sun and not the north wind. They gave me a lot of honey this summer. Did you ever taste my honey? It's darker than most. It has a lot of flavor." He turned to Qwilleran. "You've tasted my honey. Do you think it's got a lot of flavor?"

"It's the best!" said Qwilleran, wondering if Aubrey had forgotten that his bees were gone.

Brodie took a gulp of his drink. "How come this fisherman was renting your cabin last weekend?"

"I knew him a long time. He liked to come up and fish for bass sometimes. I always let him use my cabin, and the old man would let me sleep in the big house. He's in the hospital now. Did you know he's in the hospital, Andy?"

"Yes, I heard he was in a bad way."

"It's the kidneys and pros—pros—"

"Prostate," Qwilleran said.

"When he kicks the bucket, I'm gonna get his Bible. That's what he told me. It's German. I can't read it, but it's got gold edges and gold letters on the cover." He turned to Qwilleran again. "You saw it. Is it real leather?"

"Yes, it's real leather and a very handsome book." Then, to get the story back on track, he asked, "Aubrey, didn't you say your friend spent his honeymoon in your cabin, some years back?"

"Yeah. He married a nice lady, but she di'n't like fly fishin', so she never come up again. He always come alone. He tied his own flies. He was real good at it. D'you like fly-fishin', Andy?"

"Can't say that I do. Had your friend ever had trouble with the bees before?"

Aubrey shook his head solemnly, and Qwilleran reminded him, "Didn't you mention that he'd been drinking heavily Saturday night? From what I've learned of honeybees, that might have antagonized them . . . Tell Andy how you met this guy, Aubrey."

"Yeah." Without a flicker of emotion he related the story of his near-drowning and the heroic act that saved his life. "Vic always said I owed him one for saving my life. That's why I always let him use my cabin for free any time he wanted. His name was Victor, but I called him Vic. He'd call up from Down Below and say, 'How's about usin' your shanty for a coupla days, Big Boy?' He always called me Big Boy. He'd fly up here, and I'd pick him up at the airport. He'd do some fishin' and I'd do my chores, and we'd eat his catch for supper, and I'd boil some turnips. I make 'em like my mom does—mashed with butter and salt and pepper." He turned to Qwilleran. "D'you like turnips?"

"No!" was the vehement reply.

"You'd like 'em mashed with butter and salt and—"

Brodie interrupted. "What did Vic do for a living?"

"Electronics. That's what I wanted to do, but I di'n't get a chance. I hadda come home."

"Another Scotch, Andy?" Qwilleran asked. "How about you, Big Boy? Some more coffee? Then tell us about seeing Vic's wife at the Black Bear Café a couple of weeks ago."

"Yeah. They weren't married anymore. She got a divorce. I don't know why. She was a nice lady. I saw her at the Black Bear. She was with some man. Her hair was different, but I could tell it was her. She di'n't see me. When Vic called me long distance next time, I told him. He was surprised. I knew he'd be surprised. Coupla days after, he called me up again. I like gettin' long-distance calls, don't you?" He looked at his two listeners, who nodded. "He told me to meet him at the airport."

"But at Lockmaster, not Mooseville," Qwilleran said with a significant glance at Brodie.

"Yeah. Lockmaster. Nice airport. Bigger'n ours. Takes longer to get there, but I di'n't care. He was my best friend. I owed him one. That's what Vic always said. He was kinda quiet when I picked him up. He said he still loved his wife—I forget her name— and he wanted to make up. He had a birthday present for her. He said he paid a lotta money for it. It was all wrapped in silver paper and fancy ribbons. He said it would be a big surprise."

"Damn right it was a big surprise," Brodie muttered.

"Go on, Aubrey," Qwilleran encouraged.

"Next day, he borrowed my truck and drove around. Don't know where he went, but he put a lotta miles on it. I hadda buy gas. Come afternoon, I drove him to the hotel so he could leave the present and a bunch of flowers he bought somewheres. Then I drove him back to Lockmaster."

Brodie asked, "When did you find out the birthday present was a bomb?"

"Goin' to the airport. I di'n't know what to think. I di'n't know what to say. I asked him why. He said he loved her and di'n't want nobody else to get her. He told me to keep my mouth shut or I'd be arrested. He said I hadda buy a paper and see what they printed about it. I hadda cut it out and send it to him. I wanted to call him long distance, but he said no. I di'n't feel good about it, but . . . I owed him one."

"How did you feel when you learned the bomb killed the housekeeper?"

"I felt sick. She was Lenny's girlfriend—Lenny Inchpot. They were gonna get married." Aubrey jumped up. "I hafta go outside a minute."

"There's a bathroom right off the kitchen," Qwilleran said, but Aubrey had rushed out.

Brodie said, "I hope he's not gonna steal my car and go fugitive."

"He'll be back. He's accustomed to outdoor plumbing."

"Can we believe this story?"

"Wait till you hear the rest of it, Andy. It fits together like a jigsaw puzzle: mystery woman in room 203—battered wife with scarred face—divorced and trying to escape a stalking ex-husband—coming to this remote town for refuge—never thinking she'd be recognized. That's where she made her mistake."

"And he made his mistake by buying flowers; he killed the wrong woman," Brodie said grimly. "Aubrey seems to enjoy telling the story."

"It's doing him good. A few hours ago he was in a suicidal depression. Now he's blabbing like a guest on a TV talk show with an audience of millions. I think he likes the attention. He's lived a lonely life since getting out of the Navy."

"Strange guy. Strange situation."

When Aubrey returned, he said he had walked around the barn; he'd never seen a round barn before. Qwilleran offered him more coffee and said, "Tell us how Vic came up again the next weekend."

"Yeah. I picked him up in Lockmaster again. He said two people described him to the police—that's what it said in the paper. He wanted to know if I could get at the old man's guns."

"How did he know about them?"

"He seen 'em the week before—and the Bible—and the cuckoo clock. He liked the clock. Did you ever see a cuckoo clock, Andy?"

"My mother-in-law has one," the chief said gruffly.

"Okay," Qwilleran said. "Tell us about the handgun."

"Yeah. Vic took one and loaded it, and I drove him to the flower shop on Main Street. He wanted to go there. Wasn't nobody around. They was all at the fireworks. When he come out, I wanted to stay and watch the fireworks, but he wanted to get outa there. That's when he told me I hadda get rid of the gun or I'd be arrested. I di'n't know what to do."

"Whose idea was it to hide it in a turkey?"

"We talked about it. I hadda go to work at midnight. They hadda get a shipment ready for Down Below. Vic said it'd be funny if somebody bought a turkey and found a gun in it."

"Very funny," Brodie growled.

"When I come home from work, I hadda get some sleep. I dunno what Vic did, but he had it all figgered out. He said we hadda get the hotel clerk. That meant Lenny. We hadda hide in the woods and pick him off with a rifle when the bikers went by. The paper printed Lenny's number, and there was a map. Then he said it was my turn to do it because I'm a good shot with a rifle. He was drinkin' whiskey, and I thought he di'n't mean it, but he did. I said I couldn't kill anybody, and he said I hadda do it."

"Because you owed him one," Brodie put in.

"Yeah. I didn't know what to do. I got all hot and sticky, so I went down and talked to my bees. When I come back, the whiskey bottle was empty and he was workin' on the old man's schnapps. Pretty soon he was dead drunk. I hadda lug him to the cabin in my truck and dump him in the bed. There was a quilt that my mom made—red stars and green circles—but he had the cold shakes, so I got him the old man's heavy German blanket. He won't need it no more. He's gonna kick the bucket."

"Did the blanket help?" Qwilleran asked, urging him on.

"I dunno. He'd been sick, and the cabin stunk. I opened a window and got outa there."

"And the next morning?"

"He di'n't come up for cornflakes, so I went to the cabin, and he was dead. His hands and face was all swelled up. I ran outa the cabin and cried. I cried because I wouldn't hafta shoot Lenny."

His two listeners looked at each other. Brodie said, "If you had shot Lenny, you'd be the next victim. Vic would steal your truck and disappear. Nobody but you knew he was here, and nobody but you knew *why* he was here. You can thank your bees for what they did."

"They're gone," Aubrey said. "I smoked 'em out."

"You can hive another wild swarm," said Qwilleran, displaying his recently acquired knowledge.

"Yeah. I know where there's some in an old tree."

"And now I'll play you a tune before I go home," Brodie said. He carried his bagpipe to the top balcony and then spiraled down the ramp at a slow rolling gait as he piped "Amazing Grace." The bagpipe wailed like a banshee, the sound bouncing off the vast interior. Koko howled, and Yum Yum buried her ears in Aubrey's armpit.

When Qwilleran accompanied Brodie to the parking lot, the chief said, "I remember that kid when he was in high school and played football and worked the fishing fleet on weekends. He was a helluva rifle shot. He sure changed, and now he's got himself in a pickle, but when he makes his statement to the prosecutor, it'll wrap up the whole damn case."

"He'll never be charged—under the circumstances," Qwilleran predicted. "It's a clear-cut case of exploitation and coercion. I'm calling George Barter in the morning. He's handled other sensitive legal matters for me, and we're on the same wavelength . . . Thanks for coming over, Andy."

"Glad to see this nasty business come to a head." Brodie stepped into his car and then rolled down the window. "Say, how much was your smart cat involved in this case?"

"Well . . ." Qwilleran said. "More than I thought."

Indoors, Aubrey was on his hands and knees, frolicking with both cats on the Moroccan rug. Yum Yum squirmed deliriously as he pummeled her and spun her around. Koko attacked Aubrey's other hand, wrestled with it, bit it gently, and kicked it with his hind legs. Then the big man rolled on his back, and they climbed all over him. They had never paid so much attention to a stranger.

Qwilleran thought, Do they sense that he needs friends? Or have I been doing it all wrong—too many intellectual pursuits and not enough roughhouse?

He let Aubrey give them their bedtime snack, then sent him up to the guestroom on the second balcony. With the Siamese locked up in their apartment above, Qwilleran settled down for some quiet reading. He was just beginning to feel drowsy when the phone rang, and he heard the brisk, wide-awake night editor of the *Something* saying, "Qwill, this is Dave on the night desk. Sorry to call so late, but there's a long-distance call for you on the other line—from California. It's a woman. She doesn't realize the difference in time zones."

"What's her name?"

"It's a tricky one. I'll spell it. O-n-o-o-s-h."

"Get her number and tell her to hang up. I'll call her immediately."

Within minutes he was talking with Onoosh Dolmathakia.

"Oh, Mr. Qwill! I hear about it!" she said breathlessly. "I see little thing in *USA Today*—man stung to death. He was marry to me. Is too bad I not feel sad. Now I go back to Pickax and start new restaurant with partner. I cook Mediterranean."

"How soon can you get here?" Qwilleran asked.

"We fly. We stay at Hotel Booze."

"Get in touch with me as soon as you arrive." He gave her his phone number and hung up with a sense of satisfaction. Now he would get his stuffed grape leaves.

In the morning he phoned Celia first thing, saying, "I have a houseguest, and I need to rustle up some kind of breakfast. Could you come down here and make pancakes for a couple of starving castaways? Lois has left her customers beached and desperate."

"Sure," she said. "Do you have a griddle?"

"There's a large, oblong stainless-steel thing in the top of the range—is that what you mean? It has pawprints on it, but I'll clean them off. There's plenty of butter and honey here. What do you need to make the pancakes?"

"Don't worry about that. I'll mix the batter here and bring it down there. How soon?"

"Soonest."

Qwilleran went to the second balcony to wake Aubrey. The guest room door was wide open, and the guest had gone. But there were sounds of hilarity on the third balcony; he and the Siamese were having a ball.

Celia arrived with her infectious laugh and bowl of batter, and while she flipped pancakes, Qwilleran phoned the attorney.

The first thing Aubrey said to George Barter when he arrived was: "I'm gonna get me a cat."

CHAPTER 19

In all, Aubrey Scotten told his story five times: first to Qwilleran, again to Brodie, next to the attorney, then to the prosecutor, and finally to a sympathetic judge at an open court hearing. He spoke with gravity and simplicity. The facts never varied— only the digressions about the cooking of turnips and the quality of Lois's flapjacks. Listeners were spellbound by the man's rambling tale and his ingenuous way of telling it. Onoosh Dolmathakia, the former wife of Victor Greer, made an appearance to corroborate certain details, and Nick Bamba, Aubrey's employer, vouched for his honesty, reliability, and value to the community. No charges were brought against the beekeeper, who was entrusted to the guardianship of his mother.

The "old man" in the case did not appear in court. Gustav Limburger had died, leaving a will in the hands of his Lockmaster attorney. To the surprise and consternation of the locals, his entire estate was bequeathed to a daughter in Germany.

Meanwhile, Wetherby Goode was predicting a severe winter. "We shall have snow, and what will poor robin do then, poor thing?" Merchants reported a run on snow blowers and long johns.

After the first frost nipped the air, Moose County experienced a brief but glorious Indian summer. Polly was preparing to return to the workplace, half-days, and Qwilleran was taking her to Boulder House Inn in Trawnto for a celebratory dinner and overnight.

Trawnto was a quiet lakeside resort with large old summer houses on a bluff. It had been settled in the 1800s by Canadians, ship-wrecked on the rocky shore. They wanted to name their tiny village Toronto, but local officials misunderstood their pronunciation and spelled it T-r-a-w-n-t-o in the county records.

En route to Trawnto on that festive Saturday afternoon, Qwilleran kept glancing at his passenger. "Polly, you look great! Absolutely great!" She was wearing a fuchsia silk blouse with her gray pantsuit, and it gave her face a radiant glow.

"I feel wonderful!" she said. "I'm down to a size fourteen, and I'm in the mood to buy some new clothes. Also, when I return to work, I'm applying to the K Fund for public access computers. I believe we're the only library in the U.S. that still uses a card catalogue exclusively."

"I like card catalogues," he said. "I used to fantasize about being locked up overnight with the card catalogue in the New York Public Library . . . Why don't you also ask the K Fund for some chairs with padded seats?"

Polly said, "I've been reading about Edward MacDowell. He was a very handsome man, with a moustache just like yours. You'd look exactly like him if you'd part your hair in the middle."

"I'll do that," he replied dryly. "I've always wanted to look like a nineteenth-century composer. What else have you been reading?"

"The 'Qwill Pen.' Your column on cheese made me hungry."

"I didn't begin to cover the subject. Do you realize its importance in colloquial speech? *Cheese! What a narrow escape! . . . Cheese it! The cops! . . . Who's the big cheese around here? . . . This is a cheesy hotel!* And there are more that I won't mention."

There was nothing cheesy about the Boulder House Inn. It had been the summer residence of an eccentric quarry-owner, and it was constructed of rough boulders, some as big as bathtubs, piled one on another. Windows were recessed in stone walls two or three feet thick. The floors were giant flagstones, and the staircases were chipped out of rock.

"A house designed for giants," Qwilleran said. "I hope the food is good."

"It's advertised as nouvelle cuisine," Polly said with approval. "I suppose that means light sauces, small portions on large plates, cosseted vegetables, and glamorous fruit desserts."

"Something tells me I should have packed a lunch."

When they checked in, the author of the "Qwill Pen" was greeted as a celebrity, and a hospitable innkeeper conducted them personally to adjoining rooms upstairs.

"I have a four-poster bed!" Polly announced as she unpacked her overnight case.

"I have a refrigerator!" he called back.

"I have a fireplace."

"I have an overstuffed sofa and a chess set."

They spent the afternoon walking on the beach and browsing in shops on the boardwalk, then dressed for dinner and had apéritifs on the stone terrace: dry sherry for her, Squunk water for him.

Although they had talked non-stop during the drive from Pickax, they now lapsed into tranquil silence as they contemplated the turquoise lake, the boundless blue sky with billowing October clouds, and their good fortune in being there together, in good health.

After a while Polly said, "I've missed Koko and Yum Yum."

"They've missed you, too . . . So have I."

"Are you still reading Aristophanes to them?"

"Yes, we're reading *The Frogs*. Their favorite line is *Brekekekex ko-ax ko-ax.*"

"I imagine you read it with amphibian authority," she said.

"Thank you. I did the play in college and still remember some of my lines. The translation we used then was more poetic than the one I'm reading now, but not as humorous. In the comic scene where what's-his-name keeps saying *Lost his smelling salts,* my present translation reads *Lost his bottle of oil,* which somehow seems funnier to me. Don't ask why."

"For the same reason that a plate of sardines is funnier than a slice of bread," she said. "A donkey is funny; a horse is not. Pants are funny; shoes are not."

A large gray cat walked solemnly across the terrace, and Qwilleran said loudly, *"Brekekekex ko-ax koax."*

Other guests looked inquiringly in his direction, but the cat kept walking.

"He doesn't understand frogspeak," Qwilleran said.

"He's hearing-impaired," Polly suggested.

"He's missing a few whiskers."

In the dining room she said she would have an amusing piece of trout. Qwilleran decided on a serious steak.

Then she asked, "Did you ever find out who surrendered Iris Cobb's cookbook?"

"No one has confessed," he replied truthfully but evasively, protecting Madame Fetter's reputation as well as Celia's cover.

"It surprised me that Aubrey Scotten's statement to the court was printed verbatim in the *Something*."

"Possibly the editors wanted to cool the gossip."

"Why did the bees attack the man? Was it the foul odor?"

"Who knows?" Qwilleran said with a shrug. "Bees are sensitive and intuitive creatures—and even more mysterious than cats."

"Everyone is hoping Aubrey will go back into the honey business."

"He will," Qwilleran said. "I understand his hives have been moved to his mother's farm, and he's found a new swarm of wild honeybees. He'll continue to work at the turkey farm. His mother will feed him well and cut his hair. Aubrey will be all right . . . Too bad Limburger didn't leave him the Bible and the cuckoo clock."

"We were shocked to hear he had a daughter in Germany. What will she do with the hotel?"

"The K Fund is negotiating with the estate for the purchase of the hotel and the house, which will make a good country inn. If the Scottens agree to sell the cabin, the inn property will extend to the river, where the bassfishing is said to be the best anywhere around."

Accompanying the entrées were tiny brussels sprouts with caraway; spinach and toasted almonds in phyllo pastry; and an herb-flavored soufflé, which Qwilleran pronounced excellent.

"Of course, you know it's turnip," Polly informed him.

"Well, they've done something to it—something underhanded," he said grudgingly. "Do you remember my recent anti-turnip column? I took a lot of flak from readers who are turnip freaks, and someone mailed a large box to me at the office. There was no return address, so the police were notified. There's a way of defusing a bomb with a firehose, you know, so that's what they did. It turned out to be a ten-pound turnip, largest ever grown in Moose County."

The salad course was Bibb lettuce with lemon zest dressing and toasted sesame seeds, garnished with a sliver of Brie.

"Don't eat your cheese," Qwilleran instructed Polly. "It's double-cream. I'll relieve you of it."

"That's so thoughtful of you, dear," she said. "By the way, I saw the video of the cheese party, and the catchase is hilarious! What caused Koko's catfit?"

"Your guess is as good as mine." He wanted to tell her about the handgun in the turkey, but there were topics he never discussed with his two best friends. Both Polly and Arch Riker discouraged him from "getting involved" in matters that were police business and not his. There were long hours spent with Polly when Qwilleran had to hold his tongue. Neither could he reveal Koko's uncanny ability to sense wrong-doing and sniff out wrongdoers. The practical librarian looked at him askance, and the cynical publisher suggested he was cracking up.

Over dessert (poached pears stuffed with currants and pistachios and served with cherry coulis), Polly mentioned a subject that emphasized Qwilleran's predicament.

"Lisa Compton is spearheading a program to help battered women," she said. "Apparently there is a great deal of abuse going unreported in Moose County. Remember the wild rumors circulating about the mystery woman? No one dreamed she was a victim, being stalked and threatened by an ex-husband."

Qwilleran huffed into his moustache. Her statement was not true. Koko had sensed the situation. He had tried in his catly way to communicate. He started stalking Yum Yum. He drove her crazy. One might think they were playing games. Cats go through phases; they invent new games and then tire of them. But Koko also developed a sudden interest in *Stalking the Wild Asparagus*. Wild coincidence—or what? Was it a coincidence that Koko lost interest in Euell Gibbons and stopped stalking Yum Yum *after Onoosh revealed her plight in a frantic letter?* Was it a coincidence that Koko howled at the exact moment that Franklin Pickett was shot? Or that he chewed up Lenny's pledge card when the biker was in danger? Or that he campaigned for a ride to the beach on the very afternoon that the mystery woman was trespassing there? And how about the many times Koko pushed *A Taste of Honey* off the book-shelf?

Polly broke into his reverie. "You're pensive, dear."

"I was thinking . . . that these pears could use some chocolate syrup."

"There's a rumor that we're getting a Mediterranean restaurant. Do you think Pickax is ready for such exotic fare?"

"They'll like it," he predicted, "especially the meatballs in little green kimonos."

After dinner they joined the other guests around a roaring blaze in the stone fireplace and listened to the innkeeper relating the history of the building. During Prohibition it had been headquarters for rum-runners ferrying whiskey from Canada. There were tales of subterranean chambers with sealed doors and Federal agents who mysteriously disappeared. Hollow footsteps were sometimes heard in the night and apparitions hovered outside the windows.

"Pleasant dreams, everyone!" Qwilleran said, standing up. "We're going for a walk in the moonlight."

It was indeed a moonlit night, highlighting the surf that broke on the beach and giving the craggy inn an eerie otherness. Polly was tired, however. It had been an exciting day; she had walked a great deal; she was still in an early-to-bed hospital mode.

They retired to their rooms. Polly left a window open in order to hear the crashing of the surf. Qwilleran, after replacing a 40-watt light bulb with a 70-watt that he always carried in his luggage, sat up reading. It was quiet—unnaturally quiet—in that fortress of massive boulders, until . . . he heard a scream!

He rushed into Polly's room. She was sitting in bed, petrified and speechless. In her bed was a large gray cat.

"Easy, Polly! Easy!" he said soothingly as he grabbed the gray hulk. "It's only Dumbo. He climbed up the side of the building. He was looking for a warm bed." Qwilleran put the cat out on the wide sill and closed the window.

"I was sleeping soundly," Polly said. "It was a terrible scare—to wake and see that animal in my bed. I'm still shaking."

"Come and sit with me for a while," he said gently. "Curl up on my sofa. Calm down. I'll read to you."

In the breakfast room on Sunday morning, Qwilleran was in a playful mood, and Polly giggled at all his quips. Their waitress had a spectacular hairdo that looked, he muttered to Polly, like a bale of barbed wire. To the young woman he said, with a show of wonder and admiration, "I like your hair! It's different!"

She beamed with pleasure.

"You must have it done by a very good professional."

"No, I do it myself," she said modestly.

"Remarkable! It must take a long time and a great deal of skill and patience."

Polly was suppressing her mirth with difficulty, while kicking him under the table, but the waitress was overwhelmed. She brought extra muffins, extra butter, and extra preserves to their table, as well as an endless supply of coffee.

After another walk on the beach, they checked out. Monday would be Polly's first day at the library after several weeks of medical leave. She wanted to get herself together and switch roles—from convalescent to boss-lady, as the young clerks called her.

On the way home, they stopped at Indian Village. Since apartment leases stipulated no pets, Polly had bought a condominium. It was a two-story unit, and Bootsie would have stairs for exercise and a small screened porch for bird-watching. Under consideration was the possibility of acquiring a companion for him.

As they neared Pickax, both of them enjoying the comfortable silence of a happy couple, Polly startled Qwilleran by saying, "Qwill, have you been keeping a big secret from me?"

A dozen possibilities flashed through his mind. "What do you mean? Give me a clue."

"Well, there's a woman in Lynette's bridge club who does the bookkeeping for Scottie's Men's Store, and she says you've just been billed for a tailor-made kilt in the Mackintosh tartan."

He gripped the steering wheel and stared stonily ahead. The gossip was true. In a weak moment, when he feared he was losing Polly, he had ordered a full Scottish kit to please her—perhaps to speed her recovery. Now she was alive and well, but he winced at the thought of wearing a short pleated "petticoat" with gartered socks and bare knees. "Is this a Congressional investigation?" he asked. "I take the Fifth."

"Oh, Qwill! You're an incorrigible tease!" she said. "Well, anyway, you'll look magnificent in a kilt."

After taking her home and witnessing her emotional reunion with Bootsie (they had been apart for twenty-four hours), Qwilleran drove to the barn, where he was met by two cool, calm, and collected cats. It meant they had breakfasted, and it was too early for dinner pangs. It also meant: no message on the answering machine; no domestic crisis; no gunshot or other incident to report.

"Hi, guys!" he said cheerfully. "How's everything? Did Celia take good care of you?" She had fed them before going to church, according to a note left on the kitchen counter.

Koko acknowledged his greeting with two flicks of the tail, and Yum Yum purred when he asked, "Are you still my little sweetheart?"

After changing into a jumpsuit, Qwilleran settled down in the library with a mug of coffee and some cheese and crackers.

"Gruyère, anyone?" he asked, expecting a yowl from Koko. When there was no response, he said, "All the more for me! . . . How about some double-cream Brie?" Still there was no reaction. Qwilleran reeled off a list of the world's great cheeses, including goat's-milk feta, but Koko—who had become a cheese gastronome during the Explo—was silent.

What did it mean? He never did anything—hardly anything—without a reason. Abnormal behavior on his part always signified an attempt to communicate information. Now the answers were known; the case was closed; and Qwilleran realized, in retrospect, the meaning of Koko's messages:

The cat had sensed that the evildoer could be identified by a sound like Gruyère, and Brie suggested the unwitting, unwilling accomplice. To a cat's ear Gruyère, Brie, Greer, and Aubrey would be merely sounds, like TREAT or BOOK; to Koko's ear they had significance. If the scientists Down Below ever found out about the psychic cat, they would charter flights to Pickax to test Koko's brain and count his whiskers . . . No way! Qwilleran thought.

Then he slapped his forehead as another possibility occurred to him. "Oh, no!" he said aloud. "Feta . . . Fetter . . . cookbook . . . Iris Cobb . . . meatloaf!" The Siamese had been fond of their former housekeeper, and they missed her special meatloaf, the secret of which . . .

Qwilleran's ruminations were interrupted by a low rumble in Koko's chest, followed by a leap to the bookshelves.

"Okay, we'll have a read. *Brekekekex ko-ax ko-ax!*" With Koko on the arm of his chair and Yum Yum on his lap, he continued his reading of *The Frogs*.

The dialogue brought back memories. He had played Dionysus in the college production. His mother was living then, and she had attended three nights in a row. He had never forgotten his line: *Who knows if death be life and life be death, and breath be mutton broth, and sleep a sheepskin?* He remembered his costume, too: heavy robes befitting an Olympian god, but they were hot under the lights, and he thought he would drown in his own perspiration. That was a long time ago. Now he was living in a barn and reading *The Frogs* to an audience of two cats.

When he reached his favorite line, he found the translation quite different from the one he had known. He read it seriously, with meaningful pauses: *"Who knows whether living is dying . . . and breathing is eating . . . and sleeping is a wool blanket?"*

"Yow!" said Koko with equal seriousness.

Qwilleran felt a tingle on his upper lip as he guessed the answer to a puzzling question: Why did the bees attack Victor Greer? It was the wool blanket, of course! The old man's heavy woolen blanket from Germany! Did Aubrey realize what he was doing? Did he know the blanket was wool? In the confusion of the situation, did he forget that bees are antagonized by wool? . . . Or did Aubrey purposely take the wool blanket to the cabin? Later, when he found the body, he wept because, as he said, he would not have to shoot Lenny.

"How about that, Koko? Do you have an opinion?"

The cat was sitting in a tall, stately pose on the arm of the chair. He swayed slightly. His blue eyes were large and fathomless.

"Okay, we'll play a game. If Aubrey purposely caused Victor Greer's death, blink!"

Qwilleran stared into Koko's eyes. Koko stared back. It was eyeball to eyeball. The trancelike impasse between man and cat went on and on. Qwilleran forgot to breathe. With all thought and feeling suspended, he was crossing over into hypnosis; he had to blink.

Koko had won. Aubrey was absolved. But then . . . Koko always won.